WAR IN PEACE

WAR IN PEACE

AN ANALYSIS OF WARFARE TO THE PRESENT DAY

Consulting Editor Sir Robert Thompson
Introduction by John Keegan

BLACK CAT

Consultant editors

Sir Robert Thompson KBE, CMG, DSO, MC is a world authority on guerrilla warfare, on which he has written extensively. He was directly involved with the Emergency in Malaya in the 1950s and rose to become permanent Secretary for Defence. From 1961 to 1965 he headed the British Advisory Mission to Vietnam and since then he has advised several governments, including the United States, on counter-insurgency operations. Sir Robert Thompson is a Council member of the Institute for the Study of Conflict, London. His books include *Defeating Communist Insurgency* and *Revolutionary War in World Strategy, 1945–69.*

John Keegan MA, who wrote the introduction, is Senior Lecturer in the Department of War Studies and International Affairs at The Royal Military Academy Sandhurst, England. The brilliant and original analysis displayed in his book *Face of Battle* immediately established him as a profound military thinker. He is the author of many other books on military matters, including *Who Was Who in World War II*, and he was general editor of *Encyclopedia of World War II*. John Keegan was consultant for the series *The Illustrated History of the Violent Century* and wrote the volumes *Dien Bien Phu, Waffen SS* and *Barbarossa.*

The authors

Ian Beckett is a lecturer in the Department of War Studies and International Affairs at The Royal Military Academy Sandhurst, England. He is the author of *Politicians and Defence.*

Major F. A. Godfrey MC served in Malaya, Cyprus, Malta, Libya, Aden and Berlin before retiring from the British Army in 1969. From 1973 to 1983 he was a Senior Lecturer at Sandhurst.

Peter Janke is a specialist on Africa and has lectured in the United States, Britain and Spain. He has been head of research at the Institute for the Study of Conflict, London, and wrote the study papers 'Southern Africa: End of Empire' and 'Southern Africa: New Horizons'.

Eric Morris was Deputy Head of the Department of War Studies and International Affairs at Sandhurst up to 1984. His books include *Blockade: Berlin and the Cold War, The Russian Navy, Myth and Reality* and a history of tanks.

Jonathan Reed is a historian whose special interests are revolutionary wars and wars of counter-insurgency. He has contributed a number of articles on Vietnam, Central America and weapons technology to military publications.

John Pimlott is the author of a book on the B-29 Superfortress and co-author of *Strategy and Tactics of War.* He has also written a book on the Battle of the Bulge and was consultant editor on *The Middle East Conflicts* and *Vietnam: The history and the tactics.* He is Senior Lecturer in War Studies and International Affairs at Sandhurst.

David Rees is a Senior Research Fellow of the Institute for the Study of Conflict in London and writes for its publications on strategic affairs. He is the author of *Korea: The Limited War* and a biography of Harry Dexter White. He was consultant editor on *The Korean War: History and Tactics.*

Michael Orr has been a lecturer at Sandhurst since 1969. He is the author of *Dettingen 1743* and has contributed many articles to military publications. He is a specialist on the Soviet Army.

H. P. Willmott, Senior Lecturer at Sandhurst, has a special interest in guerrilla warfare. He is the author of several books, among them *Pearl Harbor, A6M* and *B-17.*

First published in Great Britain by Orbis Publishing Limited, London 1981
Revised edition 1983, second revised edition 1985

Reprinted 1988 by Macdonald & Co (Publishers) Ltd under the Black Cat imprint

Macdonald & Co (Publishers) Ltd
3rd Floor, Greater London House
Hampstead Road, London NW1 7QX

a member of Maxwell Pergamon Publishing Corporation plc

ISBN 0-7481-0113-6

Printed in Spain

Contents

Introduction

by John Keegan

Both the great wars of this century left behind them a trail of unresolved local and civil wars which took time to settle. But those which followed the victory of the Allies in 1918 were comparatively short-lived. Almost all were the by-products of the collapse of the defeated empires, the German, Austro-Hungarian, Turkish and Russian, and turned on the delineation of new frontiers between the successor states and their old overlords. Russia, convulsed by civil war between Reds and Whites, a war complicated by Allied intervention originally designed to sustain Russian resistance against the Germans, was the centre of conflict. Defeated in her efforts to retain the Baltic states, she was eventually successful in quelling separatist movements in the Ukraine, Armenia and Azerbaijan and in defeating Polish efforts to annex most of White Russia. But she was obliged to accept the victory of separatist White over Red forces in Finland and to abandon a client Bolshevik regime in Hungary. The Hungarians were themselves the losers in territorial struggles with the Romanians and Czechs. Turkey successfully opposed a Greek invasion of Anatolia, but was unable to profit from the squabbles of her former Arab subjects over the partition of the Middle East. There, desert wars were to drag on until 1925. But by that date most of the world had returned to peace. Only in China, racked by the collapse of its imperial system which antedated the Great War, did large-scale fighting continue.

This swift return to normality may be ascribed to three main causes: unity of interest between the victor powers; the continuing strength of the imperial idea; and the under-development of what today is called the Third World. Africa was still a continent asleep. India, though chafing under British rule, had not yet found the will or means to throw it off. South-east Asia was a backwater, which had been untouched by the war. Latin America remained firmly insulated from disturbing influences by the Monroe Doctrine. The Middle East was swiftly re-colonised, in the vacuum left by the Ottomans, by Great Britain, France and Italy. Such political differences as they had did not extend to interference in each other's affairs, least of all in their empires. Russia, the only enemy of the imperial idea, was too occupied in transforming the Tsarist empire into a modern industrialised state to propagate effective revolution outside her borders.

None of these factors were wholly present after 1945, and the emergence of the Soviet Union as a major world power, dominating eastern Europe and fundamentally opposed to the ideologies and status of the western allies, was a crucial difference. Although the tension between the Soviet Union and the West has not resulted in open warfare (partly no doubt because of the threat of nuclear devastation), the polarisation of world politics during the late 1940s has had a continuing effect, and underlay or added to conflict all over the globe. The subsequent assertion by China of its role as a third, independent great power has complicated rather than disturbed this pattern. Both ideologically (in the close identification with and encouragement of certain parties and regimes) and physically (in the widespread provision of arms) the mutual hostility of the great powers abetted and sponsored the spread of warfare, especially in a Third World which nationalism was making ripe for conflict by 1945.

Underdevelopment persisted in the economic sense. But most colonial territories had by 1945 at least the makings of a political elite. These elites owed their existence to the implantation of western educational systems, whose development was evidence of the imperialists' early confidence in the unshakeability of their power. That confidence was by 1945 much diminished, in part by American disapproval of colonialism but in greater measure by Japan's overthrow of the British, Dutch and French empires in the Far East in 1942. The spectacle of that humiliation had much encouraged the local nationalists. And its effect had been heightened by the steps taken by the Japanese to transfer political power in the ex-colonies to the nationalist movements between 1942–5. Vietnamese, Indonesians and Burmese had all experienced some degree of self-government in the years of Japanese occupation. They were accordingly all the less ready to welcome the return of the Europeans in the aftermath of Japan's defeat.

But it was not only the Japanese who had sown disturbing ideas in the underdeveloped world. Local communist parties had grown sturdily in the Far East during the 1930s and had been nurtured by the Soviet Union even during the years of its co-operation with the western allies in the war against Hitler. In China and Vietnam they embarked on open struggle for mastery while Russia continued to maintain the façade of alliance with the British and Americans. When alliance turned to Cold War – partly as a result of American suspicions that the success of the Chinese communists was an anti-American campaign willed by Moscow – the Asian communist parties grew bolder. In Malaya, in Burma, in the Philippines, eventually in Indonesia, each party proclaimed policies of national and economic liberation and took to arms, in the last three cases against governments which had already won their independence from European rule.

An understandable paranoia came to afflict western governments in their attitudes towards other national liberation movements which came to life in the fifties and sixties. It seemed natural to perceive the hand of Moscow or Peking in all of them. In some – notably in Cuba and in the Portuguese African possessions – it was undoubtedly present, and it dabbled energetically elsewhere. But the majority of the movements, though influenced by communist methods and rhetoric, were clearly autonomous. The Algerian Liberation Front was nationalist in inspiration, Mau Mau in Kenya tribal, EOKA in Cyprus irridentist.

Moreover, as western power retreated, and communist power advanced only erratically to take its place, the immediate violence of the post-war years was sustained by the rebirth of old local animosities buried by one or two hundred years of colonial rule. This was first and most notably apparent in the Indian sub-continent, where India and Pakistan rekindled the quarrels between Hindu and Muslim which had been quashed by British conquest in the eighteenth century. But similar outbreaks were to occur in South-east Asia, in Arabia and in Africa, some fuelled by the old imperial ambitions of local powers now restored to dominance, some by religious differences, some by tribal or racial antipathies. Empire, for all its faults, had at least had the virtue of making the world a simpler place during the years of its heyday.

Empire had also, as America ruefully came to admit, mightly served the fundamental strategic interests of the

Atlantic world at a range where maritime power attenuated into ineffectiveness. This was first demonstrated in Korea in 1950, where the local communist regime came within a hair's breadth of capturing the whole peninsula, and would have done so but for the presence of an American army in Japan. The message was reinforced at Suez in 1956 (even if that operation may now be judged an overreaction), by the Vietnam war and, most recently and threateningly, by the destabilisation of the Gulf region, on which all the industrialised western nations have come to depend for the oil supplies essential to their economies. It is only a little consolation to the maritime states that the causes of the destabilisation threaten also the integrity of the neighbouring Soviet Union, whose essentially imperial character – most marked in the Central Asian Soviet Republics closest to Afghanistan and Iran – it has successfully disguised ever since the Bolshevik Revolution.

In one area of the world, comparison between the outcomes of the First and Second World Wars fails: that is in the former territory of Palestine, centre of the most spectacular and dangerous of all the fighting since 1945. It is fashionable among Arab intellectuals and Palestinian propagandists to depict the establishment of the state of Israel as a deliberate attempt by the western powers to sustain an imperial presence in the Middle East – a version of events to which the communist world also at times chooses to lend support. A time traveller would be unlikely to accept such an oversimplification. Historians, indeed, search almost in vain for parallels to the story of Israel's foundation and role. The closest found has the same geographical focus, that of the crusading kingdoms of the Holy Land. They also were brought into being through the power of an idea, were maintained only at the cost of constant warfare against surrounding Muslim states and depended for survival upon external military and economic support.

But the chief help given by Christendom to the resident crusaders came in the form of manpower. Israel has found her soldiers from within her own population. It is the weapons with which to equip them for which she has looked to help from her foreign supporters. Her enemies too have depended upon foreign armaments for their own equipment. The result has been to invest the four Arab-Israeli wars, in particular those of 1967 and 1973, with qualities of the greatest interest for analysts concerned to measure the relative strength and combat-readiness of the opposed superpower blocs from which the armaments have come. All agree on a number of salient features of the fighting: the continuing importance of the tank and the strike aircraft; the significance of novel precision-guided weapons; the very high attrition rates inflicted, on material rather than, as in the past, on personnel; the enormous financial cost of such high-technology warfare; and the difficulty, verging on the impossibility, of making good equipment losses out of current production, perhaps even of accumulating war-reserve stocks of the least adequacy.

Because of the success of Israel's surprise attack on the assembling Arab armies in 1967, the losses inflicted then, though devastating to the Egyptians, could be dismissed as atypical. The same could not be said of the 1973 war, a much more evenly matched contest. Intense fighting lasted only three weeks, most of it concentrated into the period 5–19 October. Short though the time was, both sides nonetheless lost over half their tank strength, Israel about 800 out of 1700 tanks, Egypt and Syria 2000 out of a combined total of 4000. Proponents of the guided missile had to take note of the fact that most disabling hits had been made by tank gunnery. In the first few days of the war, however, guided missiles had scored perhaps fifty fatal hits on Israel ground-support aircraft, while radar-controlled, multi-barrelled cannon had made the lower airspace of the battlefield almost impermeable to air intrusion at critical points. Aircraft losses were therefore also very high on both sides; a fifth of Israel's air force was destroyed, a third of the Syrian-Egyptian: about 400 in all. Such figures reveal their significance when they are put in the context of aircraft costs and production rates. American first-line single-seat aircraft are now approaching a price of twenty million dollars each, and maximum monthly output of any type from the factories is about thirty.

Equipment losses in the Indo-Pakistan wars of 1965 and 1971 were also of a size to warn how difficult the sustenance of high-intensity operations in modern warfare was becoming. The trend was made all the clearer if comparisons were drawn with the earliest large-scale conventional war of the post-war years, that fought in Korea in 1950–53. Air fighting over the whole peninsula, much of it dedicated to the interdiction of the communist supply routes, was heavy and continuous and aircraft losses proportionately large. But tank combat was negligible; both offensive and defensive operations took the form of infantry and artillery battles closely reminiscent of the fighting on the Western Front in the First World War. After two periods of rapid movement in the first year, the war settled down to a struggle of attrition across the waist of the country, in which both sides lost men heavily in local attacks on points of vantage and observation. By the end of the war over a million Chinese and North Korean troops faced three-quarters of a million United Nations soldiers across a permanent no man's land. As many communist soldiers again had become casualties; the South Koreans suffered 400,000 casualties and the Americans over 100,000, of whom 34,000 were dead.

Most had been killed at the front. But the character of the war had an ominous other side to it, contributed by the active guerrilla campaign waged behind United Nations lines by communist soldiers cut off during their retreat from the south in 1950. The Chinese People's Liberation Army which intervened (technically on a volunteer basis) in Korea, and had won the Civil War of 1946–9 against Chiang Kai-shek, had transformed itself into a conventional regular army. But its founding philosophy, formulated by Mao Tse-tung, was that of a guerrilla movement and it had propagated its strategy, by example and direct instruction, to other communist parties in the region. The Hukbalahaps of the Philippines and the Malayan Communist Party, an overseas Chinese organisation, both instituted guerrilla campaigns in the 1940s, which were eventually to be suppressed. Another, to be crowned ultimately with spectacular victory, was initiated in Vietnam against the French by the Viet Minh in 1946. The Viet Minh was a coalition of nationalists and communists, with the latter dominating, which had been sponsored by the Japanese in the last months of their occupation of the territories in 1945. After the surrender, the French treated with the Viet Minh, but negotiations broke down and, on the return of a French army, fighting broke out all over the country.

It was to set a pattern for wars of national liberation all over the world during the next thirty years. Guerrilla warfare is one of the oldest means of expressing violent opposition to an unloved government or a foreign occupier. But, without direct support from a conventional army, it has rarely achieved more than the nuisance effect of chronic banditry. Mao Tse-tung's genius was to suggest, and then to demonstrate, means by which a guerrilla army might, from small beginnings, progressively raise the level of its operations until it forced its conventional opponent to meet it on equal terms and then undergo defeat. The essence of his method was to organise the army both as a political and military instrument. Its soldiers were to be not merely men of the sword, but also of the word, whose mission was as much to indoctrinate the civilian population among whom they lived and operated as to fight the enemy. Hence his famous slogan, 'The army must be in the people like the fish in the water'. Unlike regular armies, which live apart from the populations which they defend, or traditional guerrillas, whose life is spent in mountains and forests, the communist guerrillas were to make the villages their habitat and the peasants their pupils and protectors.

The method had been tried in China, at the end of the Long March to Yenan in 1934, but its validity had not been proved, since Chiang Kai-shek's army had been so exhausted by its war with the Japanese that it easily succumbed to conventional attack in 1946–9. In Vietnam, however, the Viet Minh were to invest Maoist doctrine with almost magic power. It envisages three stages of operations, guerrilla operations, then 'protracted warfare', and finally the general offensive. Giap, the leading Viet Minh general, twice anticipated his army's readiness to move to the last stage, and suffered serious setback in consequence. But by 1953 he had so tantalised the French by his ability to refuse them pitched battle, while at the same undermining their rule in the countryside, that they fell into the trap of offering him battle on favourable terms. At Dien Bien Phu, in the spring of 1954, the best of the French expeditionary force was besieged and forced to surrender. The establishment of a communist government in North Vietnam almost immediately ensued.

It had to be noted, however, that after 1949 the Viet Minh had enjoyed support from and, when necessary, sanctuary in China, which supplied them with the bulk of their weapons, many captured in Korea. When in 1965 heavy fighting again broke out in Vietnam, with the Americans reinforcing the South Vietnamese army against invasion from the north, Giap was able to make even better use of sanctuary on his home territory. Despite the committal of over a hundred manoeuvre battalions to stand beside nine South Vietnamese divisions, the Americans were unable either to check the inflow of communist units and supplies or to suppress insurgency in the countryside. A heavy air campaign over North Vietnam, running at 12,000 sorties a month at its height, was also ineffective in weakening the northern government's will to continue the war. In the end it was the American government's will which crumbled. Their policy of 'Vietnamisation' sustained the Saigon regime for only three years after their withdrawal in 1972.

Many other national liberation movements attempted to adopt Maoist methods, without necessarily converting to his ideology, after the Viet Minh victory of 1954. The most notable to do so was the Algerian National Liberation Front, against which the French fought a bitter war from 1954 to 1960. Militarily successful, in that it eventually broke the Front's army, French policy failed to carry political conviction. For, in going down to defeat, the Front had so deeply embedded its organisation and ideas in the Muslim population as to rob French rule of credibility. FRELIMO in Mozambique was also Maoist-inspired, and achieved some success in creating 'liberated areas' from which Mao had taught that successful rebellion would grow. But there, as in Angola, it was to be a revolution in the home territory of Portugal, motivated by war-weariness, which would eventually bring the nationalists independence. Elsewhere the essentially tribal nature of most armed African nationalist movements made the high degree of unity necessary to the Maoist method difficult of achievement. This was most notably to be demonstrated in the war between the white Rhodesians and the various guerrilla groups of the Patriotic Front, whose differences provided the Rhodesian army with its principal means of prolonging the conflict.

Maoist guerrilla doctrine, regarded and proclaimed as an almost magic formula for insurrectionary success in the fifties and sixties, may now be seen in a more objective light. It requires a variety of complementary predisposing conditions if it is to be made to work: a homogeneous population, a well-established sense of grievance, a certain level of political consciousness are all necessary. Hence the failure of the various attempts by Latin American Marxist groups to foment rebellion among the backward Indian populations of the interior. Che Guevara's efforts to repeat in Bolivia what he and Castro had achieved in Cuba may be seen as doomed to failure by the Andean peasants' incomprehension of his message.

Low-level warfare of an insurrectionary, sectarian, tribal or secessionist nature may nevertheless be judged to have become endemic all over the formerly colonial world, and likely to persist as long as political frontiers fail to coincide with cultural boundaries and the arms industry leaks its wares into the pools of discontent. A regrettable function of industrialisation has been the progressive depreciation of unit-costs in weapon manufacture and a consequent superabundance of supply. High-technology warfare threatens to bankrupt whatever nation embarks on it. Low-intensity warfare can be fought more cheaply than ever before. If the small-arms and ammunition which are its principal means were vended chiefly second-hand from centres outside the control of the great powers, the ease with which they are acquired and used might be a subject merely for the plaints of leader writers. Analysis of sources of production reveals, however, that most weapons, even of the simplest type, and, more important, most munitions, are still produced by a handful of countries in the developed world. In Africa, for example, only Egypt and South Africa have the means to manufacture small-arms ammunition. The bitter secessionary and irridentist fighting within, and between Ethiopia, Eritrea and Somalia is therefore entirely sustained by foreign supply, furnished for reasons which serve the producers as much as the users.

Arms control since 1945 has principally come to mean the control of the development and deployment of nuclear weapons. And it has had its effect in limiting the strategic arms race between the nuclear powers. Arms control as it was understood in League of Nations days has been almost entirely neglected. It may be that, given the adversarial relationship of the superpower blocs, the limitation of the supply of simple conventional weapons to troubled areas of the Third World is impossible of achievement. But in the absence of any concerted international effort to bring it about, the official deploring of the chronic violence to which it gives the means of expression is merely hypocritical. Certain post-war endeavours, notably the Tripartite agreement of 1950 to limit the flow of arms to the Middle East, and the Geneva accords of 1954 to demilitarise Laos and Cambodia, which had short-term effects, give hope that pacification is not wholly beyond the great powers' reach. The temptation to avoid their responsibilities offered by the competition for strategic resources so widely located in unindustrialised but contentious regions will be increasingly hard to resist. But, while it is not resisted, 'post-war' conflict seems destined to drag on into eternity – perhaps, given the all too well-proven tendency of small wars to precipitate great wars, quite literally so.

Red Star in the East

From 1945 to 1949 a civil war which had begun in China in the 1920s reached its climax and ended in a sweeping victory for the communists

David Rees

THE CHINESE CIVIL WAR saw the victory of communism in the world's most populous nation, and unveiled to the world a new method and philosophy of warfare. The war was fought on a massive scale, with millions of men involved on both sides, and its effects have been equally immense – not only on Chinese society and world politics but in the way that all wars have been fought since then.

Although the war came to its climax from 1945 to 1949, the origins of this historic conflict date back to the brief alliance between the Chinese Nationalists and the Soviet Union in the 1920s. After the abdication of the last Manchu emperor in 1912, and an abortive experiment with parliamentary democracy, effective central authority collapsed in China. Real power lay with the military governors or warlords. The Western powers and Japan, which held extensive trading and extra-territorial rights in China, acted on the premise that the warlord holding the former imperial capital of Peking (now known as Beijing) headed the *de facto* Chinese government. But by the early 1920s a new, different regional power centre emerged at Canton (Guangzhou) which was led by the Chinese Nationalist Party or Kuomintang (KMT).

Under the charismatic leadership of Dr Sun Yat-sen, the KMT had become a revolutionary nationalist party which promised the unification of China, modernisation, eventual democracy, and the curtailment of Western influence. But the KMT needed effective political organisation and reliable military forces. The Chinese Communist Party (CCP), meanwhile, founded in 1921 on Marxist-Leninist principles, had no mass following. The leadership of both the KMT and the CCP believed that they alone would rule the new China.

By 1923, Sun Yat-sen had come to believe that the KMT could rely on disinterested Soviet Russian help to achieve its objectives. In January of that year Moscow promised to help the KMT unify China. Later in 1923 a senior Soviet emissary, Michael Borodin, was sent as adviser to Sun Yat-sen. Intensive political and military preparations now began for a decisive campaign by the KMT which would eliminate the warlord system from at least south and east China. Soon there were more than 1000 Soviet military advisers with the KMT. The Chinese communists, while keeping their own organisation intact, were allowed to join the KMT only as individuals. By 1925 the KMT had become the dominant political force in China.

The struggle begins

Following Sun's death in March 1925, Soviet and communist influence in the higher echelons of the KMT greatly increased. Stalin envisaged that under Soviet guidance the CCP would take over the KMT leadership and so control the revolutionary movement in China. Given military success, communist rule over the whole country would follow. However, Sun's close disciple and former military assistant, General Chiang Kai-shek, considered that Soviet objectives in China were essentially imperialist and that CCP influence would have to be curbed.

In March 1926 Chiang carried out a limited purge of the communists in Canton, and three months later was elected chairman of the KMT and commander-in-chief. On 9 July 1926 he launched the Great Northern Expedition which, within six months, eliminated warlord influence from central China up to the Yangtze (Changjiang); in early 1927 the KMT took over Shanghai, China's largest commercial city.

On 12 April 1927 Chiang's troops and

'Marching to Victory' is the title of this modern poster which idealises the Chinese revolution. Mao Tse-tung's communists defeated the Nationalists through superior tactics, better organisation and greater dedication.

armed supporters carried out a massive purge in Shanghai during which thousands of communists were killed. Their organisations were proscribed. A new Kuomintang government was proclaimed at Nanking (Nanjing) and in July 1927 Borodin and other advisers were expelled from China. The strange alliance between Moscow and the KMT was over.

The rise of Mao Tse-tung

Leaving China, Borodin advised the CCP to go underground and to resist the 'capitalist regime' of the KMT. Three abortive communist risings occurred before the end of 1927. The first was in Nanchang, Kiangsi province, on 1 August. Although the insurrection was crushed, the date is now celebrated as the anniversary of the Chinese People's Liberation Army (PLA). Western historians regard 1 August 1927 as the beginning of the civil war proper between the KMT and the CCP.

A few weeks later in rural Hunan, Mao Tse-tung, already a veteran of the failed KMT-communist alliance, directed the 'autumn harvest' uprising on 9 September. This, too, was repressed. Finally, in December 1927, Stalin ordered an urban insurrection in Canton which was crushed after four days' fighting. With the liquidation of the Canton 'commune' all Soviet organs remaining in China were closed, Russians were killed or driven out of the country, and relations between Nanking and Moscow broken off. The policy of urban armed insurrection, which had influenced Soviet strategy in China, was hopelessly discredited. The CCP would now have to work out a completely new blueprint for the Chinese revolution.

Meanwhile the KMT consolidated its power. During 1928, Peking fell to the KMT, and in October Chiang Kai-shek was installed as president of the National government in Nanking. The regime had the support of China's cities, of Western interests, and even of the middle peasants, for order and stability were now needed. But from 1928 to 1931, despite Chiang Kai-shek's undoubted successes and the elimination of the CCP underground in the cities, a sizeable nucleus of Chinese communist rural guerrillas survived in the Chingkang mountains on the Hunan-Kiangsi border.

Chiang Kai-shek was aware of the implications of this resistance and in 1930 launched the first of a series of 'bandit extermination' campaigns. But by November 1931, when Mao's forces controlled an area with a population of about 50 million, a Chinese soviet republic was proclaimed at Juichin (Ruijin) with Mao Tse-tung as president.

A decisive phase of China's civil war was now at hand. Nationalist forces, aided by a German military advisory group, began to close the trap on the communists. The CCP was faced with annihilation and on 15 October 1934 a communist column of 100,000 men headed west on the epic of the Long March.

Crossing mountains, deserts and the sheer gorges of the upper Yangtze, Mao's guerrillas founded a new base area and capital at Yenan (Yanan) in Shensi province, north China. About 20,000 guerrillas had survived the 9660km (6000-mile) trek. But these men were now a seasoned, hardened élite and directed by a leader whose Leninist authority was unquestioned. Mao was now chairman of the CCP politburo, and during the Long March the supporters of urban, as opposed to rural, insurrection had been eliminated from the leadership.

A united front against Japan

With Mao's forces quartered in the loess caves of Yenan during 1936–37, the civil war continued in a new setting. Shensi was much less fertile than south China, and by 1937 the Red Army numbered probably less than 100,000 effectives. But external events now came to Mao's help. Following Japan's Manchurian conquests of 1931–32, war between Japan and China seemed inevitable. Anti-Japanese feeling mounted throughout China.

The KMT laid down terms in early 1937 for the inclusion of the Communist Party in

LEFT *Peasants file across Shentung peninsula bound for the battlefield. These PLA volunteers were to carry supplies.* BELOW *Buildings blaze after fierce fighting as a PLA soldier helps a distraught woman and child to escape the chaos in a rubble-strewn street.* OPPOSITE *PLA units march through Peking (top). In October 1949 Mao formally announced the setting up of the People's Republic (far right).*

an anti-Japanese 'united front'. These terms included dissolution of the Chinese soviet republic, the suspension of the class struggle, and the incorporation of the Red Army in the Nationalist military chain of command. The CCP accepted these provisions.

On 7 July 1937, two months before this agreement, Japan had invaded China. By the end of 1938, the Nationalists had been driven out of the cities of east and central China, and Chiang had been forced to remove his administration to Chungking (Chongqing) in the western province of Szechuan. There the Nationalist government remained until 1945.

These developments closely affected the eventual outcome of China's civil war. The Sino-Japanese War ripped apart the traditional social structure of the country, diminished the civil and military authority of Chiang's regime, and led to an irresistible inflationary spiral in which prices rose 2500 per cent between 1937 and 1945.

Given these conditions, the 1937 agreement soon became little more than an armed truce. Moreover, from 1938 until 1941 the CCP improved its position relative to the Nationalists in two significant ways. Militarily, communist forces infiltrated eastwards across the Yellow (Huanghe) River into north and central China, setting up 'liberated' base areas. Politically, the CCP increasingly made use of mass organisations and 'front' groups within the Nationalist-held areas.

All these developments were accelerated by the mounting inefficiency and corruption of the KMT. In Yenan, on the contrary, the CCP emphasised the necessity of strict doctrinal and military discipline.

In this seminal period immediately before Japan's defeat, the United States began to

work for the reconciliation of the two parties in China, fearing future Soviet intervention in the civil war. Yet there is little doubt that in 1945 both Chiang and Mao thought only of eliminating their opponents rather than of joining them in an American-sponsored coalition.

Futile peace moves

On 4 September 1945, two days after the final, formal surrender of Imperial Japan, the New China News Agency announced from Yenan: 'We hold the entire region stretching from Kalgan [Zhangjiakou] to the Yangtze, and from Shensi to the China Sea, except for the largest cities and some fortified points along the railroads.' To offset this development, the United States organised a massive sea-and-air lift of some 500,000 Nationalist troops into the seaports and cities of east and north China.

Meanwhile, the Soviet forces which had entered Manchuria (and Jehol) in the closing days of the Pacific War now began to transfer large quantities of Japanese arms, including heavy weapons, to the Chinese communist troops that had infiltrated the region. The Russians also prevented the landing of Nationalist troops in south Manchurian ports. Soviet withdrawal from Manchuria was also postponed until early 1946, by which time the communists controlled the countryside.

In December 1945, the Truman administration, fearing the outbreak of major hostilities between the KMT and the CCP, had decided to dispatch General George C. Marshall, the former US Army Chief of Staff. His mission was to work for the unification of China by peaceful and democratic means. Marshall soon arranged a truce between the contestants, effective from 13 January 1946. But the communists captured Changchun and Harbin (Haerbin) by April and the truce had clearly broken down. The Nationalists now went over to the offensive in Manchuria, took Szeping (Siping) and reoccupied Changchun. At that point General Marshall arranged a truce, which lasted from 6 until 30 June.

During July, however, the truce broke down and hostilities spread to all parts of China, marking the beginning of general civil war. The Marshall mission had failed, and in January 1947 the general was recalled by President Truman. China's future would be decided by war. The decision came sooner than most observers predicted.

Opposing strategies

At the outbreak of general civil war in July 1946 the Nationalist armies numbered about 3 million men, as opposed to about 1 million deployed by the PLA, as the communist forces were known after May 1946. By sheer force of numbers the Nationalists had occupied most of China's provincial capitals and the Manchurian cities south of the Sungari (Songhuajiang) River. But the PLA remained deeply entrenched in the entire countryside of north China and Manchuria. The civil war's final phase was thus a test of Nationalist manpower and firepower against PLA discipline and morale. In this crucible, Mao's doctrine of 'man-over-weapons' would be fought to a finish.

Both sides pursued rival strategies. The KMT hoped to implement a 'vertical' strategy of controlling all south–north routes from the Yangtze to Peking and the Great Wall. In this way, Chiang hoped to fragment the communist armies and push them to the west for mopping up. The PLA, on the other hand, aimed at a 'horizontal' strategy of expanding eastwards from Shensi province to

the China Sea, splitting China in two.

Two major campaigns decided the outcome of the war. In September 1948 the PLA opened a Manchurian offensive which led to the fall of Changchun and Mukden (Shenyang). By now President Truman had decided that no American forces would be used to sustain the Nationalist regime.

The second closing campaign was the prolonged battle for the vital rail junction of Hsuchow on the north China plain. Following the final capitulation on 10 January 1949 after a two-month battle, it was estimated that the Nationalists had lost 500,000 troops. The PLA armies under Chu Teh now outnumbered those of the KMT; on 21 January 1949 Mao Tse-tung entered Peking at the head of his victorious troops. The People's Republic of China was proclaimed in Peking on 1 October and the Nationalist regime moved to Taipei on Taiwan (Formosa) where its standard was raised in December.

Power from the People

FOLLOWING THE COLLAPSE of the Kuomintang-communist alliance in 1927 and the virtual extermination of the Communist Party (CCP) apparatus in China's cities, Mao Tse-tung and his followers retreated to rural Kiangsi to carry on the fight. There, in the late 1920s and early 1930s, Mao began to codify the theory and practice of agrarian guerrilla warfare, or 'people's revolutionary war'.

He reviewed the failure of the CCP's operations during the 1924–27 period of coalition. There were three main errors: the CCP had subjected itself to formal Kuomintang (KMT) leadership and so made itself vulnerable; inadequate emphasis had been given to the place of the peasantry in the revolution; and insufficient stress had been placed on the armed struggle. The most important general lesson for the future was that there must always be 'proletarian leadership' (that is, complete direction by the CCP) if the revolution were to succeed.

Organisation of a guerrilla company

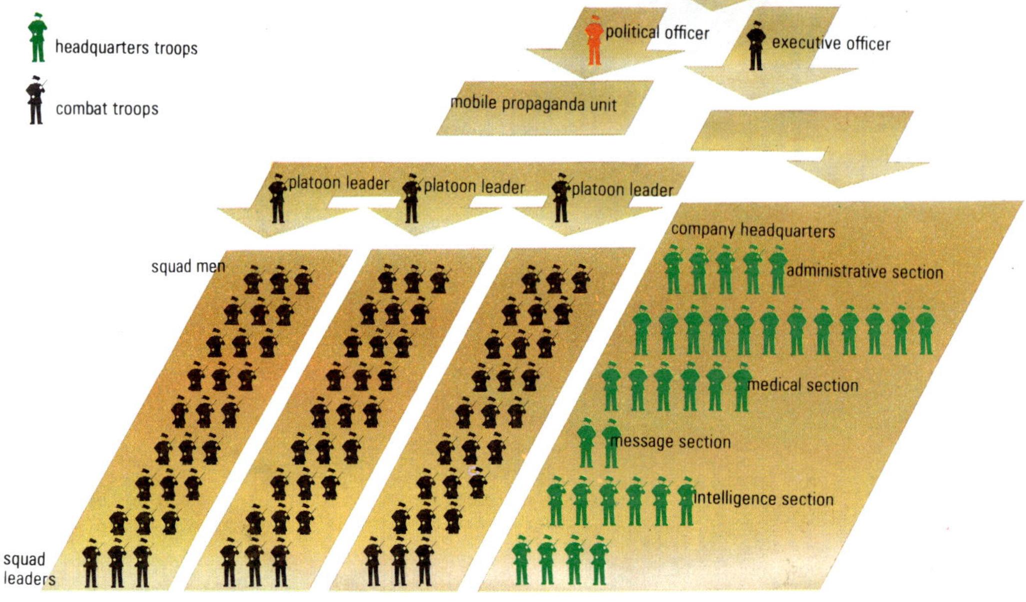

Whereas in the past, guerrilla warfare had been envisaged as ancillary or secondary to main military operations, Mao stressed that his version of guerrilla warfare had the primary strategic value of ensuring by itself the opponent's defeat. In this process, therefore, 'political power grows out of the barrel of a gun. . . . Whoever wants to seize and hold on to political power must have a strong army . . . we are advocates of the theory of the omnipotence of revolutionary war.' Maoist guerrilla warfare is therefore strategic warfare, not tactical warfare.

Within this context of complete party control and the need for total victory, Mao outlined three strategic concepts for the prosecution of the people's war in China.

Since China was a vast, underdeveloped country which had been in the throes of an unresolved social upheaval for decades, the correct course for the CCP was protracted guerrilla war in both time and space. Only through mobilising the peasantry would the initial strategic superiority of the KMT be neutralised. The first objective, therefore, would be to consolidate in the countryside. The cities would have to be the last to fall. As China had been exploited by the Western powers and Japan, so Chinese nationalism could be harnessed to the CCP's cause.

Secondly, operations would have to be conducted in three stages (see pp6–7). As a third central concept, Mao stressed that protracted war is decided by individual morale and not by weapons. The CCP must ensure the total political mobilisation of the masses under its control, as the revolutionaries are not concerned with attempting to win a quick victory separated from political goals.

The peasantry formed the basis of communist strength. LEFT *Recruits train with spears.* INSET *Mao chats with peasants in Yenan, 1939.* BELOW *This poster urged the militia to use grenades and mines in fighting the enemy.*

Leadership and ideology

Mao's central emphasis on the political nature of a people's war resulted in a two-pronged political strategy. Most emphasis was given to the indoctrination of new CCP leaders for carrying on the armed struggle.

The selected recruit was subjected to CCP propaganda, which focussed on the individual's own aspirations. The underlying assumption was that these aspirations could be satisfied only within the party context. Ideological, political and personal factors all converged to make the new recruit place membership of the CCP above everything else in life.

During 1942 a further refinement was added. An intense 'rectification campaign' was begun, aimed at 'correcting unorthodox tendencies' among CCP members.

The process of social mobilisation involved the party in setting up local organisations for the young, for farmers, and for other groups. The CCP was presented as the party of modernisation and equality, and simple drama productions brought home the message to the remotest villages under communist control. During this process the CCP stressed that the new life could be brought about only by the deployment of complete political power. Individuals had to submit to the wishes of the party for the good of all.

Complementing the process of creating a reliable elite was the basic political strategy of identifying for the masses one main enemy during each changing situation. In the 1930s the main enemy was the KMT, then later it became Chiang Kai-shek himself. From about 1935 to 1945 it was Japan but in the later 1940s the CCP began increasingly to identify the 'US imperialists' as the main enemy. Here the party looked forward to the new international situation that would face the communists when they became the government of the new China.

BELOW *The party inspired and directed the revolution. Plays, films and interest groups helped gain support in rural areas. Bases were then set up and the people mobilised for battle.*

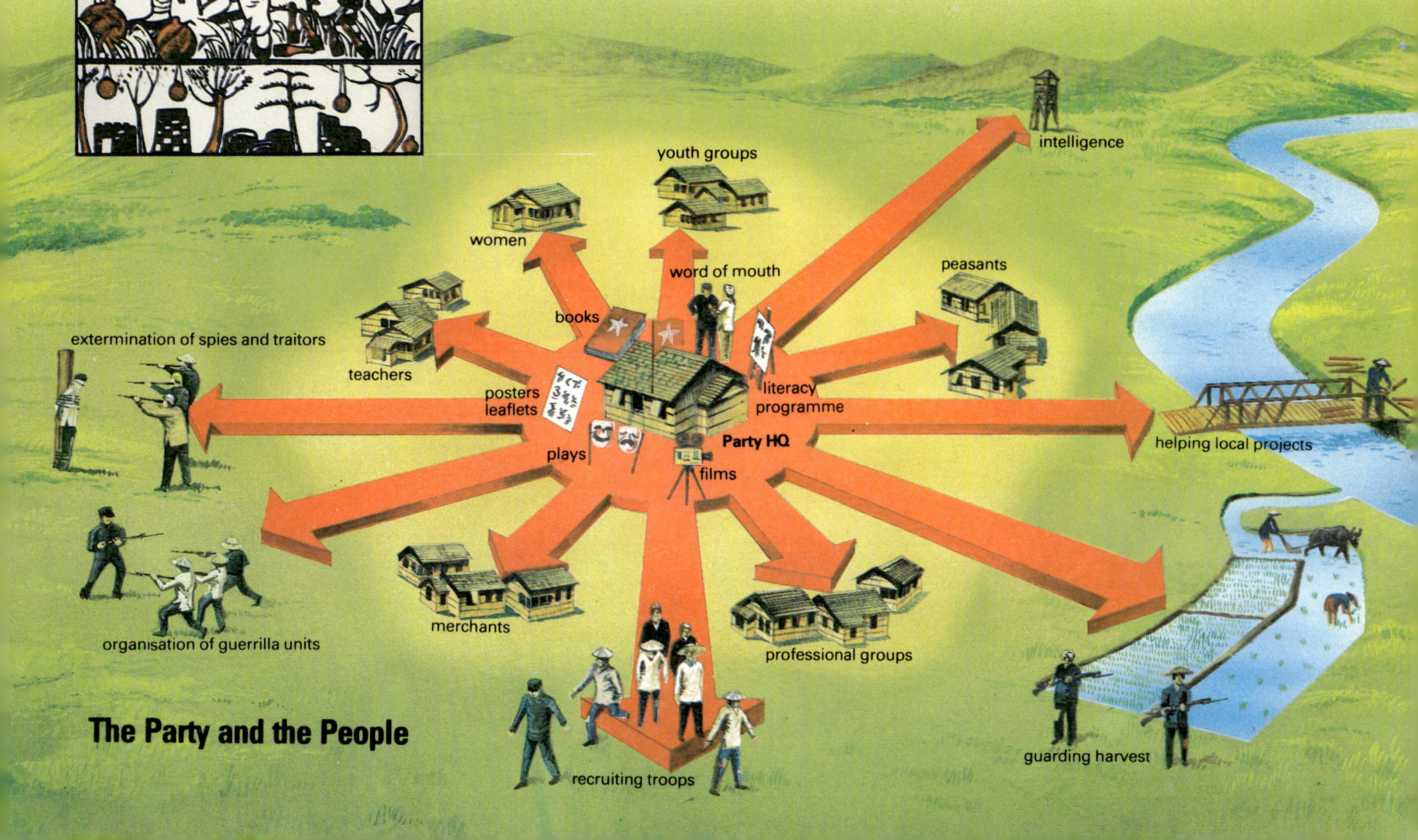

Guerrilla Warfare

Mao's 10 Principles

Attack dispersed and isolated enemy forces first, concentrated forces later

Win control of extensive rural areas and small and medium-sized cities first; take big cities later on

The main objective is to wipe out the enemy's effective strength

In battle employ superior numbers to annihilate the enemy; in this way inferior numbers overall will ultimately triumph

Do not go into battle unprepared

Fear no sacrifice or hardship

Use mobile warfare to defeat the enemy

Seize cities that are weakly defended

Use captured arms and troops to replenish strength

Use the periods between engagements to rest, regroup and train

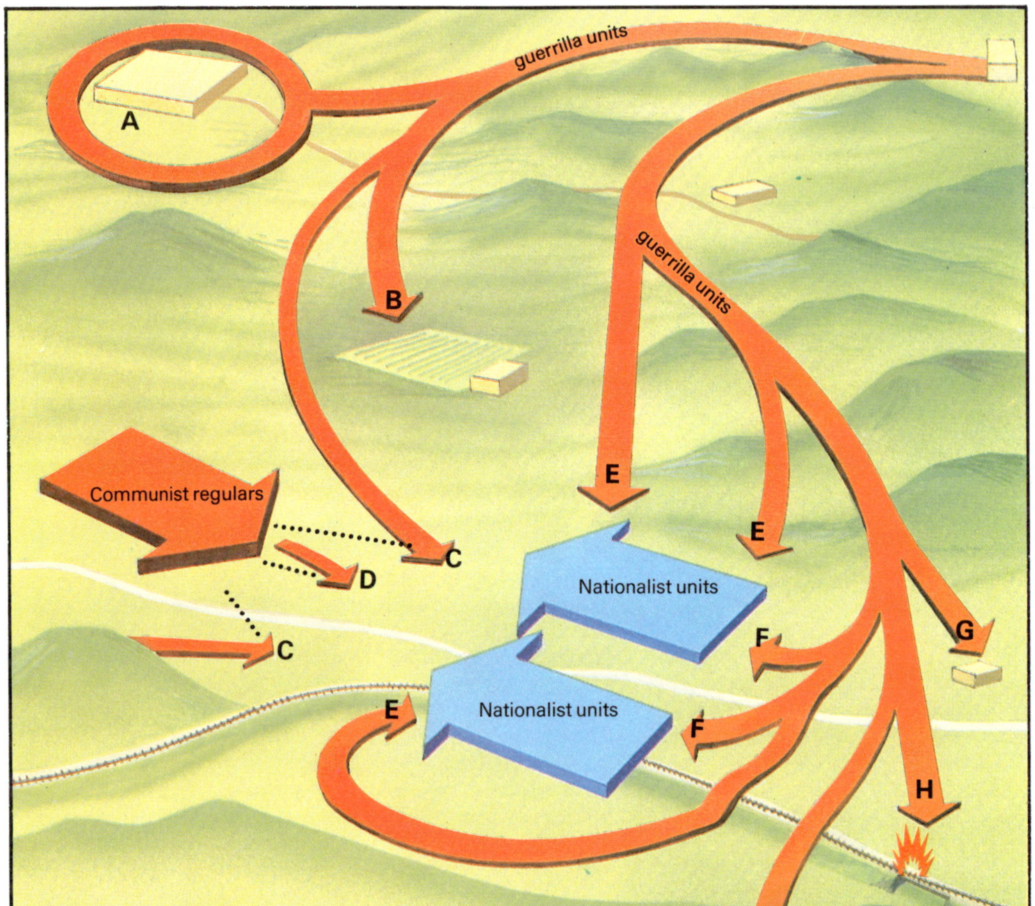

Operational tasks

A Confining enemy in towns
B Harvesting crops
C Reconnaissance
D Guiding regular units
E Harassing enemy
F Making front out of enemy's rear
G Attacking supply depots
H Disrupting communications
I Establishing new guerrilla base

IN HIS WRITINGS on guerrilla warfare Mao Tse-tung defined succinctly the difference between strategic and tactical operations. During the initial period of the people's war in China, he stressed, the Communist Party (CCP) forces would be outnumbered overall by as much as 10 to 1 by their opponents *strategically*. But by capitalising on their mobility, discipline and local support, the guerrillas could concentrate their effectives so that enemy detachments would be outnumbered 10 to 1 *tactically*.

The sum of these tactical victories over a prolonged period, combined with political work, would enable the guerrillas to improve their own strategic position.

The three stages

In this regard Mao foresaw three stages of guerrilla warfare. The first would be defensive, when the CCP was strategically weak. But in tactical operations the guerrillas must achieve local superiority, harass the enemy and capture weapons. Hit-and-run attacks would predominate.

The second stage is that of the strategic stalemate, when the enemy has reached his maximum effort. In this period the CCP would set up base areas, refine political and military strategy and begin equipping a semi-conventional army. This stage corresponds to the 'united front' period in China between 1937 and 1945.

Finally, the third stage is the strategic counter-offensive, when guerrilla operations escalate into mobile conventional warfare, corresponding in practice to the closing years of the civil war, 1945–49. The strategic initiative is now with the communists. The enemy has been worn down, his political, military and social infrastructure is collapsing, and all sections of his society are desperate for peace. In this stage Mao envisaged that the political defeat of the Kuomintang (KMT) would be already complete, and this factor explains the mass surrenders of the KMT armies in 1948–49 prior to actual military conquest. It is in this political, and even psychological context that the final phase of a Maoist people's war must be seen.

Guerrilla tactics

Mao elaborated on the guerrilla tactics to be employed, and which were used with mounting success against the Nationalists and the Japanese between the late 1920s and the 1940s.

When the limits of the enemy offensive were reached, guerrilla tactics should not only aim at concentrating a big force against a smaller force. The insurgents should also aim at a quick decision. To achieve this, enemy forces should not be attacked in a defended position but while they are on the move. Positional warfare should be avoided at all costs as it plays into the enemy's hands. The guerrillas must concentrate their forces under the maximum cover and camouflage along the predetermined enemy lines of communication. Then the guerrillas 'suddenly descend on him when he is moving, encircle and attack him before he knows what is happening, and conclude the fighting with all speed'.

Mao stressed that it is best to attack the enemy when he is on the move precisely because surprise is then easier to achieve. And surprise is essential to gaining the initiative. In achieving surprise the terrain must be carefully chosen. For maximum advantage the guerrillas must do everything to lure their opponents deep into their territory as far as possible.

These military tactics had, in one way or another, been used by guerrilla fighters from time immemorial. But Mao also taught that without accompanying political tactics, military tactics by themselves were inadequate. The objective of political tactics was to facilitate the social mobilisation of the peasantry by the Red Army.

The politics of war

The tactics of social mobilisation were necessary for a variety of reasons. Kuomintang leaders claimed the people's support, and were thus a competitor for the peasants' loyalty. It was necessary for the CCP forces to set a good example. Perhaps most important, a politically mobilised peasantry could supply the Red Army with recruits, food, transport and, above all, good intelligence in the fight against the enemy.

Although the development of the CCP's political activity began in the late 1920s it was only after the Long March of 1934–35 that a systematic programme was developed. Once based in north China the political department of the Eighth Route Army (as the Red Army was known after 1937) ordered that the local peasantry should be helped by the CCP forces whenever and wherever possible. CCP soldiers, for example, were told to pay for all goods and services requisitioned during military operations, and to assist the peasants with their own resources if the situation allowed.

Small landlords, who the CCP hoped to recruit for both political and military purposes, were not dispossessed. But the CCP made use of Sun Yat-sen's famous slogan 'Land to the tiller'.

Between 1935 and 1945, by means such as these, the CCP had not only organised a social base in north China, but also a village militia of 2 million. By 1945 CCP soldiers and activists were becoming the fish who swam in the sea of the people, as prophesied in Mao's famous analogy.

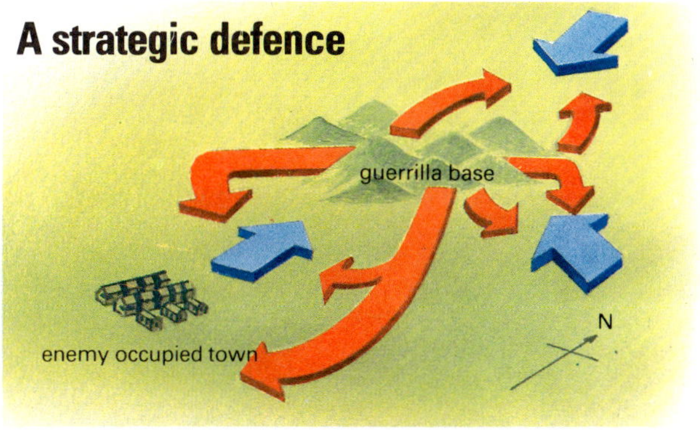

*Employing a strategic defence against a converging enemy attack often brought victory to the communists. The main guerrilla force would concentrate superior numbers against a single column (*ABOVE*, from the south) while secondary units contained the others. To prevent the column from obtaining supplies, an enemy-held town would be encircled (*BELOW*) and retreat would be impossible. Attention would then switch to each of the other enemy columns which would be wiped out one by one.*

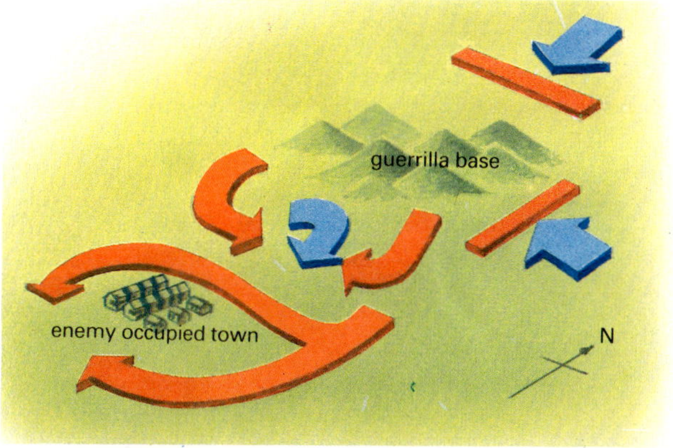

OPPOSITE *Guerrillas had to be mobile and carry their gear (and wounded) whatever the terrain.* ABOVE *Villagers overturn a section of railway at night.* BELOW *Peasants built straw men in order to confuse distant Nationalist observers as to the size of the communist armies.*

The Communist Armies

THROUGHOUT THE CHINESE CIVIL WAR, and for many years afterwards, the Chinese communist armed forces were distinguished by an extremely close relationship with the party. From the establishment of the Workers' and Peasants' Red Army in 1927, the events of the civil war made the political and military functions of the Communist Party (CCP) inseparable. Structurally army and party were virtually one.

From 1927 to 1935, the formative period of the Kiangsi soviet and the Long March, the communist movement was denied a permanent territorial base. In practice this meant that the functions of the party and army necessarily became intertwined. The Red Army was at the same time a personal bodyguard for senior party members, an offensive-defensive guerrilla force, an agency for civil administration and, officially, the armed forces of the CCP. The CCP leaders all performed military and political functions, and politburo members acted as generals. The party became increasingly militarised.

The party and the army

In the Yenan period, 1935–45, the civil-military union was reinforced as the party spread into north China and prepared for the final, conventional phase of the civil war. Army and brigade commanders were invariably senior CCP leaders. The party's chairman, Mao Tse-tung, was also its chief strategist.

As the civil war spread throughout China during 1946 the communist forces were designated the People's Liberation Army (PLA). In early 1948 the PLA was divided into six field armies corresponding to a major theatre of operations. The field army commanders performed political as well as military roles. Thus Lin Piao's 4th Field Army ruled Manchuria, and Chen Yi's 3rd Field Army governed the communist areas of north China. The system of six civil-military districts corresponding to field army commands survived the civil war.

Operationally, the growing fusion of the civil and military functions greatly enhanced the morale and the cohesion of the communist forces during the difficult period of the Kiangsi soviet and the Long March. The Sino-Japanese War and the Kuomintang-communist united front of 1937–45 gave the CCP an opportunity for both military and political mobilisation in north China.

Under these circumstances a remarkable growth in the communist forces occurred in the years preceding the end of the Pacific War. In 1937 the Red Army numbered not more than 100,000 effectives based at Yenan (now Yanan). These forces controlled a population area of about 4 million. In deference to the united front with the KMT, the Red Army became the Eighth Route Army; communist forces in the lower Yangtze (Changjiang) area were later designated the New Fourth Army. The change of nomenclature probably helped recruitment under the new 'anti-Japanese' slogans of the CCP.

Postwar growth

Under the aegis of the communist forces, the party's writ now spread to a network of 'liberated' base areas in

LEFT *Chu Teh, commander-in-chief of the communist forces.* BELOW *PLA troops pose with captured tanks of Japanese manufacture.*

north and central China. By 1945, according to Mao Tse-tung's later figures, the communist army had expanded to about 900,000 effectives, controlling a population area of about 95 million. The mobilisation of a village militia of about 2 million had by this time released from rear-echelon duties regular front-line combat troops. All these successes meant that the morale of the communist forces was high as the CCP faced the final phase of the civil war in 1945.

Not only troop morale, but organisation and leadership were of high quality as communist forces began to spread over north China and Manchuria in late 1945. These positive elements compensated for the fact that by mid-1946, 1.2 million communist troops were outnumbered by 3 million Nationalists.

More serious was the fact that with the ending of the Pacific War, the communist forces were under-equipped as they began to extend their essentially guerrilla operations into semi-conventional warfare. During the Kiangsi and Yenan periods, the CCP had captured many rifles and machine guns from the Nationalists. Increasingly, communist armouries in Yenan had manufactured light weapons and ammunition. But the final showdown underlined the need for modern arms.

The Soviet Army in Manchuria now came to Mao's help. During their *blitzkrieg* demolition of the Japanese Kwantung Army in August 1945, the Russians had captured vast quantities of Japanese arms. Most of these arms were now transferred, in one way or another, to Chinese communist forces during the winter of 1945–46. Other Japanese equipment was taken by communist forces in north and central China. According to figures later released by the Chinese communists, the Soviet Army provided from Japanese stocks more than 1200 cannon and over 360 tanks. The communists were also given 300,000 modern rifles, 4800 machine guns, and 2300 trucks. In aggregate, arms and equipment from nearly 600,000 Japanese troops were provided during the winter of 1945–46.

Moreover, as the PLA went over to the strategic offensive in 1947, ever-increasing quantities of military equipment were captured from the disintegrating Nationalist forces. In May 1947 the communists captured 20,000 rifles in Manchuria alone. By mid-1948, when the Nationalist armies numbered more than 2.5 million to 1.5 million deployed by the PLA, the two sides were equal in rifles and artillery.

The trend continued when in September 1948 the PLA captured 50,000 rifles and large ammunition dumps at Tsinan (Jinan). During the last four months of 1948 the Nationalists lost over 140,000 American rifles to the PLA. Losses of other rifles were several times this figure. By early 1949 the PLA was superior to the Nationalist armies in manpower, equipment and morale. The communist forces had triumphed.

The net result was that when the Chinese Civil War ended, the 20,000-strong guerrilla force which survived the Long March in 1935 had grown to an army of 4 million men. This force was capable of mobile and positional warfare alike, and was the largest army in Asia.

ABOVE *PLA soldiers wade through ankle-deep mud past artillery pieces dating back to World War I.* RIGHT *Cavalry cross flooded country in central China, 1947.*

Communist troop strength – regular soldiers

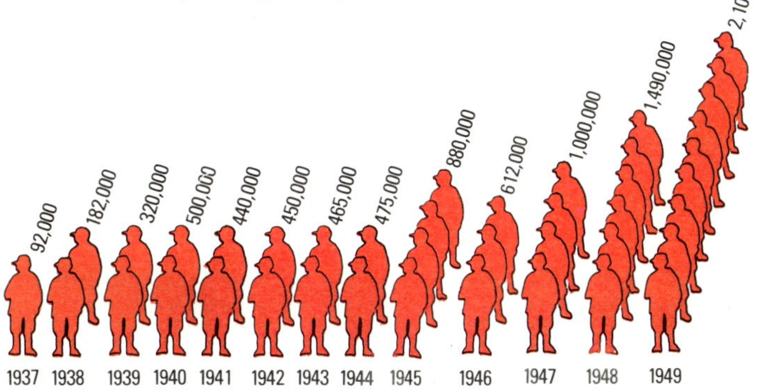

Communist troop strength – guerrillas

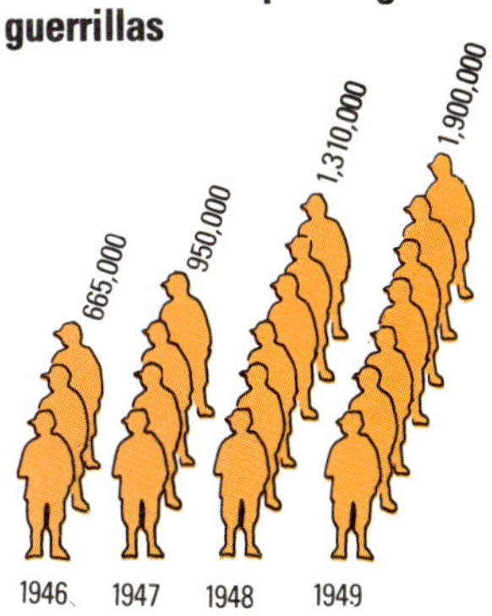

The Nationalist Forces

LIKE THE KUOMINTANG (KMT) ITSELF, the Nationalist Army had originally been restructured on the Soviet model by the Russian advisers in China during the mid-1920s. The KMT had emerged as a centralised Leninist organisation, and 'party representatives' or commissars had been attached to the Nationalist Army. In 1924 Chiang Kai-shek himself had been appointed the first director of the KMT's Whampoa Military Academy in Canton (now called Guangzhou), with the task of creating a politicised officer corps and a 'party army'.

Following the break with the communists in 1927, and the extension of his rule over most of China in 1928, Chiang set out to create a new Nationalist Army. This army was directly subordinated to Chiang's own GHQ as commander-in-chief. As Chiang became chairman of the Nationalist government's military affairs committee, the army soon became virtually autonomous within the Nanking (Nanjing) regime. Chiang's authority was reinforced by the creation of a military bureaucracy staffed by Whampoa graduates, politically reliable and absolutely loyal to Chiang.

Structurally and doctrinally the new Nationalist Army was to be patterned on the standard European model. In the early 1930s Chiang Kai-shek recruited a German military advisory group led by the former *Reichswehr* commander, General Hans von Seeckt. These advisers stressed high officer quality and formal line-of-command organisation through corps, division and brigade. They also stressed the virtues of positional warfare as practised in World War I.

Expansion in the 30s

By 1934 Chiang controlled a crack force of 300,000 men which drove the communists out of south China. But Chiang's essential military doctrine emphasised firepower rather than mass mobilisation and popular support. Moreover, the mobile guerrilla warfare which the communists were already perfecting in the mid-1930s

Nationalist and Communist Zones 1945

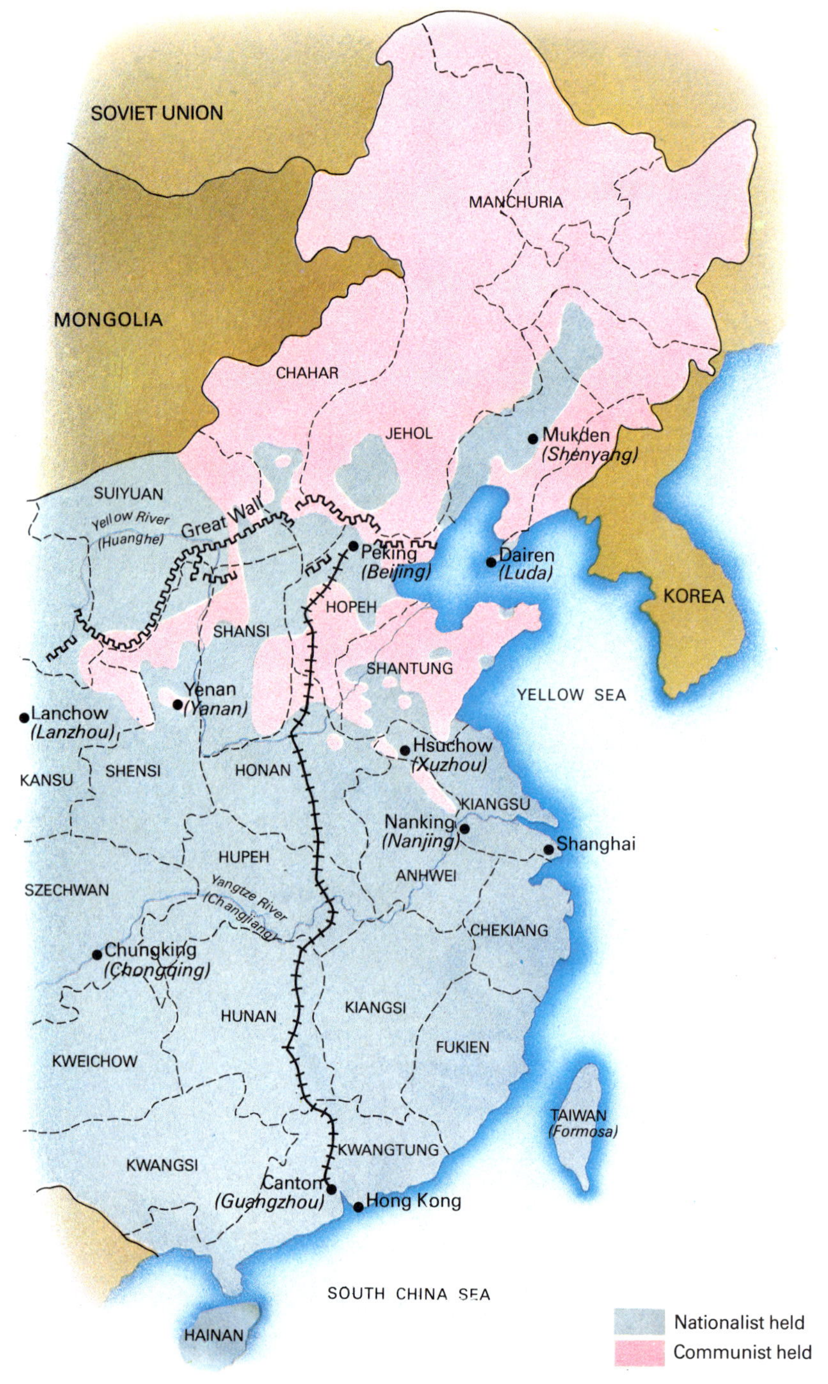

ABOVE *Chiang Kai-shek led a government and army that were riddled with mediocrity and of brittle loyalty. His own military direction was often erratic.* BELOW *Nationalist guns at Hsuchow in November 1948. The Nationalists' defeat at Hsuchow set the seal on eventual communist victory in China.* OPPOSITE *Nationalist wounded are transported from the battlefield to receive medical care. The lower photograph shows wounded troops huddled in a plane before being flown to a treatment centre.*

was the antithesis of the conventional Nationalist military approach.

Following the Japanese invasion of China in 1937, the Nationalist Army was expanded to about 1.7 million men. At first they fought well against the Japanese, leaving about 250,000 troops to contain the Chinese communists in the Yenan (Yanan) border region. But Nationalist China was cut off from its ports and cities, the regime was pushed into the poverty-stricken western provinces based on Chungking (Chongqing) and the relative military efficiency of the Nationalist forces began to collapse.

Against this background Chiang still managed to mobilise an army of about 4 million men during the later stages of the Pacific War between 1943 and 1945. But inflation eroded morale, it was impossible to supply the men with modern Western equipment, and the Nationalist forces inexorably turned into badly-led, badly-equipped and badly-fed levies. Nevertheless, Chiang Kai-shek was determined to husband his best forces for the coming showdown with Mao's communists when the Japanese war ended.

With the formal surrender of Japan in September 1945 American Lend-Lease equipment now flooded into Nationalist China. The KMT re-established itself in east and north China. The United States had promised to equip a 39-division core of the Nationalist Army and this was completed in the winter of 1945–46. For the rest of the civil war the Nationalist Army was primarily equipped with US 0.30-inch rifles, US artillery ranging up to 155mm howitzers and standard US Army trucks and other heavy equipment which had served well in the European and Pacific wars. By early 1946 it was estimated that Nationalist troops had a 3-to-1 numerical superiority over the communists. They also had an overwhelming advantage in equipment.

Reasons for defeat

Two specific weaknesses increasingly limited the effectiveness of the Nationalist armies as they occupied the cities of north China and Manchuria during 1945–46. Firstly, they were badly led. During the Sino-Japanese War of 1937–45 more than 100,000 of Chiang Kai-shek's best officers had been lost. Accordingly, during the critical military operations in 1945–47, the Nationalists lacked the drive to implement their strategy.

Secondly, the Nationalists suffered from overconfidence which radiated outwards from Chiang Kai-shek. Much of the American equipment supplied to the KMT regime after VJ-day needed time for familiarisation and effective deployment. In practice, full use was not made of the American equipment, because the troops could not handle it correctly.

These specific weaknesses were compounded by the over-extension of Nationalist resources in Manchuria in 1946–47. American vehicles and other quartermaster equipment were used, against expert American advice, to occupy Manchurian cities. Chiang's best forces were soon tied down. There was not the personnel available to the Nationalists to administer Manchuria, exploit its resources or to fight increasingly mobile communist columns which were now effectively armed with transferred Japanese weapons. Meanwhile the KMT was increasingly losing the political war.

The collapse

The net result was that by 1947–48 Nationalist forces in north China and Manchuria were encircled in the cities and only willing to wage positional warfare which they could not eventually win. Moreover, their numerical strength declined as a result of desertions, and large amounts of American equipment fell into the hands of the PLA. By early 1949 the Nationalists were outnumbered in men, rifles and cannon.

This disintegration of the Nationalist forces was compounded by the rigid command structure through which Chiang Kai-shek directed remote-control operations from Nanking. During the decisive battles in north China and Manchuria in late 1948 Chiang increasingly intervened over local commanders and threw in Nationalist divisions piecemeal. The alternative strategy of a strict regrouping south of the Yangtze (Changjiang) was never seriously considered.

In this way, the collapse of the Nationalist forces was complete by mid-1949, although three years earlier they had seemed far superior in men and equipment. The mobile political war that the communists were prepared to wage had proved itself the better of the brittle, conventional forces of the Nationalists.

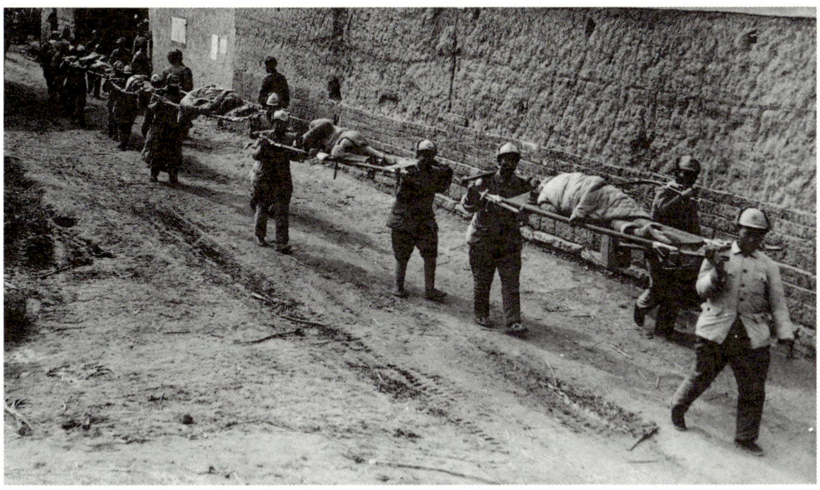

Nationalist equipment captured by communists 1946-49

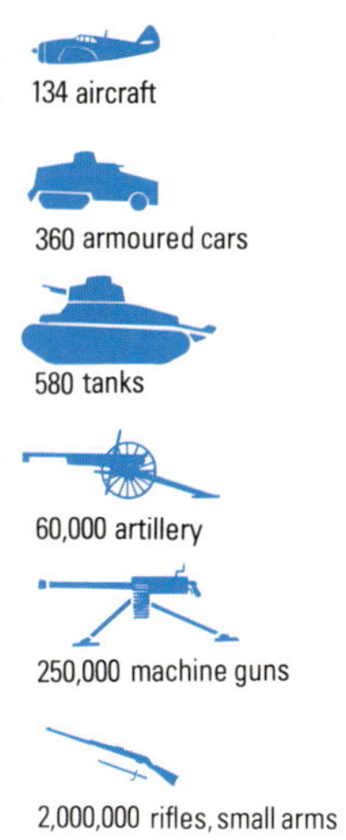

Strength of Nationalist forces

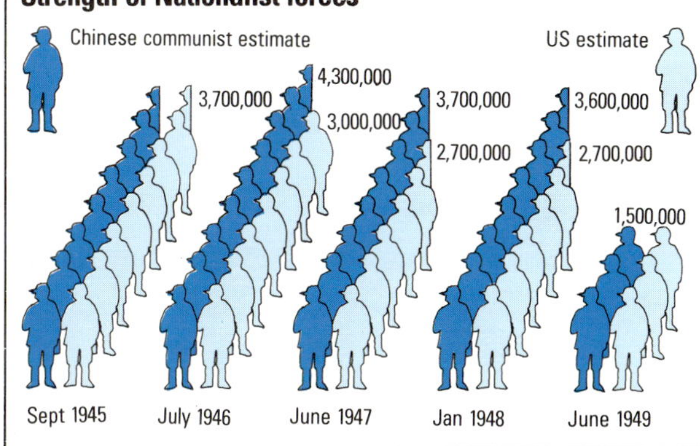

Manchuria

conquest of the north

THE BATTLE FOR MANCHURIA in October 1948 was the decisive phase of the Chinese Civil War. After it, communist victory was inevitable.

The roots of the Nationalist catastrophe went back to decisions taken by Chiang Kai-shek in November 1945, shortly after the Kuomintang (KMT) reoccupied north China. At that time, the generalissimo took the decision to move into Manchuria in force with his best divisions as soon as the Russians withdrew.

ABOVE *The rival commanders in Manchuria: Lin Piao (left) and Wei Li-huang.* BELOW *Troops storm a walled city near Mukden.*

A fatal error

In November 1945 General Albert Wedemeyer, the commanding general of American forces in China, firmly opposed Chiang's Manchurian decision on the grounds that it would lead to a potentially disastrous overextention of Nationalist forces. He argued that Chiang Kai-shek should consolidate his forces south of the Great Wall before attempting major entry into Manchuria. He also considered that the communists in Manchuria were already strong enough to harass Chiang's forces, so leading to 'a costly and extended campaign'.

Yet early in 1946 the Nationalist government began to pour its best troops into Manchuria in cities such as Changchun, the capital, and Mukden (now known as Shenyang). Logistically, all these forces were dependent on the 1600km (1000-mile) long railway which ran from Peking (Beijing), through the Great Wall to Chinchow (Jinzhou), Mukden, Changchun and across the Sungari (Songhuajiang) River to Harbin (Haerbin).

In May 1946 Nationalist troops routed the communists south of the Sungari and prepared to move on Harbin. But General Marshall's truce intervened and the communists regrouped. By January 1947 the PLA began a series of probing attacks along the Sungari while the Nationalist divisions were forced to dig in and guard the railways. In a matter of months Chiang's divisions had turned into garrison troops preoccupied with positional warfare, and wary of venturing into the countryside.

The isolation of the Nationalist garrisons was aided by the hostility of the province's inhabitants. They had welcomed Chiang Kai-shek's forces in 1946 as liberators from the Japanese and the Soviets. But the Nationalist forces were recruited chiefly from south and central China and soon began to behave like occupation troops. By the end of 1947 the setting of the final battles was already emerging. The Nationalist forces could not withdraw from Manchuria, but neither could they engage in effective military operations as logistical factors precluded real mobility. The result was a completely defensive mentality.

In late December 1947 Lin Piao's PLA forces cut all rail links into Mukden and isolated all other Nationalist garrisons. These garrisons still had enough firepower to repel direct

Nationalists return enemy fire. In the initial stages in Manchuria the Nationalists held major towns but the communists controlled the countryside.

attack. But the PLA continued to gain ground outside the perimeters, and in March 1948 the KMT forces in Kirin and Szeping (Siping) were evacuated to Mukden.

The siege of Mukden

This city, with its arms dumps and factories, now became the biggest Nationalist 'hedgehog' in China with a garrison of 200,000. A smaller force held Changchun, which was equally isolated. Resupply of the two cities continued by airlift.

In mid-September 1948, PLA forces under Lin Piao began the final phase of the Manchurian campaigns. Mobile columns feinted towards Mukden, as if preparing for direct assault. But the initial objective was the Nationalist base of Chinchow in southern

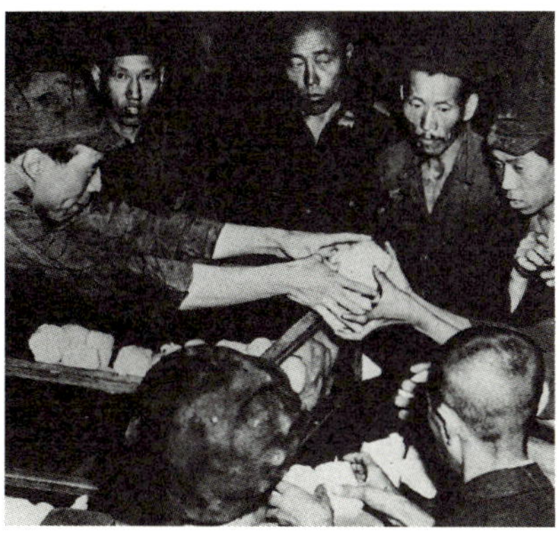

During the siege of Mukden food had to be rationed. Here bread is being distributed to factory workers.

Manchuria. Chinchow was on the main supply line that ran from Peking to Changchun. Here the Nationalists had stockpiled large quantities of arms, stores and food for the supply of their Manchurian divisions.

The commander of the Nationalist forces in Mukden, General Wei Lihuang, was ordered by the Nationalist high command on 25 September to relieve Chinchow. But Wei hesitated and delayed his departure from the Mukden perimeter until 9 October. In addition he used 11 divisions in the breakout and not 15 as ordered. General Wei ordered the Changchun garrison commander, General Cheng Tung-kao, to coordinate his own breakout towards Chinchow at the same time, but there was no acknowledgement of this order from the Changchun commander.

As the PLA stepped up the momentum of their attack, the Chinese Nationalist 93rd division defending Chinchow defected to the PLA and on 15 October 1948 this southern bastion of Manchuria fell to the communists. Chiang Kai-shek now flew from Nanking (Nanjing) to Peking and began giving direct orders to divisional commanders. The evacuation of all Nationalist troops in Manchuria was ordered.

On 19 October 1948, after further fighting, Changchun and 40,000 prisoners fell to the PLA after a partial defection of the garrison. Some Nationalist units in the region now attempted to reach Yingkow, on the Gulf of Liaotung, with the object of naval evacuation.

Field operations in the Mukden area were directed by General Liao Yao-hsiang. But Liao was killed in a PLA attack on his command post, which added to the general confusion.

The last ten days of October 1948 saw a general disintegration of the remaining Nationalist armies in southern Manchuria. On 27 October the last hope of breakout for the Mukden garrison vanished when General Wei's forces were defeated west of the city. Eventually Mukden itself, with its huge supply dumps, surrendered with about 200,000 prisoners on 2 November. Total Nationalist casualties in the final battle for Manchuria were 300,000 men. About 20,000 Chinese Nationalist troops managed to reach Yingkow for naval evacuation before its fall on 5 November marked the end of the Manchurian campaign.

The Battle for Manchuria

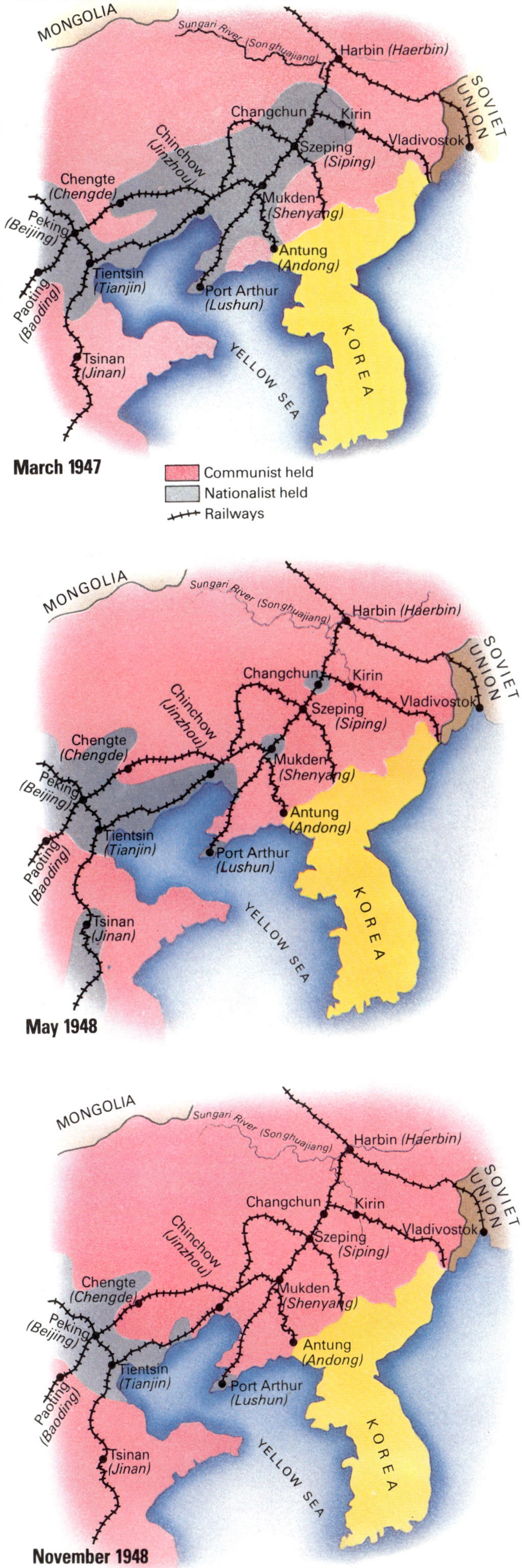

Hsuchow and Final Victory

FOLLOWING THE VICTORY of the Communist Party in Manchuria, the tempo of the Nationalist collapse increased dramatically. As divisions of the People's Liberation Army (PLA) moved south from Manchuria to the Great Wall and Peking (modern-day Beijing), large communist forces in north China began driving south to Nanking (Nanjing) and the Yangtze (Changjiang). General Chen Yi directed the PLA's 3rd Field Army.

The communist north China offensive was under way in November 1948. Opposing the communists were at least 50 Nationalist divisions, the bulk of Chiang Kai-shek's remaining forces, which were concentrated around the strongpoint of Hsuchow (Xuzhou) on the north China plain. On 11 November 1948 Nationalist spokesmen in Peking stated that the greatest battle of the Chinese Civil War was in progress around Hsuchow. It was claimed that the scale of operations was bigger than anything before and that 1 million men were in action on both sides.

From the Nationalist viewpoint, Hsuchow was a good place to make a stand. The city stood on the vital east-west railway where it intersected the north-south line from Peking to Nanking. A Nationalist garrison of some 150,000 was stationed there under General Tu Yu-ming. But if the communists could capture Hsuchow and the surrounding railway network then the PLA would command north China down to the Yangtze. Control of the Hsuchow area was thus essential for the PLA's final campaigns.

The communist offensive

In mid-November 1948 the initial communist advance was halted by strong Nationalist resistance. But, with great flexibility, the PLA continued to develop mobile strategy, and by the end of November Hsuchow was enveloped from east and west. Four Nationalist Army groups, amounting to more than 300,000 men, were now in danger of complete encirclement. Communist forces had also advanced south to Suhsien (Suzhou), 65km (40 miles) below Hsuchow on the line to Nanking. The town was soon surrounded, together with its garrison of 140,000 troops.

In early December Hsuchow city was abandoned by the Nationalists as they tried to fight south to Suhsien. But on 6 December the PLA claimed that these relief forces had themselves been surrounded west of the Hsuchow–Nanking railway. Nationalist capitulation was inevitable. There was no escape.

Several outstanding reasons may be given for this final military catastrophe for the Kuomintang (KMT). The theatre commander-in-chief, General Liu Ch'ih, was an incompetent officer who had been rewarded merely for his loyalty to Chiang Kai-shek. There was no unified command and Nationalist divisions had been committed piecemeal to the fighting. Again, as in Manchuria, the Nationalist strategy was dominated by positional factors while the communists were determined to exploit their mobility. The result of these cumulative factors was that the Nationalists were unable to make effective use of the modern American equipment they still pos-

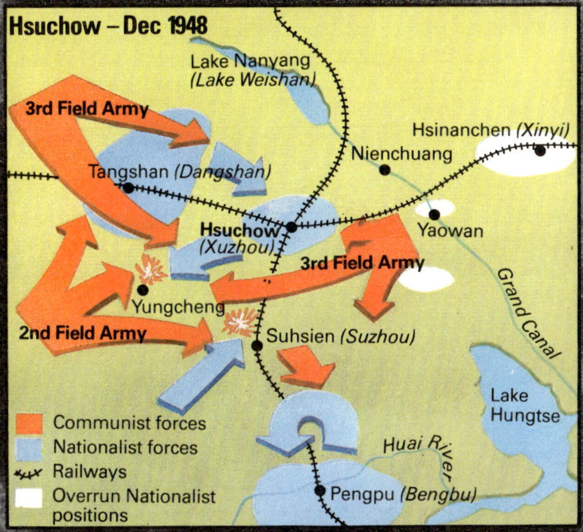

OPPOSITE *Victorious PLA troops, confident and well armed.* LEFT *The Hsuchow campaign began in November 1948 with the 3rd Field Army forcing the Nationalists north-east of Hsuchow to retreat towards Nienchuang before defeating them. In the west Nationalists around Tangshan fell back to Hsuchow. The city was evacuated in December but the retreating armies were encircled near Yungcheng. Support divisions from the south, bound for Suhsien, were beaten in battle or turned back.* BELOW *The communists take Lanchow in north-west China in August 1949.*

sessed. In addition, General Liu Fei, Chiang Kai-shek's military assistant, informed the PLA of the general Nationalist strategy. Later, General Liu defected.

In early January 1949, Chen Yi finally closed the trap on the Nationalist forces south of Hsuchow. The final surrender was made by the Nationalists on 10 January. The PLA claimed 320,000 prisoners in the campaign, and total Nationalist casualties were estimated at more than 500,000. So ended the biggest prolonged battle of the Chinese Civil War.

After the Hsuchow débâcle, the PLA continued to advance south to the Yangtze. By the end of January forward communist units had reached the north bank of the river. At this stage, on 20 January 1949, Chiang Kai-shek resigned the presidency of the republic, transferring his powers to Vice-President Li Tsung-jen. During the next two months as the communist armies prepared for the final occupation of China south of the Yangtze, the new Nationalist cabinet of Sun Fo attempted to negotiate with Mao Tse-tung and his politburo.

While these negotiations proceeded, the Nationalist government moved during February to Canton (Guangzou). That same month, Chiang Kai-shek, using his authority of director-general of the KMT, ordered the transfer of Nationalist China's gold reserves from Shanghai to Taipei on Taiwan (Formosa). Preparations continued for the creation of a Nationalist redoubt on the island.

On 19 April 1949 the negotiations between the Nationalist regime and the communists broke down. Resuming their offensive, PLA forces now crossed the Yangtze at several points, preceded by a tremendous artillery barrage. The Nationalist defence line south of the river crumbled, and on 23 April the former Nationalist capital of Nanking surrendered. Following the fall of Nanking, the PLA advanced on Shanghai, which was entered by the communists on 27 May. During the next four months PLA armies moved into east, south and west China meeting little or no resistance. Inner Mongolia and the province of Sinkiang (Xinjiang) were likewise occupied. In this way, by the end of 1949, the whole of mainland China came under communist rule.

After the proclamation of the Chinese People's Republic in Peking on 1 October, Canton fell to the communists on the 15th. The Nationalist government now moved to Chungking (Chongqing), China's wartime capital, and then briefly to Chengtu (Chengdu). As the communists advanced on Chengtu, the Nationalist government formally decided on 8 December 1949 to transfer their administration to Taipei. There the regime has remained ever since.

When Greek Meets Greek...

The Greek communist challenge of the 1940s was defeated by local antipathy, American aid and ructions within the communist movement itself

Sir Robert Thompson

THE GREEK CIVIL WAR, which in effect lasted from 1945 to 1949, was a defeat for communist guerrilla forces. The communists had, on some occasions, appeared to be heading for certain victory. But they made serious strategic mistakes; campaigns of terror rebounded against them, and the government forces, under General Alexandros Papagos, undertook a spirited and sensible campaign. The critical factors, however, lay outside Greece itself: massive American aid to the nationalist government and the gradual reduction in the support given the guerrillas by the neighbouring communist states of Yugoslavia, Albania and Bulgaria.

In 1941, when the Germans invaded, King George II and his government had gone into exile. The Greek Communist Party (KKE), led by George Siantos, became the core of the resistance movement and established a broad front organisation (EAM) which raised a Liberation Army (ELAS). Towards the end of the occupation ELAS began to form regular units and its commander, Stephanos Saraphis, prepared to take over the country. Churchill and Stalin had agreed in 1944 that Greece should come within the British sphere of influence, however, and ELAS never won Western support.

ELAS forces, now about 40,000 strong, attempted to take Athens after the German withdrawal; but British units defeated them in early 1945. Terms were accepted and signed as the Varkiza Agreement. EAM broke up as a front organisation and ELAS was destroyed as a fighting force. Thousands surrendered but a few hard-core elements took to the hills.

The Communist Party was divided between counsels of a political struggle or a continuation of the armed uprising, but the Siantos view prevailed and the party agreed to operate legally in Greek politics. It chose, however, to boycott the March 1946 elections, and in September King George returned to Greece after a plebiscite had decided in his favour.

Preparing for the main struggle

The stage was now set for the main civil war between the KKE and the Greek government, between the communists and the nationalists. The major difference from the previous period was that the KKE's support and training bases were now over the border in the new communist states of Yugoslavia and Albania, which were to be a complete sanctuary. A 'Democratic Army of Greece' (DSE) was established under General Markos Vaphiadis, probably the best of the communist generals, who was a firm believer in guerrilla warfare and the gradual wearing down of the Greek government.

The years 1945–46 were a build-up period for the communists, restricted to recruiting, obtaining supplies, sabotage of communications and general harassment by hit-and-run

BELOW *Countryside typical of the Greek Civil War. A government soldier, equipped with British uniform and armed with a British Bren gun, looks out over the fighting in the Vitsi mountains.* INSET *Communist guerrillas (one a woman) operate a water-cooled Vickers heavy machine gun. Such weapons could be difficult to move quickly and needed a large crew, but their high rate of fire over long periods made them invaluable for a sustained defence.*

tactics, with emphasis on control of the frontier area, especially the corner nearest Lake Prespa; but activity was spread throughout the country down to the Peloponnese.

By 1947 DSE forces were estimated at about 23,000 with 8000 in reserve and more in training over the border. Of these nearly 20 per cent were women. The underground organisation (YIAFAKA) was reputed to be 50,000 strong with 500,000 sympathisers. Government forces totalled about 180,000 but were deployed in small and scattered groups in defence of towns and villages. The Greek National Army (GNA) was static because the politicians refused to allow units to be moved from their own local sphere of interest. More than 700,000 people fled as refugees from the rural areas to the towns and the situation rapidly deteriorated without any major battles taking place. In the words of General Papagos: 'The national forces were in danger of losing the war without fighting it.'

The fighting in Athens in January 1945. A British private prepares to fire at ELAS troops trapped in a burning house.

American aid

The government appealed to the United States and President Harry Truman, in March 1947, went before Congress and asked for 400 million dollars in aid for Greece and Turkey. 'It must be the policy of the United States,' he said, 'to support free peoples who are resisting attempted subjugation by armed minorities or by outside pressures.' So was born the Truman Doctrine. An American Military Advisory Group was established in Athens and by August American supplies and equipment had begun to arrive.

This caused the Communist Party to accelerate its programme. On 24 December it decided to establish a 'Free Democratic Greek Government' and attempted to capture Konitsa as a capital on Greek soil. This failed as had similar previous assaults on both Konitsa and Florina. The Soviet Union did not recognise the new government and no international brigades materialised to fight on its side.

The year 1948 was, nevertheless, touch and go. The GNA went over to the offensive and tried to destroy the ELAS base areas in the Grammos and Vitsi mountains, but with only temporary success. The DSE extended its guerrilla activity into populated areas, murdering government sympathisers and kidnapping recruits, including over 10,000 children aged under ten years, who were abducted across the border. These abductions, condemned by the United Nations, lost the communists much sympathy around the world. The government was able to take harsher measures and pressure to make terms with the Greek Communist Party was reduced.

The communist failure

Circumstances on both sides changed dramatically in 1949. General Papagos was appointed commander-in-chief of the GNA with full powers to deploy the army as required, while General Markos, allegedly on grounds of ill health, was relieved of command of the DSE and was succeeded by Nikos Zachariades. Whereas Markos had favoured the continuation of political and guerrilla warfare Zachariades preferred conventional warfare to defeat the Greek Army before its reorganisation and the build-up of American aid had become fully effective. This strategy was premature, however, and the DSE conversion into conventional brigades, divisions and corps simply presented the Greek Army with easier targets.

The intention of the Cominform (an international body established by nine national communist parties) to create an independent Macedonian state rallied many nationalists and doubters to the Greek government's side. Yugoslavia's defection from the communist bloc also gradually deprived the DSE of its best outside supply and support, and Marshal Tito finally closed the Greek–Yugoslav frontier to the DSE in July 1949.

Some causes of the communist defeat were therefore of their own making but that should not detract from General Papagos's brilliant campaign. Using the minimum forces to contain the communists in their mountain bases he concentrated first against the Peloponnese. Just as important, he directed that the initial attack should be against YIAFAKA to destroy its intelligence network and control over the population. All known communist sympathisers in the designated area were rounded up so that communist units, deprived of support and intelligence, were soon broken up.

The last stages

By early spring the Peloponnese had been cleared and by mid-summer the same tactics cleared central Greece. In August, having feinted first against the Grammos base area, Papagos launched a concentrated attack against the Vitsi base. The DSE forces, about 7500 strong, decided to defend their base in the conventional tactics of positional war instead of withdrawing when faced with superior strength. This was a fatal error and by the middle of the month they were routed. A few remnants escaped through Albania to reinforce the Grammos base, which Papagos attacked on 24 August. By the end of the month it was all over.

The communists lost not only their military forces but also any claim to popular support within Greece. The Communist Party attempted to save face by announcing that it had ceased operations in order to preserve Greece from destruction. The war, however, left a bitter legacy from which Greece is only just recovering.

Mountain Warfare

THE BITTEREST FIGHTING of the last phases of the war took place in the mountains. Although mountainous terrain favours hit-and-run guerrilla tactics, the government forces, making full use of air power, showed that guerrilla forces had to be wary of risking any confrontations, even in such seemingly favourable terrain.

Many of the mountain ranges of Greece rise to more than 1500m (4920 feet), and some to over 2700m (8858 feet). About 40 per cent of the population, a hardy peasant stock, lived in scattered villages in the mountain valleys where roads were poor or non-existent. In the winter the mountains were made even more inaccessible by rain and snow. This was not, however, always to the advantage of the guerrillas because government forces were better equipped and clad and could recover afterwards in warm barracks, whereas many guerrillas died of cold and exposure.

Only one main-line railway ran north from the Peloponnese through Athens to Salonika, after which it branched to Yugoslavia, Bulgaria and Turkey. It was an important means of supply for German forces in Crete and North Africa and almost the whole of its length was vulnerable to sabotage. During the occupation, British demolition squads, assisted by EDES and ELAS guerrillas, twice dynamited one of the three viaducts south of Lamia which were guarded by Italian troops, putting the line out of action for several weeks.

In the final stage of the civil war the most important geographical feature was the long border with Albania, Yugoslavia and Bulgaria, which the Greek Army was unable to defend. It provided the communist forces with a reliable sanctuary and secure lines of logistic support within a few miles of many government-held towns, often shelled from across the border.

The Greek government neither crossed the border nor retaliated for fear that these communist countries might intervene on behalf of the Greek guerrillas. The communist

The Grammos mountains gave the guerrillas a quick escape route to Albania. ABOVE *A government border lookout.* BELOW *GNA troops scale a hill held by the communists.*

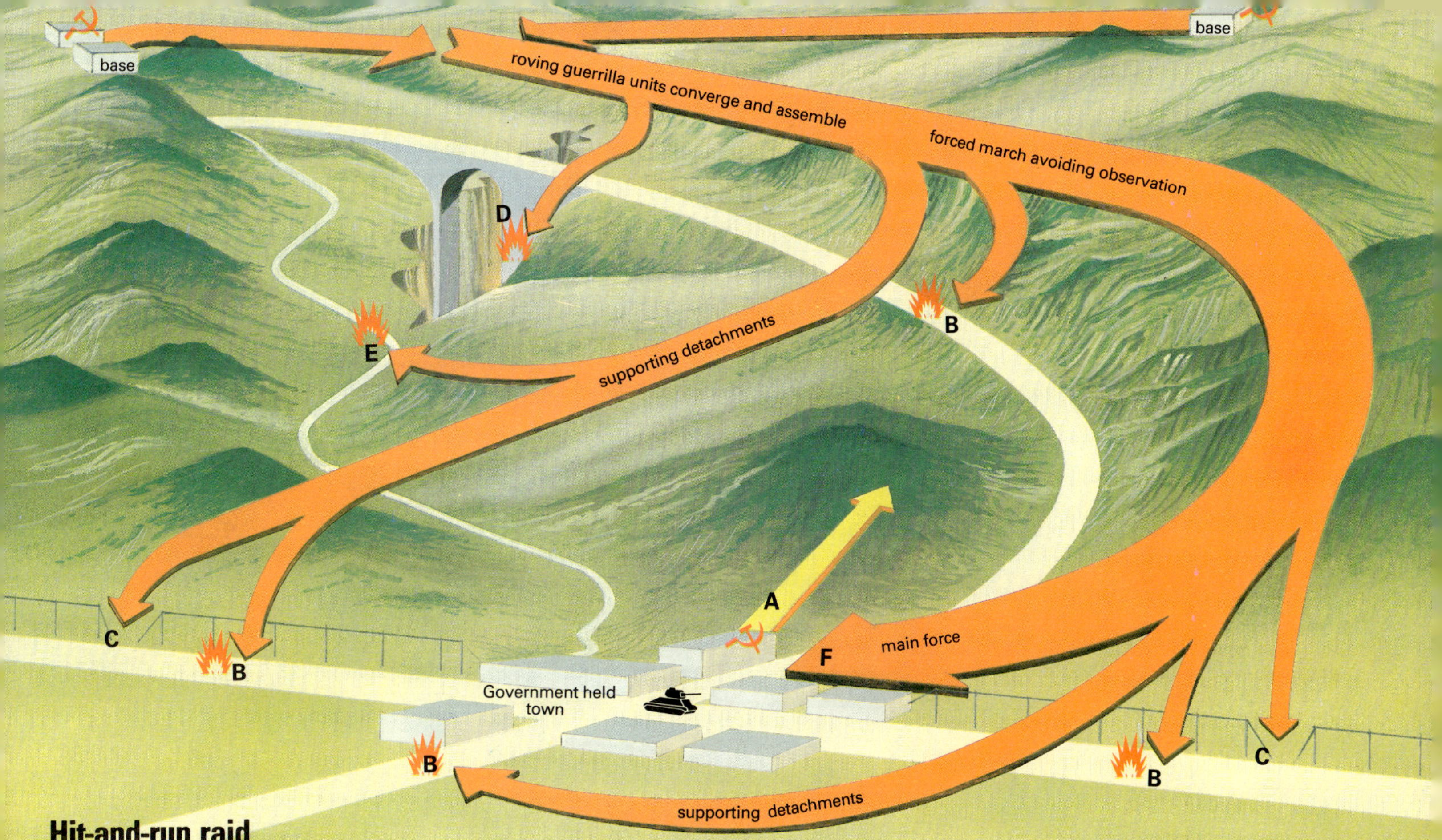

Hit-and-run raid

- **A** Communist agents inform guerrillas of town layout
- **B** Roads mined
- **C** Telephone lines cut
- **D** Bridges dynamited
- **E** Mountain trail mined
- **F** Main attack force enters town

neighbours were, in turn, equally restrained (for example, no aircraft from over the border ever supported the guerrillas) for fear of provoking greater American aid or even intervention.

Weapons and tactics

During the occupation the guerrillas' weapons, mostly gleaned from the battlefields, were a mixture of Italian and British origin. As a result there was a constant ammunition re-supply problem. When ELAS was defeated in 1945 it handed in more than 40,000 rifles, 2000 machine guns, 160 mortars and 100 pieces of artillery. These were all old weapons; newer German weapons were cached.

Later, Soviet supplies became available including rifles, mortars, flamethrowers, field guns up to 105mm and anti-aircraft guns (four or five Greek Air Force planes, including a Spitfire, were shot down). Some small naval craft were used round the coasts and even one old Italian submarine for the transport of supplies.

After 1945 the chief guerrilla offensive tactic was hit-and-run attacks on villages to capture arms and food, kill government sympathisers, abduct hostages and conscript recruits. The effect of this was to cause the government to spread its forces defensively throughout the country. Even some major assaults, with forces of more than 2000, were made on frontier towns such as Konitsa and Florina, partly for the same purpose, but also in an attempt to establish a liberated area for the newly-announced communist government. One intended effect of all these attacks was to create more than 700,000 refugees who fled into the coastal areas where they stretched government resources.

The communists adopted a totally different attitude to the villages after 1945 compared with the occupation period. Earlier on, the villages had been the main source of support, supply and recruits for ELAS, but after 1945 this was markedly less so. Supplies now came from over the border and most recruits were young men and women, with idealist and left-wing views, from the towns. Moreover, whereas the villagers were ready to support ELAS on patriotic grounds against the German and Italian invaders, they were less ready, being conservative and traditional in outlook, to support the new communist armed force, the DSE, against the constituted government (although in many cases there was a small fifth column to help the attacker).

For ELAS the villages were bases but for the DSE they were military targets. This, together with the costly casualties incurred in such attacks, especially when they failed, accounts for the fact that the DSE strength at its peak was little over 25,000.

This lack of mass popular support in the mountains was a critical element in the failure of the DSE. For although they might have some short-term success in their raids, they were basically engaging in a straightforward military struggle.

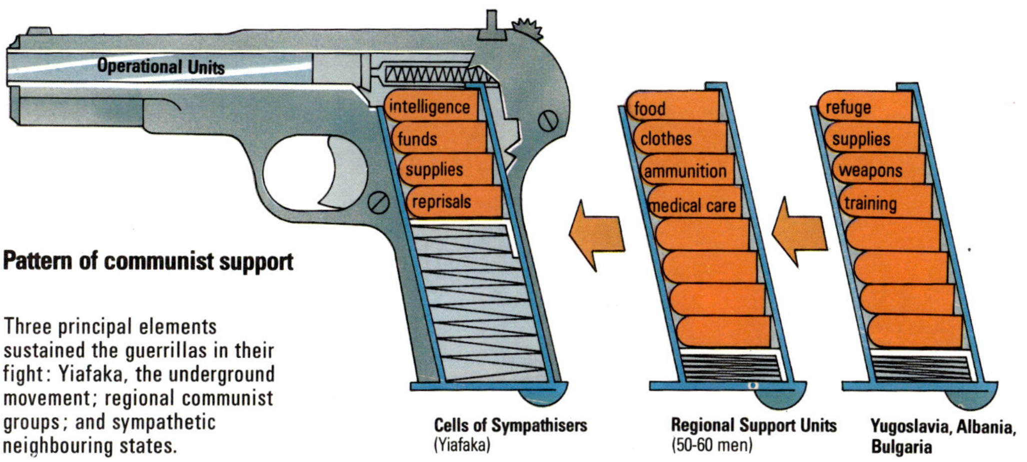

Pattern of communist support

Three principal elements sustained the guerrillas in their fight: Yiafaka, the underground movement; regional communist groups; and sympathetic neighbouring states.

Mules and dive-bombers

The Greek National Army (GNA) had to solve enormous problems in the mountains. Tanks and armoured vehicles could rarely be used, and although American aid included 8000 trucks, 4000 mules were found to be more of a help. The GNA was mainly equipped with British weapons until the arrival of United States equipment, which in the final year included 50 Curtiss Helldivers. With their cannons, rockets and two tons of bombs each, the Helldivers played a major role in the final assault on the Grammos and Vitsi mountain bases.

When on the defensive in the mountains the guerrillas usually dispersed in the face of superior government forces and returned to the area after they had left. In some districts near the border, however, the DSE refined this tactic by making an initial stand, thereby inducing the government to deploy large forces in an attempt to encircle the area, and then, at the very last moment, retreating and escaping across the border.

On one occasion in the Grammos base in August 1948, General Markos Vaphiadis almost left it too late and had to fight his way out through the last narrowing gap, carrying 3000 wounded. In this particular battle the GNA had about 40,000 men deployed against 8000 DSE.

The guerrillas were now irretrievably losing, however. They were fighting doggedly, but were basically involved in raiding against a better-equipped enemy, who realised that a patient deployment of its overwhelming force would bring victory.

In the final year, when Nikos Zachariades made the mistake of standing and fighting it out, admittedly in well-fortified positions with concrete emplacements and plenty of barbed wire, the GNA with its American firepower was too much for the DSE, as the British Army had been for ELAS when it stood and fought in the suburbs of Athens and Piraeus. Guerrilla forces are at their most vulnerable when they convert to conventional warfare prematurely.

Cost of the Civil War

In January 1951 the Greek General Staff weekly newspaper, *Stratiotika*, published a summary of losses suffered during the war. It gave Greek Army deaths as 12,777, with 37,732 wounded and 4527 missing. It said a further 4124 civilians and 165 priests had been executed by the communists. Deaths from land mines were said to be 931. Livestock lost included 114,754 cattle and 1,365,315 sheep, pigs and poultry. There were 476 road bridges and 439 railway bridges destroyed; 80 railway stations burned; 24,626 houses totally demolished and a further 22,000 partly destroyed.

Estimates of the number of communists killed vary greatly, but 38,000 is considered a reliable figure; 40,000 were captured or surrendered.

LEFT *Mules played a crucial role in supplying GNA troops.* TOP *Captured communist guns.* ABOVE *US-delivered Curtiss Helldivers inflicted heavy damage on the DSE.* BELOW *General Markos Vaphiadis (left), a skilled guerrilla fighter, led the DSE from 1946 until 1949.*

The Undeclared War

When the erstwhile allies fell out after World War II, the world teetered on the brink of nuclear disaster

Eric Morris

THE COLD WAR is the most convenient term to describe the confrontation of the late 1940s and the 1950s between the two great powers, the Soviet Union and the United States of America. Neither side made any move to threaten the other's most vital interests, and so the war never became 'hot'. But the political climate was certainly warlike in that each side regarded the other as the enemy, and on the minor level of propaganda and spying the contest was virulent. The Cold War also provided the essential backdrop to other wars of the period; all were seen as relating to this wider conflict.

The struggle was between two unevenly balanced contestants. The Soviet Union was a great land power whose army was capable of overrunning America's closest allies, the western European states. At the same time, American bomber and missile forces could – at any time – obliterate the main centres of the Soviet Union while the United States was, until the late 1950s, relatively invulnerable to a Soviet counter. These mutual threats maintained a constant level of tension.

The United States had a strong navy and worldwide power, but a major weakness in that her European allies were in the throes of losing colonial empires. While the United States disapproved of these empires it feared they would fall under communist control, as happened, for example, in North Vietnam in 1954. The collapse of these great empires was another complication which added to world tension by providing an element of uncertainty about the future of large areas of the globe.

A further general aspect of the Cold War was the perception each side had of the other as a monolithic system attempting to dominate the world and destroy the very essence of the other's civilisation. The concept of a world defined merely by the clash of two unified state systems bore some relation to the situation in the late 1940s, but by the early 1960s the world was clearly a more complicated place. European colonialism was seen to be a spent force and there were many new independent nations, such as India, taking a more prominent place in international affairs.

Most important of all, China's split with the Soviet Union had added a new dimension to big-power politics. The broader vision of a more 'pluralistic' world coincided with general acceptance of the division of Europe, and this can be said to mark the end of the Cold War. Tension and rivalry remained, but no longer in quite the same polarised manner.

A German cartoon from the last years of World War II looks toward the postwar world. The former Allies prepare to take each other on in order to assert final world dominance.

Origins of world tension

Where do the origins of the Cold War lie? Some maintain that it can be traced back to the Russian Revolution of 1917, which brought into being a nation state with a set of philosophical and political values that was bound, in time, to rival the creed of countries with parliamentary political systems and capitalist economies. This school of thought believes that the ideological incompatability between Marxist-Leninism and Western democracy is central to the Cold War period.

Opposed to this is another view, the one taken here, which sees the origins of the Cold War in much more recent times. In this view the challenge posed by the Soviet Union was evident in 1941 after Nazi Germany's invasion of the USSR, when Josef Stalin presented Anthony Eden, the British Foreign Secretary, with the Soviet Union's territorial demands in postwar Europe. A period of accommodation followed in the joint effort to defeat Germany, and Stalin's demands ultimately became reality. The Soviet demand for territory sprang from the fusion of imperialism with Marxism and the insistence on security.

More than 30 years have elapsed since the defeat of the Axis powers and, as more documentary evidence is publicly released by governments in the West, there is increasing opportunity to reassess international affairs in the Cold War period. Nevertheless, untampered Soviet archives are not available for scrutiny, so it is difficult to apportion 'blame' for the hostility that marked relations between the two superpowers.

Two schools of thought are worthy of mention. One sees in Russian foreign policy a mixture of old-style imperialism and the desire to extend the influence of communism in Europe. It was to this challenge that the West responded.

The other viewpoint lays the blame on the United States as a nation that was boastful of its economic and military strength at a time when other countries were trying to recover from the ravages of war. Its sense of power was bolstered by its possession of the atomic bomb. The determined anticommunism of President Harry S. Truman, runs this argument, reflected his desire to expel the Soviet Union from east Europe. Such an attitude provoked what was essentially a defensive response by Stalin.

Neither of these opposing viewpoints are wholly satisfactory. Both the United States and the Soviet Union acted in ways that promoted tension during these years.

Europe in 1936

Big-power politics

Although the Western allies held genuinely free elections in the areas of Europe they controlled after the end of World War II, the Soviet Union failed to do so despite promises that it would. Western powers protested at the progressive 'Sovietization' of eastern Europe and Poland in particular, and this became a fundamental cause of apprehension in the West. Sir Winston Churchill's reference to an 'iron curtain' in Europe echoed widespread anxieties.

Stalin's conception of security was not just confined to the physical protection of the Soviet Union. He saw the east European satellites as a military buffer, it is true, but even more did they form the outer lines of defence against the ideological and psychological challenge that he saw emanating from the capitalist West. These states would need to conform to Soviet ideology.

Stalin feared capitalist subversion and insisted that the nations of the newly formed Soviet empire be utterly loyal and subservient to Moscow. He never lost his 'siege' mentality, his fear of encirclement by a hostile power. Accordingly, internal repression – manifest in purges of the party, armed forces, the intelligentsia and racial minorities – was considered a necessary expedient in order to be able to meet a possible military challenge.

By the time of Stalin's death in 1953 the potential rival of 1945 had become a declared enemy. By then western Europe had been consolidated into an anti-Soviet coalition under American leadership. From 1947 American policy was directed at 'containing' communism and rebuilding western Europe to enable it to withstand any challenge that the Soviets might launch. The Marshall Plan provided American aid on a huge scale to help the struggling economies of Europe (and provide a market for American goods). The North Atlantic Treaty Organisation (NATO) sought to build an integrated military defence force. And from 1953 John Foster Dulles, the American Secretary of State, warned the world in strident tones of the dangers of communism and the determination of the free world to resist its advances. The threat posed by the Soviet Union may have been exaggerated by American spokesmen but it seemed real enough at the time. Particularly was this so after mainland China had fallen to the communists and a Sino-Soviet bloc took shape.

Stalin's heirs, Nikolai Bulganin and Nikita Khrushchev, inherited satellites that had become a heavy burden on Soviet resources. The Warsaw Pact, formed in May 1955, was in part a response to a growing NATO, which West Germany had joined shortly before. But it also fulfilled another function as a vehicle for reform within the communist bloc, updating the relationship between Moscow and the satellites to make it appear more of a partnership.

The Warsaw Pact brought about much-needed improvement in the armed forces. Under Stalin, Soviet personnel had held key posts in the armies of Russia's allies. This, together with the obsolete equipment used, undermined morale and self-respect among national forces. The changing military climate, in particular the development of tactical nuclear weapons, placed greater emphasis on mobility and professionalism. The armies of the satellite countries would have to be modernised, and the Warsaw Pact was seen as a vehicle for reform.

United States policy-makers looked at the world in terms of possible armed conflict and sought to maximise military effectiveness. America wooed and armed its allies and sometimes tried to intimidate neutrals. All the while it built up its military strength, especially its nuclear strike capacity.

Secure in its nuclear monopoly and with the United States continent geographically invulnerable, the credibility of the American nuclear guarantee was unassailable – even

Communist expansion in Europe 1939-49

Before World War II (OPPOSITE TOP) *Europe faced a Soviet Union that was still preoccupied with domestic affairs. But from 1939* (TOP LEFT) *the Soviet Union boundary expanded and the westward advance of the Red Army later eased the way for communist takeovers in eastern and central Europe. Yugoslavia early established its independence, however.* OPPOSITE *Hiroshima after the bomb. The terrible possibilities of nuclear warfare added a new dimension to strategic planning.* RIGHT *The fireball of an American nuclear test, 1956.* ABOVE *Soviet troops link arms with Americans on the Elbe in 1945.* TOP RIGHT *Soviet T34s were used to put down rioting in East Berlin in 1953.*

with a strategy of massive retaliation, which threatened the Soviet Union with total destruction for even a minor incursion.

In announcing the principle of 'massive and instant retaliation' in January 1954, Dulles looked toward a global commitment in defence of freedom. America, he said, must be prepared to 'fight in the Arctic and in the Tropics, in Asia, the Near East and in Europe; by sea, by land and by air'. As Senator Joseph McCarthy pursued his witch hunt of communists, real or imagined, the United States pledged support for South Vietnam and prompted the formation of the Southeast Asia Treaty Organisation and the Baghdad Pact, alliances to prevent territorial gains by communists in Asia and the Middle East.

Conferences and crises

In such a manner did the United States and the Soviet Union dominate world politics in the 1950s, confronting each other from behind entrenched positions. The leaders met quite frequently, nevertheless. It was an age of 'summit' conferences. Invariably these meetings were concerned with such dominant issues as Germany and the position of the Western sectors in Berlin, but agreement proved elusive. These intractable problems reached a logical conclusion with the building of the Berlin Wall in August 1961.

On his inauguration President John F. Kennedy had caught the imagination of the free world by his clarion call of commitment to world freedom. 'Let every nation know, whether it wishes us well or ill, that we shall pay any price, bear any burden, meet any hardship, support any friend, oppose any foe, to assure the survival and success of liberty.'

When the Soviet Union began erecting missiles in Cuba in 1962 Kennedy acted with vigour and succeeded in having them removed. The Cuban missile crisis brought the world to the point of nuclear war and marked the high point of Cold War tension. But as in 1956 during the Hungarian uprising, when America respected the fact of Soviet eastern Europe, so, in 1962, the Russians learned that military involvement in the Western Hemisphere would never be tolerated. An understanding of sorts had been reached.

Problems of Peace

DURING WORLD WAR II, the major powers of East and West were drawn together in an alliance of necessity against fascist Germany. The collapse of this alliance marked the first stage of the Cold War.

Whatever the ideology of the participants such an alliance would inevitably have been placed under great strain, simply because the destruction of Germany – one of the most powerful states in Europe – left a vacuum which other powers naturally wished to fill in various ways. And the major powers involved were so different that sheer misunderstanding alone was likely to be an important factor.

The Western states, for example, had never understood the nature of Russian society, even under the tsars, and now the progress of the war brought this 'mighty Asiatic enigma' into central Europe and closer contact with the West than ever before. There, by 1945, the Soviet troops confronted those of the United States. Although she had attracted thousands of immigrants from diverse areas of central Europe, the United States had never had a long-lasting relationship with Europe. Through the accident of war the United States entered mainland Europe with unprecedented military strength and political influence.

Wartime arguments

Areas of discord had existed from the earliest days of the Grand Alliance. Many of these came to the fore in February 1945 when the Big Three – Winston Churchill, Josef Stalin and Franklin D. Roosevelt – met in conference at the Black Sea resort of Yalta.

Churchill and Stalin disagreed violently over Poland. Roosevelt, anxious not to upset Stalin lest it delay the Soviet Union's entry into the war against Japan, refused to support the British leader. Russia was allowed to retain the eastern third of pre-1939 Poland and promised 'free and unfettered elections' that never took place; Poland's destiny was consigned to Soviet tutelage. Nevertheless Yalta was not all rancour and dispute. With victory in sight the leaders agreed arrangements for the military occupation of Germany once the Nazis had capitulated.

On 12 April 1945, one month before Germany's surrender, Roosevelt died. His successor, Harry S. Truman, had not been involved in any of the great decisions or the strategic planning of the war effort. He had to read himself into the job and one of the first documents he studied was the Manhattan Project, the secret programme for building an atomic bomb.

At Yalta the Big Three had agreed not to meet again for at least two years until order and stability had been restored to Germany. But the death of Roosevelt and increasingly strained relations between the armies of occupation, caused in part by the Russian intransigence over Western entry to Berlin, changed all that. Truman was determined to meet with Stalin in an effort to heal the ever-widening breach between East and West.

The Potsdam conference

A summit was convened on 17 July in Potsdam. On the day the conference opened news reached Truman that an atomic test device had been successfully exploded in the Nevada Desert. The dawn of the nuclear age presented the Western leaders with all sorts of uncomfortable dilemmas: should Stalin be told; should the bomb be used against Japan; if so, did that remove the need for Soviet participation in the Far Eastern War?

Stalin had proved so awkward over Europe and Berlin that the Americans had no intention of allowing the

LEFT *Josef Stalin took a stubborn stand on Poland and Germany at the 1945 conferences. He wanted to ensure friendly states on the Soviet border and feared the resurgence of a strong Germany.* BELOW *A Soviet T34/85 attacks near the River Spree during the drive to Berlin in April 1945.*

same thing to happen with Japan. They informed Stalin of the bomb, though the Soviet leader displayed no emotion at the news. He did not have to, since some of the scientists working on the project were Soviet agents. Stalin was probably better informed than either Churchill or Truman.

From the very first there had been disagreement over the question of reparations. The Russians were extreme in their demands and they were supported by the French. They wanted the best of both worlds – a regular flow of reparations from the three Western-controlled areas of Germany and unfettered control over their own zone. Anxious to avoid the mistakes of the past, the Anglo-Americans did not wish to so paralyse Germany that she could no longer pay her way in the world. They also believed that Germany should be treated as a single unit.

An agreement of sorts was hammered out, but represented the worst of compromises. It would provide ample grounds for future trouble.

Poland, too, caused further dissent. Western leaders protested in the strongest terms over what they saw as the Russian abuse of power and presence, together with the arbitrary manner in which the borders had been redrawn; but Stalin was unyielding. When the conference finally came to an end on 2 August, little in reality

ABOVE *and* INSET *Berlin in ruins, 1945. Repatriated POWs prepare a meal amidst the wreckage.* LEFT *The city's division into sectors was an expression of European friction and tension.*

had been achieved.

Potsdam had done nothing to resolve the enormous problem of the future of Germany and thus, by implication, of Europe as a whole. German sovereignty, for all intents and purposes, passed into the hands of the victors with a four-power occupation which soon lost all semblance of unity and cohesion. The Americans, anxious to forgive, were determined to embark on a policy of rehabilitation. The Russians, mindful of the havoc wreaked upon their people, were equally determined that Germany should never again be able to make war on others. This was a viewpoint shared by the French, while American insensitivities to European fears served only to raise new doubts. Britain emphasised the overriding need to secure stability in Europe.

As memories of the fighting gave way to the urgent problems of peace, so relations deteriorated. The system of reparations had broken down completely by May 1946 when the West stopped all further shipments to the Russians in the eastern zone. The decision by the United States, Britain and France to amalgamate their zones and promote local government was seen by the Soviets as an attempt to undermine the agreements reached at Yalta and Potsdam. Germany was now divided in two – an American-dominated western zone, and a Soviet zone in the east.

When, in March 1946, Churchill made his famous 'iron curtain' speech in Fulton, Missouri, he voiced the unease of many. 'From Stettin in the Baltic to Trieste on the Adriatic an iron curtain has descended across the Continent.' It had been caused in part by the failure of the superpowers to work together in the pursuit of agreed aims. He wanted a tougher stand against the Soviet Union and a Western alliance supported by atomic weapons. The Grand Alliance had evaporated. The Cold War had definitely begun.

The European Divide

AS THE GRAND ALLIANCE of World War II dissolved in the emerging Cold War, the economic and political situation in war-torn western Europe got worse. Desperately cold winters created fuel and food shortages and national economies laboured under the rigours of slump and recession. To an extent, through newspaper articles and speeches, such as those made by Churchill, the American people had already been conditioned to the problems of western Europe.

In China the communists were making headway against Chiang Kai-shek and in eastern Europe the Soviets were consolidating their hold on Romania, Poland and Hungary. But it was the civil war fought between royalist and communist in Greece, together with the need to sustain a crippled Turkey, which provided the catalyst for a new direction in American foreign policy.

The Truman Doctrine

Up to 1947 Greece and Turkey had been sustained by Britain, but in February of that year Ernest Bevin, the British Foreign Secretary, made it clear that Britain, hovering close to bankruptcy, could no longer afford the scale of assistance required. He urged the United States to take up the task before strategically important territories in Europe came under Soviet control.

On 12 March 1947, in an historic departure in American foreign policy, President Truman went before a joint session of Congress and asked for $400 million in economic and military aid to enable Greece and Turkey to halt the spread of communism in the Balkans. 'I believe that it must be the policy of the United States,' he said, 'to support free peoples who are resisting attempted subjugation.'

The United States was now constitutionally equipped to assume its new role as the chief supporter of countries threatened by communist insurgency. It acknowledged that a contest of rival ideologies was being waged in the world.

Truman's words gave faith and hope to the west Europeans but did nothing to stop the continued decline in their economies. The United States recognised that a massive injection of economic aid was needed to bolster western Europe's precarious position. Only if it was economically strong could western Europe stand up to any communist threat.

General George Marshall, a distinguished soldier and now Truman's Secretary of State, offered in a celebrated speech to share America's bounty with the less-fortunate nations of Europe. The offer was open to all countries, communist as well. An international body would co-ordinate national demands and distribute the aid. At a conference to discuss the idea, the Western powers readily acquiesced though the Soviets walked out, taking the east Europeans with them. So the price for American aid and economic salvation under the Marshall Plan became the political division of Europe. Churchill's iron curtain had now become a reality.

It was hardly surprising that in an atmosphere of suspicion and mistrust Stalin should see the Truman Doctrine and Marshall Plan as a threat. The Marxist in him viewed with dismay the rejuvenation of Europe through the capitalist philosophy of Marshall Aid, while the tsarist in him saw in the Truman Doctrine the abandonment of American isolationism and the start of a brand new balance of power in Europe. For Britain these initiatives were exactly what Bevin had hoped for, although it marked the passing of Western leadership from Britain to the United States.

By the beginning of 1948 the Cold War had begun to intensify into sharply defined confrontation. The German question once more became prominent and the attention of the world focused on the first clash of the postwar superpowers. It was over Berlin.

Blockade of Berlin

For the West, failure to reach agreement with the Soviet Union over a single Germany policy had set in motion a train of events that were to lead to the partition of Germany into two states. Matters worsened in April when the West announced plans for currency reform in order to place the West German economy on a more secure footing. Then the decision was taken to set up an independent West German republic. The Soviets viewed this as an attempt to create a new German state which could one day pose a threat to Russia.

In a series of moves the Russians put pressure on road and rail links with Berlin, which lay inside the Soviet zone, and by June 1948 had effectively sealed off the Western sectors of the city. It was clearly the intention to force the Western powers out of Berlin. East and West came close to war. The American commander, General Lucius Clay, favoured driving an armoured regiment through to Berlin and American B-29s armed with nuclear bombs were deployed to East Anglian airfields. Britain, however, proposed an airlift to circumvent the blockade.

The Berlin airlift lasted for 318 days (the restrictions were lifted on

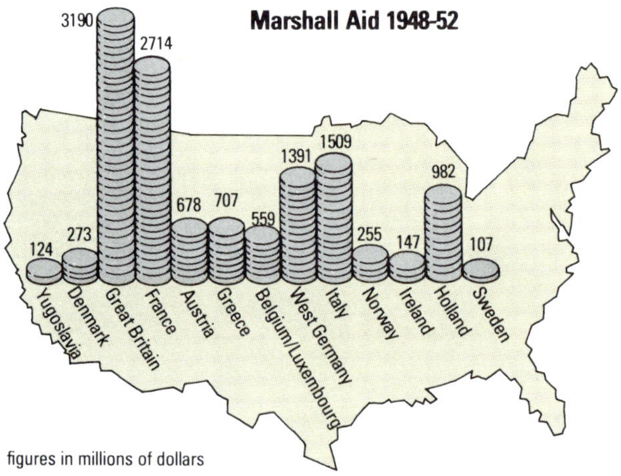

TOP *President Truman spells out the Truman Doctrine to Congress in 1947. It committed America to worldwide containment of communism.* ABOVE *Marshall Aid to Europe totalled $13,000 million.* BELOW *The communist takeover in Czechoslovakia: Klement Gottwald is sworn in by President Beneš (left foreground).*

12 May 1949). During that period Allied aircraft lifted 1,500,000 tonnes of supplies into the beleaguered city in more than 200,000 flights.

The year 1948 was crucial. Not only was Berlin blockaded but Czechoslovakia was finally brought into the communist bloc when the democratic constitution was stifled in February. To the western European states, Russian intentions seemed unmistakeable.

Bolstering western Europe

The Soviet Union maintained some 25 divisions in central Europe. To counter this threat west European governments and the United States took steps towards forming a military alliance. The North Atlantic Treaty, signed in Washington on 4 April 1949 by 12 nations, stated that an armed attack on any one member would be regarded as an attack on all. The North Atlantic Treaty Organisation had the task of co-ordinating the various military forces. Again the United States had demonstrated its support for a policy of containment, this time backed by military alliance.

The last step in formalising the division of Europe was the emergence of the Federal Republic of West Germany. For some months a specially convened constituent assembly had been negotiating a constitution with the Allies. Though the Russians sought to obstruct the process, the Allies were determined that the creation of West Germany should not become a bargaining point. On 12 May 1949 Konrad Adenauer, the chief German spokesman and soon to become the republic's first chancellor, learned that the new constitution had been approved. Almost four years to the day since the formal surrender, a new Germany was on the point of emerging from the ashes of defeat.

LEFT *A pamphlet cover shows NATO's role as a shield against attack.* BELOW *At the height of the Berlin airlift 1400 flights entered West Berlin daily. The most common planes used were Dakotas, Yorks, Sunderlands and Haltons. Each air corridor was 32km (20 miles) wide.*

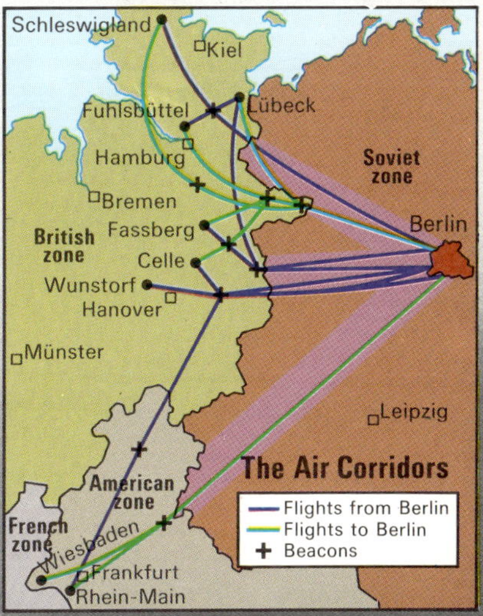

The 50s: A Decade of Tension

FOR AMERICA'S LEADERS the Berlin blockade vividly demonstrated the need to encourage the economic rebuilding of postwar Europe and the evolution of a political and military system to contain the Soviet threat. Throughout the decade the first priority in the containment of communism was Europe, even though American policy became increasingly more active in Asia and the Middle East.

The communist victory in China in 1949 caused some shift of emphasis to Asia. The Nationalist regime on Formosa faced a very real threat of invasion from the mainland. This threat was averted primarily by the decision of American President Harry Truman to send the US Seventh Fleet for protection upon the outbreak of the Korean War in 1950. At this time and for many years after, the United States refused to formally recognise the Chinese communist government.

The communist threat

America, and perhaps to a lesser extent her allies, perceived the communist threat in black-and-white terms. There now existed a single Asian monolithic bloc with Peking allied to military masters in Moscow. In the view of the State Department this new force would seek to expand into nations both friendly and important to the free world unless it was prevented from doing so. Accordingly, the United States stifled its doubts over French policy in Indochina and increased its aid to French forces fighting the Viet Minh.

The British were less convinced by this international interpretation of the communist menace and had made an attempt at recognising the new Chinese regime. But its resources were stretched to the limit in the counter-insurgency campaign against communists in Malaya.

Members of the Western alliance saw the Korean War as an attempt by the Russians to lure them into an 'Asian cul-de-sac' before they renewed their political (and possibly military) offensive in Europe. The fact that a communist nation had attacked a client of the world's sole nuclear power shattered the illusions the Europeans had had about the atomic bomb.

Europe now contributed forces to the UN Command in Korea and looked afresh at their neglected armies. The Lisbon conference of 1952 reflected this new sense of urgency as NATO embarked upon an ambitious programme of rearmament destined to balance the conventional strength of the Soviet bloc armies in Europe. At the same time the alliance itself was transformed from a multi-guaranty pact into an integrated military organisation.

In the United States the refusal of the electorate to support any longer the war in Korea cost the Democrats the 1952 presidential contest. The new hard-line Republican Party was epitomised by General Dwight D. Eisenhower who, upon election, appointed John Foster Dulles as his Secretary of State.

The Dulles style

Dulles was totally uncompromising in his stand against communism. He was determined to lead rather than follow public opinion. He wanted the Europeans to adopt a more decisive stand against the Soviet Union. In particular he promoted the cause of the new West German Republic. In Konrad Adenauer, Dulles found a ready ally and kindred spirit. When France vacillated over West German rearmament Dulles declared that the United States would have to make 'an agonising reappraisal' of its policies. France acquiesced.

His determination not to compromise in his dealings with the Russians or the Chinese was widely attacked. He was dubbed the Cold War Warrior by critics who accused him of being inflexible and stubborn. He refused to accept the path of non-alignment that some emergent states chose to follow, but in 1956 would not support France, Britain and Israel in their attack on Egypt.

For many leading statesmen the firmness Dulles displayed succeeded in checking communist Cold War strategy. Despite this, however, even Dulles was impotent when the Hungarian uprising was brutally put down by the Soviet Union in 1956.

Anti-communist alliances

The Americans attempted to construct a ring of alliances around the communist world. This began in 1954 when the situation in Indochina deteriorated rapidly. In order to prevent the collapse of Asian states like dominoes, Dulles took the initiative in creating the Southeast Asia Treaty Organisation (SEATO).

In December 1954 the United States signed a defensive treaty with the Nationalist Chinese government and pledged itself to defend Formosa and the Pescadores, for the mainland Chinese had begun to bombard the off-shore island garrisons of Quemoy and Matsu. The bombardment died away and there followed a lull until September 1958 when Peking demanded the surrender of the islands and renewed the bombardment. Dulles declared that the United States would fight to protect Formosa and attracted heated criticism for pursuing a policy of 'brinkmanship'.

American diplomacy tried to plug the 'gap' between NATO and SEATO with a Middle East security alliance, called the Baghdad Pact, in 1955. The following year the Suez crisis threw the Middle East into chaos, so America tried to make a fresh start with what was later to become known as the Eisenhower Doctrine. The president announced that with congressional approval American troops would be deployed

against any communist-sponsored aggressor in the Middle East. States that accepted this offer of protection would also receive economic and military aid. Only the pro-Western and strife-torn Lebanon responded.

On 14 July 1958 a bloody and left-wing coup toppled the Hashemite monarchy in Iraq. King Feisal II and members of his family were executed. The Americans and British, horrified by this turn of events at the centre of the Baghdad Pact, reacted at once. On the same day American marines stormed ashore in the Lebanon while British paratroopers were dropped on Amman to support King Hussein in Jordan. It was a brave move full of risk, but the intervention stabilised a highly dangerous situation. It demonstrated, too, the global nature of Cold War diplomacy in a decade when tension ran high.

OPPOSITE TOP *Crowds confront T34s in East Berlin during the 1953 riots.* OPPOSITE *John Foster Dulles (left), US Secretary of State, and Soviet leader Nikita Khrushchev (right) symbolised the verbal rancour of the Cold War. Konrad Adenauer (centre) was West Germany's first chancellor.* ABOVE RIGHT *US Marines advance against enemy positions in Korea. The Korean War highlighted the communist threat in Asia.* BELOW *Members of the British 16th Independent Parachute Brigade with mortars in Jordan. Britain sent in troops after the 1958 coup in Iraq.*

The Divided World

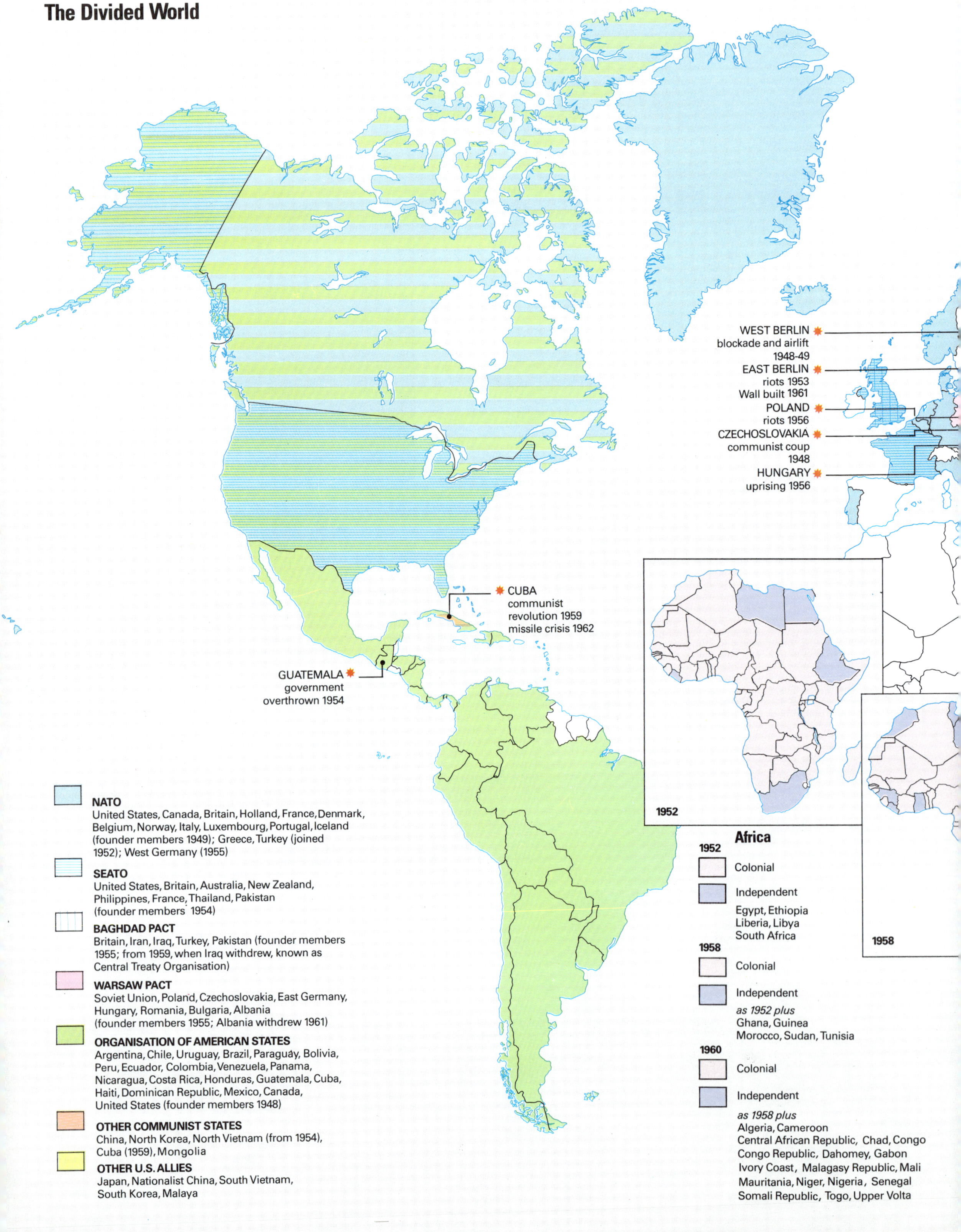

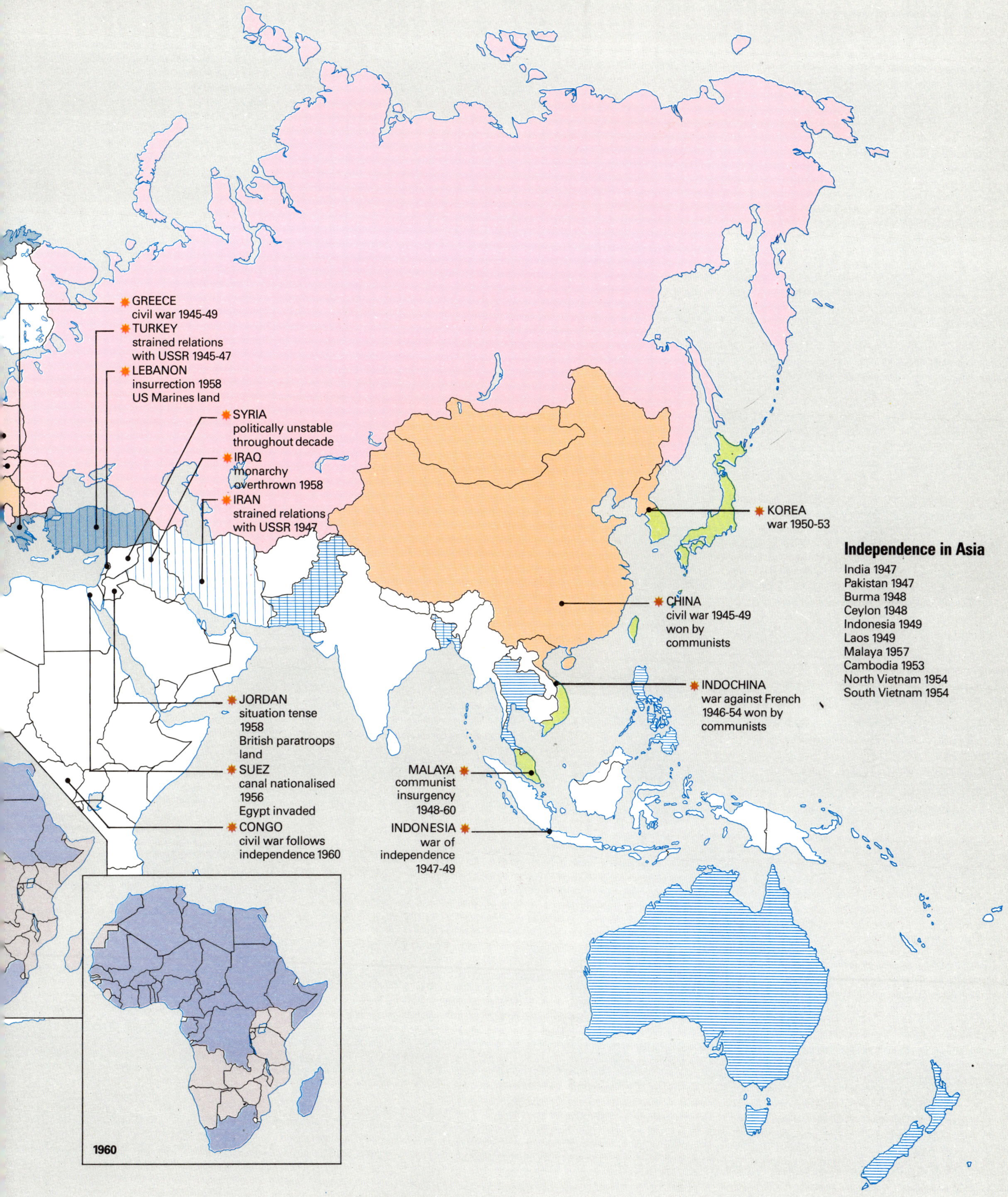
GREECE
civil war 1945-49
TURKEY
strained relations
with USSR 1945-47
LEBANON
insurrection 1958
US Marines land
SYRIA
politically unstable
throughout decade
IRAQ
monarchy
overthrown 1958
IRAN
strained relations
with USSR 1947
JORDAN
situation tense
1958
British paratroops
land
SUEZ
canal nationalised
1956
Egypt invaded
CONGO
civil war follows
independence 1960
MALAYA
communist
insurgency
1948-60
INDONESIA
war of
independence
1947-49
KOREA
war 1950-53
CHINA
civil war 1945-49
won by
communists
INDOCHINA
war against French
1946-54 won by
communists
Independence in Asia
India 1947
Pakistan 1947
Burma 1948
Ceylon 1948
Indonesia 1949
Laos 1949
Malaya 1957
Cambodia 1953
North Vietnam 1954
South Vietnam 1954
1960

The Balance of Terror 1: The Soviet Union

AT THE OUTSET OF THE COLD WAR the Soviet Union found itself at a serious disadvantage. The United States, its rival superpower, could strike at the very heart of the Soviet Union but was itself largely invulnerable to a Soviet response. As a continental power Russia was used to dealing with foes across land borders. Now for the first time, an ocean divided her from her enemy.

To counter the American strategic threat the Soviet Union retained large numbers of armoured formations and ground forces in satellite countries to threaten western Europe. Forward deployment gave them the possibility of a surprise attack. The Soviets then sought to overhaul the American nuclear lead as quickly as possible.

A nuclear weapons research programme of sorts had begun in 1942 and, like the Americans, the Russians had captured stockpiles of German V2s and a number of scientists. In December 1946 the first graphite reactor became functional and on 29 August 1949 the Russians first exploded an atomic device. In 1953 a Soviet hydrogen bomb was detonated.

It was from the stocks of V2s that the Russians, like the Americans, developed their first generation of nuclear missiles. The SS-1 (surface-to-surface), code-named Scunner, was the first short-range ballistic missile produced after the war.

The main Soviet effort, however, went in the development of a manned strategic bomber. In 1946 the Tupolev bureau produced the Tu-4 Bull, a bomber whose technology was derived directly from the B-29. (In the latter part of World War II four Superfortresses were forced to make crash landings in the far eastern USSR and the Russians learned much from these aircraft.) From 1945 to 1953 the Tu-4 was built in large numbers.

Changes in Soviet policy

Nikita Khrushchev came to power in February 1955 and ordered a new military doctrine to be prepared which would take account of the rapidly changing military scene. In a thermonuclear age Khrushchev believed that a war would begin with a strategic nuclear exchange causing vast damage. The High Command was reorganised and a new strategy emphasised the need to prepare for that kind of war. The size and budget for ground forces were reduced.

By the late 1950s Khrushchev had taken more drastic steps. With the support of generals loyal to him (and now holding critical command appointments), he created the strategic rocket forces as a separate command. In a number of speeches in 1959 and 1960 Khrushchev made it clear that he saw these forces as the single most important component of the Soviet ground forces. All missiles with a range of more than 970km (600 miles) came within the command of the strategic rocket forces.

New missiles and bombers

In terms of weaponry the Russians had made significant progress. In 1955 they deployed the SS-3 Skyster, a medium-range ballistic missile, and followed it two years later with an intermediate-range ballistic missile, the SS-4 Sandal, which was stationed in large numbers in the western provinces and along the Sino-Soviet border. It was Sandal missiles that Khrushchev tried to station in Cuba.

Khrushchev believed that the greatest emphasis should be placed on intercontinental ballistic missiles (ICBMs). The first was ready in August 1957. It was the SS-6, code-named Sapwood by NATO. In the early 1960s the Soviet strategic rocket forces moved into their second generation of ICBMs with the SS-7 Saddler and SS-8 Sasin. Deployments were often attempted before all the faults and teething troubles had been ironed out. These were huge and cumbersome liquid-fuelled rockets on 'soft' and unprotected launch pads. They needed ample warning time for a long countdown. But by now the Americans were moving into solid-fuel propellants.

The tactical or short-range battlefield support missiles first made their appearance in the armoury of the Soviet ground forces in the late 1950s. These missiles, known to NATO under the code-name FROG (an acronym of Free Rockets Over Ground), are a family of unguided, spin-stabilised artillery rockets. The first, FROG-I, was seen in 1957 and mounted on a JSIII amphibious reconnaissance vehicle. The warhead was optional nuclear or high explosive and the missile had a range of 24–32km (15–20 miles).

BELOW *The propeller-driven Tu-20 Bear jet bomber dates from the mid-1950s. Wing sweep on the original model was 35 degrees.* BELOW RIGHT *A Tu-16 maritime reconnaissance aircraft. The model has also served as a jet bomber and missile carrier.* BOTTOM *Soviet FROG-I rockets take part in a May Day parade in Moscow.*

RIGHT *Soviet military doctrine stressed the importance of the offensive in conventional warfare. The elements of this offensive were threefold. Firstly (top), Soviet forces would approach enemy positions preceded by an intense bombardment (including the use of nuclear weapons) and air strikes. Secondly (centre), armoured forces would either burst through the first line of defence or skirt strongpoints in a flanking attack, while paratroops were dropped onto strategic objectives in rear areas. Finally, overwhelming tank forces would crush the enemy's main concentrations and drive on to link with the paratroops while motorised rifle divisions came up in support (bottom). Any enemy forces outflanked or screened could be destroyed later. This emphasis on crushing offensive tactics naturally worried the NATO states which, in the narrow confines of western Europe, could not match the power and speed of the Red Army.*

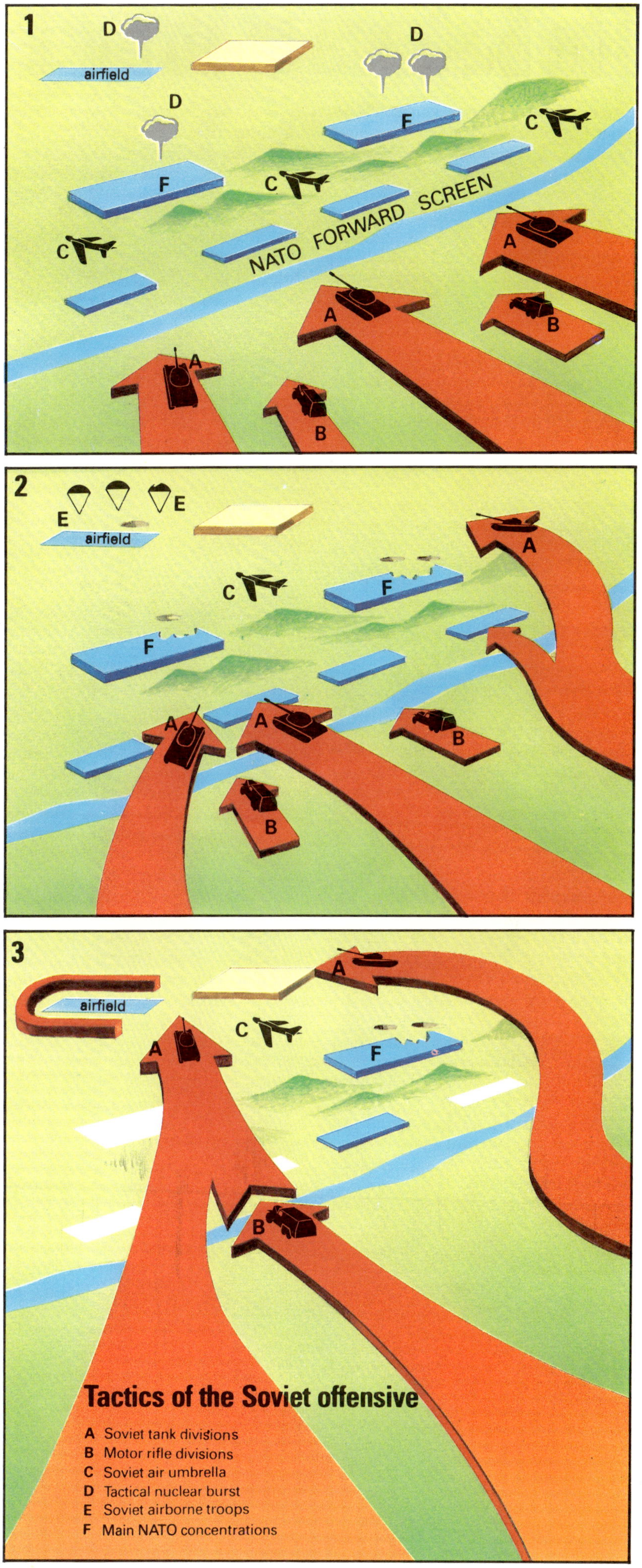

The Russians displayed their new generation of strategic bombers at the Moscow Air Show in 1955. The Myasishchev Mya-4 Bison was a four-jet bomber and only a modest number were built and deployed to the army and naval air arms. The real surprise was the Tu-20 Bear. It displayed very advanced avionics in its huge swept wing (it had a span of 48.5m or 159 feet) which formed integral tanks, and the massive turbo-prop engines with their eight-blade contraprops. Though smaller in range and payload it was the Soviet answer to the Boeing B-52 Stratofortress. There was also the Tu-16 Badger, a medium-range turbo-jet regarded as the Soviet equivalent to the British Valiant.

These planes, however, had technical shortcomings which made them inferior to their Western counterparts. Throughout the Cold War, in fact, the Soviet strategic force could not match that of the Western powers.

The Balance of Terror 2: The West

PRODUCTION OF THE ATOMIC BOMB by the United States and the subsequent development in the early 1950s of the thermo-nuclear or hydrogen bomb had revolutionised air power. Now a squadron of nuclear-armed bombers could do what the air fleets failed to achieve in World War II, namely to threaten massive and unacceptable devastation to an enemy in a single raid.

The Boeing bombers

The first atomic bombs were carried by specially adapted B-29s, the Superfortresses. The B-29 had an operational ceiling of more than 9200m (30,000 feet), a pressurised hull and radar-controlled defensive fire. This formidable weapon became the mainstay of the United States Strategic Air Command (SAC) in the early years of the Cold War. From the Superfortress the Americans developed the B-50, and this became SAC's frontline strike bomber throughout much of the decade.

The first jet bomber to enter service with the SAC was the B-45, which was soon replaced by the heavier six-jet B-47 medium bomber. Due to the range limitation of the plane, bases were established overseas and an air-refuelling technique was developed. By the time production of the B-47 was completed, more than 2000 had been built.

The B-52 Stratofortress, perhaps the most famous heavy bomber of the postwar era, made its first flight in 1952 and entered frontline squadron service a couple of years later. This huge aircraft, with a wing span of 47m (155 feet) and powered by eight Pratt and Whitney turbo-jets, can fly at transonic speed and above 15,250m (50,000 feet). The B-52 could hit a target in the Soviet Union and return to the United States without refuelling, a total journey of some 16,000km (10,000 miles). Though a formidable fighting machine, no-one envisaged when it was first introduced that it would still be in frontline service 30 years later.

The manned bomber remained the chief nuclear delivery system throughout much of the 1950s, while the long-range missile languished through lack of funds. Germany had led the world in rocket technology and when, in the last days of World War II, the top planning and technical staff of Peenemünde, headed by Major-General Walter Dornberger and Wernher von Braun, fled and surrendered to American troops, the priceless experience of the German rocket experts became available to the Allies. Also captured was an underground V2 factory at Niedersachswerfen and sufficient components to build more than 100 rockets. Yet the manned bomber was preferred, and from 1947 to 1950 all research into long-range rocketry was cancelled.

Missile development

By the mid-1950s the concerted effort of the 'missile lobby', clear evidence of a Soviet effort in this field and a number of technological developments in rocketry caused the Eisenhower administration to give much higher priority to the strategic missile programme. The long-range missile became viable with the miniaturisation and refinement of inertial guidance systems that permitted the warhead of an intercontinental ballistic missile (ICBM) to be directed close to a target more than 8050km (5000 miles) distant.

The development of solid-fuel propellants opened up all kinds of strategic options with missiles poised in hardened silos on 'short-fused countdown'. It also offered the chance to develop a seaborne missile system using nuclear-powered submarines. The US Navy had been experimenting with the nuclear-propelled *USS Nautilus* and now proceeded to test missiles and hull design. The first nuclear-powered fleet ballistic submarine, *USS George Washington*, was completed in 1959.

The rapid pace of this programme was spurred by the shock produced in America by the launching of the Soviet Sputnik spacecraft in October and November 1957. All thought of economy was forgotten as the United States sought to close 'the missile gap' with the Soviet Union. Liquid-fuelled Atlas and Titan I ICBMs were deployed as an interim measure together with the shorter-ranged Thor and Jupiters. The last-named, with a range of less than 3220km (2000 miles), were deployed to Britain, Italy and Turkey.

At the other end of the scale were the tactical nuclear warheads of the American arsenal. As early as 1949 General Omar Nelson Bradley, chairman of the Joint Chiefs of Staff, proposed the deployment of tactical nuclear weapons in Europe to balance the Soviet superiority in armour. Testing began in 1951 and the first weapon deployed, two years later,

Rival Nuclear Weaponry

	United States	Soviet Union
1945–48	American monopoly of atomic weapons Means of delivery: overseas-based B-29 bombers on borders of Soviet Union	
1949	Stockpile 100+ About 500 B-29s	First Soviet atomic weapon test
1953	1000+ atomic or hydrogen weapons B-36 and B-47 operational	100–200 weapons Means of delivery: Tu-4 Bull incapable of reaching USA; no in-flight refuelling or overseas bases
1956–57	7000–10,000 weapons B-52 operational; B-58 introduced	2000+ weapons Tu-16 Badger with range of 6450km (4000 miles), Tu-20 Bear with range of over 11,200km (7000 miles) and Myasishchev Bison with range of 9700km (6000 miles) First successful ICBM launch
1962	63 ICBMs 186 MRBMs 600 LR bombers 2200 MR bombers	50+ICBMs 200 MRBMs 190 LR bombers 1100 MR bombers

ABOVE *and* OPPOSITE *Throughout the 1950s America enjoyed a clear superiority in nuclear strike capacity, although later Soviet missiles had, individually, greater destructive power.* BELOW *A Regulus I missile is launched at sea.*

Nuclear Capacities

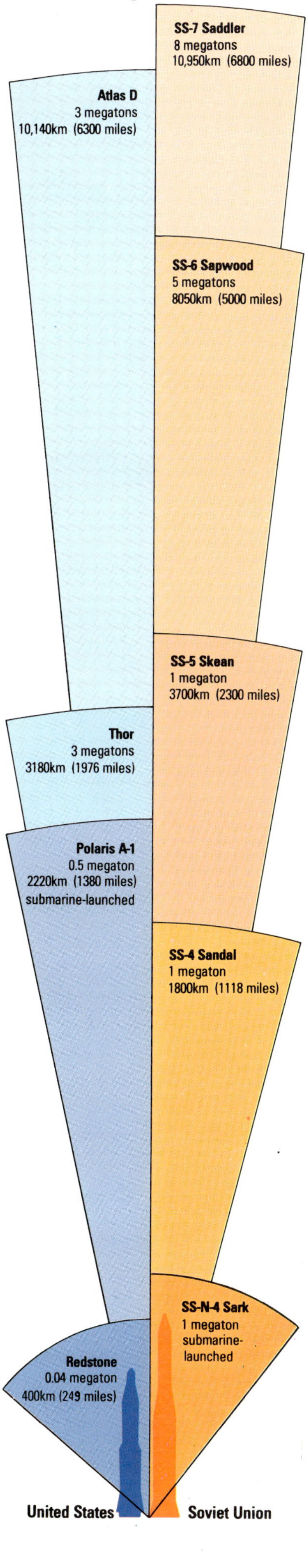

was a 280mm 'atomic cannon'. It was followed by Regulus and Honest John missiles.

The British strike force

In Britain the Labour government emphasised conventional forces, but when Churchill led the Conservatives back to power in 1951 the aversion to nuclear weapons dissolved and the pendulum swung in favour of a nuclear bias. Britain tested her own independently researched A-bomb in October 1952.

As in America the British strategic force consisted of freefall bombs carried by medium-range transonic bombers. First came the Vickers Valiant in 1956 and then the Handley Page Victor two years later. Neither, however, could match the performance of the Hawker Siddeley Vulcan, which entered service in 1957. With its distinctive delta shape, it soon became the most effective bomber, mainly because it proved to have excellent low-flying capabilities at a time when low-altitude attack was the main counter to air defence missiles.

TOP *The B-52 Stratofortress was the first jet bomber to have a fully global range. The B-52G shown has AGM-28 Hound Dog missiles underwing.* CENTRE *The Centurion tank dates from 1945 and has won an enviable reputation. The 105mm gun was introduced in 1957.* ABOVE *The Hawker Siddeley Vulcan B Mk 2 bomber could carry a free-fall nuclear weapon or 21 1000lb bombs.*

Treason and Espionage

THE IDEOLOGICAL BATTLE which had played its part in the conduct of World War II was renewed in a more virulent form by the two great superpowers in the early days of the Cold War. Each sought to retain the allegiance of its allies, convert the uncommitted and subvert the supporters of the other side. The intense and unremitting wave of propaganda disseminated to the population of each side did much to create the Cold War atmosphere of mutual fear. And every now and then, sensational spy scares would be reported.

The Soviets and their satellites had quickly established over-large staffs at their Western embassies, and these became a base and haven for espionage. In addition the Kremlin encircled the globe with agents of the Cominform, the international agencies of the Communist Party. Their task included infiltration, fomenting strikes and subverting the state.

The atomic spies

In September 1945, Igor Gouzenko, a young cipher clerk in the Soviet embassy in Ottawa, defected and revealed to British intelligence the existence of an elaborate network of spies. It involved agents not just in Canada, but, what was more alarming, spies among the Anglo-American scientists who were engaged in building the atomic bomb. Skilled and patient counter-espionage resulted in the trials of Dr Nunn May and Dr Klaus Fuchs, the latter a German-born physicist. In 1950 Fuchs was found guilty of espionage and sentenced to 14 years in prison. Fuchs had an American collaborator, Harry Gold, who was sentenced to 30 years imprisonment.

Part of the network were Julius and Ethel Rosenberg who were brought to trial in 1951 for handing over atomic secrets to the Soviet Union. Found guilty, they were executed in 1953 after a number of appeals had been rejected. They were the first civilians in American history to suffer the death penalty for espionage.

Earlier, a series of sensational espionage cases had been brought against American government employees. The most celebrated case involved Alger Hiss, a former State Department official, who was found guilty of perjury and sentenced to five years imprisonment.

McCarthy's crusade

The revelation of agents working in government departments spurred Senator Joseph McCarthy to embark upon a well-publicised witch hunt of communists in high places. Sometimes working alone, both in and out of office, but mostly through his chairmanship of the Senate investigations committee from 1953, he charged that communists and fellow travellers had infiltrated the highest levels of government, especially the State Department. The Republican Senator for Wisconsin drove people from their jobs, and those against whom he failed to secure a conviction or public confession were invariably

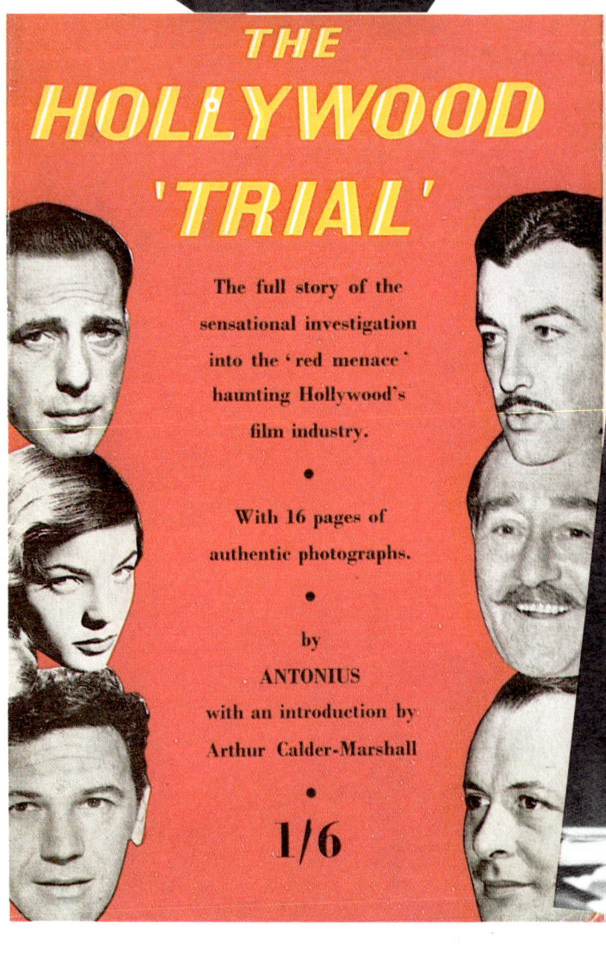

In the early 1950s American spy trials and hearings into communist influence in show business, government and the army gained huge publicity. Atomic spies Ethel and Julius Rosenberg (ABOVE) *went to their deaths in the electric chair in 1953. Klaus Fuchs* (ABOVE RIGHT) *served nine years for spying. Alger Hiss* (TOP RIGHT) *was accused of spying by Whittaker Chambers, a self-confessed former Soviet agent. He was jailed for perjury in 1950.* RIGHT *Hollywood came under the scrutiny of Congress in 1947 and a blacklist of suspected 'subversives' was drawn up by employers. The ill feeling lasted for years.* OPPOSITE *Senator Joseph McCarthy destroyed the careers of many Americans by wild allegations of communist allegiance and sympathies. He was censured in 1954 and died three years later a discredited man.*

DAILY EXPRES
THURSDAY JUNE 7 1951
CONTROLLING SHAREHOLDER LORD BEAVERBROOK
Weather: Mainly fine, cloudy at first
No. 15,901
ROW Tories protest over late vote
PRICES Some baby clothes to cost double
PERSIA The first rift in the oil grab
HUNT British Government employees sought on Continent
Phone warns 'Murder
YARD HUNTS 2 BRITONS
'On way to Russia'
'He talked and died like a gangster'
HERO WITH D.C.M. AND M.M.
KILLER'S
FROM FOREIGN OFFICE?
TORY M.P. 'HELD SOCIA LOB
Express Staff Reporter
SCOTLAND YARD officers and French detectives are hunting for two British Government employees who are believed to have left London with the intention getting to Moscow.
According to a
journey to

Britain's most notorious postwar spy case brought criticism of the 'old boy network' and the security service. Donald Maclean (ABOVE) *and Guy Burgess* (ABOVE RIGHT), *both of whom had served in the British Embassy in America, defected to Russia in 1951, having been tipped off by 'Kim' Philby* (LEFT), *a former colleague who himself fled to Moscow 12 years later.*

broken by the attendant publicity. McCarthyism later became synonymous for accusation without proof.

McCarthy himself was broken publicly in 1954 as a result of a sensational and nationally televised hearing against high ranking army officers and government officials. In December of that year McCarthy was formally censured by the Senate for conduct 'contrary to Senate traditions'.

The big stories

On the other side of the Atlantic, in 1951, the British establishment was severely shaken by the revelation of treachery in high places with the defection to Russia of senior diplomats Guy Burgess and Donald Maclean. The belief that they were able to make good their escape largely through the incompetence of British intelligence services strained Anglo-American relations.

In April 1956 Commander Lionel Crabb, a Royal Navy officer and an expert in underwater sabotage, disappeared while Nikita Khrushchev and Nikolai Bulganin were on a state visit in Britain. Crabb had dived into Portsmouth harbour on a secret mission near the Soviet cruiser *Ordzhonikidze* which had brought the Soviet leaders to Britain. Some 14 months later a headless body was washed ashore near Chichester. An inquest, on the thinnest of evidence, proclaimed the torso to be that of Crabb. Rumours have persisted that Crabb is alive and now living in the Soviet Union.

At about this time in the United States, Colonel Rudolf Ivanovich Abel was found guilty of espionage and in November 1957 was sentenced to 30 years in prison. He was destined to serve but a fraction of his sentence for in 1962 he was exchanged for Francis Gary Powers, who had been in prison in the Soviet Union since 1960 when his U-2 high-altitude reconnaissance plane was shot down over Russia. Powers's trial, film of which was released to the West, was used to discredit the United States.

Another man who was destined not to serve his full sentence in prison for espionage, but for different reasons, was George Blake. A British intelligence operative, Blake was brought to trial as a double agent and in May 1961 was found guilty of spying for the Soviet Union. He was sentenced to 42 years in prison but in October he escaped from Wormwood Scrubs and got clean away.

H. A. R. (Kim) Philby, a former senior Foreign Office official and double agent *par excellence*, had his cover blown in May 1963 when he was revealed as the 'third man' in the Burgess and Maclean scandal. By then Philby was safely in Moscow. The entire affair brought strong criticism of the competence of the British intelligence services, for Philby had survived a decade of rumour and official scrutiny arising from questions asked in the House of Commons.

U-2, Berlin and Cuba

TWO GRAVE CRISES of the Cold War came in the early 1960s. After they had taken place world politics seemed much more stable because each marked a definite assertion of the extent of one side's power which the other proved itself willing to accept. The construction of the Berlin Wall and the brinkmanship of the Cuban missile crisis resulted in a safer world.

For the Soviet leader, Nikita Khrushchev, the main issue that dominated relations with the United States in Europe was the German question. He believed that America's support of West Germany would lead to the creation of a strong pro-Western power which would threaten the communist eastern bloc. To prevent this occurring Khrushchev embarked upon a diplomatic offensive that led to summit conferences in Vienna, Geneva, Paris and Washington.

The Berlin Wall – with its barbed wire watchtowers and tank barriers – was a grim monument to communist repression in East Germany.

The Russian theme was invariably the same – the wish to have a single Germany with a string of demilitarised and neutral states running from the Baltic to the Adriatic. The West saw in this scheme all the dangers inherent in the creation of a vacuum in central Europe and opposed it.

Berlin continued to be the most sensitive spot. West Berlin was a convenient 'bolt hole' through which East Germans were able to flee to the West with comparative ease. In the ten years to 1960, 4 million had done so. As the flow continued unabated East German stability was threatened.

In August 1961 central Europe had reached a crisis point. Soviet tank divisions were reported to be deploying around Berlin, the West responded by reinforcing their garrisons, and the East Berlin authorities instigated a campaign of terror against the citizens in the West. On Sunday 13 August the first makeshift barriers were erected and within a short while the Berlin Wall, dividing East and West, became a grim reality.

There was little the West could do about the Wall since the Soviets possessed overwhelming superiority of force in the area. It was simple and crude but an effective method of preventing the flight of East Berliners. In this sense the Wall was a force for stability at a time when the situation looked as if it might get out of hand.

The U-2 affair

If the Berlin Wall amounted to an admission of failure by the communists, the U-2 incident the year before had proved to be Khrushchev's greatest propaganda victory and a humiliating episode for President Dwight D. Eisenhower and the State Department. On 5 May Khrushchev said that an American U-2 aircraft had been shot down over the Soviet Union. The State Department passed it off as a 'weather flight', whereupon Khrushchev revealed to the world that the plane had been on a spying

mission and that the pilot, Francis Gary Powers, had been taken alive.

Washington replied that the flight had not been officially sanctioned, but a week after the event Eisenhower was forced to admit personally that the mission had, in fact, been authorised at the highest level. Powers was put on trial and imprisoned. He was swopped for Colonel Rudolf Abel, the nuclear spy, in 1962.

Soviet missiles in Cuba

Eisenhower's successor, John F. Kennedy, began his period of office rather badly. In April 1961 he sanctioned the Bay of Pigs invasion of Cuba by American-trained Cuban exiles, a venture he had inherited from the previous administration. This disastrous operation humiliated the United States and enhanced the prestige of Fidel Castro. It was bound to make the Americans more reluctant to try military intervention. And it encouraged Khrushchev in his policy of testing America's resolve. He sought, now, to convert Cuba into a Soviet missile base.

The Soviet Union was increasingly worried by America's superior strike capability. The development of solid fuel propellants, the deployment of Minuteman missiles in armoured silos and the new strategies of counterforce proposed by Defence Secretary Robert McNamara had caught the Russians napping. Lacking an adequate intercontinental nuclear force, Khrushchev saw the need to diversify his strategic arrangements as a stopgap measure until nuclear parity could be attained. Thus Cuba simultaneously became the focus of American sensitivity and a temporary Soviet resolution to restore the strategic balance.

Throughout the summer months of 1962 Cuban refugees told American intelligence experts that missile sites were being built on the island, so air surveillance was intensified. On 14 October aerial photographs gave conclusive evidence of the construction of medium-range ballistic missile bases, some nearly completed on the north coast around Sagua La Grande and at the western end of the island

The shooting down of a U-2 spy plane (BELOW) *over the Soviet Union in 1960 greatly embarrassed the United States. The pilot, Francis Gary Powers* (RIGHT), *was tried, imprisoned, and released in 1962, the year of the Cuban missile crisis.* BOTTOM *Soviet equipment leaves Cuba after Khrushchev's climbdown.*

near San Cristobal. These sites, just 145km (90 miles) from Florida, exposed nearly all of the United States to attack. For President Kennedy the objective was clear: the missiles must be removed within 14 days, before they became operational.

Quarantine imposed

As missiles were still en route to Cuba by sea the decision was taken to impose a 'quarantine line' patrolled by the US Navy. Ships carrying 'offensive military equipment' were to return to their home port or a non-Cuban port; Soviet ships would be sunk if they failed to comply.

In a dramatic nationwide broadcast on 22 October Kennedy informed the Russians of the imposition of the quarantine and warned them: 'It shall be the policy of this nation to regard any nuclear missile launched from Cuba against any nation in the Western Hemisphere as an attack by the Soviet Union on the United States, requiring a full retaliatory response upon the Soviet Union.'

During the crisis United States strategic forces went on to a Condition Two Alert and preparations were made for a nuclear attack. Emissaries were dispatched to keep the NATO allies fully informed of America's actions while in the Security Council of the United Nations Adlai Stevenson, the American ambassador, confronted the Soviet delegate with photographs of the Soviet missiles and sites in Cuba.

The crisis resolved

The high point of the crisis occurred when a group of Soviet freighters known to be carrying missiles approached the American vessels on 24 October. Then they reversed their course without challenging the quarantine and headed for home. Four days later, on Friday 28 October, Khrushchev announced that the missiles would be removed. The 13-day crisis was over, and the world breathed easily again.

The Cuban missile crisis was significant on several counts. It raised, for the first time, the genuine and frightening prospect of nuclear war. It brought home vividly to Kennedy and Khrushchev and other world figures the immense responsibilities of leadership in a nuclear age. And it demonstrated to Khrushchev that Kennedy's commitment to strategic interests could never be underestimated.

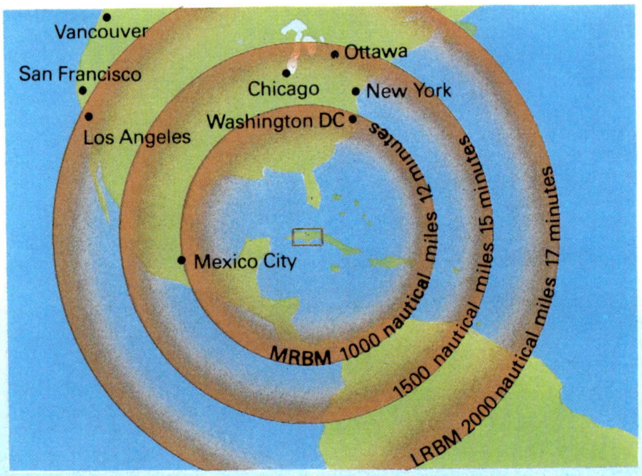

RIGHT *President John F. Kennedy's decisive action during the crisis took Soviet leaders by surprise.* BELOW *When the blockade took effect about 60 US vessels ringed Cuba. The blockade was lifted only after the missiles were withdrawn from the island.*

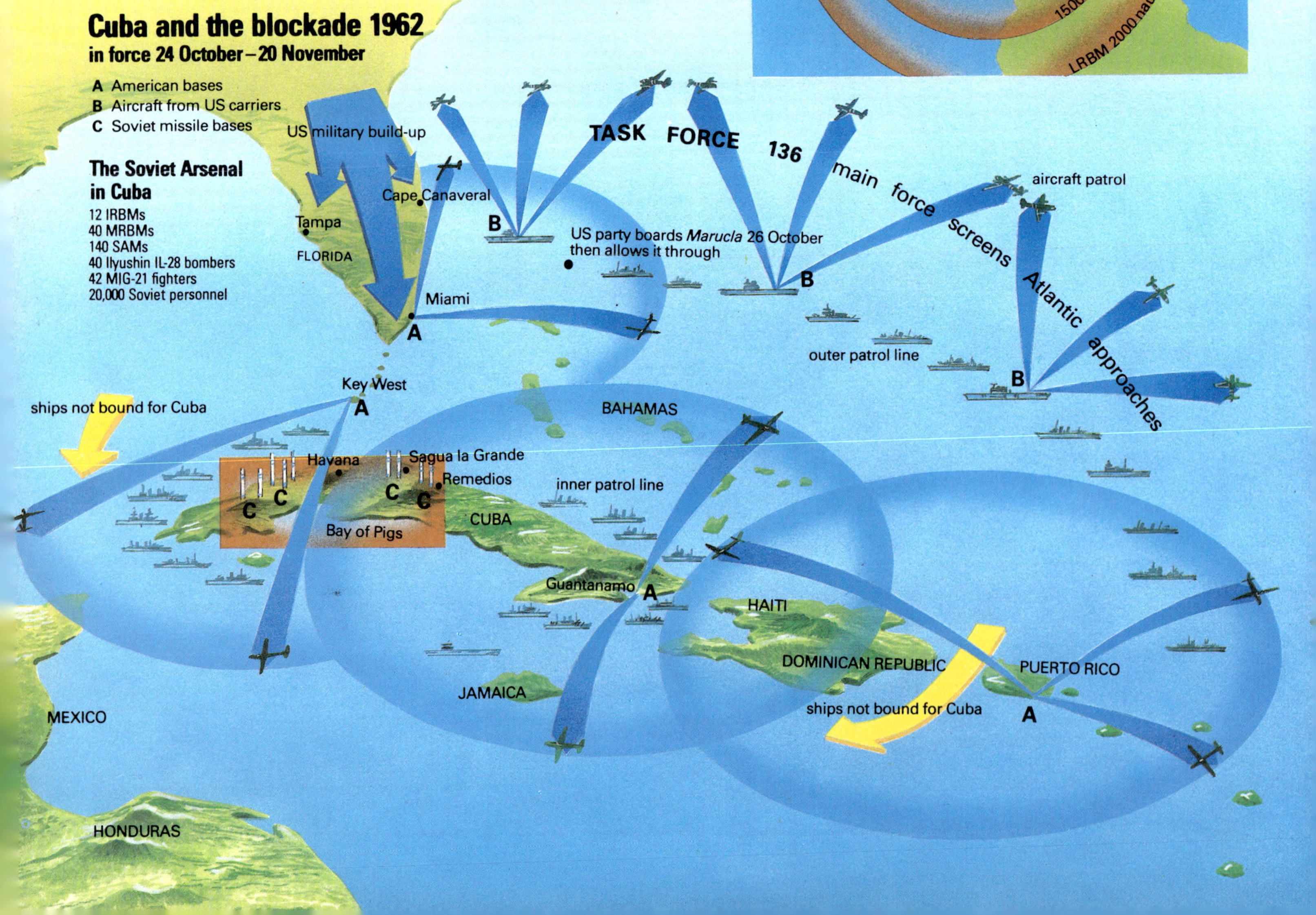

Crisis in Korea

The communist invasion of South Korea in 1950 set alarm bells ringing in the West, and the conduct of the war caused bitter rows between American military and political leaders

F. A. Godfrey

THE WAR IN KOREA exerted an influence far beyond the region in which it was fought. Beginning with an armed attempt by the communist North to overrun the South, it was quickly transformed into an international conflict involving the United States and its Western allies on one side, and communist China on the other. It showed the determination of President Harry S. Truman to contain communism through limited objectives without, as General Douglas MacArthur wished, extending the war into communist China.

The importance of Korea

To the Western world Korea seemed a far off country of little significance in the summer of 1950. A small peninsula lying off the east Asian land mass it was some 950km (600 miles) long with a rugged chain of mountains extending almost its whole length. There were scarcely any natural resources and agriculture was of a primitive nature. Indeed, the peninsula had all the attributes of an underdeveloped Asian country with a particularly inhospitable climate of harsh winters and scorching summers.

And yet, in that summer, a war of major proportions, which involved many nations of the Western world and might have led to World War III, broke out. It was not that Korea itself was so important but rather its strategic location in relation to its powerful neighbours. No fewer than three wars had been fought over Korean territory in the previous 60 or so years. In a brief conflict from 1894 to 1895 Japan fought China in a successful attempt to bring Korea into her sphere of influence, and in 1904–5 she fought Russia to establish once and for all her authority over the peninsula. In 1910 Korea became a Japanese colony and in 1942 an integral part of Japan.

Background to war

Events leading to the outbreak of conflict in Korea in 1950 can be traced back to decisions taken in the closing stages of World War II. Planning for the eventual collapse of the Japanese began in early 1945. Once the Soviet Union agreed to declare war on Japan it was decided that US forces would accept the surrender of Japanese units in the southern part of Korea but the Soviet Army would do so in the north. An arbitrary line – the 38th parallel of latitude – was chosen to delineate the American and Soviet areas of operation.

The dropping of the atomic bombs on Hiroshima and Nagasaki precipitated the Japanese collapse and the Russians belatedly declared war on Japan on 8 August. The Japanese capitulated two days later. United States forces landed in Korea on 8 September to supervise the Japanese surrender, but even by 26 August the Soviet Army had reached the 38th parallel.

To try to forge a new and independent Korea the United Nations General Assembly voted in November 1947 to establish a UN

UN infantry trudge through North Korean hill country. The biting winters and often difficult terrain posed problems for foreign soldiers.

Temporary Commission on Korea with the task of supervising the election of a national assembly from which would come a government. From the outset the Russians refused to accept the authority of the commission in the part of Korea they occupied. They had already formed an interim government in the north much as they had in the east European countries in the immediate aftermath of hostilities in Europe.

Foiled by the Soviet Union the UN commission supervised an election south of the 38th parallel in May 1948 and a national assembly of 200 representatives was created. Syngman Rhee, an elderly, patriotic figure, was elected president and a constitution for the Republic of Korea (RoK) was proclaimed on 13 July 1948. The political organs thus created claimed jurisdiction over the whole of Korea.

North of the 38th parallel an election was held on 25 August to produce a Supreme People's Assembly of Korea. On 8 September the constitution of the Democratic People's Republic of Korea (DPRK) was adopted. Two days later Kim Il Sung became premier of a government which, like its southern counterpart, claimed to rule over the whole of the country.

In December 1948 the UN General Assembly recognised as lawful the constitution of the RoK and called for the Soviet and US forces to withdraw from the country. Russia announced the complete evacuation of all her troops on 25 December and made much propaganda capital out of the event. Then, in July 1949, the United States removed her last soldiers from the peninsula, having surprisingly decided in an appraisal of the developing Cold War that Korea was of little strategic importance.

From the summer of 1949 the North and South Koreans engaged in an increasingly vitriolic propaganda campaign against each other. Linked with it were continual incidents along the 38th parallel and frequent acts of sabotage and terrorism carried out deep in each other's territory.

The opposing forces

In this developing confrontation there was considerable cause for alarm in the West. The US Army had, before its departure, trained and equipped the RoK Army, but it was little more than a para-military police force. In June 1950 it comprised about 95,000 men organised into eight divisions, of which only four were fully equipped and up to strength. These full-strength divisions were deployed along the 38th parallel in the summer of 1950.

The army was equipped with old US rifles, carbines and light mortars. It had a quantity of anti-tank weapons (2.36 inch bazookas) but these were out of date and not effective against modern armour. For artillery the South Koreans possessed 140 light anti-tank guns and some worn out US M3 105mm howitzers. There were no medium guns, no tanks, no fighter aircraft or bombers, and ammunition stocks were small.

In contrast to this unimpressive army the North Korean People's Army (NKPA) had eight infantry divisions at full strength, two more at half strength, a motorcycle reconnaissance regiment and an armoured brigade. It was estimated to be in the region of 135,000 men. All its formations contained seasoned troops who had fought with the Russians in World War II and even more who had fought with Mao Tse-tung against the Nationalist Chinese.

The NKPA possessed 150 Soviet-made T34 tanks. Each division had a towed artillery regiment (122mm howitzers) and a self-propelled-gun battalion (76mm guns). The Soviet Union had trained and equipped the NKPA since 1945. The NKPA was, in Asian terms, a highly effective, well armed and trained military force, although this was not fully realised in the West. Western intelligence agencies had no evidence that it was about to attack, nor did they report any signs of mobilisation.

It is not clear when the decision was taken to invade but it seems highly probable that Josef Stalin discussed such a possibility with Mao Tse-tung in Moscow in the winter of 1949–50. With Japan still suffering from her defeat in World War II and America showing little interest in the area, the time was certainly opportune. Although it is unlikely that China was involved in the exact timing of the event, there were, on the other hand, large redeployments of troops from the southern and central provinces of China to Manchuria in the spring of 1950.

Invasion by the North

However the decision was made, the NKPA crossed the 38th parallel in force before first light on the morning of 25 June 1950. The South Koreans were caught unprepared. It was a Sunday and many soldiers were away on weekend leave. At 1100 hours as the invasion progressed Radio Pyongyang announced that the North Korean forces were attacking in response to an invasion of the North by Syngman Rhee's army.

The attack was launched in the west, followed by a major thrust down the Uijong-bu Corridor, the traditional invasion route leading to the capital, Seoul. A further assault took place in the central mountains and another down the east coast supported by a landing south of the 38th parallel.

President Harry Truman immediately ordered his Far East Commander, General of the Army Douglas MacArthur, to send ammunition and equipment to help the RoK Army, and to send experts to study the situation. He also ordered the US Seventh Fleet to move to Japanese waters. On learning from MacArthur that there was no hope of holding Seoul and that the RoK Army was on the verge of collapse the president authorised him to use American air and naval forces to support the RoK Army south of the 38th parallel.

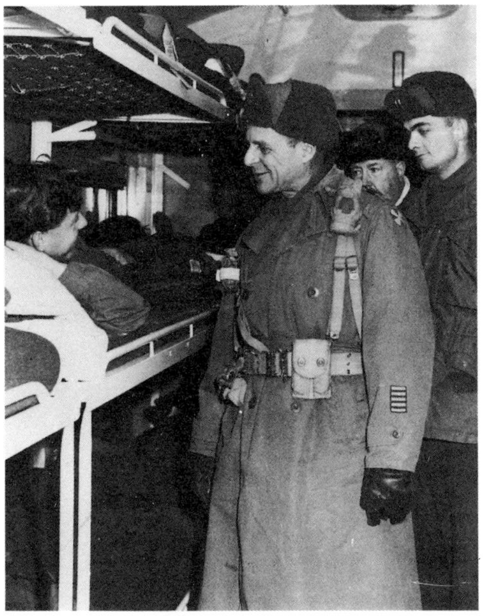

OPPOSITE *A Chinese poster portrays the capture of enemy troops in Korea. China committed herself to the war when UN forces approached the Chinese border.* TOP *General Matthew B. Ridgway visits the wounded. Ridgway became commander-in-chief in Korea after MacArthur had been sacked by President Truman.* ABOVE *Lashed by sub-zero gales, men of the 1st Marine Division retreat southwards near Chosan following the dramatic Chinese offensive of late 1950.* RIGHT *Street fighting in Seoul, September 1950. By this time the North Koreans were being driven out of the South.*

Meanwhile the UN Secretary General, Trygve Lie, called a Security Council meeting. On 25 June the council voted unanimously (with Yugoslavia abstaining and the Soviet Union absent) on a resolution declaring a 'breach of the peace' and calling for an immediate ceasefire and the withdrawal of the NKPA north of the 38th parallel. Two days later the council passed a second resolution calling on member states to give military aid to the RoK to help repel the attack.

By 29 June the situation in Korea had become critical. Seoul had been lost and the NKPA was moving swiftly southwards, driving before it the disintegrating remnants of the RoK Army. General MacArthur flew that day to the peninsula to make an on the spot assessment. He had, on his own initiative, already ordered his air force commander to bomb targets north of the 38th parallel, and on returning to Japan he informed Washington that without the use of US ground troops Korea would be lost.

On 30 June, Truman told MacArthur to use elements of the US forces in Japan to combat the NKPA. This made the four divisions of the US Eighth Army in Japan available to the commander-in-chief, who had also been appointed commander-in-chief of the UN forces in Korea.

The battle joined

The first units of the 24th US Infantry Division arrived in Pusan on 1 July and moved rapidly north to engage the North Koreans. By 18 July two more divisions had arrived from Japan. All three were commanded by Lieutenant General Walton Walker, one of Patton's corps commanders in World War II. Walker's HQ was to be known for the rest of the war as the Eighth United States Army in Korea (EUSAK).

The newly arrived US troops, badly equipped and in poor shape following occupation duties in Japan, were no match for the NKPA tanks and infantry. Despite some heroic American actions supported by the few South Korean units still intact, the UN forces were remorselessly driven back towards Pusan. By 4 August they found themselves in prepared positions to the south and east of the Naktong River, forming what came to be known as the Pusan Perimeter. Here, despite a grave threat from a North Korean thrust from the west, they stood firm. Reinforcements from the United States as well as units from Britain and the Commonwealth arrived in July and August, and the final desperate offensive by the NKPA in September was repulsed. In mid-September an amphibious landing took place at Inchon on the west coast. It was immediately successful and cut off the North Koreans' supply route. The NKPA offensive changed into a disorderly retreat, and by the beginning of October the UN forces were across the 38th parallel and heading for the Yalu River, the frontier with China.

China storms in

At the end of October, quite unexpectedly, the Chinese entered the war. Thousands of so-called People's Volunteers suddenly swamped the UN forces. Caught off-balance and unnerved, the UN troops hastily plunged southwards in headlong retreat across the 38th parallel. Only the strong personality of General Matthew Ridgway, the new Commander of EUSAK, brought the situation under control. By the end of January 1951 the Chinese outran their supply system and came to a halt. They were forced to withdraw, driven back in the face of a massive concentration of UN firepower.

The intervention of Chinese forces led to a major confrontation between Truman and MacArthur. It centred on the crucial issue of whether the president's policy of limiting the war to Korea should be maintained, or

whether China herself should be attacked. MacArthur insisted that if his forces were to be successful and not to be asked, as he put it, to die for a tie, they must be allowed to attack targets in China. Truman, however, was worried that such an escalation could lead directly to conflict between America and China and might also ultimately involve the Soviet Union. The disagreement reached its climax when MacArthur made his side of the argument public. In April 1951 Truman took the only course open to him and sacked his commander-in-chief.

Two months later armistice talks began while the fighting settled down to the vicious stalemate astride the 38th parallel predicted by MacArthur. The talks stalled interminably as the casualties on both sides mounted. Newly elected President Dwight D. Eisenhower threatened to bring the war to a conclusion by using whatever means might be necessary. His hard line had an effect, and the armistice was signed at Panmunjom and Munsan on 27 July 1953.

Inchon 1: The Plan

THE DECISION TO LAND at Inchon was one of the most audacious and inspired of 20th-century warfare and confirmed General Douglas MacArthur's place as one of the great commanders. Already on 4 July, only nine days after hostilities had begun, MacArthur was considering the possibility of an amphibious landing somewhere on the west coast of the peninsula. His aim was to create a second front and to seize the city of Seoul. Besides being of great significance politically as the capital of South Korea, Seoul was of considerable strategic importance. MacArthur argued that the lightning dash of the North Korean People's Army southwards would have stretched their supply lines almost to breaking point. A strike at Seoul, which stood at the centre of Korea's road and rail communications, would greatly weaken the North Korean efforts to capture Pusan.

ABOVE *General Douglas MacArthur, Commander of the UN forces, conceived the Inchon plan. He had to win over most of his colleagues, to whom the operation seemed a dangerous gamble.* BELOW *A Vought F4U Corsair about to take off on a sortie.*

Plans are laid

MacArthur's original plan, codenamed Operation Blue Heart, was to land at Inchon, the port for Seoul, on 22 July. This allowed only 18 days for the preparation of the amphibious force. A shortage of troops, combined with the critical situation developing at Pusan, forced him to cancel this operation on 14 July.

The dispatch of the whole of the 1st Marine Division to Korea from the United States was authorised by the US Joint Chiefs of Staff Committee (JCS) on 25 July. One of its three regiments which had been committed earlier arrived in Korea in the first week of August.

Planning for MacArthur's assault on Inchon got under way in mid-August. It was to be known as Operation Chromite. It would involve the 1st Marine Division and the 7th US Infantry Division (the last remaining US division in Japan brought up to strength with South Korean soldiers), which together formed the X US Corps.

The landing was arranged to take place on 15 September. It was planned by the Joint Strategic Plans and Operations Group (JSPOG), part of the operations staff of the US Far East Command of which MacArthur was the commander-in-chief. Certain officers of the JSPOG formed the nucleus of X Corps staff for the landing; the corps was to be commanded by Major General Edward Almond who was MacArthur's Chief of Staff.

The plan was that the 1st Marine Division would seize Wolmi-do, an island controlling Inchon harbour, then the city of Inchon itself, Kimpo airfield and finally the capital city, Seoul. The 7th Infantry Division, landing after the marines and to their right, was to cover their flank and then move south towards the town of Suwon. With Seoul in UN hands the corps would then hold their ground and await the advance of Lieutenant General Walton Walker's Eighth Army from the south.

There was a great deal of opposition to the landing taking place at Inchon,

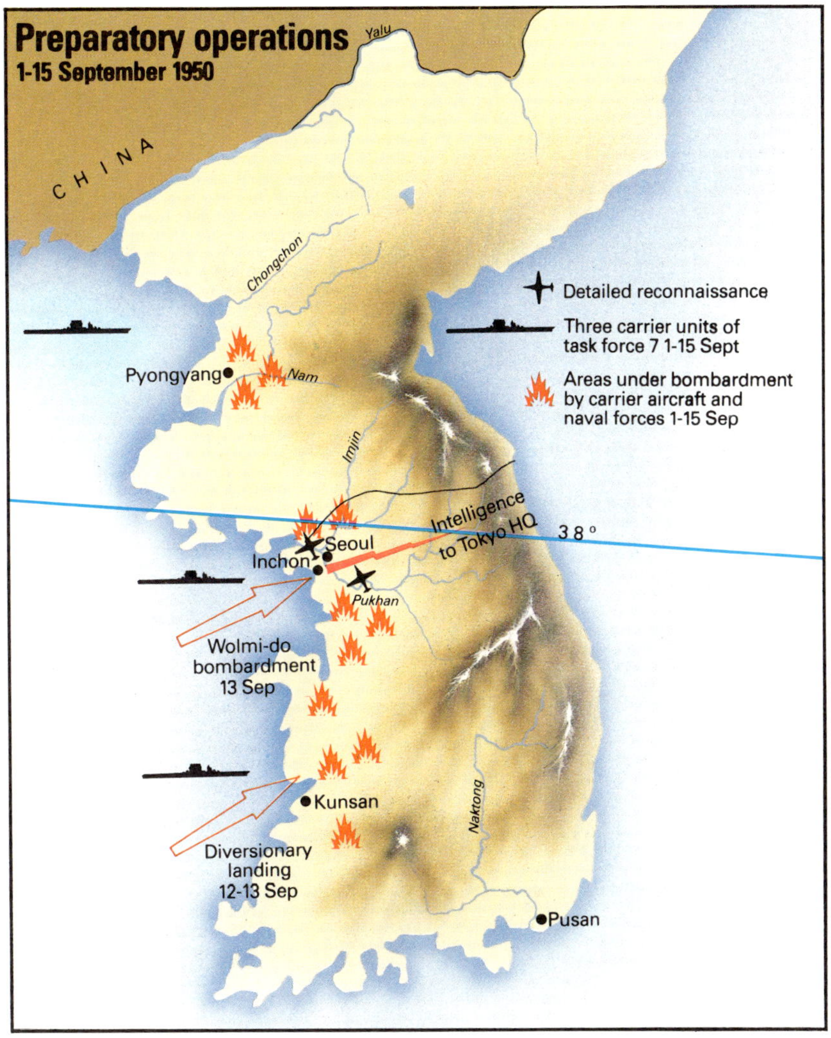

both on technical grounds and with regard to its effectiveness in relieving the pressure on the embattled Pusan Perimeter. An American naval officer said afterwards: 'We drew up a list of every conceivable and natural handicap and Inchon had 'em all.'

To reach the harbour a narrow channel scattered with reefs, islands and rocks had to be negotiated. To make matters worse there is at Inchon a very large tidal range, which meant that at low tide the harbour was cut off by some 5km (3 miles) of mud flats, creeks and streams. Worst of all, there would only be three hours of high water sufficient to allow Tank Landing Ships into the harbour on one day a month. Finally, the landing would have to take place not on beaches, as had always been the case in World War II, but at harbour walls 3.6m (12 feet) high which would have to be scaled by ladders and which led directly into the city. All possible landing sites were clearly visible from enemy-held hills surrounding the harbour.

Anxieties regarding these natural difficulties only confirmed the view of many that it would be madness to take away possible reinforcements for the Pusan Perimeter to engage in an enterprise fraught with such danger and uncertainty. Others who saw the value of surprise in such an audacious stroke baulked at the numerous disadvantages posed by landing at Inchon and argued for more suitable landing points further south or even north.

The final decision

All the objections were raised at a conference in Tokyo at MacArthur's HQ on 23 August. Two members of the JCS were present, the Chief of Naval Operations and the army Chief of Staff. Both became increasingly sceptical of success as the naval and military experts from MacArthur's staff listed the difficulties. However, the JCS members and MacArthur's planners were completely won over to the general's side when he justified his plan in the course of a 45 minute exposition without the use of a single note and during which he calmly smoked his pipe.

MacArthur argued that he based his choice of Inchon not on logical grounds but on his own intuition. The very arguments used to dissuade him only confirmed him in his belief that his choice was the correct one. As he saw it the difficulties were so many and so diverse that the enemy would consider a landing at Inchon to be highly unlikely, and complete surprise would thus be achieved.

The JCS signified their approval of the landing on 28 August and the final plans for the assault were completed on 4 September. Eleven days later the invasion got under way as troops were landed on the morning tide.

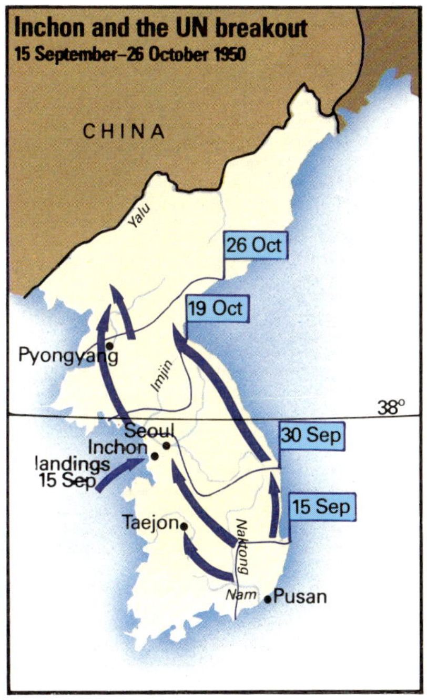

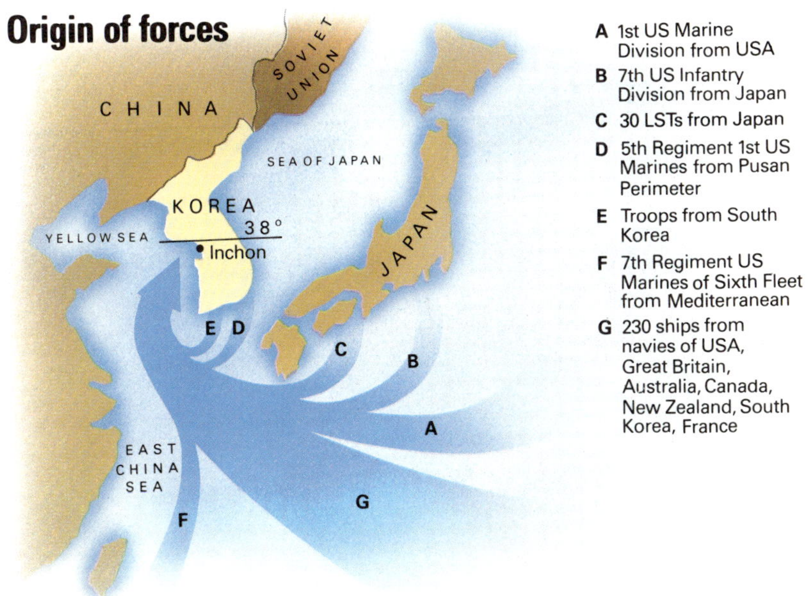

Inchon 2: The Landing

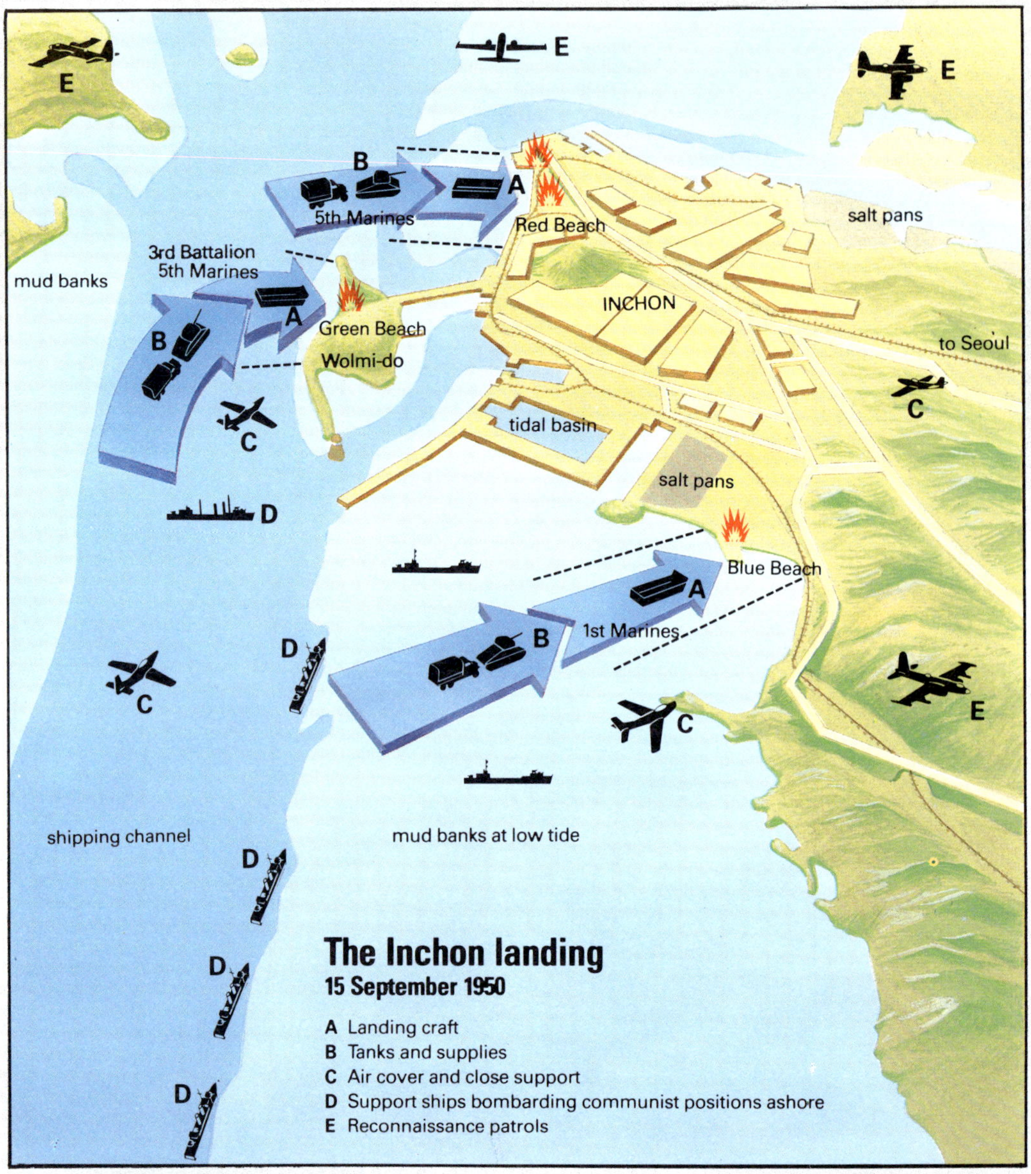

OPERATION CHROMITE, the landing at Inchon on 15 September 1950, was the largest amphibious operation undertaken since World War II. Preparations were made in extreme haste and the choice of landing site confronted the attacking force with physical conditions both on land and sea such as had never previously been experienced.

Overall command was in the hands of Admiral Arthur Struble, Commander-in-Chief of the US Seventh Fleet. Once the intial landing was secure, command of the ground forces would be assumed by Major General Edward Almond, Commander of the X US Corps.

In late August and early September enemy strength expected in Inchon was estimated at about 2000 and in Seoul, some 30km (18 miles) inland, at approximately 5000. In the event these figures were proved to be substantially correct.

On 31 August an experienced American naval lieutenant was landed, with a small team of men, on an island at the mouth of the shipping channel to Inchon harbour. He dispatched friendly local inhabitants into the harbour itself where they gathered detailed information on the enemy dispositions, water depths and the

Up the ladder and over the top: marines go ashore at Inchon. The speed at which the invasion was carried out was notable and losses were few.

delineation of the mud flats as the tides receded. A radio transmitter relayed this information to the planners in Tokyo. This daring adventure was, despite some narrow escapes, completely successful and the officer even managed to activate a lighthouse on the night preceding the landing to guide in the advanced attack group.

Choice of troops

It was decided to use the 1st Marine Division and the 7th US Infantry Division for the landing. The 1st Marine Division comprised the 1st, the 5th and the 7th Marine Regiments. The 1st and 7th (less one battalion) came from America with the divisional HQ and arrived in Japan between 22 August and 6 September. The 5th Regiment, which had been deployed in the battle for the Pusan Perimeter, was extricated from the mainland fighting on 6 September, and the additional battalion for the 7th Regiment arrived in Pusan from the US Sixth Fleet in the Mediterranean three days later.

The 7th Infantry Division was the sole remaining formation of the US occupying troops in Japan. The other three divisions were already fighting in Korea and the 7th Division had been constantly milked to build up their numbers. When the division was alerted for the Inchon landing on 26 July it was short of 290 officers and more than 8000 men. As a result, all reinforcements to the Far East from the United States went straight to the 7th Infantry Division. A total of 390 officers and 5400 men, almost all from training establishments in America and of high quality, were posted into the division. The numbers still had to be made up by press-ganging 8000 South Korean civilians who were given only the most basic training.

The plan was for the 1st Marine Division to make the initial landings in order to seize Inchon town. The division would then advance on Seoul. The 7th Infantry Division would land the following day and advance inland to the south and east of the city.

It was decided that a battalion of the 5th Marines would land on Wolmi-do ('Green Beach') on the morning tide of 15 September and capture the island. The main body of the division would land on the evening tide, the remainder of the 5th Marines at Inchon itself ('Red Beach') and the 1st Marines to the south of the town at 'Blue Beach'.

Supply and fire support

The total number of men involved was about 70,000 coming from the US Marine Corps, US Army, US Navy and the RoK Marine Corps. An armada was needed to carry these men, equipment and supplies, and to provide protection and fire support. More than 230 ships were assembled. Most came from the United States, but others came from the Royal Navy, the Royal Australian, Canadian and New Zealand Navies, the RoK Navy and the French Navy, as well as specially chartered merchantmen.

Direct fire support for the landing was provided by the naval and air forces. Diversionary bombardments and air attacks were carried out well to the north and south of Inchon to mislead the enemy. Naval bombardment of Wolmi-do and Inchon began two days before the landing and virtually neutralised opposition.

Going in

On the appointed day the advance attack group comprising the 3rd Battalion of the 5th Marines arrived 1.6km (1 mile) off Wolmi-do at 0530 hours and loaded into landing craft. The first line set off at 0625 and reached the island unopposed eight minutes later. Within half an hour their tanks had landed and by 0730 the island was secure at a cost of only 17 wounded. Thereafter the battalion remained marooned for the rest of the day as the tide went out.

At 1530 hours troops of the 1st and 5th Marines loaded into their landing craft. At 1733 the first men of the 5th Marines landed on 'Red Beach' and, despite encountering resistance, reached the high ground dominating Inchon by midnight.

The 1st Marines landed on 'Blue Beach' at 1732. There were intially some problems of location caused by heavy smoke clouds and the pitch darkness as night fell, but by 0130 on 16 September the regiment had reached the main road from Inchon to Seoul, having met little opposition.

LSTs unload men and equipment on the beach. Some 47 LSTs, most of which were rusty and scarcely seaworthy, took part in the operation.

At the end of D-day all objectives had been taken for the loss of 20 men killed, 1 missing and 174 wounded. By the end of D+1 the 1st and 5th Marines had linked up and advanced to secure and establish a perimeter 10km (6 miles) inland from the landing sites. MacArthur's bold stroke paid off fully when Seoul was captured on 22 September and the demoralised remnants of the North Korean Army fell backwards after X Corps linked up with the Eighth Army four days later.

From Inchon to Seoul

15–22 September 1950

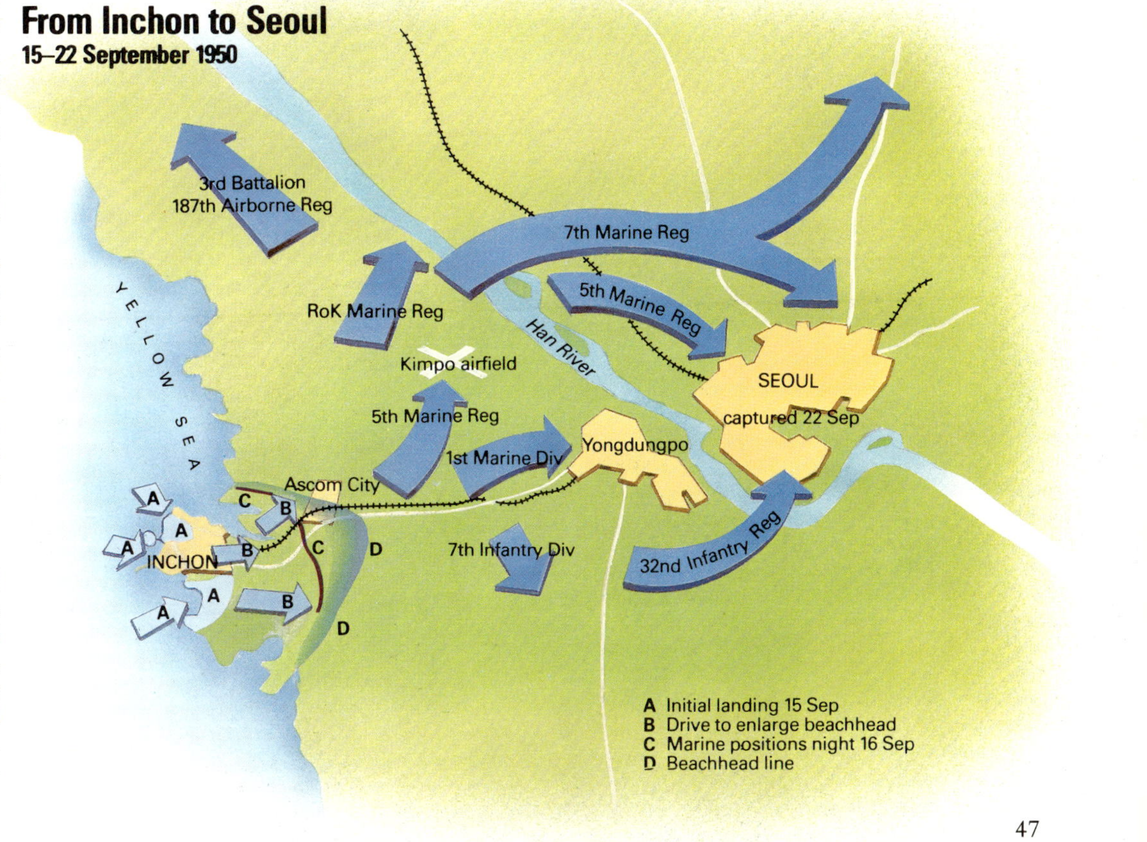

China's Commitment

ON 14 OCTOBER 1950 General Douglas MacArthur's intelligence experts reported a total of 38 Chinese divisions in Manchuria but concluded that none had entered Korea and, indeed, that the opportune moment for them to do so had passed. In fact, on the day this assessment was published, six Chinese armies began to march into North Korea. They comprised the 38th, 39th, 40th, 42nd, 50th and 66th Armies of the XIII Army Group, one of the five army groups of Lin Piao's IV Field Army. By the end of October almost 200,000 men were deployed in close proximity to the UN forces.

By late November China's IX Army Group had moved into Korea. This was deployed against the X US Corps east of the mountain range leaving the original XIII Army Group to oppose Eighth US Army in the west. In the following months some of these formations were badly mauled and were relieved by fresh troops. Numbers, however, never dropped below 200,000. After the armistice talks began and the front line became static, Chinese troop levels rose to about 300,000.

Tough and seasoned troops

The Chinese armies in Korea were largely composed of simple, scarcely literate peasants: sturdy men who had lived through the Japanese occupation and the civil war. They were used to hardship, used to living rough and understood the climate and countryside of Korea. Political officers sustained morale. Almost all their officers had fought the Japanese and even the junior officers were veterans of the Chinese Civil War.

That this army could enter Korea virtually unnoticed was largely due to expert planning and organisation. To avoid detection by constant daylight air reconnaissance, all movement was carried out at night. Groups of battalion or company size marched from after dusk until just before dawn over desperately rugged and rocky terrain. One army is known to have marched some 460km (286 miles) in this way in 19 days. Movement in daytime was forbidden so small units of troops took shelter in scattered peasant huts or in bushes and scrub.

Chinese weaponry

Each of the six Chinese armies comprised three divisions. Each division was made up of some 10,000 men. The divisions were normally composed of three regiments, a pack artillery battalion, engineers, transport (donkey, mule or horse), medical and communication companies. There were no vehicles, tanks or towed artillery. To overcome the lack of anti-tank weapons each platoon was issued with TNT which was packed in 2.25kg (5 pound) 'satchel charges', each of which was sufficient to blow the track off a tank. The lack of heavy equipment allowed divisions to move across country in complete secrecy and gain great advantage from surprise.

Some artillery crossed into Korea but it was scarcely used in the early stages of the fighting. Once, however, the stalemate set in on the 38th parallel in the summer of 1951 the Chinese became far more effective in their use of artillery and heavy mortars.

No uniformity existed among the personal weapons carried by soldiers.

ABOVE *Chinese soldiers around a camp fire in North Korea. China's entry into the war saved North Korea from total defeat.* BELOW *Piped on by a military band, Chinese troops march to battle.*

The only standard weapon was the PPSh ('burp gun') of Russian origin. Otherwise men carried old US rifles, carbines, pistols, submachine guns and some light and heavy machine guns – all obtained from the defeated Nationalist Chinese. In addition there were large quantities of Japanese weapons acquired during World War II.

Communications were primitive. There were no radios below regimental level and few, if any, telephones. At battalion and company level, control was maintained by the use of flares, bugles, horns or whistles.

Each soldier in contact with the enemy carried, as well as a personal weapon, 80 rounds of ammunition, four or five grenades and also extra clips and magazines for others who carried automatic weapons. Most carried one or two mortar bombs or TNT anti-tank satchel charges. Emergency rations of rice, tea and salt,

ABOVE *Amidst the smoke of gunfire Chinese troops advance against UN forces. The Chinese relied on numerical superiority but also used guerrilla tactics.*

sufficient for five days, were in each man's pack. Soldiers were expected to supplement this sparse diet with vegetables or anything else they might be able to obtain locally.

Supply and tactics

The Chinese Army's administrative 'tail' was practically non-existent. It was estimated that a division needed only 40 tonnes of rations, water, clothing, equipment, fuel and ammunition a day. This compares with a UN figure of something in the order of 350 tonnes a day for a similar number of troops. Such figures help to explain the Chinese ability to move and fight with scarcely any material support, but to fight effectively they had to be able to live off the land or their enemy to a certain degree. If this was not possible their offensive capability could not be sustained for long.

The Chinese continued to use the railways for supply and replenishment despite repeated destruction from the air. Gangs of workers lined each railway. Hidden during air attacks they emerged afterwards and using stores, also well hidden, replaced lines and rebuilt culverts within hours.

Only half the Chinese supplies travelled by rail; the rest were carried by thousands of porters. Large groups of these sturdy peasants, moving only at night and carrying their loads in two bamboo baskets supported on the ends of a pole on their shoulders, kept up a seemingly tireless loping trot. Each man carried a load of about 35–45kg (80–100 pounds).

The tactics used by the Chinese armies were largely those developed from Mao's campaigns against the Japanese and Chiang Kai-shek's Nationalists. Units and larger formations were highly disciplined and drilled almost into machine-like effectiveness. Mobility, deception and surprise lay behind their success as did their capacity to concentrate rapidly and deliver an unnerving, noisy, rapid attack from which they would disengage and quietly disappear.

The method of attack most frequently used followed a tactic developed by Lin Piao in which the unit to be attacked was assaulted from two sides while heavy fire was brought to bear from a third group covering the attack. If it was possible to bypass the enemy position and bring the fire to bear from the enemy's rear, so much the better. Adept at reconnaissance and night movement the Chinese units dismayed UN forces by their ability to locate the junction points of UN units and to attack these at the weakest point or, as frequently happened, to infiltrate unseen to the rear and mount an attack from there.

The Chinese turned their weaknesses to their own advantage and achieved some success against an enemy better armed and equipped.

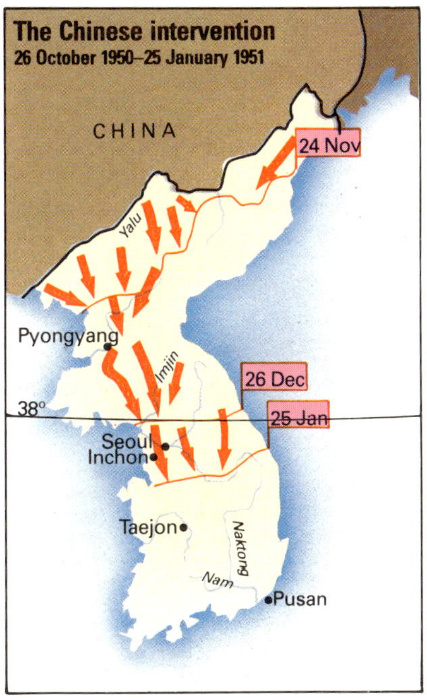

Rival Troop Strength in Korea July–August 1951

Chinese	248,000	American	230,000
North Korean	211,000	South Korean and other UN forces	356,000
	459,000		**586,000**

The American Contribution

AFTER WORLD WAR II the argument that the atom bomb delivered from the air precluded the need for other major defensive forces strengthened America's inclination to withdraw from worldwide military commitments and led to a drastic rundown in the US armed forces throughout the world. This rundown was particularly evident in Japan, where the Americans retained just four under-strength divisions on occupation duties. As a result, although the United States assumed the greatest military burden when hostilities broke out in Korea she was ill-prepared to do so.

Troops from Japan and America

It was General Douglas MacArthur's insistence that US forces be committed to the peninsula that led to elements of the 24th US Infantry Division being dispatched from Japan to Korea within a week of the start of the war. They were followed before the end of the month by the 1st US Cavalry Division and the 25th US Infantry Division. Only the 7th US Infantry Division remained in Japan.

All the divisions sent to Korea were very much under-strength, poorly trained, physically unfit and very badly armed and equipped. Except for the 24th Infantry Division all were short of three of their establishment of nine battalions of infantry; and the artillery battalions (three to a division) had only two batteries of guns instead of the normal three. In the 24th Infantry Division one regiment had its three infantry battalions and its artillery battalion was also up to strength, so it was this regiment that was sent first.

Each division had a tank battalion which was equipped with the M24 light tank (Chaffee). Nearly all of the equipment, guns and tanks in Japan had seen service in World War II. Much of it was very worn. When the 24th Infantry Division was made ready for Korea a total of 2108 men were transferred to it from the other divisions in Japan to bring it up to its proper establishment.

In the United States, reservists were drafted into the army and the marines in a hasty attempt to build up further reinforcements for Korea. By 3 July the order had gone out to form a Marine Brigade (the equivalent to a US Army regiment of three battalions). This brigade, 6500-strong, disembarked at Pusan on 2 August. In early August, also, the 2nd US Infantry Division arrived in Korea from the United States together with an additional regiment from Hawaii.

The remainder of the 1st US Marine Division, formed largely in America but with battalions drawn from other parts of the world, arrived in the Far East in September. Together with the 7th US Infantry Division it carried out the landing at Inchon in the middle of September.

The build-up of the US forces

The straight-wing F9F Panther was the first US Navy jet fighter to be used in war and it entered service in Korea in July 1950. The Panther carried four 20mm guns, had a maximum speed of 932km/h (579mph) at 1525m (5000 feet) and a range of 2092km (1300 miles). BELOW *Two Panthers fly over Wonsan, North Korea, in July 1951.* INSETS *A Panther on board the USS* Philippine Sea *(left). Pilots undergo briefing (right) before leaving on a mission against North Korean targets.*

fighting under the United Nations flag was complete. The divisions now assembled were to continue to serve with contingents from other nations until the armistice was signed in July 1953.

Disposition of forces

Although the distribution of forces changed from time to time, all the American divisions were grouped together under three corps: I Corps, activated on 13 September; IX Corps, activated on 23 September and X Corps, activated to command the Inchon landing. These corps came under the command of the Eighth US Army in Korea (EUSAK) except in one case when, after the Inchon landing and before the initial Chinese onslaught, X Corps came directly under General MacArthur's command.

After Inchon, X Corps deployed on the east coast and the division of command between EUSAK in the west and X Corps to the east beyond the mountain range led to major problems in command, communication and co-ordination which undoubtedly facilitated the Chinese success. EUSAK was commanded by General Walton Walker until he was killed in a vehicle accident on 23 December 1950, when General Matthew Ridgway took over. When Ridgway relieved MacArthur after the latter's dismissal in April 1951, General James Van Fleet assumed command of EUSAK.

Supplies of men and weapons

Throughout the early months of war the one overriding problem for the commander-in-chief was finding sufficient men to form an army. All the divisions arriving from Japan were brought up to strength in turn by denuding those that remained. When it became necessary for the last division to go, it was not possible to build up the manpower of the division without recourse to a most unusual measure. Many thousands of Korean civilians were shipped to Japan, clothed, armed, equipped and given a few days' training. They were then allocated, 100 to each company and battery in the division. This 'Korean augmentation', as it was known, was meant ultimately to lead to the infusion of 30,000 to 40,000 Koreans into all the US divisions in Korea. But so severe were the problems of language, custom and training that the system lapsed by the end of 1950.

All the US divisions, including the 1st Cavalry Division, arrived in Korea as infantry divisions and thus possessed only one tank battalion each. The North Koreans' effective use of tanks demanded that more tanks be made available and on 7 August an additional three tank battalions arrived from the United States equipped with more modern medium tanks. A further three battalions arrived later in the month and even before the Inchon landing there were some 500 tanks in Korea.

From 23 July an ever more effective logistic system operated from Japan to Korea. Initially by means of air lifts and then by sea and rail the UN forces were sustained very effectively. Indeed, such a system coupled with developing naval and air support went a long way to sustaining the fumbling efforts of the ground forces in the early stages of the war and provided the massive build-up of equipment, guns and ammunition which provided the UN forces with the ability to break successive Chinese infantry attacks.

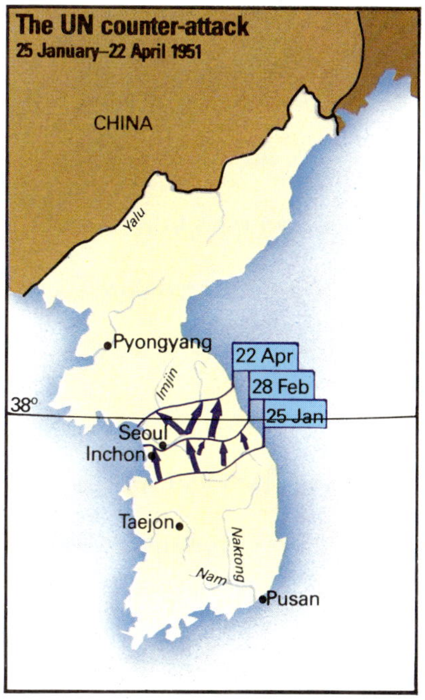

BELOW *Long Toms fire at communist positions across a frozen landscape.*
BOTTOM *Men of the 25th Infantry, newly flown in from Japan, head for the front in the first weeks of the war.*

Troops from Many Nations

FIFTY-THREE COUNTRIES out of a total of 59 member states of the United Nations approved the Security Council resolution of 27 June 1950 calling for members to aid the Republic of Korea to resist the attack from the north. Of those states 40 offered help in one way or another but only 15, apart from the United States, actually sent military forces to Korea; a further 5 sent medical units.

The military forces sent by the participating countries were scarcely more than a token and amounted in total to 44,000 men. This is in stark contrast to the American contribution, which at its peak stood at more than 300,000. However, though the number of men produced by other countries was small, their presence boosted American morale and did much to demonstrate the effectiveness of the United Nations when faced with a grave crisis. Leadership of the United Nations Command in Korea was vested in the Commander-in-Chief of the US Far East Command (General Douglas MacArthur at first and later General Matthew Ridgway).

The ground forces were slow to arrive and none reached Korea in the first two months of the war. The first to come were the British who sent the 27th Brigade HQ, the 1st Battalion of the Argyll and Sutherland Highlanders and the 1st Battalion of the Middlesex Regiment from Hong Kong. This contingent numbered about 2000 men. They arrived in Pusan on 29 August and soon found themselves committed to the defence of the Perimeter.

The 3rd Battalion of the Royal Australian Regiment joined 27th Brigade in September and by December the brigade was completed with the arrival of a New Zealand artillery regiment. Henceforth it would be known as the 27th Commonwealth Brigade.

A further (and complete) British Brigade, the 29th, reached Pusan in November. It brought with it the 1st Battalions of the Gloucestershire Regiment, the Royal Northumberland Fusiliers and the Royal Ulster Rifles.

The first battalion of a Canadian contingent reached the front in early January 1951, and the remainder of the 25th Canadian Brigade was in action by May. There were now sufficient troops from the Commonwealth to form a full division, and in July 1951 the 1st Commonwealth

ABOVE *Thai troops disembark at Pusan.* BELOW *A Canadian light machine gun team in field training in Korea.* OPPOSITE TOP *Australian troops, wearing characteristic slouch hats, enjoy a brew during a break in a wintry march through rugged country.*

Division was formed under the command of Major General James Cassels. At its highest strength the Commonwealth contribution amounted to 20,000 men.

Forces from Europe

The next largest contingent came from Turkey. The Turks produced a complete brigade of about 5000 men who arrived in Korea in October 1950. They earned a reputation second to none throughout the war, proving both fearless in attack and stalwart in defence.

Of the other NATO countries the French, with problems enough of their own in Indochina, contributed only a battalion. The French were well known throughout the peninsula for their dash and cheerfulness. On one occasion the battalion commander was reprimanded for allowing his men to cook after dark, thereby giving their positions away. His response was immediate: 'If they fire on us we shall then know where they are; if they attack us we shall kill them.'

A battalion each from Greece, the Netherlands and Belgium together with a company from Luxembourg's small army arrived in the Far East in October 1950 and were allotted roles within the American divisions. Only two Asian countries provided fighting contingents. The Philippines sent an infantry battalion and a tank company while Thailand dispatched an infantry battalion. Ethiopia was the one African country to contribute infantry soldiers.

South Africa, Britain, Australia, Belgium and France provided air force fighter and transport contingents. Naval forces from Britain, Canada, Australia, New Zealand and France which happened to be stationed in Japanese waters at the outbreak of the war, were in action off the coast of Korea from early July 1950.

The other major contributing country was, of course, the Republic of Korea (RoK) itself. The army she put into the field at the outbreak of hostilities numbered some 95,000 men forming eight divisions. The RoK Navy, operating as a coast guard, comprised 6000 men. The air force, equipped with liaison aircraft and some fighters, for which there were no fully trained pilots, had 1800 men.

By 4 August, following the North Korean onslaught, the disorganised remnants of the RoK Army were reduced to 45,000 men. Yet after the UN forces seized the initiative in September and October the army was reorganised and restored to 91,000 troops under arms.

The Chinese tactic of almost always beginning major attacks by descending on less well equipped RoK divisions meant that the South Koreans suffered very great casualties. Despite this, however, the South Korean Army remained a numerically strong force and at the close of the war comprised some ten divisions with a total of well over 100,000 men.

World War II equipment

The forces of all the countries that took part in the war were mostly well armed and equipped though weapons, tanks and vehicles inevitably dated back to World War II. The British and Commonwealth infantry were armed with the No 4 Rifle, and the Bren Light Machine Gun, with some Sten Machine Carbines and an Australian equivalent, the Owen Machine Carbine. The field artillery from Britain, Canada and New Zealand, of which there was a regiment of three batteries allocated to each brigade, were equipped with the 25-pounder field gun which had been used so successfully in North Africa and Europe. The World War II Cromwell tank was used by Commonwealth armoured units initially, but later the new British Centurion tank was tested in Korean conditions.

Non-Commonwealth units were, for the most part, equipped with American weapons and vehicles. As they were almost invariably brigaded with US divisions they relied for fire and armoured support on American units.

A Royal Artillery 25-pounder blasts away at the enemy. This gun was highly rated for versatility and reliability.

Contributors to the UN Command

Australia	Two infantry battalions, naval forces, one fighter squadron
Belgium	One infantry battalion
Canada	One reinforced infantry brigade, naval forces, one squadron of transport aircraft
Colombia	One infantry battalion, one naval frigate
Ethiopia	One infantry battalion
France	One reinforced infantry battalion
Great Britain	Two infantry brigades, one armoured regiment, one and a half artillery regiments, one and a half combat engineer regiments with supporting ground forces, the Far Eastern Fleet, two squadrons of Sunderlands
Greece	One infantry battalion, transport aircraft
Holland	One infantry battalion, naval forces
Luxembourg	One infantry company
New Zealand	One artillery regiment
Philippines	One infantry battalion, one company of tanks
South Africa	One fighter squadron
Thailand	One infantry battalion, naval forces, air and naval transports
Turkey	One infantry brigade
medical aid	Denmark, India, Italy, Norway, Sweden

Armoured Warfare

WORLD WAR II had been the war of the tank, and the confrontation in Korea again brought large tank forces into action. But their use was to be very different to what it had been in the early 1940s.

To achieve their full potential tanks must have good visibility, firm ground on which to move, and open country which will allow them to manoeuvre and strike at an enemy unsuspected. So Korea, with its rugged mountains, narrow passes, steep valleys and waterlogged rice fields, was a tank commander's nightmare. And yet, surprisingly, tanks did play a singularly effective, if sometimes unorthodox part in the first year of the war, during which it took the form of a swiftly moving campaign.

North Korean tank tactics

When the North Korean People's Army (NKPA) launched their attack on 25 June 1950 their tanks were used very effectively against the Republic of Korea (RoK) Army. The NKPA initially possessed 150 Russian-built T34s armed with an 85mm gun while the RoK Army had no tanks of their own nor even effective anti-tank weapons. In these circumstances the approach of tanks on the battlefield had a particularly demoralising effect upon the South Koreans.

During the whole of the advance southwards towards Pusan the NKPA deployed their tanks in much the same tactical manner. They would advance along a road or track in column, one behind the other, move straight into the enemy infantry position, pass through it and beyond its rear. Co-ordinating with this, infantry would bypass the enemy position on both flanks, closing in at the rear to cut off any chance of withdrawal. The tanks would bring fire to bear on the enemy as they passed in order to introduce as much disorder and panic as possible. These tactics, so successful against RoK units, were also deployed against American and British troops after their arrival at the battlefront in July and August.

In the first assault against an American-held sector of the front on 5 July, 33 NKPA tanks advanced towards the American positions in groups of four, all following in column. They fired their 85mm guns and machine guns as they advanced, but as usual did not deploy. The American commander had artillery fire directed on the tanks but it had no effect.

One US team armed with a 2.36 inch anti-tank weapon (bazooka) fired 22 rockets at 14m (15 yards) into the rear, more thinly armoured parts of the tank hulls as they passed but caused only slight external damage. It was only when artillery fired high explosive anti-tank (HEAT) shells in the direct role that two of the leading tanks were stopped. After the six HEAT rounds available had been used the gunners continued to fire high explosive but without effect. The shells were observed to ricochet off the tanks' armour.

Countering the T34

Such success did the T34 tanks have in this early stage of the war that the Americans rushed tank units to Korea to support their divisions from Japan which had brought only light reconnaissance tanks and armoured cars. By the third week of August there were more than 500 medium tanks in Korea. They included a mixture of M4A3 Shermans, M26 Pershings and M46 Pattons. Although they were never used in large numbers in decisive actions they were very effective in providing punch for infantry assaults and in the fire support role in static defensive positions.

Other weapons were used to perhaps greater effect to combat the menace of the North Korean tanks. As the war progressed the UN air forces developed their capability to rocket and bomb tanks, and napalm bombs were found to be particularly effective. But not until late July 1950 was a really useful anti-tank weapon put into the hands of the infantry.

This was the 3.5 inch rocket launcher (bazooka). The weapon had been developed towards the end of World War II but ammunition for it had not been perfected until just before the outbreak of the Korean War. On 20 July, during the NKPA assault on the city of Taejon, ten T34 tanks were destroyed by 3.5 inch rocket launchers – and this on the first day they were brought into action.

'I got me a tank'

In the early stages of the war the North Koreans used their tanks to considerable advantage in built-up areas. Individual tanks would patrol along streets, bringing their main armament and machine guns to bear against UN troops attempting to hold out in buildings.

ABOVE *Men and tanks of the 17th Royal Corps of Tanks, 7th Division, near the Chinese border at Hyesanjin, November 1950. UN tanks were almost exclusively used to support artillery assaults and provide defensive fire.* BELOW *M4A3 Shermans in North Korea, 1951.*

The tanks that attacked Taejon on 20 July entered the city, which was defended by units of the 24th US Division, at dawn. They moved singly or in pairs and carried large numbers of infantry soldiers on their decks. On reaching the city centre the infantry dismounted and established strong points in buildings from which snipers persistently disrupted the US troops' attempts to dislodge them.

One tank rumbled past a regimental command post where the divisional commander, Major General William Dean, happened to be at the time. He took two men armed with a 3.5 inch rocket launcher in pursuit of this tank. For an hour they laboriously stalked it as it moved from street to street. They climbed over walls and fences and took short cuts through houses, subject all the time to sniper fire. Finally, they found themselves looking down from a two-storey building directly onto the tank, stationary, 6m (20 feet) below. It took three shots from the rocket launcher to kill the crew and immobilise the tank.

General Dean let it be known to his division that he had personally destroyed a tank. 'I got me a tank' became a much-quoted phrase; and in getting a tank the general made the point that well-armed infantrymen were more than a match for armour in a built-up area. From then on the North Koreans used their tanks much more circumspectly as it became common practice for tank-hunting parties to move through towns with considerable success.

Rarely in Korea were tanks matched against each other in any quantity. One of the largest actions recorded was between a unit of the North Korean Army and a company of the 70th US Tank Battalion supporting the break-out from the Pusan Perimeter by the 1st US Cavalry Division. In this action the Americans lost two Sherman tanks and succeeded in destroying only one T34 with tank gun fire. An additional five T34s were destroyed in the same battle by infantry teams using 3.5 inch rocket launchers.

Estimates by UN forces made at the end of September 1950 showed that a total of 239 T34s (their total force at that date) had been lost by the NKPA, whereas the UN forces by that time had lost just 60 tanks.

TOP *A T34 with an 85mm gun. The T34s had no difficulty in smashing through the RoK Army but met a stiffer test once UN armour arrived.* ABOVE *A Centurion in an ice-covered stream.* BELOW *M26 Pershings fire on a North Korean observation post across the Naktong River.*

T34/85
weight 32 tonnes (31.5 tons) **length** 7.5m (24ft 6in) **height** 2.38m (7ft 10in) **armament** 1x85mm gun, 2x7.62mm machine guns **ammunition carried** 56 rounds for 85mm, 2745 rounds for machine guns

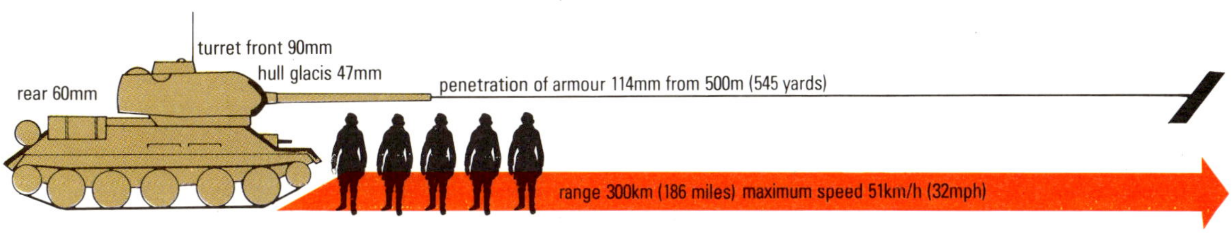

Sherman M4A3
weight 31.5 tonnes (31 tons) **length** 7.53m (24ft 9in) **height** 2.93m (9ft 7in) **armament** 1x76mm gun, 2x0.30in machine guns, 1x0.50in machine gun **ammunition carried** 89 rounds for 76mm, 7750 rounds for 0.30, 6250 rounds for 0.50

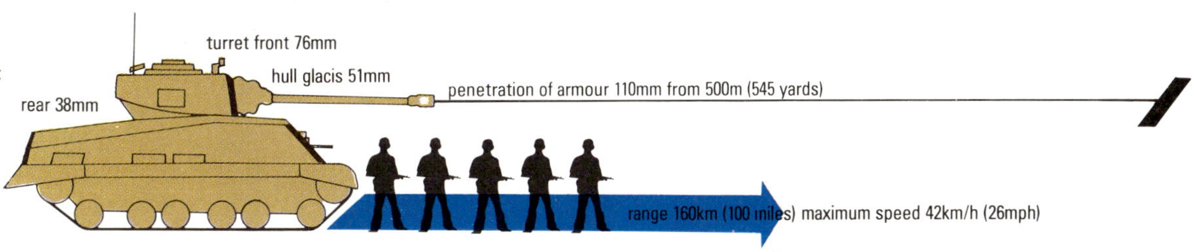

The Glosters at Imjin River

AFTER THE RAPID RETREAT of the UN forces following the intervention of the Chinese, the line was eventually stabilised. Then, slowly, making use of a massive weight of firepower, the UN forces gradually pushed northwards again. By 15 March 1951 Seoul was recaptured for the last time and General Matthew Ridgway ordered the advance to continue to establish a line slightly north of the 38th parallel. The I US Corps had advanced on the left of the UN formation and the British 29th Brigade found itself occupying temporary positions on the line of the Imjin River.

The opposing sides

While it had been intended to continue the advance further north from there it was known that large Chinese forces were grouped to the north of the UN positions preparing for a major attack. Despite the rapid advance of the Eighth US Army these enemy forces had managed to extricate themselves and had not suffered any severe losses.

The 29th Brigade comprised the 1st Battalion of the Gloucestershire Regiment (the Glosters), the 1st Battalion of the Royal Northumberland Fusiliers (the 5th Fusiliers), the 1st Battalion of the Royal Ulster Rifles (the RUR) and a Belgian battalion. In support of them were the 8th King's Royal Irish Hussars (KRIH), 45th Regiment of the Royal Artillery (45th Field) and the 170th Independent Mortar Battery. The brigade was part of the 3rd US Division of the I US Corps.

The Glosters were the left forward battalion with the 5th Fusiliers in the centre and the Belgians, the only battalion deployed to the north of the river, on the right. The RUR were in reserve. The brigade covered an unusually long frontage of about 11km (6 miles) and had been in these positions since 30 March. Because of the temporary nature of the positions and the expectations of moving north, no mines had been laid nor barbed wire defences constructed. At that season the Imjin was fordable almost everywhere on foot.

On 22 April patrols out north of the river contacted the enemy. Aerial reconnaissance that same afternoon reported that roads and tracks leading south towards the Imjin were packed with vehicles and troops on foot.

By dusk forward elements of the enemy had reached the river and had been engaged by 45th Field. By 2100 hours that night all three forward battalions were in contact with the enemy. The standing patrol from the Glosters on the river bank opened fire on large numbers of Chinese troops grouped closely together, who began fording the river at 2130 hours. The whole valley was well illuminated by a full moon in a cloudless sky.

After the intial contacts the enemy infantry continued to advance in an attempt to overrun the British positions. The full attack came before midnight, preceded by heavy artillery and mortar fire not previously available to the Chinese forces. By 0100 hours on 23 April the forward companies of all battalions were under heavy attack.

Forward companies of the 5th Fusiliers and the Belgians had been withdrawn by first light, and confused fighting continued throughout the day. By dusk the RUR had been deployed to the rear of the Belgians and succeeded in covering their withdrawal south of the river. By midnight, 23/24 April, the Glosters were effectively surrounded. All companies had suffered severe casualties and the whole battalion was concentrated on one main hill feature (later to be known as Glosters Hill).

Pressures for withdrawal

During daylight on the 24th repeated attempts were made by tank units from the Philippines and Britain, supported by American, Puerto Rican and Belgian infantry, to relieve the Glosters, but without success. There were equally unsuccessful attempts to drop ammunition and supplies by parachute and to evacuate casualties by helicopter. Air strikes on the enemy were continuous throughout the day but still the Chinese built up their attack.

On the night of 24/25 April the 5th Fusiliers and the Belgians withdrew, covered by the tanks of C Squadron 8 KRIH. The withdrawal was very difficult and costly but was

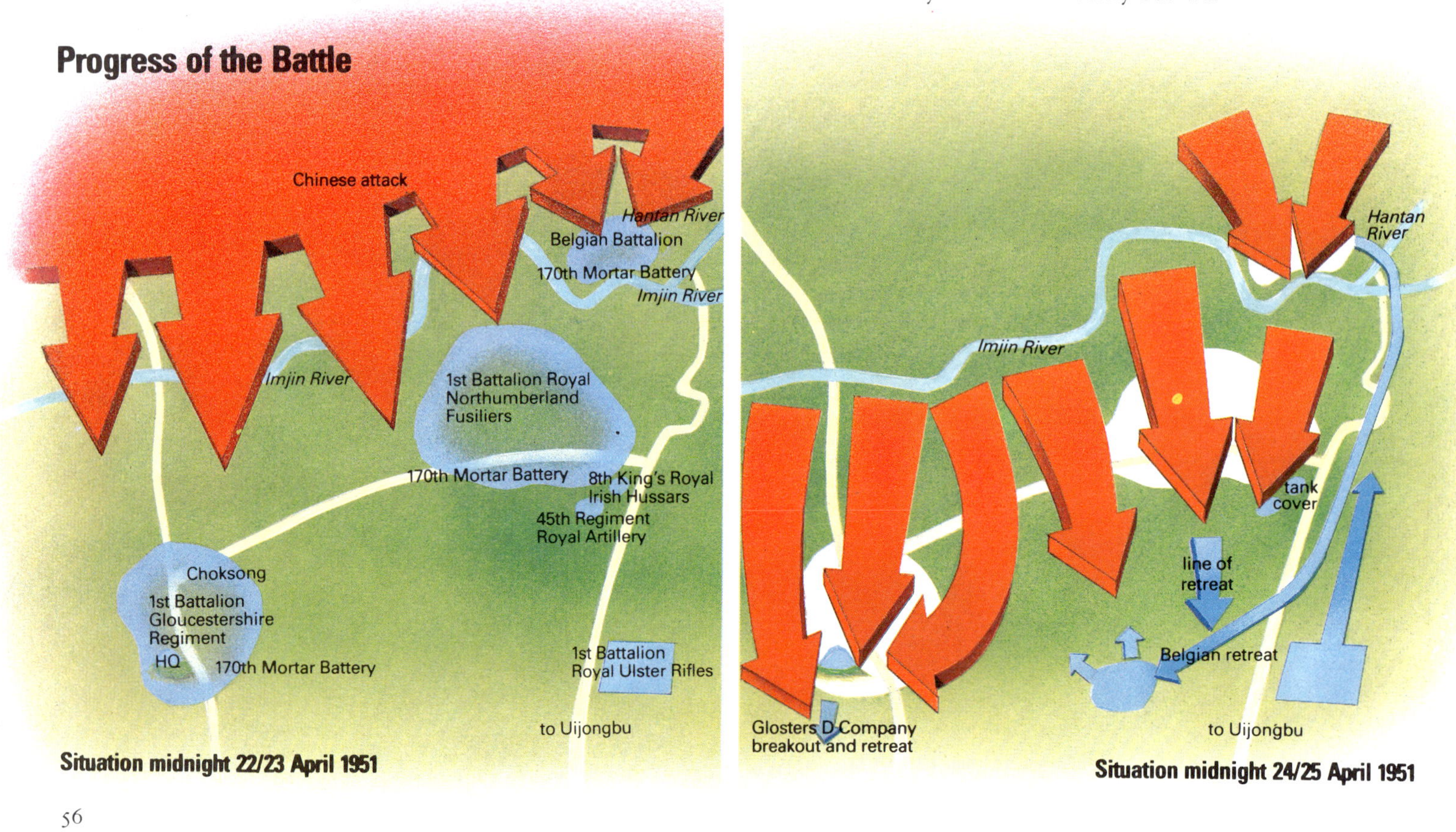

finally completed by midday on the 25th. The Glosters, however, were totally surrounded and could not withdraw.

At 0930 hours that morning the commanding officer of the Glosters ordered his company commanders to fight their way out independently. Three companies failed and all were either killed or captured. D Company succeeded and, despite coming under friendly fire, 39 men made it to UN positions. They were the only Glosters to escape the battle.

The Glosters bore the brunt of the attack on the brigade and as time was to show the brigade had taken the main force of the Chinese attempt to secure Seoul. The Chinese generals' promise of a May Day present for Mao Tse-tung could not be kept and the whole offensive petered out.

In the early stages of their intervention the Chinese attempted to envelop UN positions from both flanks and hit them hard from the rear. By the time they attempted their major offensive in April and May 1951, UN troops had become accustomed to these methods and could combat them by the use of withering supporting fire. So the Chinese fell back on the tactic which maximised their only major remaining advantage, that of manpower.

TOP *The Imjin River shows the residue of war with wrecked vehicles in midstream.* ABOVE *Gloster survivors at a roll call after the battle.* BELOW *The Glosters near Seoul shortly before the Imjin encounter.*

Importance of numbers

The assault on the 29th British Brigade on the Imjin River did have the support of artillery and mortars, but it succeeded simply because the UN forces were overwhelmed by sheer weight of numbers. Some 30 Chinese divisions were used along the whole front in the April offensive and there were 40 more in reserve. The enemy attacked the brigade with more than two divisions during the course of the three-day battle. Some 20,000 men were pitted against 6000.

Leading the Chinese attack were small patrols of 10–15 men. Once they had established contact the main infantry assaulting companies would throw themselves into the fight advancing often in closely packed groups marching shoulder to shoulder. As they reached the British trenches and came under fire they would dodge from cover to cover but always continue moving forward. Once the first wave was overcome by the defenders' fire, a second would pass through – and as many more as were needed until resistance was finally subdued. The advance could only really be stopped if there was sufficient firepower to kill or wound all the enemy troops.

This mass attack eventually overwhelmed the 29th Brigade as it had the formations to its left and right. But determined defence with heavy air and artillery support delayed the enemy for up to three days and inflicted sufficient casualties to force a halt to the offensive. Along the whole front the Chinese had suffered an estimated 70,000 casualties in seven days while the UN figures were scarcely a tenth of that number.

Pork Chop and Old Baldy

ON 23 JUNE 1951 the Soviet Union suggested truce talks in Korea and many in the West thought that the war would soon be over. Yet it took two years of argument, threat and counter-threat and much recrimination before the armistice was finally signed.

In the intervening two years the Chinese and the UN forces were considerably enhanced and their front-line positions became fortified to an extraordinary degree. The situation seemed almost to resemble the trench warfare of World War II. Yet battles of considerable size were initiated by both sides. They had the aim of weakening the resolve of the enemy, seizing ground in order to improve the local tactical situation or acquiring a bargaining counter to be used in the ceasefire talks.

One particular piece of ground became the centre of much attention

LEFT *Pork Chop Hill, seen from the main line of resistance on the day it was evacuated by the 7th Division.* ABOVE *The battle for Pork Chop provided Hollywood with a good story-line and plenty of action. This 1959 release starred Gregory Peck.* BELOW *T66 multiple rocket launchers fire salvoes of rockets at communist positions.*

and strenuous efforts by both sides. Pork Chop Hill (so-named because of its shape) assumed an importance in tactical, political and even strategic terms that far outweighed its geographical significance.

The hill stood in no-man's-land on I US Corps front and quite close to its boundary with IX Corps. It was approximately 1.5km (1 mile) forward of the American positions on the Main Line of Resistance (MLR) itself, and about 80km (50 miles) north of Seoul. The communists occupied a hill roughly level with Pork Chop and to its west some 1.3km (1500 yards). From this hill (Old Baldy as it was known) the Chinese could observe the American supply route from the MLR to Pork Chop Hill. The hill itself was only about 180m (600 feet) high and virtually its whole surface was covered in a mass of trenches and bunkers which, it was thought, made it impregnable.

On 16 April 1953 the position was held by two weak platoons even though intelligence reports said that a Chinese attack was being prepared in the general area of the 7th US Division, from which the defenders of Pork Chop Hill came. The total strength on the hill including engineers and gunners numbered 96 men. Most were deployed in the main position but some manned listening posts on the forward slope of the hill, and there was one small patrol further north in the low ground and constantly on the move.

The Chinese attack

Between 2200 hours and 2300 hours that night two full strength companies of Chinese infantry advanced across the valley and up on to the hill. They had brushed the mobile patrol and one of the listening posts, but such was their speed of advance that they arrived on Pork Chop before all the troops there could be stood-to. In the mêlée that followed, the commander of the outpost lost radio contact with one of his platoons and the Chinese artillery bombardment cut his telephone communication to the MLR. He was, however, able to call for emergency artillery support by using flares.

The heavy gun and mortar fire from both sides forced the Chinese infantry to go to ground. But after it lifted, the enemy assault swamped one platoon's position and pinned down the second in about 25 minutes. By 0200 hours on 17 April the Chinese controlled most of the hill though one or two pockets of American resistance remained. At that time a US platoon moved up from the MLR to help what it thought were its own forces to defend the hill. It came under heavy fire and the movement petered out.

At 0430 hours an assault by five platoons was launched to reinforce the hill, but the Chinese had prepared themselves to defend their gains. There followed bitter fighting with much loss of life. The Americans gained the high ground but their losses were too severe for them to mop up the remaining Chinese who continued to hold out. At this stage, of the three American companies involved, only 55 men remained.

Decision to counter-attack

As the UN fortunes ebbed and flowed decisions were being taken at the highest level at the headquarters of the United Nations Command in Japan. Although the fighting clearly remained of a local nature it raised matters of much wider significance in relation to the ceasefire talks. It would, at this delicate stage of negotiations, have been a serious blow if the Chinese had been allowed to occupy Pork Chop Hill. It was decided, therefore, to regain the hill by putting in a battalion-strength attack.

At 2130 hours that night a company of US infantry stormed the feature but came almost immediately under fierce artillery fire, which effectively neutralised it. A further company attacked, unexpectedly, from the northern side and at last succeeded in challenging the Chinese hold despite fierce opposition from 'burp guns' and grenades. At 0250 hours on 18 April Chinese reinforcements arrived and at dawn another American company was added to the fray.

Throughout the day the fighting continued until at last the Chinese yielded and withdrew. In 24 hours of the battle no less than 77,000 rounds of artillery ammunition had been fired in support of the American troops.

In the following weeks the 7th US Division gradually reconstructed the fortifications on Pork Chop Hill while the Chinese indicated their continuing interest by firing as many shells and mortar bombs at it as they fired on the rest of the divisional front.

The final outcome

On 6 July the Chinese launched their biggest attack on the hill. As the Americans reinforced their defences so the enemy poured in more men and, as always, the Chinese could go one better than the Americans in terms of manpower. On 10 July, by which time there were five American battalions on the hill and the Chinese had up to a division in the field, the UN Command finally decided to evacuate Pork Chop Hill rather than escalate the fighting still further.

Just over a fortnight later the armistice was signed. Actions such as that at Pork Chop Hill had typified the two year period of negotiations. Though this period of the war was static and lacked the vivid activity of the dramatic first year of hostilities both sides lost more men during the stalemate than before.

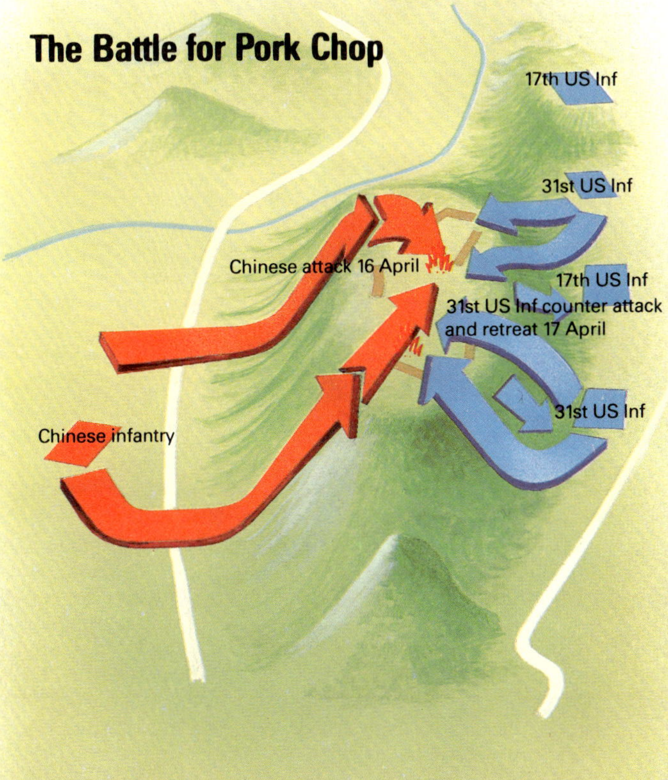

During the negotiations of 1953, hill battles became a test of wills. Every hill won by the communists made them more stubborn in their demands so that Pork Chop assumed a wider political significance over and above the purely military. On the night of 16 April the hill was held by two platoons of the 31st Regiment, 7th US Infantry Division. Despite a clear and starlit night, the Chinese surprised the US positions with their speed and stealth. Before the alarm could be sounded, they had swamped the defences. By 0200 hours Pork Chop had fallen. Attempts to relieve it during 17 April met with little success (ABOVE). The relief forces were pinned down and by the evening the situation looked grim. The decision was then made to counter-attack. Two companies of the 17th US Infantry stormed the hill and by 0250 hours Pork Chop had been retaken (BELOW).

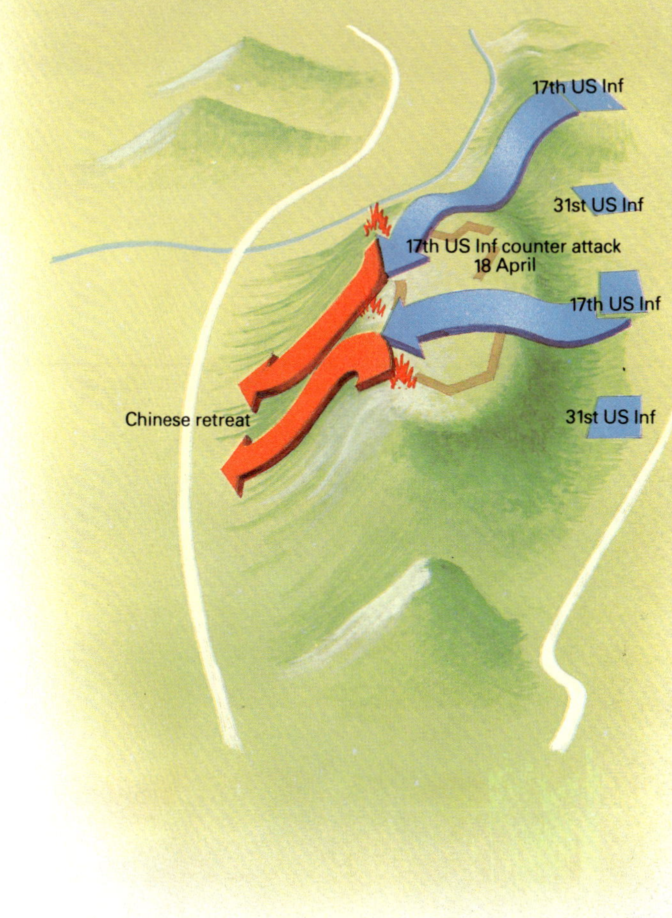

The Legacy of Korea

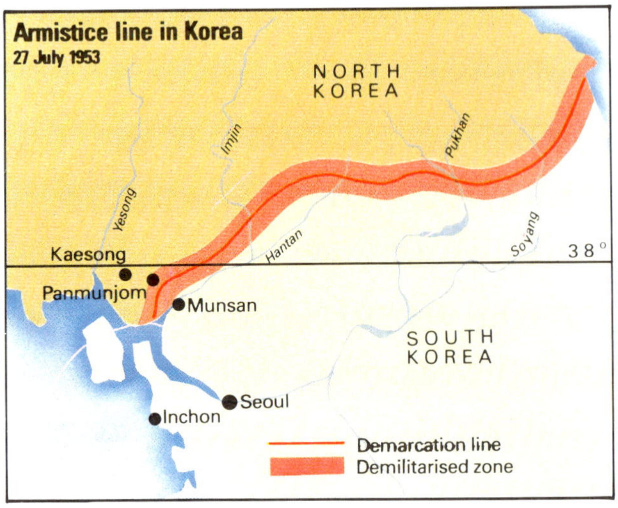

THE TWO KOREAS are ruled today by equally undemocratic governments and one is forced to wonder why the war was fought at all, and whether any of the major participants believe that the great losses they suffered were worthwhile in the long term.

After all, American deaths totalled 34,000 with 105,000 wounded. South Korean Army deaths numbered 50,000 while North Korean casualties are estimated at more than 500,000. Chinese losses were 900,000.

Yet the war did much to influence the way the world has developed since, and there were many lessons which came out of it.

Military and political differences

By far the most important question for the West, and one that has still to be resolved, was highlighted by the Truman-MacArthur controversy. General Douglas MacArthur's plea to use total resources to wage total war and win total victory was a restatement of the liberal-democratic view that sanctioned the use of force only if it was absolutely necessary to eradicate an evil – in which case it must be used without mercy.

For President Harry Truman, the situation seemed to demand an alternative strategy. From 1947, when he spelled out the Truman Doctrine, he sought only to check the spread of communism as practised by the Soviet Union and later mainland China. It was not his intention to destroy communism where it held sway.

He therefore strove – except briefly after the Inchon landings when it seemed possible to achieve the goal of uniting Korea – always to limit the extent of the conflict. He thus departed from the traditional American attitude to war and, with some justification, used the waging of war as an extension of the other instruments of foreign policy available to him.

The argument remains fundamentally important today as it was in the early 1950s. Many in the West argue that by not going all out to destroy communism at its source, when this may well have been possible, a major opportunity was lost. But others point out that had all force been used (and this would have included the atom bomb) then the conflict would have escalated to one of global proportions.

Men versus machines

A further result of the Korean War was to extend the debate on the relationship of men and machines on the battlefield. Could sophisticated technology be used in war to achieve victory by the few against immensely superior numerical odds?

In the first phase of the Korean War, the more powerfully armed and equipped North Korean forces routed the South. Then the rapid build-up of UN forces, with modern artillery, tanks and aircraft, swung the war in their favour.

With the Chinese intervention, huge armies that were poorly equipped and armed put the UN troops to flight. But the last phase of the mobile war saw the UN forces drive remorselessly northwards with the help of massive firepower. So devastating was the result that the systematic destruction of line after line of Chinese defences earned itself the soubriquet of 'the meat grinder'. Ultimately, the superiority of technique over mere numbers had been asserted – but it had been a very marginal victory.

General Mark Clark signs the armistice at Munsan on 27 July 1953 as Admiral Robert Briscoe, on his left, looks on.

Ho Chi Minh's Triumph

From 1946 France was committed to a war in Indochina against the ruthless guerrilla forces of the Viet Minh

John Pimlott

WHEN THE FRENCH sought to reassert control over their possessions in Indochina after World War II, they faced a swelling tide of nationalism that had been fostered by a well-organised communist movement headed by Ho Chi Minh and Vo Nguyen Giap. The following eight years saw a contest for supremacy between a European colonial power using conventional military tactics and indigenous Asian nationalists, led by the Communist Party, fighting a guerrilla war for independence. It was a form of warfare that held important lessons for the West which were not immediately fully learned.

The lure of the East

The area known between 1893 and 1954 as French Indochina now comprises three sovereign states – Vietnam (traditionally composed of the three kingdoms of Cochin China in the south, Annam in the centre and Tongking in the north), Laos and Cambodia (Kampuchea). Two low-lying areas – the Red (Hong) River Delta in the north and the Mekong Delta in the south – contain the major population centres.

As early as 1862 the eastern provinces of Cochin China were occupied by France and, a year later, a protectorate was declared over Cambodia. In 1867 the remainder of Cochin China was seized and in 1883, after military operations, Annam and Tongking were added. The empire was completed ten years later when Laos became a protectorate.

Ho Chi Minh and the nationalists

As the 20th century progressed nationalist groups were spawned, but not until 1930, when an Annamese, Ho Chi Minh, founded the Indochina Communist Party, were direction and cohesion imparted to the nationalist cause, although French military strength remained supreme. This situation changed dramatically in 1940. With France defeated in Europe, the administrators in Indochina suddenly became isolated and fell easy prey to the expansionist Japanese.

Ho Chi Minh seized the opportunity to draw the nationalists together, founding in May 1941 the Viet Nam Doc Lap Dong Minh Hoi ('League for the Independence of Vietnam'). The party's title was soon shortened to Viet Minh. Under this banner resistance activities were organised.

Ho Chi Minh, with his military coordinator Vo Nguyen Giap, organised the seizure of territory in the rural hinterland of

Machine guns fire in Tongking, 1947. The Indochina War was a bitter experience for France. The French discovered, painfully, that conventional tactics were ineffective against local forces, ably led, who adopted politically inspired guerrilla methods of warfare.

Postwar Indochina

the north. Co-operating with the less communist-controlled United Party in Cochin China, he was able to fill the political vacuum created by the sudden collapse of Japan in August 1945. And on 2 September the Democratic Republic of Vietnam was declared in Hanoi, capital of Tongking.

The new government was doomed to failure, however. As early as July 1945 at the Potsdam conference the Allies had decided that Indochina should be re-occupied, using Nationalist Chinese troops in the north and British in the south, meeting on the 16th parallel. By the time of the British withdrawal in early 1946, French units had arrived from Europe, most of the major towns and lines of communication south of the 16th parallel had been cleared of native opposition, the United Party had been overthrown and both Laos and Cambodia had been entered.

These events, combined with a general lack of communist influence outside Tongking, effectively isolated Ho Chi Minh in the north and set the pattern for the future war. Until 1954 the campaigns against French rule were to be largely confined to Tongking and northern Annam.

Course of the fighting

To begin with the French were numerically weak. Although an amphibious force landed at Haiphong in the Red River Delta on 6 March 1946, entering Hanoi ten days later, Ho Chi Minh's government was allowed to remain, at least for the moment.

Giap began to withdraw his regular troops from Hanoï and Haiphong, concentrating them in 'safe base areas' deep in the mountains of the north-east (the Viet Bac) and in the swamps of the southern Red River Delta (the South Delta Base), free from French interference.

The campaign opened in February 1950 with a successful attack upon the outpost at Lao Kai on the Red River near the Chinese border. Then Giap turned to the vulnerable Cao Bang-Lang Son ridge in north-east Tongking. Dong Khe was taken on 25 May but had to be abandoned when a French parachute battalion intervened. Once the monsoon eased, Dong Khe was attacked again. The garrison was overwhelmed on 18 September, isolating Cao Bang from its delta support-base and leading to its evacuation on 3 October.

It was an ill-considered move. The retreating garrison, together with a relieving force from That Khe, was ambushed and dispersed, a reinforcing parachute battalion was annihilated and Lang Son was abandoned amidst scenes of chaos and disorder. The loss of nearly 6000 troops constituted a major defeat, caused primarily by the policy of distributing small packets of military

ABOVE *Ho Chi Minh, political leader of the Viet Minh, exploited nationalist feeling against the French.* BELOW *Viet Minh suspects are kept under guard. Some carry rice baskets, which often concealed hand grenades.* OPPOSITE *French prisoners wend their way from the scene of their greatest defeat, Dien Bien Phu. This battle, which involved a 55-day siege, resulted in more than 7000 French deaths in six months.*

strength throughout an enormous area.

Giap now controlled all of northern Tongking and the crucial supply lines from China. Convinced that victory was close, he went over to the 'open battle' phase of his grand strategy and mounted an assault on the delta region. But the French, revitalised by the arrival of General Jean de Lattre de Tassigny as High Commissioner and Commander-in-Chief in December 1950, were stronger than recent events implied.

Giap tried three times to break into the delta – at Vinh Yen in the north-east (13-17 January), Mao Khe in the north (23-28 March) and Phat Diem in the south (29 May–18 June 1951) – and was badly defeated on each occasion. His troops were caught in the open against prepared defences, enabling the French to use their technological superiority to telling effect.

By this time the French had reorganised the delta defences. A series of fortified posts – the De Lattre Line – protected the approaches to Hanoi while a mobile reserve, composed of paratroops and armour-infantry 'mobile groups', was available as reinforcement should an attack materialise. The victories of 1951, however, persuaded de Lattre to go over to the offensive with the aim of destroying Viet Minh base areas. On 14 November French paratroops landed at Hoa Binh, 40km (25 miles) to the west of the De Lattre Line, and were quickly joined by mobile groups using the roads and rivers. The area around Hoa Binh was then garrisoned in the normal way.

It was just what Giap needed to restore the morale of his troops. Deploying a total of six divisions he interdicted the supply lines, isolated the garrisons and gradually increased the pressure. General Raoul Salan, who replaced de Lattre in late 1951, ordered a withdrawal on 22 February 1952.

That the French were being forced inexorably on to the defensive within a restricted area of Tongking was again demonstrated in October 1952 when Giap took the Nglia Lo ridge with ease. They now launched further attempts to regain the initiative. On 29 October 1952 in Operation Lorraine, Salan used the bulk of his mobile reserve in a pincer attack towards Viet Minh supply dumps at Phu Tho and Phu Doan, north of the Red River. The advancing French forces met minimal opposition but became dangerously overstretched and vulnerable. Salan ordered a withdrawal on 14 November.

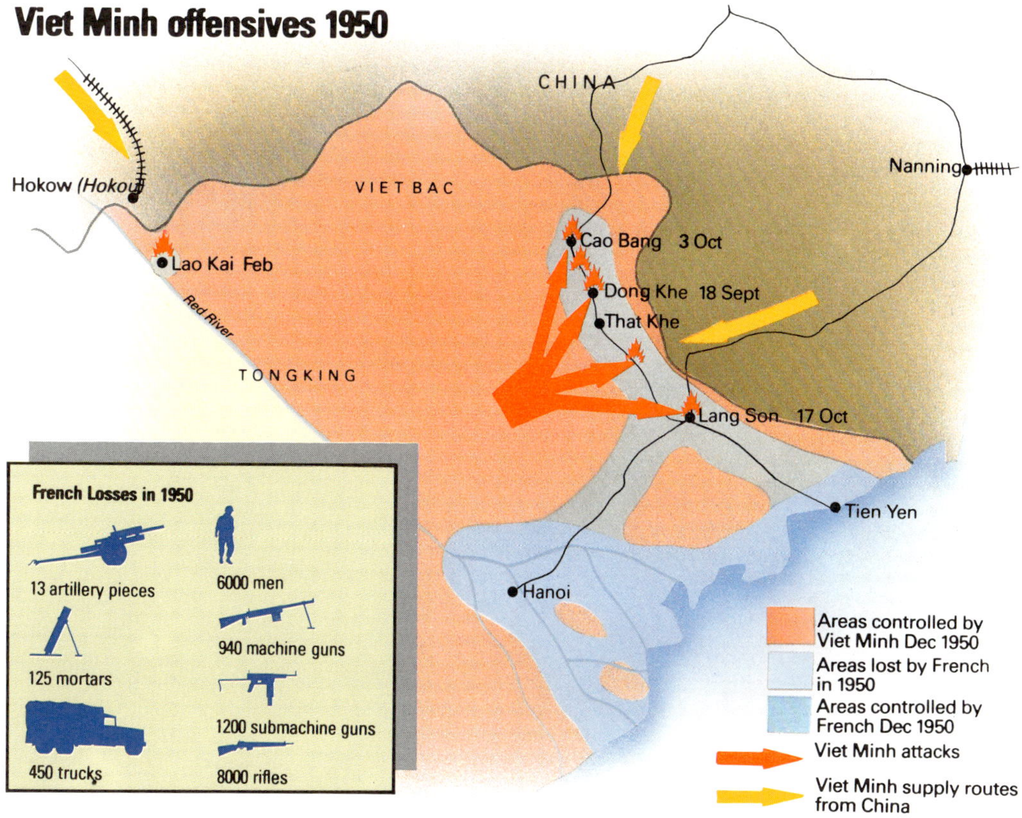

The French still possessed some trump cards, however. With undisputed command of the air it was possible to fortify, supply and reinforce 'centres of resistance' outside the delta region. This was shown at Na San near the Laotian border in November-December 1952, when wave after wave of Viet Minh attackers were beaten off by troops in prepared, entrenched positions supported from the air. Similar tactics were used in April 1953 when Giap invaded northern Laos with the twin aims of linking up with Pathet Lao guerrillas and seizing the valuable opium crop. As the invasion took shape, centres of resistance were formed by the French at Luang Prabang, Moung Khoua and on the Plaine des Jarres.

Final defeat at Dien Bien Phu

It is within this context that the decision to take the valley of Dien Bien Phu in north-west Tongking must be seen. Salan was replaced in May 1953 by General Henri Navarre and it was his idea to drop paratroops into the valley, ostensibly to create a 'mooring point' for anti-guerrilla patrols which would interdict Giap's supply lines into northern Laos. As Viet Minh divisions closed in after the paradrop on 20 November the idea began to take hold of forcing a set-piece battle on ground of French choosing, in which the advantages of artillery and air superiority could prove decisive. By December 1953 Dien Bien Phu was being organised as a fortified camp.

The weaknesses inherent within this revised plan are apparent in retrospect. Dien Bien Phu, 275km (170 miles) from Hanoi in extremely difficult country, was isolated and vulnerable. Air supply could not be guaranteed, particularly if the Viet Minh deployed Chinese anti-aircraft guns. Resources were insufficient to transform the valley into an impregnable camp, and Viet Minh strength was badly underestimated.

The results were inevitable and on 7 May 1954 the central command bunker was captured. A negotiated withdrawal was the only way out.

This was officially recognised by the Geneva Agreements of 21 July 1954. Laos and Cambodia received their independence and Vietnam was divided, rather arbitrarily, on the 17th parallel. Ho Chi Minh returned to Hanoi as leader of a new Democratic Republic of North Vietnam, comprising Tongking and northern Annam; Ngo Dinh Diem formed a more Western-orientated Republic of South Vietnam in Saigon, composed of Cochin China and southern Annam. As events were to prove, the settlement would not be permanent.

The Viet Minh

THE VIET MINH were a revolutionary army, geared more to the political task of seizing power than to that of merely defeating the more conventional French Army in open battle. So, although Vo Nguyen Giap organised his forces into the familiar formations of divisions, regiments and battalions, the strength and direction of the communist cause was firmly in the hands of political officers located at every level of command.

At the very top the revolution was co-ordinated by Ho Chi Minh and his government-in-exile in the mountains of the Viet Bac. It was to these men that the political officers owed their allegiance.

Initially, in 1946–47, the whole of Indochina was divided into 14 Viet Minh 'regions', each controlled by a committee which reported directly to Ho Chi Minh, but as the war progressed this system was confined to the area that became Vietnam. From March 1948 the number of regions was reduced to six, although the basic structure of committees remained. These regions, known to the Viet Minh as inter-zones, covered north-west Tongking, north-east Tongking (the division between them lay on the Red or Hong River), the Red River Delta, north Annam, south Annam (the division in Annam lay at Hué), and Cochin China. Each had a full political hierarchy, chosen and controlled from the Viet Bac, and each had responsibility for raising and training rudimentary guerrilla forces.

The village militia

The most basic of the Viet Minh military organisations was the village militia, raised from the people in areas already controlled by the communists. In November 1949 Ho Chi Minh decreed a general mobilisation of all males and females between the ages of 18 and 45 in these areas. They were unarmed, raw recruits whose time in military service was devoted to training in both political and military tasks.

They represented the lowest level of capability, but were essential to the revolution. Although they could be expected to contribute little to the armed conflict – at best they could only prepare defensive positions, gather intelligence or act as labourers – they could be inculcated with the revolutionary cause, strengthened by discipline and used as a source of partly trained soldiers. Numbers are impossible to verify but it is estimated that by 1954 there were more than 350,000 militia.

Regional troops

As soon as this introduction to Viet Minh methods had been completed, members of the militia were often transferred to units known as regional troops, controlled by the inter-zone committees. Such units were more trusted and therefore better armed (although often with nothing more sophisticated than obsolete rifles and home-made grenades). They were used as a sort of 'Home Guard', were responsible for protecting the inter-zone area and for mounting guerrilla-style attacks upon French troops nearby. Training and political education continued, building up a rigid backbone of popular support throughout Vietnam which was dedicated to the revolution.

These troops knew their local areas intimately and could merge into the background with ease, making their discovery almost impossible. As all were 'part-time' and, like their militia counterparts, bereft of uniform, they constituted the classic guerrilla fighters.

Operating in all six inter-zones, sometimes alone and sometimes in co-operation with the main, conventional Viet Minh force, they probably

BELOW *Women fighters for the Viet Minh. The communists mobilised all the able-bodied for the fight against the French.* BOTTOM *Viet Minh soldiers file out of Dien Bien Phu carrying recoilless weapons, which gave infantry great firepower especially at close quarters.*

Viet Minh zones 1949

ABOVE *Viet Minh wearing camouflaged helmets man a heavy machine gun and scan the sky for enemy planes.* LOWER RIGHT *Ho Chi Minh surrounded by young recruits to the army.* BOTTOM *A Viet Minh river patrol glides downstream with weapons at the ready.*

numbered about 75,000 by 1954. Their main effect – of causing the French to disperse their units the length and breadth of Indochina in response to guerrilla attacks – was a central factor in eventual Viet Minh victory.

The regular force

Their importance waned, however, in comparison with the Viet Minh regular force, or Chuc Luc. This was the cutting edge, a conventional-style army which was designed to meet and defeat the already weakened French forces in the open warfare phase of the revolution. Owing its origins to those units which had accompanied Ho Chi Minh into Hanoi in August 1945, the Chuc Luc was well armed with Japanese, Chinese and captured French weapons. It was also well organised. Its members were characterised by the now-familiar uniform of black 'pyjamas' and cork helmets.

In the course of 1950 an existing 60 battalions were organised into five complete divisions: the 304th, 308th, 312th and 316th in the Viet Bac, and the 320th in the South Delta Base. Borrowing ideas from the European armies, each division contained three infantry regiments, equipped with heavy mortars, anti-aircraft weapons and machine guns as well as normal small-arms; and each regiment consisted of two or three battalions.

In December 1950 a sixth division, the 351st, was formed. It differed from the others by being a 'heavy' division, comprising three regiments, two of artillery (with 57mm and 75mm field and anti-aircraft guns) and one of engineers. By 1954 over 125,000 regular troops existed and a seventh division, the 325th (infantry) was being raised in An Khe province.

The Viet Minh had neither air force nor navy. They received assistance from the Chinese, however. By 1954 regular Chinese troops – almost entirely belonging to anti-aircraft units – were operating alongside the Chuc Luc at Dien Bien Phu.

The French Forces

ONE OF THE REASONS why the French were defeated in Indochina is because they fielded a conventional army against the revolutionary forces of the Viet Minh. To French leaders, both political and military, the war was just another colonial revolt, one that could be put down by superior Western fire power and discipline. As a result, the army deployed was large, averaging about 150,000 men during the nine years of conflict, over-dependent upon constant supplies of modern, technological equipment and unsuited to the unconventional operations of its enemy. In short, despite its sophistications, it was a bludgeon of crude power, incapable of dealing with the subtleties of a communist revolution.

Political hindrance

The High Command must bear much of the blame for this short-sightedness. In the late 1940s French forces in Indochina were theoretically controlled by a local commander-in-chief, but he was so hide-bound by orders from military superiors in France and from political masters in Paris and Hanoi that he had little real initiative of his own. Even when the offices of high commissioner and commander-in-chief were combined in the person of General Jean de Lattre de Tassigny towards the end of 1950, political interference from Paris continued.

The war was unpopular at home and, with France suffering from chronic political instability in the aftermath of World War II, damaging decisions were made by politicians desperate for domestic support. In 1950, for example, as Vo Nguyen Giap's forces were taking the Cao Bang ridge, the French government reduced the size of the army in Indochina by 9000 men. Furthermore, an amendment to the Budget Law restricted the use of conscripts to 'home-land' territory only (France, Algeria and French-occupied Germany).

All ethnic-French units sent to Indochina had therefore to be composed entirely of regular, volunteer soldiers, a decision which restricted the size of the purely French commitment. At no time did such troops account for more than half the total Expeditionary Force (the norm was about 52,000 soldiers). Yet they were, by virtue of their discipline, equipment and origins, expected to bear the brunt of the fighting, a policy which led to 21,000 French deaths during the war. These units made up the bulk of the mobile reserve.

The emphasis was upon mobility. All infantry units were therefore equipped not only with the normal weapons of the foot-soldier (60mm and 81mm mortars, 0.50 inch machine guns, 9mm sub-machine guns and carbines) but also with half-tracks for rapid movement. They were supported by armoured units (with M4 Sherman and M24 Chaffee tanks as well as armoured cars), artillery (with 75mm field guns and 105mm and 155mm howitzers as well as 120mm heavy mortars) and engineer formations.

Parachute units – an élite which often acted as the very tip of French military capability – were virtually self-contained. They comprised battalions of air-portable infantry, artillery and engineers, but depended upon the air force for transport and supply.

Transport aircraft were always scarce and it was not unknown for French civilian airliners to be requisitioned, along with their crews, in an emergency. Not until 1952 did American-supplied C-47 Dakotas and C-119 Flying Boxcars replace the last of the French-built Junkers Ju-52s in squadron service.

For direct support of the ground troops B-26 Marauder bombers and

Indochinese troops accompany a French column during operation Brochet in October 1953.

F8F Bearcat fighters were widely used, together with Canadian-built Beaver and French Morane 500 Cricket observation/liaison aircraft. By 1954 the first helicopters, American-built H-19Bs, had also been deployed. The navy contributed Privateer maritime bombers and F4U Corsair fighters, as well as coastal fire support and river patrols.

Additional troops

These regular forces were never sufficient and had to be supplemented in a variety of ways. Chief amongst these was the use of colonial troops from other parts of the French Union. Throughout the war Algerian, Moroccan, Tunisian and Senegalese units served in Indochina. Organised in exactly the same way as the ethnic-French regulars, the majority were officered by Frenchmen and received normal French equipment. An exception was made in Algerian units. Because Algeria was regarded as part of metropolitan France, native officers were allowed (but Algerian losses were included in the 15,000 North Africans who died in Indochina).

Elements of the Foreign Legion, organised on the regular pattern and French-officered, fought throughout the war, invariably where the conflict was hardest. The Legion achieved particular fame at Dien Bien Phu, where it provided more than half the fighting units (seven out of 13) and two-thirds of the paratroop contingent. A total of 11,620 Legionnaires died in Indochina.

Attempts were also made to tap the enormous manpower of Indochina itself. Many French units recruited locally. At Dien Bien Phu, for example, nearly half the members of 2nd Battalion, 1st Parachute Light Infantry were native Vietnamese. A Vietnam National Army was raised under French command, but the full potential of both these methods was never realised. Similarly, although anti-guerrilla units were raised, particularly among the mountain tribes, they were never fully trusted or developed. Nevertheless, 27,000 Indochinese died fighting for the French.

French Expeditionary Force May 1953

54,000	French troops
20,000	Legionnaires
30,000	North Africans
70,000	Vietnamese
10,000	Air Force
5,000	Navy

Of this total of 189,000, about 100,000 were tied down in static defences. Seven mobile groups and eight paratroop battalions were available for offensive operations.

TOP LEFT *French naval forces in action.* TOP *French Foreign Legionnaires in an armoured unit. These tough, ruthless soldiers proved to be highly effective.* ABOVE *Heavy artillery such as this Long Tom was ultimately powerless against guerrilla tactics.* BELOW *Hardened Moroccan* tirailleurs *during a village clearing operation in 1951.*

Fighting Methods

THE MILITARY INITIATIVE was held by the Viet Minh for much of the war in Indochina. Once the French had used their superiority in weapons and firepower to re-establish control over the major towns in 1946, they were forced to stand back and wait for enemy moves. Even when they tried to assume the offensive, as at Hoa Binh in November 1951 and Dien Bien Phu two years later, their efforts invariably devolved into waiting to see how the Viet Minh would react, often with unfortunate results. This led the French to feel that they were fighting a 'shadow' war, but it was just a natural consequence of Viet Minh strategy.

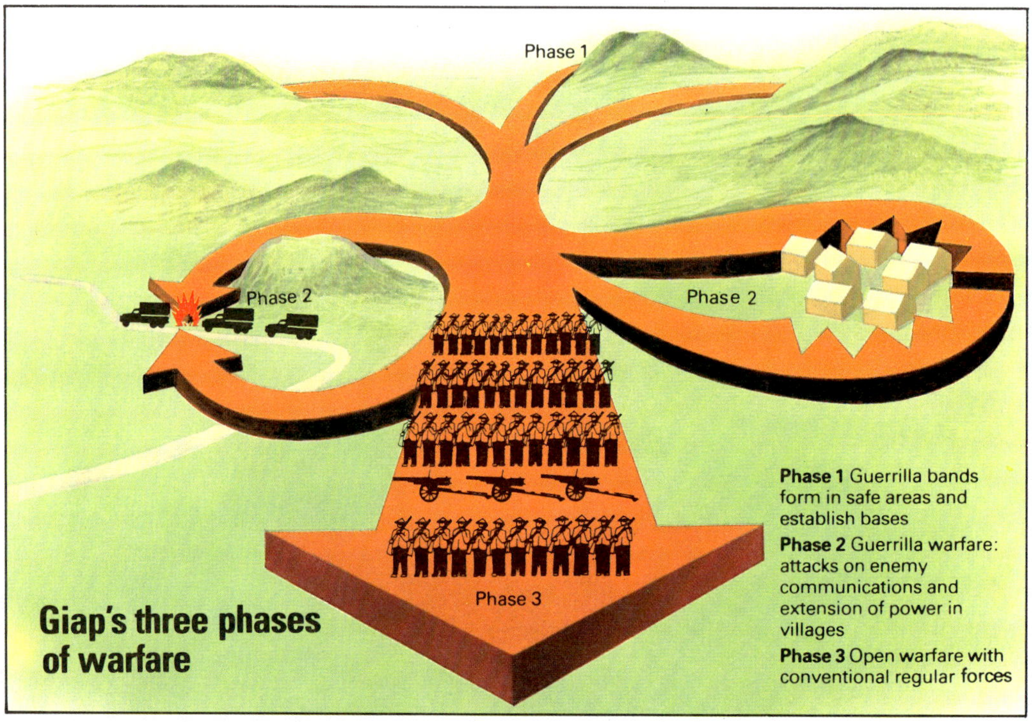

Applying Mao's theories

Ho Chi Minh and Vo Nguyen Giap were proponents of Mao Tse-tung's theory of revolutionary war and to understand that is to understand much of their success. Mao emphasised the factors of time, space and will in his writings: the revolutionary should trade space (territory) to gain time and use that time to mobilise the political will of the people. He expounded the idea of a protracted struggle for political power which would develop through three phases of activity.

These phases were important in Indochina, for all three took place simultaneously in various parts of the country. There was the preparation phase during which 'safe base areas' were established by the revolutionaries; a guerrilla warfare phase during which selected, pin-prick attacks were carried out against the French to weaken their resolve; and an open warfare phase when the guerrillas emerged to fight conventional battles. Thus, while French authorities might presume that south Annam or Cochin China were quiet because no military activity was manifest, Viet Minh political cadres could begin their infiltration of the masses, upon whose support safe base areas depended.

Similarly, as the phases were interchangeable to a large extent, French talk of 'victories' when Giap's forces were caught in the open (as in 1951 in the delta region) was premature and illogical, for the revolutionaries, realising that the time was not yet ripe for open warfare, merely reverted to guerrilla operations and waited for a fresh opportunity. In other words the French were being presented with three different types of warfare at the same time: a political campaign for popular support, guerrilla operations and open battle. They made few moves to counter the first and presumed that a mixture of static defences and mobile operations could defeat the other two. They were mistaken.

During the periods of guerrilla warfare, Viet Minh tactics stressed the twin aims of infiltration and ambush. Throughout the war French dispositions were vulnerable to both. Infiltration of political operatives and guerrilla parties behind French 'lines' (a concept which was, itself, inapplicable) was relatively easy. The Viet Minh sprang from the people and so could move amongst them, to paraphrase Mao, like 'fish in the sea'. They were literally indistinguishable from the mass of Vietnamese peasants. Short of preventing or rigidly controlling the movement of the entire population, there was little the French military could really achieve on their own.

Attempts were made to 'seal off' vital areas by building static lines of fortified posts – the garrisons on the Cao Bang-Lang Son ridge before 1950 are a good example, although

A graphic display of the dangers of Viet Minh booby traps: a boot impaled on a punji stick, which probably had a poisoned tip.

the best of all is, of course, the De Lattre Line of 1951. But infiltration was never completely halted. Political officers of the Viet Minh moved with comparative freedom wherever they desired, operating even in Hanoi and Haiphong, while guerrilla gangs were a constant menace on all lines of communication throughout the war.

The guerrilla speciality was ambush, made easy by a French preference for movement along roads and rivers at all times. Home-made land mines planted at the bend of a road or in a defile overshadowed by jungle could halt a convoy and enable covering parties of Viet Minh to pour enfilade fire down on its trapped occupants before melting back into the countryside. French operations against such guerrillas included mobile strikes into the heart of known Viet Minh territory (such as in Operation Lorraine in late 1952) but as these, too, stuck to the roads and rivers, ambush on an even larger scale was only to be expected.

Counters by the French

Once the Viet Minh emerged from rural areas and tried to take their enemy on in open battle, however, French military superiority should have tilted the balance. Indeed, when Giap entered this phase too soon in 1951, his forces were roundly defeated at Vinh Yen, Mao Khe and Phat Diem by a combination of French defensive measures – prepared, entrenched positions surrounded by barbed wire and minefields – and superior weapons.

Giap's favoured tactics were to send in small suicide squads to break through the defences and follow up with wave upon wave of infantry attackers. These tactics were countered in 1951 by artillery (often firing on to predicted target areas), machine guns, aerial strikes (particularly those using napalm) and, of equal importance, the tenacity of French defenders.

But when these advantages were undermined, as at Dien Bien Phu where artillery was useless against Viet Minh positions in the surrounding hills, aerial supply and support was curtailed by the deployment of Chinese anti-aircraft weapons and French defences were weakened by a policy of encroaching entrenchment, the Viet Minh could, and did, prevail. The French were, in the final analysis, out-fought.

BOTTOM RIGHT *French paratroops on a night patrol search for arms in a flooded cave.* BOTTOM LEFT *A convoy which has come under fire from the hills. It was eventually rescued and 100 Viet Minh were killed.* BELOW *The directors of the Viet Minh war effort: Ho Chi Minh (second from left) and Vo Nguyen Giap (standing).*

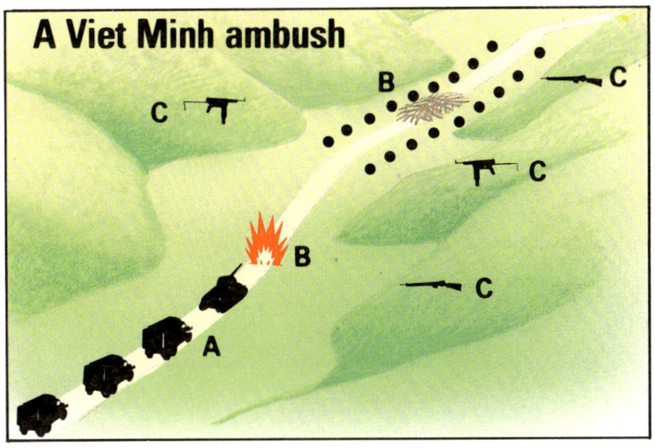

The Viet Minh used the ambush to devastating effect in thickly wooded valleys. In the destruction of a French convoy (A) the Viet Minh infantry would first halt the convoy with mines (B) and small-arms fire (C).

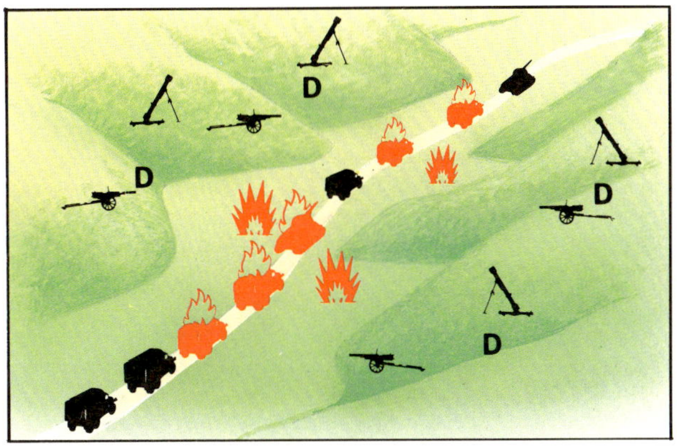

Next would follow bombardment from artillery and mortars (D) positioned in the hills. Once the vehicles were hit the road would be blocked. The final stage saw an infantry assault (E) by waves of Viet Minh, who were willing to accept enormous casualties to achieve their objective.

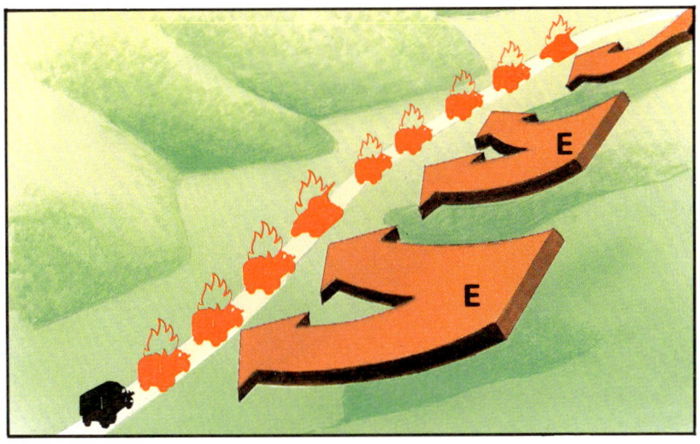

Contest for the Red River Delta

THE FRENCH RETREAT from the Cao Bang-Lang Son ridge in September-October 1950 was the first major defeat for the colonial power. To the Viet Minh it seemed like the beginning of an inevitable victory. French morale was shattered and, with the supply routes from China guaranteed, guerrilla operations in the north could now give way to open warfare against the main bastion of enemy rule, the Red (Hong) River Delta.

Vo Nguyen Giap began to deploy his forces against the delta defences as early as December 1950, determined to initiate a set-piece battle which would break through to Hanoi and ensure an early victory. He chose as his area of attack the most logical approach to the capital, the line of the Red River, and was so confident of French weakness that he did little to tie down their reserves elsewhere.

So when the 308th and 312th Viet Minh Divisions debouched from the mountains and tried to force a way through the town of Vinh Yen, 65km (40 miles) to the north-west of Hanoi, close to the Red River, General Jean de Lattre de Tassigny was free to concentrate his forces against them. The ensuing battle cost Giap an estimated 6000 casualties and a golden opportunity to end the war quickly.

Successful French tactics

It was by no means an easy French victory. When the attack began on 13 January 1951, Vinh Yen and its approaches were defended by two mobile groups (one in the town itself and the other back towards Hanoi) and a thin protective screen of infantry, a total of about 7000 men. They were assaulted by two full Viet Minh divisions, each of which comprised 11,000 troops. Giap's soldiers were therefore able to push the infantry screen back with ease and advance into the hills which lay between the south bank of the Red River and Vinh Yen. Indeed, when the first of the mobile groups moved out of the town to reinforce the infantry on 14 January, it was all but destroyed in a carefully laid ambush.

But the Viet Minh breakthrough never materialised, for de Lattre, taking personal command of the battle, concentrated his reserve in response. As the second mobile group advanced to plug the gap on the 15th, a massive airlift of French units from all over the delta swung into operation. The Viet Minh were held in the hills for 24 hours, enabling the Vinh Yen defences to be consolidated.

When Giap ordered a mass frontal assault with all available troops on the 16th, he met with disaster and was forced to withdraw. Prepared French positions, backed by air capability and a fast-moving reserve, appeared to be effective counters to open warfare – a belief which was to lead eventually to Dien Bien Phu.

Advance on Mao Khe

Success at Vinh Yen undoubtedly accelerated the creation of the De Lattre Line around the delta region. In an attempt to pre-empt this, Giap was forced to continue his offensive. He shifted three divisions to the north against the town of Mao Khe, situated a mere 32km (20 miles) from Haiphong. The attack began on the night of 23/24 March, achieving initial success against an outer ring of French defences. By the 26th Mao Khe was exposed and the 316th Viet Minh Division was concentrated for a final assault.

Before this could be fully organised, however, French naval vessels on the nearby Do Bac River opened up with a bombardment which caused chaos in Viet Minh lines. The subsequent pause in the attack enabled de Lattre to fly in reinforcements and when the

ABOVE RIGHT *General de Lattre de Tassigny, whose defensive line (although derided by some French troops) was of strategic importance.* BELOW *French paras provided valued mobility.*

LEFT *French troops with Viet Minh dead after the encounter at Mao Khe.* BELOW *Phu Ly after its re-occupation by the French in July 1951. Artillery and aerial bombardment, along with French material superiority, forced the Viet Minh to retreat.*

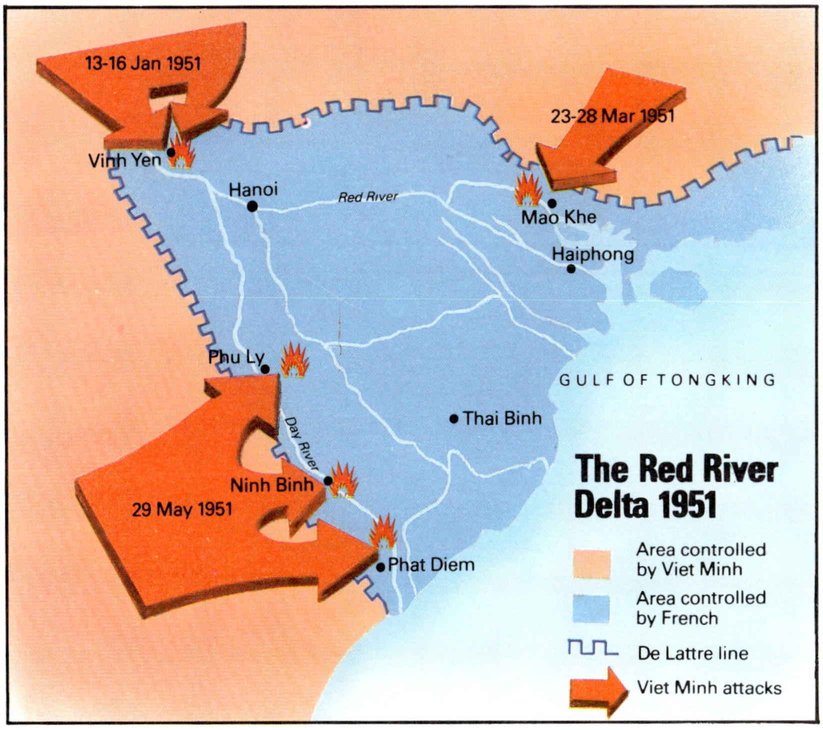

316th finally advanced on 28 March the pattern of Vinh Yen was repeated. In vicious hand-to-hand fighting the massed waves of Viet Minh attackers were beaten off, having suffered a total of 3000 casualties in five days.

Change of plan

Giap now abandoned his strategy of a direct assault upon Hanoi/Haiphong but remained determined to continue open warfare. In the third of his attacks in 1951 he altered his basic aim. He now tried to split the delta region by seizing control of provinces in the south which would draw the ring tighter around the capital, and he attempted to tie down de Lattre's reserve. Throughout April the French were kept busy in the north-west by the 312th Division while the 304th and 308th trekked south to join the 320th in the South Delta Base.

On 29 May the campaign began, with frontal assaults by the 304th and 308th upon Ninh Binh and Phu Ly on the Day River. These were designed to divert French resources while the 320th Division crossed the river around Phat Diem further south. An advance towards the coast near Thai Binh would then lop off the southern provinces of the delta, leaving the French flank exposed. The strategy did not succeed.

The French reacted quickly, moving in a total of eight mobile groups and two parachute units to blunt the attacks and deploying river patrols to cut Viet Minh lines of supply across the Day River. By 10 June, Giap had been forced to acknowledge defeat. By the 18th the last of his units had disengaged. He had lost a total of 11,000 casualties and was preparing to revert to guerrilla operations. The year 1951 had proved to be too early for victory, although it had established a pattern of French response which was ultimately to prove fatal.

Operation Lorraine

WHEN THE MONSOON ENDED in October 1952, Vo Nguyen Giap concentrated three of his regular divisions – the 308th, 312th and 316th – against French positions on the Nglia Lo ridge, between the Red (Hong) and Black (Song Bo) Rivers. As part of his long-term strategy of eliminating outlying garrisons before a decisive assault on the Red River Delta, he ordered simultaneous attacks upon Gia Hoi, Van Yen and Nglia Lo itself.

At first the French defenders held firm, but only until 17 October, when Nglia Lo fell to 'human wave' assaults by the 308th Division. This set in train an evacuation of other garrisons which was reminiscent of the Cao Bang-Lang Son disaster of 1950. Once again paratroops were sacrificed to enable the survivors to escape, most of whom made for the Black River where a makeshift defence line was set up. It was all that stood between the Viet Minh divisions and Laos.

Salan's battle plan

Initially General Raoul Salan had regarded the Nglia Lo attacks as a feint, fully expecting a Viet Minh drive on the delta as soon as his reserves were committed. When this did not materialise, he decided to strike out from the delta deep into Viet Minh territory. The aim was to force Giap to react by withdrawing his divisions facing the Black River and moving back towards the delta and his base areas, where he could be brought to battle and defeated on his home ground. This would not only destroy Viet Minh credibility with the local population but also allow the French to re-occupy the Nglia Lo ridge and protect the approaches to Laos.

Salan chose as his area of attack the line of the Clear River, north-west of Hanoi. A total of 30,000 troops (the largest French force ever gathered together for an operation in Indochina) were deployed. They comprised four mobile groups, a paratroop group and detachments of armour, artillery, engineers and river patrol craft. Their objectives were Viet Minh supply dumps at Phu Doan, Yen Bay and Tuyen Quang, nearly 160km (100 miles) outside the delta defences. The operation was given the code-name Lorraine. It was a gamble, designed to regain the initiative for the French by conventional, set-piece battle.

The French force was split into two parts, one at Trung Ha on the Red River north-west of Son Tay and the other at Viet Tri to the north-east. Both began to advance on 29 October 1952, aiming to link up at Phu Tho, about 32km (20 miles) to the north. Viet Minh regional troops fought delaying actions and the link-up did not take place until 5 November, but the absence of conventional opposition boosted French confidence, drawing them further into the jungle hinterland.

On 9 November paratroops were dropped into Phu Doan and armoured units advanced to relieve them, travelling along Route Coloniale 2. Substantial quantities of supplies were captured, including anti-aircraft guns, mortars and (a surprise to French

The remains of a French convoy which had been unable to sustain an effective defence against sudden Viet Minh fire.

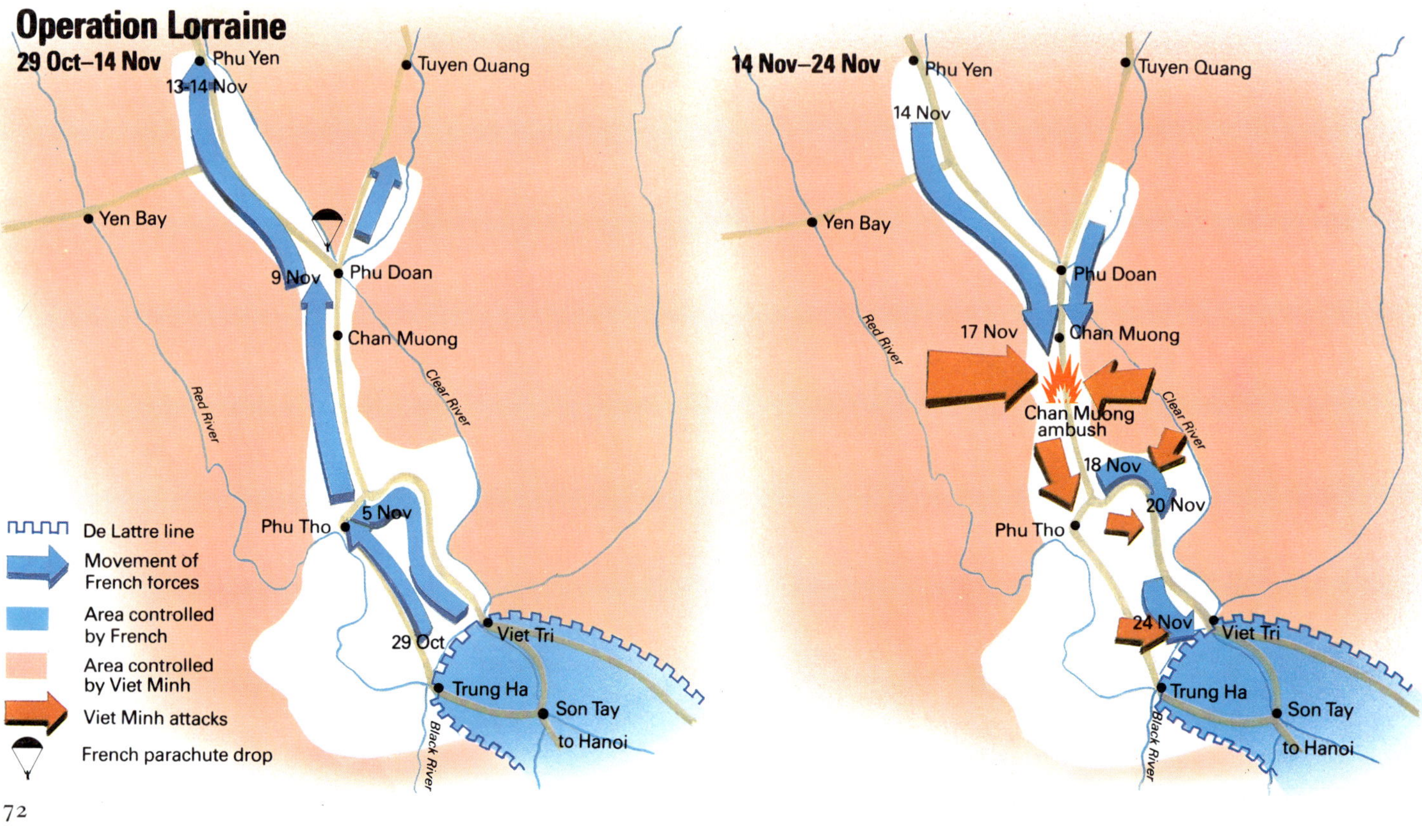

intelligence) Soviet-made Molotava trucks. Strong patrols were sent out immediately along the roads to Tuyen Quang (to the north) and Yen Bay (to the west), setting up blocking positions in anticipation of Viet Minh counter-attacks.

Reasons for withdrawal

The French plan now began to go wrong, for instead of hurrying back to defend his supply base Giap decided to bluff it out. Convinced that Salan's forces would soon become overextended, he ordered the bulk of his three divisions to stay put on the Black River, detaching two regiments only to move back towards Yen Bay. At the same time the 304th and 320th Divisions, to north and south of the delta respectively, were ordered to mount guerrilla attacks upon French positions in an effort to pressurise Salan into a withdrawal.

These were shrewd moves on Giap's part, for by mid-November Operation Lorraine had clearly run its course. The French had penetrated Viet Minh territory and taken valuable supplies, but in the absence of hard opposition the territory gained was beginning to represent a vulnerable finger of valueless land. Supplies were a particular problem. With the air force already over-committed in maintaining outlying garrisons, the new operation was beyond its supply capabilities. Road or river convoys proved costly in the face of Viet Minh ambush. Realising that the gamble had failed, Salan ordered a withdrawal on 14 November.

All went well until 17 November. On that day the two regular Viet Minh regiments reached the area between Phu Doan and Phu Tho. They took up ideal ambush positions in the Chan Muong gorge, where Route Coloniale 2 wound through a steep-sided, jungle-covered defile. Heavy mortar fire heralded an infantry assault and a French convoy was virtually wiped out.

This set the pattern for the next week as the French forces fought their way back to the safety of the delta. Some 1200 did not make it.

ABOVE RIGHT *A French infantryman moves cautiously down a road, past the body of a comrade, searching for snipers.* RIGHT *French officers captured at Nglia Lo, October 1952.* BELOW *Viet Minh troops on the march in a carefully posed photograph. Giap's command of the emplacement of his troops ensured the collapse of Operation Lorraine.*

Operation Castor

the seizure of Dien Bien Phu

THE INVASION OF NORTHERN LAOS by the Viet Minh in April 1953 was a watershed in the war in Indochina. Before it the French had faced a conflict which was contained within certain precise areas of Tongking. Now they were forced to deploy their units in 'hedgehog' positions around Luang Prabang as well as along the De Lattre Line. Although the Expeditionary Force was 190,000 strong and the Vietnamese National Army was being developed, there was a limit to French capabilities. The Viet Minh were gradually over-stretching their enemy preparatory to a final, killing blow.

This was the situation which was presented to General Henri Navarre in May 1953. His immediate concern was to nurture a viable reserve force in case Vo Nguyen Giap attacked the Red (Hong) River Delta. This he did by withdrawing outlying garrisons – Na San, for example, was evacuated without loss in August – and by attempting to clear his own base areas so that troops could be released from static defence. By November the French position was less precarious, enabling the High Command to contemplate yet again the prospect of offensive action.

Navarre had two options. The more logical was to raid deeply into the Viet Bac, threatening Giap's supply lines. This looked too much like Operation Lorraine to be taken seriously. The alternative was potentially more profitable, for if French troops could be established astride the invasion route into Laos, Viet Minh units around Luang Prabang would be isolated. Giap would have to react, either by withdrawing from Laos entirely or by devoting substantial numbers of men to containing the French incursion. Either way, pres-

ABOVE *Paratroops jump into Dien Bien Phu, November 1953. It was originally intended that Dien Bien Phu would serve as a base for raids against the Viet Minh.* LEFT *General Christian de Castries commanded the French forces at Dien Bien Phu; it was finally decided to fortify the camp for a set-piece battle with the communists.*
BELOW *French artillery in action with recoilless 75mm cannon.*

sure upon Navarre's forces would be eased elsewhere, releasing troops to create a substantial reserve for future operations.

Strategic importance

The natural invasion route into Laos ran from Tuam Giao, through Dien Bien Phu, across the border and down the valley of the Nam Ou River. It was the route used by the 312th Viet Minh Division in April. The best interdiction point was undoubtedly Dien Bien Phu, a flat valley in the midst of the T'ai mountains, a region still loyal to the French. Indeed, the T'ai capital of Lai Chau, to the north of Dien Bien Phu, was still controlled by French-officered native units, now completely cut off.

Operation Castor – the seizure of a *base aéro-terrestre* at Dien Bien Phu – was originally intended to relieve these T'ai units, distracting Viet Minh attention while Lai Chau was evacuated in Operation Pollux. Once the T'ais had linked up with the paratroops at Dien Bien Phu, the combined force would mount anti-guerrilla raids into enemy rear areas, using the new base as a central 'mooring point'. Misgivings about the isolation of Dien Bien Phu – 275km (170 miles) by air from Hanoi and lacking ground contact with other French garrisons – were countered by reference to Na San, so successfully defended a year before.

The assault

Airborne Battle Group I, comprising 1st and 6th Colonial Parachute Regiments and II/I Parachute Light Infantry, jumped into Dien Bien Phu on 20 November 1953. They met some opposition from Viet Minh regulars using the valley as a training ground. Airborne Battle Group II (1st Foreign Legion Parachute, 8th Parachute Assault and 5th Vietnamese Parachute Regiments) joined them later in the day. The area was then cleared and a rudimentary base set up.

The paras found themselves in possession of a heart-shaped valley, 19km (12 miles) long and 13km (8 miles) wide, surrounded by low, heavily wooded hills. Two airstrips, one near the village of Dien Bien Phu and the other to the south, already existed. The former was hastily strengthened to receive the first of the C-47 transports which constituted the garrison's lifeline. Patrols began to push into the hills and encountered only moderate opposition.

Giap did not react until late November, when the 308th and 312th Divisions moved towards the valley. The French now began to envisage something they had long been striving for: the possibility of a set-piece battle. This led to a basic change of plan on 30 November, altering the concept of Dien Bien Phu from 'mooring point' to jungle fortress. The destruction of the T'ai units as they withdrew from Lai Chau in December seemed to confirm the wisdom of this, for without them the original plan was useless. Dien Bien Phu was hurriedly reinforced and transformed into a fortified camp with barbed-wire, minefields and shelters on the pattern of Na San.

By the New Year the valley consisted of a series of strongpoints, all reputedly named after the mistresses of the garrison commander, General Christian de Castries. In the centre of the original village was the Command HQ, with strongpoints 'Huguette' to the west, 'Claudine' to the south, 'Elaine' to the east and 'Dominique' to the north-east. Similar posts existed some way to the north-west ('Anne-Marie'), 1.5km (1 mile) to the north-east ('Beatrice'), 3km (2 miles) to the north ('Gabrielle') and around the smaller airstrip 6.5km (4 miles) to the south ('Isabelle'). They were all isolated from the main location.

Artillery (two groups each of 75mm and 105mm weapons, plus four 155mm howitzers), armour (ten M24 light tanks) and fighter-bombers (six Bearcats, stationed on the main airstrip) supported a total of 12 battalions (10,800 men). On paper it was a formidable force; in reality it covered a range of basic weaknesses which were soon to become apparent.

The spot where the French chose to fight it out with the Viet Minh: the broad, flat valley of Dien Bien Phu.

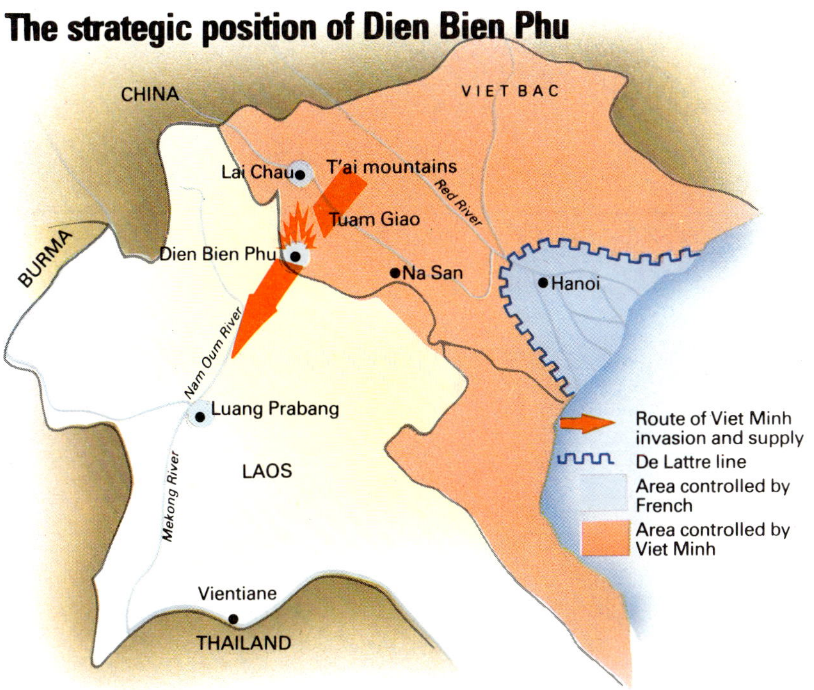

Dien Bien Phu
the French defeat

FRENCH POSITIONS at Dien Bien Phu came under artillery fire from 31 January 1954 and throughout the following month patrols encountered Viet Minh regular units in all directions. By 15 February any idea of expanding the fortress to include surrounding hill features had been dropped. The French settled down with confidence to await the Viet Minh attack.

But as Giap moved in a total of five regular divisions – the 304th, 308th, 312th, 316th and 351st Heavy – Dien Bien Phu began to look vulnerable. The French were located in positions on the valley floor, overlooked from all sides. Material for the manufacture of impregnable strongpoints had not been available, and they were dependent upon air supply for survival. The position deteriorated when the airstrip was hit by artillery fire on 10 March.

Strongpoints under attack

Vo Nguyen Giap's plan was quite familiar: he would try to eliminate the outlying strongpoints before mounting a major assault upon the main position. He began on 11 March with probing attacks against 'Gabrielle', followed two nights later by massed assaults on all three of the outlying posts in the north. The fighting was particularly heavy around 'Beatrice', and despite a gallant defence by men of the 3rd Battalion, 13th Foreign Legion demi-brigade, the position was taken.

'Gabrielle', now extremely isolated to the north, was evacuated on 15 March. This enabled Giap to concentrate upon 'Anne-Marie', the loss of which on 17/18 March troubled the French. It was supposed to cover the northern end of the airstrip and when accurate artillery fire began to sweep this vital link with the outside world, it had to be closed.

Giap immediately mounted his major assault. The blow fell on 30 March, principally against 'Dominique', but was parried by Algerian defenders in some of the bitterest fighting yet seen. The pattern was repeated as the Viet Minh turned against 'Huguette' on 1 April and 'Elaine' and 'Isabelle' two days later. By 4 April, having lost nearly 2000 men for negligible territorial gain (a minor outpost to the west of 'Huguette' that fell on the 2nd), Giap pulled back to recuperate.

The French used the lull to reorganise the defensive perimeter. They concentrated their forces into an area little over 1.5km (1 mile) in diameter, taking in 'Claudine', 'Elaine' and parts of 'Dominique' and 'Huguette', with 'Isabelle' still isolated to the south. Altogether, with three parachute battalions having joined the garrison since 14 March, more than 16,000 French Union troops were surrounded by an estimated 50,000 Viet Minh.

Closing in for the kill

Between 5 April and 1 May Giap turned away from the costly concept of massed attacks in favour of a policy of steady encroachment. Viet Minh soldiers built a complex series of trenches, gradually pushing them closer to the French positions under cover of fire from about 300 105mm guns, cleverly dug into the surrounding hills.

French air strikes, using air-to-ground rockets and napalm, failed to make much impression, particularly in the face of solid anti-aircraft de-

The siege of Dien Bien Phu lasted almost eight weeks. French entrenchments (ABOVE) *and supply planes took a severe pounding from Viet Minh artillery* (BELOW) *which forced eventual surrender.*

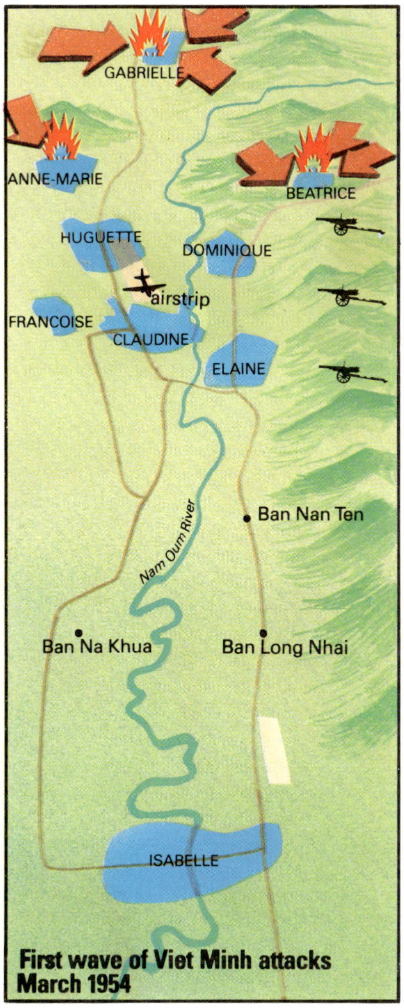

fences which included at least one complete Red Chinese regiment equipped with 64 37mm weapons. These guns, together with those belonging to the 351st Heavy Division, exacted a steady toll, especially upon the transport aircraft which were now having to fly regular sorties at the limits of their range just to keep the besieged garrison alive.

By the end of the battle 62 aircraft had been shot down or badly damaged over Dien Bien Phu, while something like 20 to 30 per cent of all supplies had fallen into Viet Minh hands, having missed the small French perimeter.

During this crucial period French units, reinforced by yet another parachute battalion on 11/12 April, mounted a number of counter-attacks but gained little advantage. On 22 April the monsoon began and as Dien Bien Phu records an average annual rainfall of 1525mm (60 inches), many of the French strongpoints soon became waterlogged. With no prospect of evacuation and with the supply situation deteriorating, Dien Bien Phu was ripe for the picking.

On 1 May Viet Minh forces attacked from all sides. Despite continued French resistance, bolstered by a 'forlorn hope' parachute battalion dropped in on 2 May, the weakened positions fell one by one. On the 7th, after a siege lasting 55 days and nights, General Christian de Castries and 11,000 of his men surrendered. The 'Isabelle' garrison followed suit 24 hours later.

The French units at Dien Bien Phu had comprised seven parachute battalions (three of them Foreign Legion), four North African battalions, four Foreign Legion infantry battalions, two T'ai battalions, an engineer battalion, four artillery groups, a tank company and a truck company. They had lost 7184 men in six months. The Viet Minh, by comparison, had lost an estimated 20,000. But they had destroyed the cream of the enemy force, leaving the French with no alternative short of political surrender at the Geneva conference two months later.

French commanders in conference. They are, from left, Botella, Bigeard, Tourret, Langlais and Seguin-Pazzis.

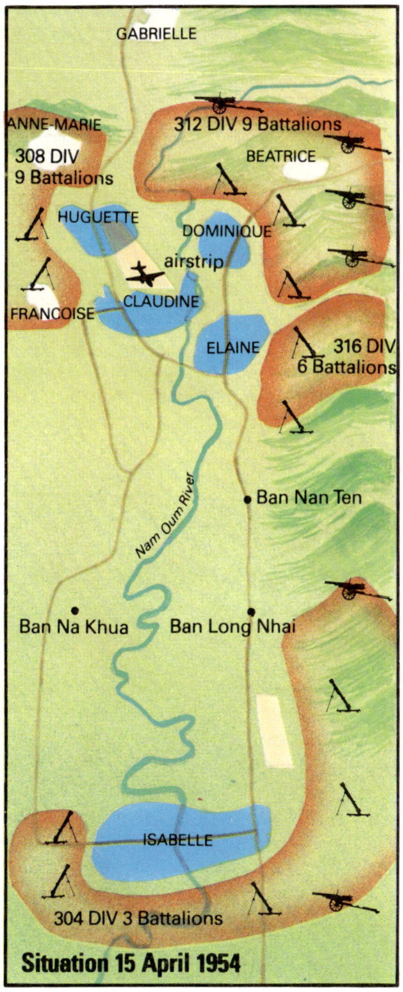

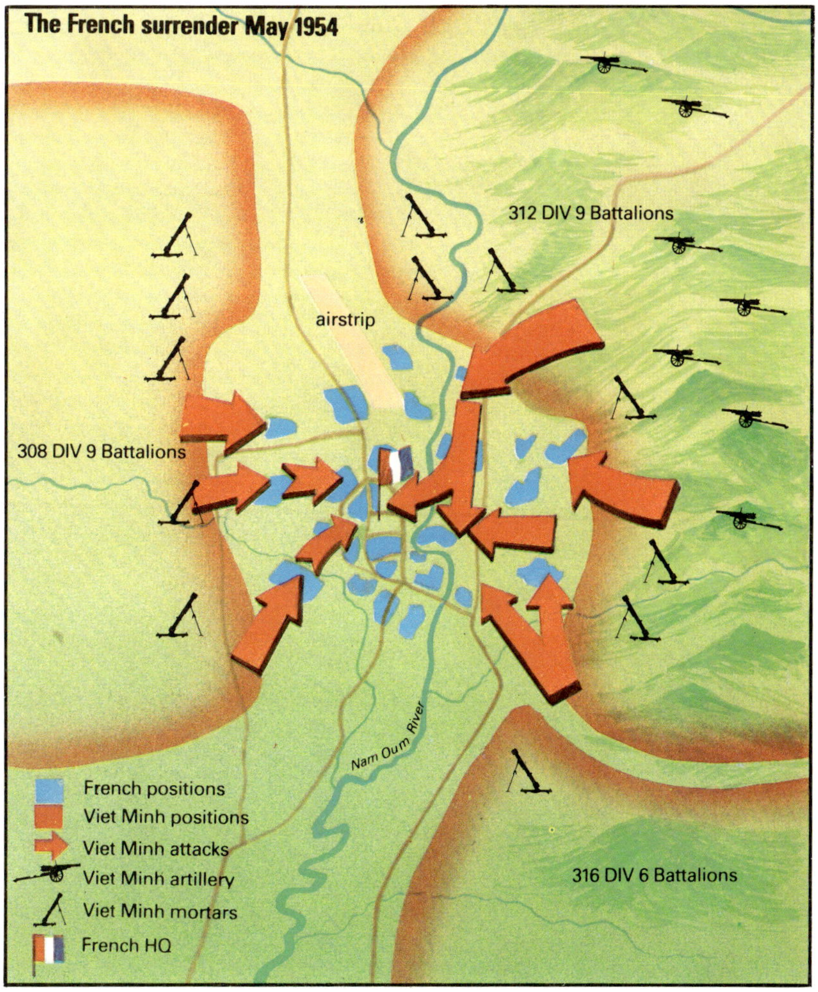

Logistics in Indochina

ALL BATTLES AND CAMPAIGNS depend, in the final analysis, upon the ability to move troops to the decisive point at the right time and then to keep them supplied with food, ammunition, replacement weapons and reinforcements. On too many occasions between 1946 and 1954 the French failed in one or the other of these respects while the Viet Minh succeeded. It is not difficult to establish why.

French difficulties

The French were maintaining a large, sophisticated army a long way from home. Their ultimate supply base, particularly so far as weapons and ammunition were concerned, was France itself. The route to the war zone was both lengthy and expensive to use. Because of political instability in France and the lack of public support for the war, supplies rarely enjoyed top priority and the High Command in Hanoi had to fight constant political battles to ensure adequate deliveries.

Nor were the French problems over once the supplies had reached Indochina, for they then had to be distributed to units in the field. Troops in the south, together with those close to supply dumps in the Red River Delta, usually experienced few shortages but, in the context of the war, they were relatively unimportant people. The crucial battles were fought in the outlying garrisons and during the various offensive operations such as Lorraine or Castor, and it was here that the major problems emerged. In all cases there were two possible distribution methods and both failed at key times during the war, with inevitable consequences.

The first was a land-based transportation system designed to create a constant link between the 'teeth' units and the delta base. As the French forces stuck rigidly to the roads and rivers, this was never difficult to organise but proved to be extremely vulnerable.

During the Hoa Binh operation in late 1951 and early 1952, for example, Vo Nguyen Giap's interdiction of the river supply chain – achieved chiefly through the destruction of barges in selected attacks – undoubtedly precipitated General Raoul Salan's decision to withdraw, exposing his forces to ambush along the roads

TOP *Bicycles were put to use to take supplies to the Viet Minh. These peasants include women and were heading for Dien Bien Phu.* ABOVE *Before large-scale movements of troops and supplies were undertaken on the Hanoi-Haiphong railway a special train made sure the track was free of explosives.* BELOW *The human supply line that kept the communist soldiers provisioned throughout the war.*

back to the delta. Similarly, the plethora of outlying garrisons which fell as the war progressed did so as much from a lack of guaranteed supplies as from direct Viet Minh assault.

The alternative was to use the air, but even here the French suffered disadvantages. For much of the war their air transport fleet was inadequate, using aged Junkers Ju-52s (known as AAC-1s), and even when the more capable C-47s and C-119s arrived in 1952 there were never more than 100 machines available. They were expected to keep all outlying garrisons supplied as well as transporting parachute units and other reinforcements. Normally they were hard-pressed; by the time of Dien Bien Phu they were extended beyond their capabilities. Some of their duties were taken over by requisitioned or contracted civil airliners, but with the losses imposed by Viet Minh anti-aircraft defence, air transport quickly lost its viability.

Supplying the Viet Minh

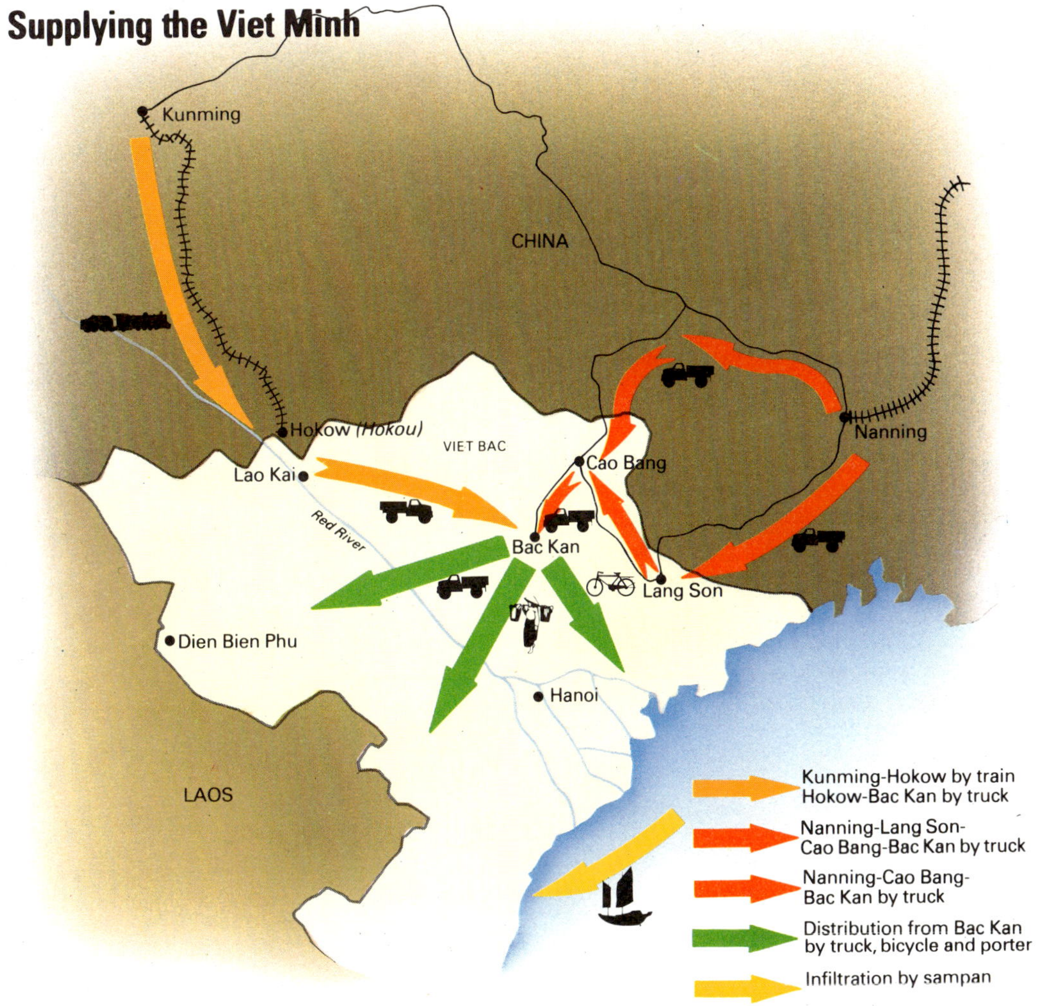

Trucks, porters and bicycles

By comparison the Viet Minh supply service, one of the three departments of Giap's War Bureau, was well organised and satisfied most of its needs from China. By 1952 Chinese aid was pouring over the border into the Viet Bac at a rate of 3000 tonnes a month, following one of three main routes, all originating from the rail-head at Nanning.

The shortest route was by road to the border town of Chan-Nun-Kwan, thence to Lang Son and Cao Bang, but this entailed excessive movement inside Indochina, vulnerable to French air attack. Because of this, an alternative road route was favoured, following the Nanning-Kunming road in an arc across the top of Tongking inside Chinese territory then crossing the border in a short hop to Cao Bang.

LEFT *Troops wait to board a transport plane at Luang Prabang in February 1954 after the city had been threatened by a Viet Minh incursion into Laos.* BELOW *French trucks crammed with troops pass a supply dump.*

In both cases trucks were the usual mode of transport and most of the movement took place at night. Finally there was a narrow gauge railway from Kunming to Hokow (Hokou) on the border, thence to Lao Kai. This was not fully developed until 1953 and probably contributed little to the war.

Once supplies had been received, they were collected at a central distribution point at Bac Kan in the Viet Bac and gradually issued to units in the field. By 1953 nearly 600 trucks were available – mostly Soviet-supplied Molotavas – and, indeed, the rapid Viet Minh build up around Dien Bien Phu in that year was achieved using these vehicles.

But for much of the war distribution was in the hands of the local peasants. As early as 1949 Ho Chi Minh had introduced conscription and by 1952 all peasants had to devote up to three months' labour service annually. This was the key to Viet Minh flexibility, for although it took about 50,000 porters, each carrying 20kg (45 pounds), to maintain a regular division in the field for a month, the man (and woman) power was available in all areas. As the war progressed, bicycles were issued to porters, increasing the load on the outward journey (to 70kg or 150 pounds each) and speeding the return. It was a most effective system.

The Reckoning

THE GENEVA AGREEMENTS of July 1954 ended nine years of war in Indochina. It had been a costly affair for both sides, the French forces (including the Vietnamese National Army) having lost nearly 75,000 dead and the Viet Minh anything up to 150,000. And a major European army had been worn down and defeated by an unconventional peasant force.

The overriding reason for defeat was that the colonial power had been presented with a totally new type of warfare for which it was not prepared. The French were used to fighting conventional wars against conventional enemies – wars in which such tangibles as possession of territory, numerical superiority and firepower were the key criteria of success.

But revolutionary war, as waged by the Viet Minh, was based on the cellular strength of the Communist Party. It aimed for political power through the support of the people, an aim which could never be satisfied by military action alone.

Political failure

Throughout the war little attempt was made by the French to counter Viet Minh politics. What propaganda there was lacked effect or relevance to the cause of Vietnamese nationalism, and was based upon the premise of continued colonial superiority. The defeats and humiliation suffered by France between 1940 and 1945 gave the Viet Minh a central propaganda theme of immense value.

The 'independence' talks of 1947–50 were undermined by the choice of the discredited Bao Dai as Vietnamese representative and were destroyed by the terms, which promised nothing that would reduce French influence. This was poor policy, particularly when it was apparent that French promises could never be backed by sufficient force to ensure their implementation.

By comparison the Viet Minh, with their efficient organisation, proven promises of reform and ruthless use of force (including terror), were far more relevant and effective.

Military ineffectiveness

A similar lack of effect may be seen in the French reaction to guerrilla warfare. With the exception of the French-officered Indochinese anti-guerrilla units in the mountains of Tongking, the military responses were stereotyped and ineffective. From past colonial experience, the French favoured the 'oil-slick' technique for countering revolt: that is, the occupation of key locations followed by a gradual widening of control through aggressive military action. This was shown by an emphasis upon static defences (such as the outlying ridgeline garrisons or the De Lattre Line) and quick-reaction strike forces (the mobile groups), but neither was particularly apt. Static defences attracted attack, and although occasionally this might lead to a 'victory' it always drained resources and manpower.

Similarly, although in theory the mobile groups could have been effective, there were never enough of them to cover all the trouble-spots; and when used, their tactics were inappropriate. Because their mobility depended upon vehicles, mobile groups stuck to the roads, exposing themselves to attrition by ambush. As few French Union troops showed any inclination towards jungle warfare, such ambushes could be mounted with virtual impunity.

So when the long-sought set-piece battle finally occurred at Dien Bien Phu, French morale – particularly at home – had already been undermined. Intelligence estimates of Viet Minh capabilities were poor or ignored by over-confident commanders; dependence upon a technological army left inadequate supply methods over-stretched; reliance on air support collapsed in the face of communist anti-aircraft weapons. In such circumstances, Viet Minh victory, both political and military, was ultimately inevitable.

TOP *At Geneva in 1954 French rule in Indochina formally came to an end. The 17th parallel provided the boundary between North and South Vietnam, and Laos and Cambodia, both of which had earlier declared independence, were now recognised as sovereign states.* ABOVE *Delegates from France and North Vietnam sign the ceasefire agreement.* BELOW *Refugees from North Vietnam queue for seats on a departing Dakota after the armistice had been signed.*

Emergency in Malaya

When communist guerrillas tried to seize control of Malaya after 1945 the British authorities responded effectively to the challenge they faced

Sir Robert Thompson

Members of a British Army patrol wade through jungle waters in the search for armed guerrillas, who used the dense jungles of Malaya as a base and refuge.

THE CAUSE of the troubles in Malaya can be traced to the activities of the Malayan Communist Party (MCP), which was of Chinese origin. Its cadres reached Southeast Asia in the many hundreds of thousands of Chinese immigrants who sought work in the fast-developing European colonies. In Malaya before World War II the party made little headway other than to set up cells in Chinese schools and labour forces in the tin mines and on rubber estates. It received support, however, among the Chinese community by exploiting nationalist opposition to the Japanese invasion of China.

When the Japanese occupied Malaya and captured Singapore early in 1942 the Communist Party, as in Greece, was the only organised underground movement and became the core of the resistance. It had a good anti-Japanese cause and gained respectability through receiving support from the Allied Southeast Asia Command in Colombo, Ceylon (now known as Sri Lanka).

A communist-led Malayan People's Anti-Japanese Army (MPAJA) was established in the jungles and British liaison officers were attached to it. Most of this army's weapons were gathered from the 1942 battlefields but more were later dropped by air. The MCP's local support came from the vast numbers of the Chinese urban population and labour forces who were compelled, by lack of employment, to squat on vacant government land in jungle valleys throughout Malaya and to seek a living from subsistence agriculture.

The MPAJA had never been tested in battle against the Japanese. Although it took the opportunity to eliminate likely political rivals during the short inter-regnum before the British returned in 1945, it was in no position to challenge for control of the country.

The communists therefore accepted disbandment of the MPAJA, which handed in most of its weapons. Many arms, however, were retained and hidden in waterproofed caches in the jungle. In return the MCP was recognised as a legal political party.

Aftermath of war

By 1948 the MCP had made no political headway but was in a strong position in trade unions, Chinese schools and youth movements. There followed a period of strikes

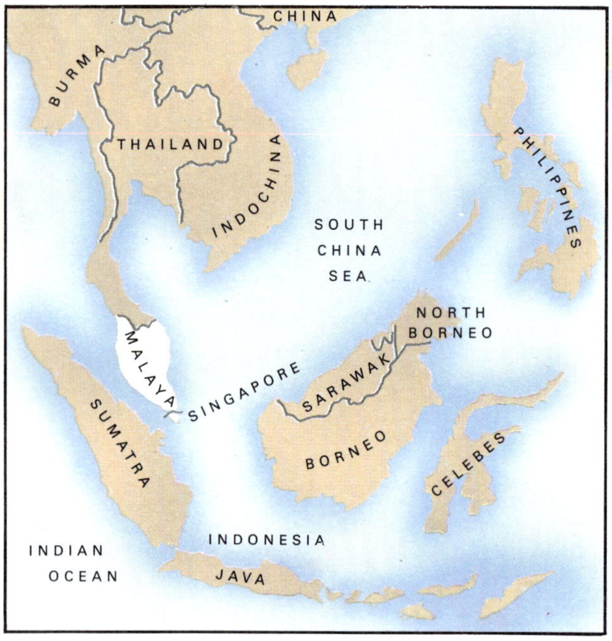

and ever increasing racial violence between Malays and Chinese. During this time a strong Malay nationalist movement, the United Malayan National Organisation (UMNO), developed in opposition to Britain's plans for a Malay Union. Because the communists were mainly Chinese they failed to penetrate it.

In the summer of 1948, with the Chinese and Greek Civil Wars in full swing, an international communist youth conference was held in Calcutta, India. Immediately afterwards, whether specifically instructed by Moscow or not (still a subject of controversy), the communist parties in Malaya, the Philippines, Indonesia and Burma all launched an armed struggle.

The decision caused conflict within the MCP. Lai Tak, the party's secretary general, who was reputed to have been both in Japanese and British pay, disappeared and was succeeded by Chin Peng. The members of the MPAJA and of the MCP now took to the jungle and formed the Malayan Races Liberation Army (MRLA). This was a misnomer, however, because its numbers were more than 90 per cent Chinese.

The Malayan Communist Party suffered from two great weaknesses. It was alien both in creed and race, so that the Malay nationalists rallied to the government. Its cause was weak because independence had been explicitly promised by Britain and was made credible by the fact that India, Pakistan and Burma had already been granted independence. The struggle which followed was less for independence than for the succession to power when the British left.

Emergency laws enacted

The first outbreak of violence occurred in Perak in June 1948 when a State of Emergency was declared and was extended to the whole of the country the following month.

The years 1948 to 1951 saw a steady increase of minor guerrilla actions and incidents. Sir Henry Gurney, the High Commissioner, made sure that the strength of the civil administration and the rule of law through the normal courts were maintained. Tough emergency laws were introduced with the consent of the Labour government in London. They were acceptable because they were effective, fair to all and enforceable through the courts. Detention of suspects without trial was authorised and, at its peak, up to 10,000 were held – but there was no public outcry. Each case had to be reviewed by a tribunal composed of a High Court judge and two non-official civilians, but the final decision to detain or release rested with the government.

Gurney requested an experienced soldier as Director of Operations and Lieutenant General Sir Harold Briggs, a former commander of the 4th Indian Division and GOC in Burma, was appointed. Briggs established

BELOW *A British truck burns after an attack by communist guerrillas. Communications were one of the main targets for guerrilla action: High Commissioner Sir Henry Gurney was killed in an ambush in 1951.* OPPOSITE TOP *A wounded guerrilla surrenders.* OPPOSITE CENTRE *The 'Home Guard' of a rubber plantation patrols through the trees.* OPPOSITE BELOW *Sir Gerald Templer, whose realistic policies proved very successful.*

an organisation (a combined civil, military and police structure at all levels down to districts) and set the priorities and responsibilities both by tasks and areas.

The major task was the resettlement into new villages of the 500,000 Chinese squatters scattered throughout the country. The objective of this was to deprive the MRLA of recruits and logistic support by isolating it from the people. A superb intelligence organisation in the police Special Branch and an efficient information service were set up to keep people informed and to conduct psychological warfare.

Because the available army units were limited, partly owing to the Korean War, the police force was greatly expanded and village Home Guards were established. The Korean War did, however, have one fortunate effect: tin and rubber, Malaya's two major exports, rocketed in price. This meant that the government, throughout the Emergency, was able to finance all expenditure from its own revenue. (The British government had only to meet the cost of its own forces on active service.) There was never any prospect of the MCP achieving victory by imposing unacceptably high costs on the government.

The Royal Navy patrolled the coasts but there was no evidence of attempted outside aid for the MRLA. Without it the MRLA had no hope of progressing beyond minor guerrilla actions.

Yet these actions were distressing enough. More than 2000 civilians were brutally murdered, property was burned and plantations damaged.

When Gurney was killed in an ambush in 1951 government morale sank to its lowest ebb. Nevertheless the foundations had been laid. Although the MRLA had expanded from 4500 to a peak strength of 10,000, government forces had increased from 21,000 to close on 90,000. Of this total the police provided 60,000 and the armed forces 30,000.

Arrival of Templer

Gurney's successor, General (later Field Marshal) Sir Gerald Templer, was appointed both High Commissioner and Director of Operations in January 1952. Templer's dynamic leadership quickly restored morale and put new vigour into the counter-insurgency programmes. Intelligence improved, the contact rate went up and, with it, MRLA casualties. More and more guerrillas began to surrender.

As the last of the great British pro-consuls, Templer was equally adroit in the political field. He laid great stress on 'winning the hearts and minds of the people'. He understood that people cannot be won solely by bribery. The key was government performance in showing that it intended to (and could) win, in protecting the population, and then in providing social and economic benefits through the normal structure of government, thereby instilling a sense of order and permanence with a promise of further progress and prosperity.

He also understood the need for reconciliation and for the adoption of measures which would help the Chinese to become loyal citizens of the country. He encouraged the formation of the Alliance Party under Tunku Abdul Rahman – comprising UMNO, the Malayan Chinese Association and the Malayan Indian Congress – and promised early elections to the legislature with independence to follow. When he left in 1954 the MCP was broken.

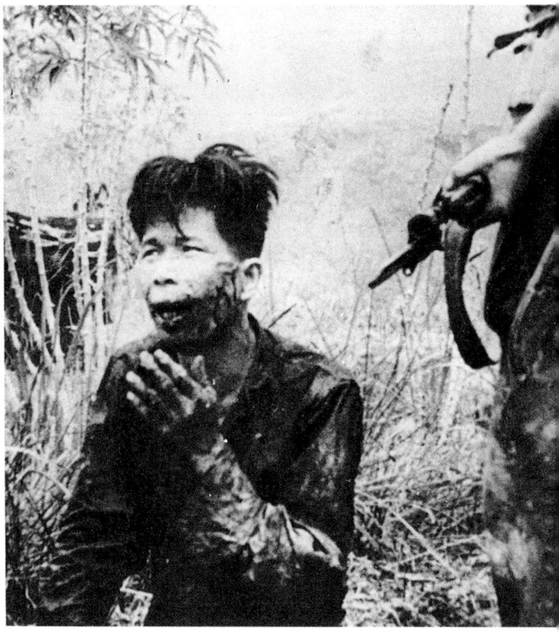

The final roundup

Under his successor and former deputy, Sir Donald MacGillivray, elections were held in 1955 and resulted in a resounding Alliance victory. In order to salvage something from defeat the MCP asked for peace talks. The MCP offered to disband the MRLA and lay down its arms on condition that it would be accepted again as a legal political party.

At this point the laying down of arms could have been enforced as the Special Branch knew, almost without exception, the names of all remaining members of the MRLA, their unit, state of health and the weapon with which they were armed. Tunku Abdul Rahman, now in a position to gain peace as well as independence for his country, refused to be tempted and offered only an amnesty. This in turn was refused by the MCP and the long mopping-up process from 1955 to 1960 began.

The MRLA was virtually driven out of the populated areas and dispersed in small groups into the jungle where its efforts were expended on survival, not on military action. These groups were slowly hunted down or starved by strict food control measures into surrender, the rate of which increased dramatically with time. Eventually the MCP central committee issued instructions for a retreat to the Thai border, but only about 500 made it. Meanwhile independence had been granted on 31 August 1957 and, after 12 long years on 12 July 1960, the Emergency was declared at an end. The insurgents had been totally defeated.

Casualties in Malaya 1948–60

	1948	1949	1950	1951	1952	1953	1954	1955	1956	1957	1958	1959	1960	TOTAL
Guerrillas														
Killed	374	619	648	1079	1155	959	723	420	307	240	153	21	13	6711
Captured	263	337	147	121	123	73	51	54	52	32	22	8	6	1289
Surrendered	56	251	147	201	257	372	211	249	134	209	502	86	29	2704
Security forces														
Police	89	164	314	380	207	58	53	47	25	5	3	1	0	1346
Soldiers	60	65	79	124	56	34	34	32	22	6	7	0	0	519
Civilians														
Killed	315	334	646	533	343	85	97	62	30	22	3	3	0	2473
Missing	90	160	106	135	131	43	57	57	26	2	0	3	0	810

Structure of the Communist Party

THE ORGANISATION of the Malayan Communist Party (MCP) was very similar to that of other revolutionary movements in the postwar years and derived from the teachings both of Lenin and Mao Tse-tung. Such an organisation is designed to achieve the political and military aims of a revolutionary movement which has been active within a country for a considerable period and which is successful enough to be able to mount an armed struggle – but not successful enough to win by disruption and subversive activity alone.

In the guerrilla warfare phase the political aim is to gain control over the population, starting in the rural areas, and to destroy the government's prestige and authority. The military aim is to neutralise the government's armed forces (not to defeat them in battle at this stage) and to render them powerless to save the state. The general strategic concept, as applied on the ground, is best summed up in Mao's saying that the 'villages must be used to encircle the towns'.

To carry out these aims in Malaya there was a joint political and military

RIGHT *Arms tied to the handle of a broom, a suspected communist is brought out of the jungle for questioning.* BELOW *A train derailed by mines. Railways and roads were prime targets for terrorist sabotage.*

organisation, with the military subordinate to the political. Support for the political aim of gaining control of the population by continued penetration, subversion and terror was a primary task of the whole organisation including the armed guerrilla units. The organisation, headed by a politburo of about ten members, was similar at every level whether region, province, district or village.

The Malayan communist political organisation within the population was responsible, with the help of the armed military units (local and regular) outside, for expanding communist control over the population under the direction of the district committee. This committee contained both political and military members and was normally located outside the population with one of the platoons. The political organisation was also responsible for providing the district committee and the armed units with supplies, recruits and intelligence.

By expanding political influence and gaining control over larger areas and more population, the flow of supplies and recruits to the armed units steadily increases. In such a way these units can be built up gradually from platoon to company and even battalion strength at the district level. With a number of districts the regular units can be built up from company to battalion and then to regimental and even divisional strength. The political organisation is in the forefront while the regular units are in the rear – the opposite of conventional warfare.

There was a natural tendency on the government side for its military commanders to regard the armed units as their main objectives in the early stages because they presented attractive military targets. Large-scale military operations and sweeps were mounted to destroy them, but guerrilla units are designed to cope with this form of reaction because they are scattered over wide areas of jungle or other inaccessible terrain. Even when a guerrilla unit was caught and suffered heavy casualties no permanent damage was inflicted because, as soon as the government forces withdrew, the whole organisation went to work to repair it with additional recruits and with transfers from local units to regular units.

Guerrilla expansion

When remoter areas of the Malayan countryside were fully under guerrilla control the political organisation then extended its operations into the next stretch of populated territory, thus allowing some of the guerrilla units to move out of the jungle areas into occupied populated territory (the 'liberated areas'). These areas were rendered more inaccessible by the cutting of all access roads and the blowing-up of bridges, so that the guerrilla-held villages began to encircle government-held towns.

In more strategic terms, to achieve its aims the insurgent movement needed, at a cost which could be indefinitely met by its organisation, to impose costs on the government which were not indefinitely acceptable because then, even if it lost every battle, it would be winning the war. That is something the communists failed to do in Malaya.

Such was the organisation and intention of the MCP in Malaya, and in the early stages it made limited headway. Because of the policy of General Sir Harold Briggs, the government did not waste too much energy in chasing armed guerrilla units. The main aim was to destroy the political organisation, known as the Min Yuen, and to cut the link between it and the guerrilla units. If this could be achieved the armed units would wither away. In this the Malayan government was wholly successful.

RIGHT *A cornered communist surrenders to security forces.* BELOW *Terrorism often had an innocent face. Simple, everyday baskets were used to carry grenades and small-arms.*

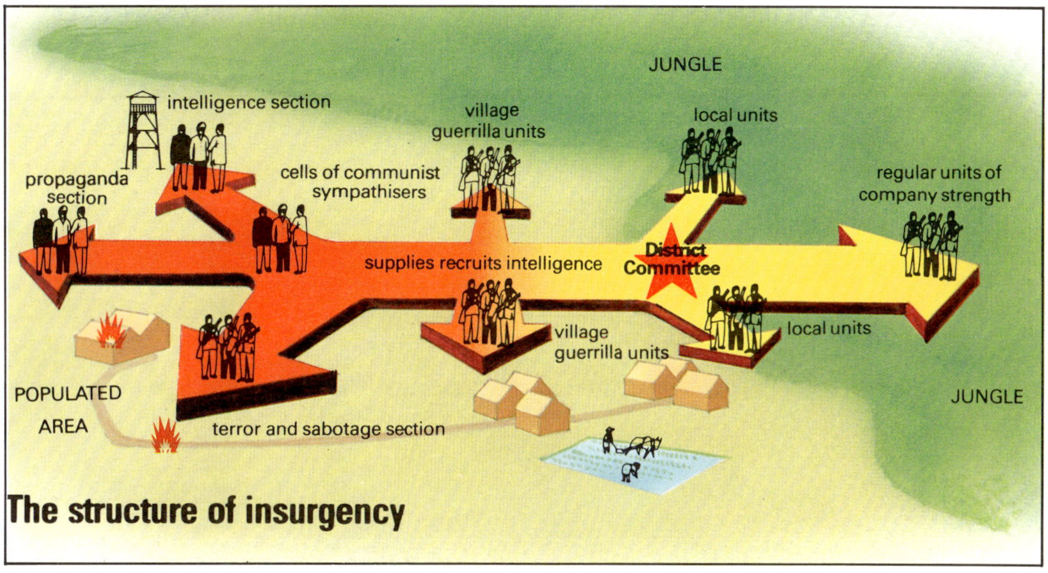

The structure of insurgency

The New Village Strategy

IN PRE-WAR MALAYA the rural population was almost entirely Malay, living in fairly substantial villages (kampongs) and cultivating rice, fruit crops and rubber smallholdings. There were few rural Chinese villages. Most Chinese were concentrated in the towns or worked on the tin mines and rubber estates, but some Chinese did have rubber holdings nonetheless.

During the Japanese occupation of Malaya urban unemployment and the closure of many mines and estates impelled thousands of Chinese to push out into undeveloped land on the fringes of the populated areas and in jungle valleys, where they cut down scrub and jungle to make a living from subsistence agriculture. It was on this population that the communist-directed Malayan People's Anti-Japanese Army (MPAJA) and later the Malayan Races Liberation Army (MRLA) depended for most of their food and many of their recruits.

Each family built a house on its clearing with jungle materials (poles, bamboo and palm leaves). The houses were well scattered, there were no villages as such. About 500,000 people squatted in this way on government land to which they had no title. When estates and mines reopened after the war and the country began to return to normal so that many of the men again became wage earners, the families remained on their clearings.

The Briggs plan

Under a plan devised by General Sir Harold Briggs, an enormous resettlement programme was launched to move these people into about 500 new villages. The entire scheme was carried out systematically as part of the campaign against the Malayan Communist Party, to deny the guerrilla bands their source of food and manpower.

The new villages were of two types. The dormitory village was for those who were mainly wage earners, while the agricultural village was for those who depended on farming. Some dormitory villages were added as suburbs to existing small towns, but many were entirely new. For the

The programme of new housing (BOTTOM) *was very successful and the protected dwellings were popular. Wall posters* (BELOW) *carried government appeals for information about terrorists.*

farmer the new village had to be so sited that agricultural land was easily accessible, not more than 4–5km (2–3 miles) from the village.

Every village was carefully planned in advance with roads, water (wells or stand pipes) and sites for shops, a school, a clinic and other amenities. The plots for house sites were carefully surveyed to allow space for chickens, pigs and vegetables. The movement of the squatters into these villages was carried out almost as a military exercise and generally in military trucks. Everything was conveyed down to the last chicken.

Each family received construction materials for a house and $100 cash, but the main attraction was that they were given a title to their new property. Parents considered it a welcome feature that the school, shops and clinic were close at hand, even though the husband might have to bicycle 4 or 5km (2 or 3 miles) to work. This neatly reversed the inconvenience of jungle life. The real test of a new village began to show after a year or two when the inhabitants began to rebuild their houses in permanent materials of brick and tiles.

Providing protection

The perimeter of each village was protected with barbed wire and a police post with six to 20 men, depending on need. As soon as the village was settled Home Guards were recruited to reinforce the police at night. Curfews were imposed outside the village at night and, if necessary, for several hours during the night within the perimeter itself.

A similar programme was carried out on estates and mines which housed their own labour forces, regrouping their housing so that they could be protected more easily. Such regrouping was generally unnecessary in Malay kampongs. Although Home Guards were recruited for local protection, kampongs were seldom attacked or penetrated by the MRLA.

Starving the guerrillas

When the resettlement programme was fully completed in a district the real campaign could be started to eliminate the Min Yuen, as the communist political organisation was known, for it was the Min Yuen on which the guerrilla units depended. Strict food control measures were introduced. Food brought into the settlement was always escorted, and none was allowed to be taken out.

MRLA sympathisers and relatives tried to carry out rice in the frames of bicycles, in cigarette tins and in false bottoms built into pig food-buckets which a Malay constable, being a Moslem, would be loath to inspect. In some areas rice was rationed and issued cooked, after which it goes sour within a couple of days; and tinned foods had to be punctured as they were

ABOVE *General Sir Harold Briggs devised the plan to resettle 500,000 Chinese living near the jungle, on whom the armed communists relied for recruits and supplies.* RIGHT *A lone sentry keeps watch outside a house on an estate.*

sold across the counter. These measures worked, and it was not unusual for a member of the MRLA to surrender with a gun in his hand and $100 in his pocket – but on the point of starving.

Local government

As conditions became more secure, particularly in 'white areas', committees were elected to run the village. The key word is 'secure', because elected members were likely to be targets for assassination.

In one case in Johore, where an election was carried out prematurely, the fearful candidates stood trembling as the votes were counted in the local school. As the results were announced those who had been elected rushed out and caught the next bus to Singapore, more than 160km (100 miles) away.

Eventually in the larger villages, or in groups of smaller villages, local councils were elected and were given legal powers to manage their villages and raise local revenue.

The ultimate test of the whole programme came at the end of the Emergency when all restrictions were lifted. Less than half a dozen new villages proved not to be viable and their inhabitants dispersed. The remainder thrived and many have now grown into prosperous towns.

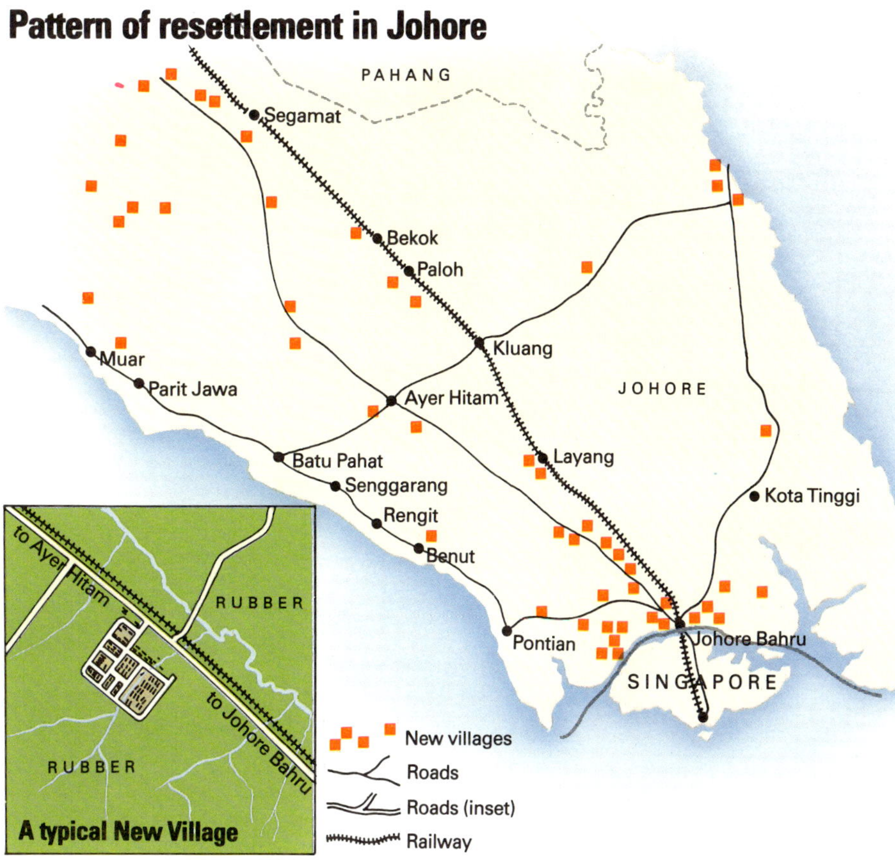

Jungle Warfare

MORE THAN 80 PER CENT of Malaya was jungle, with a central mountain spine running the length of the country with peaks up to 2130m (7000 feet) in height. Some of the worst jungle, however, was in the undrained swampy lowlands. Over most of it the canopy would be 20–25m (70–80 feet) high with dense undergrowth nourished by the heavy warm tropical rainfall. Almost the only means of access was the game trails along the ridges or up the rivers using dugout canoes. The rubber estates also provided plenty of cover with very limited visibility.

Guerrillas, therefore, could approach any objective without being seen and roads could be ambushed at almost any point. General Sir Harold Briggs stipulated that the police should operate in the populated areas while the army operated on the perimeters of the rubber estates and in the jungle fringes.

The Malayan Races Liberation Army (MRLA) had all its training camps with hospitals and armouries in the jungle but seldom, for reasons of food supply, more than a few hours' walking time from the populated areas. Some of these camps, complete with parade ground, were quite elaborate. Even so they were practically impossible to spot from the air, although a few army Auster pilots became expert at detecting them by slight changes in the canopy. It was equally difficult to approach them on foot without raising the alarm so that, while the camp might be destroyed, the unit occupying it would escape and soon build another somewhere else in the area.

Ambush tactics

The government knew, however, that the organisation of the Malayan Communist Party (MCP) had one grave weakness. At some time or other, day or night, everyone needed to move around on the ground using comparatively limited tracks and trails. Supply parties, couriers, agents and units carrying out operations were constantly on the move. The counter-guerrilla tactic most often adopted was, therefore, the ambush.

ABOVE *A para drop into the Malayan jungle. A small team would spend up to a month combing an area for guerrilla units.* BELOW *Accompanied by local scouts and boatmen, Special Air Service troops prepare for an excursion.*

Intelligence or deduction made it obvious which villages were supplying food and which trails had to be used. The only unknown was the time. The problem was to get an ambush party into position on a trail without the MRLA knowing where it was.

Many ruses were employed, such as a company operation leaving behind in the jungle four or five men. It was often necessary for such small parties to lie on a trail for days and nights before anything happened, but one alert man with a Bren gun could then create havoc. Some favoured the discharger cup with a four-second grenade. Later, Claymore shrapnel mines were frequently used.

Similar ambushes were laid by police squads in close proximity to villages where food was being obtained, for example, by sacks of rice being thrown over the perimeter wire at night. Sometimes this was allowed to continue to act as a 'honey pot' where the collectors could be ambushed.

When continual operations of this nature were carried out in an area on a reasonable scale with improving intelligence, it increased government-initiated contacts and finally denied freedom of movement to the guerrillas. This was not patrolling in the normal sense, because a moving patrol could be heard and was itself vulnerable to ambush. It was the long silent sit which got results against guerrillas who had to move and who never knew when they might be ambushed.

Retreat to the jungle

As the MRLA was gradually driven out of the populated areas it retreated deeper into the jungle where small vegetable plots were cultivated and some game could be shot. This meant that they dispersed into much smaller parties of little more than squad size. Army units, also broken down into small groups, followed and were assisted by Iban trackers from Borneo.

The Special Air Service was re-formed and perfected a parachuting technique into the high jungle canopy. The parachute caught in the tree tops with the man dangling 18–20m (60–70 feet) from the ground. He then hooked a rope carried round his waist into his parachute harness before releasing it and lowered himself to the ground. This was a far more effective means of inserting a small party (and quicker) than clearing an area with explosives for helicopters to land. Few helicopters were available, in fact, and were used mainly for evacuating sick and wounded.

Supply drops and tribal help

Many parties stayed in an area for three to four weeks at a time and had to be supplied by air. Drops were made in small natural clearings or on a river bed by Dakota aircraft releasing three parachutes on a straight run. A plane could not circle without giving away the position of the party and so, if it failed to spot the site on the first run, it had to come back again 30 minutes or more later. Such runs were often timed to coincide with a scheduled commercial flight so that supply dropping would not be suspected.

RIGHT *The Senoi guard at Fort Kemar, a remote fort and one of many that were built in the jungle to help track down terrorists.* BELOW *A Malayan patrolman, Bren gun in hand, trudges through a jungle in Selangor at night.*

Malayan jungle tribes had been much exploited by the MCP during the Japanese occupation and early stages of the Emergency so that when contacted by the government they became willing allies. Jungle forts with small air strips for STOL aircraft were set up in their tribal areas so that they could be administered and supported. An aboriginal force, the Senoi Pra'ak, numbering not more than 300, many of them armed solely with their traditional blowpipes, killed more guerrillas in the last two years of the Emergency than all the rest of the security forces put together.

Effective Persuasion

Towards the end of the Emergency, communist strength in Johore had been reduced from about 2000 to 500 guerrillas split up into groups of 10 or 20 living in the jungle but making their way north towards the sanctuary of the Thai border. Hor Lung, the political commissar in Johore and the third-ranking member of the politburo, realised that his men were doomed. One day he gave himself up at a remote police station. The sergeant in charge promptly informed the head of Special Branch in Johore and Hor Lung, with his two body guards, was whisked away until it was decided what to do about such an important surrender. It could have been publicly announced and much propaganda value obtained from it. Instead it was decided, with Hor Lung's consent, that he should be put back into the jungle to go around all his remaining units ordering them to surrender. Obviously, few people could be told what was happening in case the whole scheme was ruined. There was also the risk that Hor Lung might be shot by the security forces. So rather than ceasing security operations altogether, which would have aroused suspicion, the troops were fed information that kept them out of certain areas at particular times. The net result was that, except for a handful of individuals, all the units surrendered within a few months. Such was the sophisticated level of control achieved by the Malayan government.

The Suez Fiasco

In 1956 Britain and France tried a desperate venture: the invasion of Egypt to regain control of the Suez Canal

H. P. Willmott

THE SUEZ CRISIS of 1956 witnessed the breaking of Anglo-French power in the Middle East. It marked the occasion when two worlds came into collision and when two imperialist Western powers attempted, unsuccessfully, to reassert their authority and prestige in the face of Arab nationalism.

Moreover, the Suez crisis had wide-ranging consequences, straining Anglo-American relations almost to breaking point, dividing the Commonwealth and splitting British popular opinion so deeply that the issue remains sensitive 25 years later.

Until 1947, and possibly even as late as 1956, Great Britain was the most powerful nation in the Islamic world on account of the millions of Moslems within her empire. Even after granting independence to the Indian subcontinent, British power and influence throughout the Middle East was immense. From Libya in the west to Malaya in the east and from Nigeria and Uganda in the south to Iran and Iraq in the north, Moslems in their millions lived under either the direct control or the influence of Britain. Second only to Britain was France, with her possessions throughout the Maghreb and the Sahara in north Africa. Within ten years of Indian independence, however, Western power throughout the Middle East had been shattered beyond redemption.

The Suez campaign arose directly out of the deterioration of Anglo-Egyptian relations. Britain occupied Egypt in 1882, mainly out of concern for the security of the Suez Canal. Her period of control was, for most of the time, mutually beneficial, if distasteful to Egyptians because of British paternalism and racial disdain. In 1922 nominal independence was bestowed upon Egypt, but Britain remained in effective control of a country that was to be the base of her operations in the Western Desert and eastern Mediterranean against the Axis powers between 1940 and 1943. The defeat of the Germans and Italians removed any threat to Egypt and loosened the ties that held Britain and Egypt together.

The establishment of the state of Israel subsequently caused a major readjustment of

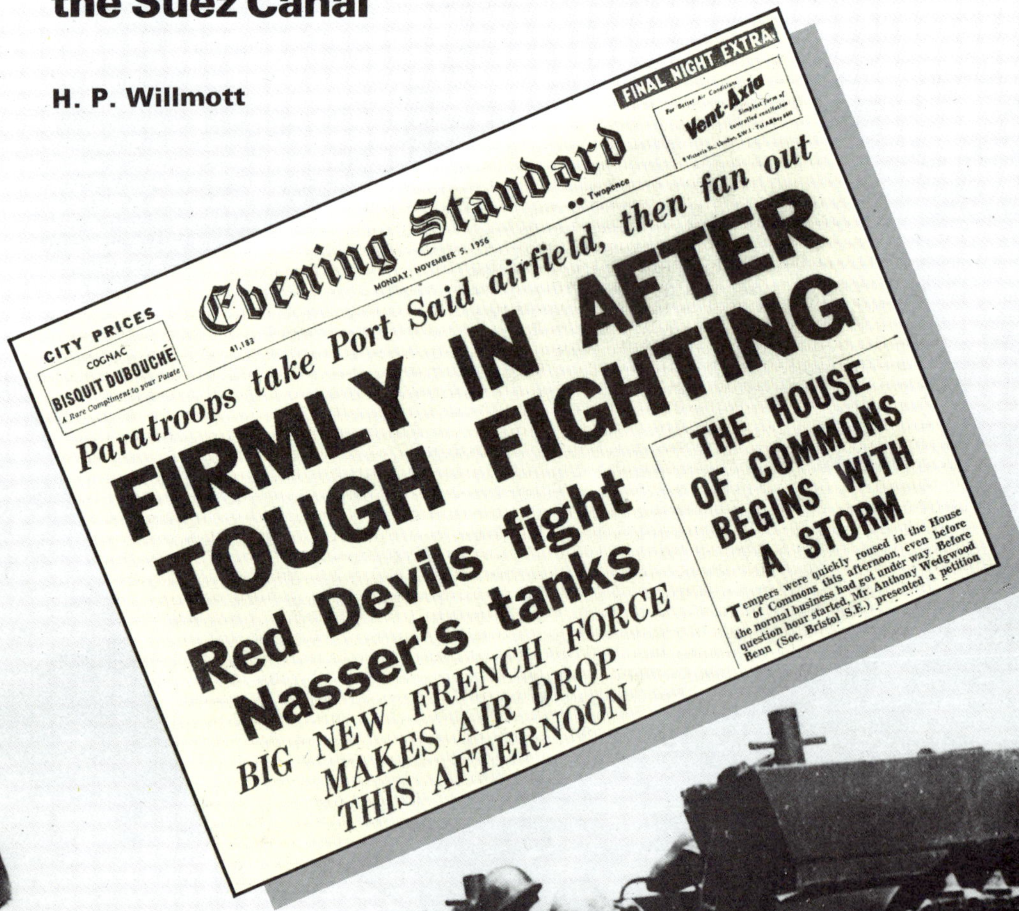
FINAL NIGHT EXTRA

CITY PRICES

COGNAC BISQUIT DUBOUCHE A Rare Compliment to your Palate

Evening Standard

41,183 MONDAY, NOVEMBER 5, 1956 •• Twopence

For Better Air Conditions Vent-Axia Simplest form of controlled ventilation 9 Victoria St., London, S.W.1 · Tel ABBey 6441

Paratroops take Port Said airfield, then fan out

FIRMLY IN AFTER TOUGH FIGHTING

Red Devils fight Nasser's tanks

BIG NEW FRENCH FORCE MAKES AIR DROP THIS AFTERNOON

THE HOUSE OF COMMONS BEGINS WITH A STORM

Tempers were quickly roused in the House of Commons this afternoon, even before the normal business had got under way. Before question hour started, Mr. Anthony Wedgwood Benn (Soc, Bristol S.E.) presented a petition

French troops leap from the landing craft and run ashore at Port Said, Egypt. The invasion was well reported in Europe, although popular opinion was deeply divided over the wisdom of the venture.

Egyptian security interests which were wholly at odds with British concerns. Even though in 1946 Britain agreed in principle to evacuate Egypt she stayed on, at least in the Canal Zone, until in October 1954 she finally agreed to leave this part of Egyptian national territory.

Nasser in control

By this time, however, one event had taken place that profoundly shaped the whole of the Suez story. The corrupt, complacent King Farouk had been deposed by a military coup in 1952, and a man who had put personal pleasure before national interest had been replaced by men who were determined to re-establish Egyptian national independence. By 1954–55 one man, Colonel Gamal Abdel Nasser, had emerged as military dictator of Egypt. He came to represent not only the cause of Egyptian self-determination but also the wider issue of Arab nationalism, both of which were certain to clash with entrenched British interests in the Middle East.

Because of this, and because he was both a military man and a dictator, Nasser quickly came to represent all that was unacceptable in British eyes. He represented a threat to British interests and to the peace of the area, and in the course of time British opinion hardened in favour of dealing with him in the manner it was felt Hitler should have been handled before 1939.

Such feelings took time to develop, however, and did not prevent Britain agreeing to partly finance the construction of the Aswan Dam, regarded by Egyptians as the symbol of national regeneration. Nor was the evacuation of the Canal Zone affected. This was completed in June 1956. But relations between the two countries were always strained and became more so during 1956 as Egypt began to arm herself with weapons supplied by the Soviet bloc.

President Nasser is cheered after announcing that Egypt had taken over the Suez Canal.

A series of retaliatory economic measures by both Britain and Egypt culminated with the British and Americans withdrawing their support from the Aswan project in mid-July 1956. On the 26th, just six weeks after the last British troops left the Canal Zone, Nasser announced the nationalisation of the Suez Canal.

The response to nationalisation

This move put Britain on the spot. It was a direct challenge to Britain's position throughout the Middle East, and everyone knew it. Britain's immediate recourse to diplomacy to try to bring pressure on Nasser to climb down was unsuccessful. Pressure began to grow inside the British government for a military operation to topple Nasser and restore British prestige. A small, quick operation, it was felt, would show that Britain had the means and will to assert her authority in an area that since 1800 had been more or less a British preserve.

But other parties were involved in these developments. The French by 1956 were increasingly enmeshed in a bloody revolt in Algeria that Cairo Radio ('The Voice of the Arabs') actively encouraged; it even claimed that Egypt was leading and directing it. The French did not question these false claims, but felt that if they could crush Egypt they would end the Algerian uprising by destroying it at its (assumed) source.

The Israelis, moreover, were concerned by Egyptian access to Soviet-bloc weapons since these would tip the balance of power in the area, already weighted against Israel, decisively in the Arabs' favour. When it became evident that Britain and France contemplated military action against Egypt, Israel saw her chance.

In the autumn of 1956, therefore, as Britain and France mobilised and deployed their forces for an attack on Egypt, the French acted as the co-ordinator of a plan of attack that involved an Israeli offensive against Egypt in Sinai followed by an Anglo-French intervention in the Canal Zone. In order to allow Israel to carry out her side of the plan France undertook a substantial re-equipment of Israeli forces. The British government has consistently denied that there was any collusion between Britain and France on the one hand and Israel on the other.

A fatal delay

Britain and France did not have the air, sea and land forces to deal with Egypt when the moment was internationally and psychologically favourable – on 27 July 1956. Months were to pass as the British and French established a joint command, redeployed their naval forces to the central and eastern Mediterranean, sent to Cyprus jet fighters capable of handling Soviet-supplied Egyptian MiG fighters, and trained parachute forces whose other duties had led to neglect of their primary role.

By October, when Anglo-French intentions were widely known, international opinion was hardening against the operation. Yet the invasion went ahead. On 29 October Israel launched an attack against Egypt, followed two days later by Anglo-French bombing of Egyptian installations. By the time the main landings were made, on 5 and 6 November, world opinion had expressed its dismay and Britain and France were compelled to agree to a ceasefire in order to conclude what had become a humiliating adventure.

Invasion Plans

THE PLANS for an Anglo-French invasion of Egypt were settled only with difficulty, partly because of the natural problems that surround any amphibious operation and partly because, until quite late, considerable confusion existed over whether or not the operation should be launched against the Suez Canal itself, or against Alexandria as a prelude to a general advance on Cairo. In the end the plan adopted envisaged a landing at Port Said with the intention of securing the canal along its entire length. To carry out this operation the French estimated they would need about four days; the more cautious British allowed a week to ten days.

This difference was small in itself but was symptomatic of very different approaches to the operation by the British and French. The French believed that suddenness and speed would ensure success. The British, on the other hand, favoured a deliberate step-by-step approach in the same manner that Anglo-American forces had tackled invasion during World War II. Because at every level command was vested in the British, the French had to give way so that the final plan of attack represented British thinking – and it was unsound.

The plan envisaged a six-day preliminary assault designed to secure air superiority over the battlefield and to allow a thorough softening-up of Egyptian defensive positions. This length of time was more than flattering to the Egyptians, but it was largely determined by the realisation that the

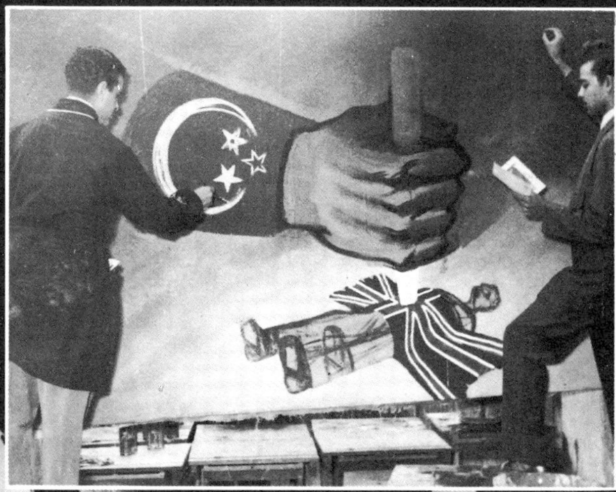

RIGHT *An Egyptian puts the final touch to a piece of anti-British and pro-Soviet propaganda. Nasser capitalised on anti-British sentiment.* BELOW *Troops bound for Suez emplane at Cyprus.*

Sir Anthony Eden went ahead with the invasion despite much opposition. Suez effectively ended his career for he quit through ill health two months later.

seaborne part of the operation would have to be staged from Malta, and Malta was six days' steaming from the canal for the slowest ships in the invasion force. Because the British insisted that the Anglo-French invasion had to appear to be a response to a conflict in Sinai between Israel and Egypt, the invasion force could not sail from Malta before the start of hostilities in Sinai.

The French were more perceptive than the British. They saw that once hostilities between Israel and Egypt began, and once the British and French made clear their intentions, the political situation might deteriorate rapidly. In the French view, the slowness that the British insisted upon constituted not a guarantee of thoroughness but a positive danger to the whole operation. Events proved the French correct, but in the run-up to the invasion proper the six-day interlude did not seem too serious a problem. Once, however, the British began to show signs of second thoughts about their intentions a very real strain developed in what was at best a hastily improvised command structure.

The forces at Suez

Phase one **Air bombardment** **31 Oct–4 Nov 1956**	Valiants, Canberras, Venoms, Hunters and Thunderstreaks operating out of Malta and Cyprus Combined naval task force of Sea Hawks, Sea Venoms, Corsairs and Thunderstreaks operating from carriers 50 miles off the coast of Egypt	
	British forces	**French forces**
Phase two **Airborne assault** **5 Nov 1956**	**main force** 3rd Parachute Battalion Group – Gamil airfield **reserve force** 1st Battalion Royal West Kent Regt	parachute battalion group of 10th Parachute Div – Raswa and Port Fouad two parachute regts 10th Parachute Div
Phase three **Seaborne assault** **morning 6 Nov 1956**	3rd Commando Brigade Royal Marines comprising 40 Commando, 42 Commando, 45 Commando C Sqn 6th Royal Tank Regt 3rd Field Sqn Royal Engineers	parachute battalion of 10th Parachute Div 3 Marine Commandos one sqn AMX tanks
Immediate seaborne follow-up **6–7 Nov 1956**	two battalions 16th Parachute Bde and supporting arms 6th Royal Tank Regt	one sqn AMX tanks one sqn Patton tanks one engineer company

Operation Musketeer

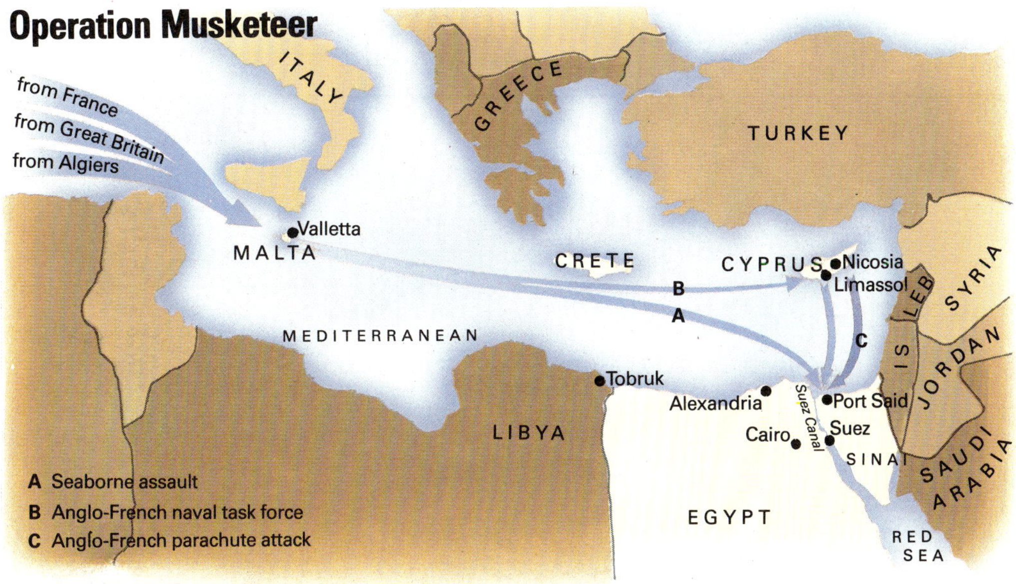

The balance of forces

The assault on the canal ultimately involved about 90,000 French and British troops, sailors and air personnel, almost equally divided between the two nations. Initially the British had undertaken to provide more than 60 per cent of the attacking force – hence Britain's cornering of the command positions – but as the French ground element was increased so a rough balance was established.

In the air and at sea, however, the British provided 300 of the 500 aircraft and more than 100 of the 130 warships earmarked for the operation. Of the warships seven were carriers, two French and five British. Two of the British carriers, the *Ocean* and *Theseus*, carried troops and helicopters. The French battleship *Jean Bart* was among the naval units that supported the seaborne landings.

Military plans

The plan of attack was for British and French jet fighters, based on Cyprus, to secure air superiority over Egypt as the first stage of the operation. This was designed to ensure the security of the invasion convoy during its long approach from Malta. The convoy was destined to bring most of the main force to the battle area, but the first troops to be committed to action were from the British 16th Parachute Brigade, planned to drop west of the canal in order to capture Port Said's airfield, Gamil, and French troops from the formidable 10th Colonial Parachute Division. The French were to land east of the canal and take Port Fouad.

A British heli-borne landing some 3km (2 miles) beyond Port Said would secure the Raswa bridges. This was intended to be the first use of helicopters for troop landings by the British Army in an assault against a conventional enemy.

The British and French airborne forces were to operate in a conventional role, securing objectives in front of an advancing force through which the latter had to pass if it was to develop its offensive. The vanguard of the main force was to be provided by the 3rd Commando Brigade and the 6th Royal Tank Regiment. These were required to make the first touchdown at Port Said, to secure and move through the town and to deploy southwards as the bulk of the forces, the 3rd British Infantry Division and the French 7th Light Mechanised Division, came ashore. The guns of the fleet and strike aircraft from both navies were to support the landings.

Airborne Operations

ABOVE *British paratroopers on their way to Egypt.* BELOW *The first men drift down and land in the dropping zone at Gamil airfield, Port Said.*

OPERATION MUSKETEER, as the Suez invasion was code-named, suffered from a series of last-minute changes, but only the initial parachute landings endured substantial changes as a result. As originally conceived the airborne landings involved a British drop at Gamil, Port Said's airfield, a French drop at Port Fouad and a British heliborne operation to secure the Raswa bridges that took the road and railway over the Interior Basin to the south. Operation Omelette, as the airborne part of Musketeer was dubbed, would involve further airborne landings along the length of the canal at El Qantara, Ismailiya and Suez while the main invading force, with the help of the paratroopers from the first wave, secured and broke out of Port Said to link up with the airborne forces to the south.

The Israeli attack on Egypt began on 29 October. The following day Britain and France delivered a joint ultimatum to both Egypt and Israel which demanded a halt to hostilities and a withdrawal of all forces to a distance of 16km (10 miles) from the canal. They demanded the right to occupy Port Said, Ismailiya and Suez to guarantee transit of shipping through the canal. Both sides were given 12 hours to agree to the ultimatum, but with the Israeli main forces 160km (100 miles) from the canal the ultimatum was clearly directed at Egypt alone, and she had no option but to reject the Anglo-French demands. On 31 October Anglo-French aircraft began attacking Egyptian installations.

Change of plan

The main force landings could not take place before 6 November because the invasion convoys did not sail from Malta until 31 October. But as the French had feared, the political situation deteriorated so rapidly that neither Britain nor France dared wait that long. On 2 November the French more or less insisted on immediate action and drew up an amended plan. It retained the Gamil drop but substituted a French drop for the heliborne landings at Raswa. The French accepted the need for an airborne force to forego supporting naval gunfire. The British agreed to launch this operation shortly after dawn on 5 November.

On paper the amended plan ran frightening risks, partly because the landing had to maintain itself for more than a day without major support and partly because a dangerously small force of less than a battalion was all that could be used in the opening assault. The operation was limited to just 600 British troops of the 3rd Battalion, the Parachute Regiment, and 500 men from the 2nd Regiment of the French Colonial Parachute Division, because of the smallness of the airfields on Cyprus from which it was launched. Parking space was severely restricted, and because the British Hastings, Valettas and Vikings were inferior in carrying capacity to the French Nord Nordatlas N2501, the number of troops that could be dropped at one time was very limited.

Early successes

The British drop succeeded despite the appalling shortcomings under which it was conducted; and the men, in spite of a lack of training, proved better than their equipment. The French operation was a model of how an airborne operation should be carried out. So successful were the French that they were able to carry out a second drop during the afternoon to secure Port Fouad. That, too,

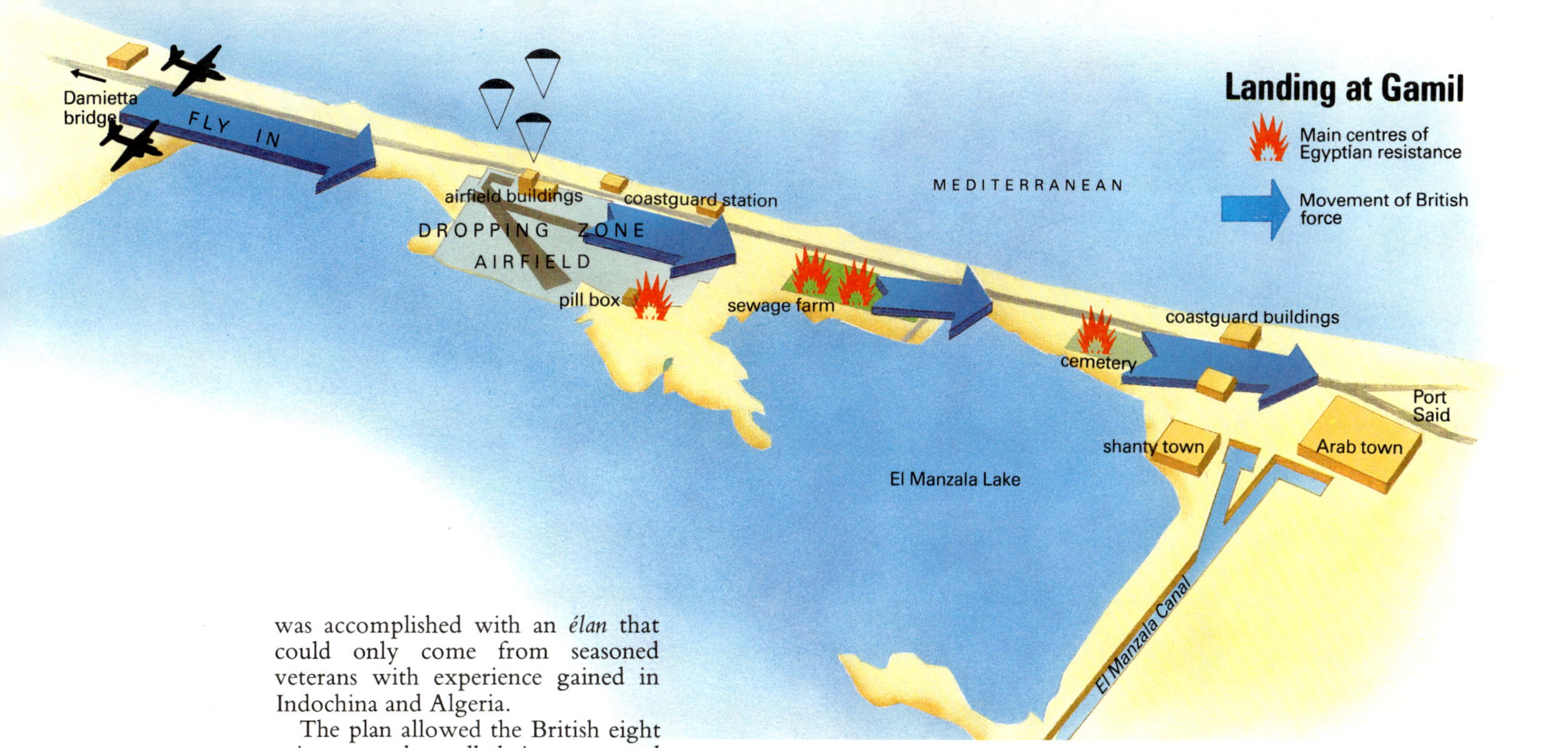

was accomplished with an *élan* that could only come from seasoned veterans with experience gained in Indochina and Algeria.

The plan allowed the British eight minutes to drop all their troops and equipment on to Gamil, an airfield that was 1600m long and 800m wide (1 mile by $\frac{1}{2}$ mile) and bound on both sides by water. To avoid drift in the air they planned to drop at 183m (600 feet). The Raswa dropping zone, by comparison, was on a neck of land 800m long and 137m wide ($\frac{1}{2}$ mile by 150 yards). The French planned to jump at 120m (400 feet) and allowed four minutes for the whole operation. The jumps were timed for 15 minutes apart, the British jumping first.

BELOW *After the drop onto Gamil airfield, British paratroops begin to assemble and to collect their equipment before going into action. Some are replacing the dropping helmet with the characteristic beret.* RIGHT *French paratroops escort defeated Egyptian soldiers into captivity.*

The French were on the ground in less than four minutes, and it took them less than an hour and cost them ten casualties to secure the one bridge over the Interior Basin that the Egyptians had not demolished. This they achieved despite being dropped on a manned Egyptian position and against an objective covered by armour and light flak. French patrols also reached as far south as 10km (6 miles) and found the road clear of Egyptian forces.

The British at Gamil had a rougher time. Unlike the French they did not carry a personal weapon for use during the descent and once on the ground they had to break open containers to secure arms and ammunition. This could have led to difficulties but for the fact that the Egyptians, fearing a landing, had blocked the runway with sand-filled oil drums. These provided cover as the British paratroopers secured arms, reorganised and moved out to attack the defenders. The airfield itself was taken inside 30 minutes, but thereafter the British ran into problems on the narrow approaches to Port Said.

Port Said holds out

Throughout the day close air support for both the British and French airborne forces was heavy and accurate, yet the British had great difficulty overcoming resistance around the sewage farm and the cemeteries. By dusk they had failed to penetrate the outskirts of Port Said, and had taken up defensive positions in the course of the afternoon.

The failure to secure Port Said on the morning of 5 November was not considered too serious. Such a view was underlined in the afternoon when the commander of the Port Said garrison sought terms, but the only terms that the British and French were willing to accept were those of unconditional surrender. This Cairo would not accept. The decision was accompanied by a general arming of the civilian population of the town, thus ensuring that some form of resistance would greet the main force invasion the following day.

Seaborne Invasion

SHORTLY AFTER DAWN on 6 November 1956, ships of the invasion convoys began to line up some 8km (5 miles) out at sea in order to let the assault craft take up position for their run-in to the objectives ashore at Port Said. An hour-long bombardment by aircraft and the fleet softened up targets before the assault, but in order to minimise damage and avoid unnecessary civilian casualties no guns larger than the 4.5 inch calibre were allowed to join in the naval attack.

The first wave of attack from the sea was formed by 40 and 42 Commando, coming ashore on either side of Casino Pier. Hard on the heels of these two units were Centurions from the 6th Royal Tank Regiment. The two marine units, with their small armoured detachments, quickly worked their way through the town to reach the southern outskirts of Port Said within a couple of hours. By noon a link-up with the French at the intact Raswa bridge had been accomplished.

Silencing the towns

Port Said, however, had not been properly occupied. The marines and armour simply did not have the means or the time to attempt to suppress opposition since their primary concern had been to secure a beachhead

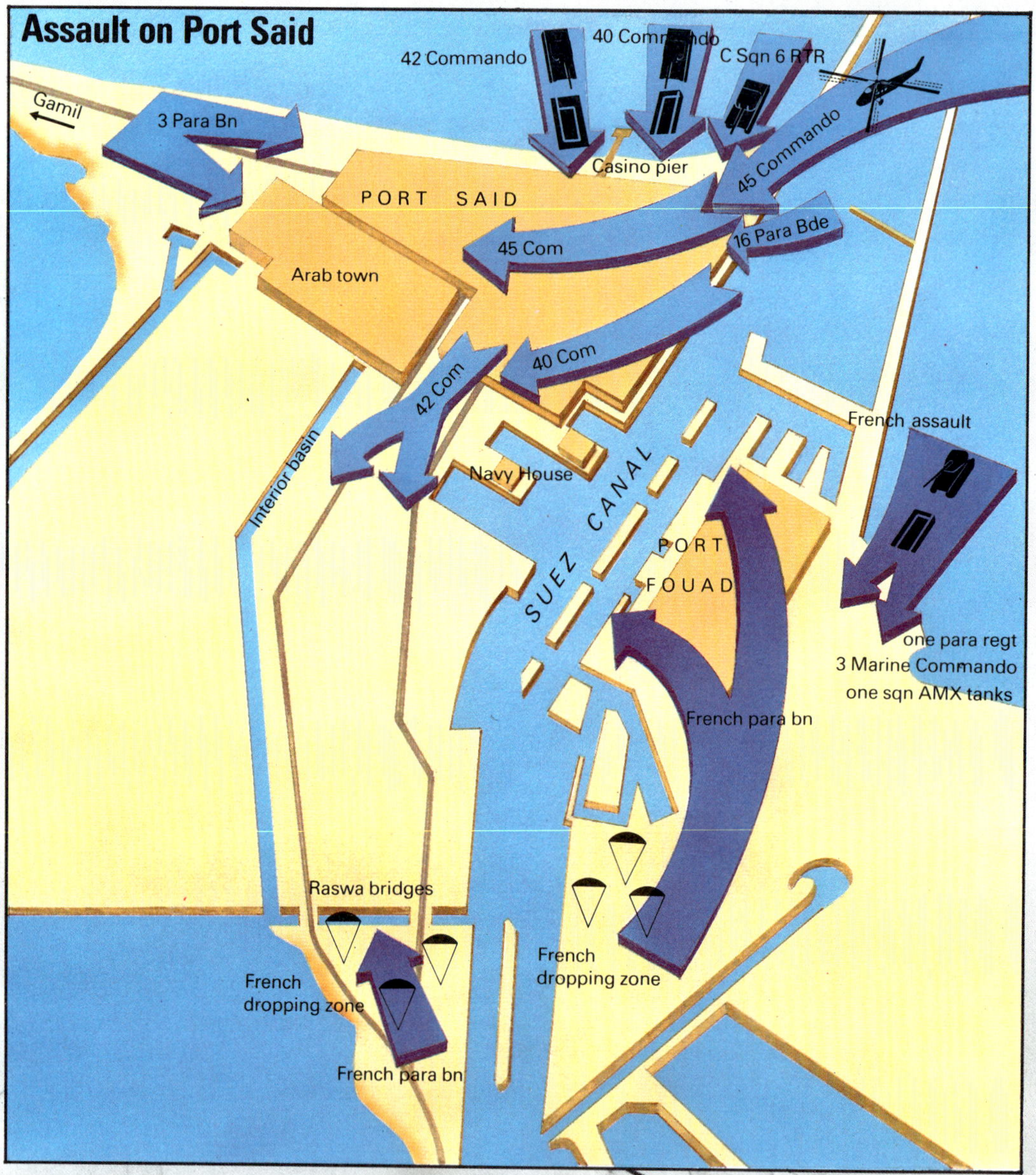

ABOVE *The carrier* Theseus, *one of the major units of the invasion force, sails from Portsmouth in 1956 with men of the 16th Independent Parachute Brigade on deck. The amount of time taken to assemble the invasion fleet was indicative of organisational weakness and serious political difficulties.* BELOW LEFT *A Centurion tank disembarks.* BELOW RIGHT *British troops in the streets of Port Said.*

and press on to link up with the airborne forces on the outskirts of Port Said. Much of the thankless task of clearing the town therefore fell on 45 Commando, brought in from the invasion fleet by helicopters, and the 3rd Parachute Battalion, resuming its attack from the west.

Throughout the 6th, operations were directed at silencing snipers, dealing with enemy positions bypassed by the first wave and collecting the thousands of rifles and rounds of ammunition that had been distributed to the population. (Nearly 150 tonnes of arms, ammunition and equipment were recovered by British forces from houses in Port Said.) Subsequently other troops had to be deployed to bring the fighting to an end, but in reality Egyptian resistance inside the town was not fully crushed before the start of the ceasefire.

At Port Fouad the French brought in a Legion airborne unit, three marine commandos and armour on the 6th. What little resistance remained there was snuffed out completely. The French, displaying a far more ruthless attitude to resistance and the civilian population than the British, remained in undisputed control right up to the time of their withdrawal.

Clearing the harbour

Concurrent with the assault landings Royal Navy ships made their way past the breakwaters at the mouth of the canal. Their objective was to secure the harbour and clear the docks and berths of wreckage so that troops and equipment could be moved directly into Port Said rather than over the beaches. This, of course, could not be done quickly because blockships had been sunk at Port Said and the harbour had to be checked for mines. Not until late afternoon were the first troops landed inside the harbour. These troops were from the 16th Parachute Brigade, used in a seaborne role because of the lack of aircraft. They had been sent by sea from Cyprus along with the French that had landed the same day at Port Fouad. These were the last troops to arrive before the cessation of hostilities and they took part in the final, bloodless, offensive of the entire operation.

The final advance

Centurions from the 6th Royal Tank Regiment, picking up French paratroopers en route, penetrated as far south as El Tina by nightfall on the 6th. There they went into defensive positions, aware of their vulnerability at night but unaware of the developments in London that were to bring a halt to the Suez adventure.

The British government, at about 1900 hours local time, announced its willingness to accept a ceasefire, effective from midnight, on condition that Israel and Egypt did the same. Even without waiting for an Egyptian reply it was obvious to commanders on the spot that the allied beachhead had to be expanded to the greatest possible extent in the few hours that might be left before a ceasefire came into effect.

The paratroopers, who knew of the ceasefire, therefore made every effort to catch up with the forces at El Tina, who did not. Through marching and 'liberating' every roadworthy and unattended vehicle in sight this was achieved, and columns of armour and infantry moved out with one hour to go before the possible end of hostilities.

In that hour the columns advanced some 11km (7 miles) to reach El Cap, about 40km (25 miles) from Port Said and 5km (4 miles) from El Qantara. There the offensive was halted without having encountered any opposition. Back in Port Said, however, fighting was still going on and the paratroopers from Gamil and the commandos in Port Said had still not linked up. But irrespective of what was happening at Port Said, the real battle had been fought and decided thousands of miles away in Washington, London, Paris and at the United Nations in New York.

The Ignominy of Suez

DESPITE ITS SUCCESSES Operation Musketeer was doomed because the French analysis of the political repercussions proved to be correct. An operation that had been planned and put into effect in order to restore Anglo-French prestige revealed only the weaknesses in the positions of Britain and France.

In 1956 both Britain and France enjoyed the status of great powers. Both were permanent members of the United Nations Security Council and still had extensive colonial territories. Britain possessed atomic weapons and one of the most powerful navies and air forces in the world. France had a large and formidable army. These two states were the leading European members of the North Atlantic Treaty Organisation (NATO).

But the Suez operation brought home to all just how stretched Britain and France were by their NATO and colonial commitments. It took them four months to mount an operation against a country regarded previously by them with disdain. All kinds of military weaknesses and unpreparedness were revealed in that period and then, when the operation got under way, Britain and France were shown to be hopelessly vulnerable to a combination of international – particularly American – displeasure and censure, the flight of capital and the cutting off of oil supplies from the Middle East.

American hostility

Long before the operation began President Dwight D. Eisenhower candidly warned Prime Minister Anthony Eden that the British were in danger of exaggerating the importance and significance of Egypt's President Nasser. The Americans had little direct interest and involvement in the Middle East. They had no intention of allowing the destruction of Israel, but their over-riding concern was to

BELOW *A Royal Navy salvage vessel attempts to clear the blockships from the Suez Canal – an ostensible reason for the invasion.* BOTTOM *A helicopter prepares to take off the wounded from the harbour at Port Said.*

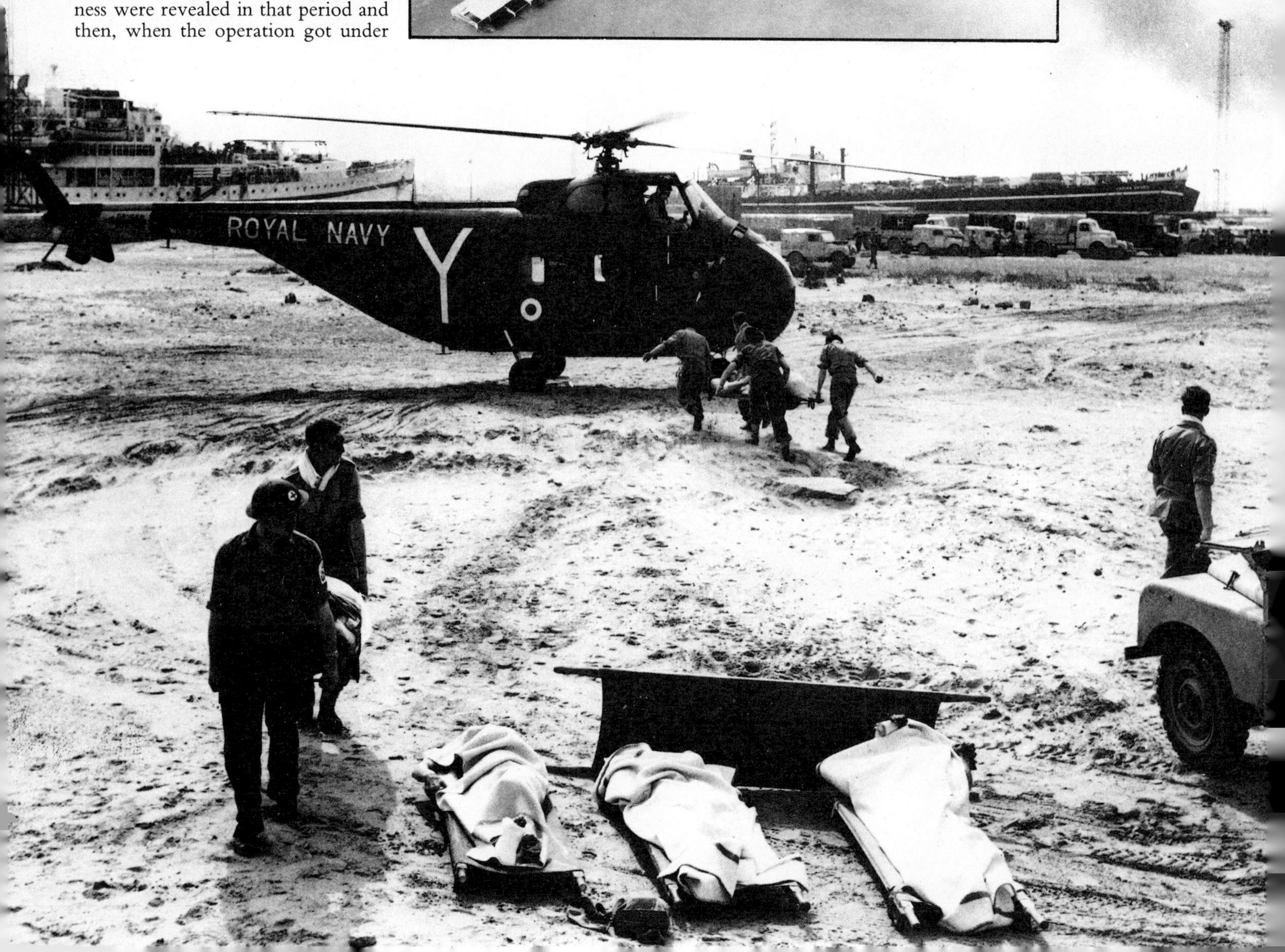

secure stability in the area.

In order to try to cool an increasingly tense situation Eisenhower insisted upon tripartite talks between Britain, France and the United States. These took place on 28 October. The British and French, giving no indication of their intentions, hoped that the Americans would stand aside as events unfolded.

The Israeli attack on Egypt on the 29th dismayed the Americans who insisted on an emergency session of the Security Council. During an adjournment, at Soviet insistence, the contents of the Anglo-French ultimatum to Egypt and Israel became known. The Americans were outraged and immediately tabled a resolution demanding the end of all operations by all four parties involved. Britain and France vetoed this resolution and a subsequent Soviet one on 30 October.

The Americans then switched their attention to the General Assembly and in the session of 1/2 November secured the passing of a resolution that demanded an end to the fighting. Ominously for Israel the resolution insisted upon a return to the armistice lines – a clear sign that the United States wanted a return to the *status quo ante bellum* and would not allow Israel to bargain any conquests in return for a general settlement. The resolution passed by 64 votes to 5, Australia and New Zealand alone in the world supporting Britain, France and Israel.

ABOVE *French tanks in the streets of Port Said. They look threatening, but UN intervention blunted Anglo-French military might.* RIGHT *Egyptians wait patiently under French guard. They were soon to be freed.*

Pressures for a ceasefire

The revelation of lack of support from the Americans, the divisions within the Commonwealth and the feeling of isolation in a hostile world thus confronted Britain long before the first troops were to land at Port Said. But the British government could hardly have been prepared for the opposition to the operation that developed within Britain itself or for the scenes of disorder inside the House of Commons on 1 November when the Speaker had to suspend the sitting.

The debate of 1 November on Suez was the third such debate in as many days, and what clearly emerged was the deep split in British public opinion between those who opposed and those who supported the attack on Egypt. Although Eden's government survived a censure motion, it could not hope to reopen the canal, it could not ensure the continued supply of oil from the Middle East and it could not stop the flow of money out of London. About 15 per cent of Britain's gold and currency reserves left London during the course of the operation and Britain had to seek an emergency loan of $1.5 billion from the International Monetary Fund to maintain the pound. Such a loan could only be funded by the Americans, and the price that the Americans set for such a loan was the obvious one.

On 3 November Britain announced its intention to accept a ceasefire provided that Egypt and Israel did the same and a United Nations force took charge of the situation in Sinai and along the canal. The following day the United Nations, by 57 votes to none, voted to set up a truce supervision team and on 5 November, when the airborne operation was mounted, Britain announced its willingness to accept the presence of this force.

Disastrous consequences

The Anglo-French operation, far from subduing Nasser, simply reinforced his position. Egyptians naturally rallied to him rather than to the invaders. But the operation also did two other things. It enabled Egypt to direct attention away from her own lamentable failure against Israel. Nasser subsequently proclaimed: 'We fought Israel, Britain and France, the three aggressors, singlehanded, relying on nobody except God and ourselves.'

The humbling of Britain and France, skilfully exploited by Nasser's diplomacy, ensured that Israel's gains would be taken away from her, that the international community would undertake clearance of the canal and that Egypt would not be made a laughing stock by her failures in Sinai. Furthermore, the Suez operation distracted attention from the Soviet Union's brutal suppression of

Losses at Suez

In the course of the Anglo-French Suez operation a total of 22 British and 10 French servicemen were killed. The Royal Marines lost 9 men, the British Army 8, the RAF 4 and the Royal Navy 1. All the French losses were sustained by the army. Wounded totalled 97 British and 33 French. Again, the marines had the highest casualties, with 60 injured. Wounded soldiers totalled 36 and there was a single RAF casualty. The French Army again suffered all casualties. A total of 10 aircraft were lost, 8 of which were British. Four Royal Navy planes were shot down and 1 of the RAF; 3 were lost in accidents. Two French planes were lost: one went missing and the other was involved in a mishap. Sir Anthony Eden estimated that the entire operation cost £100 million.

Daily Mirror
TUES AUG. 14 1956
2d FORWARD WITH THE PEOPLE No. 16,383

The 'Mirror's' Message to Eden

NO WAR OVER EGYPT!

THE 24-Power Conference on the Suez Canal is now going to be a 22-Power Conference. It opens in London on Thursday—with Egypt and Greece absent and with Russia ominously present.

the Hungarian uprising, which occurred at the same time.

For Britain and France the affair was disastrous. Their remaining interests and standing in the Middle East crumbled after Suez. The operation left a lingering poison in British political life, and it is possible to argue that Britain has never really recovered from a military adventure that it has been said resulted from the unbalanced deliberations of a sick prime minister rather than from rational calculation.

For the French, however, the effects were more immediate and drastic. To go alongside the 1940 capitulation to Hitler, Indochina, Tunisia and Morocco, Suez was yet another example, reasoned sections of the army, when the politicians 'ratted' and let the soldiers down. They would do so again in Algeria, so the argument went on, unless they were held in line. From Suez it was a very short step to the events of May 1958 that brought down the Fourth Republic, and in those events the élite of the French Army, those used at Suez and who felt the humiliation of failure most deeply, were well to the fore. Seldom can so short-lived an operation have caused such 'ripples of sorrow' as the abortive military adventure of 1956.

LEFT *This newspaper headline expresses the fears of the British public over events in the Middle East.* BELOW *The decline of Empire: British troops leave Suez.* BOTTOM *Soldiers of the UN force assemble at Suez.*

The Israeli Attack on Sinai

In 1956 Israel struck a lightning blow against Egypt and her armoured columns raced towards the Suez Canal

Michael Orr

Israeli troops take cover during action in Sinai. The Israeli attack on Egyptian positions led directly to the British and French invasion of Suez. The successful Sinai campaign boosted Israel's confidence in its army.

THE ISRAELI ATTACK in Sinai in 1956 showed the lasting importance of tanks on the battlefield, and that weapons designed with World War II in mind were still very functional.

No lasting peace had come to the Middle East at the end of the Arab-Israeli War of 1948. The establishment of the state of Israel provided a focus for Arab discontent and the borders of Israel were the scene of continual skirmishing. Border crossings were followed by more serious reprisal raids and it always seemed possible that war would flare up. During 1955 Israel faced a series of Egyptian-inspired raids from the Gaza Strip and Jordan which were answered by fierce reprisals, but the Israeli government was beginning to look for a more lasting answer.

At the same time President Gamal Abdel Nasser of Egypt turned his attention to his quarrel with the West. After he nationalised the Suez Canal in July 1956 he was more concerned about possible retaliation from Britain and France than from Israel. On Israel's eastern flank Jordan was becoming more aggressive and on 24 October 1956 it was announced that the armed forces of Egypt, Jordan and Syria would in future come under the command of the Egyptian minister of defence. Proclaimed the Jordanian chief of staff: 'The time has come for the Arabs to choose the appropriate time to launch the assault for Israel's destruction.'

It is hard to know how much empty rhetoric was involved in such statements, but the Israeli government believed that the Arabs meant business. So the Israelis decided to strike first and to strike against Egypt, the major Arab power. They acted knowing that Britain and France were also preparing a blow against Egypt. The exact extent of collusion and co-operation between Britain, France and Israel is still disputed, but it is clear that the Israeli attack was to provide the justification for the Anglo-French intervention to protect the Suez Canal.

Israel's prime minister, David Ben Gurion, also insisted that the French provide air cover for Israeli cities until the Egyptian Air Force was destroyed. This released Israeli aircraft to support their army; and the French further provided supply aircraft. On 25 October Israel began a secret mobilisation. D-day was set for the 29th.

Sinai's strategic importance

The Sinai Peninsula is roughly triangular in shape, bounded by the Mediterranean in the north, the Suez Canal and the Gulf of Suez in the west, and the Israeli frontier and the Gulf of Aqaba in the east. It is an almost entirely unproductive combination of desert and mountain, divided into three main types of terrain. In the north is a broad strip of desert, crossed only by the coastal road from Gaza to El Qantara. Further south is a stretch of rocky hills and dried-up wadis, crossed by a number of tracks. It is, therefore, passable in many places, but only at great cost in vehicle wear and tear.

There are few passes in the hills and so those that do exist, such as the Mitla Pass leading to Suez, assume great strategic significance. The boundary between the strips of sand and hills is marked by the only reasonable east-west road, running from

The War of 1948

The partition of Palestine which resulted in the formation of the state of Israel was achieved through a United Nations resolution adopted on 29 November 1947. The blueprint allotted 55 per cent of Palestine to the Jewish state and 45 per cent to the Arabs, although a large proportion of the Jewish area comprised the barren Negev Desert. Arab reaction to the resolution was hostile, and civil war ensued.

The state of Israel was proclaimed on 14 May 1948 but was almost immediately forced to defend itself against attack from its five Arab neighbours – Egypt, Iraq, Syria, Lebanon and Jordan (then Transjordan). Despite UN intervention the Arabs made gains, notably in the south and east where Israel had yet to assume *de facto* control; a sector of the old city of Jerusalem was also taken. After a period of ceasefire in June, Israel herself took Arab-allotted areas, thus setting the scene for mediation.

Temporary frontiers were fixed in early 1949 – after more outbreaks of fighting in violation of a further UN ceasefire – which corresponded roughly to those previously negotiated. Significant gains for the Israelis included a secure corridor to Jerusalem, itself in the centre of an Arab-occupied sector, and control of the vital Tel Aviv-Haifa railway line along the north-west coast.

Abu Aweigila through Bir Gifgafa to Ismailiya. South of the line between Suez and Aqaba rise the Sinai mountains, which are of no strategic interest. At the southern end of Sinai lies Sharm el Sheikh, an Egyptian base which dominates the Strait of Tiran, and, therefore, the Israeli lifeline to Elat. It is approached by a good road on the western coast and a series of tracks to the east.

Opposing strategies

By 1956 the Israeli Army, after initial neglect, was beginning to develop into a formidable fighting force with its own strategic doctrine. The leadership of General Moshe Dayan as Chief of Staff was largely responsible for the change. It was basically an army of civilian reservists with a small cadre of conscripts under training. The system was designed to ensure rapid mobilisation for a short war. The Israelis tried to avoid formal battles which required resources which they did not possess. They stressed surprise, initiative and training but on occasions they relied on headlong assaults in which high morale substituted for tactical skill or preparation.

Israeli equipment was basically World War II vintage. American Sherman tanks and M2 half-track personnel carriers and British 25-pounder field guns were the backbone of the army, though a number of AMX13 light tanks had recently been bought from France, which also supplied Israel's most recent aircraft.

The Israeli plan for the 1956 campaign was very flexible. It was divided into a number of phases and the Israelis could limit their commitment at any stage. The war would begin with a parachute raid in Sinai supported by a ground thrust. This would 'threaten' the Suez Canal and give Britain and France an excuse for invading Egypt.

If this phase succeeded the raid would be followed by an offensive in Sinai. The main attack would be against the Egyptian concentration at Abu Aweigila. Later the Israelis would increase the pressure against the Gaza Strip, where the Egyptians were expecting the main Israeli attack, and clean out the guerrilla bases there. Finally, if there was time, the Egyptian base at Sharm el Sheikh was to be taken by a two-pronged attack along the eastern and western coasts of Sinai.

The Israelis did not intend to occupy Sinai permanently but they did hope to inflict on Egypt such a military defeat that its government would halt the border war.

The Egyptian Army was by no means as weak as has sometimes been claimed. Although it had problems of leadership, particularly among middle-ranking officers, the rank and file did not lack courage. But the army had not developed a character of its own. Since 1945 its training had been supervised successively by British, German and Russian advisers and this inevitably caused confusion. As a fighting force it was best in defence and considerably less effective in any sort of offensive action.

Its equipment dated from World War II. Besides the British and American weapons also used by the Israelis, the Egyptians had recently acquired some Soviet equipment from Czechoslovakia. T34 tanks and SU100 assault guns were the most impressive of these new weapons. The Egyptian Air Force had received Soviet MiG jet aircraft which were generally superior to Israel's French planes.

The Egyptian plan for the defence of Sinai has been severely criticised. Strong forces were maintained close to the frontier but there were few reserves in central Sinai and most of the army was west of the canal. Egypt had been advised to screen the border lightly and pack the vital passes in the central mountains with the bulk of the infantry, supported by a strong armoured reserve ready to counter-attack. But this ideal military plan neglected political factors. It was essential to deter Israeli raids across the border, which light forces would not have done. Moreover, given the Egyptians' weakness in attack, it was probably better to rely on the proven defensive strength of their infantry and artillery.

Diary of the conflict

On 29 October the war began with an Israeli parachute battalion landing at the eastern end of the Mitla Pass just before dusk. The rest of the 202nd Parachute Brigade crossed into central Sinai by land, taking the frontier post of El Kuntilla and aiming to reach the pass as soon as possible. During the night Israeli ground forces elsewhere began to approach their first objectives.

Next day the Egyptians, still unsure whether they were facing a raid or a full-scale invasion, slowly began to reinforce Sinai. The 202nd Parachute Brigade hastened towards the Mitla Pass, overcoming Egyptian positions at El Thamad and Nakhl and reaching its objective at 2230 hours. On the central axis the main Israeli thrust at Abu Aweigila was halted in confusion, then a way around the position to the south was found. The 7th Armoured Brigade began to outflank Abu Aweigila by this route.

At 1800 hours Britain and France issued an ultimatum to both sides to evacuate the area 16km (10 miles) on either side of the Suez Canal. Egypt rejected the ultimatum but Israel accepted it as it did not conflict with her plans.

On the third day, 31 October, the 202nd Parachute Brigade tried to traverse the Mitla Pass but was ambushed. At the end of the day the paratroopers had driven the Egyptians out of their positions but were forced to abandon their attempt to move through. The Israeli 9th Infantry Brigade began to concentrate at El Kuntilla for its march to Sharm el Sheikh. In the centre two more frontal attacks on Abu Aweigila were repulsed by the Egyptians. However, 7th Armoured Brigade had succeeded in its flanking move and was established in the village of Abu Aweigila itself. The main Abu Aweigila position was, therefore, surrounded. In the north the Israelis had begun an attack on Rafah, between Gaza and El Arish, but it was checked by a strong Egyptian garrison in prepared positions.

The Anglo-French ultimatum had by now expired and the air forces of Britain and France began bombing Egyptian airfields after dark.

On the morning of 1 November, Nasser decided that Britain and France were about to invade so he ordered a withdrawal from Sinai to meet the greater threat. By this time the Israeli 27th Armoured Brigade had broken into the Rafah defences after a dawn attack. By 0900 the Israelis had secured Rafah and during the day they moved up to El Arish. In the centre another Israeli

RIGHT *General Moshe Dayan, Chief of Staff of the Israeli forces from 1953 to 1958, planned the Sinai invasion, which convinced him of the effectiveness of tanks as the spearhead in offensive operations.* BELOW *Israeli soldiers on the heights outside El Quseima before taking the town on 30 October.*

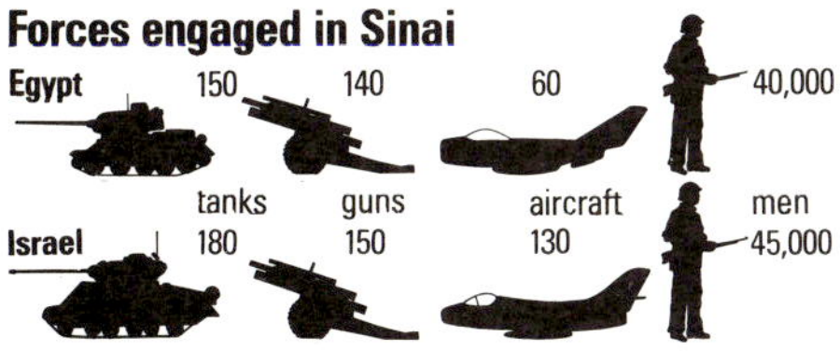

attack from the east failed to take Abu Aweigila but the Egyptian garrison was given orders to try and escape northwards to El Arish in small parties. The Egyptian armoured reserve had been deployed from Bir Gifgafa towards El Arish and there was some indecisive skirmishing before it received Nasser's order to head back across the canal.

The main Egyptian priority on 2 November was to get as much back from Sinai as possible. The air force left Sinai to the Israelis, whose aircraft harried the withdrawing Egyptian columns. In the centre Abu Aweigila had been abandoned and was occupied by the Israelis. Israeli and Egyptian

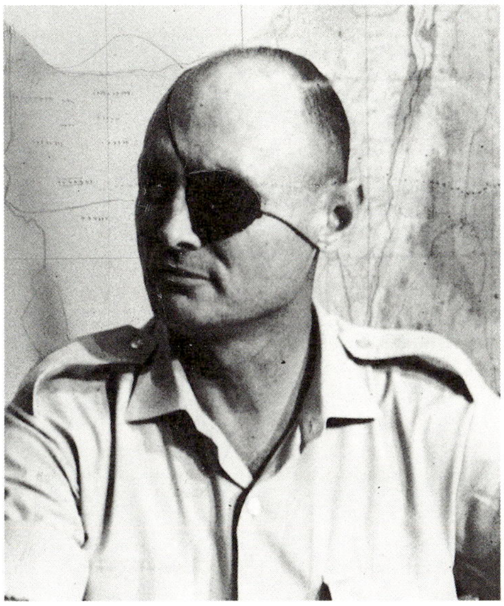

tanks clashed near Bir Gifgafa but at dusk the Egyptians broke contact and completed their withdrawal to the canal. In the north El Arish was captured at 1500 hours and the Israelis pursued along the coast road to within 16km (10 miles) of the canal. The 12th Infantry Brigade moved into Gaza and discovered that the Egyptians had gone, although a Palestinian brigade gave some resistance.

The only activity from 3 to 5 November occurred as the Israelis closed in on Sharm el Sheikh, using the paratroops and 9th Infantry Brigade. Sharm el Sheikh was captured on 5 November, the day that British and French paratroops landed at Suez. Two days later a ceasefire came into effect and a United Nations force of 6000 men was charged with supervising the truce and the withdrawal of Israeli troops.

The Israelis suffered about 800 casualties, of whom 181 were killed. Egyptian dead numbered about 1500. The Israelis captured nearly 6000 prisoners, and many other Egyptian soldiers were merely disarmed and released. They also found nearly $50 million worth of military equipment in abandoned Egyptian positions.

The Israeli victory did not end the struggle in the Middle East, although Arab guerrilla raids into Israel were reduced for several years. Perhaps the most important result was the boost it gave to Israel's confidence in her armed forces. Within the army the war led to a fierce debate about Dayan's system of command. Many argued that it was no good thing that so many senior officers were prepared to ignore orders and follow their own judgment. Dayan replied that it was 'better to be engaged in restraining the noble stallion than in prodding the reluctant mule'. The problem was one that the Israelis did not solve. It re-emerged in 1967 and by 1973 had reached dangerous proportions.

The war had unhappy repercussions in another way. Before the war the Israeli Army was basically an infantry force, and Dayan in particular was sceptical about the value of the tank except as an infantry support weapon. The 1956 war changed attitudes overnight and the Israelis thenceforth made the tank their dominant weapon. They formed more armoured brigades and the infantry and artillery were neglected until the 1973 conflict in the Middle East revealed the need for all-arms co-operation on the modern battlefield.

Advance on the Mitla Pass

IN THE SOUTHERN SECTOR, the strategic importance of the Mitla Pass was the dominant factor. The Israeli advance on the pass had two phases. The 1st Battalion of the 202nd Parachute Brigade was to land at the eastern end of the pass and so trigger the Anglo-French intervention to protect the Suez Canal. Then the rest of the brigade, under Colonel Ariel Sharon, was to advance across Sinai to re-inforce the paratroops before the Egyptians could counter-attack.

The 395 paratroops took off at 1500 hours on 29 October in 16 Dakota aircraft. They dropped at 1659, but landed nearly 5km (3 miles) short of their objective, the so-called Parker Memorial. In the rapidly falling dusk the battalion advanced until it met an Egyptian reconnaissance unit near the memorial. After a brief exchange of fire the Israeli battalion settled in to prepare defensive positions in the rocky ground.

Meanwhile the rest of the brigade had crossed the frontier at 1600 hours. It should have been supplied with civilian cross-country vehicles for its arduous journey but most of these did not arrive on time. Sharon decided not to wait for them. A strong advance guard led the way, consisting of a battalion in half-track personnel carriers, supported by 25-pounder guns and a company of 13 AMX13 light tanks. The rest of the brigade followed in a variety of vehicles.

Successful assaults

The advance guard was to capture El Kuntilla and El Thamad, by-pass Nakhl (leaving it to be mopped up by the main body), and hurry on to join the 1st Battalion. El Kuntilla was a frontier post, held by an Egyptian platoon, with two anti-tank guns. Two infantry companies in half-tracks circled the post while tanks and a 25-pounder bombarded the Egyptians. Then the Israelis assaulted from the west with the setting sun behind them. The dazzled Egyptian defenders fired back until the Israelis crossed the barbed wire, when they fled.

Although the attack was successful Sharon was already in difficulties. His vehicles were constantly breaking down and the whole brigade was already strung out along the route. Only seven tanks and one gun had reached El Kuntilla in time for the attack, but Sharon decided to press on.

His next objective was El Thamad. Here the road passed through a narrow defile in a steep escarpment, with a minefield at its foot, and an Egyptian company dug in along the road. There was no way round and no alternative to a frontal assault.

It was dawn on 30 October when Sharon reached El Thamad. He had only two tanks that were still running. His plan was simple. The tanks would close to within a few hundred yards and bombard the Egyptian trenches. Then they would drop a smoke screen and burst up the road, followed by the half-tracks. Sharon hoped the enemy would be too dazed to react quickly enough to block the road.

LEFT *Colonel Ariel Sharon, commander of the 202nd Parachute Brigade in 1956. A dashing leader in the battle for the Mitla Pass, he was later promoted to general.* BELOW *Israelis advance up a hillside during fighting in Sinai.*

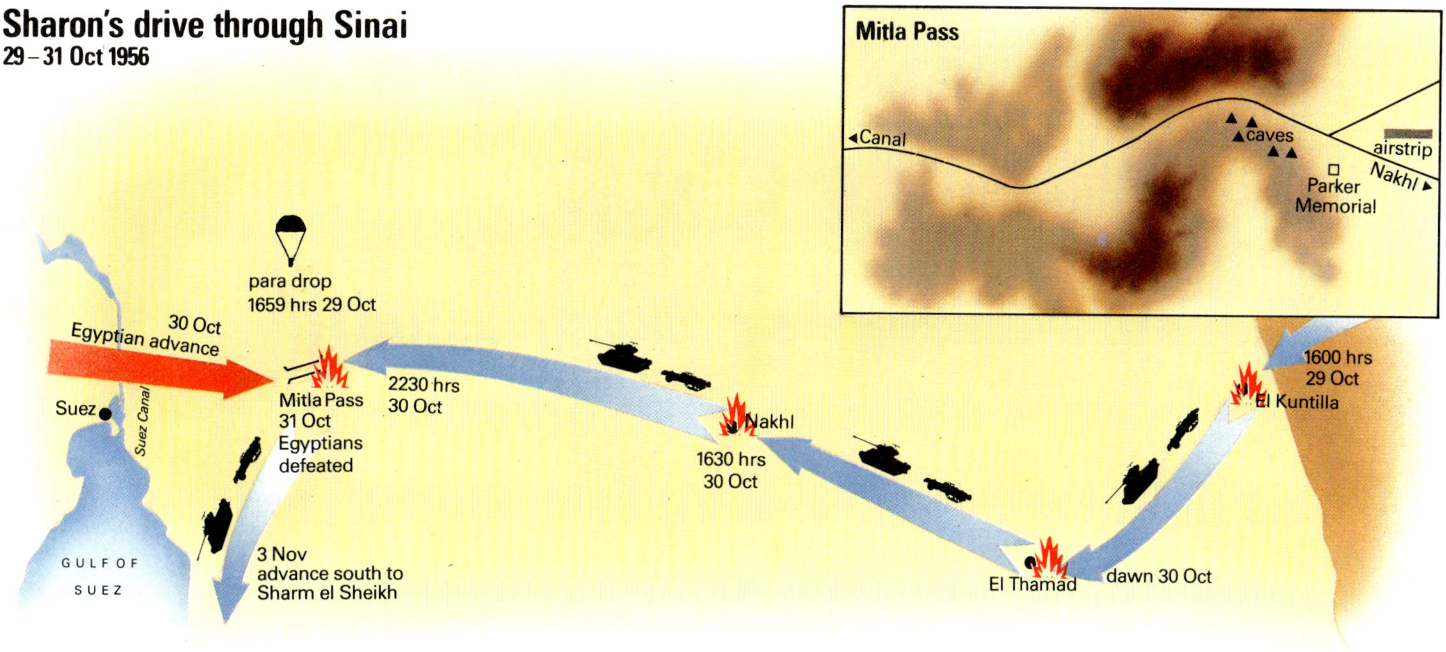

This is precisely what happened. Once the Israelis reached the top of the escarpment the Egyptians fled, leaving 50 killed. The Israelis lost a half-track and two dead. Sharon now called for a previously arranged air drop of fuel. He intended to move on as soon as his vehicles were refuelled. But at 0800 six Egyptian MiGs strafed the Israeli force and Sharon decided that his men needed to rest before advancing again.

Change of plan

During the night of 29/30 October the Egyptians had learned of the Mitla landing and two infantry battalions crossed the Suez Canal to take up prepared positions in the pass. Next morning the Israeli 1st Battalion came under air and mortar attack. Sharon decided that his advance must continue.

The original plan was changed and Sharon now chose to attack Nakhl with the advance guard. By 1630 hours he was in sight of Nakhl, a fortified village at a crossroads. Dusk was falling. Again Sharon decided that only a head-on attack would serve. As the battalion deployed, the artillery arrived and immediately opened fire. The Egyptian garrison had already been dismayed by the vast dust-cloud which hid the weakness of the Israeli force. Once more the Egyptians left their trenches as the assault went in and fled into the desert. Again Sharon moved on and at 2230 on the 30th he reached the Parker Memorial. His brigade was exhausted, having covered 300km (190 miles) in 28 hours.

Ambush at Mitla

Sharon had achieved his objective, but the fire and dash which had carried him so far now proved his undoing. Next morning he wanted to advance into the pass. General Moshe Dayan, the Chief of Staff, forbade the attack but agreed to a reconnaissance. Sharon sent a reinforced battalion, which was soon in trouble. The Mitla is a winding pass, only 45–55m (50–60 yards) wide in places. The Egyptians held ideal ambush positions on either side and the Israeli battalion was soon pinned down. Not until nightfall were the Israelis able to climb the cliffs and winkle the Egyptians out.

The Egyptians lost more than 200 dead and the Israelis 38 killed and 120 wounded. Sharon's brigade withdrew from the pass next morning and needed 48 hours' rest before it was fit for action again. When it finally advanced south to Sharm el Sheikh it cut across the desert, avoiding the Mitla Pass altogether.

ABOVE RIGHT *In hasty withdrawal the Egyptians discarded heavy clothing. An Israeli soldier reports the news by radio.* RIGHT *The Israeli flag is hoisted at Sharm el Sheikh, captured on 5 November.*

Encounters at Abu Aweigila

THE MAIN ISRAELI ATTACK in Sinai aimed to capture the vital communication centre of Abu Aweigila, which was the key to the best road across the peninsula. The road crossed the border and then passed between a sea of soft sand in the north and high ridges to the south. This road was defended by a series of positions. From east to west they consisted of lightly held border posts, two outposts and then the main position, which blocked the Abu Aweigila Pass through the ridge.

Further east a battalion was dug in around a dam just south of the road and then in the village of Abu Aweigila itself were various store dumps. These positions were all well constructed and formed a major obstacle to a westwards advance. But the Abu Aweigila defences had a weakness to the south, where there was a road through El Quseima. The Quseima Pass led to a plain which gave access to the Abu Aweigila Pass and the Daika Pass further west.

Frontal advances

The Israelis assembled a strong task force for the attack, led by Colonel Assaf Simchoni. The 37th Mechanised Brigade and the 10th Infantry Brigade were to advance directly on Abu Aweigila. The 4th Infantry Brigade was to capture El Quseima, thus allowing the 7th Armoured Brigade to progress to Abu Aweigila or to support the Parachute Brigade in the Mitla Pass.

ABOVE *and* RIGHT *Israeli troops prepare for the attack on El Quseima, which was taken en route to Abu Aweigila on 30 October.* BOTTOM *Troops set out across the desert.*

Simchoni, a tank officer, was unhappy with the plan. He disobeyed orders and gave the 7th Armoured Brigade a more important role. His decision ensured success, however, because the frontal attacks on Abu Aweigila failed. On account of the strong defences the Israelis decided to make night attacks, but slow approach marches meant that at dawn on 31 October and again on 1 November they were short of their objective, in

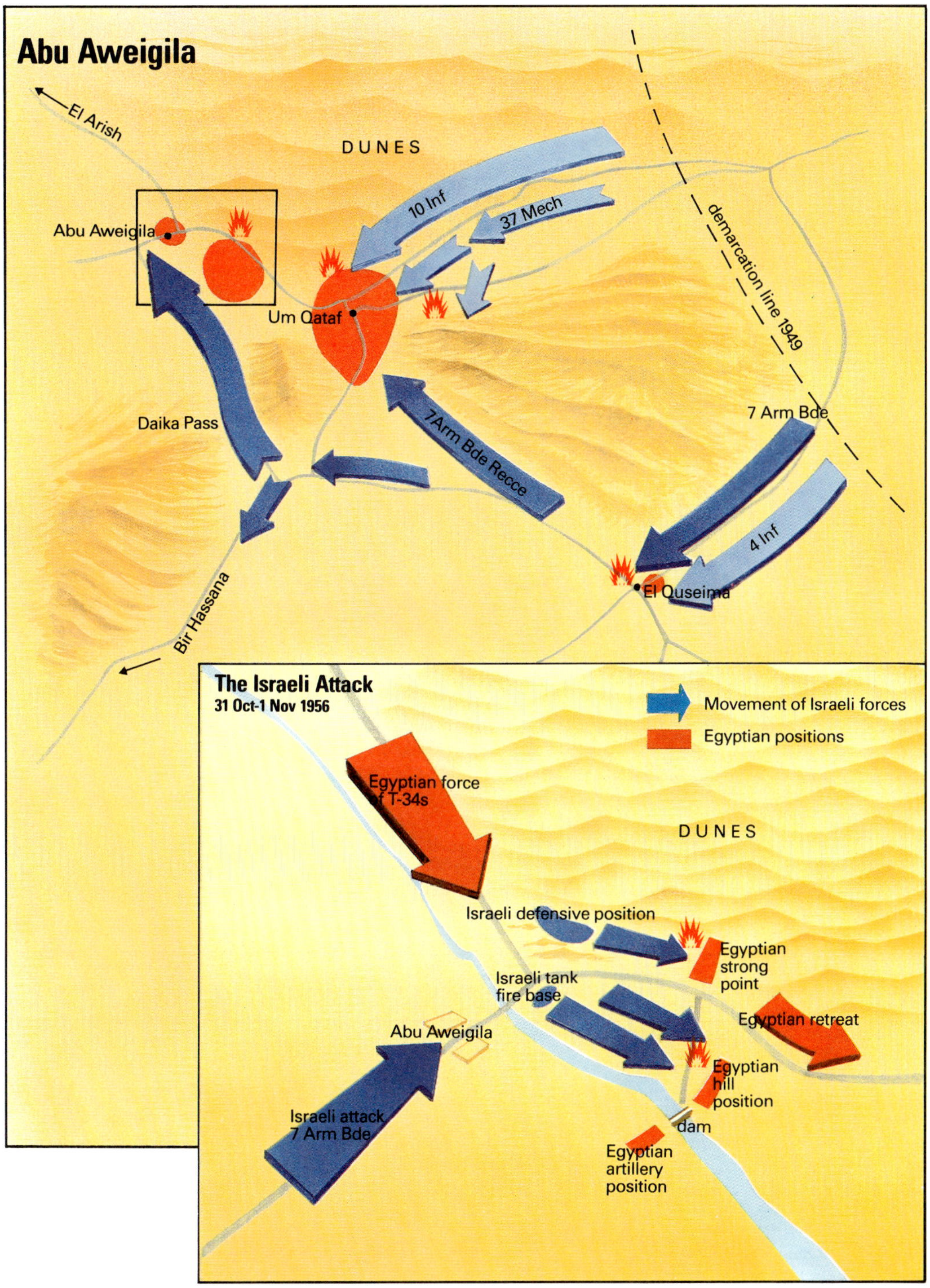

full view of the Egyptian guns. The commander of the 10th Brigade was sacked for over-caution, but the commander of the 37th Brigade was killed leading a foolhardy frontal assault in broad daylight. The main Abu Aweigila position held out until the Egyptian High Command ordered a withdrawal on 1 November.

The Israelis had greater success in the south. The 4th Brigade, after a slow march on foot across soft sand, captured the positions covering El Quseima during the night of 29/30 October. They pressed on into the village at dawn and found the weak Egyptian garrison withdrawing northwards. The 7th Armoured Brigade's reconnaissance company pursued them into the Quseima Pass until they reached the main Abu Aweigila position. A battalion of infantry in half-tracks and a company of Sherman tanks followed up and tried to rush the southern flank of the position. The attack was halted within five minutes by Egyptian anti-tank guns.

Approach from the west

General Moshe Dayan and Simchoni now began to plan a combined attack on the Abu Aweigila Pass by the 4th and 7th Brigades. Then a reconnaissance platoon reported that the Daika Pass was unguarded although the road was damaged. The Israeli commanders therefore decided to encircle Abu Aweigila from the west through the Daika Pass with the 7th Brigade alone. During the night an AMX13 battalion established a blocking position in the west, in case of an Egyptian counter-attack by armour from Bir Hassana. Then a Sherman battalion passed through the Daika Pass with some difficulty and delay. It proved impossible to attack during darkness but after dawn on 31 October the Shermans rushed into Abu Aweigila village, which was captured by 0645.

The Israeli force was quite weak, consisting of one company of Shermans and one of infantry. It soon came under heavy artillery fire from the dam position nearby. The Israelis therefore moved behind some sand dunes north of the village while they waited for the brigade's half-track battalion to move up and assault the dam. As Egyptian tanks were reported to be moving from the west the half-tracks were sent to meet the threat. This left the Sherman battalion to take the dam. First they had to meet a counter-attack by T34s and SU100s coming from the north, but the Egyptians preferred to stay at long range and did no real damage.

The final assault

The Israeli battalion commander, Lieutenant Colonel Adan (known as 'Bren'), decided to attack as darkness fell on 31 October. Two Sherman platoons were to remain in the base and keep the T34s at bay. Two more platoons were to move to a ridge from where they could give fire support. The last two platoons, with two of infantry, were to move east, break through an enemy strongpoint and roll up the dam position from the north and east. In the darkness the tanks and infantry did not co-ordinate their attack properly, but Adan used the fire-support Shermans as a reserve. The Egyptian position on a hill overlooking the dam was overrun, but the Israelis were left in confusion. Adan ordered them back north to the main road to re-group. He had lost 80 casualties and eight tanks. After taking on fuel and ammunition he moved back onto the hill, finding that the Egyptians had fled.

During 1 November Adan's battalion held a road-block to prevent a break-out from the main Abu Aweigila position. The Israelis decided not to mount another attack because the Egyptians were clearly about to withdraw. At night the Egyptians split into small parties and tried to escape across the sand, where many died from the heat and thirst. On 2 November the 7th Brigade began to move into central Sinai, skirmishing with Egyptian tanks as they withdrew from Bir Gifgafa. The 7th Brigade had made the Abu Aweigila position untenable by 1 November, but the final withdrawal owed more to the Anglo-French landing at Suez than to Israeli actions. The success of the 7th Brigade had, however, re-affirmed the importance of free-ranging armoured forces in desert war.

Kenya in Revolt

The Mau Mau troubles involved military operations throughout central Kenya

H. P. Willmott

THE KENYAN EMERGENCY of 1952 to 1960, generally referred to as the Mau Mau campaign, was an unusual affair. Though unrest and disturbances were recorded in many British territories in Africa during Britain's withdrawal from empire, only Kenya passed into independence and nationhood after a major insurgency campaign, although whether or not that campaign contributed to the process is unclear. At the beginning the campaign was directed against colonial authorities and whites, but it degenerated into a tribal civil war within the Kikuyu peoples. Even today little is really known about it. Few details of the origins of the Mau Mau are known and even the derivation and meaning of the name itself are disputed.

The State of Emergency was proclaimed in October 1952 after a period of mounting lawlessness, particularly around Nairobi, which culminated in the murder of one of Britain's staunchest friends amongst the Kikuyu, Senior Chief Waruhiu. Although it lasted technically until January 1960 the campaign was effectively brought to an end in October 1956 with the capture of the last of the major insurgent leaders still at large, Dedan Kimathi. The final British battalion was withdrawn from unit-sized operations that month. The Emergency was kept in force more to enable the continued holding of suspects and prisoners than to facilitate operations in the field.

Causes of trouble

At the start of the campaign the insurgents numbered about 12,500. The origins of the revolt lay in what many members of the Kikuyu tribe felt were the increasingly intolerable conditions in which they lived after 1945. The Kikuyu had a more developed sense of grievance against the colonial authorities than other tribes. This was because of the feeling that land traditionally theirs had been lost to them by decisions of the governing authorities. What gave the feeling shape was the worsening conditions within the Kikuyu Reserve, mainly as a result of growing population pressure on land that was already producing less and less because of over-intensive use, and the increasing obligations placed upon black labourers on white farms.

When white farms were first set up in Kenya, conditions for black agricultural labourers were very favourable. Obligation to work was not that onerous, seldom more than four months in the year, while smallholdings were often quite extensive (up to 2 hectares or 5 acres) and more than enough for a man to support his family. After the war, however, the prices of commodities and foodstuffs essential for black Africans rose markedly. It occurred at a time when the white settlers took steps to increase work obligations and to reduce the size of smallholdings. Between 1945 and 1951, at a time of growing white prosperity, the living standards of blacks on white farms fell by about 40 per cent. These elements formed the groundswell on which the Mau Mau built.

The Aberdare Forest afforded Mau Mau gangs considerable natural protection and concealment. Operation Longstop of January 1953 was a typical anti-terrorist sweep, intended to clear 260 square km (100 square miles) of insurgents. This patrol is being helped by loyal Kikuyu.

Political as well as economic factors were at work. In part this was the natural result of African emergence from a state of 'cultural shock' that had hitherto prevented coherent political development and resistance to alien rule. The emergence, of course, was gradual. Two world wars and the intervening Depression had helped to open the eyes of black Africans to the shortcomings and failures of colonial authorities.

But what played a larger part in the origins of the revolt was the growing awareness amongst blacks of their low status (second-class at best) in their own country. Black resentment grew as a result of the influx of white settlers from Britain after 1945 and attempts by the settler community to secure full internal self-government on the Southern Rhodesia model. There was also the sense of disillusionment of black soldiers when they returned to Kenya after the war.

This last was critical because the impulse and spirit of the revolt was provided by a shadowy and largely unknown body called the Forty Group, made up of soldiers who had been recruited into the British Army in 1940. There they had received good treatment, enhanced physical fitness and self-confidence, and took justifiable pride in being part of a winning combination that stressed corporate identity. On their return home they were expected to resume their former status in society.

Tribal divisions

Why the major part of Mau Mau fury came to be directed at the Kikuyu itself is not hard to fathom. The revolt was tribally based and only the Embu and Meru tribes, related to the Kikuyu, were otherwise involved in it. This in part explains the ease with which the revolt was contained and crushed. It became 'internal' because sections of the Kikuyu resisted induction into the Mau Mau and stood apart from it. Nearly all Mau Mau were Kikuyu, but not all Kikuyu were Mau Mau, even though many were involved, albeit at a very low level, mainly through fear of their lives.

Many Kikuyu resisted Mau Mau. Some tribal elders refused to support it and Christian and propertied Kikuyu stood firm. Elders resented usurpation of their traditional tribal leadership by 'angry young men' whom they and the Christians regarded as having embarked upon a campaign that was bestial, lurid and a regression to the very worst aspects of tribalism and depravity.

District Officers noted that old scores against men of substance were often settled during the troubles. The gruesome 1953 massacre at Lari, for example, in which about 100 people were hacked to pieces, was perpetrated by Kikuyu made landless by an administrative decision that went in favour of their victims.

Growing success against the communists in Malaya resulted in the adoption of many aspects of the plan followed there – particularly the fusion of military, police and civil administration at all levels. One notable difference, however, was the refusal of Britain to place in charge an official with full civil and military power. London also refused white settler demands to take charge of the counter-insurgency effort.

Jomo Kenyatta, the nationalist leader and Kenya's first president. His relationship to the Mau Mau has never been satisfactorily established but many whites regarded him as instigator of the Mau Mau campaign.

On the civil side three people made crucial contributions in the drive to win popular support and isolate the Mau Mau from would-be supporters through political and economic action. Frank W. Carpenter reported on the conditions of urban blacks and set minimum rates of pay that had to be observed. David Lidbury's report led to the breakdown of racial pay, promotion and job structures within the civil service, and Richard J. M. Swynnerton was behind a £6.5 million agrarian reform programme in which blacks were freed from restraints on the growing of cash crops, particularly coffee, new strains of cattle were introduced and the development of co-operatives and tea plantations was encouraged.

Under Harold Macmillan the major part of black political development took place. The process pre-dated his premiership, of course, because during the campaign black representation in the Legislative Council increased from being the least numerous to a position of parity with whites. Blacks advanced to majority rule under Macmillan and the ease with which Kenya passed into nationhood owed much to him, as it did to Kenya's first leader, Jomo Kenyatta.

Mau Mau Organisation

THE MAU MAU began to develop in the late 1940s within the legal Kenya African Union, a mass organisation largely dominated by the Kikuyu. What distinguished the Mau Mau from the KAU was the taking of oaths which bound its members together in a secret anti-white society.

Organisational weakness

Theoretically the Mau Mau was directed by a body that called itself the Kenya Parliament and by the Nairobi central committee which supervised district committees and sub-committees in the capital and those of other areas of the country. This part of the organisation, the 'passive wing', was supposedly organised to keep forces in the field. These forces in theory were organised into sections (10–35), platoons (35–100) and companies (100–250), and hence into battalions. The parliament, central committee and war office issued policy directives to the 'generals' fighting in the field.

In reality Mau Mau scarcely had any organisation except in Nairobi, where the central committee and its subordinate bodies functioned quite effectively until mid-1954. The Mau Mau lacked the sophistication to organise itself and the people on the lines that Mao Tse-tung would have approved, and British countermeasures quickly disrupted communications between insurgent groups themselves and also between the insurgents and their supporting agencies.

As time passed the Mau Mau groups fought and tried to survive as best they could, without any hope of respite, support from other groups or help from outside. The Mau Mau commander on Mount Kenya, Waruhiu Itote (better known as General China), was able to tell his British captors nothing about the Mau Mau groups in the Aberdares for the very good reason that he did not know anything about them.

Mau Mau groups were held together less by any formal organisation and discipline than by respect for (and in some cases terror of) individual leaders, the binding commitment of oaths and the perpetration of crime, and an often fearsome code of punishment for even comparatively minor offences.

Diverse weaponry

Mau Mau possessed very few firearms and modern weapons. In 1953 it was estimated that less than 12 per cent of the 12,000 Mau Mau were in

The Mau Mau organisation took, roughly, the form of a pyramid. Individual members formed committees in each 'location' (township) on the Kikuyu Reserve, from these were formed divisional committees and then, in turn, district groups. The central committee and war office were the top political and military planning bodies. The committees' job was to gather recruits, arms, ammunition and money. Supplies for the armed gangs included blankets, cigarettes, bandages, medicines, food and clothing.

Mau Mau organisation and supply structure

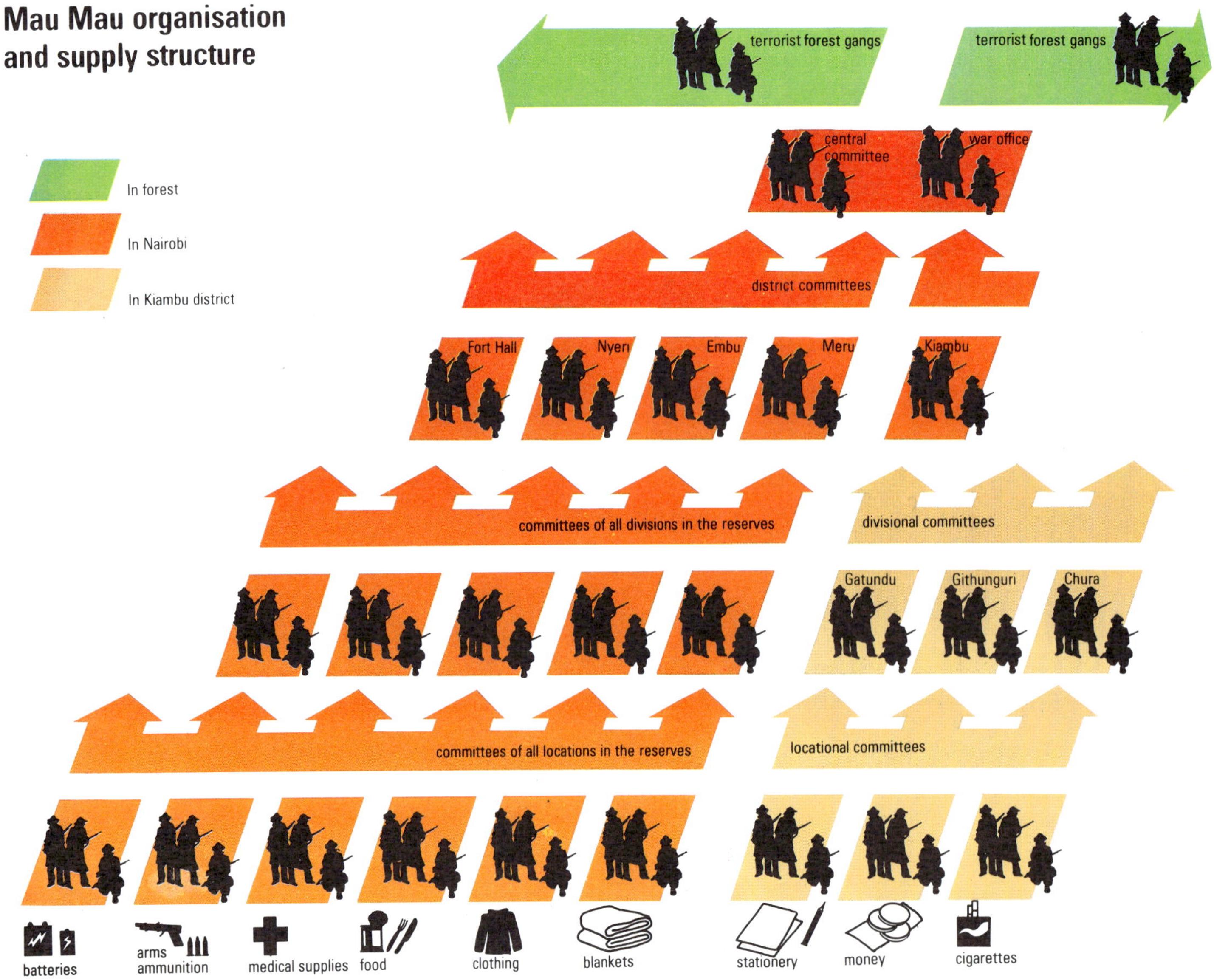

possession of any kind of firearm. What weapons they did have had normally been stolen before the start of the Emergency. After October 1952 very few weapons were captured from the security forces. The raid on the Naivasha police station in March 1953 was exceptional because it yielded guns – but the 18 automatics and 29 rifles captured did not amount to very much. In any case captured weapons quickly became useless because once the ammunition was expended no more was easily available. Although the Mau Mau tried to make their own rifles, bullets and grenades in makeshift workshops these tended to pose a greater danger to the user than to the intended victim.

The record of the East Kent Regiment (The Buffs) on its tour of duty in Kenya illustrates just how poorly the Mau Mau were equipped. The Buffs claimed 290 Mau Mau killed and another 194 taken prisoner. They themselves lost just one man killed in action. They captured 114 firearms, almost all of which were home made. Not even Mau Mau generals were able to secure for their own personal use good reliable weapons. One general was bayoneted by a British NCO after his home-made rifle jammed on him three times with the British soldier out of ammunition.

Tactics of terror

The Mau Mau were normally armed with pangas or axes, and herein lay the key to their methods and tactics. Seldom would they attack the security forces but instead tried to conduct a reign of terror, arson, rustling and general mayhem that was intended to force a British surrender. They normally worked at night and in densely populated areas that could never be fully secured.

Their basic tactic was the use of terror. Ghastly mutilation of humans and animals were the trademark of Mau Mau actions. Much of the violence fell upon women and children as the Mau Mau did not respect age, sex or race. Disfigurement and the hacking-off of limbs and sexual organs were normally a prelude to death, often by throat-slitting, and further dismemberment. The sheer ferocity and gruesomeness of these attacks discredited the organisation and played into the hands of the British. The lack of international support for the Mau Mau stemmed from the revulsion aroused by their methods.

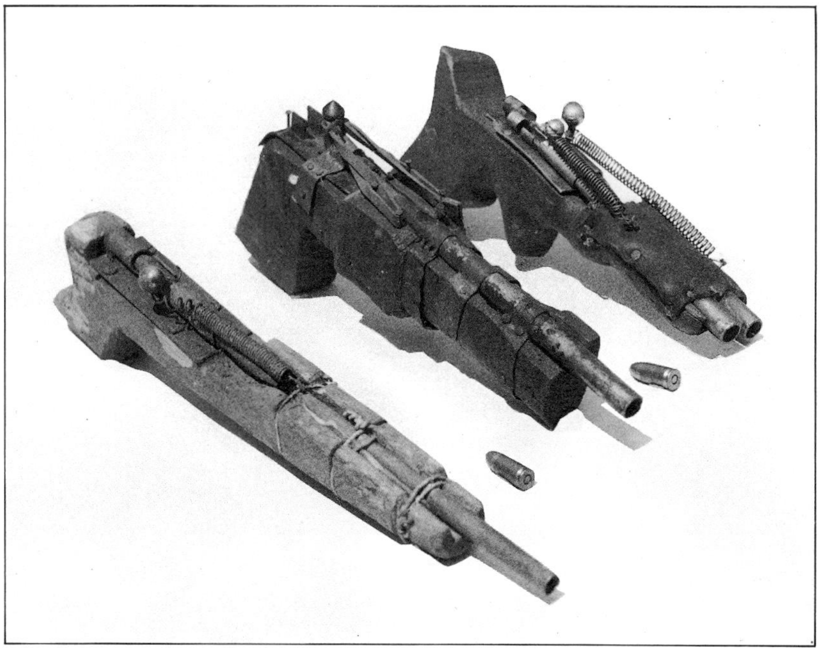

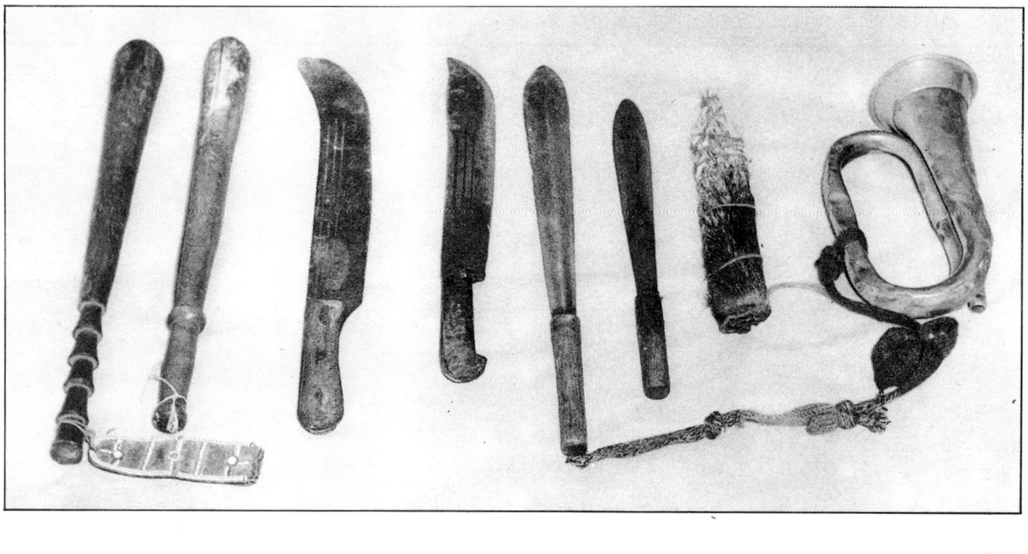

LEFT *An inspector of the Kenyan police force examines a Kikuyu for the tell-tale razor cuts of the Mau Mau.* RIGHT *Two Mau Mau weapons: a long knife or 'simis' and a strangling rope.* BELOW *Home-made guns. Fashioned from door bolts, their effectiveness was limited.* BOTTOM *A selection of clubs and pangas.*

Counter-insurgency

ALMOST A YEAR ELAPSED before the British counter-insurgency effort assumed the proportions that the seriousness of the situation demanded. The garrison had to be reinforced and Kenya eventually organised as an independent command separate from GHQ in Cairo. The police, Special Branch (personally supervised by the head of MI5) and reserve and auxiliary formations needed to be overhauled or expanded. In addition there was the fusion of administration, police and army at all levels of government.

It took time for these measures to show results, and in that period the Mau Mau achieved their two most notable successes – the Lari massacre and the attack on the Naivasha police station, both on 26 March 1953. Once the security forces were reinforced from Britain and swelled by recruitment from inside Kenya, Mau Mau effectiveness, such as it was, declined quickly.

Civil and military forces

Rapid expansion of the security forces from Kenyan sources provided mixed results. Throughout the Emergency cases came before the courts involving uniformed members of the security forces accused of offenses, including murder and perjury, against prisoners, detainees and suspects. Very few cases involved British servicemen, and the conduct of the army was of the highest standards. The police, police reserve, the whites-only Kenya Regiment and the prison service provided a steady stream of offenders, and several times the Kikuyu Guard, recruited amongst Kikuyu loyal to the government, had to be purged and re-formed.

On the military side the British Army never numbered more than six King's African Rifles and five British battalions. It was not until September 1953, nearly a year after the start of the Emergency, that the bulk of the British units arrived in Kenya. Before that time those units in the colony invariably operated in sub-units in support of the police. They were mostly engaged in resettlement and village housing programmes – which caused much suffering and bitterness and produced a substantial number of recruits for the Mau Mau.

Only in 1954 did the military effort against the Mau Mau begin to get under way in a systematic manner. Before then there were insufficient trained troops and it took more than

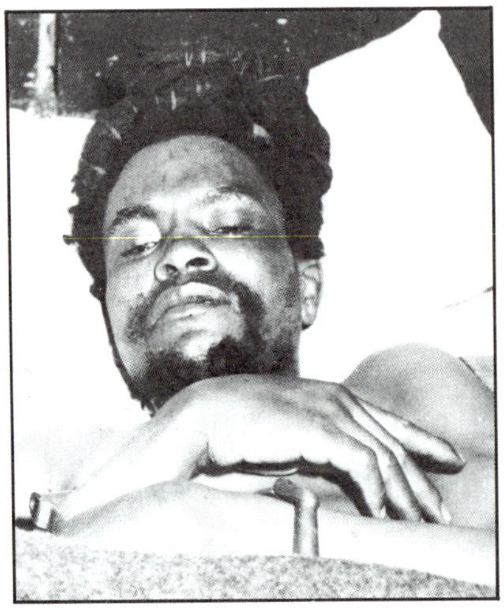

ABOVE *Dedan Kimathi led the Mau Mau in the Aberdares. This self-styled Knight Commander of the African Empire was hunted down in 1956 and executed.* BELOW *Men accused of Mau Mau terrorism enter court.*

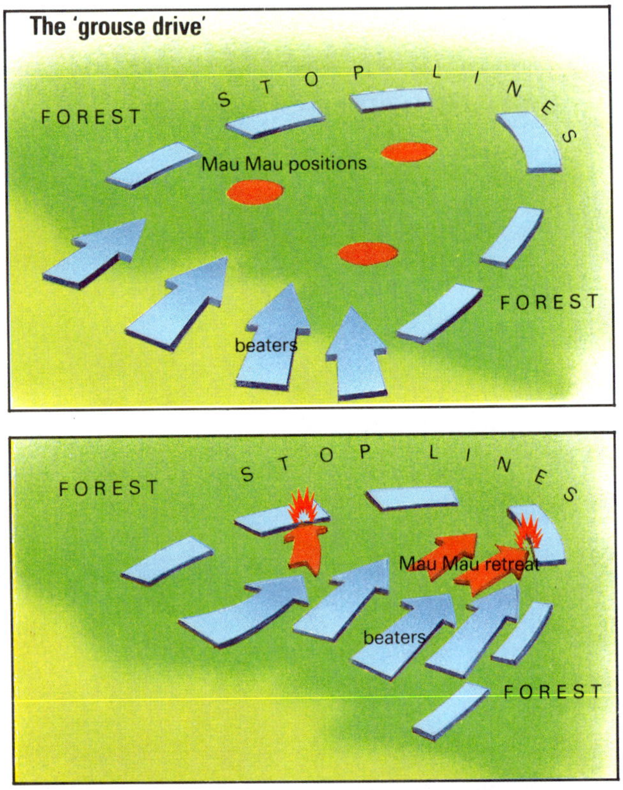

a year for intelligence activities to show results. Even by mid-1953, however, Mau Mau casualties were running at about 100 per month, but the following year British measures began to bite.

Clearing Nairobi

In April 1954 the British started their major operations and cleaned-up Nairobi with Operation Anvil. It took the form of a month-long systematic cordon and search of the capital and netted 16,500 suspects, most of whom were Kikuyu. Positive suspects were identified by hooded informers. In all, 32,000 prisoners and

detainees were held in prison camps at the end of 1956. Anvil generally had two beneficial effects. It stamped out crime in Nairobi for a long period and it broke the lines of communication and supply between Mau Mau supporters in the capital and insurgent groups in the Aberdares and on Mount Kenya.

The British then directed their efforts to clear disaffected areas near Nairobi, leaving the Mau Mau 'strongholds' in the mountains until later.

The first areas to be cleared were Thika, Fort Hall and Kiambu. Kiambu proved difficult to control, partly because of the area's strong association with the Mau Mau but mainly because its large population made enforced rehousing in villages often impossible. Later, military attention switched to the Prohibited Areas – the Aberdares and Mount Kenya.

Tackling Mau Mau strongholds

In these known areas of Mau Mau revolt, devoid of villages and settled communities, the army could use weapons on a war basis. Most of the rest of the country was designated as Special Areas, where the security forces had the right to stop and search at will but where a suspect could be fired upon only if he resisted or attempted evasion. Here the security forces had to abide by common law.

In 1955 there was an attempt to clear the forests on the mountains up to 2400m (8000 feet) with the intention of establishing stop-lines. Around the Aberdares, sappers built a fire zone 1.6km (1 mile) wide and constructed deep ditches and other obstacles to prevent escape. The British then attempted to clear the high-altitude moorland over 3350m (11,000 feet) with the intention of producing a 'Mau Mau sandwich' amidst the intervening thick bamboo.

At all three levels of vegetation the British employed three techniques to contact the enemy: massive cordon and search operations, sub-unit patrolling and ambushes, and the use of infiltration groups. Some of the cordon and search operations were enormous. It was not unknown for the army to mobilise upwards of 50,000 black Africans as 'beaters', armed with machetes, to clear the undergrowth up to stop-lines held by the military forces. Most of these people were Kikuyu, and frequently women, often with personal scores to settle.

Captured insurgents were used extensively in 'counter-gangs'. These had started as groups of loyal blacks, led by suitably made-up white officers and NCOs, that went into the forests posing as Mau Mau gangs. Their aim was to use the enemy's methods to contact and eliminate him. Many surrendered rebels willingly operated against their former colleagues.

The atmosphere of the time was very unpleasant. It may well be that the stability Kenya has enjoyed since independence in 1963 stems, in part, from the unwillingness of Kenyans to indulge in actions that could resurrect the pathological climate that marked the years of the Emergency.

Disaffected areas

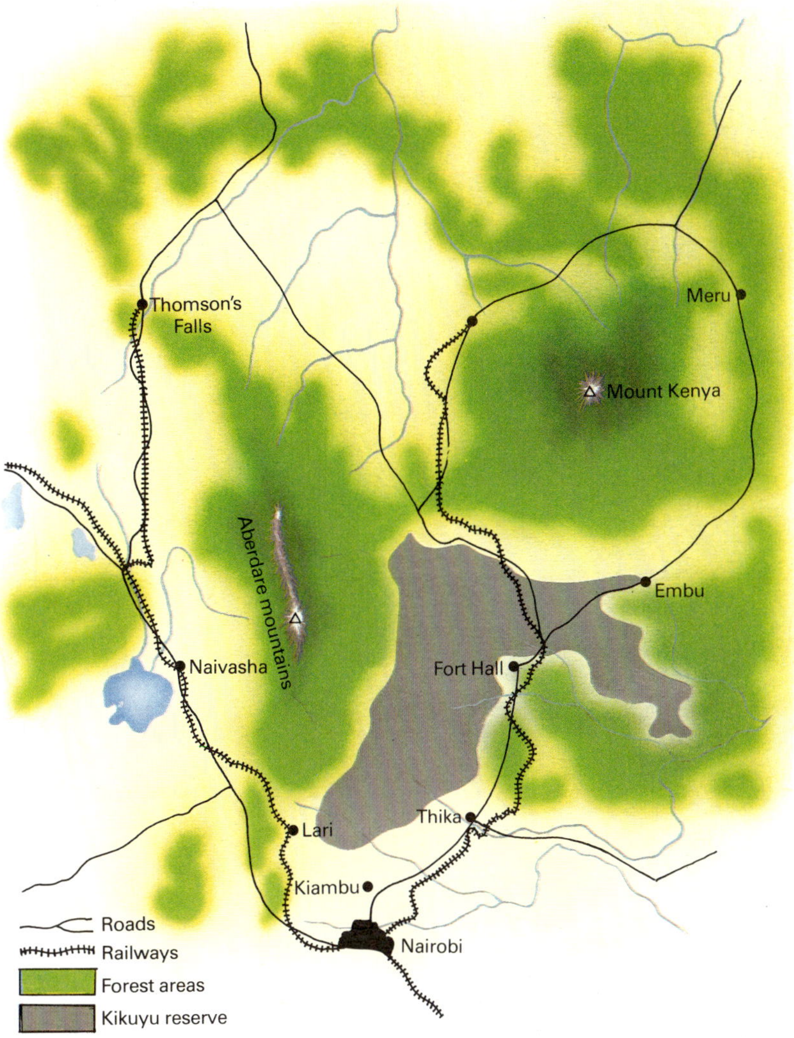

ABOVE *Members of the Kikuyu Home Guard. These unpaid volunteers – they numbered 10,000 by 1953 – killed more insurgents than the colonial authorities. They used clubs, spears and bows and arrows but were later issued with firearms. They were prime targets of the Kikuyu-dominated Mau Mau.* BELOW *A new village built to remove loyal Africans from Mau Mau intimidation.*

Counting the cost

By British standards Kenya was a rough campaign that cost the security forces about 600 deaths (63 of whom were white) and the government some £55 million. About 2000 civilians loyal to the government were killed, almost all of them black Africans. Just 32 whites were killed by the Mau Mau in the course of the Emergency. About 11,500 insurgents were killed in action while another 2500 were captured. Some 78,000 people were detained or imprisoned for various lengths of time. Up to April 1956, 1015 executions had been carried out; and a total of 402 prisoners died in captivity.

Cyprus and Aden

In Cyprus and then Aden the British Army came face to face with terrorist groups fighting for independence and political power

H. P. Willmott

British soldiers round up an Arab demonstrator in Aden. The British Army supported the Federation of South Arabia against the rival claims of the NLF and FLOSY.

THE CAMPAIGNS in Cyprus (1955–59) and Aden (1963–67) shared many common features. In both the British were opposed by insurgents who were actively supported by other states. The insurgents in both theatres sought to mobilise international opinion to force Britain to concede independence. They used guerrilla warfare tactics and in both cases elements of civil war developed.

The British, on the other hand, had no clear political aims in either Cyprus or Aden. They sought a military solution but in neither case were they successful. The insurgent movements were able to obtain a grip on the community through persuasion and intimidation that the British found impossible to break.

The two campaigns also showed significant differences. Cyprus was a racially divided community; South Arabia was not, though it did contain a significant Yemeni community. Cyprus was a single political entity, unlike the Federation of South Arabia. In Cyprus the security forces came to win a large measure of control over the military situation, particularly in rural areas, but this did not happen in Aden, which became independent and cut the link with Britain. Cyprus, because of the racial division between Greeks and Turks, became an independent state under international guarantee within the Commonwealth.

Mediterranean base

The crown colony of Cyprus possessed a strategic importance that led the British government on 28 July 1954 to announce that it could never expect to secure independence. Britain wished to retain Cyprus as a base for operations in the eastern Mediterranean and the Middle East.

Cyprus had a population of about 520,000 of whom about 80 per cent were Greek. Though it had never been part of modern Greece, the Greek government claimed the island as its own, and the main political aspiration of Greek Cypriots was for *Enosis*, union with Greece.

About 18 per cent of the population, on the other hand, were Turkish. They looked to Turkey, the legal owner of the island until 1923, as their homeland. Turkey itself insisted that Cyprus be returned to Turkish rule or be partitioned.

The Cyprus Emergency resulted from the Greek Cypriot attempt to secure *Enosis* by force of arms. Its outcome was decided when the leader of the Greek community, Archbishop Makarios III, endorsed a Greek-Turkish plan, devised in 1959, to make Cyprus an independent state.

EOKA's campaign

Makarios had been the driving force behind the *Enosis* movement and had set about creating mass support organisations needed to sustain the campaign. In 1951 he contacted a known right-wing extremist, George Grivas, a Cypriot-born colonel in the Greek Army, to organise the military wing of the movement. This became known as EOKA, the National Organisation of Cypriot Fighters.

Trouble began to develop in late 1954 with the arrival of British forces evacuated from Egypt, and the refusal of the United Nations to consider the Cyprus question. On 27 November 1955 Britain proclaimed a State of Emergency that lasted until December 1959. In that time EOKA sought to gain control over the Greek Cypriot community, harness world opinion and wear down the British until they tired of the struggle.

Two-pronged attack

The methods which EOKA used to achieve these aims were a skilful blend of propaganda and military action. On the civil front there were riots, disturbances, boycotts, civil disobedience and strikes. On the military side EOKA fought both an urban and a rural campaign. It started the campaign with no more than 100 men and ended with about 300 in the mountains, which the British managed to control.

In the urban struggle EOKA used terrorism, intimidation and infiltration to keep the issue in the headlines. EOKA never thought in terms of military victory over the British. It sought to neutralise the police, eliminate the Special Branch and neutralise the administration, thereby depriving the British of vitally needed intelligence. But the main EOKA method had to be by gun and bomb. The chief targets were British servicemen and installations.

EOKA made its main effort before March 1957. After that time the emphasis was on attempts to find a political solution. This search became increasingly complicated and urgent as Turkish Cypriots became ever more fearful of seeming British 'weakness' in

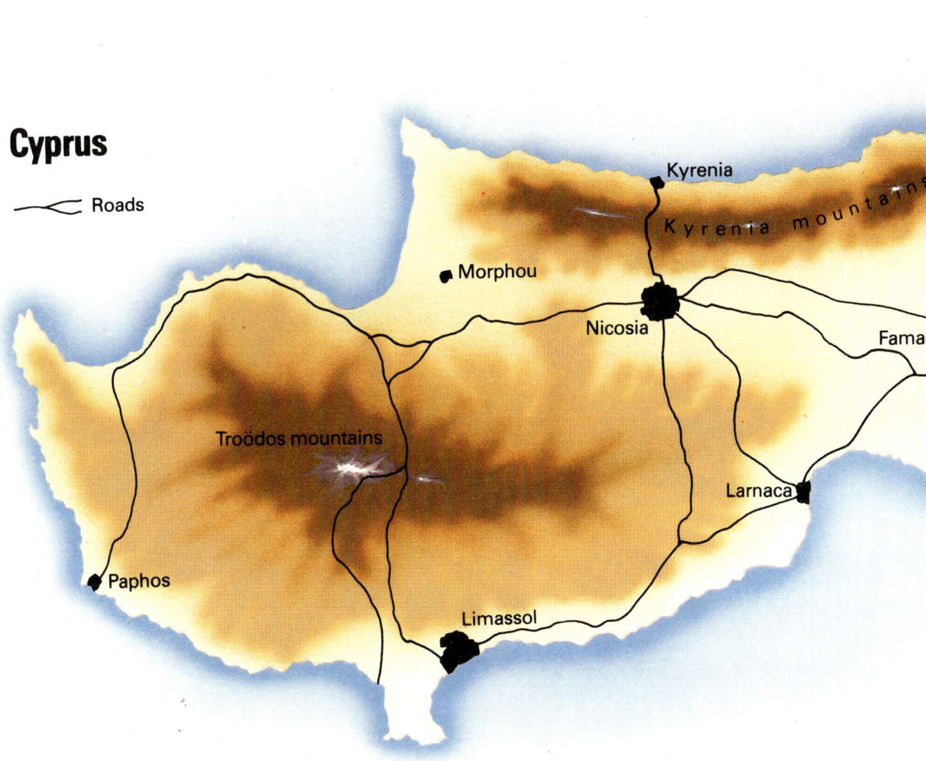

the face of Greek demands. Violent sectarian strife erupted in mid-1958 when 109 were killed. It was this development that prompted Archbishop Makarios, Greece and Turkey to accept reality and agree on the solution of independence.

In 1958 the area that is now South Yemen consisted of 20 'states', emirates, sheikhdoms and sultanates – 17 in the Western Aden Protectorate (WAP) and three in the Eastern Aden Protectorate (EAP) – and the British crown colony of Aden. Their status and political institutions varied widely. The most obvious difference was between the unruly tribes of the wild and inhospitable interior and the sophisticated and heavily populated Aden. Only Aden was British territory. Since her forces had arrived in Aden in 1837, Britain had concluded treaties with neighbouring states which recognised British sovereignty in return for protection against external enemies.

In February 1959 six territories came together as the Federation of South Arabia (FSA). By the end of 1963 another ten, plus Aden, had joined. The three members of the EAP and Upper Yafa from the WAP refused to join. The ten states that came into the federation did so on the understanding that Britain would retain a presence there even after independence. But by 1959 the balance of power and moral authority had shifted decisively against Britain and the traditional rulers with whom she was associated in favour of Arab nationalism.

The original external threat to the FSA came from Yemen, which had claims on FSA territory, but it developed as a serious menace only after 1962 when Yemen began to give active support to pro-Yemeni elements in the FSA and indigenous nationalist organisations.

The two main nationalist groups that came to dominate the insurgent effort – and which fought to the death in 1967 – were the National Liberation Front (NLF) and the Front for the Liberation of Occupied South Yemen (FLOSY). It was the NLF, formed under Egyptian auspices in June 1963, that spearheaded the anti-British campaign and which finally defeated its opponents to take control of the new state of South Yemen on independence in November 1967.

The British Defence White Paper of June 1964 looked forward to independence for the FSA before 1968 and initial nationalist violence was directed towards discrediting the FSA internationally and intimidating the population, local security forces and rival political leaders so that no one within the FSA could dispute the nationalists' claim that they alone represented South Yemen. In addition, of course, the nationalists wanted to force a total British withdrawal. This was secured by the Defence White Paper of February 1966 when Britain announced its intention to leave the area after the FSA became independent.

Insurgent violence was not the principal factor behind the British 1966 decision but the whole basis of the FSA – continued British support – was now removed, and with it any hope that the population could be turned against the nationalists. Already-inadequate intelligence sources dried up as people realised that after 1967 there would be no alternative to nationalist rule – and no escaping nationalist vengeance.

In November 1967, the last month of British rule, open war came to Aden when the NLF and FLOSY fought for supremacy until the FSA Army ordered a ceasefire and announced its support for the NLF. And on 29 November the last British forces left Aden, with very few regrets.

Waning British power in the Middle East

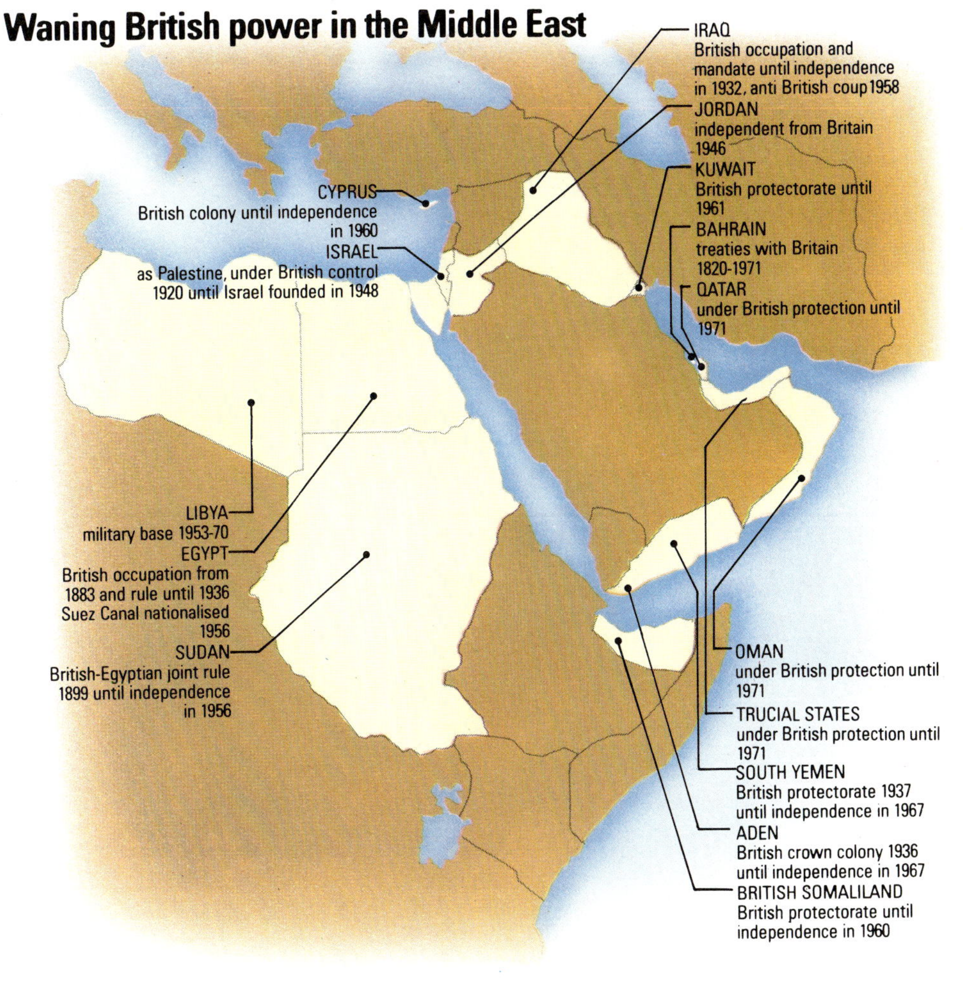

EOKA and NLF

IN BOTH CYPRUS AND SOUTH ARABIA the overall strategy employed by the insurgents was less strictly military than political. They aimed to mobilise domestic opinion and organise it in a manner that would make government impossible. At the same time they applied gradually increasing pressure through selective military action.

The insurgents sought to eliminate political opponents and manipulate the local population for economic and physical confrontations with the authorities. They employed what would now be called active service units (cells) to create and maintain an atmosphere of crisis. Violence was the critical element in presenting the insurgent cause to the outside world. It took the form of sniping and street murder, arson, sabotage and bombing, and small hit-and-run attacks on isolated and vulnerable police and military posts and patrols.

Favoured weapons

In Aden mortars and bazookas were used against the British security forces, but not frequently. Aden's airport was twice subjected to mortar attack, but on the second occasion 19 of the 20 rounds fired into the perimeter failed to explode. For the most part support weapons were not used on a large scale in the towns. They were too conspicuous, too vulnerable and imposed too great a strain on lines of communication.

Insurgents tended to favour pistols and revolvers because they were relatively easy to dispose of or conceal. Victims were identified and stalked in order that the assassin might be able to fire, at the right time, a single decisive shot and then escape to safety into a crowd or maze of side streets. Normal practice was for an assassin to be given a weapon by a woman to whom it was returned after use. (Women tended to be less rigorously searched and were better able to conceal a hand gun, such as in a shopping basket, than men.)

Because both assassin and victim lived in the same community the former had all the advantages of choosing when and where to carry out an attack. Unless a gunman was caught in the act there was very little chance of his being apprehended.

Victims of attack

Grenades were frequently used in Aden, but not in Cyprus. Officer messes were a popular target in Aden, as were parties of British schoolchildren. In Cyprus the Governor, Lord Harding, survived an attempt on his life when his servant, an EOKA agent, placed a bomb in his bed. It was one of the 2976 EOKA bombs that either failed to explode or were discovered and rendered ineffective by the security forces. A further 1782 bombs did explode and accounted for damage to the value of £10 million.

Most attacks in Cyprus were directed against British government property. Perhaps the best-known incident was the bombing of the British NAAFI at Nicosia in October 1958. Two people were killed and the 3000 Greek Cypriots employed by the British authorities were subsequently dismissed.

In Aden the Arab nationalists suffered several 'own goals' at the outset of the campaign – including one grenade-thrower who actually threw the pin – but insurgent bomb-making and the performance of operations quickly improved. Letter bombs, booby traps, pressure and release bombs as well as electrically detonated mines and bombs were used.

Riots and the Happy Hour

Both the nationalists in Aden and EOKA in Cyprus made extensive use of demonstrations and civil dis-

ABOVE *A man leaps through the flames of a fire lit by Arabs during riots in Aden.* BELOW *Bystanders in Nicosia look upon the body of a British officer shot by EOKA terrorists.*

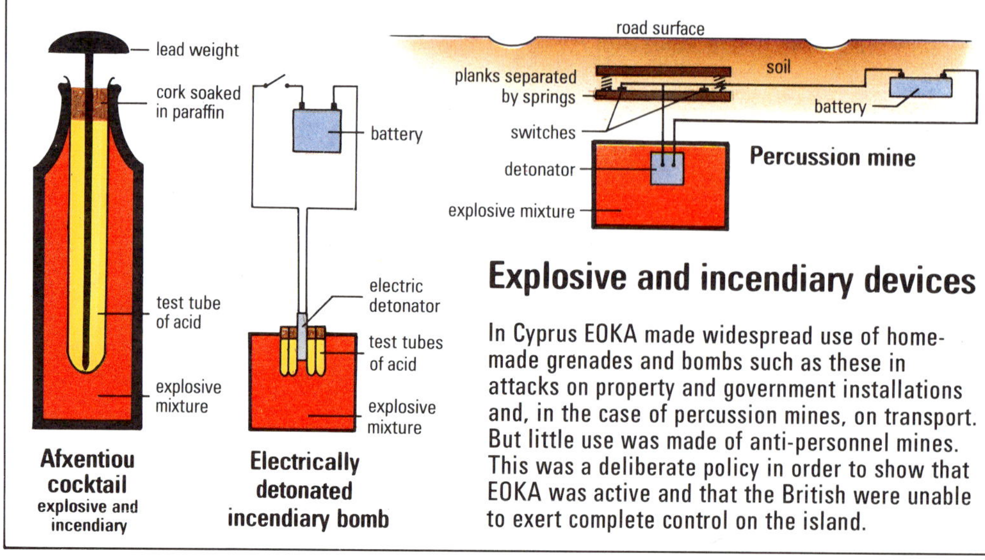

Explosive and incendiary devices

In Cyprus EOKA made widespread use of home-made grenades and bombs such as these in attacks on property and government installations and, in the case of percussion mines, on transport. But little use was made of anti-personnel mines. This was a deliberate policy in order to show that EOKA was active and that the British were unable to exert complete control on the island.

His anonymity assured, an NLF gunman stands guard in 1967, by which time the British were about to leave Aden and the main enemy was FLOSY, rival nationalists.

turbances. In Aden demonstrations were occasionally used to lure the security forces into killing zones, but demonstrations and riots were mainly employed to illustrate strength – showing that the authorities were not in control – and for propaganda purposes. In the battle for the headlines the insurgents often managed to get their slanted views across in a manner that confused issues and drew sympathy for their cause. Insurgent allegations often made great impact even though they were frequently shown, later on, to have been false.

In rural areas in Cyprus EOKA sought to survive rather than fight, although they did carry out ambushes and laid mines. In the Federation of South Arabia (FSA), insurgents had the space and an open border with Yemen that gave them much greater scope, as did the smallness of the forces opposing them in rural areas.

Insurgent activity in the FSA tended to be intermittent and involved mining roads and individual sniping. Sniping was often by machine gun at long range. Insurgent attacks were frequently timed for the last hour of daylight, giving the rebels the chance to escape under cover of darkness. In Aden itself the last 60 minutes of daylight became known as 'Happy Hour' because of the insurgent activity which occurred at that time.

The British Response

IN RESPONSE TO THE PROBLEMS posed by insurgency in Cyprus and the Federation of South Arabia (FSA), the British used techniques that had proved effective in Malaya and Kenya. In the FSA, however, it was impossible to adopt even the machinery of state authority used in the earlier campaigns and neither in Cyprus nor the FSA did the techniques yield results. This was because the nationalist organisations were extremely resilient and the security forces were unable to counter widespread public support for the insurgents.

Limits on effective action

In Cyprus it was quite easy to produce an integrated administration-police-army organisation on the Malaya pattern in order to combat EOKA, and the intelligence services were quickly formed into a single integrated organisation. But the sheer size of the FSA, the complexity of its different political bodies and the fact that the states were divided by rivalries and jealousies meant that effective integration and streamlining of government was all but impossible.

The federal authorities themselves were often at odds with the British over policy and methods of implementation, and were sensitive over the extent of their powers and status. In some cases local state authorities were less than helpful. This was especially true of the Aden state government of Abdul Mackawee which was dismissed by the governor in September 1965 because of persistent obstruction of the security forces and its support for the nationalists.

RIGHT *Armed with an FN rifle, a British lance-corporal in Aden checks a dish of food for explosives.* BELOW *A mine detector is used at the border.*

Aden

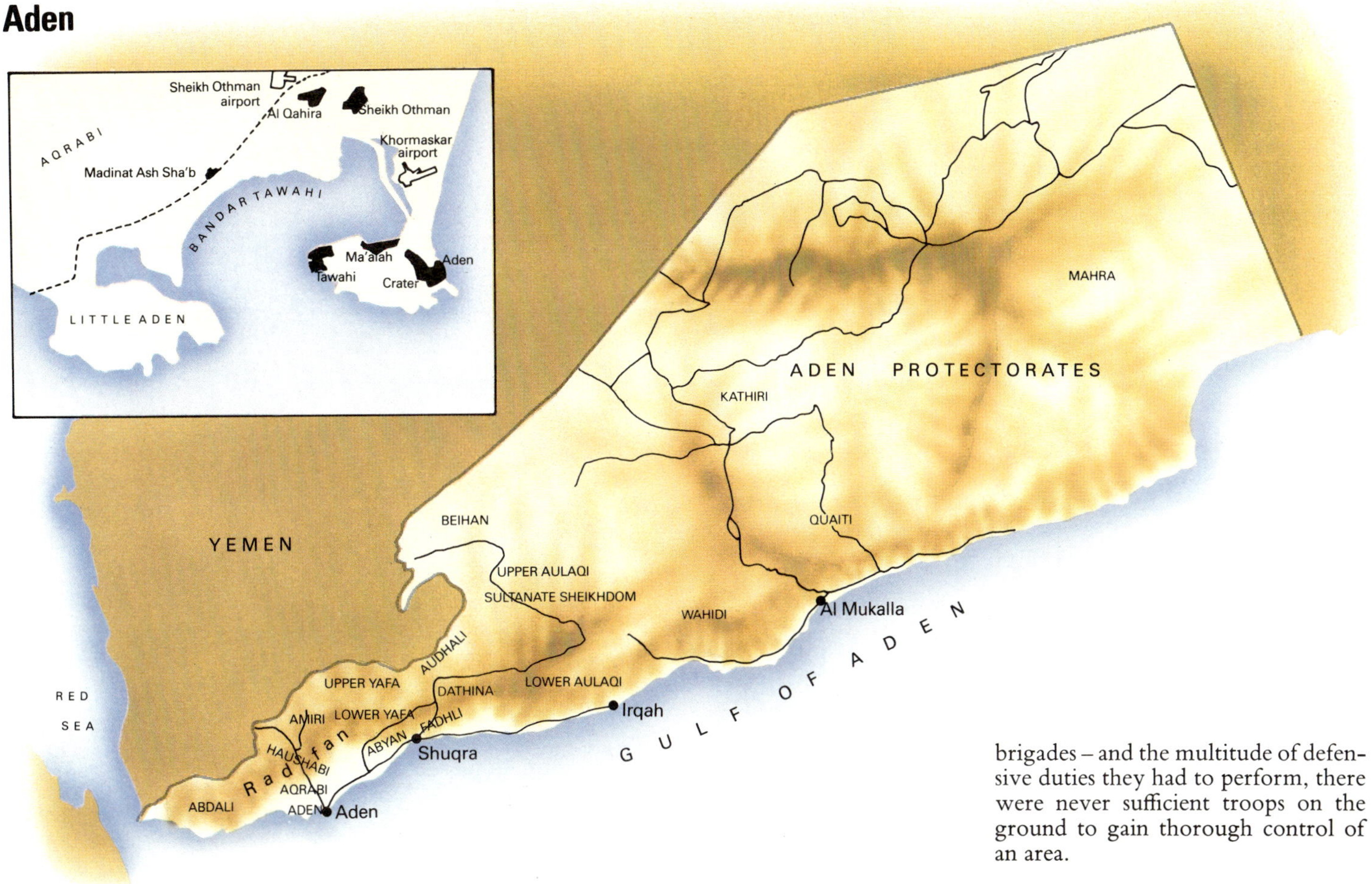

Until 1965 there were no less than ten intelligence agencies on the FSA side, but overall co-ordination and direction was lacking. Thereafter, even when a director of intelligence was appointed, the situation did not improve because the police and Special Branch had been neutralised and the population so intimidated that good intelligence was lacking.

Cypriots are searched in Nicosia's Paphos Street, part of the EOKA-dominated Old Market area.

In the absence of widespread support amongst the population and sound information on which to work, the security forces in both Cyprus and Aden had to rely on patrolling, setting up check points and manning observation posts to gain intelligence and contact the insurgents. These very basic tactics yielded much valuable, if low-grade, intelligence over a period of time. Yet, given the small number of troops involved – in Cyprus never more than 25,000 and in Aden no more than two British brigades – and the multitude of defensive duties they had to perform, there were never sufficient troops on the ground to gain thorough control of an area.

Town patrols

Most counter-insurgency activity took place in the towns. Road blocks were set up in order to search people, vehicles and animals; aggressive patrolling, cordon and searches, covert observation and specific searches were used when troops were acting on hard information. Though a system of identification checks was enforced in Cyprus this was not effective in Aden. In neither campaign did the British adopt the ruthless system of accountability by households and streets that the French adopted with great success in Algiers.

Most of the security forces' contacts with insurgents were achieved by reacting to events. In Aden the British came to adopt a 90-minute limit for men on patrol because it was felt that beyond that period troops lost their alertness and speed of reaction. Only very occasionally could the security forces operate aggressively and effectively in the towns, though in Aden covert observation posts and two-way radios often resulted in swoops and arrests that astounded and dismayed the terrorists.

In both Cyprus and the FSA troops were bound by the provisions of minimum force and common law, but during the Cyprus campaign, because of the never-ending stream of false allegations made about British troops on searches, they were freed from legal accountability for their actions during an operation. In rural areas, on the other hand, the rules

Casualties in Aden 1964–67

In the four years from 1964 to 1967 a total of 382 people were killed in terrorist incidents in Aden and a further 1714 wounded. British security personnel suffered 57 deaths and 651 wounded. Amongst local security forces the respective figures were 17 and 58. There were 290 deaths among local nationals and 922 wounded, the greatest number occurring in 1967, when fighting broke out between the nationalist groups'NLF and FLOSY. The year 1967 was easily the grimmest. Local nationals lost 240 killed and 551 were wounded. British security servicemen killed numbered 44, while 325 were injured.

governing the use of weapons by the security forces were much more relaxed.

In the mountains, cordons and searches of brigade size were not uncommon, and in the Radfan in South Arabia such operations were normally accompanied by armour or armoured cars, artillery and aircraft. Cyprus was the first major campaign where the British used helicopters on a large scale while in Aden the ubiquitous Hunter was in frequent action as, indeed, were Shackletons.

In such operations it was quite common for small patrols to take up advanced reconnaissance positions during the night in order to pass on information to units as they took part in formation-sized operations. It was common in the Radfan for units to move along mountain spurs to blocking positions in order to try and tie down tribesmen whose elusiveness had been gained from a lifetime's familiarity with the mountains and warfare against other tribes.

In the reconnaissance role the Special Air Service (SAS) was active. On several occasions the ability of the SAS and other reconnaissance parties to call up heavy and accurate air and artillery support saved British and federal forces from awkward situations.

But the rural role of the security forces in both theatres was largely a passive and unproductive one. Most of the time seemed to be spent in manning forts and patrolling the few roads.

Thus both in Cyprus and the FSA the security forces never had the numbers to control the countryside, and they never had the amount or quality of intelligence that was needed to get to grips with terrorist groups in the towns. Faced with populations that could never be reconciled to British rule and could never be induced to inform on insurgents, the attempt to find a military solution in Cyprus and South Arabia was doomed to failure.

ABOVE *Crowd control in Aden was hampered by lack of personnel and British attempts to control demonstrators made good propoganda for the Nationalists.* BELOW *Troops wearing gas masks fire tear-gas bombs and move forward to disperse protestors in Aden in 1967.*

The Algerian Revolution

Algeria was deeply scarred by eight years of vicious civil strife and the loyalty of the French Army was strained to breaking point

John Pimlott

Moslems demonstrate in the Rue de Lyon, Algiers, proclaiming their support for the FLN. The assembly was broken up by French paratroopers who opened fire, killing 61. Algeria was a battleground for many factions; European settlers and Moslems were in conflict both with the security forces and each other.

THE CONFLICT IN ALGERIA had many unusual features. It was a three-cornered contest with the French government, the European colonists and the Algerian nationalists all pursuing different aims. Caught in the middle was the French Army, still reeling from the shock of defeat in Indochina. It was an explosive mixture that led to savage fighting, mutiny in the army and political confusion within France itself.

The local dilemma

Between 1830, when French troops landed at Sidi Ferruch, and 1962, when the tricolour ceased to fly over the country, Algeria displayed all the characteristics of a colony. The majority of the population were native Moslems, dominated by a small number of European settlers known as *colons* or, more graphically, *pieds noirs*. They farmed the best land, enjoyed a virtual monopoly of political power and imposed their own educational, economic and administrative structures upon the country.

Yet, surprisingly, Algeria was not even a protectorate (a status enjoyed by her neighbours Morocco and Tunisia), for in December 1848 the country was absorbed into metropolitan France, being regarded thereafter as an integral part of the parent state. It was a decision which was to create enormous problems as Algerian nationalism burst into violence after 1954 for, constitutionally, it left no room for negotiation about the 'independence' of what was part of France itself.

FLN operations

The war began on 1 November 1954 with a series of nationalist attacks upon French and *pied noir* targets. They were carried out by guerrilla groups belonging to the Front de Libération Nationale (National Liberation Front or FLN), a revolutionary organisation created under the collective leadership of nine Moslem nationalists (Hocine Ait Ahmed, Ahmed Ben Bella, Mostafa Ben Boulaid, Larbi Ben M'hidi, Rabah Bitat, Mohamed Boudiaf, Mourad Didouche, Mohamed Khider and Belkacem Krim).

These leaders had divided Algeria into six autonomous zones (*Wilayas*), each of which was responsible for mounting selected operations on 1 November, although preference was given to *Wilaya 1* in the Aurès mountains of the east, an area chosen as ideal for the creation of a 'safe base'. Unfortunately, the attacks were not a success and drew a military response from the French which nearly destroyed the FLN. By February 1955 Didouche was dead, Boulaid and Bitat were in French prisons and the guerrilla networks were in ruins.

But the FLN was not destroyed. Despite subsequent French attempts to integrate Moslem and European populations at a

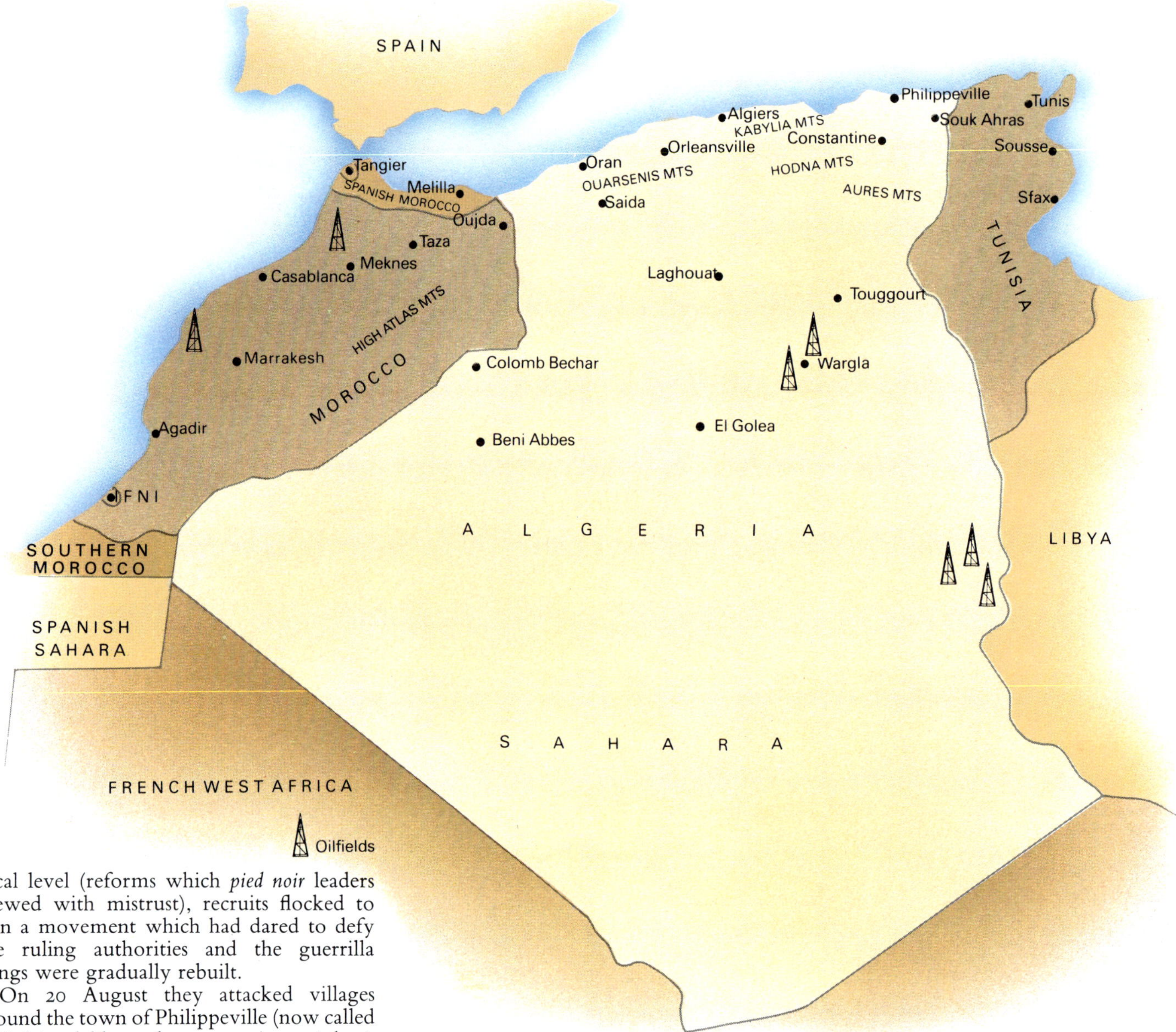

local level (reforms which *pied noir* leaders viewed with mistrust), recruits flocked to join a movement which had dared to defy the ruling authorities and the guerrilla gangs were gradually rebuilt.

On 20 August they attacked villages around the town of Philippeville (now called Skikda), deliberately massacring *pied noir* families. In horrific circumstances 123 settlers died, but for the FLN the results were encouraging. French political reforms were abandoned in favour of revenge and the army ruthlessly restored order in the Philippeville area – moves which drove a wedge between Moslem and European – while *pied noir* vigilante groups retaliated with a ferocity which shocked both world and domestic French opinion, killing an estimated 12,000 Moslems.

In March 1956 Morocco and Tunisia were granted independence, opening up sanctuary areas for the FLN to both west and east and forcing the French to divert troops to frontier protection. Eight months later the international standing of France declined as a result of the Suez crisis and a number of countries, chiefly from the Arab world, began to provide aid to the Algerian cause.

The new FLN

The FLN was now re-formed, and made more militant under a five-man Comité de Coordination et d'Exécution that had been created at a special conference held in the Soummam Valley in Kabylia in mid-1956. Moderate FLN leaders were ousted by a new generation of extremists who laid down the aims of the party in uncompromising terms, stressing the objective of complete Algerian independence. They also restructured the guerrilla gangs, forming them into an Armée de Libération Nationale (ALN), and began preparations for a new campaign. The target, based upon the lessons of Philippeville, was to be Algiers.

ALN networks in the city, centred upon the rabbit-warren of Moslem streets known as the Casbah, had been rebuilt since the setbacks of 1954–55 by Saadi Yacef, a young revolutionary dedicated to terrorism. His campaign began in 1956 with shootings and bomb attacks in the hope of producing repression against the Moslems which could be exploited on the world stage. But Yacef got far more than he bargained for. As *pied noir* vigilantes and ALN bombing teams threatened the city with anarchy, local administrators took the unprecedented step of handing over complete authority to the army.

In mid-January 1957 General Jacques Massu's 10th Parachute Division moved into Algiers with *carte blanche* so far as countermeasures were concerned. The paras proved to be as ruthless as the ALN, surrounding the Casbah, rounding up suspects and pushing patrols deep into Moslem areas. An attempted general strike was broken up by force and, as suspects were subjected to systematic torture, a remarkably accurate picture of Yacef's organisation was built up. As key personalities within it were arrested and the ALN network began to fall apart, the bombings ceased.

Despite such military success, in political terms the paras' actions were a disaster. As allegations of torture were substantiated, public opinion in France recoiled in horror, particularly when it was estimated that up to 3000 Moslems, including the FLN leader Ben M'hidi, had died or 'disappeared' under army interrogation. Moslem support for revived French attempts at integration waned dramatically and world sympathy began to veer towards the nationalist cause.

Militarily the ALN were doing badly. The destruction of the Algiers network was a major blow, but it was swiftly followed by even greater disasters on the border with Tunisia. In response to an ALN strategy of using Tunisia as a supply base and sanctuary, the French Army built an elaborate barrier – the Morice Line – down the length of the frontier. This immediately split 'interior' ALN units from their support.

Dissent in the army

By spring 1958 the French Army could, with some justification, claim that it was winning the 'shooting war', but was dismayed to find no evidence of overall victory. Elements within the army, particularly among the para units which had borne the brunt of so much action, blamed the weakness of domestic French politics and began to look around for a leader whose strength would ensure a preservation of the status quo.

An obvious choice was Charles de Gaulle, in political exile since 1946, and plots to ensure his return to office were well advanced when events in Algeria presented an opportunity for their early implementation. On 9 May 1958, following the execution of one of Yacef's bomb-makers, the ALN killed three French Army prisoners, an action which inevitably produced a *pied noir* response. Four days later about 20,000 *colons* filled the streets of Algiers and took over government offices, drawing disgruntled army units with them.

General Raoul Salan, Commander-in-Chief in Algeria, allowed himself to be appointed to an extemporised Committee of Public Safety and messages were sent to Paris demanding official support for *Algérie française*. The Paris authorities were thrown into chaos, especially when Salan openly threatened 'military incursions' into France, and by the end of the month de Gaulle had been persuaded to form a government. It marked the end of the Fourth Republic and the start of a new era in modern French history.

De Gaulle was no one's puppet. From the start he did not put himself forward as a champion of *Algérie française*, preferring to feel the political climate before committing himself to any long-term policy. In a major speech at Constantine on 3 October 1958 he announced a five-year plan of industrialisation for Algeria and promised a new military campaign to wipe out the ALN. The FLN responded by forming a Provisional Government of the Republic of Algeria (GPRA), based in Tunis, and by appealing directly to the communist world for support. They even extended terrorism to France itself to convince many French people that Algeria was not worth fighting for.

In early 1959 General Maurice Challe, who had replaced the discredited Salan, began the promised offensive against ALN strongholds in the remoter rural areas. By the end of the year most of the ALN networks within Algeria had been dispersed, while continued operations on the Morice Line prevented their reinforcement. The military threat to French rule was virtually over: it was now up to the politicians to find a lasting solution.

The path to independence

Unfortunately the politicians were following a course which was to the liking of neither the *colons* nor the army. In a broadcast on 16 September 1959 de Gaulle spoke of 'self-determination' for Algeria, a policy which threatened the very basis of *Algérie française*. *Pied noir* 'ultras' or extremists led by Jo Ortiz and ex-para Pierre Lagaillarde, organised themselves for action against de Gaulle and, when a renewed ALN bombing campaign hit Algiers in late December, tried to repeat the success of 1958. On 24 January 1960 the so-called French National Front (FNF), backed by 30,000 demonstrators and supported by dissident French paras, threatened to take the reins of power in Algiers. But de Gaulle was determined to prevent them, authorising Challe to deploy police and troops in response.

ABOVE *Civilians protesting at the fencing of a district of Algiers came under fire from French troops on 26 March 1962; 41 were killed and 130 injured.* BELOW *Former FLN leader Ahmed Ben Bella became prime minister after independence. Here he casts a vote in 1963.*

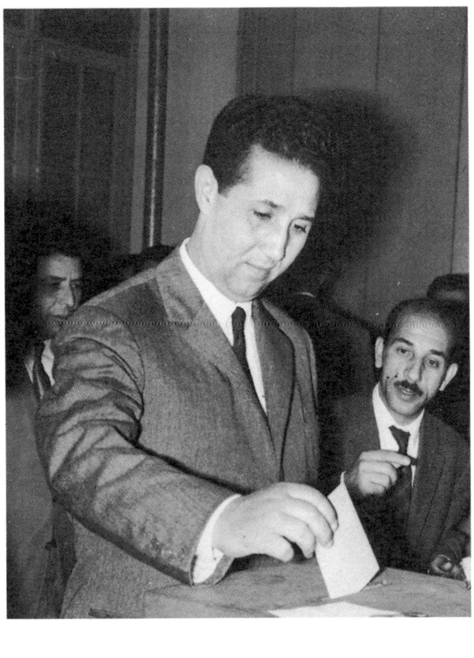

The FNF retired behind elaborate barricades, defying the authorities for almost a week. An impassioned plea from de Gaulle for loyalty from the people of France destroyed all hope of outside support, however, and the onset of rain dispersed most of the demonstrators. 'Barricades Week' was a blow to *pied noir* power, and extremists became convinced that de Gaulle was about to sell them out.

Such feelings were reinforced six months later when French representatives met GPRA delegates at Melun. This implied a willingness to recognise the nationalists and showed the desire of de Gaulle for negotiation.

At this point dissident elements within the French Army began openly to associate themselves with *pied noir* 'ultras' to preserve *Algérie française*. They turned for leadership to Salan, who was in contact with a number of other disaffected generals including Challe, discredited by the fiasco of 'Barricades Week'. The storm broke on 21 April 1961 when four of the generals – Salan, Challe, Edmond Jouhard and André Zeller – instigated a military coup in Algiers which was seen as a first step in the overthrow of the Paris government. Supported by dissident paras, they held the city for five days, but to no avail. The French public rallied to de Gaulle in an amazing display of national solidarity, forcing the generals to abandon their plans.

But the 'ultras', together with members of the dissident para units who had evaded capture, were determined to maintain the pressure. They created their own terrorist group, the Organisation Armée Secrète (OAS), and began a ruthless anti-Moslem campaign designed initially to prevent negotiations but, when these went ahead regardless, to destroy as much of Algeria as possible before independence. The war swiftly degenerated into a bloodbath as Moslem liberals and intellectuals were assassinated and Moslem areas bombed. The ALN retaliated in kind.

Agreement was finally reached at Evian in March 1962, giving Algeria complete independence under the GPRA, with no special status for the *colons*, who now began to leave the country in droves. It represented total nationalist victory, achieved at an awesome cost of an estimated 1 million Moslem lives. By comparison, the French Army lost 17,456 dead and 2788 *colons* lost their lives. The latter, however, suffered all the humiliation of defeat and exile. For all concerned it had been a bitter war.

The Aims of the FLN

ALGERIAN NATIONALISM before 1954 was fragmented. Dissatisfied Moslems had a variety of parties from which to choose, none of them offering policies with universal appeal. The Algerian Communist Party (PCA), which might have been expected to provide the organisation for revolt, was weakened by its lack of religious fervour; the religious Association des Ulemas was too preoccupied with pan-Islamic policies to find room for specifically Algerian problems. The Mouvement pour le Triomphe des Libertés Démocratiques (MTLD) under Messali Hadj did offer an anti-French stance, but was split over the question of force. The split became permanent in 1949 when Ben Bella created the more militant Organisation Spéciale (OS), a party dedicated to the use of violence which did not attract widespread support. Finally, more liberal Moslems could join the Union Démocratique du Manifesto Algéria (UDMA), led by Ferhat Abbas, but he promised little beyond political integration with the ruling authorities. The unification of these disparate elements was a vital prerequisite to successful revolution.

Towards unity

Blatant electoral frauds by the *colons* (the European settlers) after 1947, designed to prevent Moslem representation at all levels of government, provoked the first moves in this direction when, in 1951, UDMA, MTLD, PCA and Ulema leaders formed a common front. The experiment was short-lived. Within three years Messali had broken away, eventually forming the Mouvement Nationaliste Algérien (MNA), and it was this event, fraught with implications of nationalist weakness, which caused OS militants to create a new force, dedicated to armed revolt.

In March 1954 Ahmed Ben Bella and his eight co-leaders created a revolutionary committee which, seven months later, spawned the National Liberation Front (FLN). Despite a French Army belief that this was a Moscow-orientated communist organisation, fighting the West as part of a worldwide strategy, the FLN was firmly nationalistic. It turned to Ho Chi Minh as a successful example, establishing the six *Wilayas* which bore a strong resemblance to Viet Minh 'inter-zones', but was never a slavish follower of communist revolutionary theory. The organisation and tactics of the guerrilla groups which initiated the revolt on 1 November 1954 in fact owed more to the French Resistance of World War II.

In common with all revolutionary movements, the FLN needed two things if it was to be successful – strong leadership and popular support. The latter turned out to be the easier to find, for although the number of activists was small in 1954 (probably less than 400), *pied noir* reprisals, an absence of strong French political reaction and the appeal of the FLN's aim of complete independence, combined to attract substantial support.

Algerian soldiers undergo marching drill. Those that wear a triangular patch on the right breast are full members of the FLN.

The guerrilla networks were rebuilt by 1956 as recruits came in from the towns as well as the rural areas and sufficient people, prepared to risk their lives in attacks upon the French, became available. As a result, by mid-1956 both the PCA and MNA had been largely absorbed and even the moderate UDMA had thrown in its lot with the FLN, giving the movement an active strength of up to 20,000 organised into the Army of National Liberation (ALN), and the passive support of most Moslems.

The ALN eventually took the form of a regular army, containing units ranging from a section to a battalion, organised in exile in Tunisia. Its task was, ostensibly, to support rural guerrilla gangs and urban bombing teams inside Algeria, although the success of the Morice Line prevented its deployment. Nevertheless, by 1958 popular support had been gained.

Personal rivalries

The creation of strong FLN leadership was much more difficult. By the time of the Soummam Valley conference in mid-1956 only two of the original nine leaders – Belkacem Krim and Larbi Ben M'hidi – were still at large in Algeria, and they were joined by a number of new personalities whose views were more extreme. Chief amongst these was Ramdane Abane, an energetic revolutionary who had revitalised the Algiers network in 1955, bringing in the ruthless Saadi Yacef and introducing the concept of urban terrorism. Abane was one of the instigators of reform at Soummam, forming with Krim and M'hidi the co-ordinating committee (CCE) as a central governing body which could control the efforts of the newly created ALN.

But this development was made possible only by the exclusion of the 'outsiders' – those original leaders like Ben Bella, Mohamed Boudiaf and Rabah Bitat who were in prison or exile – and this split within the leadership had important ramifications. Abane attempted to gain complete personal power – a move which betrayed one of the basic beliefs of the FLN, that of collective leadership – and he was executed by his fellow-revolutionaries in December 1957. As a result, the CCE was discredited, being replaced in June 1958 by the Provisional Government of the Republic of Algeria, the government-in-exile, formed to appeal to the international rather than the purely Algerian scene.

In this it was successful, but the political emphasis of the new leadership, now in the hands of moderates such as Abbas, alienated those who believed in a military solution, a group led eventually by Ben Bella and Colonel Houari Boumedienne. At conferences in January 1960 and August 1961 these militants gradually assumed command, presenting the French with hard-line negotiations which resulted in independence. Further splits were to appear after 1962 – Boumedienne overthrew Ben Bella as president three years later – but a strong revolutionary party had been formed when it mattered most.

TOP RIGHT *Soldiers of the ALN perform a Moslem prayer ritual.* ABOVE *Hands on head, the French occupants of this vehicle are led away after an ambush by the ALN.* RIGHT *Moslem corpses are laid out in Philippeville after European reprisals for an FLN massacre of* pieds noirs *in August 1955.*

Battle of Algiers

ON 7 JANUARY 1957 Robert Lacoste, Governor-General of Algeria, met with his commander-in-chief, Raoul Salan, and the commander of 10th Parachute Division, Jacques Massu, to discuss the deteriorating security situation in Algiers. Trouble had started the previous June, when 49 *pied noir* (European) civilians had been gunned down in the streets. There followed the familiar pattern of reprisal and counter-reprisal which always threatened anarchy. On 10 August *pied noir* extremists had killed 70 Moslems in a single bomb attack; on 30 September bombs had exploded in *pied noir* cafés; on 28 December the extremist mayor of Boufarik had been assassinated.

Lacoste and Salan agreed that troops would have to be deployed to maintain law and order and directed Massu to move in his four regiments. They were given complete freedom regarding methods, merely being told to root out the National Liberation Front (FLN) networks.

Yacef's tactics

The paras were presented with a difficult task. Since late 1955 Saadi Yacef had devoted considerable effort to creating an urban terrorist organisation, dedicated to the furtherance of revolutionary aims by selected assassinations and random bomb attacks. These tactics, it was argued, would drive a wedge between the Moslem and European populations of Algiers, destroying the 'middle ground' (those who might be prepared to accept a compromise settlement), and would take French military pressure off the rural areas by forcing a re-deployment of troops.

By January 1957 Yacef controlled about 1400 activists, capable of forming small gangs of gunmen or bomb-planters (the latter often women), based in the Casbah, a maze of Moslem streets in central Algiers which the security forces had failed to penetrate.

The French response

When the four para regiments moved in during the second week of January, each was given a specific area of the city to control: Colonel Marcel Bigeard's 3rd Colonial Parachute Regiment received the Casbah. An aggressive policy of house-to-house searches, foot patrols and checkpoints was immediately instigated, the aim being to isolate the 'safe base' of the Casbah preparatory to its infiltration.

In this Bigeard's men enjoyed some success, establishing a reputation for ruthlessness by their handling of Yacef's abortive general strike on 28/29 January and making movement in the city centre difficult for all Moslems, but without an intimate knowledge of the FLN set-up, this was at best only a short-term strategy. What was needed was good, reliable intelligence, something which soon became a well-organised central theme of the paras' actions.

Colonel Roger Trinquier set up a system whereby Algiers was divided into a number of sectors and sub-sectors. Within each, one person was appointed – usually a Moslem who had served in the French Army and was still 'loyal' – and he reported all suspicious activities. At the same time, police files were used to compile a list of all suspected FLN sympathisers and they, together with Moslems arrested at the checkpoints, were rounded up. They were usually passed to the paras' Détachement Opérationnel de Protection for interrogation. This was invariably brutal, often involving the use of torture, but the results were catastrophic for the FLN.

By March, Yacef's organisation had been broken up, his bomb-factory had been destroyed and the higher command network had been forced to leave the city, with one of its members, Ben M'hidi, dead in French hands. By the end of the month, Massu's division had been withdrawn.

Yacef's final offensive

This proved to be a premature move. Despite the successes of January–March, Yacef himself was still at large, together with a hard core of his best

Algiers

LEFT *Governor-General Robert Lacoste, flanked by Generals Salan and Allard, drives through Algiers in November 1957.* ABOVE RIGHT *Saadi Yacef, FLN leader in Algiers, waged a campaign of urban terror against the French. He is shown soon after his capture in September 1957.* BELOW *A victim of FLN terrorism lies in a doorway. Gun and bomb attacks on* pieds noirs *inevitably attracted reprisals.* RIGHT *Barricades and checkpoints were used by paratroopers as a means of civil control in Algiers.*

operatives, including the gunman Ali Amara ('Ali La Pointe') and the majority of his female bomb-planters. Yacef was now in full command in Algiers and he used his new powers to prepare a fresh offensive. It began on 3 June with bombs planted in lamp standards throughout the city and reached new heights of terror six days later when a bomb exploded in the 'Casino', a popular *pied noir* night-spot, killing nine young *colons* and mutilating a further 85. The inevitable *pied noir* reprisal, involving mob attacks upon Moslem areas in Algiers, prompted Lacoste to recall the paras.

Massu now decided to concentrate on the FLN leaders in the city, building up a remarkably accurate picture of Yacef's organisation through the continued use of intelligence and torture. Simultaneously, para patrols began to operate deep in the Casbah, forcing Yacef and his colleagues underground. Here they were tracked down by a new French tactic – that of infiltrating 'loyal' Moslems into FLN areas.

The net began to close. On 26 August two FLN terrorists, 'Mourad' and 'Kamel', newly appointed by Yacef to co-ordinate the bombing campaign, were trapped and killed; on 24 September Yacef himself was isolated and captured alive. Two weeks later 'Ali La Pointe' and the remaining hard-core gunmen blew themselves up rather than face captivity. The battle was over.

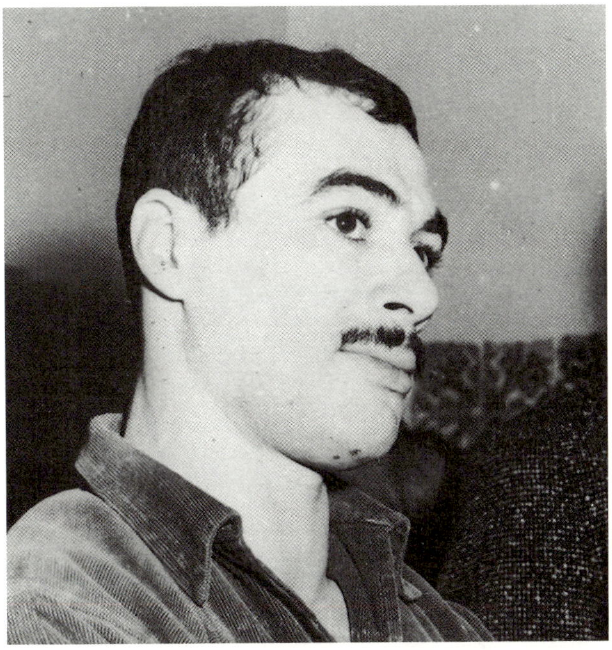

In purely military terms, this was a major French victory, but in a revolutionary situation it is politics that matter most. The ruthlessness of the paras alienated moderates on both sides, forcing them into entrenched positions which prolonged the war by making compromise unthinkable and violence the norm. It was exactly what Yacef had wanted.

The Morice Line

THE GRANTING OF INDEPENDENCE to Morocco and Tunisia in March 1956 altered the nature of the Algerian War. Before that time the National Liberation Front (FLN) had been forced to create its 'safe bases' within Algeria – a policy which had taken a hard knock in 1954–55 when French troops swamped the rural areas in response to the initial guerrilla attacks – but the sudden creation of independent Arab states on both the western and eastern borders offered new possibilities. FLN leaders fled over these borders when under pressure, there to be joined by refugees, recruits and defeated guerrillas who formed the potential for a new army which could act as a pool for the reinforcement of hard-pressed areas.

At first neither King Mohammed V of Morocco nor President Habib Bourguiba of Tunisia gave his full support – both were still heavily dependent upon French economic aid – but when, in October 1956, Ben Bella and three of his fellow FLN leaders were kidnapped by the French while flying from Rabat to Tunis, both modified their stance, providing money, training areas and arms to the National Liberation Army (ALN). By 1957 the French were presented with an entirely new facet to the war: the possibility of intervention from outside.

The death strip

The response by France was to close both borders by creating impregnable barriers from the Mediterranean to the Sahara. The more impressive, covering the border with the country giving most direct support to the ALN, was the so-called Morice Line along the frontier with Tunisia.

Named after the minister of defence in Guy Mollet's government, the Line was a miracle of modern technology. Its main feature was a 2.5m (8-foot) high electric fence, through which a charge of 5000 volts was passed. There was a minefield 45m (50 yards) wide on either side. Behind it, inside Algeria, were barbed wire entanglements and then a track, constantly patrolled night and day. The fence was designed to kill anyone foolish enough to touch it, and the fact that it was festooned with dead animals acted as a constant reminder.

The electric charge was also an alarm: if anything did get electrocuted, a break would set off bells in the nearest command post. When this happened, fire from 105mm howitzers could be brought instantly to bear and mobile forces rushed to the spot. If by any chance ALN groups did manage to make it into Algeria, helicopters, tanks, infantry and parachute units were available to pin them down and destroy them before they could link up with guerrilla gangs in the country.

The line was completed in September 1957 and involved the deployment of 80,000 French troops. They

BELOW *French soldiers question suspects at a fortress in the Aurès mountains, 1954.* BOTTOM *Construction of the Morice Line, the lethal barrier between Algeria and Tunisia, was completed in September 1957.* OPPOSITE *French troops on the Tunisian border after a French air raid across the border in 1958.*

faced a rapidly expanding ALN which, by the end of the year, could muster about 10,000 men armed with a wide variety of weapons gathered from sympathetic nations in both the Arab and communist worlds. As guerrilla groups under pressure from French units were crying out for reinforcement, a confrontation on the line was inevitable.

Challenges on the line

During the winter of 1957–58, ALN forces tried every conceivable means of breaching the wire, using high-tension cutters, Bangalore torpedoes, tunnels and ramps, while other units tried to divert French attention elsewhere. But the results were negligible. Despite a steady rise in the number of ALN troops involved (by early 1958 it was not unknown for entire battalions to rush the wire), French counter-measures proved to be decisive, even when some units tried to outflank the line through the Sahara. The latter were invariably destroyed by the air force, while elsewhere a combination of mines, electricity, patrolling and mobile strike forces gave the French a steady advantage.

Statistics were issued immediately after the battle which indicate the extent of the French victory. In January and February 1958 it was claimed that 35 per cent of all ALN infiltrators were killed; by March–April this had risen to 65 per cent and, in the last days of April, to an incredible 85 per cent.

The latter figure resulted largely from a massed ALN attack on 27 April, through wooded hills to the east of Souk-Ahras. Seven groups, totalling over 800 men, were thrown against the wire. A proportion got through but were almost immediately surrounded by French airborne troops. The ensuing battle went on for almost a week, although the eventual outcome was never in doubt. Of the 820 men who came out of the Tunisian woods, well over 600 were killed or captured. It was a loss rate which the ALN could not sustain for by that time, according to French figures, more than 6000 men and 4300 weapons had been lost. There were no more serious attempts to cross the Morice Line nor its counterpart on the Moroccan border.

This defeat affected the FLN cause considerably. Faced with such losses, the militants in exile in Tunisia decided not to deploy their army inside Algeria, but to build it up as a regular force in Tunisia which could be used to ensure FLN rule once independence had been gained. Guerrilla operations were to continue, but in the absence of outside support it was obvious that this was only a half-hearted military strategy which was gradually giving way to one of politics. The war was entering a new phase which the French, flushed with military victory, were slow to appreciate.

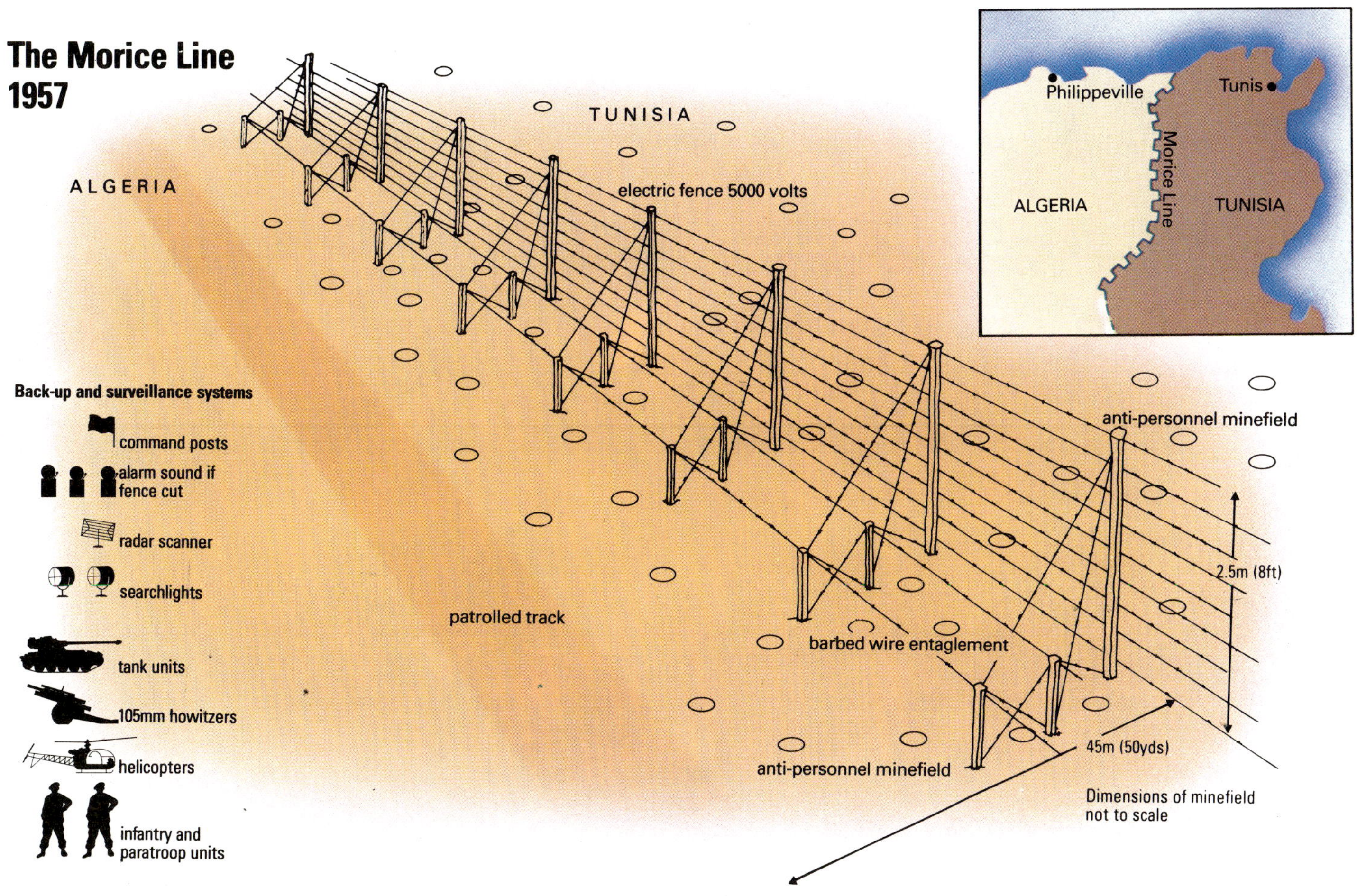

The Challe Offensive

IN EARLY 1959 the task facing General Maurice Challe, Salan's replacement as commander-in-chief in Algeria, was to complete the apparent defeat of the National Liberation Army (ALN). Since Souk-Ahras the previous April the nationalist movement had suffered enormous casualties. Although about 15,000 activists, backed up by an estimated 30,000 irregulars, were still at large in the interior, the ALN as a whole had lost more than 25,000 men in the first seven months of 1958 and the French were encountering progressively smaller units in the *Wilayas*, the zones of nationalist resistance.

In addition ALN command structures had been disrupted severely by some key losses. In November 1958 the military chief of *Wilaya 4*, Si Azedine, had been captured and two months later his field commander, Si Rachid, was killed. In March 1959 the leaders in both *Wilaya 3* (Si Haouès) and *Wilaya 6* (Ait Hamouda) lost their lives and, as an indication of growing ALN demoralisation, up to 300 guerrillas were surrendering each month. To many it seemed as if the ALN (and, by implication in Western eyes, the FLN) was so close to total defeat that the slightest pressure would cause collapse. Challe's orders were to provide that pressure.

General Challe's tactics

His first priority was to root out remaining guerrilla strongholds in the remote rural areas, where French military activity had never been strong. The main reason for this lay in the prevailing French tactics, involving a policy known as *quadrillage* in which the entire country was divided into sectors, each theoretically controlled by military presence. This required an enormous commitment of troops, spreading them out so thinly that concentration against ALN networks was impossible. It was a problem which had occurred in Indochina, but Challe was quick to see this and to introduce a solution.

He took as his major aim the destruction of ALN guerrilla gangs rather than the physical occupation of territory and reorganised his forces accordingly. In an effort to isolate the gangs he authorised the employment of pro-French Moslem units (*harkis*), who would move into an area of known ALN activity, living off the land and playing the guerrillas at their own game. Once ALN formations had been discovered, mobile Commandos de Chasse would step in, pursuing and eventually pinning down the enemy preparatory to the kill. This would be carried out by forces from the Réserve Générale, comprising high-quality troops equipped with the full panoply of modern war. It turned out to be an effective combination.

Clearing the mountains

The first phase of the Challe offensive was ready by February 1959, when it was decided to concentrate against the western end of the Ouarsenis mountains, around Saida to the south-

LEFT *French C-in-C General Challe.* BELOW *Troops rest during Operation Jumelles, Challe's successful drive against ALN strongholds in Kabylia.*

east of Oran – an area covered by the ALN's *Wilaya 5*. It was rolling, lightly wooded country, ideal for mechanised forces, so the chances of a French victory were good. The operation was spearheaded by the 10th Parachute Division, supported by *harkis* and mobile forces from the Oran sector. It was a remarkable success. By the end of April more than 1600 ALN guerrillas had been killed and the area effectively cleared.

On 18 April a follow-up operation (code-named Courroie) tackled the more difficult terrain at the eastern end of Ouarsenis. Although fewer guerrillas were killed, sufficient success was achieved to persuade the French that they had discovered a winning strategy.

Operation Jumelles

Thus by summer 1959, with a Réserve Générale of two good divisions in existence, backed by armour, helicopters and ground-attack aircraft (piston-engined Harvard T6 trainers armed with machine guns and rocket pods), Challe was ready to turn against the heart of ALN strength – *Wilaya 3* in Kabylia, to the east of Algiers.

Operation Jumelles ('Binoculars') was planned as a two-pronged attack against Little and Great Kabylia, involving 25,000 French troops. Its chances of success were enhanced when, just before the assault was due to go in, a major ALN force was pinpointed in the Hodna mountains, between Kabylia and the Aurès. Challe immediately shifted troops to that area, wiping out half the rebel band and cutting off any hopes of ALN retreat out of *Wilaya 3*.

Jumelles began in July 1959 and lasted until October. It was a stunning military success which fully vindicated the new strategy. Para units, supported by *harkis*, took crest-line villages, cleared them of people (many of whom were 'resettled' in new, protected villages away from the region) and then fanned out into the surrounding valleys. ALN units, deprived of protection and support from the indigenous population, were gradually isolated and broken up, losing 3746 men.

A further operation, this time in *Wilaya 2* around Constantine, was equally successful in November. By the end of the year much of the ALN inside Algeria was in ruins and preparations were being made to close in on the last stronghold in the Aurès mountains in early 1960 (Operation Trident). Total military victory seemed assured.

But Trident was overtaken by the events of 'Barricades Week'. Challe was recalled and General Charles de Gaulle, shocked by the intransigence of *pied noir* extremists, began to explore the policy which was to lead eventually to Algerian 'self-determination'. Such a policy played right into the political hands of the FLN, ensuring them of eventual victory regardless of the military situation. It was a development which the *pieds noirs*, together with certain members of the army, could not understand, and one which was to have far-reaching ramifications.

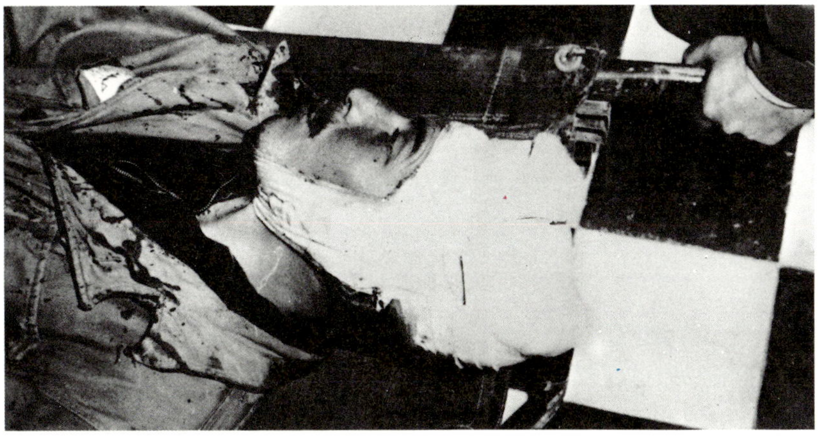

ABOVE *An ALN sentry on duty in the Algerian hinterland.* BELOW *The rebel leader Amar Driss, taken prisoner in 1959 by the French.*

Operations against the FLN

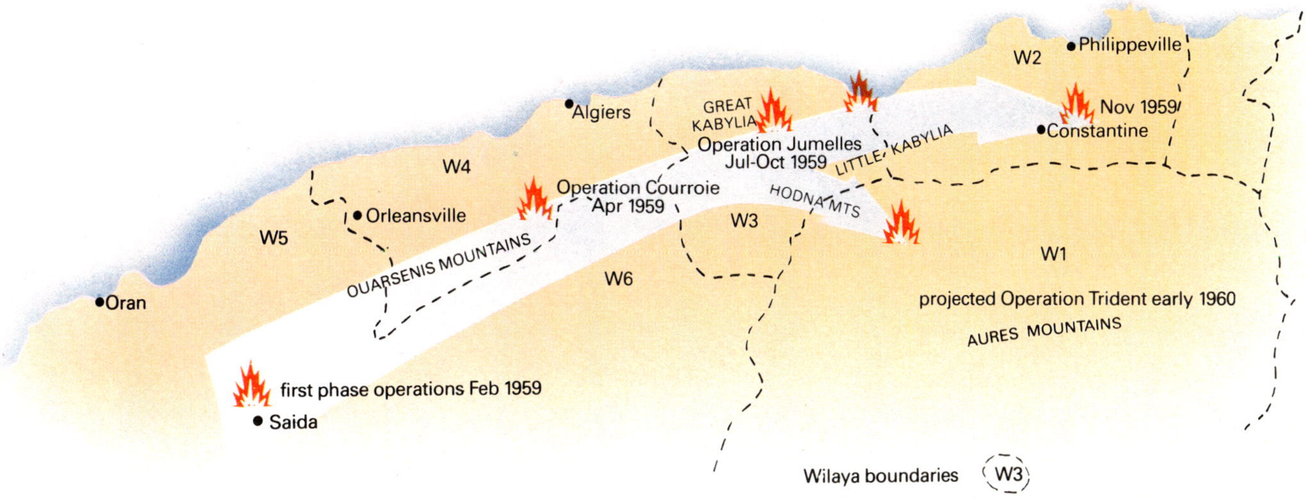

Unrest in the Army

THE FRENCH ARMY entered the Algerian War determined to win. Having only just suffered the ignominy of enforced withdrawal from Indochina, many French officers, particularly those who had experienced Viet Minh prison camps, felt a deep need to analyse their defeat and to make sure that it did not happen again elsewhere. The result was an attempt to understand the reasons for Viet Minh victory and, as a natural corollary, arrive at a theory on how best to counter such warfare in the future. Together, this became known as *guerre révolutionnaire*, a dangerously restricted view of communist warfare based almost entirely upon the strategy propounded by Mao Tse-tung and Ho Chi Minh. It bore little relation to Algeria.

The lessons of Indochina

Avid reading of everything written by Mao and his Vietnamese disciples seemed to suggest two key factors which the French had not recognised in Indochina. The first was that the Viet Minh had not been fighting a purely military campaign but one that was geared to the gaining of political power, according to the Maoist pattern. Thus even when French 'victories' had been achieved, they could never be total without concurrent operations against the political infrastructure of the 'safe bases' occupied by the revolutionaries. If the French in Indochina had developed an attractive alternative to Viet Minh policies through education and reform, then some form of lasting victory might have been achieved.

The second factor to be noted was that Mao's theories were communist. It seemed only logical to presume that all insurgencies were part of some communist grand strategy, aimed at an isolation of the capitalist West by attacking its colonial links.

To the French theorists the war in Algeria was not merely a colonial conflict but the latest in a long line of communist revolutions which it was the army's job, within a framework of strong political backing, to contain. The argument was admirably summed up by Colonel Antoine Argoud, Massu's chief of staff, in 1960: 'We want to halt the decadence of the West and the march of communism. That is . . . the duty of the army. That is why we must win the war in Algeria.'

Guerre révolutionnaire was therefore full of dangerous implications. In the

TOP *Armed French troops seal off a district of Algiers.* ABOVE *General Jacques Massu (right) talks with some of his crack paratroops.*

first place, because the Algerian War was seen as a last-ditch stand against communism, any negotiation with the National Liberation Front (FLN) was, by definition, a sign of weakness. What was needed was a strong politico-military stance based on a status quo modified only by a Western-orientated re-education of the Moslem population. Secondly, as the army was the only true bastion of the West, it naturally took on the role of political watch-dog, aware of and determined to counter any sign of weakness displayed by successive French governments. In short, it became a highly politicised body, prepared to stand firm against the insurgents even if that entailed opposing the Paris authorities.

These beliefs, half-formed in 1954, gradually hardened as the Algerian War progressed. The lack of a coherent or workable policy towards Algeria, together with a poor political response to the growing tally of military victories against the FLN, produced a feeling of deep dissatisfaction, particularly among the para officers who believed in *guerre révolutionnaire*. Men such as General Jacques Massu and Colonels Marcel Bigeard, Argoud and Roger Trinquier began to share a common desire to see a strong, pro-military leader in political power in Paris. By 1958 plots to ensure the return to office of General Charles de Gaulle were well advanced.

Salan's challenge

The crisis came to a head on 9 May, when news of the execution of French prisoners by the FLN sent shock waves through the army in Algeria. The commander-in-chief, General Raoul Salan, sent what amounted to an ultimatum to Paris, demanding that the new government then being formed (the twenty-sixth since 1945) should be dedicated to a policy of *Algérie française*, creating the wall of strength against the nationalists which the para officers were advocating. Such a policy obviously appealed to the *pieds noirs* (the European settlers) and, when they took to the streets on 13 May, this implication of military support made it easy for the extremists to organise a takeover in Algiers.

Salan and Massu were drawn inexorably into the revolt, appearing openly as members of the Committee of Public Safety and making threats of 'military incursions' into France itself if de Gaulle was not returned to power. Army units elsewhere in Algeria, France and Germany were unaffected and neither the air force nor the navy was involved, but the reality of *pied noir* rule in Algiers, backed by Massu's paras, was sufficient to influence events in Paris. By 1 June de Gaulle had formed a government.

Once this initial intervention in the domestic politics of France had taken place, there was no turning back for the officers involved. In an overt political move, they had associated themselves with the *pieds noirs* and the status quo in Algeria and, on the precedent of these events, had shown a disturbing willingness to go to extremes in pursuance of their beliefs. Unfortunately for them and for the political stability of Algeria, de Gaulle neither understood nor supported those beliefs. As he veered towards negotiation with the FLN, a repetition of military intervention, this time against him, became inevitable.

ABOVE *De Gaulle is greeted by General Salan during a visit to Algiers soon after taking power in 1958.* RIGHT *A pro-Massu* pied noir *shows her allegiance.* BELOW *Algerians who fled from the FLN were housed in French-run refugee camps.*

The Army Revolts

THE ARMY'S DISILLUSIONMENT with General de Gaulle developed quickly. In the immediate aftermath of the crisis of May 1958 de Gaulle showed little sympathy towards those involved, replacing Raoul Salan with Maurice Challe and recalling the more politically active para officers to France. He then began to develop his own policy towards Algeria. As early as 3 October 1958 his speech at Constantine, although promising political reform and a renewed military offensive against the National Liberation Front (FLN), disgusted *pied noir* (European) and army extremists by offering a *paix aux braves*, apparently treating the rebels as fellow-soldiers.

Disgust turned to anger on 16 September 1959 when, for the first time, de Gaulle spoke openly of 'self-determination' for Algeria – a policy that was guaranteed to upset the status quo. This in turn gave way to fears of a sell-out when, two months later, a ceasefire programme was laid down. The situation worsened on 18 January 1960 when General Jacques Massu, one of the few leaders of the 1958 revolt to remain in Algeria, was recalled to France after criticising de Gaulle's policies in a newspaper interview.

Extremists in control

Paradoxically, however, Massu's departure probably prevented the subsequent 'Barricades Week' from developing into full-scale military intervention. The demonstrations of 24 January and the ensuing battles between the *pieds noirs* and gendarmes were organised almost entirely by the extremist leaders of the French National Front, Jo Ortiz and Pierre Lagaillarde.

They received practical advice on the building of barricades from para officers such as Colonels Argoud, Gardes and Godard and they were not seriously opposed by units of 10th Parachute Division, disgusted at the recall of Massu, but there was never any real danger of a spread of disaffection to other elements of the army. Indeed, when 25th Parachute Division was moved into Algiers on 29 January, the barricades were soon destroyed and the revolt was crushed. De Gaulle, strengthened by the wave of popular support which resulted from his broadcast to the nation, also on the 29th, felt free to pursue his Algerian policy.

The failure of 'Barricades Week' did not destroy the opposition, it merely made it more extreme as *Algérie française* gradually lost its viability in the face of de Gaulle's continuing search for a negotiated compromise. This development, manifested at Melun on 25 June 1960 when representatives of the French government and the FLN met for talks, was clearly anathema to those army officers who believed in *guerre révolutionnaire*.

Their worst fears were reinforced

RIGHT *Pierre Lagaillarde, instigator of 'Barricades Week', acknowledges the cheers of the crowd.* BELOW *A wreath adorns the barricades after paras had ended the display of European defiance in Algiers during January 1960.*

when de Gaulle recalled Challe before he could implement the final phase of his anti-guerrilla offensive, Operation Trident. His replacement as commander-in-chief cancelled it, as he was under orders to adopt a low military profile while political negotiations began.

The growing mutiny

To many army officers this was the final straw, coming at a time when the National Liberation Army (ALN) was all but defeated. Murmurings of revolt were renewed. On 25 October 1960 Salan, retired prematurely from the army and denied permission to settle in Algeria because of his known contacts with *pied noir* extremists, declared 'total war' on de Gaulle and his policies before departing for exile in Spain. A small clique of para officers, many from the 1st Régiment Etranger Parachutiste (REP), openly associated themselves with the *Algérie française* movement. They became more and more committed as de Gaulle's policies developed.

On 4 November General de Gaulle announced a 'new course' which would lead eventually to an 'Algerian Algeria' and directed a referendum on the issue of 'self-determination' to be held on 8 January 1961. This went ahead despite the appalling riots in Algiers in December and presented de Gaulle with an overwhelming vote of support from a war-weary French population. Challe, shabbily treated since his return to France, saw this as a betrayal of all he had fought to achieve in Algeria and resigned from the army. When de Gaulle announced the decision to negotiate with the FLN at Evian, Challe offered his leadership to the military plotters.

Failure of the coup

A speech by de Gaulle on 11 April, in which he referred to 'decolonisation' in Algeria, acted as the spark for revolt. Challe, accompanied by General André Zeller, erstwhile Inspector-General of Ground Forces, flew secretly to Algiers on 21 April, made contact with an ex-air force general, Edmond Jouhard, and set up a command HQ at Zéralda, base of the 1st REP.

The plan was for that unit to seize key centres in Algiers and for the generals, soon to be joined by Salan, to take power. At the same time, disaffected units in France would march on Paris, forcing de Gaulle to resign. The generals would then rule Algeria until the ALN had been defeated, after which a *pied noir* government would be appointed.

It did not work. By 25 April, with little support from outside Algiers and a growing wave of public opposition to the *putsch* in France, Challe and Zeller were forced to surrender, while Salan, Jouhard and most of the other officers involved went underground into the Organisation Armée Secrète (OAS).

Their failure marked the end of military revolt. In its aftermath five generals and 200 other officers were arrested, trials of the leaders were hastily arranged and the 1st REP was disbanded. De Gaulle was free to pursue his policy of disengagement, which culminated with the official declaration of Algerian independence in July 1962.

ABOVE *A French Army patrol stalks terrorists in Algiers.* LEFT *Soldiers listen to a broadcast by de Gaulle, whose policy of Algerian independence enjoyed majority support in France.* BELOW *Rebel Generals (left to right) Zeller, Jouhard, Salan and Challe after the failure of their bid for power.*

Hungary in Revolt

In 1956 the Hungarian people rose up against Soviet oppression and took to the streets to fight Russian tanks

Michael Orr

THE HUNGARIAN REVOLUTION of 1956 was a turning point in the history of the communist bloc. It was the climax and, effectively, the end of the monolithic system established by Josef Stalin after 1945 when the Soviet Army occupied most of eastern Europe. Since 1956 Hungary has been allowed a measure of economic, if not political, freedom. The events of that year forced the Soviet leadership to accept that there are limits to its rule in Europe.

The Stalinist system

After World War II Stalin exploited the strength of his military position to force the states of eastern Europe into a common mould. Hungary's fate was typical of them all. Having been an ineffective German ally, Hungary was occupied by the Red Army after severe fighting in the last months of the war. A coalition government was established. The communists were a minority but controlled key posts such as internal security. Political rivals were eliminated and by April 1949 communist control was signalled by elections in which no opposition candidates were permitted. Mátyás Rákosi was First Secretary of the Communist Party and apparent dictator of Hungary.

Not all of eastern Europe followed this pattern. In Yugoslavia Marshal Tito, although a committed communist, refused to subordinate national interests to Stalin's policy. Stalin's answer was to isolate Yugoslavia within the communist bloc by suppressing any element of nationalism, or 'Titoism'. In 1949 he demanded purges and show trials in the satellite states.

Rákosi responded eagerly by disposing of his main rivals. Lázló Rajk was tried and executed for 'Titoism'. Imre Nagy, popular because of his land distribution programme in the postwar coalition, was stripped of office. About 1000 people suffered in this purge.

Thus Hungary and the rest of the Soviet bloc were remoulded in the image of Stalin's Russia. Stalin's death in March 1953 was the first crack in that mould: the Hungarian leadership was called to Moscow. There they were told it was necessary to forestall unrest in Hungary by revising policy. Rákosi was criticised but allowed to remain as first secretary of the party. However, the Soviet leaders decreed that Imre Nagy should become prime minister.

Nagy slowed down the pace of industrialisation and reversed the collectivisation of agriculture. But the Hungarian politburo was still dominated by Rákosi and the hardline Stalinists who hindered Nagy's reforms. Nagy suffered a heart attack and was dismissed in April 1955.

The signing of the Warsaw Pact in May 1955 indicated that the Soviet Union could no longer afford to treat the eastern European countries as totally subservient, but needed at least the pretence of an alliance of sovereign states. In June 1955 the Soviet leaders visited Tito. Rapprochement with Tito had far-reaching consequences. If Tito was no longer an outcast then 'Titoism' was not a crime and Rajk and the other victims had been innocent. Then in February 1956 Khrushchev delivered his famous 'secret speech' to the 20th Party Congress in which he denounced Stalin's mistakes.

Expression of dissent

Hungary was just beginning to ferment. Rákosi and his cronies were completely discredited. Nagy's supporters were growing, though Nagy himself moved very cautiously.

In Poland a strike at Poznań developed into a rising that was suppressed by Russian troops. Rákosi took this as an indication to crush dissent but on 18 July Anastas Mikoyan arrived from Moscow and curtly ordered Rákosi to resign. The Soviet leadership replaced Rákosi with Ernő Gerő.

In October a new crisis occurred in Poland. The Soviet Army began to move into Poland but then the decision was reversed by Khrushchev and Mikoyan. They allowed Wladyslaw Gomulka, who had been purged for 'Titoism' under Stalin, to become First Secretary of the Communist Party on 21 October.

BELOW *A symbol of oppression is toppled: the disfigured head of a statue of Stalin lies in a Budapest street. The denunciation of Stalin by Khrushchev in early 1956 encouraged Hungarian discontent.* BELOW RIGHT *Budapest youths demonstrate their support for Imre Nagy, who had formed a government the previous day, 27 October. It was a short-lived regime, however, for by the end of November Nagy was in Soviet custody. Two years later he was shot.*

Open revolt

The news that a communist country was to be allowed to find its own path to socialism brought the Hungarian crisis to a head. On Monday 22 October a student meeting at the Technological University produced a 14-part manifesto. Its demands included the withdrawal of Soviet troops from Hungary, a new government including Nagy, elections based on a secret ballot, freedom of the press and economic liberalisation. The meeting also decided to join a march organised for the next afternoon to express solidarity with Poland.

The march was to go from the statue of poet Sándor Petőfi to that of General Józef Bem, a Polish general who had fought for Hungary against Austria in 1849. The demonstration was first banned and then permitted. It passed off quietly but by 6pm a crowd of over 200,000 had moved on to the parliament building, calling for Imre Nagy. Nagy spoke but his confused and hesitant speech did not satisfy them.

Budapest

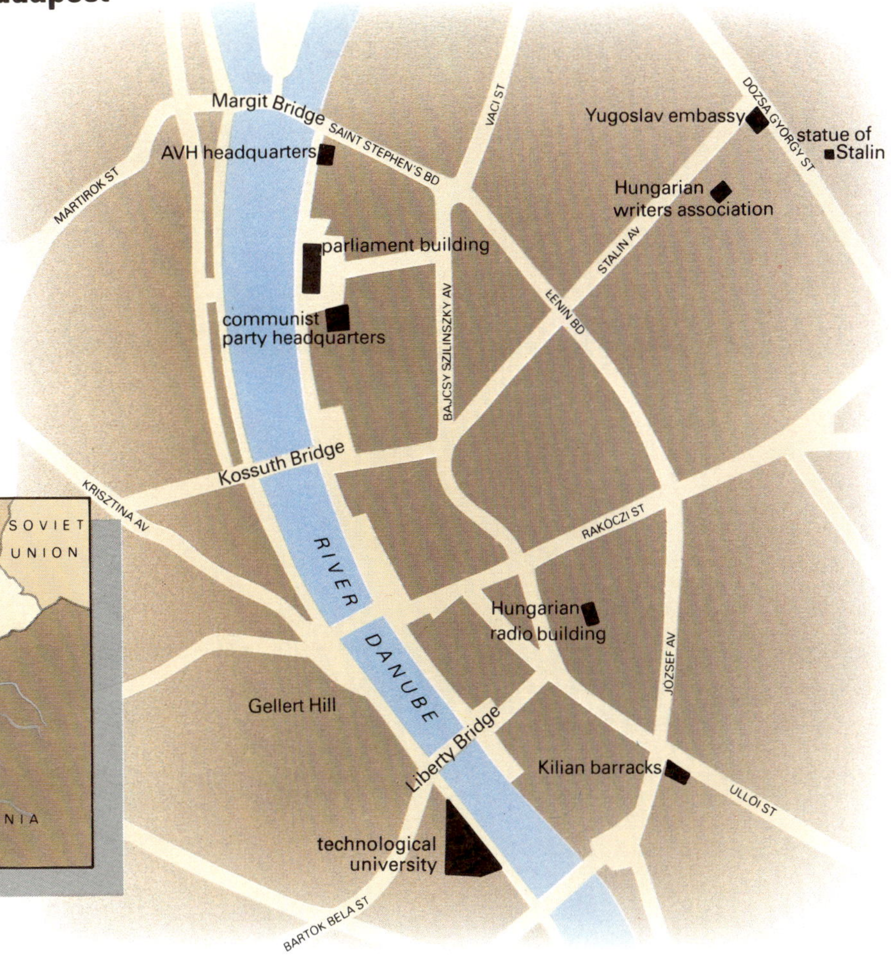

At 8pm Rákosi spoke on the radio. His threatening speech incensed the crowd. Many moved to the radio building to insist that their demands should be broadcast. The building was garrisoned by AVH (state security) troops and the situation got out of control. Tear gas was used, blanks were fired and then the AVH shot into the crowd.

The politburo was meeting all this while. Soviet troops had been sent for to overawe the demonstrators. It was also decided to appoint Nagy prime minister, although Nagy had refused to endorse the call for Soviet troops. Russian tanks arrived at 2am on 24 October and their presence only made matters worse. When a delegation from the Soviet politburo – Mikoyan and Mikhail Suslov – arrived from the airport in an armoured car, Russian tanks had already been destroyed by petrol bombs. Nagy was surrounded by AVH and could not act independently.

In the politburo Mikoyan and Suslov had insisted on Gerő's removal. He was replaced by János Kádár, a former victim of the purge. Outside Budapest other demonstrations took place and on 26 October AVH troops fired on a crowd in the town of Magyarovar, killing 87 people. In Budapest, fighting was concentrated on centres such as the Kilian Barracks where a Hungarian Army colonel, Pál Maléter, took command.

Mikoyan and Suslov returned to Moscow on the 26th, leaving Nagy trying to form a cabinet. By 27 October he was able to announce names which included leaders of the old non-communist parties. By 29 October Soviet tanks were leaving Budapest and Mikoyan and Suslov returned to Hungary the following day with a declaration respecting Hungarian national sovereignty.

Soviet volte-face

It seems most likely that the Soviet leadership had not yet made up its mind how to react to the Hungarian problem. But no decision had been taken when events in the Middle East changed the Soviet perspective. Israel attacked Egypt in Sinai and Britain and France announced their intention to intervene. This proof of Western aggressiveness was enough to persuade the Soviets to close ranks in Europe.

By 1 November it was clear that, despite their protestations, the Russians were not leaving Hungary. Instead more than 75,000 men were crossing from Russia, Romania and Czechoslovakia. Kádár, after promising to fight Russian tanks with his bare hands if necessary, hastened to the Soviet embassy and thence to Romania. The Soviet Union began to promise concessions. Negotiations on withdrawal from Budapest began on 3 November, but at midnight Soviet secret police arrested the Hungarian delegation led by Pál Maléter. Pretence was over; the Russians had been buying time to complete their invasion preparations.

At 5am on 4 November Nagy broadcast to the nation, announcing a Soviet attack on Budapest. The Battle of Budapest continued until 14 November, but it was a hopeless struggle. At the end Budapest had been reduced to the devastation of 1945. Nagy and his government took refuge in the Yugoslav embassy. Kádár returned with the Russians and on 22 November Nagy was persuaded to leave the embassy with promises of safe conduct. His party was immediately seized by the Russians and taken to Romania. There they were kept until June 1958, by which time the Kádár government was firmly in control. Nagy and the other leaders of the revolution were then shot.

Street Fighting

THE FIGHTING IN HUNGARY began on the night of 23 October when state security (AVH) troops opened fire on the crowd demonstrating at the radio station in Budapest. During the night elements of two Soviet motor rifle divisions from the normal garrison in Hungary entered Budapest and two more divisions moved across the Hungarian-Romanian border. These troops were not able to crush the rebellion and by 29 October were beginning to withdraw. This was partly because the troops stationed in Hungary showed considerable sympathy with the population.

The second phase of the fighting began on 4 November when a new wave of troops invaded Hungary from the Soviet Union, Romania and Czechoslovakia. This invasion may have involved as many as twelve divisions, with 3000 tanks. The second wave came prepared for a full-scale battle and they quickly gained the

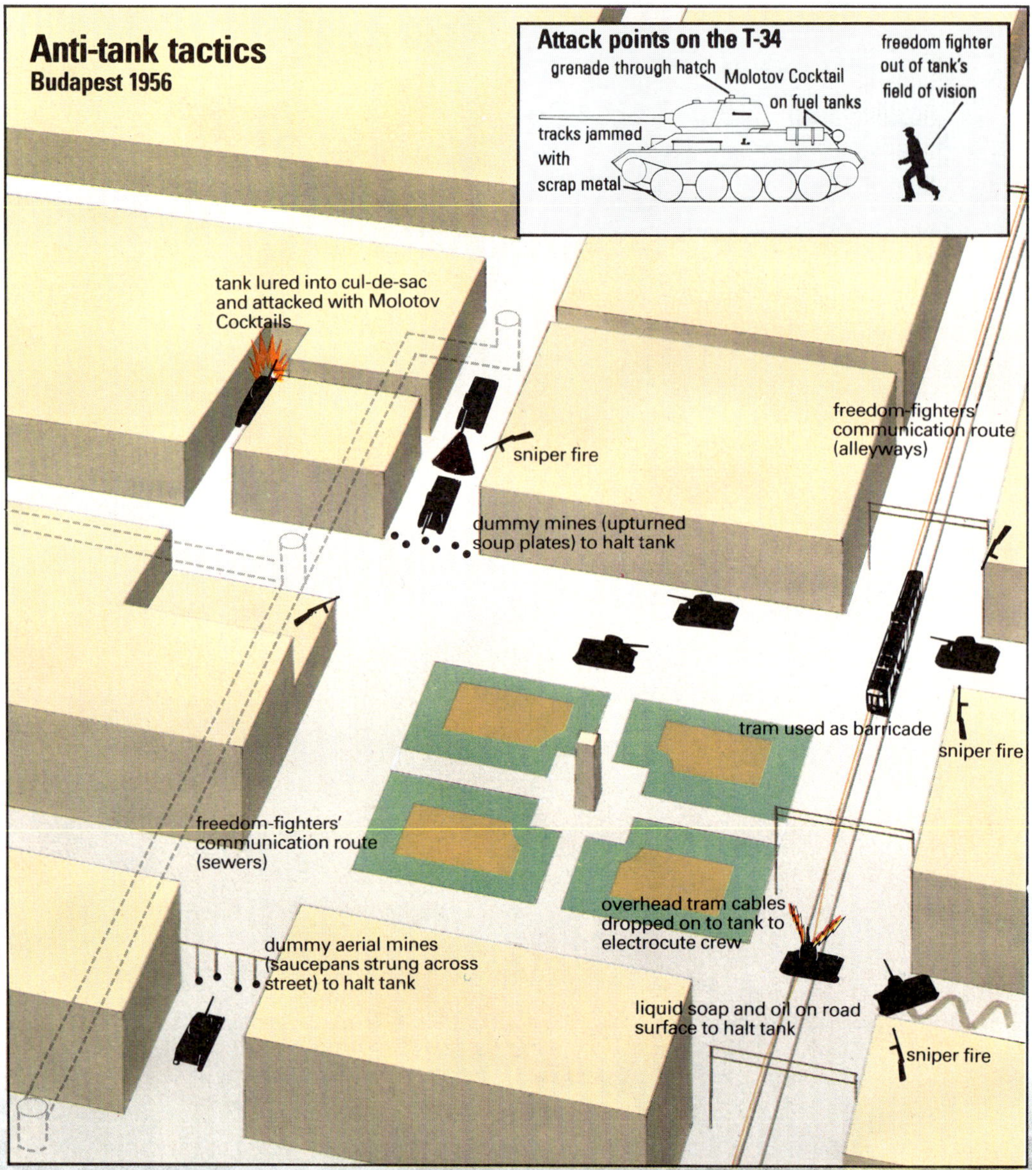

Soviet tanks crowd the centre of Budapest. What they lacked in mobility they made up for in crude firepower.

ABOVE *Freedom-fighters raise the Hungarian flag on a captured T54 in Budapest.* RIGHT *Insurgent Hungarian soldiers are transported to do battle with the Soviet invaders.* BELOW *Smoke rises behind a knot of onlookers as Soviet armour swings into action in the centre of Budapest, two days after the military intervention.*

upper hand. By 7 November victory was assured, although some resistance continued until 14 November in the towns and until the end of the year in the southern hills. In the fighting about 2000 Hungarians were killed in Budapest and about 1000 elsewhere. The Soviet casualties are unknown.

Tanks in the towns

Most of the fighting took place in the towns, especially Budapest. Although the final result was never in doubt the Russians were often at a disadvantage in this kind of fighting. The first units into Budapest were tank units. They must have been ordered to move before the fighting started and were intended to frighten the crowds into submission by a display of force. When faced with actual fighting in the streets the tanks had several weaknesses. There were not enough infantry with them and they could not stop the freedom-fighters dodging through alleys and sewers. This phase was characterised by tanks running up and down the main streets in search of their elusive enemy. It has been compared to a bull-fight.

The freedom-fighters were mostly armed with rifles and sub-machine guns and grenades. With these they could kill any Russian soldier who ventured out of his tank or even opened a hatch. Closed down in their tank the Russian troops were almost blind, able to see only out of the tiny vision ports in the driver's and commander's hatches. Their field of view upwards was particularly limited, so it was impossible to spot snipers in the upper floors of buildings. The Russians became jumpy and shot at anything they saw moving.

In the second intervention more balanced forces were used. The invading army surrounded Budapest, seizing the dominating ground of Gellert Hill on the west bank of the Danube. Here they installed artillery and rocket

Soap, saucepans and soup plates

While a tank was moving it was least exposed to attack so the Hungarians became very cunning at halting tanks. Barricades of trams were used to block boulevards and squares. Tanks were lured into cul-de-sacs and then surrounded. Liquid soap was poured onto roads, so that tank tracks could not grip. Bales of silk were unrolled on the roadway and covered with oil, which sent tanks sliding hopelessly.

Freedom-fighters built dummy mines out of bricks covered with planks and rubbish; an even simpler method was to leave upturned soup plates in the road. Too frightened to leave their tanks the Russians could not investigate these strange devices. One road was blocked to tanks for two days by rows of upturned soup plates which were taken for anti-tank mines. Another trick was to suspend saucepans full of water from cables across the roads, which the Russians took for some sort of aerial mine. At night freedom-fighters would tap on the sides of tanks. If the crew were foolish enough to open a hatch a grenade was dropped in.

Russian tactics were basically simple – to employ the maximum firepower against any target. If it was suspected that a sniper was hiding in a building tank guns destroyed the building. In the last stages of the battle the Russians relied on indiscriminate terror to end resistance. Queues of housewives were shot down by machine guns; aircraft and artillery levelled buildings. When the last 30 defenders of the Kilian Barracks surrendered they were shot down as they emerged.

launchers and began their attack with a bombardment. Then tank forces sped down the main roads to seize the river bridges and the main buildings. Finally tanks and infantry were used to clear the main areas of resistance. This was a conventional military operation in which the Russians used the same techniques as they had in the last battles of World War II.

Weapons of the insurgents

Against this military might the Hungarians had very little more than courage and ingenuity. Most of the Hungarian Army stayed out of the battle, though some individuals did join the fighting. Pál Maléter, a Hungarian Army colonel, added five tanks to the defences of the Kilian Barracks when he joined the fight. A few anti-tank guns were available but to deal with the tanks the freedom-fighters had to rely mostly on home-made weapons. They were helped by the training in guerrilla warfare which was part of the Soviet-imposed curriculum in schools and universities. The Russians had also insisted that factory workmen should be formed into a sort of Home

ABOVE *Hungarian freedom-fighters man a machine gun and use the cover provided by a burned-out vehicle in Budapest.* RIGHT *The face of insurgency: a teenage girl cradles a captured Soviet sub-machine gun.*

Guard and the factory armouries and the police stations provided most of the insurgents' weapons. It was reported that Russian soldiers were willing to sell their personal weapons and even their tanks for food after the failure of supply arrangements.

The Molotov cocktail was the Hungarians' basic anti-tank weapon. It was easily made by filling a bottle with petrol. A loose cork, wrapped in rag, was fitted in the neck. When a tank approached, the bottle was turned upside-down to soak the rag which was then lit and the bottle thrown at the tank. The rear deck was the best target, in the hope of igniting fuel tanks or the engine compartment.

The first wave of Russian tanks were mostly T34s, a World War II design which was quite vulnerable to such weapons. However the second wave mostly consisted of T54s, which were not so easy to disable.

The Congolese Bloodbath

The bloody civil war in the Congo quickly took on a wider significance as outside forces became involved

Peter Janke

Katangese soldiers take cover during fighting in Elisabethville, the capital. Katanga seceded from the newly independent Congo in July 1960 but its revolt was ended in 1963 after United Nations forces defeated Moise Tshombe's army.

SEVERAL THOUSAND PEOPLE died in the Congo crisis, a conflict marked by political and tribal violence rather than conventional warfare. The murderous events that followed independence from Belgium hold distinct lessons for history. They exposed, for instance, the grave inadequacies of parliamentary institutions in post-colonial Africa. Furthermore, not only did the Soviet Union unmask its intent to fill the political vacuum left by departing colonialists, but private capitalists sought to carve financial fiefs from the mineral-rich province of Katanga. For the United Nations the Congo provided a test case for military intervention.

A bloody independence

On 30 June 1960 King Baudouin presided over the independence celebrations of the vast territories of the Belgian Congo. Even at the time, independence was considered precipitate. It was the hasty response of a small European country determined to rid itself of responsibility for growing colonial disorders. Congolese representatives from a disparate but élite corps of black civil servants, teachers and priests had reached agreement in Brussels earlier in the year on a constitution. Embodying a bicameral legislature, it divided authority between one central and six provincial governments, but scarcely survived the elections, which were marked by violent skirmishes between the major divisions of the country's 200 ethnic groups.

Elections served, nonetheless, to bring to the fore Patrice Lumumba, who two years before had founded the Congolese National Movement, which emerged as the strongest single party, although with nothing like a majority. Lumumba was exceptional in that he looked beyond tribal politics towards pan-African unity, but he failed to prevent the outbreak of civil strife on the very day following the independence ceremonies. Black troops mutinied against their Belgian officers; in the towns whites were intimidated causing a sudden, panicked flight. Thousands crossed the river from the capital, Leopoldville (now known as Kinshasa), to Congo-Brazzaville, while others left by air.

Those unlucky enough to be caught without transport in Katanga (Shaba) province were rescued by 800 Belgian paratroops flown in at the request of the provincial premier, Moise Tshombe, on 10 July. In the confusion Tshombe declared independence for Katanga, accusing Lumumba of wishing to sell out to the Soviet Union. In desperation Lumumba appealed for assistance to the United Nations, which within days flew in 3500 troops from Tunisia, Morocco, Ghana and Ethiopia, and 625 Swedish troops from the UN emergency force in the Gaza Strip.

Part of the urgency was to forestall Soviet intervention, for on 14 July the Congolese

government appealed to the Soviet Union for aid against Belgium, which thereupon increased its troop levels. Nikita Khrushchev responded with a 'hands off' warning to the West. 'The Soviet Union,' he said, 'will not shrink from resolute measures to curb the aggression.'

After the event it was clear that Khrushchev had simply taken advantage of confusion to establish a Soviet presence in Africa. He pushed his candidate, Lumumba, who used a dozen Soviet Ilyushin Il-14 twin-engined aircraft to ferry loyal troops to the secessionist areas. The Soviet presence was short-lived, however, for the UN occupied and closed the Congo's airports to all but their own flights. More than 100 Soviet trucks had already been landed on the coast at Matadi in support of Lumumba's centralist government. President Dwight D. Eisenhower 'deplored' such interference which seemed, he said, 'to be motivated entirely by the Soviet Union's political designs in Africa'.

Lumumba deposed

Deprived of his backing, Lumumba succumbed to a military coup on 14 September. The coup was led by the Congolese Army Chief of Staff, Joseph Mobutu, who expelled Czech and Soviet Army personnel and closed European communist bloc embassies in Leopoldville. Lumumba remained under house arrest until late November, when he escaped in a dramatic attempt to rejoin his supporters in Oriental province. Troops loyal to Mobutu captured him and returned him to the capital, where he was imprisoned.

Lumumba's supporters threatened to cut off the heads of whites in Stanleyville (Kisangani) in retaliation unless he were freed. Antoine Gizenga, Lumumba's closest associate, proclaimed a new government in Stanleyville on 13 December 1960, again backed by Soviet air power.

Far from vanishing, Lumumba's support grew in Oriental and Kivu provinces so that clashes with Mobutu's forces became more frequent. The engagements, however, seldom involved more than 100 men. In early January 1961 Lumumbist officers invaded northern Katanga to support a revolt of Baluba tribesmen against Tshombe's secessionist regime. The transfer, therefore, of Lumumba from Leopoldville to Katanga, allegedly for 'safety' reasons, in fact sent him to his death. Tshombe ordered him to be shot on arrival.

The murder shocked the world. Belgian embassies were attacked by angry demonstrators in some countries. President Nasser confiscated all Belgian property in Egypt and on 14 February led the first moves, with the Soviet Union, to recognise the Lumumbist government in Oriental province. East Germany, Ghana and Yugoslavia followed suit.

This action was accompanied by a call for a new all-African force to replace the UN troops in the Congo. Khrushchev took the initiative, backed by India's prime minister Jawaharlal Nehru, and the heads of 66 other governments. Khrushchev accused UN Secretary General Dag Hammarskjöld of playing the role of 'chief assassin'. Inside the country, 300 troops supporting Gizenga seized control of the capital of Kasai province on 24 February but failed in a bid for Katanga. Very few lives were lost: central government forces either withdrew or temporarily sided with the rebels. Such advances probably gave the Lumumbists control of three of the country's six provinces.

Communist support for Gizenga

Gizenga had assumed Lumumba's mantle, although lacking the qualities which had distinguished the latter from his bureaucratic colleagues in the old civil service. Backed by the communist states, Gizenga expelled the consular authorities of those countries which had not recognised his government. In July he agreed to join a central cabinet under Cyrille Adoula and to participate in a parliament in which

Lumumbists held the key posts. Anticipating his early dominance of the new government, Gizenga dissolved his Stanleyville base on 18 August, encouraged by Adoula's socialism and neutral stand in world affairs. Both men were determined to end Katanga's secession, which was largely made possible by Belgian mining interests, particularly the Union Minière du Haut-Katanga.

However, the new partnership did not last long. In November, Gizenga returned to Stanleyville and mutinies against both central authority and the UN military presence broke out. In one instance at Kindu, pro-Gizenga forces captured 13 Italian airmen, whose bodies were cut into pieces and distributed to bloodthirsty bystanders. Such atrocities were part of a more general picture of tribal massacres, set off by the sudden withdrawal of colonial authority.

Although repudiating the central government, Gizenga failed to consolidate his base in Stanleyville. His own party split, and fighting broke out in January 1962. Some 300 followers surrendered on 14 January and Gizenga was taken prisoner.

China's involvement

Stanleyville provided a base for opposition to Leopoldville which outside forces could take advantage of. In 1964 Pierre Mulele took up the challenge, having spent 18 months abroad in Cairo and Peking. He led a revolt in January and took control of most of the eastern Kwilu district. Further uprisings extended a tenuous hold over Kivu province and even north Katanga.

This time outside support came from Red China, through its embassy in Brazzaville. Since the United Nations had ended its operations in June 1964 the central government, now headed by the Katangan separatist Tshombe, sought and received aid from Belgium and the United States. On 13 August four US Lockheed C-130 transport planes carrying three helicopters arrived in Leopoldville. On 7 September the Chinese-backed rebels announced the formation of a Congolese People's Republic, dedicated to overthrowing Tshombe's government. Heading the movement was Christophe Gbenye, who had worked with Gizenga in 1961, Pierre Mulele and, in charge of military operations, Nicholas Olenga. In Stanleyville they held some 500 Europeans hostage against possible central government air raids.

Tshombe hits back

Tshombe's offensive began in November. Unable to rely upon black troops he engaged mercenaries from Europe, South Africa and the United States to recapture the Kamina base in north Katanga and to press on along the road to Stanleyville. On 24 November 600 Belgian paratroops re-took Stanleyville in a combined assault with ground troops led by 150 mercenaries. The rebels fled, but not before killing 29 hostages. In all, 1800 whites and 300 blacks were rescued from rebel captivity before the paratroops withdrew on 1 December 1964.

Dramatic as this action was, it merely served to save European lives. The rebel hold on the Bunia-Wamba-Watsa region remained. Tshombe's mercenary-led forces continued to flush out rebel support and to rescue white hostages in the outlying areas near Yangambi and Wamba. During this particular phase of the conflict more than 150 white hostages, including priests and nuns, were slain.

Responding to Tshombe's campaign, the Soviet Union agreed to finance and supply a joint Egyptian-Algerian military airlift to the rebels. Meanwhile the rebel leadership had fled to Sudan, and during the first half of 1965 Tshombe succeeded in consolidating the central government position. In exile the rebel movement split and by September Egyptian and Sudanese support was largely withdrawn. In all, this running rebellion probably cost the death of 9000 people, black and white. Mulele, the principal inheritor of Lumumba's position, was lured back in 1968 and executed, while Gizenga lived on in exile.

Patrice Lumumba (TOP LEFT), *deposed after less than three months in power, was shot on the orders of Moise Tshombe* (TOP RIGHT), *who took Katanga out of the republic in protest at Lumumba's policies.* BELOW *A government paratrooper on alert in Stanleyville, scene of many revolts against General Mobutu's regime.*

In the elections of 1965 Tshombe attempted to form his own national party (CONACO), but lost. The president dismissed Tshombe, but before the newcomers could settle into office General Mobutu deposed President Joseph Kasavubu on 25 November and assumed power himself. Opposition to Mobutu surfaced in 1966, but the leaders were arrested in May and hung after having been found guilty by a special military tribunal. Once again, Stanleyville revolted in July; behind the resistance were 2500 Katangese gendarmes who supported Tshombe. Mobutu recovered control of the town in September, however.

For this, and for further attempting to recruit mercenaries abroad, Tshombe was tried *in absentia* the following year and sentenced to death. An attempt to hijack him failed in 1967, and he died in Algeria two years later of heart failure. The six leaders of the mutiny faced trial at the same time: two were subsequently shot, three were sentenced to 20 years imprisonment and one was acquitted. Thereafter, Mobutu ruled the Congo, which he renamed Zaire, in comparative peace.

Looking back on the conflict, three facets stand out prominently – Soviet involvement, United Nations intervention and the use of mercenaries. The first factor occurred again in subsequent conflicts, particularly in Ethiopia. The United Nations was assailed on all sides, but endeavoured to support the central government, both against the secession of Katanga – to the irritation of Belgium, Britain and France – and against Stanleyville, to the annoyance of the communist bloc. Its total force amounted to 20,000 men drawn from 34 nations, of whom 126 died in action.

Mercenaries and their Masters

MERCENARIES flew into Katanga (now known as Shaba province) in 1960 at Moise Tshombe's request. They were to reassure fearful and beleaguered whites, upon whom local mining operations – and thus the prosperity of Katanga – depended. Mercenaries were the answer to Tshombe's secessionist dreams, as well as the ambitions of the Belgian-owned Union Minière company, his principal supporter.

They arrived at the same time as Major Crèvecoeur, a Belgian whose task was to create a Katangan gendarmerie based upon Belgian junior officers and police. With the gendarmerie in being and numbering some 10,000, the 400 or so mercenaries acted as an élite spearhead, operating in columns of eight to nine jeeps and receiving weapons and uniforms from the gendarmerie.

An international force

Most of the men were Belgian ex-servicemen recruited in Brussels, while others had answered advertisements in Johannesburg, Salisbury and Bulawayo. Only on arrival were they issued with their service contracts. Basic pay was up to £180 a month, plus allowances and other inducements. Some were Frenchmen who had seen service in Algeria while others were British. The Compagnie Internationale, as the outfit was known, was commanded by a British officer. They were tough men, physically fit, who had joined up for a variety of personal and political motives. Their assignments were hard, and there is no doubt that they saved the lives of missionaries in isolated areas. They were present in Elisabethville (now called Lubumbashi), Kolwezi, Jadotville and Albertville (Kalémié), indeed wherever the United Nations forces were not.

In March 1961 Katanga appeared threatened by the penetration in the north of some 400 Lumumbists who captured Manono. The gendarmerie was used to repel the invasion, but the mercenaries spearheaded the attack which recaptured the town. However, they were not prepared to fight the UN forces which were being drafted into Katanga to bring an end to secession. Pressure, both internationally and from their home governments, was applied to the men, and most were repatriated. By early September 1961, 273 had left and a further 65 were waiting to go.

A year later the Katangan gendarmerie had also largely disappeared, with most of the recruits returning to the land. Some were integrated into the central government forces while others left for Angola to fight with the Portuguese. When Tshombe came to power in Leopoldville (Kinshasa) in 1964, as leader of a reunited nation, he had need again for the service of gendarmes and mercenaries.

TOP *Anti-government mercenaries and Katangan gendarmes at a mortar and machine-gun post at Bukavu, which they captured in August 1967 and held for two months.* ABOVE *A mercenary demonstrates machine-gun technique.*

Mercenary activity – Belgian Congo

'Mad Mike's' men

The year 1964 saw some of the worst atrocities in the Congo conflict, largely involving tribal rivalries. Assailed by Soviet-backed forces from Stanleyville and opposition from socialist Congo-Brazzaville, Tshombe made use of Major Mike Hoare. Most of these mercenaries were recruited in southern Africa and were offered well in excess of £100 a month for a six-month contract and a payment of £7000 to next-of-kin in the event of death. On this occasion no more than 250 mercenaries were involved, mostly under the command of Hoare who, for his services in the Congo, was promoted to Lieutenant Colonel in January 1965.

He engaged further recruits that year, once the original contracts had expired, and was active on the Sudanese border to prevent communist arms getting through to the regime in Stanleyville (now called Kisangani). Hoare's mercenaries successively recaptured Mahagi, Aru, Aba, Faradje and Watsa in March. The operation sealed the border, a major blow to the rebels who never recovered the initiative. In April, Hoare declared the war in the north-east finished. He then turned his attention to Bondo, which fell on 30 May. A French-speaking mercenary group occupied Titule. When the last pockets of resistance had died out, some 35 mercenaries were dead.

That was not the end of the mercenary story in the Congo. In 1965 General Joseph Mobutu assumed power in a bloodless coup; in the following year, a mutiny of some 2500 Katangese gendarmes supported by mercenaries broke out in Stanleyville on 23 July. While about 30 Belgian mercenaries promoted the coup, a further 70 under the command of the French Colonel Bob Denard stood by Mobutu. Behind the attempted coup was Tshombe, then in Madrid, and certain Belgian interests.

Mobutu and Denard thrashed the rebels.

In 1967 Mobutu's rule was again troubled by mercenary commandos, who landed at Stanleyville on 5 July. An aircraft carrying Tshombe had been diverted to Algiers, whence Mobutu was seeking his extradition since sentence of death had been passed on him, and the mercenaries' landing appeared to be related to this. Colonel Denard, who was involved with about 200 colleagues, was wounded in the fighting and was flown out to Salisbury, Rhodesia. Stanleyville and Bukavu were retaken by government forces. The mercenaries left behind under Belgian Major Jean Schramme took hostages, most of whom were later evacuated by the Red Cross.

The mercenaries moved to Schramme's estate about 240km (150 miles) from Stanleyville in a convoy of 27 trucks. With them went 40 to 50 white civilians, some as hostages. Schramme wanted to replace Mobutu with Tshombe's associates. On 9 August his men captured Bukavu with the help of some 900 Katangese gendarmes. All whites had left the town,

ABOVE *The end of the road for Katanga: UN forces lead away captured mercenaries near Elisabethville in January 1963.* LEFT *Mike Hoare (right) with his bodyguard and a Belgian pilot after restoring Albertville airport to government control in 1964.*

which became Schramme's headquarters. Skirmishes continued with disastrous consequences for black and white civilians alike. Bukavu was retaken in early November, when Schramme and his followers retreated.

As the government concentrated its attention upon Bukavu, a further mercenary attack, from Angola into Katanga, occurred on 2 November, capturing 16 trucks and a train. Dilolo was a target for a second attack led by Denard, but the intrusions came to nothing. So ended an inglorious chapter in individual enterprise.

Castro's Revolution

Fidel Castro came to power in Cuba by exploiting the unpopularity of a corrupt and high-handed regime

H. P. Willmott

ON 1 JANUARY 1959 the dictator of Cuba, General Fulgencio Batista, fled the country for the safety of the United States. His forces had disintegrated as a result of reverses at the hands of insurgents led by Dr Fidel Castro, who entered Havana on 8 January to a tumultuous reception from a population weary of the corruption and tyranny of successive regimes. Cubans were confident that the fall of Batista would usher in a new period of open and honest democratic government in the manner suggested, before his suicide, by Eddy Chibás. Public support for Castro stemmed in large part from his claim to be the embodiment of Chibás's ideas.

The Cuban revolution turned out very differently from the notions so readily expressed in the days following the flight of a harsh dictator. Not merely were most Cubans surprised by events, but so, too, were many revolutionaries in Latin America who saw the Cuban revolution as an inspiration and model for their own attempts to overthrow conservative and reactionary regimes. They were actively encouraged in this by Castro himself for he viewed the revolutionaries as a means by which he might break down the blockade that the Organisation of American States had placed on Cuba as a result of his growing alignment with the Soviet bloc.

The revolution was much misunderstood, both at the time and subsequently. To a large extent this arose from too ready an acceptance of the 'three lessons' projected by one of Castro's lieutenants, the Argentinian Ernesto ('Che') Guevara. These lessons were, firstly, that popular forces could defeat established authority; secondly, that the countryside was the natural area of insurgent activity and, thirdly, that revolutionaries did not have to await a crisis in their society before acting – what Lenin termed waiting for the 'revolutionary moment' – but could provoke a political and social upheaval by vigorous action. This, he believed, could be accomplished by a small, heavily armed and hard-hitting force, moving quickly and registering military successes against the security forces. This was a concept that Guevara tried to apply in Bolivia, and other revolutionaries tried to put into effect with equally disastrous results.

Castro's landfall

Castro and 81 followers landed in Cuba on 2 December 1956 from the yacht *Granma* in an attempt to raise revolt in the eastern provinces against the dictatorship of Batista. The landing was late and therefore failed to coincide with a series of armed actions that had been planned for 30 November in various parts of the island. These actions were quickly suppressed by the security forces, who also discovered Castro's party. Within a matter of days Castro's small force was surrounded and most of its members were killed. When the survivors regrouped in the Sierra Maestra, it was found that about 15 were left to carry on the struggle.

Castro's forces in the Sierra never exceeded 300 in the first year of the campaign. That they finally won was the result more of the failures of the Cuban Army and the shortcomings of the Batista regime than any strength on the insurgents' part. With such a small force throughout the whole of 1957, the task of eliminating the insurgents should have posed no problem to a trained and

Castro attends a training session for his troops. By patiently building support in the countryside and choosing carefully the encounters he fought – and then winning them – he undermined Batista's shaky regime and completely demoralised the Cuban Army.

Castro's forces, riding on captured tanks, enter Havana in triumph on 8 January 1959, a week after Batista had fled the country.

properly led force. But Batista's army lacked effectiveness, for the dictator placed loyalty above professional competence.

The ordinary rank-and-file had very little proper training and even less enthusiasm for either campaigning or Batista's regime. The officer corps was equally bad. The one really good officer in the field against Castro, Colonel Barrera Perez, made himself *persona non grata* with his superiors, and was removed from his command. The corps suffered from blatant favoritism, and many members opposed the regime.

The defensive mentality that came to cripple the Batista army in part derived from the ability of Castro's men to pick off scouts in those relatively few contacts that took place in the Sierra in the course of 1957. Battlefield successes for Castro were few in 1957, however. Though some barracks were raided and arms captured, in that first year Castro's forces generally tried to avoid contact with the security forces. The operations they did carry out were usually against economic targets such as sugar mills.

Batista loses support

From the very start of the campaign Batista's answer to insurgency was casual and brutal, the security forces murdering and torturing on a wide scale, often indiscriminately. The response to some scattered insurgent activity just before Christmas 1956 in Oriente province was the murder by the army of 22 members of opposition parties, two being hanged and their bodies left on public display at Holguín. In the aftermath of the attack on the presidential palace in Havana in March 1957, Batista allowed his forces to kill and torture seemingly at will. The naval officers' mutiny at Cienfuegos in September 1957 saw the same cycle of action and counter-terror repeated. The assassination of individuals closely associated with the regime, such as Colonel Fermin Cowley in Holguín in November, was answered by the reprisal killing of six men.

Such brutality became widespread. It alienated the Batista regime from the large professional middle class, which should have been its firmest supporters. The counter-terror programme divided society and led to an exodus of able-bodied men to the hills. It was safer for those with radical sympathies to be in the mountains than on the streets of the major cities.

In the course of the campaign, many prominent people in Cuban public life gave information, money, support or direct aid to the anti-Batista forces. This support was invaluable to Castro, but it was not enough in itself to win the campaign. Not until the beginning of 1958 did Castro really begin to develop firm support among the peasantry of Oriente province. Individual peasants had earlier joined the insurgents and there was goodwill for Castro among those who had been cleared off their lands by the army or by landlords who used the insurgency as an excuse to drive out peasants and steal from them what little they had. From mid-1958 onwards, however, the support of both the peasantry in Oriente and the urban middle classes proved decisive.

By then there was a rough balance between the insurgents and the security forces. In numbers the latter were overwhelmingly superior, but in terms of morale, determination, concentration and effectiveness the balance increasingly lay with Castro. The army had become badly demoralised by its failure in May to eliminate Castro once and for all. Seventeen battalions, with armoured and air support, embarked upon Operation Verano, but it was a fiasco. Failure resulted mainly from the poor control exercised by both staff and field officers, but Castro's forces did achieve one major success when an entire battalion, the 18th, was destroyed as an effective fighting unit in an ambush.

Castro then prepared to launch a series of offensives into eastern and central Cuba in order to divide the island before making a general advance on Havana. Events quickly assumed a momentum of their own, and what few armed encounters there were took on a significance and importance out of all proportion to their individual size or military effect. Batista's army often fled in the face of Castro's troops. Batista made one last effort to rally his forces around Santa Clara in December; a series of actions were fought, the tactical aspects being determined largely by the presence of an armoured train on which Batista pinned great hopes. He saw the writing on the wall even before the 'battle', however, since he had given orders to keep an aircraft on standby to take him – and as much gold and foreign currency as he could assemble – into exile. And that is what happened.

Reasons for Victory

IT IS EASY to see the basis on which Che Guevara framed the 'three lessons' that he drew from the outcome of the Cuban revolution. The revolution contained all the ingredients of a real-life adventure story with a strong hero, through sheer force of personality, leading a small group of men to success against overwhelming odds. From a rural base this man conducted operations that gained widespread support for his cause and, ultimately, victory in the field over a superior enemy. Such is the picture that can be drawn, but it is a misleading one.

The truth is that Cuban society was deeply divided and ripe for revolution well before the start of Fidel Castro's campaign. Castro's great achievement was in bringing various opposition factions together under his control. He orchestrated and gave leadership to what had hitherto been a hopelessly fragmented opposition. He drew it all together in the last three months of 1958.

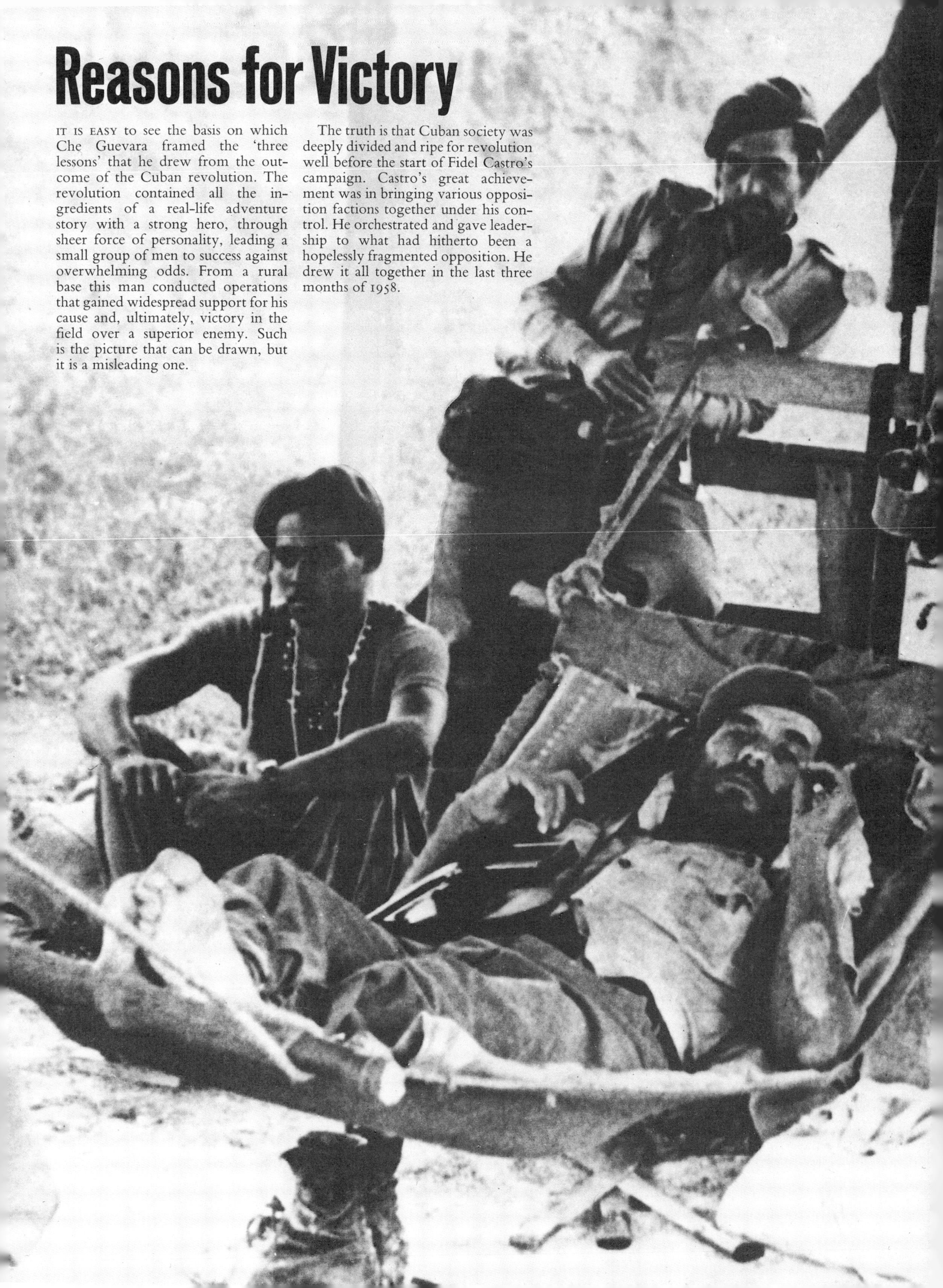

Cuban society in the early 1950s was very volatile and in the process of disintegration, mainly because of growing disenchantment with the government of General Fulgencio Batista. Probably the most important single cause was the staggering, blatant corruption carried out by those in government. Democratic government in Cuba was almost totally discredited between 1944 and 1952, and Batista's rule was no different. At one time ex-President Grau San Martin stood accused of misappropriating $174 million. Corruption was practised at every level of government activity, and deputy ministers finished up as multi-millionaires. 'Clean' government was the critical issue in the presidential elections scheduled for April 1952, but these elections never took place because of a coup in March that brought Batista to power.

Growing dissatisfaction

Batista had once been popular. As a sergeant he had led the 1933 coup that overthrew the venal regime of General Gerardo Machado. Batista retired from office in 1944, loaded with self-bestowed honours, rank and wealth. By Cuban standards he had been capable and reasonably honest – the wartime boom certainly helped him – and he restored the country to democracy. Despite democracy's failures, the coup of 1952 ended the prospect of a more honest type of government. Once in power, Batista ruled Cuba as if it was his personal fief. Middle-class sensitivities were more than a little bruised – and society's nationalist sentiments were inflamed – by the fact that the whole country was, literally, prostituted to the Americans and to Batista's self-interest. This became increasingly intolerable to Cuban opinion.

The combination of injured nationalism, outrage at government corruption and Batista's disregard for constitutional rights were at the basis of urban and middle-class resistance to the regime. This resistance was critical to Castro's success. Towns provided Castro with supplies and recruits throughout the campaign, and opposition groups in the cities tied down security forces whose participation in the rural struggle might well have proved decisive. At no time did Batista's forces have a secure base area, and the grip of the security forces on the towns became necessarily tenuous.

Critically important in the falling-away of support for Batista was the fact that the two great pillars of stability and order in Latin American society, the church and the army, were both weak in Cuba. They lacked power, influence and standing. Even the leading clerics of Havana turned against the regime in 1958 because of its disregard for the rule of law and its recourse to arbitrary powers as the insurgency unexpectedly moved into its final phase.

Throughout the campaign the armed forces totalled about 30,000 men, yet in the fighting against Castro's forces the army lost a total of only about 200 killed. As much as anything the Cuban Army was defeated psychologically, almost before any shots were fired. Certainly the unwillingness of the army to get to grips with the insurgents was a decisive factor in the outcome of the campaign and reflected the widespread dissatisfaction in Cuban society.

OPPOSITE *Members of Castro's army at a resting post.* ABOVE RIGHT *Castro fires a rifle fitted with telescopic sights at his base in the Sierra Maestra, from which he launched guerrilla raids in 1957 and 1958.* RIGHT *The bodies of armed rebels lie beside a truck outside an army barracks near Matanzas in 1956. Eleven men had attacked the base and were killed by the Cuban troops.*

An Isolated Success

IN THE AFTERMATH of the Cuban revolution it was inevitable that any genuinely popular reform programme would threaten American interests on the island, and the American and Cuban governments very quickly found themselves on a collision course. As the United States took steps to cut Cuba off from her traditional markets, Fidel Castro turned to the Soviet bloc for aid and attempted to stir up revolution throughout Latin America.

The example and success of Cuba had excited revolutionary groups throughout the continent, mainly because Castro had broken the myth of invincibility that had hitherto surrounded the Americans and the armies of Latin America. Time was to show, however, that no amount of revolutionary enthusiasm and endeavour could overcome certain basic realities that proved insurmountable obstacles to revolutionary success in Latin America.

Cuba was not typical of Latin America generally. Cuban society, its historical development and its values, the position of the church and army and the island's geography, terrain and vegetation all set it apart. The conditions that had led to Castro's success found no echo in Latin America, and Che Guevara's thesis of revolution was uncritically accepted and applied with disastrous results.

Governments forewarned

There were many attempts throughout Latin America to establish insurgent movements in rural areas, almost all of which collapsed at the outset. By proclaiming his intention of promoting revolution, Castro alerted governments and armies throughout the continent to take appropriate steps. This they did with remarkable effectiveness. It was no coincidence, for example, that just one week separated the Bolivian Army's deployment of the final elements of its one and only (American-trained) Ranger battalion and Guevara's capture and death in 1967. The armies of Latin America were tougher, forewarned and reasonably competent and hence very different from that of Batista in Cuba, and they did not give their opponents the second chance that Castro had enjoyed at the start of his campaign in the Sierra Maestra.

Obstacles to revolution

There were obvious local and minor factors in the long list of revolutionary reverses in the 1960s. The refusal of communist parties to involve themselves in insurgency, the poor field-

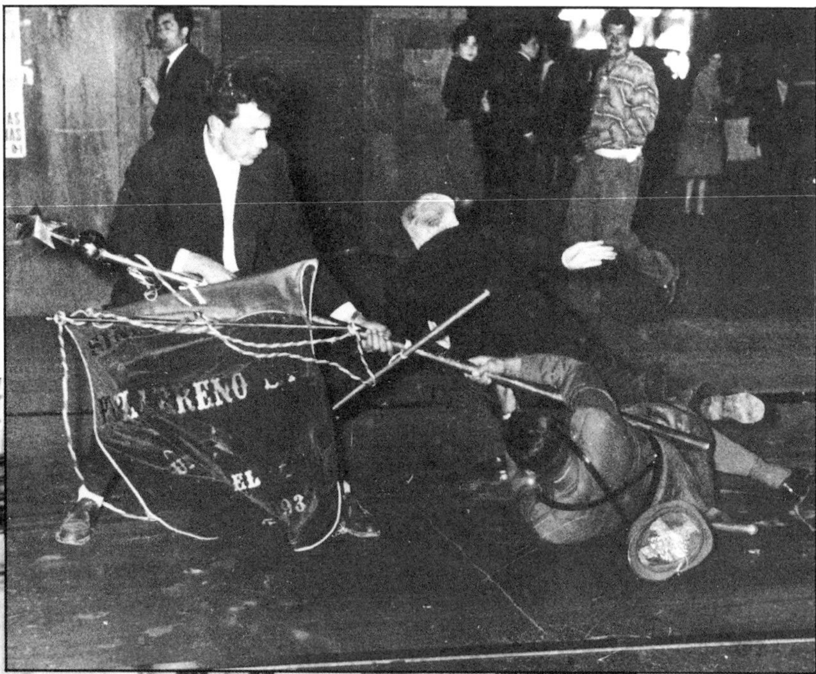

craft and proficiency in arms of most revolutionaries from urban backgrounds, the lack of good leaders, poor intelligence and planning, are just a few. Four general considerations are relevant, however.

Firstly, after Cuba the United States set out to extinguish the embers of revolution fanned by Castro. With Vietnam absorbing most attention and resources, Latin America had to be kept quiet. In the early 1960s the Americans took on the re-equipping, reorganising and retraining of Latin American armies. Moreover, the United States encouraged limited reform and propaganda programmes that helped Latin American governments and armies to keep control and crush insurgents before they had time to establish themselves.

Secondly, revolutionaries could no longer pose as the radical alternative to the established order. In Cuba, Castro received the benefit of middle-class doubts: he was an unknown and untried quantity and was preferred to a man Cubans had come to know only too well. His identification with communism, however, meant that South American revolutionaries came to be seen as embryo communist challenges to the status quo.

Social stability

Thirdly, throughout Latin America there was a deeply engrained conservatism and stability at all levels of society. Even in urban areas the combination of unemployment, under-employment, inflation and intense competition for jobs made for social stability rather than unrest. Those in employment wanted to stay in work; those coming on to the labour market had to find jobs. Neither could afford to be identified as radicals and trouble-makers. The only organisations that could have provided the basis of insurgency, the communist parties, supported the status quo while the flight of people from the countryside to the towns also served as a stabilising force in rural areas.

The depopulation of the countryside served to prevent the pressure on land becoming so great as to emerge as an explosive social and political issue. Moreover, the Indians of the Andes were not attracted to social revolution. Some even lived outside the cash economy while others – notably in Bolivia, the very area where Guevara tried to establish himself – were already beneficiaries of land redistribution programmes that were more than adequate to meet their needs. Although major unrest among the Indian peasantry in Peru did come about as a result of revolutionary activity, this was the exception to the rule.

The final reason for failure was the problem of movement on the part of insurgent groups. In the Andes the revolutionary groups found that the jungle gave immediate cover, but only at the expense of mobility, concentration and effectiveness. Steep gorges and fast-flowing rivers forced movement overland in a manner that the security forces could control with relative ease. As Guevara found to his cost in 1967, an insurgent group in the field was the antithesis of a fast, mobile, hard-hitting force. The point was not lost on those survivors of insurgency movements at the end of the 1960s as they began to drift back to the towns; and it helped lead, in part, to the development of urban guerrilla warfare.

OPPOSITE *Anti-government demonstrations in Chile (top) and Argentina (bottom). A trade union leader falls to the ground in Santiago as a worker and policeman fight for his banner during a trade union march in 1960. In 1962 in Buenos Aires, Perónist deputies barred from parliament were dispersed by troops with tear gas.*
BELOW LEFT *Fidel Castro proved a dynamic leader but other revolutionaries did not have his degree of success.*
BELOW RIGHT *Che Guevara met Castro in Mexico and went with him to Cuba. He left in 1965 to help other revolutionary groups, but two years later was captured in Bolivia and shot.*

Portuguese Africa

In Angola, Mozambique and Guinea, nationalist guerrillas fought a long struggle which eventually wore down the Portuguese Army

Ian Beckett

Portuguese soldiers in the jungles of Angola. By the late 1960s the strain on Portuguese manpower was such that the age of conscription had to be lowered and the term of service extended from two to three years.

PORTUGAL was the first European colonial power to arrive in Africa (in the late 15th century) and, with Spain, the last to withdraw, in the mid-1970s. The durability of its empire in Africa can be attributed in some measure to Portugal's neutrality in World War II, which enabled her to avoid the defeats that undermined the resolve of other powers to retain their colonies.

It can also be explained by a genuine belief in a 'civilising mission' and the determination that this historic role should be fulfilled. The colonies also contributed to the Portuguese economy, being the only sector which regularly recorded a trade surplus.

Place of the blacks

The Portuguese always claimed that their version of imperialism was unique since it was not based upon racial discrimination and it aimed at total assimilation of the African. From 1951, the colonies were officially regarded as overseas provinces electing representatives to the National Assembly in Lisbon. In reality Portuguese policy was economically and socially exploitive. Slavery was abolished in 1878 but was replaced by an equally restrictive system of contract labour. In the 1950s the number of contract labourers was greatly increased to meet the demand for export crops such as coffee and cotton.

Assimilation also fell far short of realisation. The theory was embodied in the 1933 constitution which established Antonio de Oliveira Salazar's *Estado Novo* ('New State'). The population of the colonies was divided into *indigenas* (natives) and *nôa indigenas*. The latter, who were subject to Portuguese rather than native law, included whites, *mesticos* (mulattoes) and *assimilados* (assimilated Africans). *Assimilados* could vote, travel without permission and were exempt from both contract labour and the need to carry pass cards, but the status was exceptionally difficult to obtain in view of stringent requirements and the lack of educational facilities. By 1961 barely 1 per cent of the native population of the colonies had become *assimilados*. Not surprisingly it was among *mesticos* and *assimilados* that the early leaders of the nationalist groups were to be found.

Tribalism was a prominent factor in nationalist groupings. In Guinea, PAIGC (Partido Africano da Independência da Guiné e Cabo Verde) was founded in 1956. It consisted of urban *assimilados* in the city of Bissau and members of the Balante people (approximately 29 per cent of the population), but the Moslem Fula and Mandinka peoples (approximately 22 per cent of the population) remained loyal to the Portuguese. In Mozambique there was FRELIMO, which stood for Frente de Libertação de

Moçambique. It was a coalition of several groups which united in 1962 and was predominantly Makonde (less than 3 per cent of the population).

The most complicated divisions were those in Angola. MPLA (Movimento Popular de Libertação de Angola) was founded in 1956 in Luanda. It drew its strength from the urban *assimilados* of the capital and the Mbundu people whose territory surrounded it. FNLA (Frente Nacional de Libertação de Angola) grew out of the grievances of the rural Bakongo people of northern Angola. It was led by Holden Roberto, the nephew of the heir to the kingship who had been displaced by a Portuguese nominee. FNLA also drew support from the Ovimbundu people of the south and the Chokwe people of the east. These later switched allegiance to UNITA (União Nacional Para a Independência Total de Angola), founded in 1966 by Jonas Savimbi, who broke from Roberto on political and personal grounds.

The coming of war

In Guinea in August 1959, 50 strikers at Bissau docks were fired on and killed by the Portuguese authorities. After a number of related incidents, which resulted in an authoritarian backlash against the nationalists, a flashpoint was reached in Angola. On 15 March 1961 a widespread revolt erupted in the northern coffee plantations of the Uige region led by groups crossing the frontier from the newly independent Congo. Several hundred whites were massacred, together with more than 7000 Africans.

The revolt took the Portuguese by surprise. They had barely 3000 troops in Angola and none in the north. Immediate concessions followed with the abolition of compulsory cultivation of cash crops, greater autonomy and the end of the system of assimilation; henceforth any African was theoretically equal to any European as a Portuguese citizen. The concessions came too late. Amilcar Cabral's PAIGC opened its campaign in Guinea in 1963 and in September 1964 FRELIMO made its first cross-border raids into Mozambique from Tanzania.

Guerrilla activity

Although FNLA may have had anything between 3000 and 8000 guerrillas by 1971 it is unlikely that more than 1000 were actually inside Angola at any one time, and two of the three 'fronts' were largely illusory. In fact FNLA, operating from Zaire, was only sporadically active after 1970 in the north. UNITA, operating in the extreme south from 1966 onwards, was estimated by the Portuguese to have no more than 300 activists in 1970.

MPLA had approximately 5000 to 7000 guerrillas by 1970 and accounted for some 59 per cent of guerrilla incidents that year; again, however, there were probably no more than 1500 actually inside Angola. Having begun its campaign by infiltrating the Cabinda enclave from the Congo Republic in 1963–64, MPLA diverted its attention to the east in 1966–67, attacking the Moxico region and subsequently the Bié region from Zambian bases. Portuguese operations had all but eliminated MPLA in the east by 1974, forcing it to return to

Luis Almeida Cabral, first president of Guinea-Bissau, chats with troops of the newly independent nation in 1974.

the Congo Republic as a base of insurgency.

In Mozambique FRELIMO probably numbered about 8000 guerrillas by 1971 but was unable to penetrate beyond the frontier regions of Cabo Delgado and Niassa where the Portuguese had been well-prepared to meet the threat. In 1968 FRELIMO began to infiltrate the Tete region from Zambia, posing a threat to the important Cabora Bassa Dam project, but they never seriously interrupted work.

The greatest success achieved by guerrillas was in Guinea where PAIGC, operating from Senegal and the Guinea Republic, claimed to control about 60 per cent of the country by 1970. However, the arrival in 1968 of a new Portuguese commander-in-chief in Guinea, General Antonio de Spinola, brought a change in strategy, and stalemate had resulted by 1973.

Portugal's commander in Mozambique from 1969 to 1972, General Kaulza de Arriaga, believed the war to be winnable, but Spinola had doubts as to whether a purely military solution was feasible. Defence expenditure as a proportion of the national budget rose from 25 per cent in 1960 to over 40 per cent by 1967. With the forces deployed in Mozambique, the Portuguese had over 150,000 men in Africa by 1970. In proportion to the Portuguese population this represented a troop level five times greater than the American presence in Vietnam in the same year. By 1974 the war had cost Portugal 11,000 dead and 30,000 wounded or disabled.

Withdrawal from empire

The disillusionment of the professional officer corps with Portuguese policies led directly to the formation of a group, the Armed Forces Movement, which planned a coup after Spinola had been dismissed as deputy chief of staff for criticism of government policy. Spinola was installed as president and the Armed Forces Movement pressed for complete withdrawal from Africa.

In Guinea and Mozambique power was transferred to PAIGC and FRELIMO respectively, Guinea becoming independent in September 1974 and Mozambique in June 1975. The existence of rival groups prevented agreement in Angola, where fighting broke out well before the independence date of 11 November 1975. With South African assistance, a joint FNLA/UNITA column drove on Luanda from the south in October 1975 while the bulk of the FNLA advanced from the north. On 7 November Cuban troops arrived by air in support of MPLA, supplementing those already brought by sea. The Cubans destroyed FNLA and, after discreet South African withdrawal in January 1976, rolled back the joint forces in the south. MPLA was recognised as the legitimate government in February 1976.

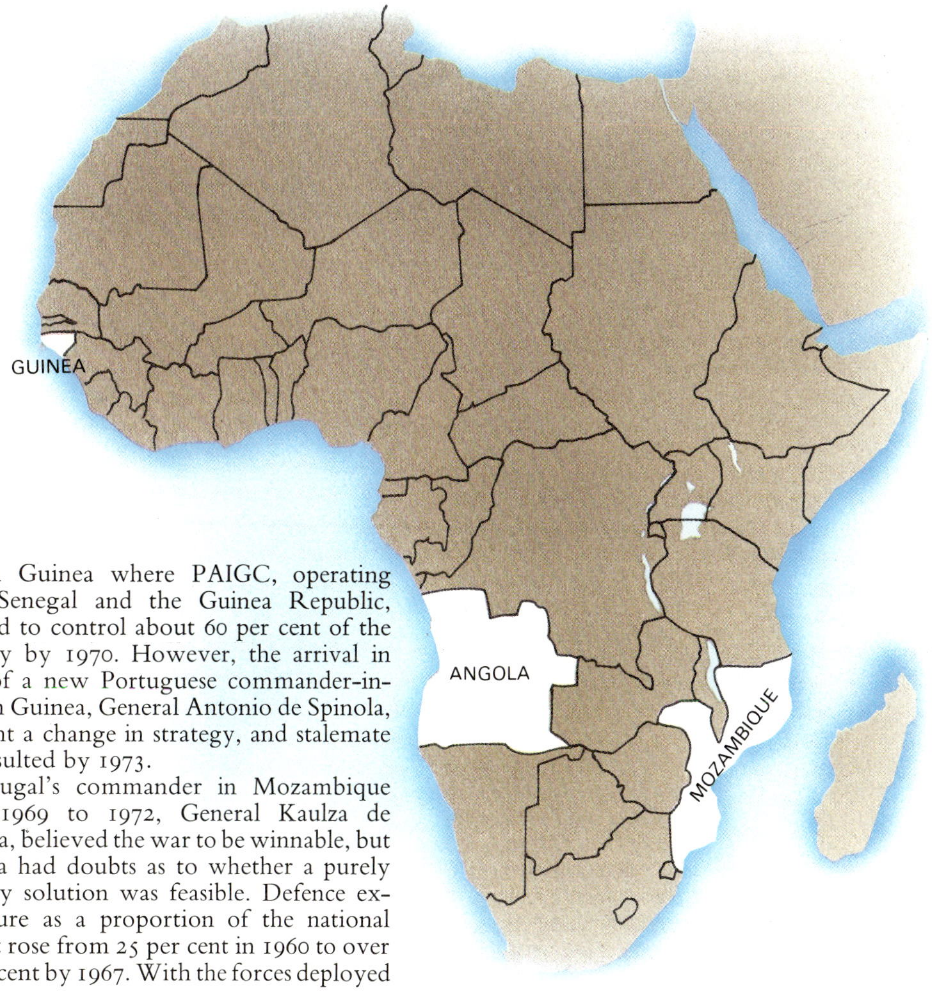

Black Guerrillas

Guerrilla activity and infiltration routes – Angola

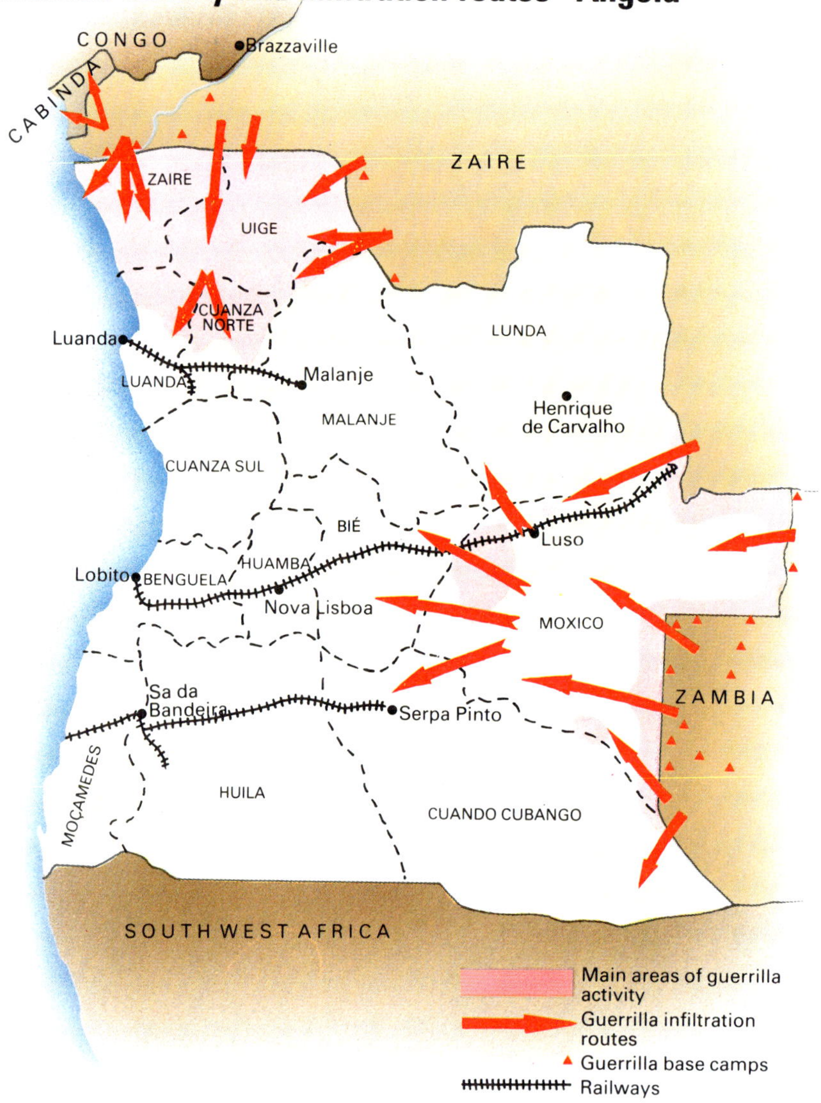

THE GUERRILLA WARS against the Portuguese in Africa were entirely rural. They were fought for the most part over vast distances in terrain which was frequently difficult. Much of FNLA's activities, for example, were conducted along the 2100km (1300-mile) frontier of mountain, swamp, jungle and elephant grass separating Angola from Zaire. MPLA operations in the Moxico region ranged over a plateau of savannah and forest covering 391,000 square km (151,000 square miles). In contrast to Angola, which was mostly over 915m (3000 feet) Guinea was entirely low-lying and 40 per cent water-covered.

Situated in tropical and sub-tropical zones, the colonies were subject to seasonal extremes – a dry cool season (April to September in Angola and Mozambique, October to March in Guinea) and a hot rainy season (vice-versa). The terrain conferred advantages on the guerrillas but could also work against them. Supplies often had to be transported long distances on foot, and while the rainy season provided relief from aerial attack through the low cloud cover, the swamps into which most of the grasslands were transformed hindered the guerrillas as much as the Portuguese.

It greatly helped FNLA that the Bakongo people were spread across both sides of the Angola/Zaire frontier while FRELIMO similarly benefited from the fact that the Makonde lived on both sides of the Mozambique /Tanzania frontier. Yet FRELIMO was unable to penetrate south of the Cabo Delgado and Niassa regions largely because of the hostile Macua peoples across northern and central Mozambique. In Angola MPLA was unable to operate out of Zaire because of FNLA's influence there. FNLA's effectiveness was itself affected by the movement of large numbers of Bakongo into Zaire during the war. FRELIMO's campaign in the Tete region from 1968 onwards was similarly inhibited by the migration of a large proportion of the native population into Malawi.

Frontier sanctuaries

Frontiers provided readily accessible sanctuaries. PAIGC operated from the Guinea Republic and Senegal, and on occasions its incursions were covered by Senegalese artillery fire. Zaire was the natural refuge for FNLA especially after Joseph Mobutu, Holden Roberto's brother-in-law, became president. MPLA found sanctuary in the Congo Republic and, after its independence in 1964, in Zambia; Tanzania and Zambia were bases for FRELIMO. Only UNITA was denied an external refuge, being expelled from Zambia at an early stage.

It was in such sanctuaries that most training was undertaken by the guerrillas themselves, by the hosts, and by other external advisers. The original nucleus of 250 FRELIMO guerrillas and the first 300 MPLA guerrillas were all trained in Algeria. MPLA guerrillas were also trained in Bulgaria, Czechoslovakia and the Soviet Union. The Soviet Union also assisted PAIGC and FRELIMO while the Chinese supported FRELIMO and FNLA, which also received tacit support from the United States. PAIGC and FRELIMO were recognised by the Organisation of African Unity which also gave its support to the FNLA provisional government until switching to MPLA from 1968.

All the guerrilla groups sought to establish 'liberated' areas with an important political purpose. The most successful was PAIGC which claimed in 1967–68 to have established 159 'schools' with more than 14,000 'pupils' inside Guinea and which formally announced a government for the 'liberated' areas in 1973.

In Angola the establishment of woodland *kimbos* ('protected villages' growing much-needed food) by

Guerrilla camps and infiltration routes – Mozambique

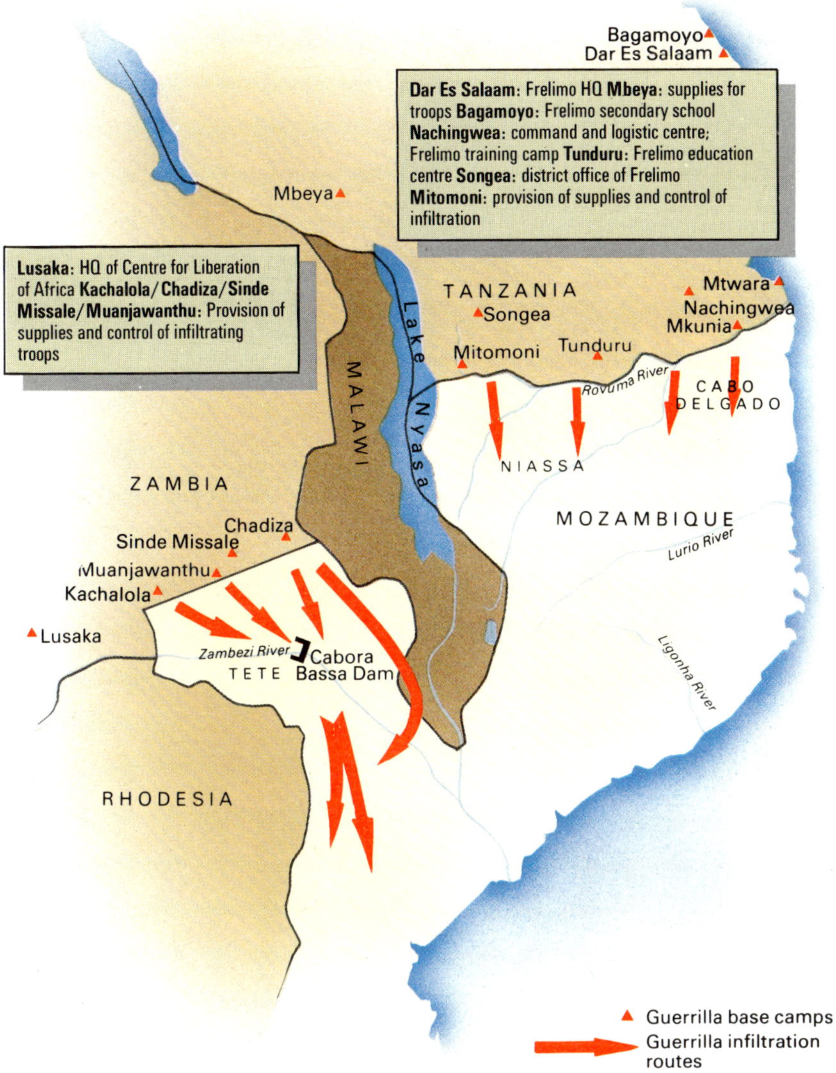

MPLA was not successful as they proved too vulnerable to air attack. Guerrilla activity generally was too remote from the centres of population to be really effective. FNLA was particularly inept at this political role, preferring outright military action. This, above all, led to the breakaway of UNITA, which claimed to concentrate on 'education' with its guerrillas operating in defence of political activities.

In 1967 PAIGC claimed to have undertaken during the course of the year some 142 attacks on camps and barracks, 22 raids on airfields and ports and 476 ambushes. They said they had captured 26 mortars, 86 submachine guns and 397 rifles. They claimed to have killed that year 1905 Portuguese for the loss of only 86 guerrillas.

'Mines versus helicopters'

Although questionable, the PAIGC figures do indicate the pattern of guerrilla activity. To a large extent this consisted of ambush of road traffic and bombardment of targets at the longest range possible. The attacks on the Cabora Bassa Dam by

OPPOSITE *Guerrilla soldiers of the MPLA, equipped with Soviet weapons, wade through a river in the Angolan jungle. MPLA won out over its rivals, UNITA and FNLA, after independence.* ABOVE RIGHT *Troops of UNITA on patrol near Luso in January 1976, shortly before MPLA's victory.* RIGHT *FRELIMO forces with an antiquated machine gun.*

FRELIMO were mostly 122mm rockets fired from the maximum 16km (10 miles). In Angola the war has been characterised as 'mines versus helicopters' with often a minimum of contact and, indeed, mines accounted for about 40 per cent of Portuguese casualties there in 1970.

Most guerrilla activities were undertaken by relatively small groups in short-range incursions with a minimum number permanently living in Portuguese territory. In Guinea, for example, the original guerrilla groups consisted of 17 to 25 men. By 1971, however, PAIGC favoured 120-man groups operating by night before withdrawing to sanctuaries and having only small, mobile commando units remaining in Guinea itself.

Simonov automatic rifles and the reliable Kalashnikov assault rifle were the usual personal weapons carried by the guerrillas. Mortars such as the Russian 82mm medium mortar were valuable for longer-range attack, but 75mm cannon and bazookas of all kinds were also carried.

Weaponry became increasingly sophisticated. By 1973 PAIGC was using ground-to-air missiles; they claimed to have shot down 21 aircraft by September, including that of the local Portuguese air commander. But better weapons and training such as that received by FNLA in Zaire after 1970 could not offset the intervention of trained Cuban troops in Angola at the war's end. Before their 90 tanks (T34s and T54s) and the devastating 122mm 'Stalin Organ' rocket launchers the guerrillas of FNLA and UNITA were powerless.

Portuguese Defences

WHEN REVOLT BROKE OUT in Angola in 1961 the Portuguese Army had little difficulty in defeating the original rebellion since the rebels were armed only with a few rifles, machetes and improvised weapons. Early use was made of air power in a ferocious response which was reported to have killed 50,000 Africans between August and September 1961. In preparing for the real guerrilla war to come, the Portuguese could draw on the recent experience in Vietnam. More than 2000 Portuguese are said to have been trained in counter-insurgency in the United States.

Yet initial Portuguese reaction to guerrilla activity was hesitant, largely through a lack of military resources, until such time as troop levels could be increased. Troops withdrew into defended outposts and relied upon air attack with bombs and napalm and occasional forays on foot all aimed at containment. In Guinea between 1964 and 1968 all initiative lay with PAIGC. The situation was much the same in Angola and even in Mozambique.

Village scheme

The first feature of Portugal's enhanced strategy from 1968 was the concentration of population in strategic hamlets or defended villages. When General Antonio de Spinola arrived in Guinea in 1968 he initiated a co-ordinated 'hearts and minds' campaign based on the villages and using the army to build 15,000 houses, 164 schools, 40 hospitals and 163 fire stations. In Mozambique there was an energetic programme of improvements with farms, medical centres, cattle dips and a road-building effort that achieved a rate of 1400km (870 miles) per annum by 1972 – more than the United States had built in six years in Vietnam or Britain in 12 years in Malaya.

The second feature of Portuguese strategy was the use of air power to seal off guerrilla supply routes across the frontiers and as an immediate reaction to guerrilla attacks. Napalm was used from an early stage and, from 1970, herbicides and defoliants, particularly against guerrilla villages

Portuguese troops move through the jungle after a successful action against a guerrilla camp in Angola during a sweep against rebel strongholds.

where crops were being cultivated. The Fiat G91 and the American F-84 Thunderjet and Lockheed P-2V were used for offensive air support, the F-86 Sabre being withdrawn from service in 1967 at American insistence. But the mainstay of Portuguese air operations were the American T-6 converted trainer and the Dornier Do27.

The co-ordination of light bombers, helicopters and reinforced ground patrols was seen at its best and most successful in large-scale dry-season operations such as those in Moxico in 1968 and 1972. One operation in Mozambique in 1970 lasted seven months, involved 10,000 troops and netted 440 dead guerrillas. Cavalry was also used to cover the flanks of patrols and where the terrain was too difficult for motor transport.

ABOVE RIGHT *A medium field-artillery piece being tested by Portuguese soldiers.* BELOW *The Portuguese forces cautiously take up positions as they prepare for an ambush.*

Portuguese objectives

The main fighting was undertaken by élite units of Portuguese paratroops, commandos, marines and naval fusiliers. Many of these were black. Extensive use was also made of units of captured or deserted guerrillas to penetrate their former localities. The Portuguese strategy and the influence of popular commanders like the monocled Spinola and Kaulza de Arriaga, known as the 'Pink Panther', was sufficient to produce stalemate in Guinea, low-intensity stalemate in Angola, though problems were increasing in Mozambique.

The price of that success was international criticism damaging to Portugal's prestige, ever-increasing expenditure damaging to the economy and expansion damaging to the army itself. By 1970 it was already noticeable in Angola that Portuguese ground patrols were entirely black or had just two or three white Portuguese with 20 to 30 Africans. Professional soldiers were faced with unenthusiastic conscripts and anti-war subalterns, growing indifference in Portugal itself, and increasing hostility from white colonists with whom the army had little sympathy. Once the army had seized power in Portugal in April 1974 the forces in the colonies showed little interest in offensive action.

The Nigerian Civil War

Biafra's fight for independence had appalling consequences for its people

Peter Janke

Nigerian troops with British equipment. In the early stages of the war the federal forces lacked proper training. Arms and aircraft from abroad proved crucial to eventual victory. INSET *Colonel Chukwuemeka Ojukwu led Biafra's bid for independence. When it failed he went into exile.*

'WE ARE ABSOLUTELY CONVINCED of the enemy's intention to annihilate us. We have withdrawn from the Nigeria which we were so proud to have built up; we, the Ibo people, the most industrious race in the federation, have been forced back into Biafra in order to survive. Genocide stares us in the face.' These were the words of Colonel Chukwuemeka Ojukwu, the man who declared Biafra independent from Nigeria on 30 May 1967.

Recent events, rather than personal ambition, had driven him to make the stand, for he led by agreement and through consultation. Indeed, only four days before he announced the breakaway, Ojukwu had called for and was given a mandate by 300 delegates representing 14 million people. The Ibos' determination sprang from their failure the previous year to abolish federalism and impose a unitary state upon a nation in which they played the dominant role.

After seizing power in a coup, General Johnson Aguiyi-Ironsi's Ibo-dominated military government had abolished the federation in May 1966, but the move set off a chain of riots against Ibos in the northern region. Terrible slaughter ensued and several hundred died. Many hundreds of thousands returned south, especially when the same Islamic leaders provoked further terror in which at least 10,000 Ibos were killed with indescribable brutality.

Oil was a further important factor. Hitherto the Ibo-dominated east had been a poor region and so favoured a unitary state; after oil was discovered, it could afford to proclaim its independence as Biafra. The Ibos' ethnic originality, encompassing their Christian faith, enterprise and high standard of education compared with their Islamic northern neighbours, gave the Biafran conflict deep cultural roots.

In 1966 General Yakubu Gowon came to power after Ironsi had been killed by mutinous troops, and he restored the federation.

The trends of battle

The war itself began in July 1967 with Biafran successes. Federal troops had heavier equipment and artillery and attacked Nsukka from the north, taking the town on 13 July. Biafran troops withdrew from a number of towns before the mechanised advance. They captured Mid-West province, taking Ore, barely 161km (100 miles) from Lagos. The column was too weak to maintain its position for long, but raids on the city by one Biafran

Douglas B-26 bomber created panic, and set off communal violence directed at Ibos.

Throughout September and October the Biafrans lost their advantage, being driven not only from Mid-West but also from their own towns. Their capital, Enugu, was occupied as was Calabar on the coast. They were effectively cut off from the sea, and access to their border with Cameroun was denied them. By mid-October these advances were checked at Onitsha, where retreating Biafrans blew up several spans of the 1370m (4500-foot) bridge over the Niger.

After the fall of Onitsha in March, Port Harcourt fell on 19 May; the Ibos were then confined to an inland area around Aba, Owerri and Okigwi. Later that summer the first two of these townships were captured and the last stronghold of Umuahia had been surrounded. The advance had involved some 25,000 men on the federal side.

Owerri was recaptured by Ojukwu's troops as Umuahia fell. Federal forces took Owerri in January 1970, and Colonel Ojukwu left the country. On 12 January a cease-fire was ordered and three days later Lagos proclaimed the end of the secession.

Troops, weapons and aid

At the start each side had around 6000 men. The Biafrans were felt to have the edge, however, because around 50 per cent of the officer corps in the Nigerian Army had been Ibo. The federal government made good this number and expanded its troop level to 80,000 men – but they were quite untrained and efficiency was poor.

The Nigerian Navy – a frigate and three patrol boats – was loyal and successfully blockaded Biafra. Three torpedo boats were later delivered by the Soviet Union. The

Reduced by the war to the point of starvation, a woman picks the last scrap of food after the arrival of aid.

federal forces possessed 20 single piston-engined Dorniers, half a dozen Alouette helicopters, a dozen Piaggio P-149D trainers and some light liaison aircraft, in addition to French jets. The Biafrans had only helicopters, until they acquired a B-26 bomber. The federal forces had some 50 armoured vehicles.

Outside support was important to both sides. Biafra was formally recognised by no state upon secession, but the tenacity of its fight led President Julius Nyerere of Tanzania to grant recognition in April 1968. The move was taken in the hope of stopping the mass killings of tens of thousands in tribal conflict. Other African states to recognise Biafra were Zambia and the French-speaking states of Gabon and Ivory Coast. The Vatican was sympathetic to Biafra's cause, as were South Africa, Rhodesia, Portugal and France.

Britain was anxious not to escalate the conflict by supplying arms. It was nudged into doing something for Lagos once the Soviet Union acted, and sent anti-aircraft guns, Belgian FN rifles and ammunition. Spain and Belgium were additional sources of federal supplies. Of much greater significance was the arrival of 15 MiGs and 10 Delfin jets.

Short of crews, Nigeria relied upon Egyptian Air Force pilots for training; European and South African pilots flew the Delfins under contract. Egyptian pilots undertook combat missions at the start of the conflict. On the other side, the Biafrans obtained three B-26 light bombers and a North American B-25 Mitchell bomber from French Air Force surplus stocks. They also purchased six French airliners, which were used to bring in supplies.

Biafra's failure

Behind the vivid images of the war and the horrors of starvation and distress relayed by television throughout the world lay the underlying motivation – tribal antagonism. The Ibo were a people who under colonialism had risen from abject poverty to outstanding educational achievements, which marked them out from other Nigerians. An entirely new sense of purpose, of control of their own destiny, strengthened Ibo determination.

Economically the backbone of Ibo resistance was broken early on, when the oil production of the south ceased and revenues no longer flowed into the eastern region. Deprived of access to the sea and of income, Biafra had no hope.

Although Biafra, the smaller contender, attracted world sympathy, General Gowon showed great courage and sound sense. Though he failed to control federalist excesses, massacre was never government policy. The subsequent history of reconstruction proves the point: Gowon will be remembered for masterly reconciliation.

Foreign Intervention

ABOVE *A federal soldier guards Biafran captives.* BELOW *Men from the federal 6th Brigade move up to the front. Russia and Britain aided Nigeria but the United States remained neutral.*

OF ALL ASPECTS of the Nigerian civil conflict the most puzzling was the international diplomatic alignment. Here were Britain and France, both Western powers and members of the North Atlantic Alliance, supporting opposite sides. In the Algerian war for independence five years earlier there had been no question of Britain trying to supplant French influence in North Africa. Yet over Biafra, General Charles de Gaulle took advantage of Nigerian weaknesses and British agonising to pursue French advantage at the tragic cost of local life.

French and British views

The French stand in 1968 was the more extraordinary considering the insistence of the Organisation of African Unity (OAU) on preserving existing boundaries in Africa. However, the OAU was but four years old and had failed in its efforts to mediate. The general calculated that bold moves might pay big dividends and, since it cost France nothing, the game was worth playing. A divided English-speaking Nigeria was less of a threat to French Africa, and Biafra might even be incorporated in the French zone of influence.

British authorities suffered agonies of conscience, not knowing how to play their cards. For the Labour government the remnants of imperial responsibilities were an embarrassment. The sale of defensive arms was allowed, but even this decision cost the party much deliberation. The government never appreciated that military victory could, or would, decide the issue; it maintained an unrealistic belief in negotiation.

Lagos needed jet aircraft, tanks and even armoured cars. Had Britain supplied these, she would have had to supply technicians and pilots too, for the necessary expertise was lacking in Nigeria. Here the Soviet Union stepped in. A Nigerian mission went to Moscow after leaving London empty-handed and found no difficulty in acquiring 10 Czech Delfin jets and, later on, 15 MiG-17s.

A new Soviet approach

The decision to arm Nigeria reflected an increasingly flexible approach to foreign policy by the Kremlin. Orthodox policy suggested the support by Russia of African liberation movements, but not military governments like that of General Yakubu Gowon, who had no pretensions of being a socialist. Yet the Soviet Union had only recently suffered a setback in Ghana, where it had heavily promoted Kwame Nkrumah, who had been ousted in February 1966. The Russians were therefore anxious to regain their foothold in West Africa.

The Soviet Union's provision of arms was made with the utmost caution, and only after other powers had made their position clear. The United States had declared its neutrality and had reaped hostility from both sides. Had Britain – alone or in conjunction with America – supplied arms of any sort to Biafra, it is most probable that the Soviet Union would not have risked arming the other side. The Soviet Union stepped into a vacuum created by Britain and the United States.

The Six-Day War

On 5 June 1967 the Israelis launched one of the most devastating offensives in the history of warfare

H. P. Willmott

Moyshe Dayan walks through the streets of Bethlehem accompanied by Israeli troops. Like other West Bank towns Bethlehem fell to the Israeli Army with comparative ease; the Jordanians put up a brave resistance in Jerusalem, but elsewhere could not hold off the Israelis.

THE ARAB-ISRAELI WAR of 1948–49 challenged the creation of the state of Israel, and the war of 1956 against Egypt served to confirm its existence. Neither war, however, led to peace, stability and security for any of the major participants in the conflict between Arab and Jew in the Middle East. The Arabs remained unreconciled to the existence of the Jewish state, since they believed that its creation had been a moral outrage. Defeat on the battlefield failed to induce the Arabs to reconsider their attitude.

These wars, therefore, did nothing to promote the sense of Jewish security that the creation of Israel had been designed to achieve. Nineteen years after its proclamation, the state of Israel remained unrecognised by its neighbours, while no peace treaty defined its relations with them and their shared borders. What passed for state frontiers were mere ceasefire lines that left Israel hopelessly vulnerable.

The state of Israel enjoyed no natural frontiers in 1967. At its narrowest point, in the coastal belt between the Judean Hills and the Mediterranean, it measured only 21km (13 miles). In area Israel covered merely 36,260 square km (14,000 square miles). These two facts conspired to spell out one simple military fact that governed Israeli strategic deliberations. Israel lacked the depth in which to manoeuvre for the counter-attack: it lacked the space in which to fight defensively against its enemies.

Defence through offence

Israel's unity of command and central geographical position could only be assets if used to fight for and secure the initiative through offensive action. Every aspect of geography ensured that Israel had to undertake offensive action in order to deploy fully, secure gains that hopefully could be used for bargaining purposes and prevent the Arabs from co-ordinating their efforts. The military logic of Israel's position pointed to the need for pre-emptive offensive action, primarily against Egypt since this was the most powerful of Israel's enemies, as the means of disrupting Arab preparations before they could be completed.

In this context, the rapid exploitation of offensive action alone would ensure the ineffectiveness of a collective Arab response and thus allow Israel to switch forces from one front to another. Speed was vital to Israel for two more reasons. Firstly, Israel could not afford protracted wars because of its small human and economic resources. Secondly, Israel had to make gains before the United Nations could intervene to deprive it of the bargaining counters the nation hoped to secure.

When tension in the Middle East began to rise during May 1967, therefore, the Israelis found themselves in a position where they had to contemplate immediate offensive action in order to destroy the Arab armies that quickly massed along their borders.

ABOVE *Egyptian troops in an advanced post in the Sinai Desert just prior to the Israeli attack.* LEFT *An Israeli tankman looks across the border into Jordan with his 0.50 Browning machine gun at the ready.*

What provoked the crisis was a series of rumours of both sides' ill-intentions, the deciding factor being Egypt's demand on 16 May for the withdrawal from Sinai of the UN Emergency Force. This force had been in Sinai since the 1956 war, and its presence had served to guarantee Israel's security. Sinai was Israel's buffer zone, and as long as the UN force was there Israel was secure. After the 17th, however, elements of seven Egyptian divisions entered Sinai. These consisted of five infantry divisions and two armoured formations, the bulk of the infantry being deployed in the coastal area forward of El Arish, and most of the armour being held back from the border. The armour took up position just beyond the Central Ridge, from where it could either support the infantry in resisting any Israeli attempt to break through the Egyptian defensive positions, or move directly against the Negev in the event of an offensive.

The citizen army

With the Egyptian occupation of Sinai came the closure of the Strait of Tiran to Israeli shipping, and Israeli attempts to lift the blockade dominated diplomatic exchanges for the next few days. The real threat to Israel, however, was not through any long-term economic blockade but directly and immediately from substantial and well-equipped ground and air forces. By 20 May Israel's call-up of reservists was complete. Yet, with such limited financial and manpower resources, Israel could not afford to keep her citizen army mobilised for more than two weeks because of the damage that would be inflicted on the economy. Israel therefore had to decide whether or not to go to war within two weeks of 20 May.

What quickly became evident was that it would be impossible for the Israelis to enter any dialogue with the Arabs. Events showed that Israel was not only very unlikely to get any help from the Western powers but that her enemies were intent on her destruction. After years of mutual animosity, the Arab states announced their intention of creating a unified command. Evidently this could not be anything other than nominal, since an improvised command could not be expected to operate effectively overnight, but the very announcement of its creation posed a serious threat to Israel. In 1956 the other states had done nothing when Israel took on Egypt and, although this might be repeated if war came in 1967, the creation of a unified Arab command posed a threat of encirclement and Arab co-ordination that the Israeli government could not ignore.

What the Arabs did not appreciate as May slipped away was the manner in which they had backed the Israelis into a corner. By re-occupying Sinai, closing the straits, forming a unified command with Jordan and Syria and demanding that Israel surrender Elat and Nizana, Egypt more or less made an Israeli attack inevitable. With the Syrians and Egyptians openly talking about the destruction of the Jewish state, Israel began to move towards the option of an attack before the Arabs had time to ready themselves.

President Abdel Nasser of Egypt seemingly miscalculated badly in two respects. It is doubtful if he expected an Israeli attack, but he was confident that even if one did develop his forces would win. On both counts he was wrong. Nasser believed that a crisis with major political gains for Egypt, a crisis which he could control, would not necessarily result in war. Because of his actions, however, the power of decision passed to Tel Aviv and on the evening of 3 June the Israeli cabinet voted for war.

Phases of the war

The June war of 1967, often known as the Six-Day War, divides into three distinct phases – the Israeli campaign against Egypt (5–7/8 June), against Jordan (5–7 June) and against Syria (9–10 June). The United Nations passed a ceasefire resolution on 7 June, supposedly with immediate effect, but the major fighting between the Israelis and the Syrians did not begin until more than two days later.

Such was the basic chronology of the war, but to all intents and purposes the war was over after three hours. In that time the Israelis inflicted a colossal defeat on the Arabs from which there could be no recovery. Once the Israelis secured air superiority, the outcome of the war was never in any doubt and, although hard fighting subsequently took place on all three fronts, there was no disputing the outcome.

The Middle East
5 June 1967

BELOW *King Hussein of Jordan (left) and President Nasser of Egypt sign the defence treaty of 30 May 1967.* BOTTOM RIGHT *Armed with a variety of weapons Israeli reservists march up to the front around Jerusalem.*

Rival Armouries

IN GENERAL TERMS the armouries of the Arab states were Soviet-supplied and that of Israel was made up from Western sources plus equipment that had been captured from Egypt in 1956 and still remained in service. Egypt and Syria, favoured states of the Soviet Union, were almost exclusively armed by the Soviets, while almost all the latest Iraqi equipment was Soviet in origin. Older Iraqi equipment was overwhelmingly of British manufacture, and it was Britain that supplied the major part of Jordan's requirements. Britain was also a supplier of tanks to Israel, but it was the French who had provided the Israelis with the backbone of their air force.

Quantity against quality

Israel was decisively outnumbered on the ground by the Arab states, and even by Egypt alone, but Egyptian strengths were somewhat misleading because a substantial part of the Egyptian armed forces was fighting in the Yemen. The imbalance of numbers was redressed by several factors: the poor maintenance of Arab equipment compared to that of the Israelis, the concentration of Israeli resources and Israel's unity of command, and the qualitative superiority of the ordinary Israeli soldier over his Arab opposite number except, perhaps, in the very professional Arab Legion of Jordan.

Israel's was a citizen army. The distinction between the civil and the military was very blurred in a society extremely conscious of its vulnerability and the need for utmost professionalism in fighting and the maintenance of equipment. It was common for reservist tank crews and service troops to train most weekends, and the standard of the 260,000 troops Israel could put into the field within three days of mobilisation was formidably high.

Much of the same was true of the situation in the air. The Arabs had more aircraft, but the Israelis had a far higher rate of serviceability. Israeli ground crews and pilots were intensively trained to a standard far beyond that of the Arab air forces, so that they could always put far more aircraft into the air than their enemies.

Under normal circumstances the Arab turn-round time for an aircraft was about two hours with an aircraft flying two missions in a day; the Israelis averaged five or six and sometimes even more missions in a day. This was possible because Israel spent nearly half her defence budget on the air force and had more than two pilots for every aircraft.

Comparative armour

The main battle tanks were the Centurion and the T54/55. Each had seen service with more than a dozen armies, but the war of 1967 was the first occasion when they engaged in major battle with one another. In 1967 the two tanks were both in service in the armies of their builders, Britain and the USSR respectively, but were in the process of being phased out.

The 1967 Israeli Centurions were of the Mark 5 and 6 varieties, both having been fitted with stabilised 105mm guns. The Mark 5 differed from the Mark 6 only in its slightly thinner armour. The T54 and T55 – essentially the same tank, but with the latter incorporating certain minor improvements over the T54 – did not command as good a reputation, but still remained formidable. In a 36-tonne tank the Soviets incorporated a splendidly reliable chassis, a very long range of over 480km (300 miles) with external fuel tanks, a reasonable offensive capability in the shape of the 100mm high-velocity gun and good defensive powers.

ABOVE *A sea-to-sea anti-submarine missile is launched from an Egyptian motor torpedo-boat. During the Six-Day War the Egyptian Navy sank an Israeli destroyer by missile action.* BELOW *Israeli Sherman tanks launch an attack.*

Its armour had been sloped to secure the maximum deflection and its low height, 2.68m (8ft 10in), made it a small target compared with the much larger Centurion. Its agility and speed (over 50km/h or 32mph) on roads were good. It was capable of climbing a 1 in 1.6 gradient and could wade to a depth of 1.36m (4ft 6in) without preparation. Because of the relatively low weight carried on its tracks, the T54/55 could move on ground the Centurion could not cross.

T54

weight 36 tonnes (35.4 tons) **length** 9.02 (29ft 7in) **height** 2.68m (8ft 9½in) **armament** 1 x 100mm gun, 2 x 7.62mm and 1 x 12.7mm machine guns **ammunition carried** 42 rounds of APHE, HEAT and HE, 3000 rounds for 7.62mm, 500 rounds for 12.7mm

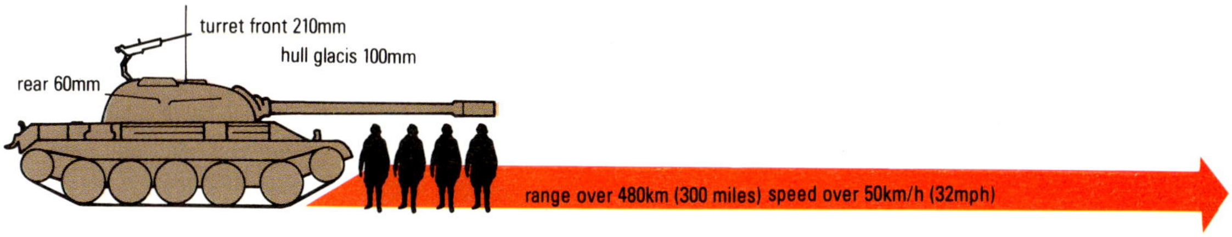

Centurion V

weight 51.8 tonnes (51 tons) **length** 9.85m (32ft 4in) **height** 3m (9ft 10½in) **armament** 1 x 105mm gun, 2 x 7.62mm and 1 x 12.7mm machine guns **ammunition carried** 64 rounds APDS and HESH, 4250 rounds for 7.62mm, 700 rounds 12.7mm

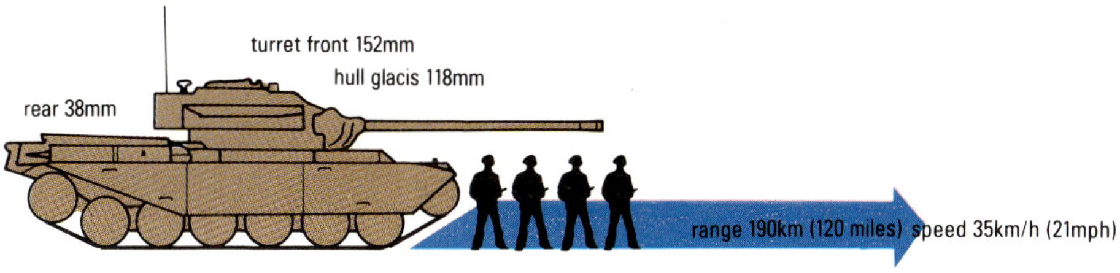

Where the Centurion decisively outscored the T54/55, however, was in its ability to kill armour beyond the range of the Soviet tank. This has to be combined with the larger internal space of the Centurion that allowed greater crew comfort and a faster rate of fire. Despite a road speed of only about 35km/h (21mph) and a range of 110km (68 miles) it was almost as fast over 200m from a standing start as the T54/55. This was an important consideration in a fast-moving tank battle where tanks had to fire and manoeuvre. The real point of difference between the tanks, however, was in gun and shell.

The Centurion carried 64 rounds of APDS and HESH compared to only 42 rounds of APHE, HEAT and HE carried by the T54/55. The latter was limited, therefore, to a range of about 1000m (3300 feet), and slightly less than that if it was to deal with a Centurion. The latter, however, had an effective killing range of up to 2000m (6600 feet) while its APDS round was far superior to anything the Soviets had produced. For shock and exploitation through massed attacks the T54/55 was good, but in a tank-killing role in 1967 the Centurion was probably unequalled in the world.

ABOVE *Centurion tanks of the Israeli Army prepare for battle. In addition to the 105mm gun the Centurion was armed with three machine guns and smoke dischargers.*

Arab-Israeli forces – 1967

country	men	tanks	aircraft
Israel	**264,000**	**800**	**350**
Egypt	240,000	1200	450
Syria	50,000	400	120
Jordan	50,000	200	40
Iraq	70,000	400	200
Saudi Arabia	50,000	100	20
Algeria	60,000	100	100
Kuwait	5000	24	9
Arab total	**525,000**	**2424**	**939**

The Israeli Air Strike

MANY ASPECTS of the Israeli opening air assault on 5 June are well known, and the strike itself ranks with some of the most celebrated operations of all time. In simple terms the war began with the Egyptian Air Force totalling 450 combat aircraft, of which about 350 were MiG fighters. The Israelis had 350 front-line aircraft, including some 200 fighters. At the end of the first day's operations about 300 Egyptian aircraft had been destroyed, and during the whole of the war the Israelis claimed to have destroyed 418 Arab aircraft for the loss of 27 of their own. The Israelis admitted to losing ten of their aircraft on the first day of the war. Subsequent photographic reconnaissance substantially confirmed the extent of Israeli claims.

Victory in the air

The preliminary Israeli air strike was against eight Egyptian airfields in Sinai, on the Suez Canal and around Cairo, but in the course of the first day's operations Israeli attacks were extended to cover a further nine Egyptian airfields. The Israelis also broadened their operations to cover the Jordanian, Iraqi and Syrian fronts, and in the course of this one day annihilated the Jordanian Air Force and inflicted such losses on the Syrian Air Force that thereafter it took virtually no active part in the war. The Israeli claim that Israel destroyed the Jordanian and Syrian Air Forces inside 25 minutes was not a vain boast but a fact.

Success against Jordan and Syria would have counted for nothing – indeed, the Israelis could not have even tried to attack these countries – had it not been for the success achieved by the Israelis in their opening attacks on the Egyptians on 5 June. Overall timing and co-ordination of the initial assault were superb.

The Israelis timed their attack for

Turn-around procedure for combat aircraft

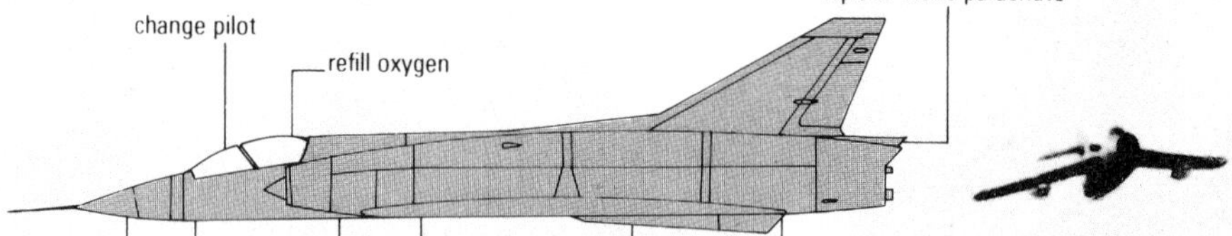

0845 hours Egyptian time. The relative lateness of the hour was chosen so that the Egyptians would be struck when they were least ready and after the early morning mists in the Nile Delta had lifted. By this hour Arab air patrols and radar surveillance had been stood down with the passing of the time for a classic 'dawn attack', and also the change-over of watches within the Egyptian air command was taking place. To ensure maximum surprise the Israelis chose not to make Arab radar stations their first objective, but used some of their aircraft on a strike that led them deep into the Mediterranean before they turned to take the Egyptian airfields from the rear.

The Israelis kept successive waves of attacking aircraft over the major Egyptian airfields until resistance was totally broken. This was achieved through very careful calculation of flight times and an allowance of ten minutes – four strafing runs – for each attacking wave before the next attackers arrived to continue the pounding. An extraordinarily fast turn-round time of 7 minutes per aircraft and a serviceability rate of 90 per cent ensured that the Israelis kept almost all their aircraft in continuous action in the first crucial hours of the war.

Expertise in execution

If the planning and timing of the attack were of the highest standard, execution was no less impressive. For 80 minutes the Israelis kept up a continuous assault on the airfields housing the cutting edge of Egyptian air power. Israeli intelligence was superb, and target identification among pilots proved to be outstanding, for dummy installations and aircraft were ignored while real targets were systematically destroyed. Most of the damage was inflicted by cannon-fire against aircraft caught on the ground, some Israeli pilots lowering their undercarriages to reduce speed and thus increase the accuracy of their fire.

The Israelis did not rely solely on cannon, however. Various bombs had been developed to make runways unuseable, including one type designed to ensure maximum cratering effect. This bomb had a drogue parachute designed to let the attacking aircraft get well clear of the blast. Forward-firing rockets then propelled delayed-action bombs deep through the concrete of the runways, some bombs being set on long delay in order to discourage ground crews from trying to repair the damage. Installations and runways in Sinai were relatively lightly attacked because the Israelis wanted to use them themselves.

It was hoped that the strike against Egypt would deter Syria and Jordan from entering the fray. In the event, Jordan did enter the battle, whereupon her small Air Force was entirely destroyed in the course of a single Israeli attack on the afternoon of 5 June. All of Jordan's 29 aircraft were lost, as were 60 Syrian aircraft. Israeli aircraft also struck at the only Iraqi air base within range and accounted for another 17 enemy planes. In the history of air warfare no operation stands comparison with the Israeli Air Force attack on 5 June with regard to effectiveness and significance for the outcome of a campaign.

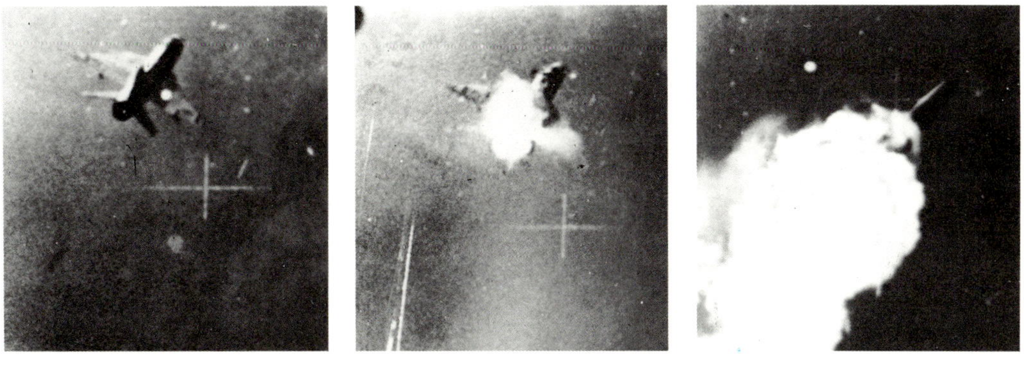

ABOVE LEFT *Three Egyptian MiG-21s lie on an airfield, victims of the Israeli air attack of 5 June 1967.* LEFT *An Egyptian MiG-17 makes a strafing run on an Israeli convoy near the Suez Canal. Although effective as a ground attack plane the MiG-17 was inferior to the Israeli Dassault Mirage III.* RIGHT *A sequence of pictures taken through the gunsight of an Israeli Mirage fighter showing the last moments of a Syrian MiG-21. In the air as on the ground the Arab states were overwhelmed.*

The Sinai Front

ON THE SINAI FRONT the Israelis had two objectives. The main one was the destruction of Egyptian field forces. A secondary objective was the clearing and securing of the whole of the peninsula by advancing to the Suez Canal and the entrance of the Strait of Tiran.

In 1956 the Israelis' objective had been a battle of encirclement through manoeuvre without having to endure a head-on attack against the Egyptians' main defensive positions. In 1967 matters were very different. Whereas in 1956 the Egyptians had not posed any immediate threat to Israel, in 1967 they did. Israel intended to use her armour to blast routes through the strongest points in the Egyptian line in an attempt to get across the enemy's lines of communication in the first hours of the war. Once on those lines of communication, relative security (from mines) and speed of exploitation were all but assured.

Three-pronged advance

In order to achieve their objectives the Israelis deployed three formations under Generals Abraham Tal, Abraham Joffe and Ariel Sharon. These were all deployed between Nizana and the Mediterranean coast – a distance of about 65km (40 miles) – directly opposite the Egyptian infantry divisions. These divisions were organised along Soviet lines, each with substantial armoured forces attached, and they employed standard Soviet defensive tactics in order to withstand assault. These proved unavailing, as the Israelis under Tal attacked at the base of the Gaza Strip, while Sharon's force made its main effort against Um Katif and Abu Aweigila. Starting from the Nizana area, Sharon directed his main effort towards Nakhl and thereafter followed the route of the 1956 advance. Joffe's force, between those of Tal and Sharon, was directed to cut the lateral El Arish-Abu Aweigila road and thereafter support either of the other two forces as the situation dictated.

Tal's force made the first breakthrough in the area around Rafah and Khan Yunis. Such was its importance that success had been ordered 'regardless of cost'. The defenders put up a bitter – but neither effective nor prolonged – resistance. The Israelis were constantly surprised by the strength of the defenders and their extremely good camouflage, but only the Egyptian gunners fought consistently well and even they had no answer to the weight of firepower and the fighting ability of the Israelis.

The Israelis enjoyed two immense advantages – possession of air superiority and Centurion tanks. The Centurions were far superior to anything the Egyptians had and were the main cutting edge of the Israeli ground forces. It was the Centurion units that made the breakthrough and by the evening of 5 June reached the outskirts of El Arish. One Israeli weakness was the lack of co-ordination between armour and other arms. On many occasions armour tended to rush ahead and leave the infantry and artillery – and even the light armour – floundering far behind, unable to overcome resistance that hardened once the heavy armour had passed.

The Israelis lost the equivalent of an

The battle for Sinai

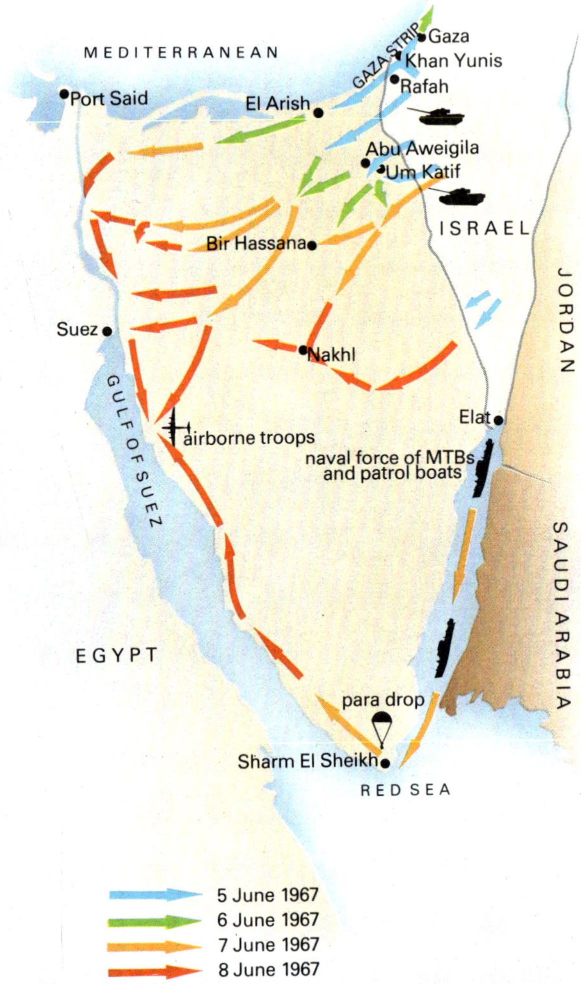

BELOW *Israeli troops equipped with jeep-mounted recoilless rifles near Ismailiya.* RIGHT *Israeli infantry, preceded by US-built M4 Sherman tanks advance towards El Arish. Although outclassed by the T54s of the Arab nations the Sherman was a useful supplement to the Israeli Centurion and M48 tanks.* FAR RIGHT *An Israeli patrol passes destroyed vehicles.*

armoured unit around Rafah and would have suffered far more heavily both there and at the Jeradi Pass had it not been for the Israeli Air Force. For what pulled the battle around in the Israelis' favour was the appearance over the battlefield of ever-growing Israeli air strength on the afternoon of 5 June. It has been calculated that, had it not been for the air force, the ground forces would never have been able to reach even the Central Ridge, still less the Suez Canal. But as it was, the leading patrols of the Tal force reached the canal just after midnight on 9 June.

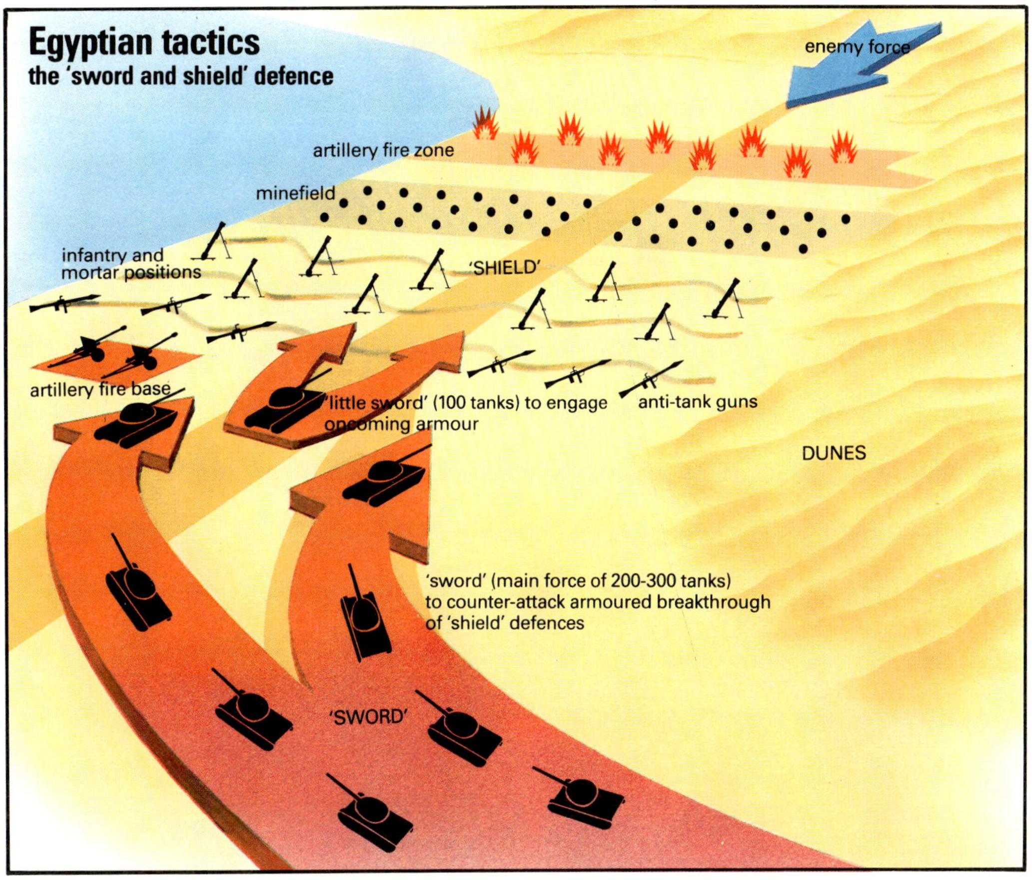

The southern front

Further south, Israeli progress was hampered by soft sand and fierce resistance. Once the first breakthrough was registered against the strongest part of the Egyptian front, however, the result was a foregone conclusion. The making of the breakthrough, however, was no easy task and needed one of the most spectacular operations of the war.

This involved a night attack by armour, artillery, infantry and paratroopers from all sides on the very strong defensive position between Um Katif and Abu Aweigila. It is believed that this operation involved the greatest artillery attack ever made by the Israelis. While heli-borne paratroopers caused massive confusion in the Egyptian artillery park, the infantry began to clear the defensive lines from the front while the armour, which encountered Egyptian tanks coming up from the Central Ridge area in support, fought its way around the flank and rear. Egyptian resistance at Um Katif was not finally silenced until after noon on the 6th, but the Israelis had made the decisive breach by dawn and within another 36 hours the advance had carried them to the foot of the Central Ridge. The Israelis reached the ridge in an exhausted state and with very little fuel for their vehicles.

By that time, there had been a general Egyptian collapse and the third and fourth days of the war saw a disintegration of the Egyptian forces as they sought safety in flight. Vehicles were abandoned in profusion, and it is estimated that fewer than 100 Egyptian tanks in Sinai managed to get back across the canal. Egyptian authorities have admitted to 10,000 casualties. What this figure did not disclose, however, was that seven divisions were totally destroyed.

Jordan and Syria

TWO LESSER-KNOWN FEATURES of the 1967 war are that nearly half of Israel's fatal casualties were incurred on the Jordanian front, and that, overall, slightly less than half of Israel's 32 brigades took part. This reflected the way Israel chose to make war. Her basic intention was to stay on the defence in the east until the issue had been resolved in Sinai. Once it had become clear that the battle in Sinai had been won, the Israelis began to pull out some of their élite troops from the south and to deploy them against the Jordanians and Syrians. One film of the war shows Israeli armour moving nose-to-tail through northern Israel towards the Syrian (Golan) Heights – a classic example of the use of interior lines of communication.

The war in the east was really two quite separate encounters. The Israelis gave unstinting praise to the Arab Legion of Jordan which lost more than 6000 of its 50,000 men and almost all its armour and artillery in a vain attempt to hold the West Bank. Jordan could not hope to withstand Israel, and would have been well advised to have kept out of the war. But Jordan chose to stand alongside the other Arab countries.

The Eastern fronts – Jordan and Syria

Israeli objectives

The Syrian affair, on the other hand, was bitter. The Israelis believed the Syrians to be largely responsible for the crisis that had led to the war and felt they had an old score to settle because of persistent Syrian shelling of Israeli settlements in the Galilee area. Israel certainly had no intention of honouring a ceasefire until enemy positions on the Syrian Heights had been dealt with.

These Heights were, indeed, a major Israeli objective of the war – far more so even than the Jordan River, which would provide a natural line of defence for her narrow central region. In the course of the war Israel secured both the line of the Jordan and the Syrian Heights, thereby achieving a much larger degree of security than before. In the fighting in the east, Israel gained one more prize, the most glittering of all: Jerusalem. The Holy City cost Israel 195 killed and 1131 wounded. Total Israeli losses in the Jordan fighting were 1756 killed and wounded, and the Jerusalem figures, high because the use of heavy weapons was impossible in such a city, show the extent to which the Arab Legion resisted overwhelming attack.

On the first two days of the war the Israelis registered very little success against the Arab Legion, and it was not until the third day, when Egyptian

An Israeli tank column of M4 Shermans advances into enemy territory. By 1967 the Sherman was both up-gunned and up-armoured.

formations in Sinai were falling apart, that the Israelis achieved their breakthroughs and dismembered the Jordanian kingdom as it had existed since 1949, taking Jericho and Nablus. As in Sinai, the decisive element was the air force which flew, it was claimed, more than 800 missions against Jordanian ground targets. The Jordanians were helpless against this kind of attack.

Defending the Heights

The Syrians should have been better able to withstand Israeli assault because their positions on the Heights were immensely strong and they had unrestricted fields of observation from various points, most notably Mount Hermon. More missions were flown against the Syrians than against the other two fronts, but the defensive lines the Syrians held were strong enough to reduce the effectiveness of Israeli bombing, even with napalm, quite considerably.

In fact, for almost 36 hours the Syrians resisted the three-pronged Israeli thrust from the Dan, Beni Yakov bridge and Haon areas. The ground strongly favoured the defenders, the Israelis having to negotiate very steep gradients with narrow fields of fire against positions which the Syrians had had years to prepare. Syrian choice of ground had been skilful, but it did not match the élan and expertise of Israeli forces who worked their way through minefields to get to grips with the defenders.

By the end of the first day's fighting (9 June) the Israelis had made a substantial inroad into the northern defences, but on the morning of 10 June, as the Israelis began to launch an all-out assault right along the front, the Syrians began to withdraw, initially in good order and then in mounting chaos. By dusk the Israelis were in possession of all of the Heights and part of Mount Hermon.

Of all the Arab performances, that of Syria was the least impressive. Only some of the Syrian forces were deployed on the Heights, and an attempt was made to withdraw even these when defeat became inevitable. In less than two days the Israelis secured the strongest natural position anywhere in the combat zone for less than 500 casualties. The Syrians lost about 100 of their 250 tanks and all but 60 of 260 guns they deployed on the Heights, but much of their material strength, including 1000 artillery pieces, was still intact when the fighting ended.

TOP *A column of M3 half-tracks moves up towards the Golan Heights.* ABOVE *An Israeli AMX 13 light tank pauses during action on the Golan Heights. Manufactured in France, the AMX13 is armed with a 75mm or 90mm gun.*

BELOW *By 1967, the Israelis combined tanks and infantry in the* ugdah *formations. Tanks advanced relentlessly with mechanised infantry support, while lorry-borne infantry cleared the way for the shuttle which kept the armour supplied and maintained.*

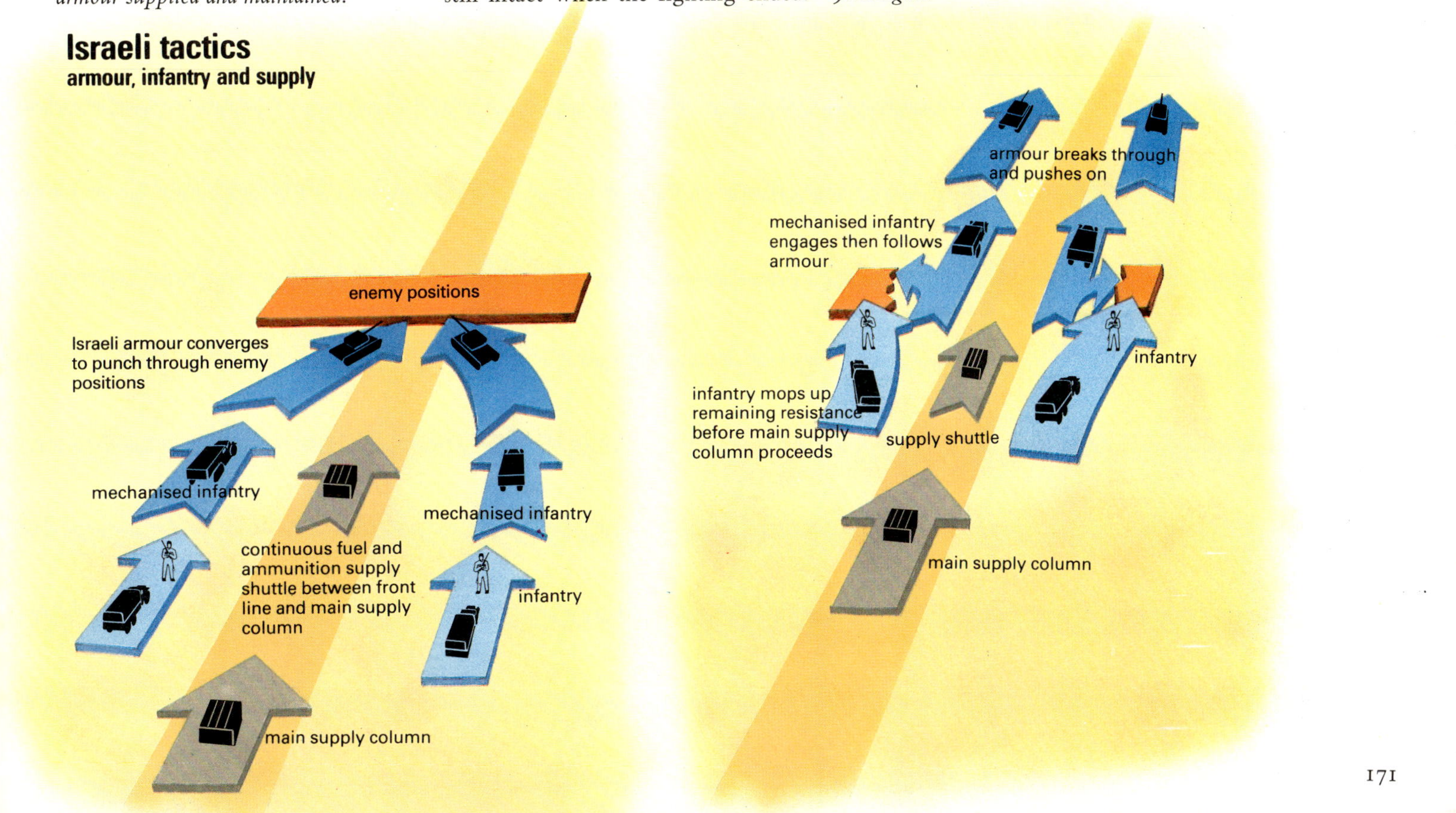

Uneasy Balance

THE WAR OF 1967 had resulted in a victory for Israel that, on her own estimation, would set the Arab states back a decade. In just six days a state that had been gravely threatened with utter destruction was transformed into one that had tripled in size and had expanded to natural and easily defended borders along the Suez Canal, the whole of the Jordan Valley and the Syrian (Golan) Heights.

Egypt lost the equivalent of seven divisions and about 800 tanks, of which 300 were captured intact. The Israelis claimed to have captured a further 450 artillery pieces and 10,000 vehicles. The Israelis captured 150 guns from the Jordanians, who lost almost all their 200 tanks and over half of their armoured personnel carriers. Syrian and Israeli losses have been recounted earlier. After the war the Israelis stood in possession of the battlefield with its booty of wrecked and semi-wrecked vehicles and equipment, material that could be adapted easily for use.

Inevitably, however, even these gains brought problems. The vast increase in size and the acquisition of buffer zones on three sides caused a major numbers-to-space problem, brought under Israeli control a vast number of disaffected Arabs and forced Israel to undertake a massive programme of roadbuilding and stockpiling in order to take full advantage of the gains that had been made. The most serious matter potentially was the acquisition of 1,500,000 Arabs who could never be reconciled to Israeli rule as long as the Arab states refused to accept their defeat.

Territorial gains

The bitterness of defeat ensured that the Arabs would remain intransigent; and, in addition, two other factors were now at work. Firstly, the Israelis took Old Jerusalem and this, because of the holy Islamic places there, was something that no Arab could ever accept. Secondly, the nature of the Arab-Israeli dispute was significantly altered by the conquests Israel had made. Prior to the Six-Day War the dispute between Arab and Jew had concerned Israel's right to exist. The

argument centred on Palestine and the establishment in 1948 of a Jewish state at the expense of the local Arab community. After the 1967 war, however, Egypt and Syria both lost national territory. They had a direct interest in recovering their former land.

There was one other factor at work – the intransigence of both sides. The Arabs adopted a stubborn 'no war, no peace' formula which meant they did not have to rethink their policies. The Israelis, on the other hand, were equally obstinate, but they failed to see the real significance of events. They neglected to explore the possibility, however remote, of a deal with Arab states by which territory was returned at the price of legitimising Israel's existence.

The Israelis thought that they could have territory and peace because they believed that the Arabs would eventually come to settle on their terms. This was a dangerous misreading of the situation, and it was made worse by an utter disdain for the Arabs as a result of the war. The Israelis came to believe that what they had done once they could do again, forgetting that a finesse seldom works twice in succession. Israel's position and calculations, seemingly so sure in 1967, contained flaws that ensured a resumption of conflict at a later date.

LEFT *Israel in victory: a Jewish soldier at the Wailing Wall in Jerusalem.* BELOW LEFT *Israeli troops in M3 half-tracks drive past a truck-load of Egyptian prisoners.* BELOW *Armed with an automatic rifle an Israeli soldier stands guard over a holy place in the newly captured Jerusalem.* BELOW RIGHT *Under the muzzle of a Browning 0.30 machine gun a group of Egyptian officers surrenders.*

The new frontiers
12 June 1967

Casualties in 1967

Israeli	Egyptian front	Jordanian front	Syrian front	TOTAL
Killed	275	299	115	689
Wounded	800	1457	306	2563
Arab(estimates)				
Killed	10,000	1000	2500	13,500
Wounded	20,000	2000	5000	27,000

The Urban Guerrillas of South America

In the 1960s South America experienced an eruption of urban terrorism as revolutionary guerrilla groups took to the streets

H. P. Willmott

Bolivian soldiers stand over the body of a colleague killed by guerrillas. Although insurgency sometimes posed acute problems for the authorities they generally were able to repel the challenge to their rule with effectiveness and speed.

SOMETIME IN THE MID-1960s Latin America became more urbanised than rural for the first time, with more people living in towns than on the land. This fact alone was a pointer to the declining importance of rural insurgency in South America and its significance was not lost upon various revolutionaries in the aftermath of a series of insurgent defeats in rural South America in the course of the 1960s. Peru, Bolivia, Colombia and other smaller states, both in Central and South America, had seen rural insurgency movements destroyed with almost contemptuous ease by the security forces. The defeats had been too consistent, too regular and too emphatic to be attributable to purely local factors. In short, by the time that Ernesto ('Che') Guevara was killed in Bolivia in 1967 the idea of emulating the Cuban Revolution by rural insurgency throughout South America had been totally discredited.

Fortunately for these survivors of rural disaster, there were individuals who had already given some thought to the problem of how to continue the struggle. There was, moreover, the example of various small campaigns that had been fought throughout the world – Palestine, Cyprus and Aden against the British, Algiers against the French – that pointed to certain possibilities for revolutionaries, and there was the revival in the late 1960s of Spanish anarchism and the general anarchist notion of securing the transformation of society by direct action. When these influences and developments were combined with the fact that even before 1967 there had been two significant urban campaigns produced by South America, the result became known as urban guerrilla warfare.

Marighela's strategies

Urban violence has always been a part of revolutionary struggle, but since 1968 the world has become familiar with a new aspect of revolutionary warfare. This is the

ABOVE *Chilean trade unionists march in favour of wage rises in 1960. Organised labour tried to exploit social unrest but support for guerrillas was never automatic.* RIGHT *Carlos Marighela propounded the idea of urban revolt arising from opposition to government repression.* BELOW *Juan and Maria Perón had little success in stemming social disorder in Argentina.*

systematic employment of guerrilla tactics in an urban setting as one part of a co-ordinated operational strategy designed to secure revolutionary objectives. In this process the name of one man – Carlos Marighela, a Brazilian communist – is all-important. Marighela wrote a booklet entitled *The Handbook of Urban Guerrilla Warfare*, and it ensured for him a fame, notoriety and influence that lasted beyond his death in 1969.

Little of what Marighela had to say was new. Much of what he wrote seems narrow, obvious and pedestrian in its presentation. What he did, however, was to take up various points concerning revolutionary warfare, guerrilla tactics and the physical conditions of fighting in South America and develop the idea of an offensive military strategy based on the towns being linked with political militancy in order to bring about change in society.

Marighela tried to solve the problem of how revolution can be promoted when all the military, political and social advantages are with the counter-revolutionaries. His answer was relatively simple, but none the less potent for being so. Insurgents had been unable to establish themselves in rural areas because the security forces had been too powerfully entrenched in the countryside. The grip of the security forces had to be broken by luring them into the towns to deal with a deteriorating situation. In this way, rural guerrillas could establish themselves in the resultant vacuum and urban and rural guerrillas thereafter would complement one another's efforts. By doing so they would keep the security forces off-balance, unable to concentrate to deal with either threat and therefore liable to defeat. Both revolutionary efforts had to be developed; one without the other would be doomed.

Propaganda of the deed

It was Marighela's next point that showed the way for a new development in revolutionary thought. Marighela was an élitist in that he believed in making revolution on behalf of people, irrespective of whether they wanted it or not. He was a committed revolutionary, and, like Guevara, believed in revolutionary violence precipitating a crisis in society that would produce the political and social conditions needed for the final revolutionary triumph.

Guevara had expounded his idea of the *foco*, a small group of mobile, aggressive revolutionaries creating, through armed victories over the security forces, a groundswell of popular support that would be self-generating and bring about victory. This was very much 'propaganda of the deed' – an old anarchist notion that had been dismissed contemptuously by Lenin. Guevara had applied the concept to rural areas, with disastrous results. Marighela applied the *foco* concept to the towns. He believed that revolutionary violence before a wide audience would get the message across to the population and at the same time provoke the authorities into adopting repressive measures that would alienate the people.

What Marighela aimed to achieve was the polarisation of society whereby public support for an increasingly repressive regime dwindled and popular support and sympathy for the insurgents rose. In this way, through provoking a crisis of confidence in society, Marighela believed that the conditions needed for the overthrow of established order would be achieved. To carry this out Marighela set out a list of tactics that could be used to discredit and ridicule the authorities. These ranged from murder and bombings to peaceful fermentation of strikes, sit-ins and demonstrations, but all had one common theme. They had to be carried out for their maximum publicity effect: every action had to be considered in the light of its psychological impact. Marighela appreciated that publicity was similar to a weapon lying in the street: anyone could pick it up and use it.

The Guerrilla Groups

THE IMPORTANCE of Carlos Marighela was that he drew together a number of ideas and produced a new concept of revolutionary war, but he was not the first South American to practise urban guerrilla warfare. At least three guerrilla groups had taken to the streets in the early and mid-1960s, more or less devising strategy and tactics as they went along. These three groups were based in Venezuela, Guatemala and Uruguay.

Venezuela probably saw the first urban guerrilla war, and it is the most urbanised of all South American states. The revolutionaries, however, realised the need for rural insurgency, but very much as a secondary effort. In the event rural insurgency proved more long-lasting than the urban campaign which, at one time, seemed certain to achieve the overthrow of President Rómulo Betancourt.

Betancourt was to become the first democratically elected president in Venezuela's history to complete a term of office, and one of the major factors in this unexpected achievement was the development of an urban guerrilla campaign waged by the National Liberation Armed Forces (FALN). This was a tactical alliance of various revolutionary groups. Much of the initial success of the FALN stemmed from the fact that though students, intellectuals and youths were heavily involved in the organisation, a large part of the leadership was drawn from officers and men from the armed forces and much of the rank-and-file was provided by the Communist Party.

Repudiation of violence

Between 1961 and 1964 the FALN conducted a full-scale insurgency campaign in Caracas that peaked in 1962–63. It involved a sustained campaign of violence primarily directed against the police (it was nicknamed the 'Kill a Cop a Day' offensive), but in September 1963 the FALN overplayed its hand and in one indiscriminate attack on an excursion train gave Betancourt the pretext for an immediate clampdown. Moreover, his insistence on elections to choose a successor in December showed to many that change was possible through the ballot box. Over 90 per cent of the electorate voted, despite FALN orders to boycott the poll. It was an overwhelming repudiation of violence and by 1964 the FALN was clearly in decline.

If the FALN turned its attention to the towns out of choice, the same was not true in Guatemala where urban guerrilla warfare developed after 1963 as a result of bloody insurgent defeats in rural areas in 1962. In the aftermath of the rural failure the Rebel Armed Forces (FAR) – a front formed by local communists, and disaffected officers and soldiers and students of the MR-13 movement (named after the abortive coup of 13 November 1960) – tried to instigate urban insurgency to bring down the venal and brutal junta that had ruled Guatemala since the overthrow of the democratic Arbenz government in 1954.

Despite some spectacular murders and kidnappings in 1965, however, the FAR never achieved much in either town or country. Internal divisions crippled the movement and the insurgents could never hope to withstand the sheer brutality unleashed

BELOW *A captured leader of the Tupamaros, Jorge Maneras Lluveras, is taken to prison in Uruguay after a police raid on guerrilla hideouts.*

LEFT *Hooded terrorists in Argentina called a press conference in 1971 to announce a new plan of action against the government.* BELOW *Left-wing demonstrators parade in Venezuela, backed up by a giant placard depicting Che Guevara, who encouraged and inspired many dissident groups.*

by the government, both by the security forces and by vigilante groups of the extreme right. Between 1967 and 1968 right-wing counter-terror accounted for possibly 10,000 deaths.

A campaign of ridicule

Fragmentation was not a problem in Uruguay where one group, the Tupamaros, conducted a four-year campaign with an aplomb that attracted worldwide publicity and sympathy. The Tupamaros began life as a protest movement in the rural and backward north-east among sugar-cane workers, but their student leader, Raul Sendic, came to realise that traditional forms of protest and insurgency had little relevance in a society where 80 per cent of the population lived in towns and half the country's population lived in the capital, Montevideo.

Sendic began to organise urban violence as early as 1963, the first public outrage being carried out in 1965. Despite reverses in the period 1966–67, by 1968 the Tupamaros were in a position to launch operations that inside four years brought Uruguay to the brink of chaos. This they did by well-publicised kidnappings (including as one of their victims the British ambassador), robberies and murder. Killings were comparatively rare, the Tupamaros in the early years aiming more to humiliate and ridicule the authorities. This they did with considerable flair. None of their kidnap victims was ever found by the security forces, while their sit-ins and certain of their raids were conducted with impudence and humour.

Uruguay is sandwiched between the two giants of South America, Argentina and Brazil, both of whom experienced urban guerrilla campaigns in the 1970s. Government reaction in both countries was very severe, far more so than in Uruguay. This was particularly true in Argentina, where politics was dominated by the Perón legend.

The return of Perón

Juan Perón was president of Argentina from 1946 until 1955, when he was overthrown by a military coup. Despite his immense popular support, his successors banned his return from exile until 1972, by which time the country was becoming engulfed in financial, social and political disorders of staggering dimensions. Perón was allowed to return only because of these crises and the violent campaign waged by his supporters, but he could do little to halt the slide into chaos. In fact he added to it by alienating groups of his own supporters, particularly the radical youth movement, and he accelerated the disintegration of his party, the Frente Justicialista de Liberacion, which itself was a fragile coalition of six national and seven provincial parties. The political fragmentation was such that the 1973 elections were contested by nine alliances.

The fragmentation continued when Perón's wife, Maria Estela ('Isabelita'), succeeded him in 1974. There was increasing recourse to street violence by the left and right, the left being dominated by the Trotskyite ERP (People's Revolutionary Army) and the Perónist Montoneros. Kidnappings and murders, armed street battles and bombings proliferated until March 1976, when a military coup overthrew Señora Perón and installed a right-wing military junta.

In Brazil such a regime was already in power when Marighela began his campaign of urban violence. He formed the ALN (Acào Libertadosa Nacional) in February 1968 from student and intellectual elements and from parts of the São Paulo section of the Communist Party. From the start, however, the ALN was but one group of a bewildering number of urban insurgency movements whose very proliferation made them hopelessly vulnerable to penetration and destruction by the security forces.

Government Reaction

URBAN GUERRILLA GROUPS survived in various countries in South America throughout the 1970s, but none was able to register the impact that the first-generation groups had achieved. They continued to pull off the occasional spectacular murder, raid or kidnapping, but had greatly declined in political influence and strength.

This can be explained in part by the insurgents' belief that violence itself could be a political force: this was shown not to be the case. The failure of the revolutionaries could also be explained in terms of the debilitating arguments over strategy and tactics that wrecked many movements. The major factor in their decline, however, was the efficiency of the security forces and the use of authoritarian measures.

In December 1977 President Jorge Videla of Argentina said of the campaign against urban guerrilla groups: 'This is really a war. In a war there are survivors, wounded, dead and, sometimes, those who disappear.' He conceded that there may have been those who 'might have disappeared as a result of repression', and that 'excesses might have occurred', but he said that excesses were not 'authorised, condoned or encouraged'. He justified repression on the grounds that it was 'directed against a minority who we do not consider Argentinians'.

Answers to repression

Videla's comments were a candid and succinct summary of one of the major characteristics of the way in which most South American states responded to the challenge of urban guerrilla warfare in the 1970s. A main aim of the insurgents was to push authorities into repression, even severe repression, in the belief that in the end it would prove self-defeating. It was much the same sort of mistaken logic that had led the German communists to welcome the rise of Hitler in the belief that it would pave the way for their own triumph. Urban insurgency generally provoked severe repression by most governments on a scale and intensity that resulted in the destruction of insurgency to a point where, even if social unrest had arisen as a result of governmental action, the revolutionaries were unable to take advantage of it.

Venezuela, as has been noted, was an exception. Of all the urban guerrilla threats, the one that developed in Venezuela probably came the closest to success, yet it was decisively crushed by a government that operated strictly within the law. The chief characteristic of President Rómulo Betancourt's approach was 'minimum force' on the part of the security forces, but this was tied in with maximum numbers. By a combination of cordon-and-searches, systematic clearing of areas, control of the population and movement and displays of heavily armed troops, the security forces were able to exhibit resolve, reassure the population and bring increasingly intolerable pressure on the insurgents.

At times civil liberties were suspended to facilitate operations and detain people against whom admissable evidence was not available, but civil rights were restored at the earliest possible opportunity. A masterly publicity campaign placed the responsibility for crisis where it properly belonged. Betancourt made it clear that the National Liberation Armed Forces (FALN) was the obstacle to change and the cause of loss of liberty, not his government.

The president's hand-over of power to Raul Leoni in March 1964 marked his final triumph and the vindication of his methods. Leoni was able to continue to use exactly the same techniques, along with carefully con-

TOP *The army guards a barracks in Lima, Peru, after anti-government strikes in 1975.* LEFT *Rómulo Betancourt's anti-insurgency policies met with success in Venezuela.*

The guerrilla campaigns of South America

CUBA
1956 beginning of guerrilla fighting by Fidel Castro
1959 Cuba Revolution; Castro in power

GUATEMALA
During 1960s revolutionary groups MR-13 (formed by Marco Antonio Yon Sosa) and FAR (led by Luis Augusto Turcios) main agents of activity
1967 urban insurgency crushed by right-wing counter-terror
1968 MR-13 and FAR merge

NICARAGUA
1979 urban guerrillas lead overthrow of General Anastasio Somoza's regime; new government follows path of non-alignment

VENEZUELA
1959 democratic government of Rómulo Betancourt elected
1960-62 urban guerrilla activity involving gun battles with police; police raid left-wing parties; students killed in campus demonstrations
1963 FALN very active, especially in Caracas (robbery, kidnapping, sabotage), but call for election boycott rebuffed
1964 Raul Leoni continues repressive policies; FALN broken
1965-68 revolutionary activity shifts to rural areas; ex-army, peasant and student involvement
1969 communist party denounces armed struggle

EL SALVADOR
1980 — guerrilla war between left-wing insurgents and US-backed government forces

COLOMBIA
1964 peasant 'independent republic' broken by army
1965 guerrilla-preacher Camilo Torres attracts widespread publicity for revolutionary views
1968 Torres killed in fighting
Throughout decade urban guerrilla activity centred on Bogota; banditry and lawlessness endemic in countryside

PERU
Throughout 1960s large-scale Indian involvement in rural insurgency; little urban unrest
1961-63 revolutionary peasant groups seize control of mountainous districts ('the land invasion' inspired by Hugo Blanco); crushed by army
1965 Movement of the Revolutionary Left (MIR) led by Luis de la Puente and Guillermo Lobaton, begins armed revolt; defeated by army

BOLIVIA
1952 military junta overthrown in revolution
1964 military seize power
1967 Che Guevara killed
Continuous unrest in mines

URUGUAY
1965 start of insurgency by Marxist Tupamaros group
1968 peak of Tupamaros activity (kidnapping, robbery, demonstrations, murder)
1972 military takes power, General Juan Maria Bordaberry suspends civil liberties in successful drive against Tupamaros

CHILE
1971-73 fighting in cities between groups of right and left reaches peak
1973 Marxist President Salvador Allende killed in military coup; General Augusto Pinochet assumes power

BRAZIL
1968-69 peak of urban guerrilla activity, centred on Rio de Janeiro and São Paulo
1969 death of Carol Marighela

ARGENTINA
1975-76 peak of street fighting; little rural unrest

ducted offers of amnesty, to complete the destruction of the FALN. Venezuela is one example, perhaps the only example, of a democracy being actually strengthened by a campaign of urban violence that was designed to destroy it.

Political counter-terrorism

Guatemala and Brazil, on the other hand, had military regimes before insurgency became established, and the reaction of these governments to insurgency is an example of what can happen in a society that refuses to accept any form of restraint in dealing with opponents. Both governments were unaffected by domestic or international opinion. In these two countries the chief characteristic of government response was terrorism, much of it directed by semi-official 'death squads' (some of which were organised from the security forces) which eliminated known liberal and radical elements. Most counter-terrorism was indiscriminate because the identity of the urban guerrillas remained unknown. This reign of right-wing terror, when combined with more selective torture and normal police techniques of gathering evidence, observation, statements and collation of material, led to the gradual elimination of left-wing terrorism. The problem, however, was that right-wing vigilante groups proved infinitely more destructive than the original guerrillas and became institutionalised in national politics.

In Argentina (and Chile, in the wake of Salvador Allende's murder and replacement by the regime of Augusto Pinochet in September 1973) a similar situation prevailed, but the movement towards the right included the overthrow of a democratically elected (if incompetent) government. The Argentinian security forces used techniques no different from their Brazilian and Guatemalan counterparts. Preserving order and national unity were the justification for the destruction of civil liberty. Extreme right-wing groups flourished, and anti-semitic groups were formed, which led some members of the Jewish community to leave the country after threats against their lives.

For the most part the Argentinian security forces did not give the 'death squads' a free hand but undertook the more disagreeable features of the anti-insurgent effort themselves. The military junta in Argentina was not deflected from its intended course of prolonged military rule, and condemnation of its methods did not lead to moderation of its police-state methods.

Downfall of democracy

Uruguay is one of the world's oldest democracies. Until 1972 her one and only coup had been conducted not by the armed services but by the

police. It is perhaps surprising that a country with such strong traditions of democratic rule and civil liberties should have experienced so serious an internal security threat.

In fact Uruguay was in economic and political crisis. Between 1962 and 1972 inflation was recorded at 6457 per cent, while political parties failed to give any form of leadership. Parliament and government seemed incapable of dealing with the Tupamaros. Widespread tax and currency evasion came to light as a result of Tupamaros activities, but the resultant crisis played into the hands of the right-wing factions of the army and air force which, in February 1973, effectively ended democratic rule.

Congress was not actually dissolved until June, but after February the armed forces, belatedly joined by the navy and still headed by President Juan Maria Bordaberry, ruled the country and within little more than a year broke the Tupamaros. This they did by suspending civil rights, by ruthless interrogation and normal police work and patrolling. It was very effective compared with four years of fumbling by the democratic parties. Uruguay has yet to return to the democratic practice that was first established in 1830. In the words of one observer: 'The Tupamaros dug the grave of democracy and fell into it themselves.'

ABOVE *General Jorge Videla has conducted a ruthless campaign against social disorder in Argentina.* RIGHT *Soldiers search civilians in Uruguay in 1970 after three public figures had been kidnapped.* BELOW *Police move to disperse crowds in Buenos Aires, 1970.*

Vietnam

The clash between the Republic of South Vietnam and communist insurgents rapidly involved the world's greatest power in a war it could not win

Sir Robert Thompson

A father holds the body of his child, killed as South Vietnamese forces pursued the Viet Cong into a village near the Cambodian border.

THE FIRST INDOCHINA WAR ended with the Geneva Accords in 1954. For Vietnam the ceasefire was signed by the French and Viet Minh military authorities and provided for a separation of forces and a Demilitarised Zone (DMZ) at the 17th parallel. The International Control Commission, with members from India, Canada and Poland, lacked the teeth to supervise it. The conference did not solve the real problems of the succession to French power in Indochina and achieved only a temporary peace.

In South Vietnam Ngo Dinh Diem, widely acclaimed as a patriotic nationalist who had been both anti-French and anti-communist, returned to become prime minister under Emperor Bao Dai. In 1955 a referendum approved the formation of a republic with Diem as president. It was recognised by all Western governments, and even the Russians were prepared to accept both North and South Vietnam as separate members of the United Nations, but the deal fell through over similar recognition for East and West Germany.

Diem refused in 1956 to countenance a combined election for the reunification of Vietnam, as proposed in the Geneva Accords, on the grounds that the election would not be free in the North and that the vote in the North, with its larger population, would automatically outweigh the vote in the South. He was supported in his stand by President Dwight D. Eisenhower, while Soviet leader Nikita Khrushchev failed to back the North on the issue because he could not have accepted a similar vote either in Germany or Korea.

To everyone's surprise there was no collapse in the South, where Diem restored order against rebellious sects and successfully absorbed 800,000 refugees who fled from the North after the ceasefire. There would have been many more if there had not been obstruction by the North until the time limit was passed. Only 80,000 moved the other way, from South to North.

Insurgency begins

The politburo in Hanoi accepted the 17th parallel, partly because it was the traditional dividing line through most of Vietnam's previous history, but mainly because, as Khrushchev later stated, it was 'the absolute maximum we would have claimed ourselves'. The North had expected, however, to achieve reunification through a collapse in the South. Instead, South Vietnam was becoming a comparatively peaceful and prosperous state with American military advisers and economic aid. There was therefore only one solution – to reactivate the Viet Minh organisation and revert to the armed struggle.

To this end Le Duan, the highest ranking member of the politburo below Ho Chi Minh, had already visited the South where many Viet Minh pockets remained. To reinforce them there were the 80,000 who had moved north after the ceasefire. There was no need for a build-up phase and in 1959 the second Vietnam War went straight into the guerrilla warfare phase.

Vietnam was ideal terrain for guerrillas, with jungle-covered mountains stretching from the DMZ down to Saigon. The population here was restricted to the coastal belt and some highland plateaux. All roads (and the coastal railway line) were interdictable and subject to ambush at any point. The Mekong Delta south of Saigon had many undeveloped swamp areas and its population was spread out along a multitude of rivers and canals in hundreds of small hamlets, many of which could not be reached by road. Unlike Malaya and South Korea, which were surrounded by sea on three sides, Vietnam had on its western flank a long 1000km (600-mile) indefensible jungle frontier with Laos and Cambodia, through which infiltration was no problem down the Ho Chi Minh Trail.

The South's reply

Drawing on their Korean experience the Americans had built up the South Vietnamese Army (known as ARVN, the Army of the Republic of Viet Nam) into a conventional force with artillery and tanks to meet an expected invasion. ARVN proved too cumbersome for guerrilla war. The brunt of the early fighting was borne by the Civil Guard (later renamed Regional Forces) of light infantry companies recruited and stationed in each province, and the Dan Ve (later renamed Popular Forces) established at platoon strength for the defence of villages.

The Viet Minh, now called the Viet Cong ('Vietnamese communists'), had an underground movement in the population and military support from village squads and regional and regular units. With American advisers present, and the Southeast Asia Treaty Organisation (SEATO) in the background, the Americans were inevitably involved. To President John F. Kennedy, meeting the Viet Cong threat became almost a crusade and, as a result of a mission under General Maxwell Taylor in 1961, American military aid was increased.

Fall of Diem

The use of the Ho Chi Minh Trail and the North's presence in Laos prompted Kennedy to send a marine brigade to north-east Thailand in 1961, where the Americans had already established air bases for the defence of Thailand under SEATO. This resulted in a recall of the Geneva Conference and an agreement to neutralise Laos. This decision, however, in effect safeguarded the North's use of the Ho Chi Minh Trail, without which it could not have pursued the war in the South. President Diem understood this perfectly and American pressure on him to sign this agreement was the first cause of the split between him and the United States.

The position within South Vietnam in 1962 was being held partly with the help of a strategic hamlet programme which had some similarities to the New Village scheme in Malaya. In 1963, however, the mutual disenchantment between Diem and the American administration was magnified by the Buddhist crisis which was badly mishandled by Diem and his family. With the self-immolation of monks on the streets and with government forces raiding the pagodas, Kennedy ensured the overthrow of Diem by letting South Vietnamese military leaders know that, if there was a change of government, American aid would still be forthcoming. The consequent coup by General Duong Van Minh resulted in the murder of Diem and a gradual collapse within South Vietnam. Minh was ousted in a subsequent coup by General Nguyen Khanh, who himself was later succeeded by Air Vice-Marshal Nguyen Cao Ky. Meanwhile, Kennedy himself had been assassinated. He was succeeded by President Lyndon Johnson, who lacked a mandate to deal with the escalating war. This was partly rectified by the Tongking Gulf incident, as a result of which Congress gave the president full powers in the Tongking Gulf Resolution. The president, however, delayed action because he was fighting the 1964 election on a peace ticket.

In 1964 the Viet Cong were undoubtedly winning. Insurgent activity had increased alarmingly and whole ARVN units were being engaged and defeated. In October the

Progress of the war

1954 **7 May** Surrender of French garrison at Dien Bien Phu.
26 April–21 July Geneva Conference: Vietnam divided into North and South at the 17th Parallel.

1955 **26 October** Ngo Dinh Diem becomes president of South Vietnam.

1956–64 Guerrilla activity by the Viet Cong supported by North Vietnam.

1961 **11 December** Direct US military aid to South Vietnam begins: two US Army helicopter companies arrive in Saigon.

1962 **February** Instigation of strategic hamlet programme.

1963 **May–August** Buddhist demonstrations against Diem's government.
1–2 November Diem deposed and murdered; short-lived governments follow.

1964 **August** North Vietnamese patrol craft attack US ships in the Gulf of Tongking; America retaliates.
7 August Tongking Resolution passed by US Congress giving President Lyndon B. Johnson extensive military powers in Vietnam.
31 December US armed forces in South Vietnam total 23,000 men.

1965 **February** Viet Cong attack US bases in South Vietnam.
7 February US Air Force starts bombing selected targets in North Vietnam, culminating in Operation Rolling Thunder.
8 March US Marine battalion dispatched to Vietnam, followed by a steady build-up of US Army forces.
19 June Air Vice-Marshal Nguyen Cao Ky becomes premier of South Vietnam.

1966 **12 April** B-52s bomb targets in North Vietnam.

1967 **8 January** Operation Cedar Falls launched against communist controlled 'iron triangle', north of Saigon.
3 September General Nguyen Van Thieu comes to power in South Vietnam.

1968 **22 January–7 April** Siege of Khe Sanh.
30 January Tet offensive launched throughout South Vietnam.
31 March Restrictions imposed on US bombing of North Vietnam.
3 May Peace overtures by North Vietnam accepted by President Johnson.
4–5 May New communist offensive against South Vietnamese towns and bases.
1 November US bombing of North Vietnam ceases temporarily.

1969 **25 January** Formal truce negotiations open in Paris.
31 January US forces in Vietnam reach peak strength of 542,400 men.
8 July Planned withdrawal of US troops begins.
November Massive anti-war demonstrations in the United States.

1970 **18 March** General Lon Nol deposes Prince Sihanouk as ruler of Cambodia and later declares a republic; receives direct military support from the United States and South Vietnam.
May Violent anti-war demonstrations in America at US involvement in Cambodia.
June–July US forces withdrawn from Cambodia.
31 December Congress repeals Tongking Resolution.

1971 **8 February–25 March** Operation Lam Son 719, the South Vietnamese incursion into Laos.

1972 **30 March** North Vietnam launches conventional invasion of South Vietnam.
May North Vietnamese ports mined by US planes; US bombing offensive stepped up.
June South Vietnamese troops hold North Vietnamese invasion; position stabilised.
12 August Last US ground troops depart from Vietnam leaving 43,000 Air Force and support personnel.

1973 **15 January** US military operations against North Vietnam cease.
27 January Peace agreement between US and North Vietnam signed.
29 March Last US troops leave Vietnam.

1974 **April** Cambodian Lon Nol regime under increasing pressure from communist forces. Phnom Penh besieged.

1975 **5 March** North Vietnamese Army launches final offensive against South Vietnam.
17 April Phnom Penh falls to communist insurgents.
30 April North Vietnamese troops enter Saigon; South Vietnam surrenders unconditionally.

LEFT *Lt Gen William C. Westmoreland visits the village of Vam Lang in 1964 shortly before taking over as US military commander in Vietnam.* RIGHT *President Nguyen Van Thieu came to power in South Vietnam in 1967 at a time of sustained military pressure against the communists.*

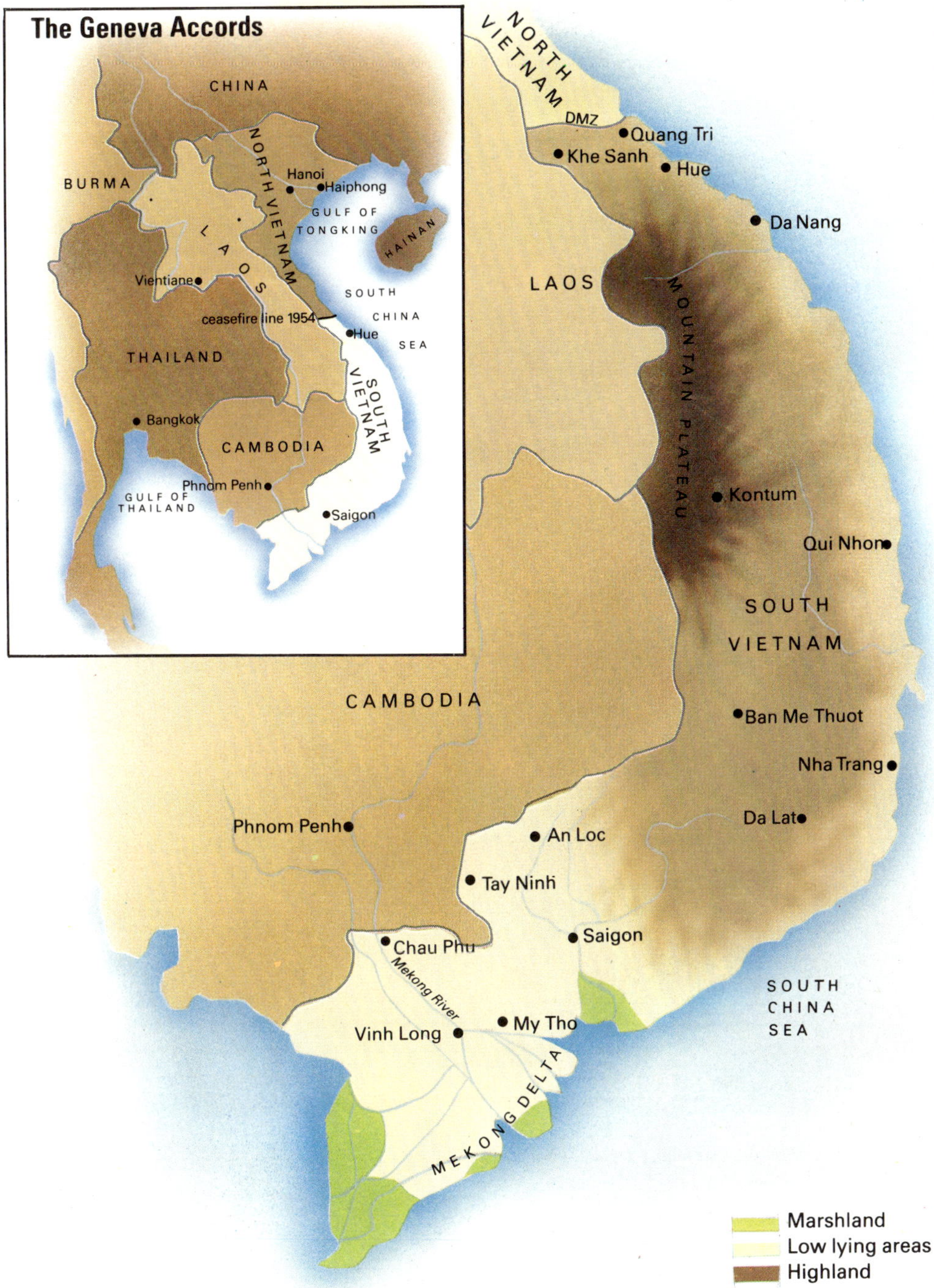

North Vietnamese began to infiltrate regular army (NVA – North Vietnamese Army) units. After re-election, President Johnson was faced with the alternative of a complete collapse of American policy, and the difficult extrication of 20,000 Americans, or of committing American combat troops to the war. The Democrats, already blamed for the loss of China 16 years before, could not face the prospect of another failure. In February 1965 American and South Vietnamese aircraft launched the first bombing attack on North Vietnam and in March American marines landed on the beaches at Da Nang.

An American war

From 1965 to 1968 the war was fought under General William Westmoreland as an American war. The bombing of the North escalated from roads, railways and bridges to supply dumps and oil installations round Hanoi and Haiphong. American losses in planes and men gradually mounted, but the fighting capability of the North was hardly impaired. The supplies came in from China and by ship from Russia and eastern Europe. The movement of troops and supplies to the front down the Ho Chi Minh Trail, which was also bombed, was slowed but never halted. Enough always got through to maintain the war at the pace which the North was dictating.

It was the task of the NVA from sanctuaries in Laos and Cambodia to keep US forces occupied. Major battles occurred at Ia Drang and Dak To on the Cambodian border and north and west of Saigon, later spreading to the DMZ and Khe Sanh. This suited the American concept of war with major units engaged and enormous firepower brought to bear. 'Search and destroy' operations were the order of the day and body counts proclaimed the victories. It was a war of attrition and statistics – much beloved by Secretary of Defense Robert McNamara.

The demoralised South Vietnamese forces were left to defend the populated areas, many of which were under Viet Cong control. Little attention was paid to pacification or to nation-building, except that in 1966 an elected constituent assembly produced a new constitution on American lines and Nguyen Van Thieu was elected president in 1967.

By the end of 1967 the Americans had won every battle and President Johnson was pressing for military victory before the election in 1968. American forces had built up to 540,000, of which less than 100,000 were operational at any one time. But casualties were mounting to hundreds a week, costs had reached $30 billion a year, dissent within the United States was increasing and emotional and political costs were rising. While the NVA's and the Viet Cong's casualties were much higher, they did not approach even half the annual birth rate. Moreover, their extent was unknown in the North and, even if known, would not in a totalitarian state have been a political liability. Nor did the supplies affect the Russians or

Men of the 3rd Marine Division rush to the aid of two radio operators wounded by sniper fire near An Hoa village in November 1966.

Chinese. The point was being reached where the NVA and the Viet Cong were imposing unacceptable costs on the United States. An army undefeated in the field was losing the war.

The Tet offensive

In January 1968 most American forces were committed to the border areas, with over 5000 marines isolated at Khe Sanh. There was, however, nothing to prevent the NVA infiltrating through this outer ring and the Viet Cong were always inside it. At the very moment when Americans were announcing more victories, General Vo Nguyen Giap's Tet offensive opened on 30 January 1968.

The offensive was dramatic in its impact, with Viet Cong units getting into the centre of Saigon and Hue and at least 30 other provincial capitals throughout the country. Although the attackers were defeated and driven out with heavy casualties (from which the Viet Cong, as opposed to the NVA, never recovered), the Tet offensive was a shattering psychological blow to the United States. It resulted in the 'abdication' of President Johnson, in the opening of 'talks about talks' and increased dissent. In early November the president halted all bombing of the North. This was a precondition demanded by Hanoi but the announcement, five days before the election, was somewhat cynically intended to boost the chances of Senator Hubert Humphrey, the Democratic candidate for the presidency.

The Nixon years

This meant that Richard Nixon, who won the 1968 election and who would therefore have to deal with Vietnam, was denied the leverage of the bombing option during the following three years. The whole emphasis was necessarily switched from an American war aiming at military victory to a longer-haul, lower-cost strategy which would gradually turn the war over to the Vietnamese and enable them to hold their own country with limited American help. The four major policies were Vietnamisation, pacification, the gradual withdrawal of American forces and the continuation of negotiations.

At this point the United States undoubtedly had its best and most experienced team in Saigon under Ambassador Ellsworth Bunker and General Creighton Abrams, the latter one of the best American generals of this century. For the first time, annual plans co-ordinated with the South Vietnamese government were drawn up. This worked fairly well; by 1971 more than half the American forces had been withdrawn and yet the security situation within the South was improving daily. The Viet Cong had been irretrievably weakened by the Tet offensive and without Viet Cong help the politburo could no longer conduct a guerrilla-type war; its strategy had to be changed to conventional invasion. The NVA's capability, too, had been temporarily spoiled by the limited American incursion into Cambodia in 1970, although this had had the advantage for the North of increasing dissent in the United States and Europe.

TOP LEFT *A US Marine drags the body of a dead Viet Cong past a Vietnamese woman cradling a child in a village near Chu Lai.* ABOVE *An infantryman aims a grenade at a Viet Cong bunker while his comrade covers with an M16 rifle.* BELOW *Marines ford a stream near Phu Bai in August 1967.*

The secret negotiations between Dr Henry Kissinger and Le Duc Tho always foundered on Hanoi's demand that the United States must first abandon Thieu and his government before there could be a ceasefire. In 1971 accordingly Le Duan visited Moscow and obtained agreement to an invasion. Massive supplies poured into the North and the Americans responded by bombing military targets south of the 20th parallel in December 1971. Although it was clear at the beginning of 1972 that an invasion was coming, the Americans could not act pre-emptively to prevent it as this would be interpreted as provocative and any invasion would then be blamed on the bombing.

The North struck on 30 March across the DMZ and almost simultaneously on two other fronts – in the central highlands towards Kontum and, north of Saigon, towards An Loc. The North, now equipped with Russian T54 tanks and 130mm guns, eventually committed 14 divisions and several independent regiments. By June the invasion was stalled on all fronts and ARVN recaptured Quang Tri.

Because ARVN had held, American tactical air power had been able to inflict great losses on the North Vietnamese and the new laser bombs were proving devastatingly effective against the North. On 8 May, Nixon mined Haiphong harbour with ten Russian ships inside. This tough response in an election year enhanced his standing and improved his negotiating position at the Peking and Moscow summits. The NVA had sustained 120,000 casualties and some of its battalions were down to under 50 men. With much fewer casualties and good reserves the South had actually increased its numerical strength. For the first time Hanoi was facing possible defeat.

Negotiations resumed

The North responded by offering to restart negotiations with all previous American concessions still on the table. As a gesture of goodwill, bombing was stopped north of the 20th parallel and ARVN's counter-offensives petered out. Hanoi gained a six-month respite and became yet more intransigent at the negotiating table, frequently going back on points previously agreed.

This caused great frustration to the president and Kissinger, who were under domestic pressure to settle at any price. On 16 December, the B-52s were turned on Hanoi for the first time, with fighter support. Within 11 days the North's defences were shattered and the whole system was breaking down. After 1242 surface-to-air missiles had been fired the US Air Force (USAF) was free to roam over the North with impunity.

The raids bore no comparison with those of World War II because, by this stage, the USAF was a surgical instrument and, except for three inevitable accidents, the targets were all military and industrial. Hanoi claimed to have suffered about 1500 civilian casualties in all – no more than Coventry in one night, and the same number as the NVA had killed when shelling the provincial town of An Loc. To get the Americans out of the war Hanoi signed the ceasefire.

ABOVE *Men of the North Vietnamese Army march to the front in December 1974.* BELOW *South Vietnamese troops carry their wounded from the battlefield.*

The ceasefire had the disadvantage that it would be neither supervised nor enforced. This greatly favoured the North because, whereas it would have a free hand with the Americans out of the war, the South would still be restrained by the need for continued American aid to survive.

The last years

Over the next two years the North completely restored its offensive capability, pouring additional men and hardware down the Ho Chi Minh Trail and into the South contrary to the ceasefire. The South on the other hand suffered a drastic reduction in American aid which, coupled with the oil price rise of 1973, reduced its forces to a static role stretched throughout the country in defence of towns and populated areas. No counter-offensive or spoiling attacks could be mounted for fear that Congress would cut off all aid. Moreover, no one-for-one replacements as allowed under the agreement were being provided.

By early 1975 the initiative was with the North. It could attack when and where it liked and could deploy overwhelming force at any point. The South had no reserves and was quite unable to switch forces or supplies from one region to another. Defeat and disaster were inevitable. In spite of Nixon's guarantee to Thieu, political pressures ensured that the US Air Force would play no part.

The first blow fell in the central highlands and the two South Vietnamese divisions there were soon in full retreat. The divisions in the north were cut off and, by NVA thrusts to the coast, were each isolated and routed. Around Saigon, only the 18th Division put up any major resistance. The remaining Americans fled in their helicopters and the NVA's tanks rolled into Saigon. The second Indochina War was over, but there was no peace.

The North lost over 1 million killed, the South about 400,000 and the Americans 47,000, but subsequent deaths in Indochina have been more than twice that total. The real cost to the United States of failure and of deserting an ally has been incalculable, and no one knows what the final price may be. Vietnam could turn out to be one of the most decisive wars of this century.

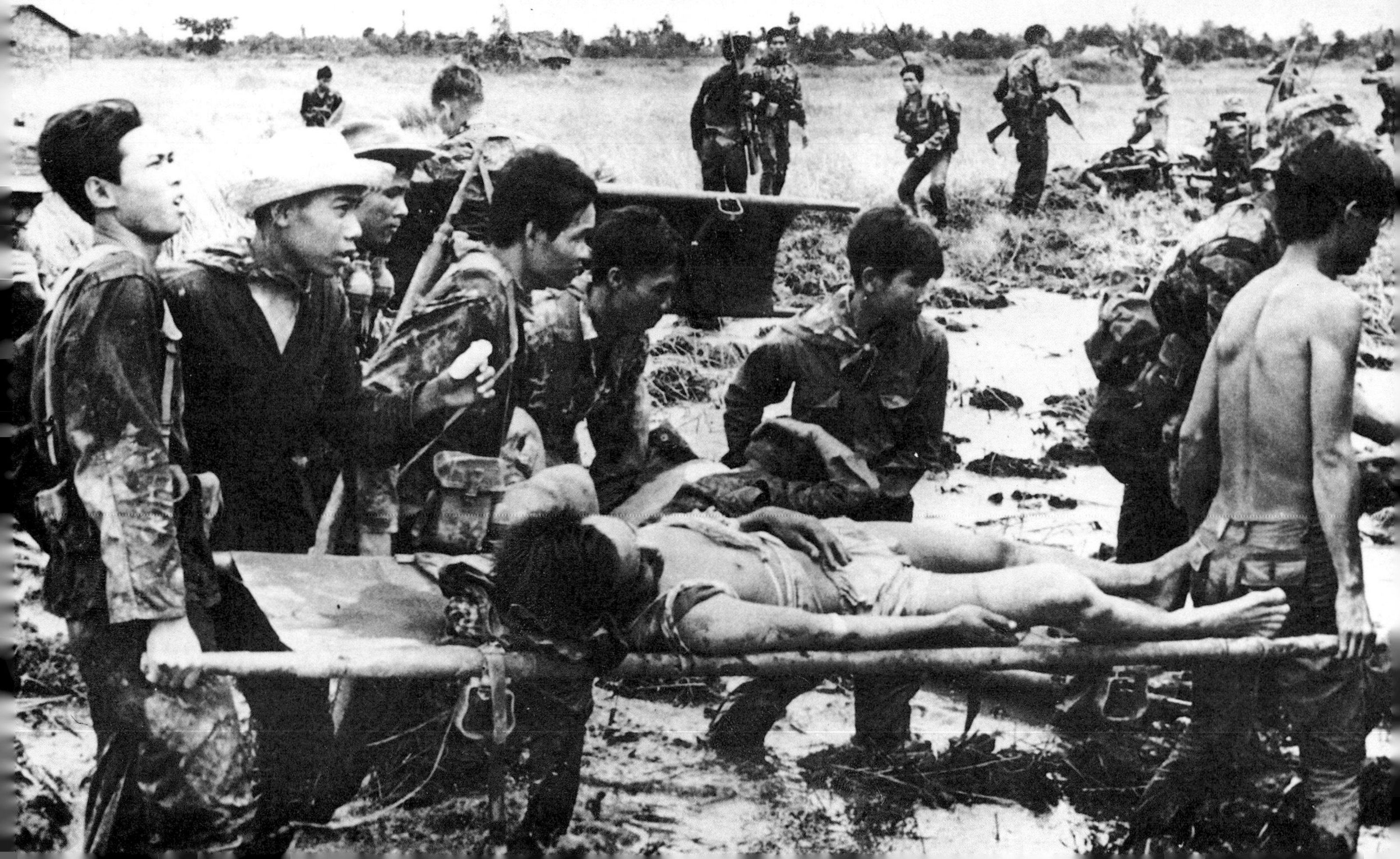

Viet Cong

THE COMMUNIST FORCES during the first Indochina War against the French were generally known as the Viet Minh ('the Vietnamese people'); in the second Indochina War from 1959 to 1975, however, it is usual to draw a distinction between the North Vietnamese and the Viet Cong. The term Viet Cong literally means 'Vietnamese communists' but, in the context of the war, refers to the Viet Minh of southern origin remaining in South Vietnam after the Geneva Accords of 1954 and includes the 80,000 withdrawn to the North after the ceasefire. This distinction was fostered by the politburo in Hanoi, which throughout tried to disclaim its involvement and to suggest that the war, at least in its early stages, was solely an uprising within the South.

Accordingly the Viet Cong were recognised by the North as a National Liberation Front (NLF) in 1960 and later, in 1972, as a Provisional Revolutionary Government (PRG) with a southerner, Nguyen Huu Tho, at its head and with, among others, the colourful character of Madame Binh as foreign minister.

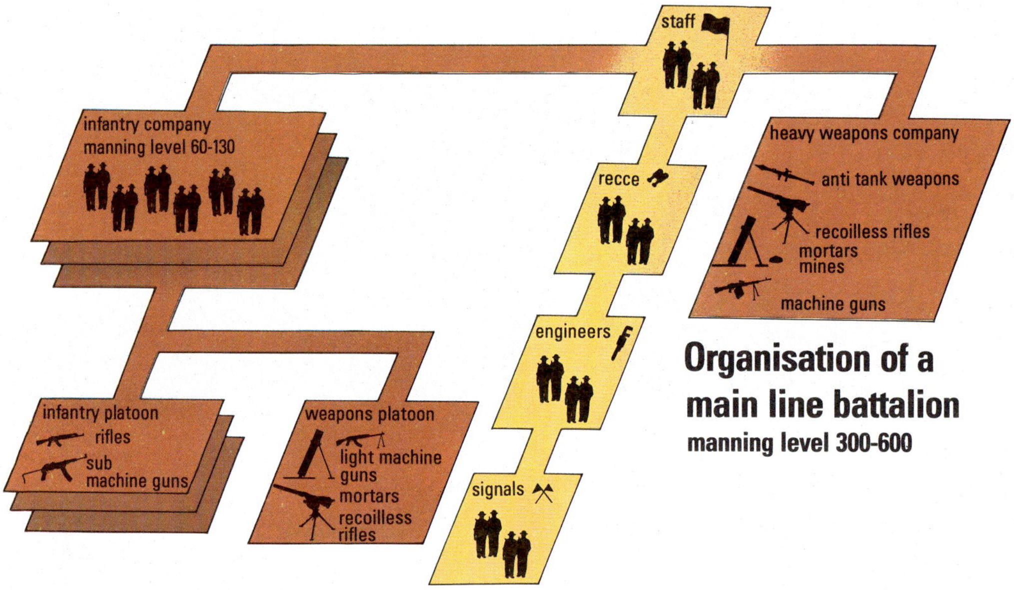

Organisation of a main line battalion
manning level 300-600

The initial armed strength of the Viet Cong in 1959 was estimated at about 5000, with 100,000 active sympathisers in the population. Steady recruitment within the South, reinforced by the infiltration of the trained cadres from the North, gradually built up their strength to about 40,000 by 1963. The Viet Cong organisation was similar to that of insurgents in Malaya.

In the early 1960s its expanding control in the populated areas enabled it to absorb 50 per cent, and in some years 100 per cent, casualties and yet to end a year with its overall strength increased. Its best regional companies and regular battalions were more than a match for equivalent government units and in 1964, after the fall of President Ngo Dinh Diem, Viet Cong

The Viet Cong were adept at using any available means of transport. This canoe-borne unit is in the Mekong Delta.

success seemed assured. The South would probably have fallen in 1965 but for the entry into the war of the United States.

A sudden decline

From 1965 to 1968, the main struggles were fought between US and regular North Vietnamese (NVA) forces, while the Viet Cong maintained their stranglehold over the rural countryside – using the villages to encircle the towns – and prevented the South Vietnamese armed forces from regaining control. In terms of armed strength and control of the population, the Viet Cong reached their peak at the time of the Tet offensive in 1968. Their losses in this offensive probably exceeded 30,000 killed and many more wounded in their best units, and the two subsequent offensives in May and August of 1968 not only broke their military strength but caused the first major defections.

Viet Cong strength then steadily declined and their units became dependent on NVA fillers, while North Vietnamese cadres (mainly Tongkingese and having little affiliation with the people in the South) were infiltrated into the political underground organisation.

The leading Viet Cong officer responsible for recruitment and training in Kien Hoa province in the Mekong Delta, with a population of half a million, surrendered in 1970 for the reason that, whereas he had previously had about 10,000 armed guerrillas under his command, this figure had dropped to 3000 and he decided that the government was winning. In another case, the famous Viet Cong 316 Company – earlier about 300 strong and a first class unit – operating about 48km (30 miles) south of Saigon was reduced by 1971 to a strength of three, all NVA fillers. The Viet Cong only survived as a revolutionary movement in remote areas of the countryside and a few defended mini-bases which they had long controlled.

TOP *Guerrillas off-duty, but with weapons (an SKS rifle and an AK47 assault rifle) close at hand.* ABOVE *Communist guerrillas in Quang Ngai province in 1965 prepare punji-stick booby-traps.* RIGHT *Smiling Viet Cong bring back captured weapons after a successful raid.*

The net result was that, when the North Vietnamese Easter invasion was launched in 1972, the Viet Cong were too weak to assist it and there were even some instances where they refused to supply guides for NVA battalions in the Mekong Delta. It was significant that, during the whole of this invasion period, not one single incident occurred in the teeming population (4 million) of Saigon, not even a hand grenade in a bar.

The PRG publicly remained in the forefront – in the open talks with the United States in Paris, for example – but took no part in the secret talks between Le Duc Tho and Dr Henry Kissinger which resulted in the 1973 ceasefire. After the fall of Saigon in 1975 and the reunification between North and South, the PRG ceased to exist and its Viet Cong members have not been heard of again. They were at one time confined to barracks at Tan Son Nhut Airbase in Saigon. Some Viet Cong have joined the boat people and become refugees.

North Vietnam

AFTER THE GENEVA ACCORDS in 1954, the Viet Minh and its guerrilla army based in Tongking and those parts of Annam north of the 17th parallel became a state – the Democratic Republic of Vietnam. As far as the 21 million people were concerned there was neither a referendum nor an election. The Indochinese Communist Party, later re-named the Lao Dong Workers' Party, under Ho Chi Minh merely took over and was recognised by all communist countries and some neutrals.

After Ho, other members of the politburo – excluding five alternates, one of whom defected to China – were: Le Duan, First Secretary of the party and a former head of the Central Office for South Vietnam (COSVN); Truong Chinh, Chairman of the Standing Committee of the National Assembly and historian of the party; Pham Van Dong, Prime Minister; Pham Hung, member of the Secretariat and head of COSVN from 1967 and ruler of South Vietnam after its fall in 1975; Vo Nguyen Giap, Minister of Defence and Chairman of the Central Military Party Committee, and Le Duc Tho, member of the Secretariat, responsible for organisation and also a former head of COSVN.

Aims and weaknesses

They were all original members of the Indochinese Communist Party, which was strictly orthodox and Stalinist in its outlook. These six men have been in power for about 35 years and are changeable only by mortality. The National Assembly, which is supposed to meet twice a year, rarely does so and even at the height of the war, between 1967 and 1970, was in session for only four days.

The first aim of the politburo was unification with the South and any opposition to this aim became, under Article 7 of the constitution, an act of treason. Its second aim was a Federation of Indochina and, throughout the war up to 1975, the North Vietnamese supported both the Pathet Lao communist forces in Laos and the Khmer Rouge in Cambodia.

The fundamental weakness of the North was its dependence on outside aid, not just for arms and military equipment from Russia and China but also for food. Even in a good harvest year it still needed to import about 400,000 tonnes of rice and other cereals. This weakness was not helped by its socialist economy, the collectivisation of agriculture and a total direction of manpower. These reduced production and led to a peasants' revolt in 1956 in which (according to some reports) more than 500,000 were killed.

LEFT *Vo Nguyen Giap, the man who guided the communist armies to victory.* RIGHT *Ho Chi Minh, whose precise, ruthless planning provided a firm foundation for the communists' strategy during the war.* BELOW *North Vietnamese troops move forward in a typical massed attack during the fighting in Laos.*

million men were lost. In terms of cost this made no impact politically or economically on a totalitarian state and was acceptable to the politburo in a country with a rising male annual birth rate of over 250,000.

It is unlikely, however, that General Giap alone made the major war decisions or ultimately controlled the strategy. A number of actions were pointless in military terms but had an enormous psychological impact overseas. Political, long-term objectives were always at the root of North Vietnamese strategy; this aspect suffused the North's conduct of the war, and Giap's colleagues on the politburo were equally, if not better, qualified in the higher strategy of revolutionary war and in the art of negotiation. They knew that they could not defeat the United States in the field, but that there were other channels to victory.

Long-term strategy

The first instrument for taking over the South by armed struggle already existed in the Viet Cong, over which control could be exercised through COSVN with its headquarters in the jungle north of Saigon and later in north-east Cambodia. It was always headed by a member of the politburo. The second instrument was the North Vietnamese Army (NVA), eventually built up to over 20 divisions under the leadership of General Vo Nguyen Giap, the victor over the French at Dien Bien Phu.

He was responsible for training and tactics, and was a great believer in artillery bombardment followed by mass infantry attacks regardless of casualties. These were horrendous during the course of the war and at a conservative estimate, more than 1

ABOVE LEFT *A SAM missile (the SA-2 Guideline model) is prepared for action.* BELOW *North Vietnamese anti-aircraft gunners await the next American attack.*

Hanoi's Strategy

IT IS NOT DIFFICULT to understand the strategy of guerrilla warfare on the ground as expounded by Mao in terms such as 'using the villages to encircle the towns' or the 'strategy is to pit one man against ten but the tactics are to pit ten men against one'. The higher strategy of revolutionary war, however, is more complex and is based on the concepts of time, space and cost. Time means a gradual wearing down of a government and its allies' will to resist through protracted war until a collapse finally occurs.

If time is to be gained then space must be held, not in the sense of holding territory as in conventional war, but by being in a position to threaten a government throughout its territory, from attacks on outposts to hand grenades in the capital city and by penetrating into all groups of its society so that there is no complete security anywhere. A protracted war of this nature then imposes enormous waste and costs – for example, many men are required to defend bridges, some of which may never be attacked. Eventually a situation is reached when a revolutionary movement is, without necessarily winning any battle, imposing costs on a government and its allies which are not indefinitely acceptable. At that point it is winning the war.

The four channels

Through this strategy Hanoi had four possible channels to victory: a failure of American resolution; a failure of South Vietnamese resolution; a failure of the Americans and South Vietnamese to adopt the correct counter-strategy, and a failure of the South Vietnamese to build, with American help, a stable and self-reliant state and government. These channels were all inter-related and could be combined to achieve victory. Throughout most of the war they were all open and, in the end, victory came mainly through the first one.

That this might be so was always understood by Hanoi, and General Vo Nguyen Giap expressed it thus: 'The enemy will be caught in a dilemma: he has to drag out the war in order to win it and does not possess, on the other hand, the psychological and political means to fight a long drawn out war.'

Nevertheless throughout the 16 years of war Hanoi had to make some fateful decisions. When the Viet Cong were clearly winning in 1964, Hanoi began to insert regular North Vietnamese Army (NVA) units, partly to accelerate victory but mainly to be in place to reap the reward of reunification under the politburo. On American intervention in 1965 Hanoi had two options: it could withdraw and retreat to the status quo of 1959 or, by applying the same concepts of

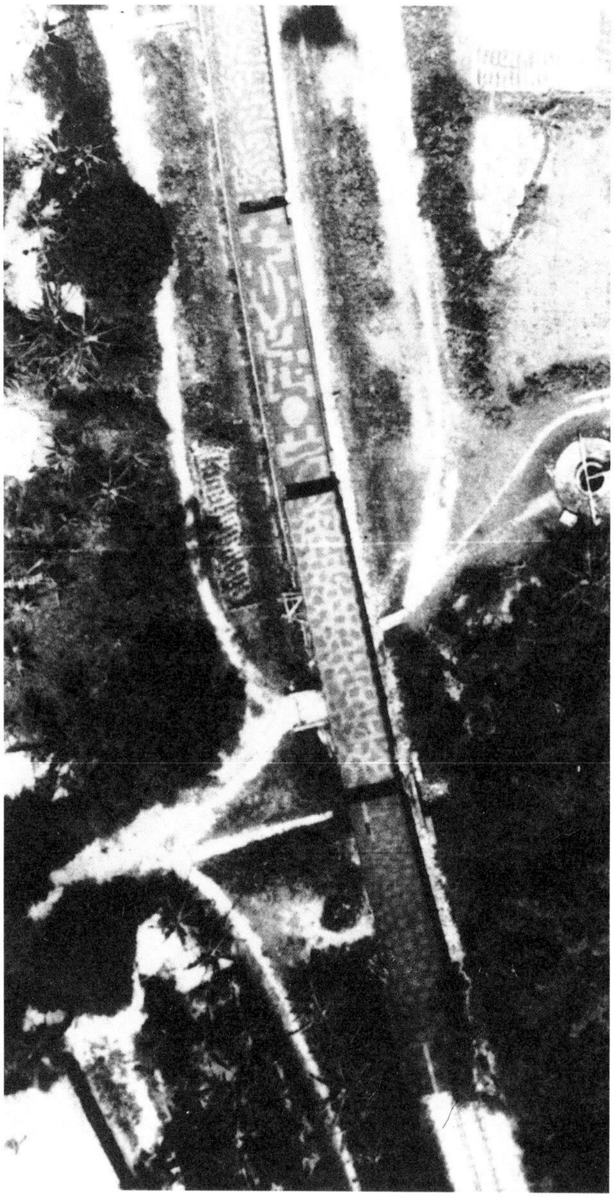

North Vietnam felt under constant threat from US air and sea power. RIGHT *A train is camouflaged against aerial spotters.* BELOW *Soldiers place mines on a beach near Dong Hoi.*

war, it could take on the might of the United States which would require greatly increased costs in manpower and greater support from Russia and China.

The second option was acceptable, because Hanoi could dictate the pace and intensity of operations either by engaging the Americans or by fading away across the borders. Later, by conducting the Tet offensive in 1968, Hanoi destroyed the Viet Cong militarily as a possible rival in the South and gained a great psychological victory within the United States. The former meant that the remainder of the war had to be fought almost entirely by the North Vietnamese Army in conventional terms, as in the Easter invasion of 1972 and the final offensive of 1975. It should be noted that 1964, 1968 and 1972, the major decision years, were all presidential election years, when American political resolution was at its weakest.

The use of negotiations

Hanoi's major psychological weapon was negotiation as expressed in the phrase: 'Fighting while negotiating is aimed at opening another front'. The negotiations were held solely with the United States, which implied that the United States was prepared to settle well short of victory and make concessions at the expense of South Vietnam. Moreover, the very possibility of a negotiated settlement – whatever its terms – steadily sapped any remaining American resolution, as indeed it was designed to do. There was no need for Hanoi to make any concessions at all until after the failure of the 1972 invasion, when the mining of Haiphong (threatening food supplies) and the devastating accuracy of the new American 'smart' bombs, made it clear to Hanoi that, if victory was to be achieved, it must get the American Air Force out of the war.

Limited concessions had thus to be made without ruling out a continuation of the war and an eventual takeover of the South by force. Even the principle of international supervision was acceptable provided that it did not work. In reaching a ceasefire agreement in January 1973, Le Duc Tho proved more than a match for Henry Kissinger. The Americans were out and, as for the agreement, the members of the politburo knew that at the right moment they could drive tanks through it.

ABOVE *North Vietnamese fighter pilots undergo briefing. Air defence against US bombers posed great technical problems.*
BELOW *The moment of triumph after a war of attrition: grim-faced North Vietnamese troops in Saigon, 1975.*

The ultimate protest: a Buddhist is enveloped in flames after an act of self-immolation. Civilian dissent was an unwanted burden for the government.

South Vietnam

IN 1955, one year after the Geneva Accords, South Vietnam became a separate sovereign state as the Republic of Vietnam following a referendum in which well over 90 per cent of the population voted in favour. Its constitution was similar to that of the United States with an elected President, Senate and Assembly. Beneath these the country was divided into over 50 provinces and cities with a population of 19 million – 2 million less than in the North – rising steadily at 3 per cent a year.

South Vietnam was almost entirely agricultural with a few rubber estates and some minor industries. The main crop was rice, and the rice fields of the Mekong Delta were the richest in Asia. Experts estimated that, with the introduction of the new 'miracle' rice strains and given peace, South Vietnam would have been able to export up to 5 million tonnes a year. But because of the war and its economic disruption the South needed imports of cereals in most years.

The first president, Ngo Dinh Diem, was overthrown and murdered by generals in November 1963; thenceforth, there were constant changes of leadership until General Nguyen Van Thieu was elected president from ten other contestants in 1967, with 34.8 per cent of the votes. He remained president until within a few days of the final collapse in 1975.

A remarkable feature of the war was the number of elections held, not only for the presidency but for the Senate and the Assembly and later for provincial councils. In spite of Viet Cong intimidation, the turnout of voters was better than in most Western democracies and in one election in

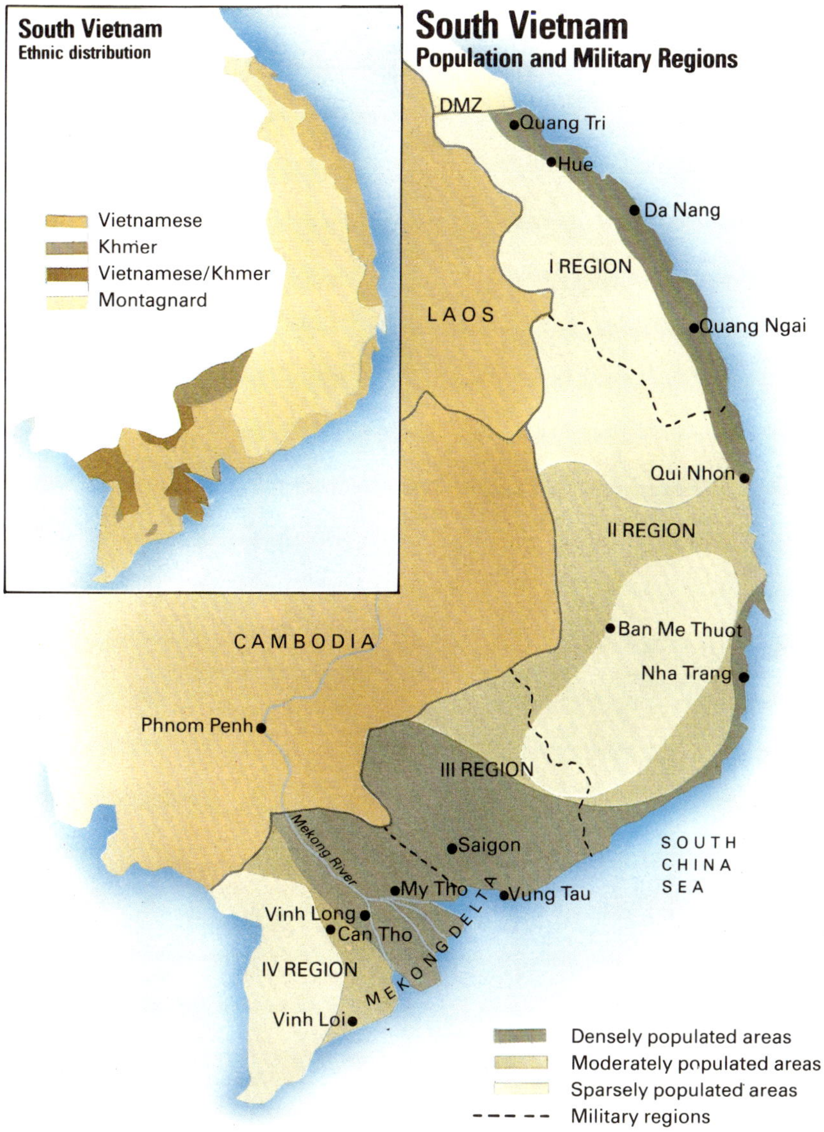

August 1971 for the Assembly there were 1239 candidates for 159 seats.

A divided nation

The great problem was cohesion. South Vietnam lacked the efficient administrative structure and wealth of, for example, Malaya. It was a newly created nation under great stress and with many divisive elements. The ethnic Montagnard tribes in the hills disliked all Vietnamese, while religious sects such as the Hoa Hao and the Cao Dai resented central government interference. There was also antipathy between Buddhists and Catholics partly because of the policies of President Diem and partly because Catholic villages, particularly those which had fled from the North with their priests, were resolute in defence and tended to receive greater support. A million Chinese in the cities added to the mixture.

The country inherited an army of about 170,000 built up by the French against the Viet Minh, a Civil Guard in each province of light infantry companies, various hamlet defence forces and a small ineffective police force which until its reorganisation played little part in the war. The army (ARVN) was built up by the United States on conventional lines, with a small navy and air force. ARVN proved a cumbersome and inflexible structure to cope with an insurgency and was only saved in 1965 by direct American intervention.

After the Tet offensive in 1968 all the armed forces were completely re-equipped and their fighting quality greatly improved. There were always bad units but there were also some remarkably good ones. By 1972 the 1st, Marine and Airborne Divisions were three of the best in the world. The individual soldier, conscripted at 18, was fighting all his life with little respite and, at one-tenth of the population, Vietnamese casualties were higher than American casualties in every week but three of the war.

ABOVE RIGHT *A South Vietnamese soldier takes cover during close fighting in the delta region, 1975.* RIGHT *Summary execution of a Viet Cong officer by a Saigon police chief.*

America's Involvement

ABOVE *A Patrol Air Cushion Vehicle (PACV) patrols the Mekong Delta.* BELOW *The first wave of infantry follows amphibious LVT ashore at Tam Quan during 1965.*

THE UNITED STATES became involved in support of the French in the first Indochina War for two reasons. When the negotiations to end the Korean War remained unresolved for two years at Panmunjom, Secretary of State John Foster Dulles said that the communists could not 'stall it up here to have a free run down there [in Indochina]'. Secondly, after NATO had just been founded, the French alone had a standing army in Europe but that army was being stretched by its overseas commitments; the Americans therefore decided to aid the French. This action also fitted in with their general policy of preventing communist aggression in terms of the Truman Doctrine enunciated during the Greek Civil War and of containing China. Moreover, the three new sovereign states of Laos, Cambodia and South Vietnam, although not members of the Southeast Asia Treaty Organisation (SEATO), were included in its defence provisions as 'the protocol states'.

When the French withdrew from South Vietnam after 1954, the Americans inevitably and naturally took over the advisory role and training of the South Vietnamese forces as allowed under the Geneva Accords. President Dwight D. Eisenhower also provided the necessary economic aid both to pay these forces and to prevent South Vietnam from collapsing.

Although once mooted at the time of Dien Bien Phu, no one envisaged the direct involvement of American combat units. This was still the view of General Maxwell Taylor when he visited Saigon in 1961 on behalf of President John F. Kennedy as the second Vietnam War was beginning to escalate. It was decided, however, to give Vietnam additional aid, increase the number of advisers, and send in American transport helicopters, mainly as a means of supplying remote and isolated outposts.

This breach of the Geneva Accords was justified on the grounds that North Vietnam had already broken them; ample evidence for this was soon forthcoming in the International Control Commission Report of 1962. President Kennedy had also made his policy in Southeast Asia very clear by the deployment of a marine brigade in north-east Thailand in 1961.

The build-up

When Lyndon Johnson succeeded to the presidency in 1963 on the assassination of Kennedy, the situation was deteriorating rapidly. In the summer of 1964 there occurred the Tongking Gulf incident in which North Vietnamese torpedo boats attacked Ameri-

Ratio of combat to support troops in the US army

	combat	support
World War II	36.2%	63.8%
Korea	33.0%	67.0%
Vietnam	22.2%	77.8%

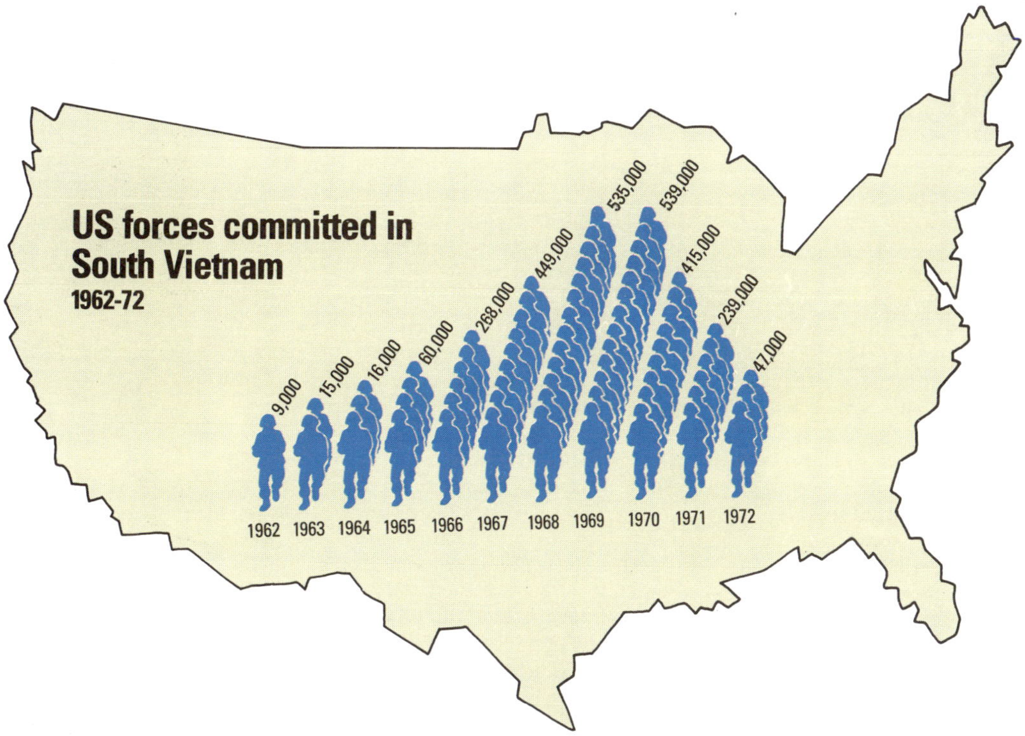

can destroyers in international waters. The congressional resolution which followed gave the president full powers and was the legal basis for all subsequent American action.

The president, however, was in the middle of an election campaign, in which he defeated Senator Barry Goldwater on a peace ticket. After the election the situation got worse; a number of Viet Cong attacks took place on US compounds. This led to the decision in February 1965 to start bombing the North as 'a measured response', and was followed in March by the landing of marines.

As United States troops became involved in battle, the original intention was soon lost. That summer the president stated: 'If we are driven from the field in Vietnam, then no nation can ever have the same confidence in American promises or American protection. We will stand in Vietnam.' That statement made the American commitment absolute. Over the next three years, American troop strength grew to just under 550,000 men, plus far eastern air force and offshore navy units.

BELOW *Troopers of the 101st Airborne Division repulse the enemy from old Viet Cong trenches in Operation Hawthorne, June 1966.* RIGHT *A wounded 25th Infantry trooper is helped to a rear area for evacuation.*

This required, because the individual soldier only did one year in Vietnam, a massive draft programme. Casualties mounted to hundreds a week and the cost reached $30 billion a year. After the Tet offensive, the opening of talks and the election of President Richard Nixon in 1968 the commitment steadily declined, becoming in effect a rearguard action with a final burst of air activity at the time of the North Vietnamese Army's Easter invasion in 1972.

After the ceasefire in January 1973, the American commitment was reduced to the provision of military equipment supervised by the Defence Attaché in the embassy in Saigon. The only other outstanding commitment, contained in a letter from President Nixon to President Thieu dated 5 January 1973, was a promise by the American president 'to take swift and severe retaliatory action' if North Vietnam violated the ceasefire. Congress, the War Powers Act, Watergate and the resignation of Nixon changed the perspective, however, and in 1975 the promises of the previous ten years came to nothing.

American Strategy

VIETNAM was of no use to the United States either economically or geographically. It was, however, of great political importance and acquired a moral significance for both opponents and proponents of the war. American strategy must be viewed basically in the context of the Truman Doctrine of preventing the expansion of communism; the American outlook was defensive and was aimed at preserving the status quo, rather than toppling the North Vietnamese communists or altering boundaries.

Strategy was also conditioned by the Americans' experience in the Korean War and little heed was paid either to the French experience in Indochina or to the lessons of the civil war in China. The Americans had no clear idea of what winning meant and there was, therefore, no coherent strategy other than to react to Hanoi's initiatives.

Under President John Kennedy American strategy was expressed in somewhat simple terms: 'Give President Diem what he needs to win his own war' and 'We will sink or swim with Diem'. Diem's 'strategic hamlet' programme was supported, but American impatience for quick results led to its becoming overstretched. It was conducted haphazardly instead of being directed as a strategic advance in clear priority areas. Kennedy also failed to see the strategic significance of the Ho Chi Minh Trail in Laos.

By agreeing to the coup against Diem, the Americans were automatically hooked to his successors. The Democratic administration, having already been blamed for losing China, could not risk losing Vietnam too. This compelled President Lyndon Johnson to intervene, and between 1965 and 1968 the war was fought as an American war in which overwhelming firepower and material wealth would be decisive. The real

RIGHT *US soldiers of the 25th Infantry Division question a Viet Cong suspect in Quang Ngai province, May 1967.*
BELOW *1st Cavalry troopers and South Vietnamese children hide from sniper fire south of Da Nang.*

The new US response 1969-72

ABOVE *A hut wall is smashed in a search and destroy mission. Such operations sought to locate Viet Cong food caches.* RIGHT *A marine sets fire to a Vietnamese hut in the course of a sweep against the Viet Cong in March 1967.*

nature of the war was ignored and only lip service paid to control of the rural areas and nation building. The pressure was on for a military victory before the 1968 election through a strategy of attrition. One major operation followed another and all battles were won. As one general remarked, however: 'I can go on killing Viet Cong for ever but where's that going to get us?'

Attrition no answer

The aim was, through inflicting an unacceptable 'quotient of pain' and through the 'five minutes more' syndrome, to force Hanoi to the conference table ready to settle. The costs were mounting alarmingly, however, and when, after the Tet offensive in 1968, General William Westmoreland asked for 200,000 more men, the strategy was bankrupt. How could attrition possibly have worked when, in the final score, the North accepted more than 1 million killed and the United States could not accept 47,000?

President Richard Nixon switched the strategy in 1969 by emphasising Vietnamisation – which involved improving the performance of the South Vietnamese government and forces so that they could take over the greater share of the war – and pacification (regaining control of the populated areas). He started the withdrawal of American forces and later cancelled the draft to dampen dissent. He opened secret negotiations with Hanoi to secure a 'just peace'. It became the task of the remaining United States forces merely to keep the NVA from interfering with these policies.

This strategy was successful to the extent that it left Hanoi with no alternative but to launch a conventional invasion in 1972. Its failure and Nixon's tough response in mining Haiphong harbour, thereby threatening food supplies, and in bombing the North, faced Hanoi with defeat. No matter what happened in Vietnam, however, the war was already lost within the United States. Domestic pressure compelled Nixon to accept a ceasefire which would inevitably give ultimate victory to the North. The Americans had failed to secure their own rear base.

The Ho Chi Minh Trail

AN ESSENTIAL FEATURE of success in war is the security of the rear base and a secure line of communication to the front. This gives a side the strategic initiative and flexibility in attack. China had been the great rear base in the first Indochina War after 1950 and North Vietnam, with supplies coming from Russia and China, was to be the secure rear base in the second Indochina War. The secure line of communication to the front was the Ho Chi Minh Trail.

The trail began in the mountain passes linking southern North Vietnam and southern Laos and then wound down through an area sparsely populated by hill tribes to Sepone and Attopeu. It was later extended to Stung Treng and Kratie on the Mekong River in north-east Cambodia.

It was never a single trail, but rather a spider's web of tracks initially for men and bicycles but gradually improved in places by all-weather roads and bridges to take trucks, artillery and tanks with an oil pipeline to supply them. Indeed, by 1973 it had become a freeway rather than a trail. In the conduct of the war, its security as a line of communication was as vital to North Vietnam as the Atlantic had been to Great Britain and the United States in World War II.

Neutrality of Laos

When it became clear in 1961 that the North Vietnamese were operating in Laos and using the trail (contrary to the Geneva Accords) President John F. Kennedy deployed a marine brigade in north-east Thailand, thereby threatening to intervene in Laos. This prospect horrified the North Vietnamese and their Soviet and Chinese supporters, who willingly accepted the re-convening of the Geneva conference in 1962.

Averill Harriman, the chief American negotiator, was fascinated by the irrelevant prospect of establishing a neutral government in Laos and ignored the military aspect of the new agreement, one provision of which was that there should be no foreign troops in Laos. This automatically barred the Americans, who were monitored by Senator J. W. Fulbright and the Senate Foreign Relations Committee. There was no such sanction on the North Vietnamese because the supervisory International Control Commission was rendered completely ineffective by the actions of its Polish member. North Vietnam's line of communication to the front was secured.

It was down the trail that most of the 80,000 personnel withdrawn to the North in 1954 were returned to the South, followed later by North Vietnamese units. The number of men coming down the trail gradually rose to 7000 a month between 1965 and 1968, the total for 1968 alone being estimated at 100,000. American air attacks, with the agreement of the Laos government, could do no more than slow down the speed of movement, most of which was at night with men and vehicles being dispersed and camouflaged during the day. From the time of leaving North Vietnam it sometimes took men three to four months to reach their destination in the South. After the ceasefire in 1973, the journey took just a few days by truck.

In the period between 1967 and 1970 a second secure line of communication for supplies to forces in the southern portion of South Vietnam was through the port of Sihanoukville in Cambodia. The supplies were then trucked quite openly (and to the financial advantage of Cambodia's ruler, Prince Sihanouk) up to north-east Cambodia, where four NVA divisions were located. When Sihanoukville was closed to this traffic after the fall of Sihanouk in 1970, the extension of the Ho Chi Minh Trail into Cambodia below the 12th parallel and the need to re-route supplies down it reduced NVA capabilities for about eighteen months.

During this period, a number of South Vietnamese raids were made on the trail, the most important of which was Operation Lam Son 719

in 1971 in which the South Vietnamese captured Sepone. Unfortunately they delayed their withdrawal too long until it became a rout. Thereafter, except for air attacks, the trail was secure. It is an interesting speculation that, if American units in 1965 had occupied southern Laos and completely blocked the trail, the major battles would have been fought there and the war might have taken a very different course.

BELOW *Lorries pour along the Ho Chi Minh Trail in the mass logistics operation which kept the forces in the South supplied. The individual lorries* (INSET) *were often heavily camouflaged to protect them from US air power.*
BELOW RIGHT *North Vietnamese infantry, armed with bazookas, on the march in Cambodia.*

Supplying the Viet Cong

Communist Weapons

THE VIET CONG were originally armed with a mixture of small-arms picked up from the battlefields of World War II and the first Indochina War against the French. These included the old French Indochina rifle, the Mas 36, and even shotguns. The heaviest weapon was the mortar, with which the Viet Cong proved to be very accurate. As the insurgency progressed, US weapons were captured from the South Vietnamese.

It is interesting to compare figures on weapons lost and recovered in Malaya and South Vietnam. In Malaya, between 1948 and 1960, 2829 weapons were lost and 8464 recovered. In South Vietnam, in $2\frac{1}{2}$ years between August 1962 and the end of 1964, 24,537 were lost and 12,642 recovered.

Booby-traps and tunnels

Meanwhile, as the Ho Chi Minh Trail was extended and improved and a new supply route opened through the port of Sihanoukville in Cambodia, Soviet and Chinese small-arms began to appear. The Viet Cong were completely re-equipped before the Tet offensive with AK47 rifles and B40 rockets, which temporarily gave them a higher firepower than the South Vietnamese. In defence of their own areas the Viet Cong placed great reliance on mines and booby-traps, including poisoned bamboo stakes. For example, during the pacification period from 1969 to 1971, in one province alone the South Vietnamese territorial forces suffered 320 casualties in six weeks, of which 290 were caused by booby-traps.

One unusual feature of the war was the Viet Cong tunnel system. In the dry laterite areas north of Saigon extensive underground tunnels, partly for defence against air attacks, were used by headquarters such as the Central Office for South Vietnam, but tunnels were also used tactically to conceal forces in populated areas before an attack and also in defence against American or South Vietnamese Army sweeps. Frequently, when an area had been ostensibly cleared, a Viet Cong unit would emerge from its tunnels and create havoc in the rear. The entrances were very narrow, well camouflaged and hard to find and, even if found, the twists and turns made them difficult to deal with. A hand grenade was not enough.

Viet Cong booby-traps were ingenious and deadly. ABOVE RIGHT *A spiked trap suspended above a door to swing down at chest height.* RIGHT *A grenade attached to a trip-wire.*

Punji sticks
concealed underground bamboo spikes or nails to trap victim's foot, piercing boot and leg

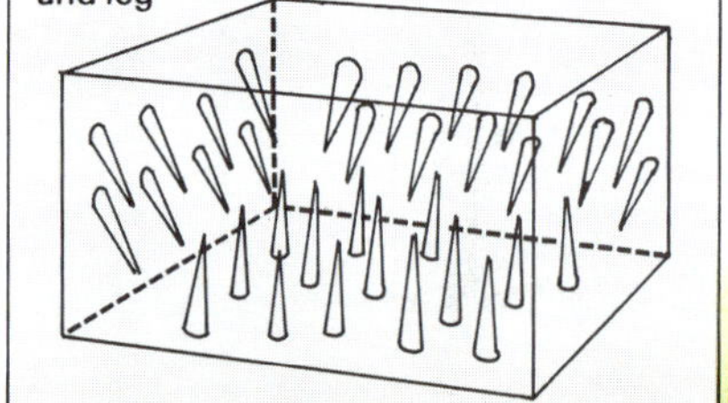

Mines
mines concealed around obstacle across path

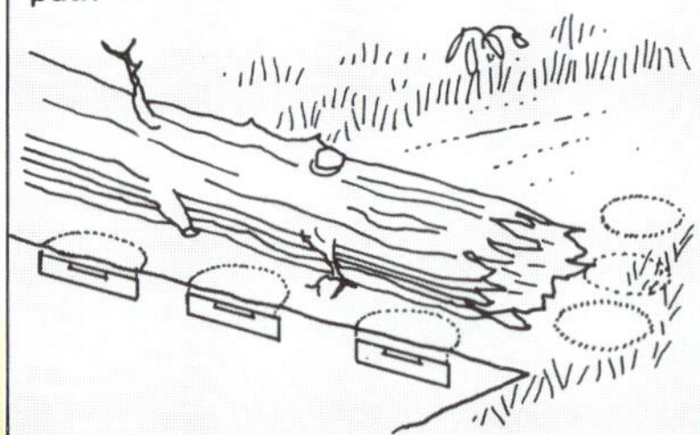

Grenades
grenades with pin extracted, concealed in cans and linked to trip wire

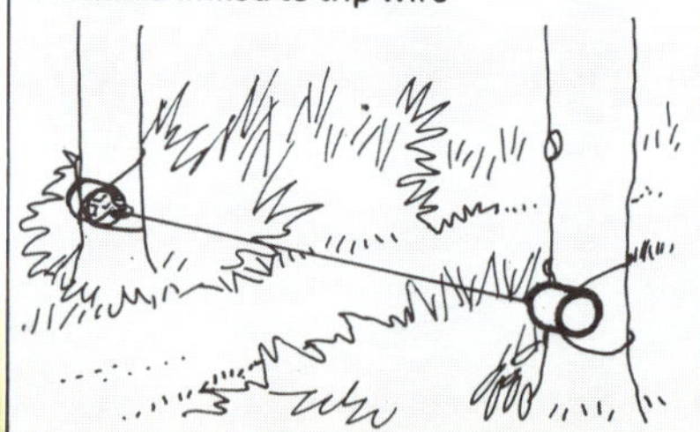

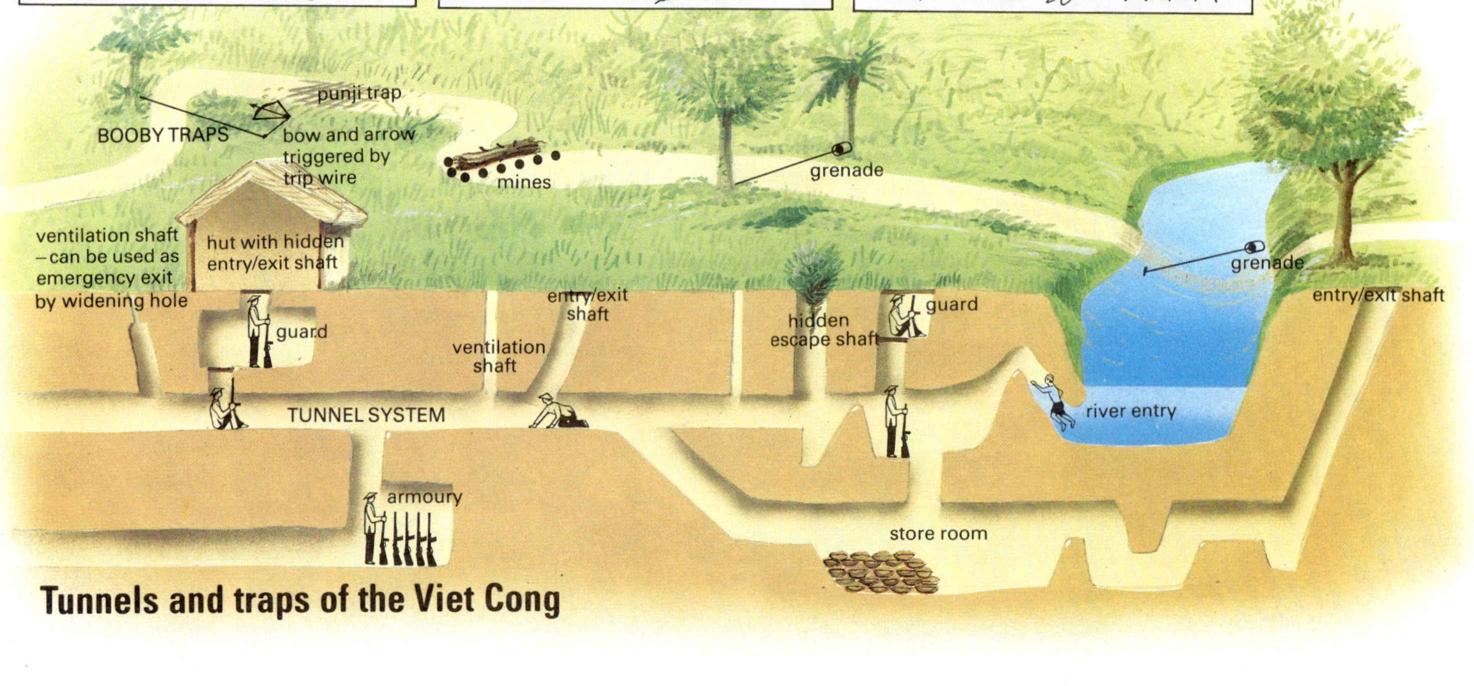

Tunnels and traps of the Viet Cong

Rockets, tanks and artillery

The North Vietnamese Army (NVA) was equipped throughout with Soviet weapons, some of which, mainly small-arms, were made in China. Before 1972 these were almost entirely infantry and anti-aircraft weapons, except for a 122mm rocket with a range of about 18km (11 miles) for indiscriminate firing into cities. At that range it was too inaccurate to be used on military targets.

In the 1972 invasion the whole picture changed; the NVA was equipped with tanks and artillery. The tanks included the Chinese PT76 and the efficient Soviet T54 fitted with infra-red sights and a 100mm gun. While some captured US 105mm guns and 155mm howitzers were used in the An Loc area, the main artillery weapon used was the deadly Soviet 130mm gun, which was mobile and accurate and easily out-ranged the American guns. It was the outstanding weapon of the war.

In their set-piece attacks, the NVA placed great reliance on artillery and mortar (also up to 130mm) bombardments. More than 70,000 rounds were fired into An Loc (population 20,000) in five weeks with 7000 rounds on each night of the two main attacks.

The NVA was already heavily equipped with mobile anti-aircraft weapons such as the 57mm and 0.5in machine guns but in 1972 the SAM-7 (the Strela heat-seeking missile), capable of being carried by one man, was introduced and immediately restricted low flying and all helicopter operations. This neutralised South Vietnamese superiority in the air and, by 1975, the NVA was superior in both weaponry and supplies on the ground. A war which had been begun by ill-equipped guerrillas was finally won by an army which was technologically superior to its enemies.

ABOVE *The Soviet-built M1946 field gun of 130mm calibre had exceptional range and could outdistance its American equivalents.* RIGHT *Captured North Vietnamese arms of Soviet and Chinese design and manufacture.* BELOW *Crew prepare an SA-2 Guideline surface-to-air missile for launching in North Vietnam. The SA-2 was a medium altitude weapon.*

The US Armoury

THE SOUTH VIETNAMESE ARMY (ARVN) was originally equipped by the United States to meet a conventional invasion with tanks, armoured personnel carriers (APCs) and artillery. It was often said that the tanks were used only for *coups d'état*, but many were used in a defensive role, dug in to form a pillbox. The APCs could be used only in dry weather, but were hampered by the network of canals. The artillery, however, were much used in defence and were eventually deployed to district towns to give support to local forces and outposts. During the early part of the war ARVN tended to be too encumbered by its equipment, and the lightly equipped regional forces were more mobile and effective.

As part of the Vietnamisation programme after the Tet offensive of 1968, all forces were equipped with the new light Armalite M16 rifle, capable of more rapid fire than the communist AK47 but not as robust.

Artillery duels

Excluding aircraft, helicopters and the normal infantry weapons, the main US weapon was artillery tactically grouped in fire-bases. Batteries of 105mm and 155mm were lifted by helicopter into small fortresses on

The US Army's fire support bases provided a comprehensive and flexible backup for infantry operations.

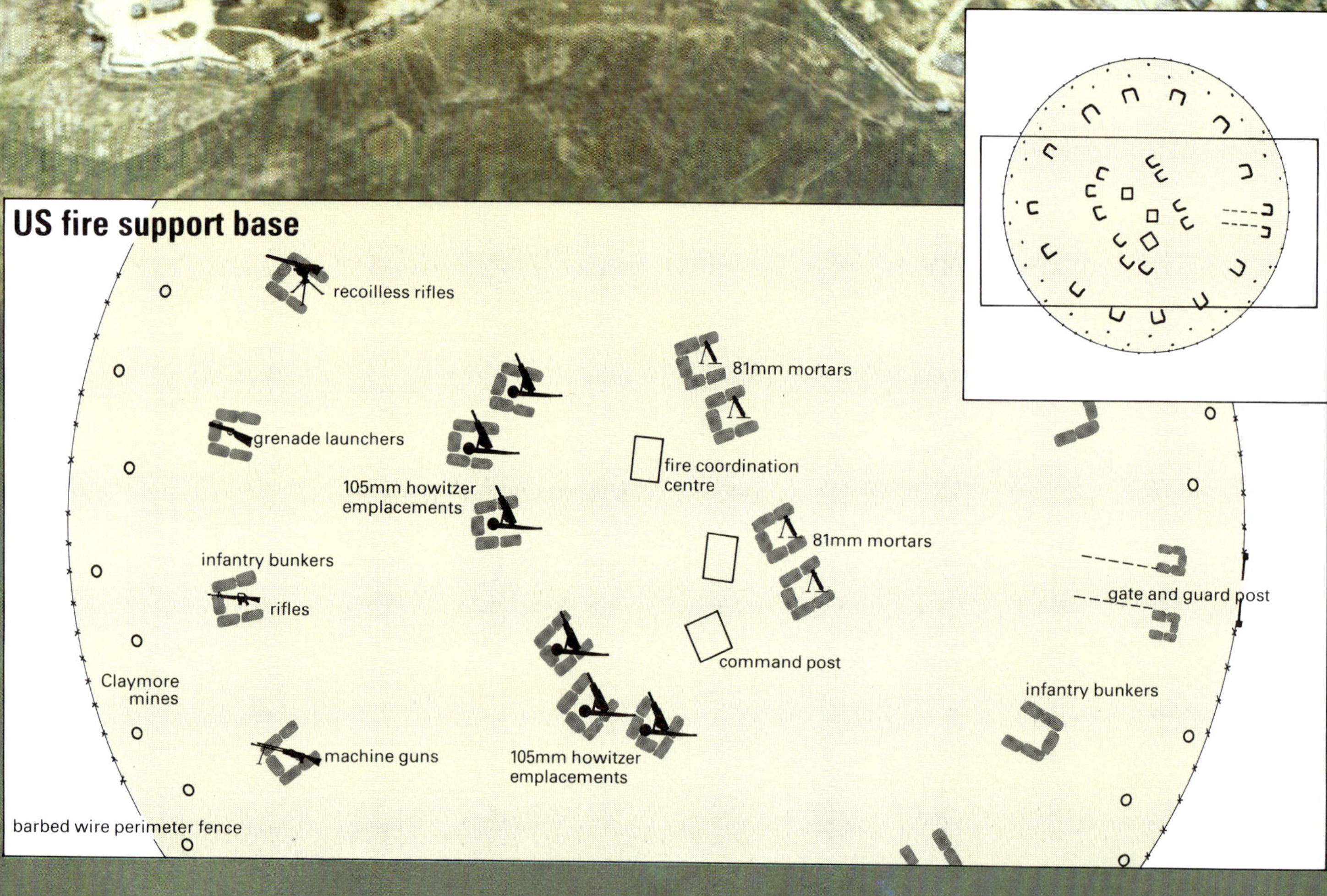

prominent features so that they could dominate the surrounding countryside and support ground forces operating within their range. This was very effective between 1965 and 1968 when there was no NVA artillery to oppose them.

ARVN adopted similar tactics after 1968, but in 1972 the NVA's 130mm guns, with greatly superior range, blew the fire-bases to pieces. Some of them, like Camp Carroll with a diameter of little more than 275m (300 yards) across, took over 2000 rounds on the first morning of the invasion with no means of reply. From that moment the gun batteries had to be kept constantly on the move to avoid destruction. The only US gun capable of engaging the 130mm was the 175mm, which was far from mobile and required both radar and computers to operate in a counter-battery role.

During these later battles the light anti-tank weapon (LAW) carried by the South Vietnamese did, however, prove a match at short range for even the T54 tank. In An Loc, 39 were destroyed within the perimeter. The South Vietnamese were later equipped with the TOW anti-tank missile and heavier American M48 tanks.

ABOVE *The M48 medium tank had a 90mm gun and was capable of competing with the larger Soviet T54 of the North Vietnamese.* LEFT *Mortars were inaccurate weapons but their rate of fire and mobility were valued by air-dropped infantry.*

Special weapons

Much of the fighting and activity took place at night. Apart from flares, all sorts of night devices including infra-red and radar were used to pick up movement on the ground. Sensors were also dropped further afield to monitor traffic on the Ho Chi Minh Trail. Mines, including Claymores, and barbed wire were much used in defence and there was even talk of emulating the Morice line (as built by the French on the Tunisian-Algerian frontier) on the DMZ.

The use of chemicals – especially defoliants such as Agent Orange – was common. They were designed to make infiltration routes vulnerable to reconnaissance and bombing, but their effect was probably small.

The weapon most commonly associated with Vietnam, however, no doubt partly because of its dramatic effect on colour television, was napalm. Burning oil has been a weapon of war for centuries, and napalm had proved more effective than high explosive against Japanese bunkers in World War II. It was also useful on marshy ground where high explosive was ineffective, for clearing an area of booby-traps, and for clearing underground tunnel networks.

Soviet M-46 130mm Field Gun

calibre 130mm **weight** 7700kg (16,975lb) **barrel length** 7.6m (24ft 11in) **depression/elevation** −2.5° to +45° **rate of fire** 5-6rpm **ammunition** HE, APHE **crew** 9

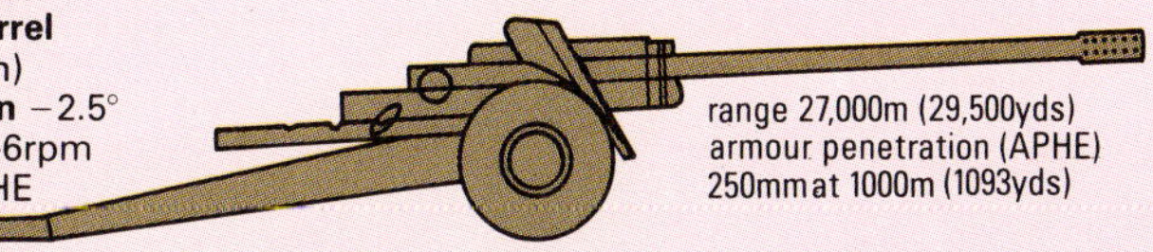

range 27,000m (29,500yds)
armour penetration (APHE)
250mm at 1000m (1093yds)

American M-101 105mm Howitzer

calibre 105mm **weight** 2222kg (4899lb) **barrel length** 2.57m (8ft 5¼in) **depression/elevation** −5° to +66° **rate of fire** 1st 4 mins 4rpm, 1st 10 mins 3rpm, sustained fire 100 rounds per hour **ammunition** HE, HEAT, smoke, illuminatory, gas, chemical **crew** 8

range 11,000m (12,000yds)
armour penetration (HEAT)
102mm at 1500m (1640yds)

Tactical Bombing

THE US ARMY was supported in Vietnam by the US 7th Air Force. At least nine enormous air field complexes, complete with concrete aircraft shelters, were built along the South Vietnamese coast from Hue in the north to Can Tho in the south, with nearby bases in north-east Thailand at Udorn and Ubon. Fighter aircraft were available, but North Vietnamese MiGs were not used over the South.

As part of the attrition strategy which required the maximum firepower and as a means of reducing friendly casualties, particularly in operations where artillery could not be brought to bear, tactical air support was nearly always called for in ground operations. A high sortie rate was maintained by aircraft ranging from the old North American T-28 to the F-4 Phantom and there was hardly a day when aircraft were not in action. The cost was enormous and, to justify it, communist casualties from air attack were always counted in fives or tens.

The major development was the first use of Boeing B-52 and General Dynamics F-111 bombers in a tactical

TOP *A flight of B-52 bombers pounds a North Vietnamese target near Bien Hoa in 1966.* ABOVE RIGHT *The aftermath of an American fighter bomber attack.* RIGHT *US Air Force C-123s spray defoliant over a valley in 1967. Vast tracts of land were laid waste by the Americans in this controversial bombing campaign.*

role. They were originally used on infiltration routes near the Cambodian and Laos borders and on suspected jungle base areas, which probably took as much high explosive as was dropped in World War II. Some areas north of Saigon were so cratered as to resemble a moonscape.

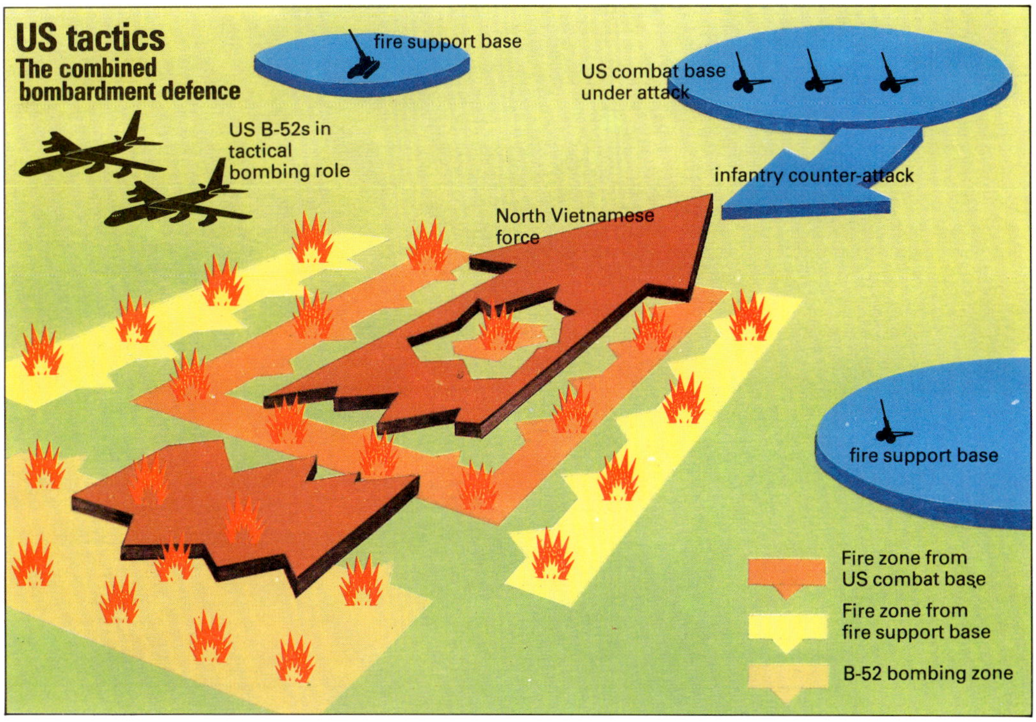

Support for defenders

When Khe Sanh was besieged and isolated at the end of 1967 the B-52s were used in a closer tactical role. It was not difficult to work out the area in which NVA forces would be massing for an attack. These concentrations were carpet-bombed by B-52s in groups of three, with each aircraft dropping at least 40 500lb bombs. Although no firm figures are available, heavy casualties were inflicted and no major attack ever developed. This technique proved decisive during the 1972 invasion. Both at Kontum and An Loc, because ARVN held its ground, the NVA was compelled to launch set-piece attacks.

American advisers with ARVN could calculate the lines of attack and the forming-up areas. These could be accurately hit by the B-52s from about 9000m (30,000 feet), day or night and irrespective of the weather, provided the correct off-sets to the fixed marker beacons were set in their computers.

On many occasions large bodies of NVA troops were caught before they got into action. For example, at An Loc one column including 15 tanks was engulfed in a B-52 raid as it was moving in to attack the southern perimeter. The NVA constantly switched its forces in an attempt to avoid being caught in such raids. One obvious ploy was to move a unit into an area which had just been bombed but, since this could often be deduced, such areas might be bombed again. Ghastly accidents did take place: in Cambodia in 1973, one B-52 in a flight of three hit the beacon itself which was in the town of Neak Leung because the off-set from the marker beacon had not been fed into the B-52's computer.

RIGHT *A Douglas A-1E Skyraider of the South Vietnamese Air Force takes off armed with six napalm bombs.*

BELOW *US Navy pilots recount their exploits in shooting down a MiG-17. US naval aviation operated from carriers in the South China Sea.*

When the NVA became equipped both with the SAM-7 and with radar-controlled anti-aircraft guns all but the most modern aircraft became obsolete. This was a decisive factor in the final offensive of 1975 when the South Vietnamese tactical air force, equipped mainly with the twin-jet Cessna A-37 which was not fast enough at a low altitude, was neutralised.

Khe Sanh

KHE SANH, on Route 9 leading from Quang Tri to the Laos border and Sepone, was a quiet mountain village where a Special Forces camp for training Montagnards had originally been established. After the battles in the Demilitarised Zone (DMZ) in 1967 it was occupied by United States Marines as a means of blocking North Vietnamese infiltration routes through the DMZ to Route 9 and thence to Sepone and the Ho Chi Minh Trail.

By the end of the year this force was built up to nearly 6000 men and was surrounded by superior NVA forces. All patrolling ceased and the marines were cut off and confined to their perimeter. Khe Sanh was shelled from Laos and the number of supply aircraft able to land was severely restricted. It began to resemble a miniature Dien Bien Phu, except that the marines were not as well entrenched as the French and were being used in a role for which they were not trained. There was a great deal of sniping and some hand-to-hand combat at night. It became a Mecca for journalists.

A valueless symbol

Khe Sanh soon lost its original purpose – the NVA bypassed it easily – and became instead almost a symbol of the American military presence and effort. After the president had extracted pledges from his chiefs of staff as to its importance and impregnability, its defence became top priority. While General William Westmoreland could claim that it was acting as a honey pot for the B-52s to inflict heavy casualties on the NVA besiegers, there is reason to believe that General Vo Nguyen Giap did not really want to take it.

Psychologically, there was no knowing what the reaction in the United States would have been to the

RIGHT *US Marine tank crews observe the results of American air support on the Khe Sanh perimeter, 1968. Land-based US Air Force units combined with carrier-based Navy jets to repel the North Vietnamese.* BELOW *An armed helicopter prepares to airlift marines from the beleagured base.*

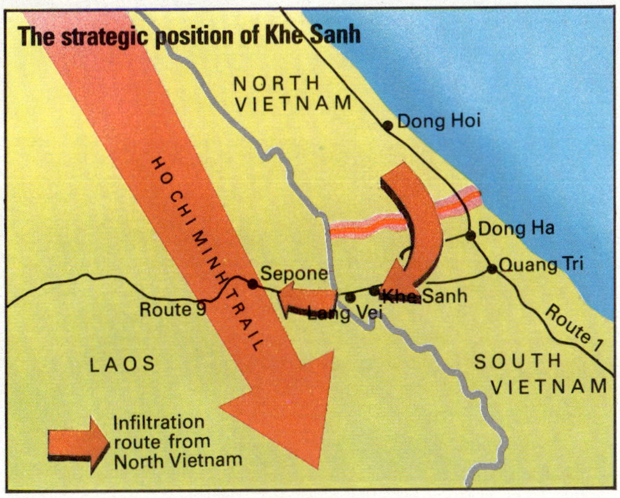

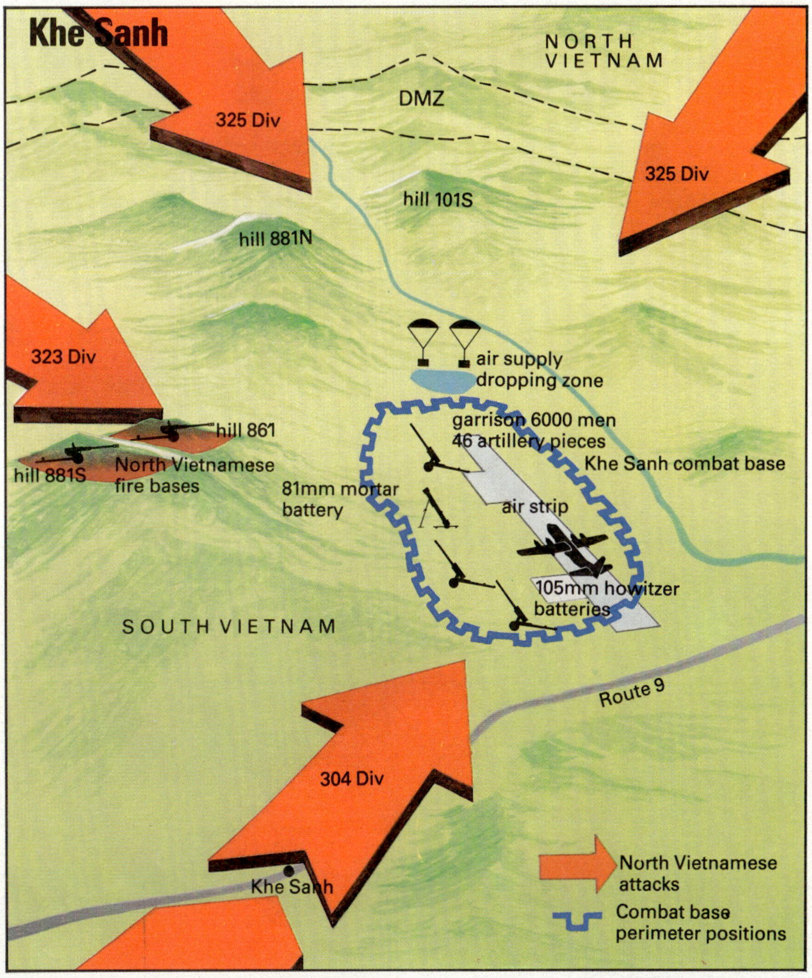

capture of nearly 6000 marines. There might have been an overwhelming demand for revenge and all dissent to the war could have been swept aside. Moreover, not only was a large force bottled up but several American divisions were tied down to go to its rescue if attacked; and these dispositions left open the NVA's route to Hue for the Tet offensive in 1968. No attempt was made to interrupt the water supply and just enough aircraft were allowed in to enable the garrison to be kept there.

The holding of this outpost, its subsequent relief and its evacuation after the Tet offensive in 1968 were all claimed as victories. It remained in NVA hands until temporarily recaptured by ARVN during Operation Lam Son in 1971. Thereafter, it was entirely in NVA hands and by 1973 the American supply aircraft strip had been converted to an all-weather MiG runway.

BELOW *A Fairchild C-123 Provider transport of the US Air Force comes under mortar fire on the runway at Khe Sanh. A group of marines use the cover provided by a metal storage box on the offloading ramp to await a lull in the bombardment before boarding.*

The Tet Offensive

BY THE BEGINNING OF 1968 the Americans were claiming great military victories. Every battle had been won and casualty rates were running at least 4 to 1 and sometimes as high as 10 to 1 in their favour. They claimed that their forces were pushing the NVA back across the borders into Laos and Cambodia. Khe Sanh seemed to be firmly held. There were rumours of an impending offensive, but no one expected anything to happen at the end of January during Tet (the Buddhist New Year) when there had usually been an informal if unrecognised truce. Only the air force at Tan Son Nhut, the Saigon airbase, was on full alert.

The attack goes in

The Viet Cong and NVA forces struck on 30 January. The main attacks occurred in Saigon and Hue, where the old citadel was captured, but more than 30 provincial capitals were also attacked. It is probable that 50,000 troops were involved, including all Viet Cong regular and regional forces with NVA support. Most South Vietnamese forces were withdrawn into the towns and fierce urban fighting followed with the Americans directly involved in both Saigon and Hue. Small groups of Viet Cong penetrated into the centre of Saigon, but General Fred C. Weyand, US commander in the Saigon area, had realised that there were powerful enemy forces in the area and had several battalions in reserve near the city.

Except for Hue, which took a month, other towns were cleared within a week but suffered considerable damage – 'destroying to save', not unusual in war, as Stalingrad and Caen (in 1944) had shown. The offensive was resumed in May with the NVA and Viet Cong adopting a more intelligent tactic of infiltration by small units on a more widespread basis so that they were much harder to clear out. A final attempt to renew the offensive in August failed dismally.

The Tet offensive was a major turning point in the war and had traumatic

RIGHT *A captured Viet Cong is disembarked from a PACV.* BELOW *A medic and two aides run to help a wounded marine during fighting in Hue.*

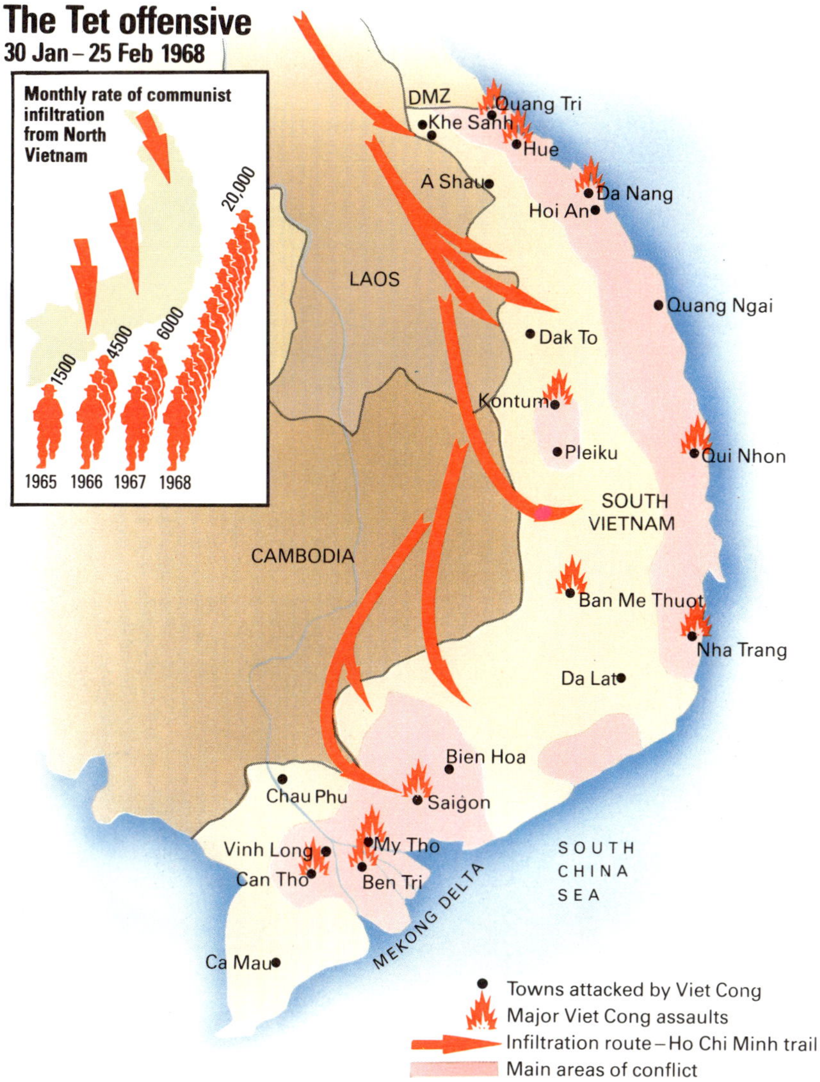

effects. The Viet Cong regular and regional forces suffered nearly 30,000 casualties, and there were high-ranking defections when the offensive was pressed later in the year.

There was no mass uprising as had been expected and planned by the politburo; in fact, the South Vietnamese were more effectively mobilised after Tet when it became a war against the NVA rather than the Viet Cong. As a result of the move into the towns, there was a vacuum in the countryside and, with the decline of the Viet Cong as a military force, this was filled by the South Vietnamese forces.

But, if the offensive resulted in a military defeat within Vietnam, it achieved a striking psychological victory abroad. The credibility of the American administration was destroyed and the strategy of attrition was bankrupt. It had a dramatic political effect when President Lyndon Johnson announced that he would not stand for re-election. It also brought him to the conference table and he was compelled to halt the bombing of the North and to open negotiations or at least 'talks about talks'. The myth was created that the war was unwinnable; and that had a decisive effect on American resolution.

ABOVE RIGHT *Men of the 2nd Battalion 5th Marines take cover behind a wall in the citadel during the battle for Hue.* RIGHT *US Navy forces leap from their patrol boat to raid a Viet Cong base in Kien Hoa province immediately prior to the Tet offensive.* BELOW *Marines shelter from sniper fire in Hue on 1 February 1968, two days after the start of the Tet offensive.*

Choppers and Gunships

VIETNAM was the first war in which the helicopter played a dominant role. The original helicopters provided by President John F. Kennedy in 1961 were intended for supply purposes but were soon being used to ferry troops into minor operations. Units were lifted from their barracks to the operational areas in the morning and then returned again in the evening. These became known as 'picnic lunch' operations and were not generally very fruitful.

With the commitment of American combat forces the Bell UH-1 Huey helicopter arrived in large numbers until eventually about 5000 were operational. In previous wars, helicopters had normally been used for communications, small unit operations and the evacuation of wounded personnel. The last was an important role in Vietnam too, and very great courage was shown by the Medevac helicopter crews landing and taking off under intense fire to get the wounded out. The Australian Brigade in Phuoc Tuy province claimed that a wounded man would be in hospital on the operating table within 40 minutes.

Choppers into battle

From the first deployment of US ground forces, helicopters brought large forces into battle, with helicopter gunships in support firing machine guns and rockets to suppress enemy fire. As soon as contact was made on the ground with a Viet Cong or NVA unit, reinforcements and blocking forces were immediately deployed, often against intense small-arms fire, including 0.5in machine guns, to which the helicopter was very vulnerable.

The US Air Cavalry Division, stationed at An Khe on Route 19 between the port of Qui Nhon and Pleiku, was particularly designed for this type of operation and frequently had hundreds of helicopters airborne at one time. Boeing CH-47 Chinook twin-bladed helicopters were used to lift heavy loads, such as artillery pieces into fire-bases and even caravans into remote outposts as living quarters. They also rescued damaged Hueys, carrying the downed helicopters by means of under-fuselage hoists.

The helicopter certainly enabled

Bell AH-1G HueyCobra gunship

range 574km (357 miles) **mission** fire support of ground operations **cruising speed** 352km/h (219mph)

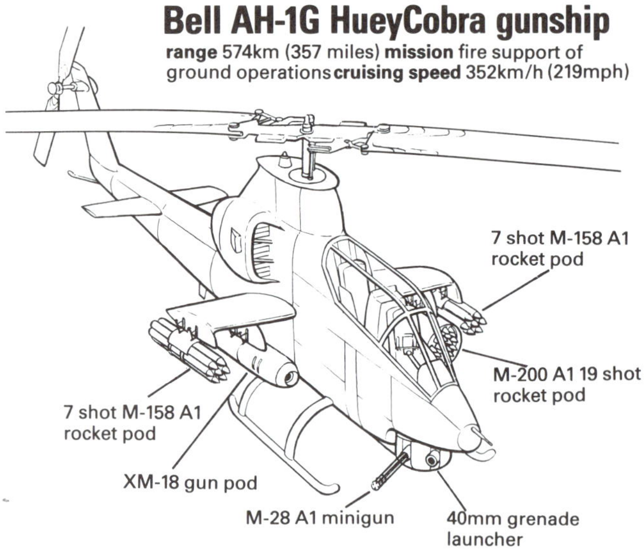

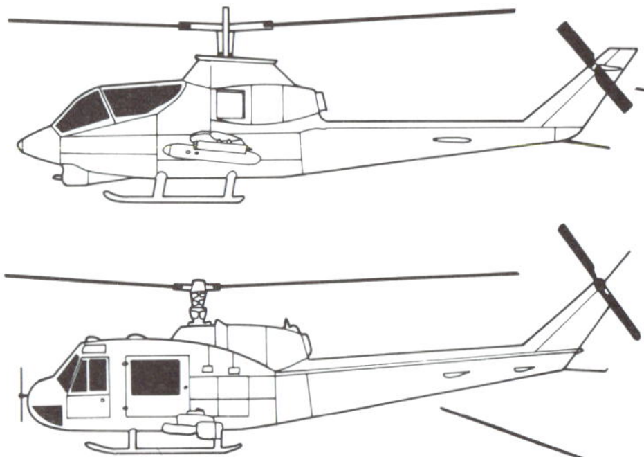

Helicopter deployment

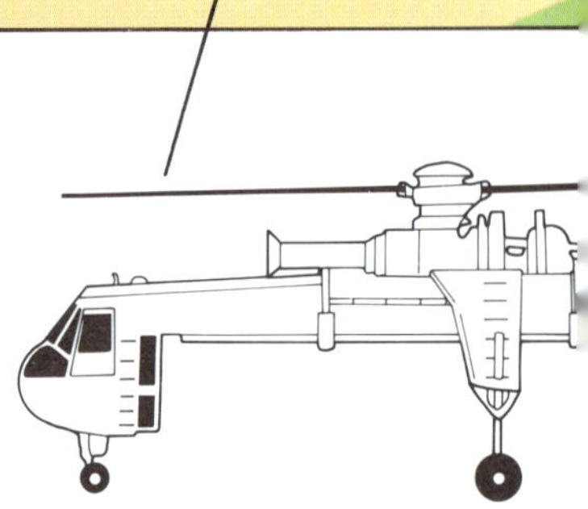

RIGHT *A Bell UH-1E evacuates wounded marines during an operation in July 1966.* BELOW *Army UH-1D troop transports prepare to disembark men of the 1st Air Cavalry Division into the Bong Son district in a drive against the Viet Cong in February 1965.*

ABOVE LEFT *A heavily armed Bell AH-1 HueyCobra escorts a UH-1 over Quang Ngai.* ABOVE *The gunner of a US Navy UH-1 fires at a target in the Mekong Delta.* BELOW *A CH-47 Chinook supplies a 101st Airborne Division base.*

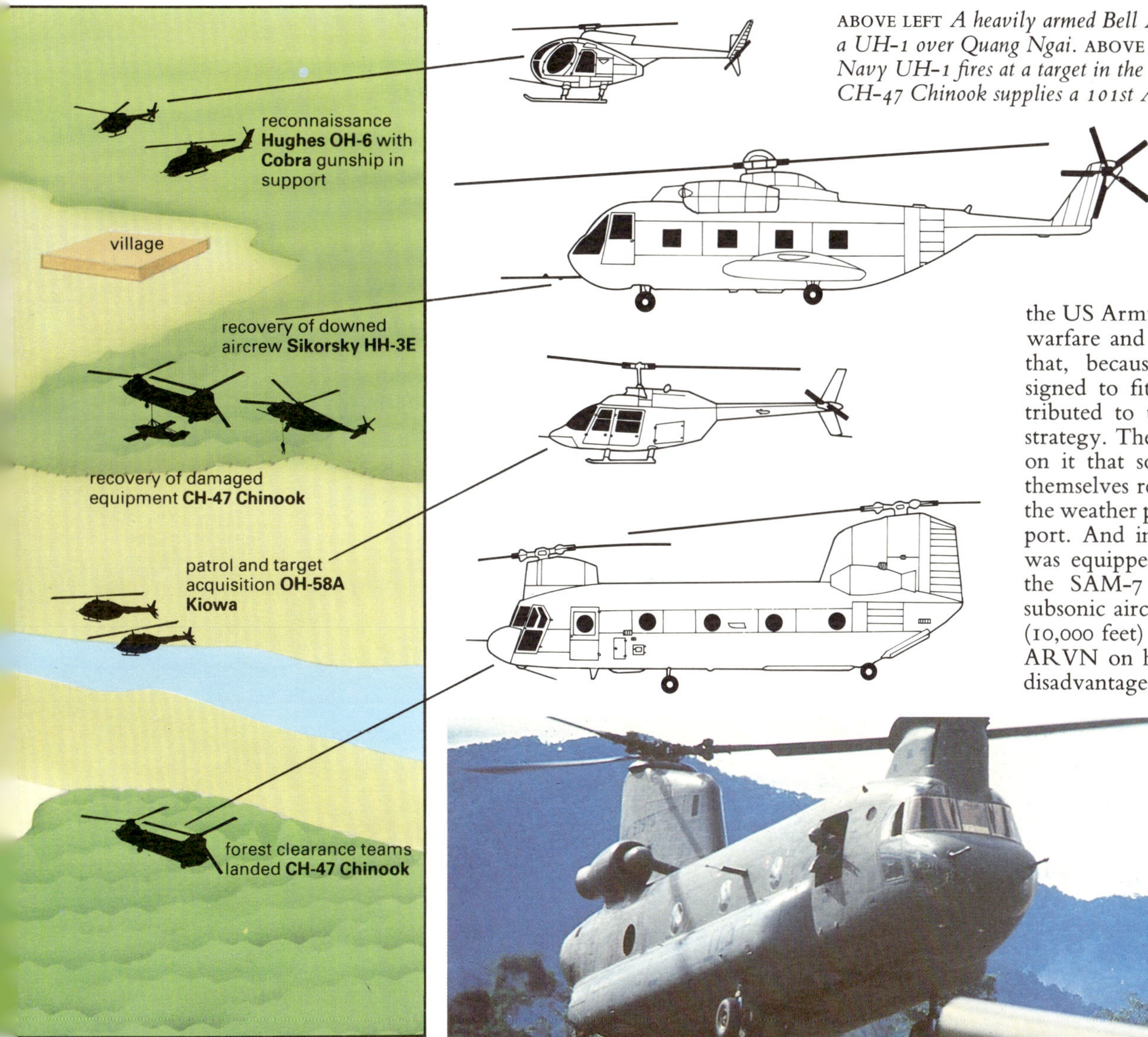

the US Army to fight its own type of warfare and a case can be made out that, because operations were designed to fit the helicopter, it contributed to the failure of American strategy. There was such dependence on it that some operations were in themselves rendered hazardous when the weather prevented helicopter support. And in 1972, when the NVA was equipped by the Russians with the SAM-7 – effective against all subsonic aircraft below about 3050m (10,000 feet) – the dependence of the ARVN on helicopters was a serious disadvantage.

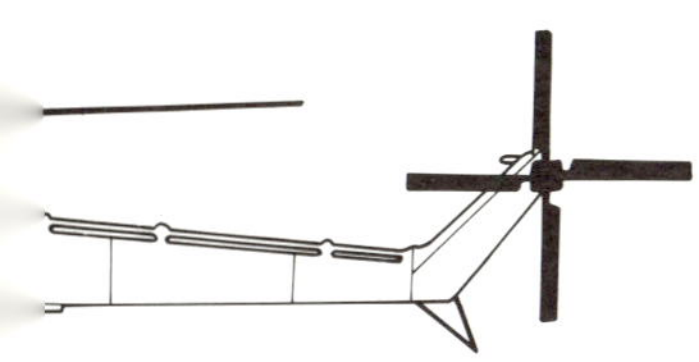

Bombing the North

ON 7 FEBRUARY 1965 the United States and South Vietnamese air forces first bombed North Vietnam; the main target was communications in order to reduce infiltration into the South. By May one pilot reported that the air force was running out of bridges and when, later in the year, it was found that infiltration had actually increased, there were demands for a massive campaign to bomb the North 'back into the stone age' and to bring Hanoi to the conference table.

President Lyndon Johnson first called a 37-day bombing pause at the beginning of 1966. When this had no effect, the bombing resumed. In July oil depots round Hanoi were attacked, as later were the iron and steel complexes close to Hanoi and Haiphong and the road and railway to the Chinese border.

The problem was that at this stage there were no targets, other than the Red (Hong) River dykes and perhaps Haiphong harbour, which affected Hanoi's capacity to carry on the war. The North Vietnamese were very adept at repairing bridges or establishing small boat ferries so that, while the speed of movement was slowed, the monthly rate of men and supplies moving into South Vietnam steadily increased.

The bombing became an air war between the American Navy and Air Force and Russian anti-aircraft defences largely manned by the Chinese. American losses mounted, and their prisoners of war became a major issue. Cessation of the bombing, however, was always Hanoi's pre-condition for the starting of talks. After the Tet offensive and in an election year it was President Johnson who gave way and halted the bombing on 1 November 1968.

A new accuracy

His successor, President Richard Nixon, maintained the bombing of the Ho Chi Minh Trail both in Laos and north-east Cambodia. All sorts of devices were tried for hitting NVA troops moving at night including transport aircraft fitted with multiple machine guns firing downwards at several thousand rounds a minute. Then, when the invasion occurred in 1972, Nixon delayed for one week before the bombing of the North was resumed.

The new campaign was very different from the previous air attacks.

BELOW *F-105 Thunderchief fighter bombers release their loads over a North Vietnamese target.* INSET *A Thunderchief attack on the Xuan Mai barracks and ammunition storage site in 1967, with bomb bursts visible.*

First, the United States Air Force was equipped with the laser-guided 'smart' bombs which were devastating in their accuracy. For example, over 800 sorties had been flown against the Thanh Hoa bridge south of Hanoi between 1965 and 1968 without hitting it. In the first sortie by four laser-equipped Phantoms, it was hit at once by a 2000lb 'smart' bomb.

Within a few weeks no bridge was left intact and the air force was able to attack with precision military targets in and around Hanoi without inflicting civilian casualties. Five 'smart' bombs were dropped through the concrete roof of the transformer house of the Lang Chi hydroelectric plant, providing 47 per cent of the country's electrical power, without causing any damage to the dam or spillway a few yards away.

Secondly, Hanoi was now conducting a conventional invasion with T54 tanks and heavy artillery. This required several thousand tonnes of supplies a day carried by trucks. For the first time the air force really had some significant targets and could make its power tell. When talks were resumed, however, the bombing was halted south of the 20th parallel and Hanoi gained a respite. When the talks stalled at the end of 1972, B-52s and F-111s were used on Hanoi for the first time.

Eleven days of hell

After 11 nights of raids it was reported that 'virtually all industrial capacity was gone. Power generating plants and their transmitting grids were smashed. Gas and oil storage dumps were burned-out shells. Railroad marshalling yards looked like lunar landscapes. Roads and canals were clogged with shattered transport. SAM storage areas, tank, artillery and truck parks were pulverised. Military traffic dwindled to a trickle.'

The raids were carried out against the most intensive air defence so far seen in war. B-52 losses reached their peak on the third and fourth nights, when six were lost, but the defences then began to crumble. By 28 December the United States Air Force was free to roam over the North with impunity. Hanoi could no longer track them with radar. Its MiGs could no longer take off and the re-supply of SAMs was negligible after 1242 had been fired at the American raiders in the course of the 11 nights.

The whole system was breaking down, including the radio communications on which a communist regime was particularly dependent for control. Radio transmitters could be pinpointed by direction finding and then destroyed by 2000lb delayed-action laser bombs.

The air force went to extreme lengths, at greatly increased risk to both aircraft and crews, to avoid civilian areas; there were only three accidents, excluding one B-52 which crashed in the centre of the city. Some casualties were caused by falling SAMs. According to Hanoi's own estimate the number of civilians killed was about 1500. This was the most successful sustained air bombardment ever; but it is a measure of the nature of the Vietnam War that it did not decide the outcome of the conflict.

TOP *An anti-aircraft flak gun mounted on a dyke east of Hanoi opens fire on the approaching aircraft.* ABOVE *A Vought A-7 Corsair attack bomber prepares for catapult launch aboard the aircraft carrier* USS Constellation *in the Gulf of Tongking, 1968.*

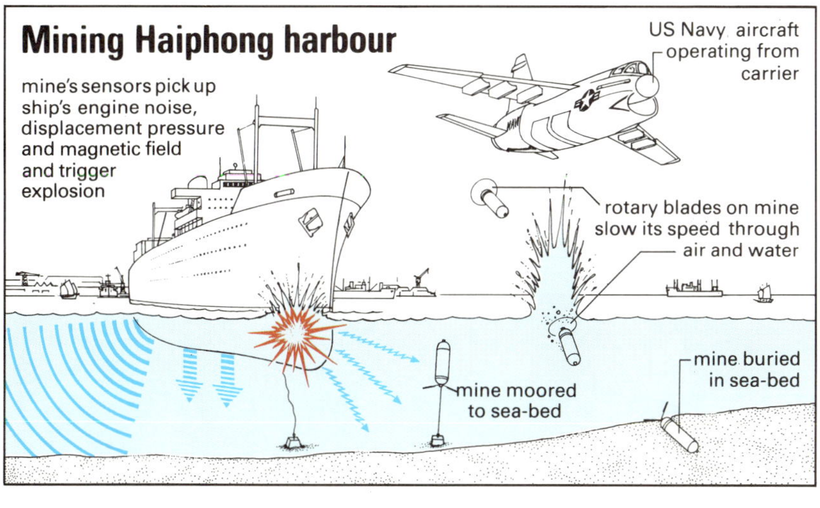

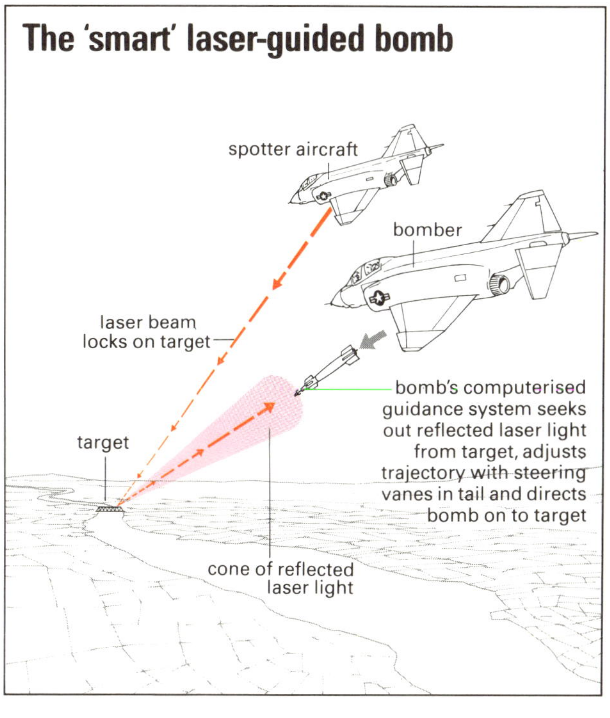

The Easter Invasion

BY EARLY 1971 the politburo realised that it was losing ground within the South because the NVA could not conduct a guerrilla war there, as it had between 1965 and 1968, without strong Viet Cong support which was no longer available. As a result of the successes of Vietnamisation and pacification the South was gaining strength; even agricultural production (with the introduction of new strains of 'miracle' rice) was improving. The green revolution was defeating the red revolution. There was no alternative but to invade.

Accordingly, Le Duan visited Moscow for several weeks in the spring of 1971, obtaining both agreement and the necessary equipment for a conventional invasion. By early 1972 it was clear that the invasion was coming and that it would be on three fronts – across the Demilitarised Zone (DMZ), in the central highlands against Kontum and from north-east Cambodia towards Saigon. While for political reasons it was desirable for the timing to be close to the American presidential election, the monsoon weather dictated that it would have to start well before May. It was not clear in advance how hard Hanoi would press it. It was thought that the communists might be prepared to take 60,000 killed; in the event 120,000 of the communist forces died.

At 0200 hours on 30 March 1972 the invasion started across the DMZ and soon after on the other two fronts. The 130mm guns demolished ARVN's artillery fire-bases and the whole 16km (10-mile) stretch between the DMZ and the Cua Viet River was lost within six days to the NVA's 304th and 308th Divisions and their T54 tanks. At the same time the 324th Division attacked eastwards from Laos towards Hue. Sixteen kilometres (10 miles) in a week was not exactly an impressive initial thrust with 40,000 men and armour, however.

All was not entirely well on the NVA side; there were frequent reports of tanks running out of fuel, for

example. There was a lull on this front for three weeks before, as a result of a command snarl up, the ARVN 3rd Division collapsed and the provincial capital of Quang Tri was captured by the NVA. Thousands of refugees fled south but the front was stabilised by General Ngo Quang Truong north of Hue when the South Vietnamese Marines and Airborne divisions were committed.

In the central highlands the ARVN 22nd Division was routed at Tan Canh but the 23rd Division was rushed in to hold Kontum against the NVA 320th and 2nd Divisions. North of Saigon the NVA 9th Division reached An Loc and was joined there by the 5th and 7th Divisions. An Loc with 5000 to 6000 men was then besieged for several weeks, but all attacks on it failed. The NVA eventually committed 14 divisions and there were many diversionary attacks by individual NVA battalions against district towns, but these were held except where the NVA 3rd Division got through to the coast north of Qui Nhon and cut Route 1. It was later turned out by the re-formed 22nd Division.

Air power and counter-attack

When the invasion was stalled on all three fronts, the American Air Force came into play both tactically and strategically. By July the South Vietnamese were able to conduct counter-offensives and Quang Tri, the only provincial capital to be lost, was recaptured by three ARVN divisions against six NVA divisions.

ABOVE LEFT *A North Vietnamese heavy machine gun fitted with rudimentary anti-aircraft sights. Small-arms and machine-gun fire accounted for many US aircraft in the earlier years.* LEFT *A group of civilian refugees carrying the South Vietnamese flag are escorted from a devastated sector of Quang Tri.* BELOW *An Loc in June 1972 after having borne the brunt of the NVA artillery offensive.*

General Vo Nguyen Giap, if he it was, had made the same mistake as Hitler in Russia by attacking on three fronts without deciding which was to be the vital thrust and reinforcing that. The NVA also lacked the experience to co-ordinate attacks by artillery, tanks and infantry. Tanks were misused by attacking rubble-strewn towns without supporting infantry. In both An Loc and Kontum they became easy targets for infantry anti-tank weapons. If An Loc had been sealed off and by-passed, the tanks, with some supporting infantry, would have been able to travel along a wide flat spur of hard laterite into the heavily populated areas between Saigon and Bien Hoa where they would have created panic and confusion in the capital.

All the numerical advantage at the initial points of attack was thrown away by frontal assaults, with the following infantry suffering a casualty rate of 4 or 5 to 1 against. For the first time there was evidence of NVA desertions and of hasty retreats leaving equipment behind – something quite unheard-of in the past. One tank crew in Quang Tri bailed out and fled when they saw the marines approaching, and the tank was captured with its engine running.

One result of the invasion was that the manpower balance shifted in favour of ARVN with most of its battalions, thanks to its training reserves, up to 600 men whereas many NVA battalions were down to 50. Plans were being made for a counter-offensive on all fronts. To halt this and gain a respite the North reopened negotiations with the Americans.

Laos and Cambodia

IN EXPANDING SOUTH over the centuries the Vietnamese destroyed the Khmer Empire and by the middle of the 19th century had captured Phnom Penh. Cambodia and Laos both owed their existence to the French, first as protected states in the colonial era and then as independent sovereign states after 1954. They were, however, always indirectly involved in the Vietnam War (as they had been in the first Indochina War) because of Hanoi's aim to create an Indochina Federation and its support for the Khmer Rouge and Pathet Lao communist movements in the two states. They were more directly involved by Hanoi's use of the Ho Chi Minh Trail and the Viet Cong's need for cross-border sanctuaries.

Under Cambodia's Prince Sihanouk, NVA and Viet Cong forces were allowed to occupy north-east Cambodia and were supplied with arms through Sihanoukville and with Cambodian rice. This force eventually built up to four divisions (the 1st, 5th, 7th and 9th). As the NVA's demands, and control of territory, increased so did the Cambodians' historical hostility to the invader.

Sihanouk's fall

In 1970 Sihanouk was overthrown by his Prime Minister, Lon Nol, and Prince Sirik Matak and the accommodation with Hanoi abruptly came to an end. The subsequent American incursion into Cambodia, limited in both time and depth, not only spoiled the NVA's offensive capability for nearly two years but also saved Phnom Penh and gave Cambodia time to build up its forces from 28,000 to 200,000.

There was extensive fighting over the next two years but, with American aid and help from South Vietnamese forces in the border areas, all the main towns were held and the Mekong River to Phnom Penh remained open to navigation. After the Vietnam ceasefire in January 1973, however, aid was limited and American air support ceased a few months later. South Vietnamese forces were no longer allowed to cross the border to assist, while Hanoi had a free run.

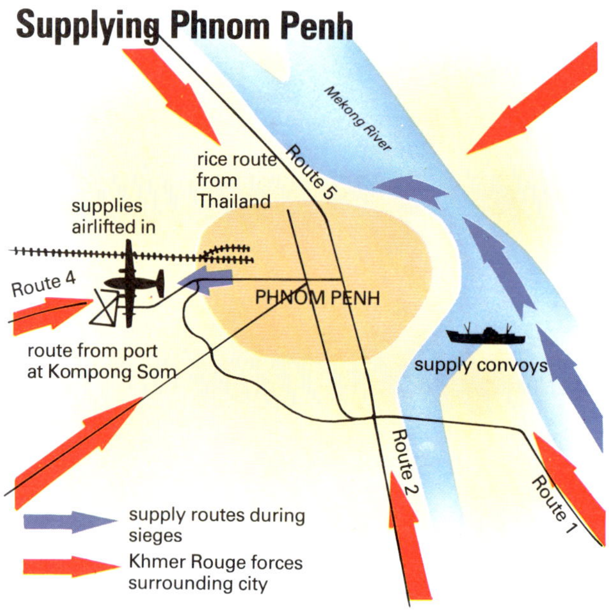

North Vietnamese troops overrun a South Vietnamese paratroop base during the fighting in Laos in 1971.

Prince Norodom Sihanouk, the ruler of Cambodia until his overthrow by Lon Nol in 1970.

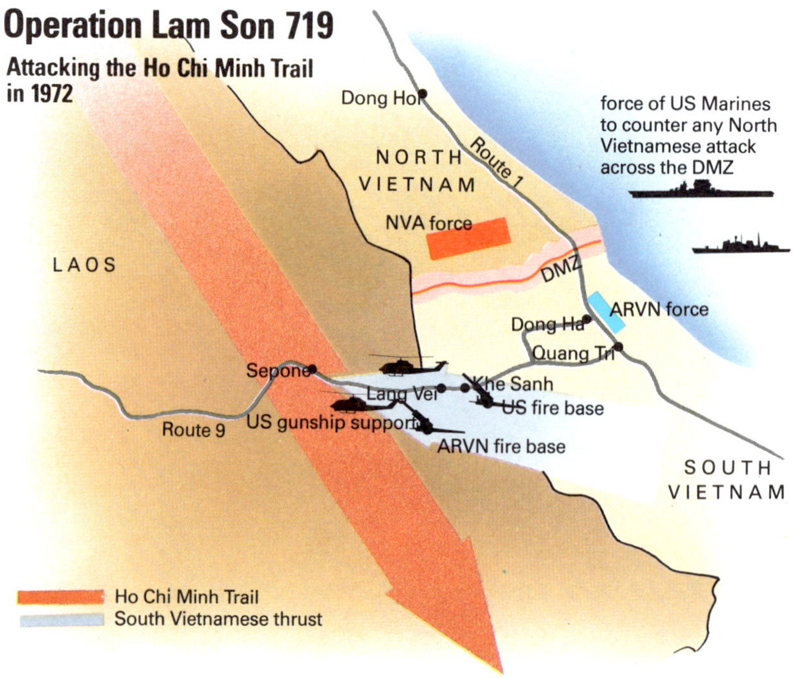

Because Hanoi needed rice for its forces in the south, which were being built up again after the ceasefire, it encouraged the Khmer Rouge to take Phnom Penh and end the war. The city was besieged in the dry seasons of both 1973 and 1974, but just managed to hold out although bursting with hundreds of thousands of refugees fleeing from the Khmer Rouge. In 1975 the Mekong was finally blocked by mines and the city fell in April. Cambodia was subjected to the horrors of Pol Pot and finally a Vietnamese invasion, in which 3 million died.

Pathet Lao victory

Laos was comparatively quiet after the 1962 agreement, except in the area of the trail. The Chinese in Phong Saly province built a road down towards the Thai frontier, while Souphanavong, the leader of the Pathet Lao, confined his activities to the Plaine des Jarres. The fighting did not really hot up until the arrival of the NVA 315th Division before the Easter invasion in 1972. The Laos were greatly assisted by the Meo hill tribes under Vang Pao who successfully held Long Cheng, which controlled access to the capital of Vientiane. After the Vietnam ceasefire Pathet Lao troops entered Vientiane, the king abdicated and Laos became the first domino under Hanoi control.

ABOVE *US B-52 bombers unload their deadly cargo over Cambodia. The bombing of Cambodia attracted worldwide condemnation.* RIGHT *Khmer Rouge troops parade through Phnom Penh, which fell to the communists in April 1975.*

War and the Media

VIETNAM was the first major war to be completely televised. Journalists and camera crews were granted every facility, including helicopter transport. For the first time the close-up horrors of war were brought into the sitting room daily. But the camera has a very limited view, less even than the cameraman, and argues always from the particular to the general.

The most spectacular pictures are those of destruction and that is where the camera went. Vietnam provided an unlimited supply of scenes, particularly during the Tet offensive. The coverage turned full circle at Hue when one BBC correspondent described American aircraft bombing the citadel as 'just like watching television'. As Robin Day has subsequently remarked: 'Television is a medium of shock rather than explanation. It is a crude medium which strikes at the emotions rather than the intellect. And because of television's insatiable appetite for visual action, for violence very often, it tends to distort and trivialise.'

It certainly shocked the sitting rooms of the United States, particularly with scenes like the ghastly American massacre of villagers at My Lai. Equivalent acts by the NVA and Viet Cong, as at Dak Son where they incinerated more than 250 villagers with flame-throwers, or the massacres at Hue in 1968 where over 5000 people were executed and buried in mass graves, were not shown as the cameras concentrated on the American involvement.

A wave of protest

Dissent started with sit-ins in 1965 and soon developed to demonstrations, moratoriums and candle-lit processions which were as much part of the war as any battle. Demonstrations were not confined to the United States and spread to Europe. At all times the opinion polls showed a majority of the American people in favour of the administration, however. As late as 13 October 1972 President Richard Nixon's Vietnam

RIGHT *Chicago police struggle to control anti-war demonstrators during the 1968 Democratic Party convention.*

BELOW *South Vietnamese children flee the horror of a napalm strike. For many people this now-famous photograph, published around the world, was the most telling image of the war.*

ABOVE *A protester offers a symbol of peace to a military policeman during an anti-war rally in October 1967.*
RIGHT *At Kent State University, Ohio, in 1970 four deaths occurred when students and National Guardsmen clashed on campus.*

policy was supported by 58 per cent to 26 per cent undecided and, even in the 18 to 29 age group, he had a majority of 52 to 33. This came through in the presidential election when Senator George McGovern, who favoured withdrawal, was defeated in every state except Massachusetts and the District of Columbia.

The minority opposed to the war was, however, still large, and vociferous. The atmosphere in the United States was comparable to that in Europe during the Spanish Civil War: the war itself became the symbol of something broader, irrespective of the precise truth or relevance of the events reported there. The moral issues at stake in Vietnam were extremely complex, and events subsequent to 1975 have indicated that the slogans of the 1960s were often the product of an idealised and over-simplified view. Nevertheless, millions of people in the United States did oppose the war for reasons which were sincerely felt, and their activities were an important element in the failure of the American involvement.

The Fall of the South

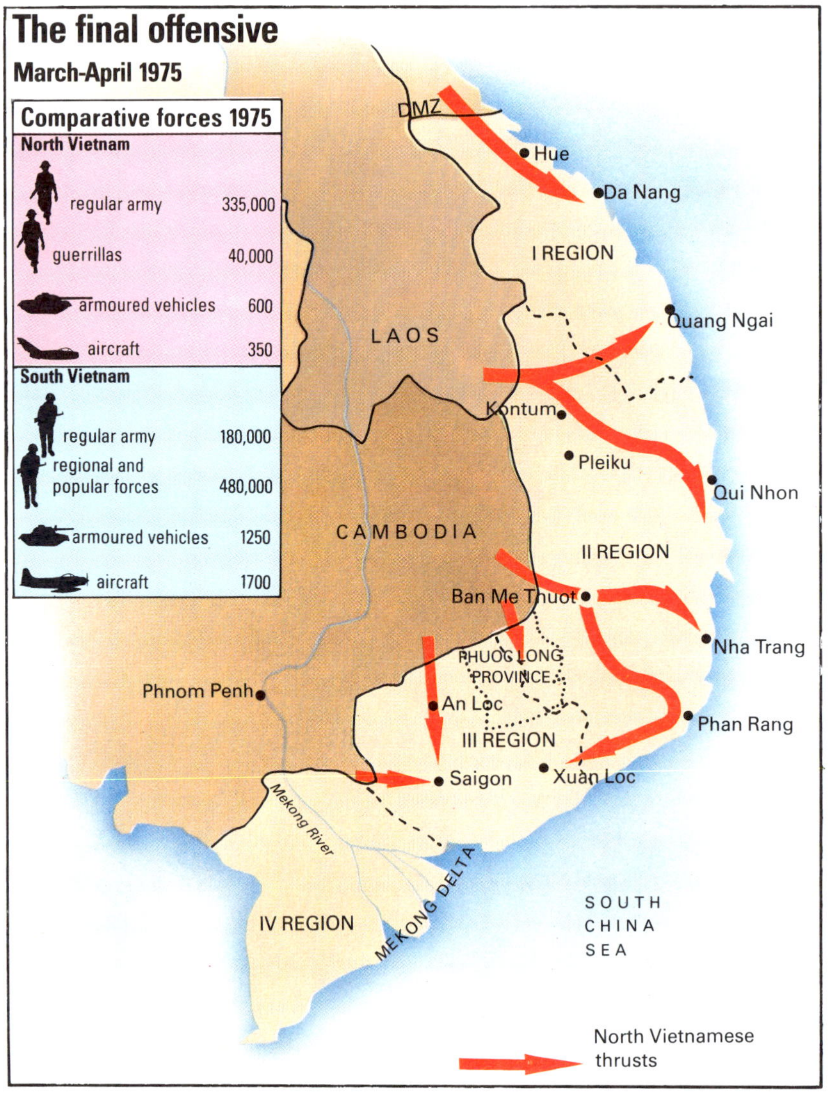

AT 0800 HOURS on 28 January 1973, the morning of the ceasefire, the NVA shelled several South Vietnamese airfields, including Tan Son Nhut in Saigon. This, and their order of the day referring to the 'Difficult, complex and violent struggle ahead', made it clear that the war would continue.

In 1974 the war escalated as the NVA consolidated its in-place positions and eliminated South Vietnamese outposts. The main activity, however, over these two years was the reinforcement and re-equipment of NVA forces in the South. By the end of 1974 the total NVA forces had been built up to 20 divisions, plus armour and artillery with estimated stocks for over 12 months of intensive combat. The South Vietnamese on the other hand had reduced their forces by about 100,000, partly because of the reduction in American aid.

The general strategic situation was now entirely in the North's favour. Its forces had a free run along the whole border and in parts of South Vietnam, and not a single man had to be wasted on defence. It could attack at any chosen point with overwhelming superiority because South Vietnamese forces, stretched throughout the length of the country, were tied down in a static defensive role and, owing to the petrol price and shortage, were even less mobile than before.

Thieu's dilemma

At the beginning of 1975 South Vietnam was facing absolute disaster. President Nguyen Van Thieu was presented with the choice of maintaining his present untenable positions or of attempting to improve his military situation by withdrawing all the regular ARVN units from Military Regions 1 and 2 in the north and defending Saigon and the Mekong Delta alone. This was both politically and practically impossible. It would have meant deserting millions of people and all the local forces.

On 6 January 1975 the NVA overran Phuoc Long province in a trial run to test reactions. There were none, and General Van Tien Dung, now commanding the NVA as Vo Nguyen Giap's chosen successor, set out on his 'beautiful road to war'. Having cut all road communication in Regions 1 and 2, three NVA divisions overwhelmed two ARVN brigades and captured Ban Me Thuot in the highlands on 10 March. Thieu ordered the corps commander to withdraw all his forces from the highlands to the coast using Route 7.

Meanwhile, too late, he ordered the withdrawal of the airborne division from Region 1 back to Saigon to form a reserve. This caused panic in the north. Hue was abandoned and all forces fell back with thousands of refugees on Da Nang, which fell at the end of March and all of Region 2 soon after. Only the ARVN 18th Division fought magnificently at Xuan Loc north of Saigon to stem the advance.

It proved quite impossible to withdraw other divisions from the delta area for the defence of Saigon, which was ringed by 13 communist divisions. Thieu resigned and General Duong Van Minh (Big Minh), who had overthrown and murdered President Ngo Dinh Diem, became president to preside over Saigon's unconditional surrender on 30 April. The Americans fled in their helicopters to the waiting Seventh Fleet. The second Indochina War was over.

The flag of North Vietnam is waved in victory over a Saigon base in April 1975 after the South's unconditional surrender.

Birth of a Nation

In 1971 the Indian Army overran East Pakistan in a lightning campaign

H. P. Willmott

IN 1971 a new nation state was born as a result of the dismemberment of Pakistan at the hands of her giant neighbour, India. It amounted to more than a revision by force of the territorial division of the Indian subcontinent that dated from independence in 1947. The war established India as a great military power and ended a series of humiliating defeats she had suffered in the 1960s from her Chinese and Pakistani neighbours.

The 1947 settlement lay at the heart of the 1971 war because it established two separate states, a Hindu-dominated India and a Moslem Pakistan that was divided into two parts separated by India. West and East Pakistan shared a common religion but they were divided by distance, culture, race, language and economics. Since independence Pakistan's leaders had failed to forge a strong sense of national identity between West and East.

From its creation Pakistan was plagued by the imbalance between its two parts. West Pakistan was almost six times larger than East Pakistan and contained the nation's capital. Political power was concentrated in the west, and West Pakistanis held an almost total monopoly of appointments in the civil service, armed forces and the diplomatic service, despite being outnumbered by eastern Pakistanis by three to one.

By contrast East Pakistan, established in the rich alluvial plains formed by the confluence of three major rivers – the Brahmaputra, Ganges and Meghna – and their tributaries, accounted for 75 per cent of exports and foreign earnings. In return it received less than 30 per cent of the nation's imports and investment. To the rulers of Pakistan the east was a colony that was milked to the extent that per capita income in the west exceeded that in East Pakistan. Such discrimination became increasingly intolerable to East Pakistan.

East Pakistanis celebrate India's victory against Pakistan which brought into being the new state of Bangladesh.

Challenge to the army

Between 1947 and 1958 Pakistan had a veneer of parliamentary democracy but was increasingly controlled by a faction of landowners, industrialists, bureaucrats and the army, mainly drawn from the Punjab. Real power was exercised by the army, which openly ruled from 1958 to 1969 under the presidency of Field Marshal Ayub Khan. The provincial elections of 1954 in East Pakistan saw candidates of the establishment decisively repudiated, and the subsequent democratic government was quickly suppressed by the military authorities.

In 1966 the leading political figure in East Pakistan, Sheikh Mujibur Rahman, put forward a six-point programme that proposed the establishment of a federal Pakistan with a central government having very limited powers. The two federal parts would be self-financing and self-supporting. The sheikh was arrested and in January 1968 it was announced that he was to be tried for treason. By its action the government made the sheikh a martyr and turned eastern demands away from autonomy within Pakistan and towards total separation.

What finally pushed the East Pakistanis to demand the break-up of the nation came about between March 1969 and March 1971 amid the events that surrounded the fall of Ayub Khan and his replacement by General Yahya Khan. In March 1969 Ayub Khan promised to hold general elections but his personal popularity had sunk so low that even this manoeuvre failed to satisfy the population. He was forced to hand over power to the army commander, Yahya Khan, the same month. Yahya confirmed the promise of free elections. He banked on no clear majority being obtained by any of the political parties, thereby allowing the army to remain effectively in control.

Sheikh Mujibur Rahman's Awami League dominated East Pakistan, and East Pakistan had a majority of seats in parliament. So when elections were held on 17 December 1970 the results were catastrophic for the military junta. In East Pakistan the Awami League captured 298 of the 310 seats in the provincial assembly and 167 seats in the national parliament. This meant that Sheikh Mujibur had a decisive majority in Pakistan

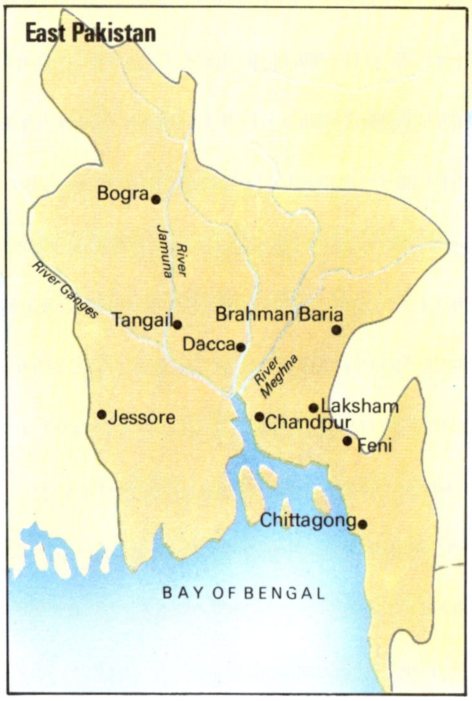

as a whole.

The Yahya regime put pressure on the sheikh to come to an arrangement, but he refused. On 1 March, Khan announced the indefinite postponement of the opening of parliament. Rioting broke out in East Pakistan and a general strike was called by the sheikh on the 2nd. Yahya arrested the sheikh on 25 March and gave orders to the Martial Law Administrator in East Pakistan, Lieutenant General Tikka Khan, to 'sort them out'.

Tikka Khan began a policy of overkill with a vengeance, the aim being to intimidate the population into submission. The course of action that he pursued has been dubbed 'élitocide'. The intelligentsia and Hindus living in East Pakistan were singled out for specially atrocious treatment, but anyone and everyone was a potential target in the army rampage that even now seems hardly credible. Murders have been placed as high as 1 million. Not the least revolting of the army's practices was organised, systematic rape, the helpless women usually being bayonetted when new victims were herded into the military barracks.

By April the outrageous behaviour of the army in East Pakistan had unforeseen results. Firstly, with nothing to lose the local inhabitants began to fight back. This led to reinforcements being sent from West Pakistan and the reign of terror intensified. Secondly, thousands of refugees began to cross into India.

Yahya hoped that Pakistan's understandings with China and the United States would enable him to counter any threat that India might pose. If war came he could use the Chinese link to tie down large parts of the Indian Army, and gains made against India in the west could be traded against any losses in the east.

But the Yahya regime miscalculated. By

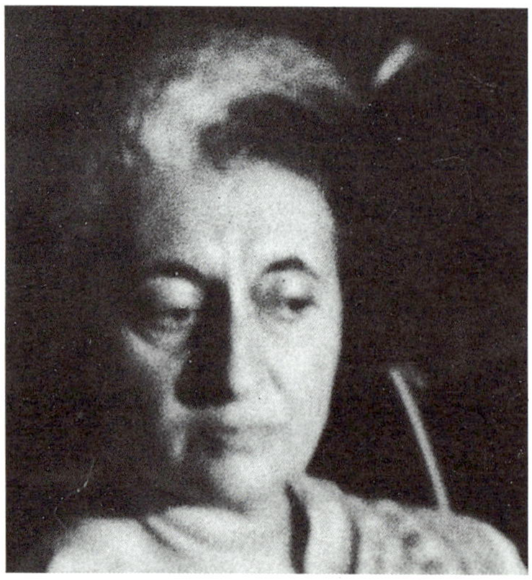

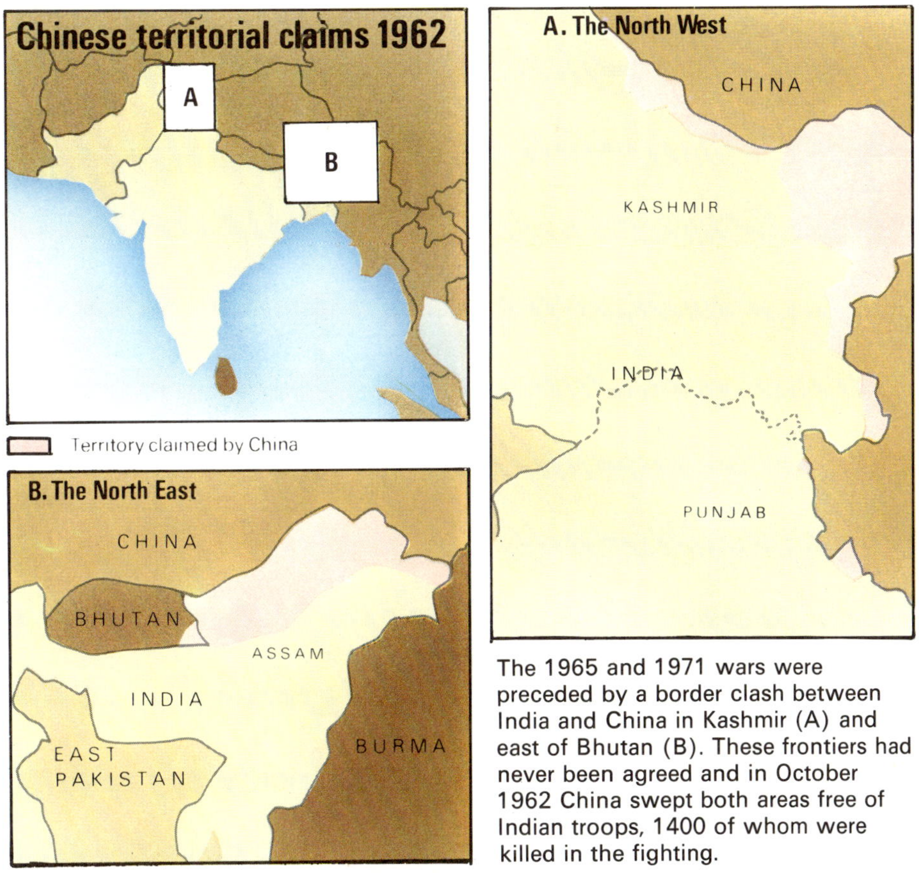

The 1965 and 1971 wars were preceded by a border clash between India and China in Kashmir (A) and east of Bhutan (B). These frontiers had never been agreed and in October 1962 China swept both areas free of Indian troops, 1400 of whom were killed in the fighting.

OPPOSITE *The three political leaders involved in the war: from left, General Yahya Khan of Pakistan, Sheikh Mujibur Rahman of East Pakistan, and India's Indira Gandhi. Pakistan and India were old foes and the Indians supported the independence claims of Pakistan's eastern province.* ABOVE *Indian troops move forward near Jessore, East Pakistan, on 16 December 1971, the day that Pakistan signed an unconditional surrender.*

1971 the Chinese had their own problems in the form of the Soviet Union and now that she was beginning to emerge from isolation and was looking for friends, China had no wish to become associated with events in East Pakistan. As the sub-continent drifted towards war the Pakistan government was clearly on its own. Furthermore, India in 1971 was far stronger militarily than in 1965, when Pakistan won major gains in the west during a fierce border war.

India believed that events in East Pakistan posed the most serious threat to her security since 1947. Thousands, then millions, of refugees streamed into India, a country that already had enough social and economic difficulties of its own. In the United Nations indifference met Indian demands for international action to deal with the crisis. The refugees had to go back because eastern India threatened to fall apart under the strains that they imposed. Once diplomacy had failed India looked to her own resources, and that could only mean war.

No intervention could occur until November at least. By then the monsoon would be over, the ground in East Pakistan dry enough to allow large-scale operations, and the onset of winter would close the Sino-Indian frontier. The intervening time was therefore spent in getting the armed forces ready for war.

India in 1971 could deploy one armoured, 13 infantry and ten mountain divisions and a variety of independent brigades. She had about 600 combat aircraft, the largest naval force in the Indian Ocean, the capacity to wage a two-month war and, after August 1971, an understanding with the Soviet Union as a counter to a possible Chinese move.

Border incidents

Throughout 1971 the steady drift to war became increasingly deliberate on India's part as Pakistani military operations in East Pakistan spilled over into India. In carrying out 'hot pursuit' of the Mukti Bahini guerrillas, the Pakistan Army became embroiled with the Indian Army – most notably at Kamalpur (20–22 October), Boyra (21 November) and Hilli (26–28 November) – as the Indian government allowed its forces to carry out retaliatory action.

India had to avoid losses in the west and overrun East Pakistan before possible international intervention. At all costs she had to prevent Pakistan making substantial gains in the west and holding out in the east, which would force India to accept the status quo.

India needed to win a war in East Pakistan quickly, but with rivers up to 8km (5 miles) wide to cross in East Pakistan the extent of India's problems can be realised. The Indian Army also had to prevent the Pakistan Army from slipping back into the Dacca Bowl, a triangle of land around Dacca formed by the chord across the confluence of the Meghna and Jamuna Rivers. In the aftermath of the monsoon Dacca was almost an island fortress.

In the event, the Indian victory was indeed swift, and the war lasted barely 13 days, from 3 to 16 December. In the west, where India had suffered heavy defeats in 1965, both sides made gains and there were large-scale tank engagements. The balance of the fighting was in India's favour, however.

In the east, the decisive sector, Indian success was complete. The Pakistan Army, deployed forward to provide defence in depth against the expected Indian attack, was swept away by the initial assaults. The rivers proved a major obstacle to Indian progress, but by 16 December the Indian Army had reached Dacca and a new state – Bangladesh – was in being.

Comparative forces

	army-men	tanks	guns	aircraft
India	860,000	1450	3000	625
Pakistan	365,000	820	1100	285

The Air War

PAKISTAN had very little to gain and potentially much to lose in a full-scale war with India. The lack of United Nations interest in East Pakistan's plight showed that as long as Pakistan kept the affair a domestic concern, she had a good chance of getting away with the excesses that were being perpetrated against the local population. It was in the interests of President Yahya Khan to avoid a widening of the East Pakistan problem.

Yet war, when it came, was the result of a deliberate Pakistani attack on India. The Indian Prime Minister, Indira Gandhi, in talks with world leaders, had made it clear that time for a peaceful solution in East Pakistan was running out. With about 6 million refugees in India by November 1971, and faced with the prospect of the figure doubling during the winter, India could not afford to do nothing – especially as border incidents in the east were increasing as Pakistani military operations spilled over into India.

For Pakistan the implications were obvious. If war was inevitable then it was in Pakistan's interests to start one at a time and in a manner of her own choice – and the lessons of the 1967 Arab-Israeli War were still fresh in everyone's memory. In that war Israel had profoundly altered the balance of power, hitherto against her, in one dramatic pre-emptive attack. By shattering the Arab air forces in one all-out offensive, Israel had transformed a potentially disastrous situation into decisive and overwhelming success.

The Pakistan air strike

Pakistan thought in terms of emulating the Israelis. In order to surprise the Indian Air Force (IAF) the Pakistan Air Force (PAF) carried out a series of attacks on 3 December 1971 around dusk. By choosing such a late hour on a Friday – the Moslem sabbath – the PAF hoped to catch the IAF at its least ready, but the attack failed to achieve any real success.

The IAF subsequently claimed to have lost just three aircraft in the first hours of the war. This may seem an understatement, but there were good reasons why the PAF could not emulate the Israeli achievement of 1967. The lateness of the strike and

ABOVE *Houses in Sialkot suffered heavy damage from Indian bombing.*
LEFT *Pakistani ground crew rearm a Mirage between sorties in 1971.*

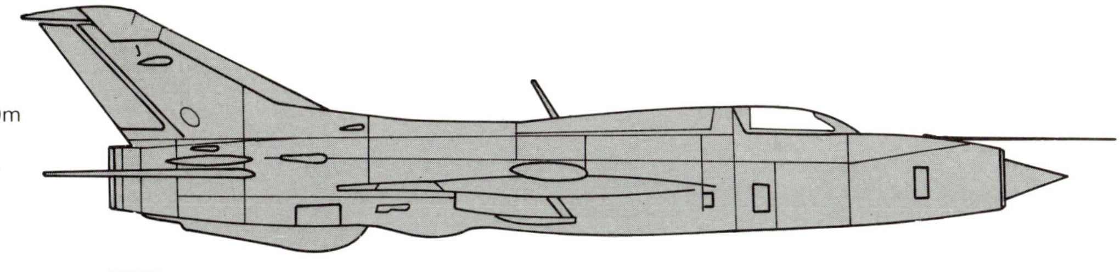

MiG-21PF
type all weather interceptor **range (combat radius)** 600km (375 miles) **speed (fully armed)** Mach 1.5 at 11,000m (36,000 ft) **armament** 1 or 2 30mm cannon, 2 x Atoll AAMs **radar** spin scan, search and track **crew** 1

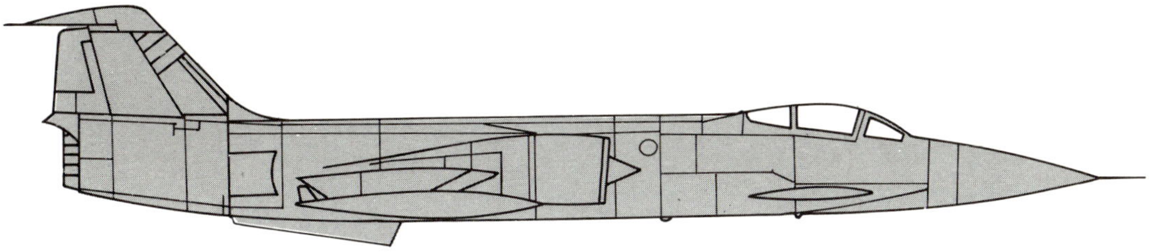

Lockheed F-104A
type day interceptor **range (combat radius with 2 x 166.5 imp gall tanks)** 930km (580 miles) **speed (fully armed)** Mach 1.9 at 11,000m (36,000 ft) **armament** 1 x 20mm Vulcan M-61 rotary cannon, 2 x AIM-9B Sidewinder AAMs **radar** AN/ASG-14TI **crew** 1

the rapid fall of night, notwithstanding the full moon, meant that the PAF could not repeat one of the salient characteristics of the Israeli attack – total and sustained effort until the whole of the enemy's strike force was destroyed.

Reasons for failure

The individual attacks achieved little, mainly because the PAF conducted its offensive on too narrow a frontage and without sufficient depth. Two airfields in Kashmir, five in the Punjab and three to the south were hit in the initial assault, apparently in the belief that the IAF was deployed well forward near the frontier. In fact the IAF had done its homework. It had taken care to disperse its aircraft, most of which were housed in concrete shelters that were invulnerable to anything other than a direct hit.

Moreover, the PAF does not seem to have committed more than 30 per cent of its 300 combat aircraft to its initial attacks between 1740 and 1815 hours on 3 December. This may have been the result of a low serviceability rate on the part of the PAF, but there were demands after the war for an inquiry as to why PAF strength was persistently withheld from the battle. It may be that, with the Yahya regime trying to provoke international intervention in order to restrain India, the Pakistanis tried to ensure that as much of their forces as possible remained intact at the end of the war for political and diplomatic purposes.

Such seemingly contradictory concepts of politics and strategy may explain the PAF's indifferent performance, but there is another possible explanation: the IAF was assisted by Soviet Moss aircraft. These were AWACS (Airborne Warning and Control Systems) aircraft and this war seems to have been the first conventional war when such aircraft were used to fulfil their detection, control and communications functions. Every move that the PAF made was immediately known to the IAF, and the AWACS aircraft, in conjunction with active electronic counter-measures, threw a blanket over Pakistani radar and communications. The IAF was able to operate between 320 and 480km (200 and 300 miles) behind the front line with impunity.

The exact events of the air battle are impossible to disentangle, but the Pakistanis claimed to have accounted for 81 aircraft, the Indians for 94. The Indian authorities admitted to the loss of 45 aircraft. What is clear, however, is that the air battle went decisively in India's favour and that the PAF, except in the Chamba sector, played very little part in supporting the ground forces.

RIGHT *A Lockheed F-104A Starfighter of the PAF over the Karakoram mountains.* BELOW *MiG-19s also served Pakistan in the 1971 war.*

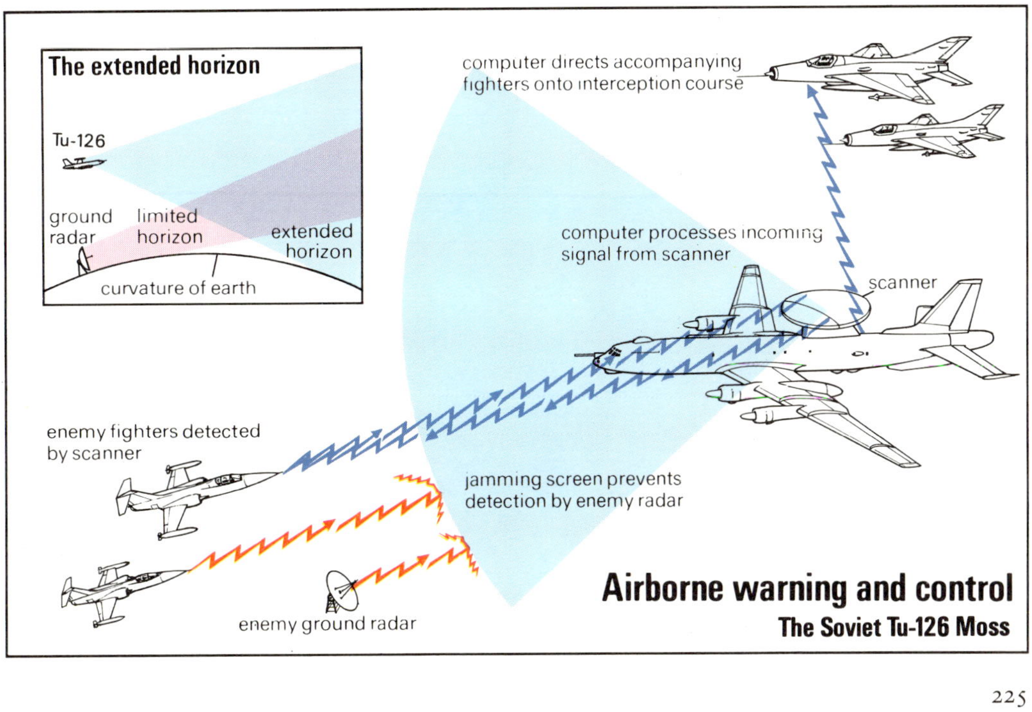

Airborne warning and control
The Soviet Tu-126 Moss

The War in the West

THE FRONTIER between India and Pakistan in the west followed no natural feature. It was a compromise that had been settled in 1947 on the basis of borders of old states and took no account of topography. On both sides of the frontier there were dangerously exposed salients that were coveted as much for tactical as for political reasons. In the 1971 war both combatants sought to 'rationalise' the front to their advantage, although the balance of gains ultimately favoured the Indians.

At best the Pakistan High Command could hope to delay defeat in the east, but it was in the west that it had to make the effort to ensure it avoided total defeat. In West Pakistan the government deployed ten infantry and two armoured divisions, various brigades and almost all their combat aircraft.

In Kashmir the Pakistan Army deployed the 12th and 23rd Infantry Divisions. Southwards to the sea it deployed II Corps (the 8th, 15th and 17th Infantry and 6th Armoured Divisions), IV Corps (the 10th and 11th Infantry Divisions), I Corps (the 7th and 33rd Infantry and 1st Armoured Divisions) and the 18th Infantry Division in the Sialkot, Lahore, Multan and Hyderabad sectors respectively. Except in Kashmir the Pakistani command had brigades attached. (The Indian order of battle in the west remains unknown, but Indian accounts of the war have admitted that their forces were not inferior to those of Pakistan.)

Kashmir and the Punjab

In Kashmir the Pakistanis moved against Punch at the same time as they mounted their pre-emptive air strike, but they made virtually no progress in operations that attracted heavy Indian Air Force attack on 4–6 December and the Indians finished by taking some of the Pakistani outposts in front of Kahuta. Around Kargil the Indians took all the Pakistani outposts and observation posts overlooking the Zoji La Pass in battles that were fought at heights above

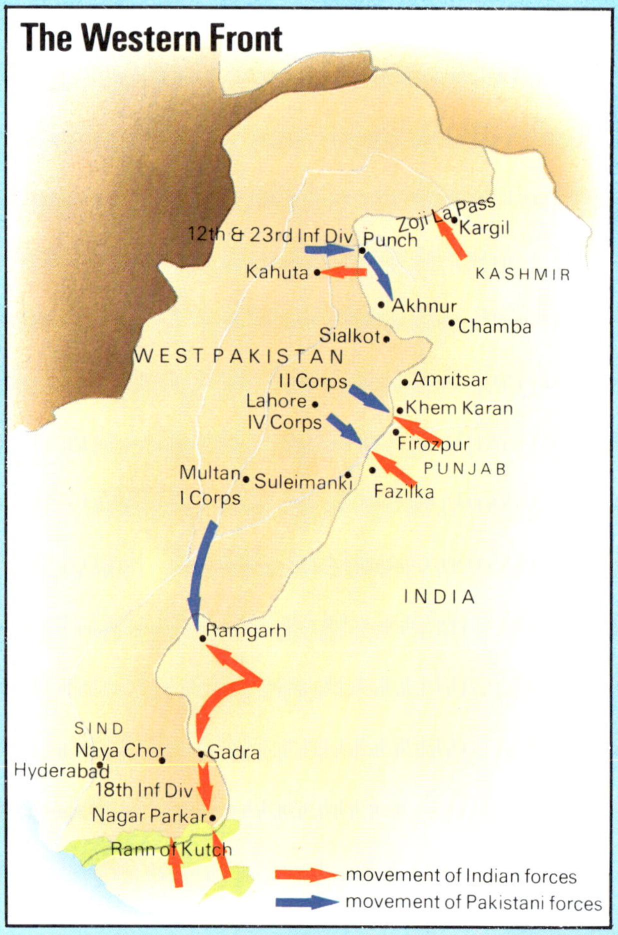

Pakistani regular troops with mortars and small-arms take up defensive positions facing the Indians.

Indians moved on but failed to take Naya Chor (because of the ceasefire coming into effect, according to the Indians). It seems probable, however, that the sheer difficulty of moving armour across the desert played its part in this failure though the attack did pull Pakistani forces, particularly their armour, down from the north and centre.

LEFT *An Indian artilleryman loads a gun in the Punjab sector.* BELOW *This T54 tank was abandoned by Indians withdrawing from Chamba.* BOTTOM *A recoilless rifle on an Indian jeep.*

4800m (16,000 feet) and in temperatures well below zero. Around Chamba, however, the Indians had to give ground, withdrawing across the Munawar Tawi on 7 December. The II Pakistani Corps, under Lieutenant General Tikka Khan, who had been recalled from the east, was badly defeated in its attempts to cross the river. It was also unable to prevent the Indians pinching out the Pakistani salient over the Munawar around Akhnur, directly below Chamba.

In the Punjab there were fierce exchanges in the Amritsar-Lahore, Firozpur-Hussainawala and Fazilka-Suleimanki sectors, with the largest single tank engagement of the war taking place around Shakargarh. The Indians claim to have destroyed 45 Pakistani Pattons in this battle, and they made gains both here and around Khem Karan. In all, the Indians finished in control of some 1000 square km (400 square miles) of Pakistani territory in the Punjab. Their own losses were insignificant.

India's gains in the south

In the north and centre, therefore, the Indians took about nine times as much territory as they lost, and they certainly secured the better ground. In the south, in the Sind, their territorial gains were much larger and the Pakistani failure even more marked since the Indians ended the war in control of over 2600 square km (1000 square miles) of Pakistani territory, although most of it was desert and salt marsh.

In this area the Pakistanis came to grief quite badly. An armoured thrust on Ramgarh literally ran itself into the ground (or rather sand), and was subjected to punishing air attack. The Indians claimed the destruction of 34 tanks and nearly 100 vehicles in turning back this abortive attack.

Further to the south the Indians took Gadra on 5 December and moved to secure Nagar Parkar and the territory in the Rann of Kutch that had been ceded to Pakistan in 1968. The

Nevertheless, at the end of the war, the Indians had come out decisively on top. There had been none of the failures of 1965 and even in Chamba, where in 1965 the Pakistanis had won a decisive victory under Yahya Khan, the Indians had abandoned the salient and town in an orderly manner and inflicted heavy losses on the enemy. Overall Pakistani losses are unknown, the Indians announcing their casualties in the west to be 1426 killed, 3611 wounded and 2149 missing.

Victory in the East

TO CONQUER EAST PAKISTAN the Indian Army set up four commands under Lieutenant General Jagjit Singh Aurora. These were, in West Bengal, II Corps with two divisions and three armoured and artillery units; in Bihara, XXXIII Corps with one division, two brigades and two units; IV Corps in Tripura with three mountain divisions and three supporting units; and 101 Communication Zone with a single brigade in Assam. Overall the Indian Army deployed about 250,000 men for this invasion and it could rely on the active support of about 100,000 Mukti Bahini and the help of the local population. The plan of campaign envisaged attacking from all directions to break East Pakistan into fragments and then driving directly on to Dacca as fast as possible.

Deployment of forces

The Pakistan Army in East Pakistan totalled about four-and-a-half divisions (approximately 40 battalions of regular infantry) with about two light armoured units in support. Since this force had to hold an area with a population of about 70 million and a border nearly 2250km (1400 miles) long, its task would have been utterly impossible had it not been for the fact that with so many rivers dissecting East Pakistan the Indians had to make all their efforts along narrow and restricted fronts. Strongly defended positions, held in depth, could be used to block Indian advances. The Pakistan Army was therefore deployed forward in order to hold the Indians at the border, the intention being to strengthen the Pakistani diplomatic position.

To meet the Indian Army the Pakistani command deployed the 9th Infantry Division opposite II Corps, the 16th Infantry Division between the Ganges and Jamuna Rivers opposite XXXIII Corps, the 36th Infantry Division opposite IV Corps and the 14th Infantry Division in the northern part of the province opposite 101 Communication Zone.

The Indian attack began with 23 thrusts to eliminate, surround or bypass salients and strongpoints held by the Pakistan Army. The main purpose was to infiltrate and get behind Pakistani positions in order to ensure that enemy formations could not withdraw to Dacca. The rigid policy of trying to hold forward and deny the Indians ground proved physically and tactically disastrous for the Pakistanis and, in the end, self-defeating.

The attack began on the morning of 4 December. IV Corps took Akhaura and Laksham on 5 December and Feni the next day, thereby cutting the road between Dacca and Chittagong, but it bypassed the strongpoints at Mainamati and Brahman Baria and pressed on to reach the Meghna River at Ashuganj, Dandkandi and Chand-

ABOVE *A Pakistan border post at Benapol, where Indian batteries were just 70m distant.* BELOW *Indian troops head towards Dacca in the assault that resulted in Pakistani surrender.*

The PT76 light amphibious tank

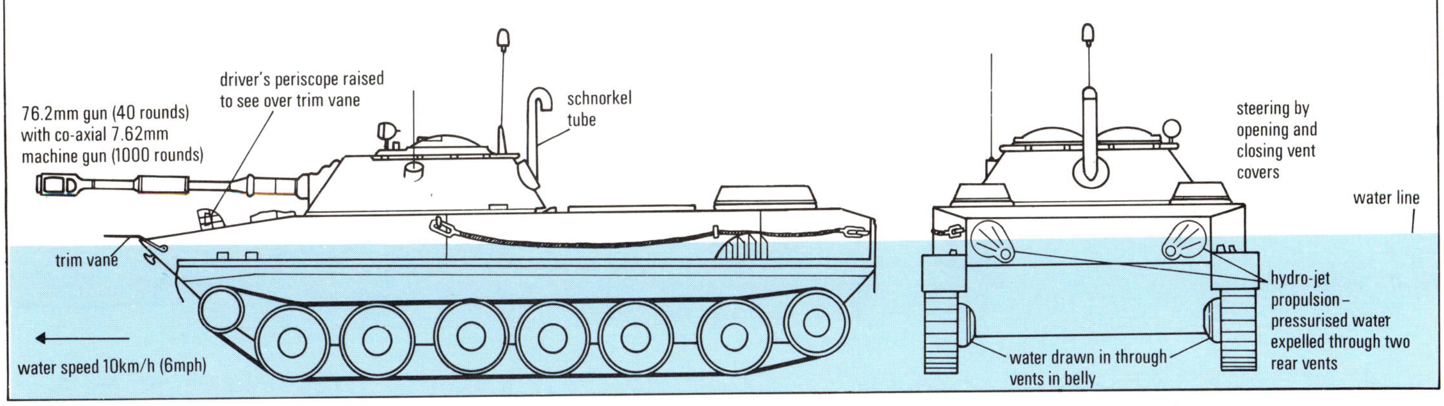

pur on the 9th. The following day IV Corps crossed the mile-wide river by steamer, backed up by helicopter assault landings, and firmly established itself within relatively easy striking distance of Dacca.

Pakistani losses

In the west of the province the first success was registered on 4 December by the Mukti Bahini when they took Darsana after a hard fight. Jessore was taken by II Corps on 7 December, the Pakistanis abandoning a strong, well-stocked position that the Indians considered might take a week to reduce. Jennida also fell on the 7th. In general the advance of II Corps tended to slow down because of the problems of crossing the formidable rivers in its line of advance. Not until the 14th did II Corps secure the general line of the Ganges.

One of the problems that the Indians found was that their Soviet-supplied reconnaissance tank, the PT76, the only tank in the world capable of amphibious operations, overheated after 30 minutes in the water – and some of the rivers required a three-hour crossing. Such armour had to be towed, and the Indians were forced to rely on helicopters to make assault crossings and establish air bridges. In general Soviet bridging and amphibious equipment served the Indians very well – as did the 130mm field gun which had been used extensively in Vietnam – but there were obvious limitations in a region where rivers were so enormous.

In the north the Indians met their fiercest opposition. Bogra, HQ of the 14th Division, was not taken until 14 December. A Pakistani withdrawal to the Dacca area was forestalled not by the infiltrating ground forces but by a battalion paradrop (later reinforced) on Tangail on 11 December.

By that time the defenders' resolve was beginning to crack. The Pakistanis knew full well the degree of hatred they had incurred. On 7 December India called for a surrender in the east. After an attack on Dacca by field artillery the Pakistanis formally requested a ceasefire on the 15th. The Indians, anxious to avoid a bloodbath in Dacca and concerned to prevent the Pakistan Army taking final revenge on the civil population, demanded unconditional surrender. The surrender was signed on the 16th, and amid delirious scenes in Dacca, Bangladesh became the world's newest state.

Battle for Bangladesh

The Indian invasion

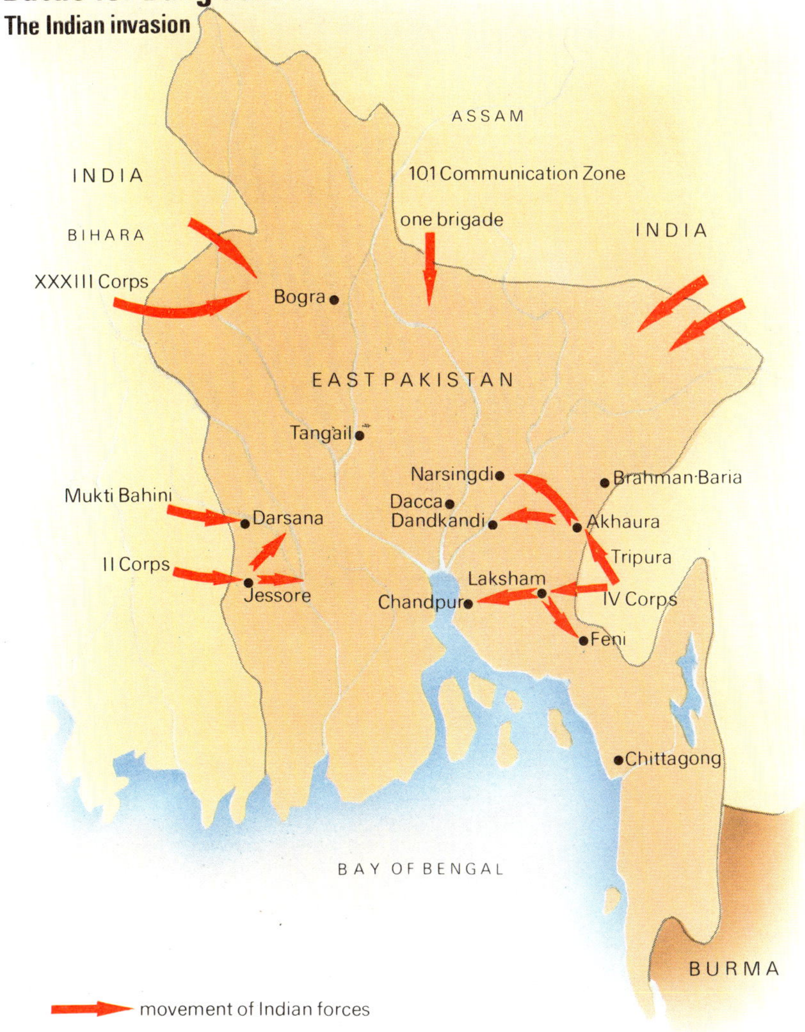

A Soviet-built T54 tank of the Indian Army on the outskirts of Dacca shortly before Pakistan's surrender.

The Yom Kippur War

The Arab attack of October 1973 threatened to bring Israel to its knees

H. P. Willmott

BELOW *The body of a Syrian tank crewman lies beside a T54 knocked out during an Israeli counter-attack in Syria. The opening Syrian advance met with initial success but the Israeli riposte proved decisive. More than 860 Syrian tanks were destroyed or abandoned.*
OPPOSITE *Israeli prisoners take orders from their Syrian captors as a TV camera films the scene.*

THE ARAB-ISRAELI WAR of 1967 brought an end to Israel's immediate anxieties regarding security. Israel was as secure as a state of 2.5 million ever could be when surrounded by more than 100 million enemies. But a lasting guarantee of security could only come from binding peace treaties that reconciled her neighbours to her existence – and these were impossible. Yet Israel believed that Arab disunity was so great and Israeli military superiority so marked that the Arabs would be forced ultimately to settle on her terms.

Having conquered large areas of Arab territory in 1967 Israel saw no good reason to give them up while the Arabs refused to contemplate a peace settlement. And the Arabs refused even to consider a settlement unless Israel relinquished her gains.

Both Lyndon Johnson and Richard Nixon wanted stability in the Middle East. Ideally the Americans would have liked a general settlement, but if that was impossible then they were prepared to accept the status quo and an avoidance of conflict. At this time American power was floundering in the morass of Vietnam and the United States was making strenuous efforts to prevent an

Israel 1973

epidemic of revolt in Latin America. The United States armed and supplied Israel in the belief that the very imbalance of power between Jew and Arab would prevent conflict.

After 1967 there emerged the full extent of Arab disunity, so often concealed or over-shadowed by the Arab-Israeli dispute. Incessant feuding occurred throughout the Arab world, but this development was itself over-shadowed by the death of Nasser.

President Gamal Abdel Nasser of Egypt was without equal in the Arab world. He was the only Arab leader to attain world stature. Anwar Sadat, his successor, seemed insignificant and destined for only a short time in office, yet Sadat quickly showed his mettle.

During 1972 the summit meeting between President Nixon and Leonid Brezhnev proved critical in the events leading up to the 1973 war. It came after more than a year of intense diplomatic action by Sadat to get the superpowers to exert pressure on Israel to agree to a settlement. Egypt needed peace, but not peace at any price.

War option

Sadat had called 1971 the 'year of decision' when diplomacy would yield results. He was pro-West by sentiment and wanted to persuade the Americans to promote a settlement. His attempts were unsuccessful. When Nixon and Brezhnev met in 1972 the two leaders seemed prepared to maintain the status quo in the Middle East. The official communiqué at the end of the talks made no reference to Resolution 242, the UN framework for all the abortive peace efforts since 1967.

The failure of diplomacy in 1971 and early 1972 forced Sadat towards the conclusion that he would have to resort to war. But Sadat and every other Arab leader knew that in open battle the Israelis were too good to be beaten. The problem for Sadat and the Arabs, therefore, was a difficult one. There was no prospect of a settlement by peaceful means, and no chance of winning a war.

Sadat came up with a subtle analysis: he realised that the Arabs did not have to win a war. They had to win two battles – one against the Israelis and the other for the newspaper and TV headlines around the world. What the Arabs needed were favourable political conditions for a superpower intervention. The start of a war and initial success could produce this result, particularly if they coincided with threats to oil supplies for Western countries. Sadat was after the benefits of victory without letting war escalate to a level where the Arabs would lose – and, as it happened, he very nearly succeeded.

One conclusion drawn from the experience of the 1967 war shaped Arab plans. This was that the Arab disaster had stemmed from Israel's initial air attack. The Arabs therefore wanted to strike the first blow in overwhelming strength on more than one front. Egypt and Syria planned to launch simultaneous attacks along the whole of their respective fronts with all strength while the Jordanians tied down Israeli forces and secured the Syrian left flank, not by participating in the attack but just by mobilising.

The Arabs intended to secure surprise so that Israel would not be mobilised at the time of the assaults. A surprise attack along the whole length of the front lines would mean that Israel would be unable to detect the direction of the main Arab effort and unable to concentrate effectively for the counter-attack.

The Arabs' strength lay in their numbers, their weakness in their lack of technical expertise and flexibility on the battlefield. In any fluid situation the Israelis were certain to show greater flair and initiative than the Arabs. But the Israelis had their weaknesses. Manpower was scarce and Israel lacked the financial means to fight a long war. These considerations came together in an Arab plan that envisaged the Syrians using Soviet-styled mass armour attacks on the Syrian (Golan) Heights and the Egyptians using Soviet river-crossing techniques to cross the Suez Canal. Once across the canal and established firmly on the eastern bank, the Egyptians intended to fight a static battle in an effort to wear down the Israelis.

The Egyptians intended to fight a set-piece battle in which weight of fire, tenacity and numbers prevailed over superior training and technique. They planned to rely on their superiority in artillery, their armour, new Soviet-supplied anti-tank guided weapons and, for the infantry, a profusion of anti-tank RPG-7 grenade launchers, to blunt the cutting edge of Israeli armour in a battle fought under the protective shield umbrella of the SAM batteries massed on the west bank of the canal.

The question of timing

Timing had to be a compromise. The Syrians wanted a dawn attack when the sun would be behind them; the Egyptians wanted a late-afternoon attack for the same reason. Although 1400 hours pleased neither, it was a fair compromise. The date, however, was inspired. October was the month when tidal conditions in the canal were best suited to an attack. Operations could not be delayed beyond October because of the onset of rain and snows on the Syrian Heights. But 6 October was the anniversary of the Prophet's victory at the Battle of Badr in 626, and was mid-way through Ramadan, the Moslem month of fasting. Furthermore, 6 October was also Yom Kippur, the Jewish fast day, when the Israelis could be guaranteed to be at their least prepared.

The initial Egyptian attack across the Suez Canal was very successful, and by 8 October substantial forces were established there and fought off the Israelis' desperate attempts to dislodge them. Meanwhile, in the northern sector, the Israelis were early rocked by fierce Syrian attacks but by 9 October had emerged victorious.

On 14 October the Egyptian forces made the mistake of advancing deep into Sinai; a more open battle followed and the Israelis' success was such that their forces crossed the Suez Canal on the 16th. An effective ceasefire was proclaimed on 24 October. The fighting had been very different from 1967; new weapons had added a new dimension to warfare; defensive tactics had been shown to have great strength when correctly applied; but Israel had again triumphed.

Comparative forces 1973

	men/army	tanks	aircraft
Israel	275,000	1700	432
Egypt	285,000	2000	600
Syria	100,000	1200	210

Crossing the Canal

THE SCALE of Arab prepations could not be concealed from the Israelis who had, on both the Suez Canal and Syrian (Golan) Heights, good positions from which to monitor Arab moves. But by very careful control of movement under the guise of exercises, plus preparations to meet an Israeli attack after an air battle over Syria in mid-September, the Arabs succeeded in obtaining a large measure of strategic and tactical surprise.

The Arabs therefore secured their initial objective, and thereby ensured that they won two political points of utmost significance. Firstly, they destroyed the American notion of stability in the Middle East by imbalance. Secondly, the first the world knew of the war was Egypt's successful crossing of the Suez Canal. In political and psychological terms this was critical. It broke the myth of Israeli invincibility and showed that the Arabs could organise themselves. Subsequent events never took the edge off this achievement.

Israel had only one division, with some 280 tanks in three brigades, along the canal to face an attack from five Egyptian infantry divisions and assorted brigades. Five more Egyptian divisions were in reserve. About 1600 Egyptian tanks were deployed along the Egyptian front, about half of them with the five forward divisions.

Tactics of attrition

The Egyptians planned for a deliberate step-by-step attack. It was designed first to cross the canal, reduce Israeli fortifications on the eastern bank and firmly establish divisional bridgeheads, to meet and defeat Israeli counter-attacks and finally to link up the various bridgeheads in order to wage defensive warfare that would grind down the Israelis in a massive battle of attrition.

Plans existed for the development of offensives towards the passes of the Central Ridge and down the Gulf of Suez coast towards Sharm el Sheikh, but these were vague compared with the detailed plans for the canal crossing and the defensive battle in Sinai. The Egyptians placed their faith in relatively shallow penetration and a defensive battle.

The offensive opened with an hour-long artillery and air attack on Israeli positions along the canal and against various key installations in Sinai. Then, in accordance with Soviet practice, the infantry assaulted across the canal between the Israeli fortifications. The Egyptians did not intend to attack directly against the strongpoints of the Israeli line, but the Israelis hoped that the fortifications would impede the Egyptians more than they did. The presence of fortifications at 8–13km (5–8 mile) spacings down the length of the canal tied down Israeli armour in the gaps in small, relatively ineffective, numbers and caused the Israelis to consider the relief of these positions as their immediate aim. It was only when the Israelis accepted the loss of the fortified bases and freed their armour from trying to effect their relief that many of Israel's immediate problems in Sinai began to ease.

On 6 October the Egyptians fought their way across the canal in dozens of places. In two days they managed to get ten bridges into service to bring armour, guns and equipment over the canal to forces that had to withstand 23 Israeli counter-attacks

Egyptians raise their flag on former Israeli positions across the canal.

The Egyptian attack

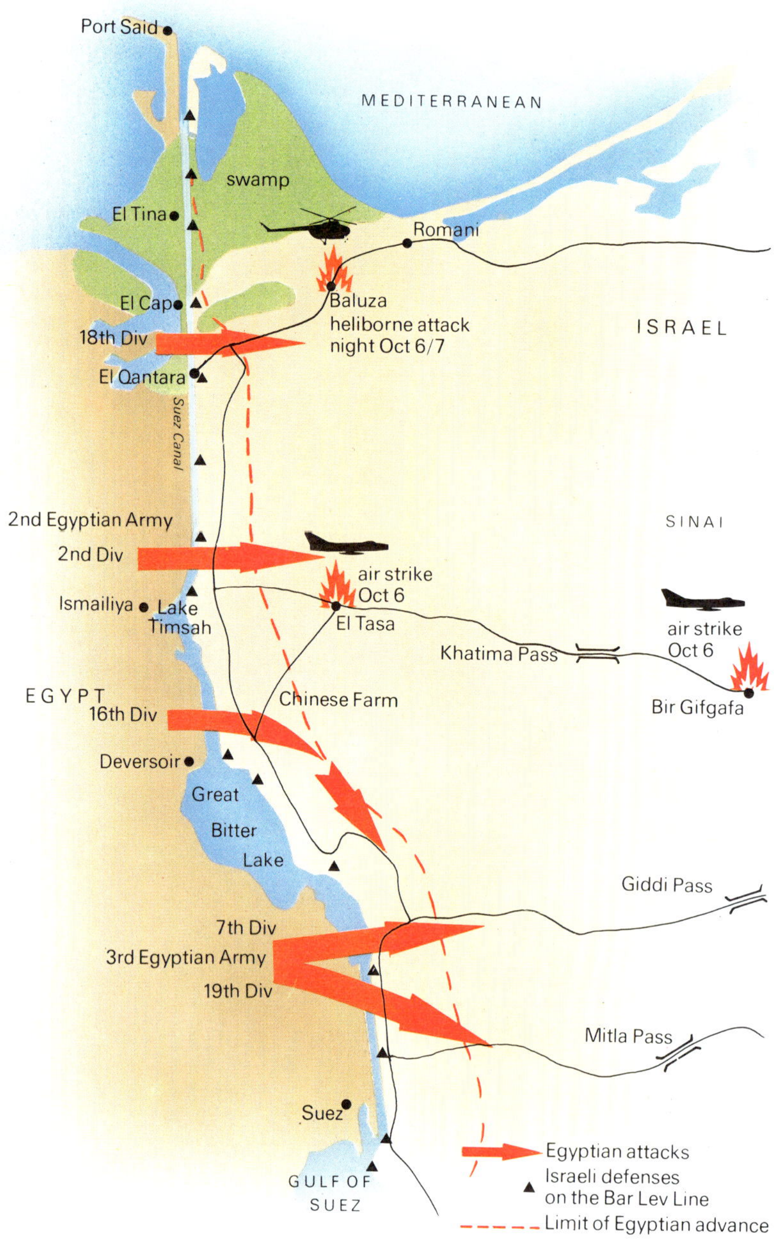

between 6 and 8 October. None of these attacks were made with less than a battalion of armour and they grew in size as the hours passed. Yet all were unco-ordinated and were made in insufficient strength.

Each of these Israeli attacks was broken by the formidable combination of artillery, anti-tank guided weapons and RPG-7s. Losses amongst Egyptian infantry on the east bank were heavy – though only 208 had been killed during the actual crossing of the canal – but Israeli confidence was badly shaken by failure and heavy losses.

Counter-attacks repulsed

On 7/8 October a series of Israeli assaults in the northern sector against the 2nd Egyptian Army were severely handled, mainly because the Israelis, through faulty navigation, attacked across the front rather than into the positions of the 18th and 2nd Divisions. In the south the 3rd Egyptian Army dealt with an ill-supported attack by the 14th Armoured Brigade in a pre-emptory manner.

With their own supporting armour coming across the canal in increasingly large numbers the Egyptian position seemed a strong one, but this was deceptive. The Egyptians had failed to secure vital roads which would have denied the Israelis their depots and lining-up positions for subsequent operations. Israeli forces were arriving on the battlefield in larger numbers. The Israelis had gone over to the defensive so as to contain the Egyptians while events elsewhere were resolved. Moreover they had seen the need for fresh tactics to overcome Arab anti-tank weapons – and on 9 October they found that near the Chinese Farm the Egyptians had failed to tie in their joining flanks effectively.

TOP *Egyptian vehicles cross a pontoon bridge erected over the Suez Canal.*
ABOVE *Soviet-made amphibious vehicles were used to bridge the canal. The top unfolded to provide a platform.*
BELOW *Troops of the Egyptian 3rd Army are supplied with food.*

Battle for the Heights

THE MAIN REASON why the Israelis went on to the defensive in Sinai was not the situation on the battlefield but the course of events on the Syrian (Golan) Heights. However badly the situation in Sinai developed for the Israelis, 190km (120 miles) of desert separated the Egyptian forces from Israel. In the north there was no comparative depth to the Israeli positions, and this, coupled with the strength of the initial Syrian assaults and the fact that these advanced almost to the River Jordan, prompted Israel to make her initial effort in the north on the Syrian Heights.

Tanks versus tanks

The Syrians envisaged an attack that would clear the whole of the Heights in 2–3 days. Unlike in 1967, when much of their army had been held back, they committed almost all their forces to the attack. They employed two armoured divisions. three infantry divisions and a variety of brigades on a 50km (30-mile) front. In all about 1200 tanks were deployed for the operation. The Syrians planned to attack along the full length of the front with their infantry divisions (each of which had about 180 tanks), the two armoured divisions being detailed to exploit the breaches made by the first-echelon attack.

Opposing the Syrians on 6 October were two Israeli brigades with a total of about 180 tanks. One of these brigades had been deployed to the Heights after the September air battle as a purely precautionary measure, and its presence proved the difference between victory and defeat.

Both Israeli formations were all but totally annihilated in the course of the two days' fighting, but in that time they exacted such a toll of the attackers, both in casualties and time, that hastily mobilised Israeli forces, rushed to the Heights, were able to contain and then throw back the final stuttering Syrian assaults. By the time the Syrians had decisively breached the Israeli positions they no longer had the strength to exploit, or even consolidate, their positional gains. The Israelis subsequently counted 867 destroyed or abandoned Syrian tanks and hundreds of vehicles and guns.

Such losses – in a battlefield less than 16km (10 miles) deep – point to the ferocity with which the Israeli-Syrian battle was conducted and the bravery shown on both sides. The Syrians relied solely on numbers and weight of firepower to overcome resistance (there was no room for manoeuvre), but this proved inadequate in the face of an opponent that had had six years to prepare his positions. Israeli forces had trained for a defensive battle and they knew the ground, the fields of fire and the ranges intimately.

It was this high degree of technical and tactical expertise that enabled Israeli armour, fighting from defensive positions, to exact a crippling toll of Syrian armour. All along the front on the first two days of the war small groups of Israeli tanks faced battalions, brigades and even divisions of Syrian armour and inflicted huge losses on the attackers. The 7th Armoured Brigade alone accounted for over 250 Syrian tanks in the Valley of Tears between Hermonit and Kuneitra.

ABOVE *Israeli guns score a direct hit on a T55 tank.* BELOW *Israeli 155mm artillery pound enemy positions in Syria. Although outnumbered, the Israeli artillery units gave a good account of themselves during the fighting on the Syrian front.*

By the time reinforcements arrived to support the 7th one of its battalions was down to six tanks and another group of Israeli armour had no more than two rounds per tank. Miraculously for the Israelis it was just at this point, with the Jorden less than ten minutes' drive for the Syrian armour, that the Syrians began to break off the action and Israeli reinforcements began to arrive.

In the south the story was much the same, though there the sheer weight of the Syrian attack penetrated more deeply and posed the most serious of all the crises that beset Israel on 6 and 7 October. The very number of Syrian tanks involved in the attack ensured that some would survive battle with the Israelis. The assault penetrated almost as far as El Al, Nafekh and the Bnot Ya'akov bridge as Syrian tanks lapped round the edges of isolated Israeli defenders, yet as they did so the first Israeli forces to come up in support – the 50 tanks of the 17th Armoured Brigade – took them in their flank. The 17th Armoured alone destroyed more than 200 Syrian tanks around Yehudia.

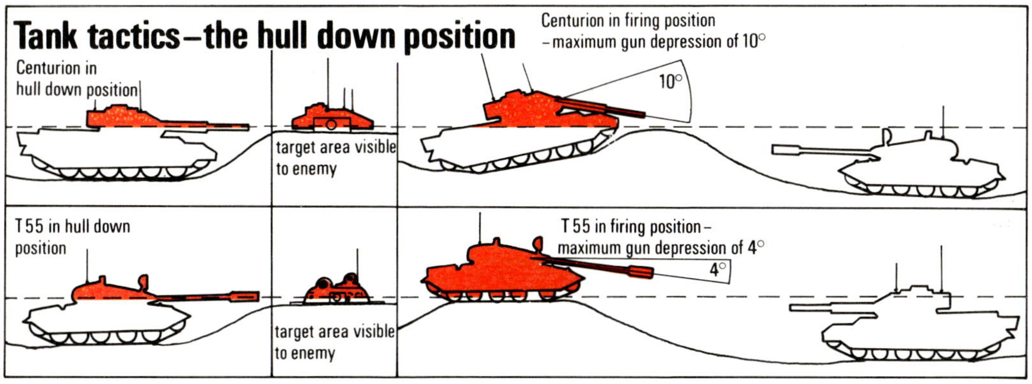

Further Israeli gains

By the evening of 9 October the Syrians had accepted defeat on the Heights and had begun to break contact with the Israelis all along the front. Further losses of both territory and military resources could not be averted because, with the arrival of fresh Israeli formations, the balance had shifted decisively against Syrian units drained of their strength and cohesion.

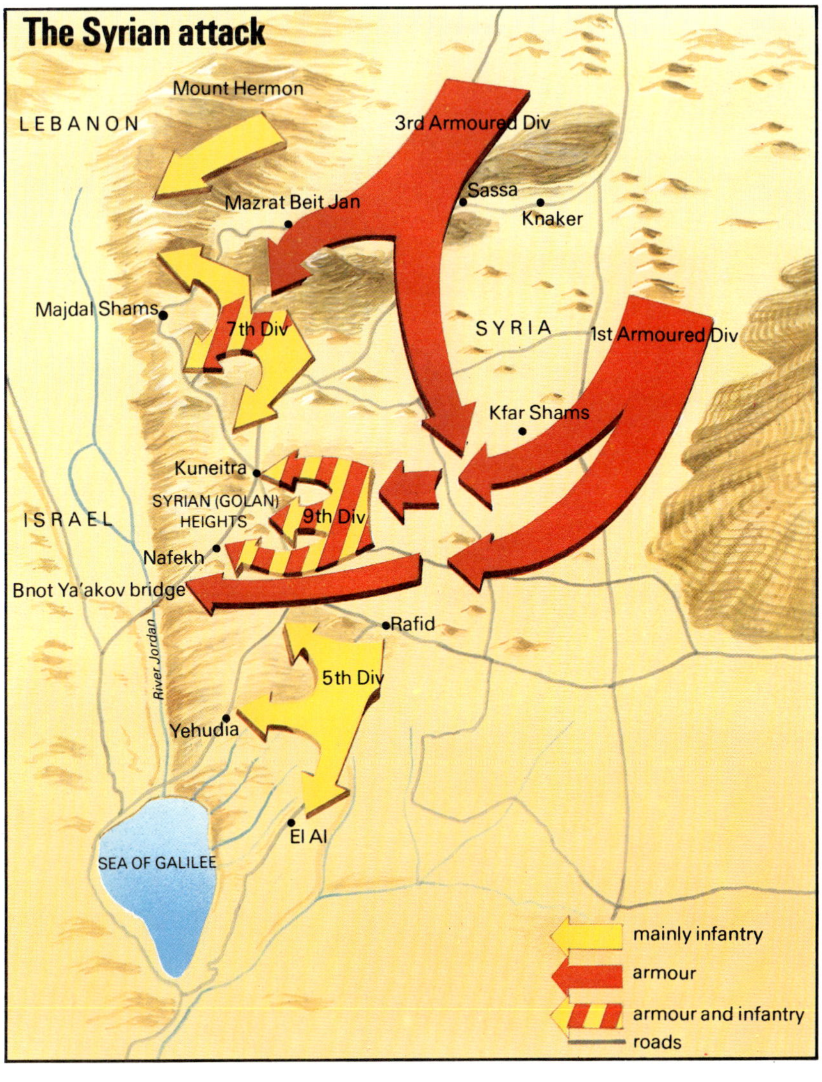

A gunner overlooks Syrian territory from the Israeli lines. His weapon is a 0.3 inch Browning light machine gun.

Operations on the Heights continued until Syria accepted a United Nations ceasefire on 22 October. The Israelis, who had retaken all the ground that they had lost by 10 October, subsequently added further territorial gains to go alongside their 1967 conquests, thereby giving their positions on the Heights greater depth and security. The Israeli advance took them almost to Kfar Shams (despite opposition from the Jordanians, Syrians and Iraqis), Knaker and Mazrat Beit Jan while in the centre their advance secured Tel Shams on 13 October.

The last battles on the Heights were fought on the slopes of Mount Hermon, where Israeli forces re-took observation positions that had been lost in the first hours of the war. Overall, the battle on the Heights cost the Arab armies more than 1400 tanks. The Israelis lost 250 tanks, but 150 were recovered from a battlefield, with all its invaluable booty, that remained firmly in Israeli hands at the end of the war.

Missiles and Fighters

ONE OF THE OLDEST military clichés is that victory breeds complacency whereas defeat encourages innovation. The experience of the 1967 war confirmed its truth. The Arab defeat of 1967 led to a fundamental reappraisal of every aspect of Arab strategy and tactics. Victory, on the other hand, confirmed Israel in her disdain for Arab military capabilities and led the Israelis to assume that what had been achieved in 1967 would be repeated in any renewal of hostilities.

An unexpected surprise

Early on in the war, Israel learnt that the forces on which she relied for victory, the Israeli Air Force (IAF), and the armoured arm, could not dominate the battlefield as they had done in 1967. And now, too, the Arabs had new weapons. After the 1970 'War of Attrition' fought over the Suez Canal, the IAF earmarked Arab radars and surface-to-air missile (SAM) batteries as their primary targets. It recognised the real threat posed by the Soviet-supplied missiles and anti-aircraft guns. The 1973 war began in such a manner, however, that the IAF was called upon to mount all-out attacks on the Arab ground forces in an effort to ease the pressure on the dangerously outnumbered Israelis on the ground. This the IAF had to do before it tackled the SAM batteries and radars.

The result was disastrous for the Israelis. The IAF had failed to appreciate the extent of its aircraft's vulnerability to the inter-locking air defence system provided by the SA-2, SA-3, SA-6, SA-7 and SA-9 and the ZSU-23-4. For the IAF the SA-2 was a familiar enemy, but most of the remainder were unknown quantities. To evade the SA-2 Israeli aircraft found they had to enter the zone of operations of the SA-6, and the only effective counter to it was to dive inside and below the missile before it had time to reach high altitude and speed. To do so the evading aircraft ran straight into the range of the SA-7 and SA-9 and the massed array of ZSU-23-4s.

In the whole of the 1967 war the IAF lost about 26 aircraft. In the 1973 war the Syrians alone handed back 63 Israeli aircrew. The Israelis admitted to a loss of 115 aircraft, including 60 in the first week of the war. Other estimates of Israeli losses are much higher, the Americans placing them at about 200.

Whatever the true figures, Israeli air losses were substantial. They were particularly heavy in the first two days of the war when the IAF committed its best elements against the Arab ground forces.

Israeli counter-measures were often helped by the Arabs themselves. To meet incoming Israeli aircraft and to ensure that the enemy would be hit, the Arabs fired off missiles in salvos, thereby rapidly depleting their ammunition reserve.

Israeli ground forces aided the IAF by their advances on the ground. On

The Egyptian anti-aircraft screen

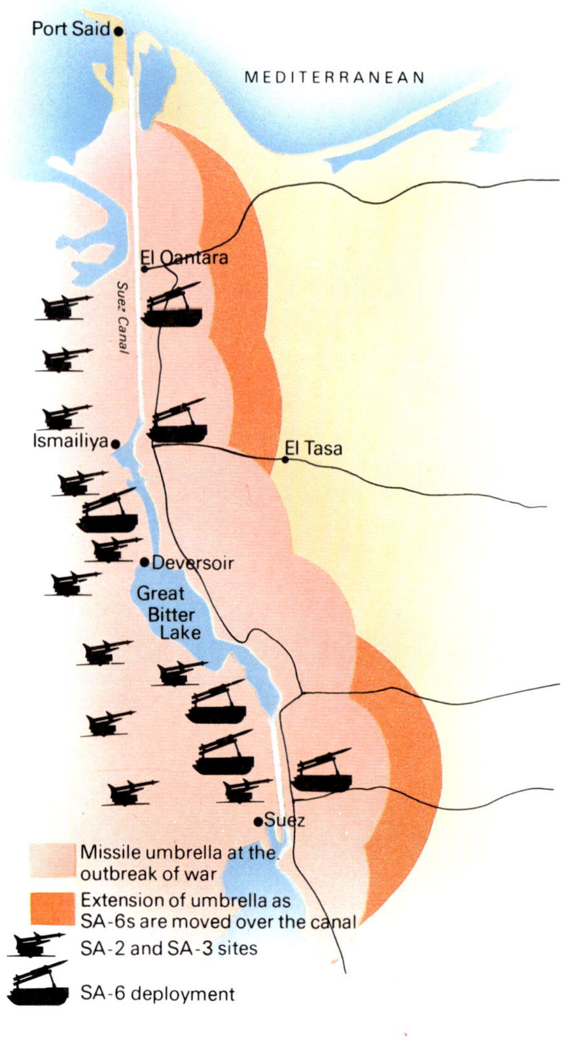

the Suez Canal and on the Syrian (Golan) Heights the Israeli Army opened up breaches in the Arab air defence systems. Once a breach was made and Arab batteries were deprived of air support the IAF was able to attack what may be termed an 'open flank'. The Israelis were able to blast corridors through Arab air space and 'roll-up' the Arab batteries, and when this was achieved the Israelis began to register increasingly impressive results.

Massed attacks and ECMs

The IAF overcame the problems posed by Arab salvo tactics with massed attacks of their own. Instead of using four aircraft for an attacking mission as was their usual practice, the Israelis used up to squadrons in blanket attacks. Increasing accuracy against targets was obtained by use of

LEFT *Despite its age, the subsonic MiG-17 remained the principal close-support fighter of the Egyptian Air Force in 1973.* ABOVE RIGHT *An SA-2 Guideline on its launch pad in Egypt. The Egyptians reinforced their surface-to-air missile positions on the west bank of the canal by establishing emplacements on the other side.* BOTTOM *A Soviet-built missile radar station, set up in Sinai by Egypt and later captured by the Israelis.*

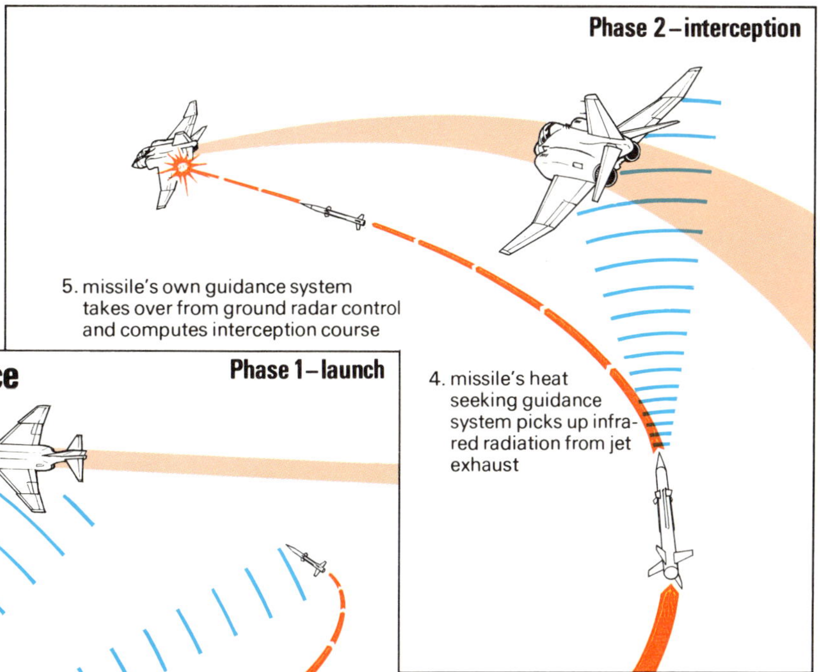

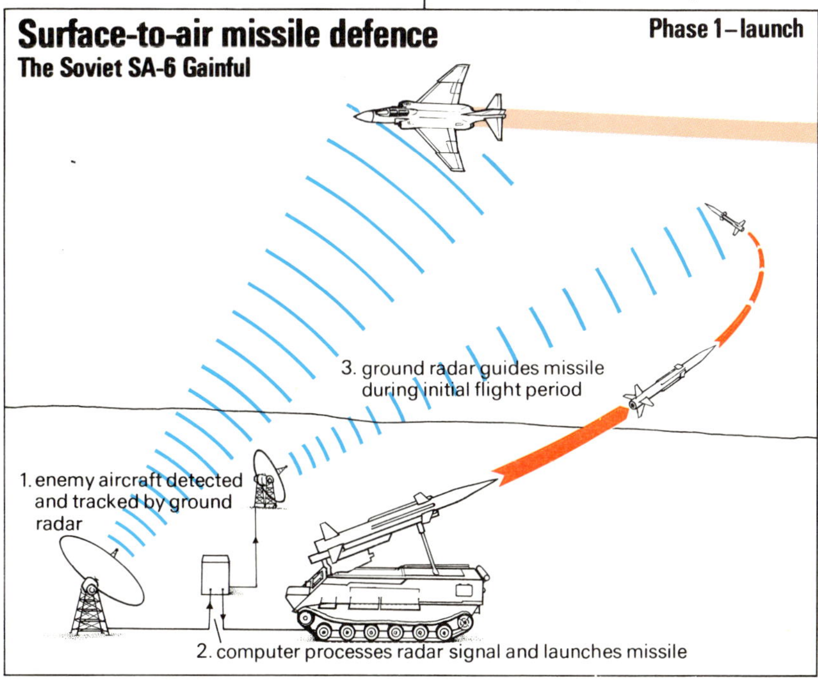

American-supplied 'smart' bombs, notably Walleye, while Israeli aircraft were given increasing protection by the acquisition of new active and passive electronic counter-measures (ECMs).

The most widely employed ECMs involved deception and the jamming of Arab frequencies. 'Chaff' – the modern equivalent of World War II 'Window' – was a method of scattering small strips of metal, fibreglass and other materials that had been cut to a metallic dipole corresponding to Arab radar frequencies. This provided a missile with a host of decoy targets. Even if the missile managed to detect the real target from its 'cover', it then had to distinguish between the aircraft and decoy flares and deflected exhausts with which Israeli aircraft were fitted. Active ECMs included noise production and jamming, mainly achieved by special ECM aircraft flying well behind the battle lines. With these measures in force, the IAF was once again able to dominate the air.

Attack and Counter-attack

AFTER THE SITUATION on the Syrian (Golan) Heights had eased and the counter-attack brought her more gains, Israel's main attention began to focus again on Sinai. There the position had improved considerably for Israel once she had abandoned her costly armoured and air attacks and adopted instead a defensive role in order to contain the Egyptians.

Decision to attack

By about 10 October the Egyptians had approximately 800 tanks and 75,000 men in Sinai and they had secured a strong but shallow bridgehead along most of the length of the Suez Canal. The initial Egyptian plan had been to fight a defensive battle but by the 10th pressure was mounting on both sides for offensive operations.

The disasters that had befallen the Syrians required a response, and it was evident that Egypt had much to gain, politically and strategically, if her forces could advance and secure the passes over the Central Ridge. Israel, likewise, had much to gain by crossing the Suez Canal and carrying the war into the Egyptian heartland. The Israelis had made plans and preparations for such an advance even before the war, and on 11/12 October the Israeli High Command and cabinet discussed whether or not to embark on the operation.

The Israelis decided against going over to the offensive, mainly because they were convinced that the Egyptians would be forced to attack in Sinai. They were prepared to let the Egyptians come forward, beyond the cover of their SAM batteries, in order to defeat their armour in open battle before finally deciding whether to take the war to the west bank of the canal.

Events confirmed the Israeli analysis. While the Israeli leadership decided their future moves, the Egyptians were moving most of their armour from the west bank to the east bank of the canal in preparation for a general offensive along the length of the front. This Egyptian offensive, along the coastal roads on the Mediterranean and the Gulf of Suez and towards the Khatima, Mitla and Giddi Passes, began on the morning of 14 October.

Israeli successes

So the Egyptians began the fluid battle that they had been determined to avoid because they believed that they would lose it. One day's fighting showed that their initial analysis had been correct. The Israelis proved more than a match for the Egyptians in a type of battle that the Israeli armour understood and knew how to fight. As the Egyptian armour came forward it moved into ground commanded by Israeli tank guns. By continual fire and movement the Israeli armour and infantry fought frontal holding actions while Egyptian flanks were repeatedly assaulted by armour when the Egyptian advances stalled.

Instead of relying on armour operating in sections, the Israelis concentrated into companies with a strong leavening of infantry in APCs. These were plentifully supplied with heavy machine guns and mortars in order to put down a heavy volume of fire on suspected Egyptian anti-tank guided weapon (ATGW) positions.

The Israeli answer to precision weapons was increased general fire. In order to spoil the aim of Arab ATGW firers the Israelis relied on saturation fire over an area. After 16 October the Israelis increasingly relied on ATGWs of their own, mainly the hastily supplied American TOW (tube-launched, optically-tracked, wire-guided missiles), to counter Egyptian armour. Moreover, while the Israeli armour increasingly relied on the infantry to deal with enemy infantry and armour, the air force and the artillery were tied in more effectively to the Israeli battle formations in order to help blast a path through enemy defensive positions.

On 14 October possibly as many as 800 Egyptian tanks, with infantry and artillery support, had moved into the attack. By the evening perhaps as many as 300 had been lost, and the survivors were in retreat. Egyptian positions began to lose their cohesion, and worse was to follow. Israeli reconnaissance indicated that the east bank around Great Bitter Lake was very lightly held and that the west bank was almost deserted. On the 15th, as they followed up their previous day's success, the Israelis decided to cross the canal in the Deversoir area.

On the night of 15/16 October, Israeli formations fought their way down the Tasa road and paratroopers crossed Great Bitter Lake in assault

ABOVE *Israeli soldiers pose triumphantly on a self-propelled gun.* BELOW *Israeli tanks attack a SAM missile base while being shelled by the Egyptians during an encounter in Sinai.*

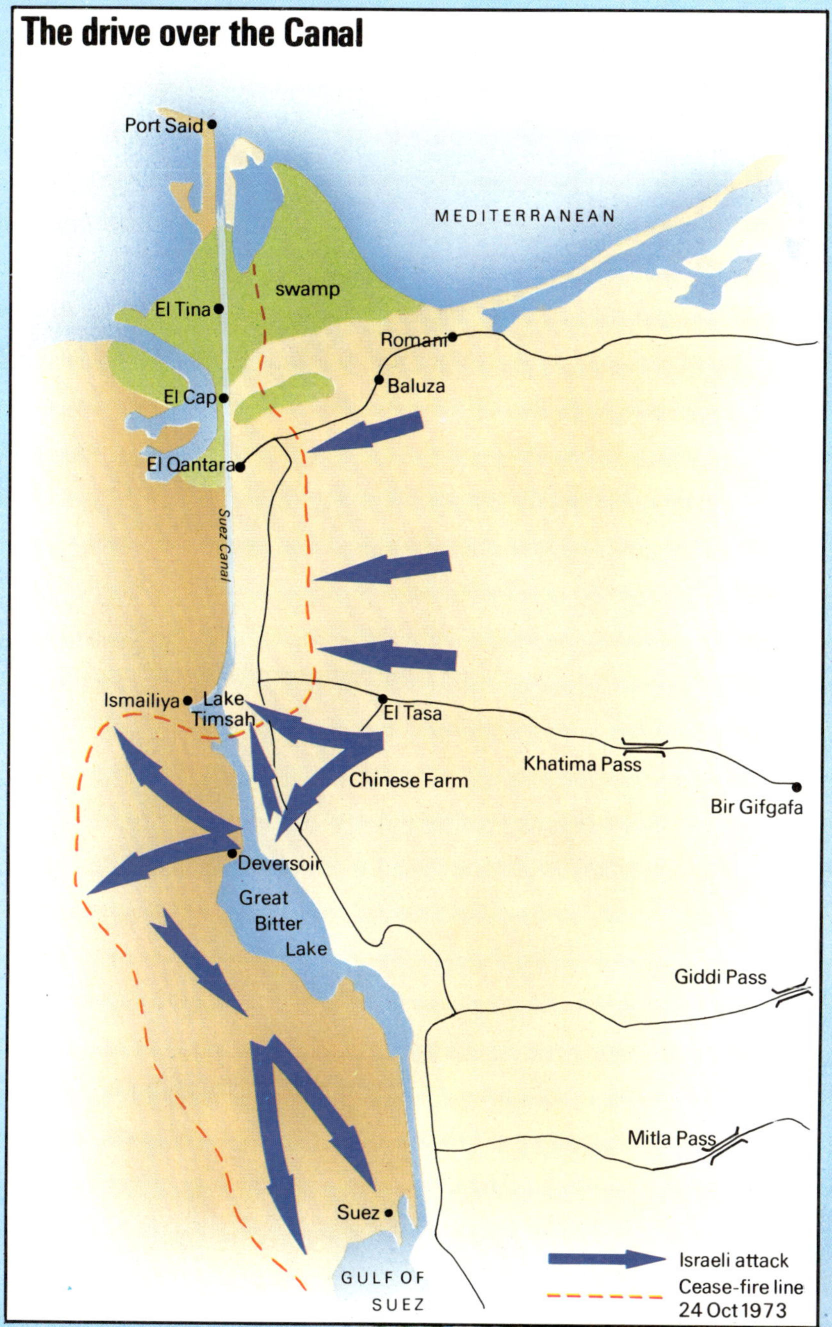

boats in the early hours of the 16th. SP pontoons brought armour across the northern part of the lake during the morning. Thereafter, Israeli crossings halted for nearly two days as a series of battles raged on the east bank in and around the breach the Israelis had made in the Egyptian positions along the Tasa-Deversoir road.

From the 16th to the 18th Israeli forces struggled to roll the 2nd Egyptian Army back from its positions south of Lake Timsah, particularly around Chinese Farm, and to hold attacks from the 3rd Egyptian Army. These attempts were successful despite stiff opposition, and with the passing of the hours the bridgehead gradually widened.

On the west bank the Israelis, despite a couple of costly initial failures, began to develop their offensive after 17 October when they managed to bridge the canal securely.

BELOW *Egyptian soldiers surround a damaged Israeli M48 tank in Sinai.* BOTTOM *A Sagger anti-tank missile of Soviet origin is displayed on an Egyptian vehicle.*

An attempt to get around the rear of the 2nd Army and take Ismailiya via the back door was halted when the Egyptians flooded the Sweet Water Canal, making the ground impassable, but the Egyptian command, which was slow to appreciate the extent of the breakthrough, lacked the means to stop the Israelis coming south against the rear of the 3rd Army.

By 20 October the Egyptian situation on the west bank of the canal had become critical, but on that day Saudi Arabia put a stop to oil exports to the United States, and Egypt, unable to halt the Israeli advance, announced its willingness to accept a ceasefire, which came into effect at 1852 hours on 22 October. The ceasefire did not stop the Israelis over the next six days mouting a series of operations designed to complete the encirclement of the 3rd Army. In the end American pressure forced the Israelis to desist on 24 October.

Ironically, the intervention that Sadat had wanted to confirm initial Arab gains came about in order to ward off an impending Arab defeat. Yet the Egyptian successes of 6–10 October, plus the cutting off of oil, remained powerful political assets for the Arabs. Both sides claimed victory; but the Israelis had the more tangible rewards to show, having defended or extended their gains of 1967.

ABOVE LEFT *The peace negotiation tent at Kilometre 101 in Egypt. Israeli troops are in the foreground with armed UN soldiers behind.* ABOVE *Israeli commandos cross the canal as Egyptian tracer fire illuminates the skyline.* BELOW *An M48 medium tank in Israeli service crosses into Egypt.*

War in the Bush

The fighting in Rhodesia arose from black demands for majority rule in a colony governed by whites

F. A. Godfrey

Equipped with FN rifles, infantrymen of the Rhodesian Army race to a target area during a training exercise. In the 1970s the strain on the army and police became acute as black guerrilla activity intensified.

THE GENESIS of the conflict in Rhodesia may perhaps be traced back to the decision by the British government to grant responsible government to the white settlers in Southern Rhodesia in 1923. Although legally they could only govern their own affairs, in practice they were frequently left, as the people on the spot, to interpret and put into effect laws applicable to the whole population.

In 1923 there were some 35,000 whites and 900,000 blacks living in Southern Rhodesia. Inevitably there grew up a bitterness on the part of the few educated blacks when they saw, for example, the results of the 1931 Land Apportionment Act which allocated 28 million acres to 1 million blacks and 48 million acres to 50,000 whites. In 1953 the colonies of Southern Rhodesia, Northern Rhodesia and Nyasaland were linked together in what came to be known as the Central African Federation. From the beginning the white settler government of Southern Rhodesia dominated the federation politically and economically.

Nkomo and the ANC

By 1957 the blacks in Southern Rhodesia had formed their own political organisation, the African National Congress (ANC) which was led by Joshua Nkomo. The ANC attempted to pursue moderate policies so as not to alarm the white population: they campaigned for an end to racial discrimination and more economic progress for the blacks. Nkomo was seen by the whites as a moderate and initially participated in the politics of the federation. But despite its policy of moderation the ANC was banned in 1959. Nkomo was out of the country when this happened but many of the movement's leaders were detained and the government of Southern Rhodesia introduced a series of measures to control the growth of black nationalist disaffection.

A new nationalist political group was formed in 1960: the National Democratic Party (NDP) led by Joshua Nkomo, the Reverend Ndabaninge Sithole and Robert Mugabe. Their supporters hoped that the federation would soon collapse and majority rule would be forced on the Southern Rhodesian government by the British government. At the constitutional conference of 1961 (to which the NDP was invited) the existing government in Southern Rhodesia was given almost complete authority over the colony's affairs, however.

Attempts to disrupt elections under the new constitution led to the banning of the NDP, and in December 1961 the Zimbabwe African People's Union (ZAPU) was formed. Nkomo went abroad to seek support from Britain and the United Nations, leaving the remainder of the leadership in Southern Rhodesia. Under criticism because of his moderate stance, he hastened back home and began to campaign for the use of violence, as a last resort, to achieve ZAPU's aims. In September 1962 ZAPU was, in its turn, banned.

The growing militancy of the nationalists

Rhodesia–population distribution

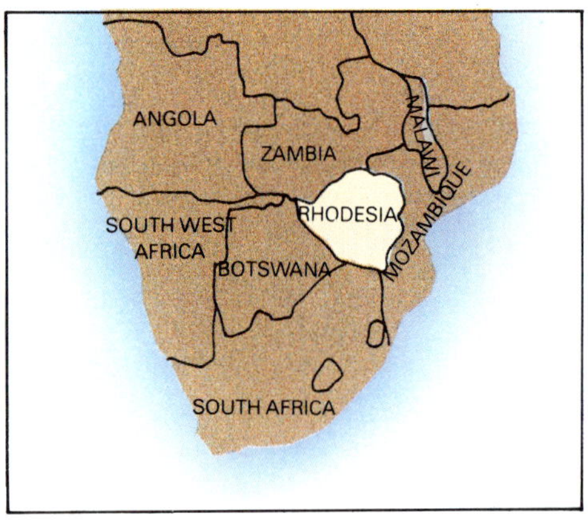

led to a strong reaction on the part of the white population. A new political party of the right – the Rhodesian Front (RF) – was swept into power in the 1962 election, mandated to resist any 'sell out' to the black population. Once in power the RF crushed the nationalist movement and established a strong, often harsh, system of law and order. As a result, when the Central African Federation collapsed in 1964 and out of the ensuing turmoil Northern Rhodesia became Zambia and Nyasaland became Malawi, both independent, the only really stable regime in the area was that presided over by the RF in Southern Rhodesa.

In the early 1960s the black nationalist leaders were in disarray: they could not agree on the best policy. Nkomo wanted to establish a government in exile while the others, fearful of a loss of internal support for their cause, sought to remain in Southern Rhodesia. In August 1963 Sithole formed the Zimbabwe African National Union (ZANU), a rival party to ZAPU but with the same broad aims of majority rule. Gang warfare broke out between the two parties and there were clear signs of a split based on tribal allegiances, a factor which was to continue to plague the nationalists' cause and to restrict the support for the Zimbabweans from other black southern African states.

The Smith regime

Ian Smith became Prime Minister of Southern Rhodesia in 1964 and he immediately promoted the idea of independence on the basis of the existing constitution. The British government, however, was resolute in its determination to withhold independence without safeguards for the black population. After the breakdown of negotiations Smith announced a unilateral declaration of independence in November 1965. Discussions between Smith and Harold Wilson in 1966 and 1968 were unsuccessful and Britain, later followed by the UN, imposed economic sanctions on Southern Rhodesia. Sanctions were, however, never fully effective, largely because South Africa and the Portuguese government (the latter still in control of Mozambique) were sympathetic to the Smith regime.

After being banned in 1964 both ZAPU and ZANU moved their headquarters to Zambia and began to build up guerrilla armies. Initial penetrations into Rhodesia by guerrillas failed completely and attempts to infiltrate in co-operation with South African National Congress guerrillas met with a similar fate. Indeed, the latter made matters worse for the nationalists as co-operation with South African guerrillas provided the excuse for the Rhodesian government to invite South African para-military police contingents into the country to bolster the Rhodesian security forces.

In the late 1960s ZAPU and ZANU quarrelled incessantly; there were further signs of a breakdown within each organisation on tribal grounds, and the Zambian government grew more and more irritated and then anxious about the ill-disciplined, numerous but ineffective armed guerrillas in its country.

Muzorewa's moderate line

In 1971, the Smith government accepted the terms of a British proposal to resolve the crisis and it was agreed that the settlement should be tested by a British Commission in Rhodesia before it was finally approved. The Salisbury government was confident of a 'yes' vote and was amazed by the support for a 'no' vote whipped up by a new black political group – the African National Council – formed in 1971 and led by a then little-known figure, Bishop Abel Muzorewa. The Methodist bishop had until then always contented himself with moderate criticism of government policies from his pulpit.

The 1971 settlement attempt failed, largely as a result of Muzorewa's efforts and in 1973 there followed a strong upsurge in guerrilla activity which forced Rhodesia to close the Zambian frontier. This mounting guerrilla campaign marked the beginning of the real war between black nationalists and the white government. By now, the guerrillas had gained access to more and better

ABOVE *Ian Smith resisted black demands for majority rule until international pressure forced his hand.* OPPOSITE *Joshua Nkomo's supporters at an election rally in 1980. Nkomo was defeated by Robert Mugabe, but joined his government as a cabinet minister.*

weapons; they were rather better trained and, of greatest importance, were assured of more sympathy and support from the black population in Rhodesia whose political awareness had been sharpened, paradoxically, by the success of Muzorewa's non-violent methods.

The next development of critical importance was the end, in 1974, of Portuguese rule in Mozambique. The appearance on the scene of a black government in Mozambique favourably inclined towards the aspirations of the Zimbabwe nationalists had a number of effects on the situation, not only in Rhodesia, but in southern Africa generally. South Africa, now the only neighbouring country friendly to Rhodesia, grew more anxious to disengage from obvious support for the Smith government. Pressure was brought on the white Rhodesian leader to reach a settlement with the nationalists and all South African police units were withdrawn in 1975.

Reacting to this South African pressure and fearful that the war might intensify, the Rhodesian government attempted to negotiate with Bishop Muzorewa. The initiative failed but other nationalists were released from detention and, following an apparently successful attempt to link Muzorewa's ANC with ZAPU and ZANU, Smith conducted negotiations with the complete group. Nothing came of the talks and a proposed ceasefire arrangement collapsed. The attempt to unify ANC, ZAPU and ZANU was opposed by some black nationalists, notably Robert Mugabe and also the guerrilla army leaders of both ZAPU and ZANU. As a result the ZANU faction with its army, the Zimbabwe African National Liberation Army (ZANLA), established itself in the now friendly territory of Mozambique. In 1976 a renewed campaign of guerrilla activity was initiated from Mozambique and further attempts by the Smith government to negotiate with Nkomo's ZAPU ended in failure.

Supplying Rhodesia

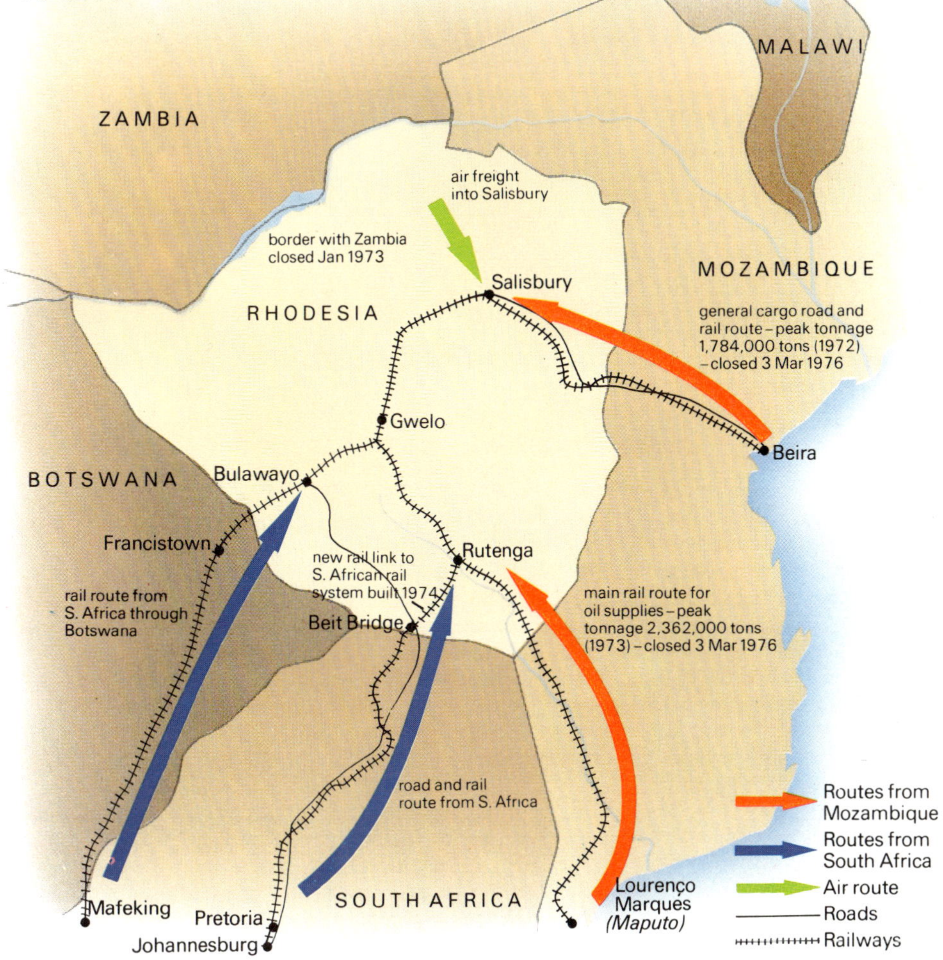

Smith under pressure

Mozambique closed its frontier with Rhodesia in 1976 and the country was now effectively reduced to relying on South Africa's goodwill in all matters. South Africa, however, was now anxious to end the war in Rhodesia, and through the mediation of Prime Minister John Vorster of South Africa a meeting was arranged between Ian Smith and Henry Kissinger, the American Secretary of State. At the meeting the pressure was on Smith, now effectively facing the world alone, and he was forced to announce that he had at last conceded the principle of majority rule. Kissinger put forward a joint American/British plan to implement their agreements and it was arranged to hold a conference to which all factions would be invited.

At the conference which followed in Geneva the nationalists proved to be once more in disarray, in spite of an agreement merging ZAPU and ZANU into a new alliance called the Patriotic Front. They could agree to nothing except a bitter dislike of Ian Smith and the rejection of the Kissinger proposals unless they were modified. Smith, himself, refused to enter into discussion of the Kissinger plan which he would only accept as it stood, unamended. Stalemate was almost instantly reached and the meeting disintegrated.

Now the Rhodesian government rejected further American or British initiatives and decided to go for an agreement with Bishop Muzorewa on the basis of 'one man one vote' in what came to be known as the 'internal settlement'. A mixed white and black transitional government came into being on 3 March 1978 and was bitterly opposed by Nkomo and Mugabe. Nonetheless elections, held in April 1979, led to Bishop Muzorewa becoming the first black prime minister of what was now called Zimbabwe-Rhodesia on 1 June.

The Muzorewa government was, however, doomed to failure. By seeming, too readily, to adopt the policies advocated by the whites, the bishop had left himself wide open to criticism from ZAPU and ZANU who gained increasing popularity among the black population in the country, partly because they were suspicious of the outcome of Muzorewa's tactics and partly because the guerrilla armies were becoming more and more successful.

Zimbabwe is born

Throughout 1977 to 1979 the guerrilla attacks, especially out of Mozambique, increased in intensity. Despite extremely effective, if on occasion over-ruthless retaliatory attacks by Rhodesian security forces into Mozambique, Zambia and even Angola, there was no doubt that the government was finding it increasingly difficult to maintain its authority throughout the country. Large tracts of land, especially in the north-east, were dominated without challenge on a permanent basis by the guerrilla organisations.

Recognising that the Muzorewa government would be faced with a continuing war that it could not win and that the surrounding black African states were beginning, for political and economic reasons, to weaken in their resolve to support ZAPU and ZANU, the British government seized the opportunity to promote the idea of a new conference to resolve the deteriorating situation. By forthright bargaining and persuasion of all the parties involved, which included seeking support from the interested black African states, a solution was found.

The plan was one of an extremely delicate nature involving the assembly of the guerrilla armies at rendezvous on Zimbabwe-Rhodesian territory under the supervision of Commonwealth troops while the existing security forces retained responsibility for law and order. This daring enterprise worked and elections were held under British supervision which resulted in a government based on one man one vote being formed in March 1980 under the leadership of Robert Mugabe, who had won a resounding victory. The following month Rhodesia formally became the independent state of Zimbabwe.

The Selous Scouts

THE SELOUS SCOUTS was a unit of some 1000 men and formed part of the Rhodesian Special Forces which included the Rhodesian Special Air Service (SAS) and Grey's Scouts (a horse-mounted infantry patrol unit of approximately 200 men). The unit took its name from Frederick Selous, a white hunter and explorer, a friend of Cecil Rhodes who was involved in much of the exploration and pacification of the territory which became Rhodesia. Selous remains to this day something of a heroic figure among whites in southern Africa.

The Scouts were formed soon after the black nationalist guerrilla forces began launching increasingly effective raids into Rhodesian territory from the sanctuary of neighbouring Zambia and Mozambique in the 1970s. The force was recruited from all races in Rhodesia but as time passed more and more black soldiers were brought into the organisation because of the specialised nature of the tasks it had to perform.

Colonel Reid-Daly, who had served with the SAS in the Malayan Emergency, commanded the Selous Scouts and all his officers were white. Initially, most were Rhodesians but one or two American and British officers joined the unit bringing with them experience gained in Vietnam and Northern Ireland. The unit was based in Inkomo Barracks in Salisbury but there was also a field training camp located at Wafa Wafa near Kamba.

The training that new recruits received was generally considered to be particularly rigorous, even by SAS standards, and the methods used achieved a remarkable degree of realism. Much emphasis was placed on preparing men to survive in small groups in the arduous physical circumstances in which they would be required to conduct operations.

While the conventional units of the security forces were well-trained and highly-skilled in bringing the enemy to battle it became crucial that accurate intelligence should be acquired so that these forces, usually air or helicopter borne, could be deployed in the right place at the right time. The provision of this intelligence was the task of the Selous Scouts. As a 'combat-tracker' unit their role was to locate the enemy, ascertain his strengths and intentions and to pass this information back.

In all counter-insurgency operations a major problem for the security forces centres on the question of how to move into an area of insurgent activity

ABOVE *The Selous Scouts travelled light, this soldier carrying only an FN rifle, a knife and water canteen.*
BELOW *Blacks served alongside whites and were in a sizeable majority.*

undetected. Unusual transport movement by road or using aircraft (especially helicopters) always warns the enemy. Even unusual movements of troops on foot are often detected. The Selous Scouts were trained to live for extended periods without reliance on any form of transport or the need for resupply. In their reconnaissance role they operated in very small groups ('sticks' as they were called) of four to five men which further enhanced their ability to remain undetected.

'Sticks' would establish observation posts in known areas of enemy activity and they would remain there, completely self-contained, for long periods of time always reporting back, by radio, information on guerrilla movements which would be acted on by the more conventional units of the security forces.

Tracking and disguise

Many of the officers and men of the Selous Scouts, coming as they did from rural surroundings in Rhodesia, were past masters in the hunting of wild and game animals. It was a comparatively simple matter for them to switch to tracking groups of enemy and they achieved a high success rate. It was not unknown for the Scouts to follow the tracks of an enemy group for anything up to a week, moving only in the morning and evening when the slanting rays of the sun tended to highlight the minute signs of human movement for which they were looking.

Another method of gleaning intelligence on the enemy's activity used by the Selous Scouts was to dispatch small groups of men into remote and often hostile areas disguised as guerrillas. They would, in this way, make contact with village communities and attempt to glean snippets of information on enemy movements, intended targets and rendezvous. This type of clandestine operation was often carried to its logical conclusion when careful training enabled 'sticks' of men in the guise of guerrillas actually to penetrate enemy camps and thereby neutralise a complete enemy group.

Counter-measures

Toward the end of the war in the late 1970s, when the guerrillas had succeeded in winning friends or pressuring unwilling supporters in the villages to provide them with information on security force movements, life for the Selous Scouts became more and more difficult. Villagers would, themselves, patrol the country around their homes in an attempt to locate the whereabouts of the security forces. These guerrilla helpers were known as *majubis* and many were young boys who would in any case normally be out on the hills tending the herds of cattle. If in their wandering they discovered an observation post they would deliberately move their herd right onto the Scouts' position and thereby pinpoint the exact location of the security force patrol. These helpers also gave false information to the patrols in order to conceal the intentions of the guerrilla forces.

Another ploy by the guerrillas designed to fox the Scouts was to change their clothing whilst out on patrol. A group of guerrillas might be seen to enter a village carrying weapons and wearing uniforms. By concealing their arms and exchanging their camouflaged shirts for white or red ones they became extremely difficult to identify from a distant observation post. On occasion guerrillas were known to begin an operation wearing several layers of different coloured clothing.

Because of the inevitable secrecy which shrouded their activities the Selous Scouts became the object of much curiosity during the war. Their enemies depicted them as a gang of bandits and ruffians while their supporters were prone to see them as a group of experts providing the eyes and ears of the main body of the security forces.

ABOVE *Selous Scouts cross a river during a tracking expedition.* BELOW *Scouts were often required to live off the land. This man lays a trap to catch a rodent.*

The Rhodesian Army 1977

Regulars

Rhodesia Regiment 8 battalions (600–700 men, all white) with recent addition of coloured and Asian reserve
Rhodesian Light Infantry 3 commando units and 1 weapons support group (about 1000 men, all white); between one-quarter and one-third mercenaries
Rhodesian African Rifles 3 battalions (600–700 men, all black) with white officers
Rhodesian Artillery (1st Field Regiment) 1 regular battery of 105mm howitzers and 1 reserve battery of 25-pounders; white officered
Support and administrative troops (signals, engineers, pay corps etc) all white officered
Rhodesian Armoured Car Regiment About 400 men, black and white; duties include reconnaissance, patrolling, convoy escort, crowd control and manning road blocks

Irregulars

Special Air Service 3 squadrons (60 men each, all white); specialise in laying counter-insurgency ambushes
Selous Scouts About 1000 men, large majority of blacks; some mercenaries
Grey's Scouts 150–200 men, black and white; horse-mounted infantry for tracking, pursuit and patrolling

ZAPU and ZANU

TOP *The bodies of two Red Cross workers killed by guerrillas in 1978. Terror was often indiscriminate.*
ABOVE *Black recruits to the Rhodesian Army on parade. Despite the guerrilla war blacks continued to enlist.*

IN THE EARLY STAGES of the confrontation between black nationalist groups and the government of Rhodesia (Southern Rhodesia until 1965), the aim of the nationalists was to use what political pressure they could muster, inside and outside Rhodesia, to influence the government, peacefully, to change its policies. As these methods met with little success they turned in the early 1960s to the use of violence. The campaign in 1960–62 was restricted to cases of minor sabotage, arson and intimidation which could be carried out with the use of explosives, stolen from mining companies, and home-made petrol bombs.

The decision was taken in mid-1962 to go out in search of foreign sources of support in the provision of arms and training in their use. From 1963 there was increasing evidence of the nationalists' success in the pursuit of these policies. February 1964 saw the first attempt at mounting a guerrilla operation by a group of insurgents which called itself the Crocodile Commando. A police post was attacked and later a white farmer shot dead. However, the group was successfully broken up by security forces acting with the benefit of good intelligence.

In the period 1964 to 1965, just prior to the unilateral declaration of independence by the Rhodesian government, training for the members of the nationalists' embryonic guerrilla armies got under way on a proper basis. Arrangements were made for training, carried out by foreign experts, in some African countries and even further afield. Between March and October 1964, courses were organised for ZAPU guerrillas in the USSR, the People's Republic of China and North Korea. Men from ZANU received training in the same period in Ghana and Tanzania.

In 1966 and 1967 there were many attacks mounted by armed and uniformed groups crossing into Rhodesia from Zambia, and although the security forces got early warning of the movements and were quickly able to respond it was accepted that the guerrillas were by then rather better trained and prepared. Perhaps of even more importance, a perceptible rise in the guerrillas' morale was noticed at this time despite the neutralisation of the vast majority of their attempted operations.

In early 1968 a major attempt to infiltrate guerrillas was once again foiled and later, in August, a complete group of 28 well-armed men was destroyed by security forces. Details of the weapons and equipment captured from these men were publicised and they are extremely interesting in providing an insight into the types of equipment the guerrillas were now

able to obtain directly or indirectly from other countries. The list is a formidable one:
3 light machines guns (RP-46) with 9 magazines
3 RPG-2 anti-tank rocket launchers with 24 projectiles
19 Kalashnikov AK47 rifles
6 Simonov carbines
6 automatic pistols
112 grenades
150 slabs of explosive
40,000 rounds of ammunition (most 7.62mm).
The bulk of the weapons were identified by Rhodesian security forces as being of Soviet manufacture.

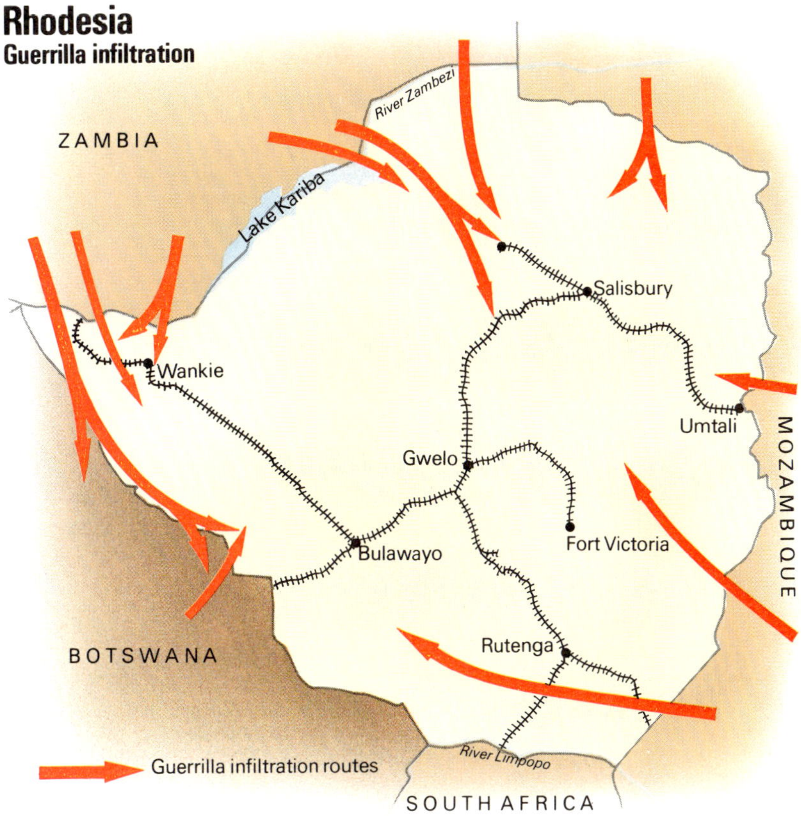

The war escalates

From 1969 onwards the guerrillas conducted operations from sanctuary in Zambia across the Zambesi into Rhodesia in ever increasing numbers. Groups of anything from 30 to 100 uniformed men, armed with PPSh sub-machine guns, Simonovs and Kalashnikovs, would make their way into the tribal trust lands and game reserves. A new piece of equipment – the land mine – was introduced in the 1970s and at first it caught the security forces napping. The mines were used to disrupt traffic on roads and tracks most frequently used by the army, police and administration. As operations by the guerrillas became more sophisticated they would use the mines in conjunction with attacks on government offices, police posts and isolated farms. By placing the mines on roads and tracks leading to the target it was hoped to take the reacting security forces by surprise. The army and police quickly responded to this threat and approached with caution but vital minutes, sufficient to allow the guerrillas to escape, were thereby lost.

After 1974, when Mozambique became independent, the guerrillas were provided with another sanctuary from which to launch their attacks into Rhodesia. From then onwards the ZANU faction of the nationalists made use of Mozambique and its guerrilla arm, by then known as the Zimbabwe African National Liberation Army (ZANLA), directed operations in that area. The forces of ZAPU, now known as the Zimbabwe Peoples Revolutionary Army (ZIPRA), continued to train and launch their operations from Zambian territory.

It was from the mid-1970s that Soviet support, in particular, escalated. It is generally accepted that by 1979 there were some 1400 Russian, 700 East German and 500 Cuban military instructors working in Mozambique and many were directly supporting the efforts of the guerrilla forces. In the same way in Angola over 19,000 Cuban soldiers, 6000 East Germans and a few Czechs and Bulgarians provided, via Zambia, the same sort of service. Arms and equipment were shipped into southern Africa at this time via the ports of Beira in Mozambique and Luanda in Angola.

Such a strong system inevitably tended to take the initiative from the Rhodesian security forces and give it to the guerrillas. Despite punitive raids by the Rhodesians into Mozambique, Zambia and even Angola to strike at the base camps of the guerrillas, by the end of the war Rhodesian resources were stretched almost to the limit. Towards the climax of hostilities, guerrilla capability was enhanced even further by the acquisition of SAM-7 anti-aircraft guided missile launchers, medium mortars and a new version of the anti-tank rocket launcher, the RPG-7.

BELOW *Refugees cook a meal at a camp in Mozambique, which provided a base for ZANU guerrillas.* BOTTOM *Former guerrillas move to an assembly point prior to the elections of 1980.*

The Horn of Africa

The 1974 revolution in Ethiopia unleashed forces which provoked a renewal of war in Eritrea and the Ogaden

Peter Janke

BELOW *Members of Ethiopia's People's Militia parade through Addis Ababa in 1977. Soviet arms and supplies enabled Ethiopia to defeat the Somali invasion and turn back the challenge from Eritrean separatists.* OPPOSITE *Mengistu Haile Mariam, Ethiopia's ruler, swung the country into the Soviet orbit of influence.*

THE OVERTHROW of Emperor Haile Selassie in 1974 had its immediate origins in the inability of the emperor's administration to meet the needs of his people during the catastrophic drought which affected the Sahel region of Africa in the early 1970s. Not only were people dying but the relief aid from international organisations was squandered by corrupt officials. No one group in Ethiopia laid claim to the revolution, which was not inspired from outside but rather resulted from internal collapse.

A confused period followed the emperor's downfall on 12 September 1974. The power of the feudal landlords crumbled before a Provisional Military Administrative Committee, better known as the Dergue ('committee'). No one had a constitutional blueprint for one of the world's poorest nations ($100 per capita annual income), the vast majority of whose population could neither read nor write.

The confusion was compounded by the secessionist war in Eritrea, which had been dragging on for 14 years. Opinion in the capital, Addis Ababa, was divided on whether or not to reach an agreement with the rebels, even though the coastal province provided Ethiopia with her only ports, Aseb and Mits'iwa.

Decision came finally from the lower ranks of the military. Two majors, Mengistu Haile Mariam and Atnafu Abate, played key roles in wresting power from General Anam Amdom, who was killed 'while resisting arrest' on 23 November 1974. Amongst those who were summarily shot at this time were two former prime ministers and two former defence ministers.

They were replaced by the former chief of staff, Brigadier Teferi Bante, who became head of state. Henceforth the revolution, which had been popular, turned sour in the hands of a coterie of ambitious soldiers. The original support withered and, wider afield, African sympathy was alienated. In time Mengistu disposed in a bloody manner of both Teferi Bante and Atnafu Abate to emerge as sole ruler of Ethiopia.

Lurch to the left

To achieve this end he embraced Marxism-Leninism, and by so doing qualified for the whole-hearted support of the Soviet bloc. To begin with, the philosophy of the revolution amounted to no more than a form of idealistic socialism. Above all the revolution meant land for the peasants, for all land was nationalised in 1975. In the course of 1976 a People's Democratic Republic was created. An office was set up to 'politicise' the masses and moves were made to establish a workers' party. The declared task of the party was to bind 'genuine Marxists to the workers, thereby extending Marxist ideology'. There was to be no alternative to the 'long march to the victory of socialism'.

The leftward drift of the revolution was not uncontested, nor was there a commonly shared view on ideology. Democrats fought back in the capital and in the countryside, especially in the north-west on the Sudanese

border. In Eritrea, the separatists took advantage of the revolution to attack and capture the main towns.

The Dergue, comprising 140 members and which supported Mengistu, came under attack in the capital – a city of 1 million people – from the virtually clandestine Ethiopian People's Revolutionary Party (EPRP), a Marxist-Leninist group opposed to military government. Other Marxist-Leninists saw the military as the promoters and guardians of the revolution and offered support. They grouped themselves around a French-educated Marxist son of an imperial general, Haile Fida, who subsequently established the All Ethiopia Socialist Movement (MEISON).

Fighting for control

On the streets of Addis Ababa MEISON supporters fought the EPRP. There was summary execution of youngsters who were guilty of nothing more than the distribution of pamphlets. Both sides were armed and terrorised the inhabitants, drawing them into the violence. By mid-1977 Mengistu was more firmly in control and could dispense with Fida, who was then arrested. To further consolidate his hold Mengistu made murderous terror on the streets into an official campaign. The cruelty and violence was a fact; instead of attempting to stop it, he promoted it and swamped his rivals.

On 3 February 1977 Mengistu had seized power from Teferi Bante, who probably died in hand-to-hand fighting in the Grand Palace. The following day Mengistu's triumph was hailed by Cuba's leader, Fidel Castro, and subsequently by the Soviet Union, which in the course of the year signed 13 co-operation agreements with Mengistu. The Ethiopian leader consolidated the relationship in May, when he spent five days with Soviet leaders and secured firm support for the revolution. He returned from Moscow via Tripoli, and Libya later delivered Soviet arms to Mengistu.

Diplomatic realignments

The Ethiopian Revolution was a remarkable event. But even more remarkable was the diplomatic revolution which took place in the Horn of Africa in 1977. Under the emperor, Ethiopia had been aligned with the West and had afforded the United States military facilities. All this changed under Mengistu. The Americans left in April 1977, and the Soviet bloc was invited in to help Ethiopia quell an invasion from Somalia in the southern Ogaden region and to resist separatist pressures in Eritrea.

To the south, Somalia, which had signed a friendship treaty with the Soviet Union in 1974, found that Moscow was not prepared to back it in a war with Ethiopia aimed at extending its borders to include Somali-speaking areas occupied in the last century by an expansionist Ethiopia. The Soviet Union saw greater advantage in aligning itself with a larger country in the Horn, which might provide it with a firmer base for its activities in Africa and the Middle East.

For a time Moscow found itself in the position of supplying two countries in the Horn which were increasingly at war with one another. The position became untenable and on 13 November 1977 the Somalis asked the Russians to leave and terminated the 20-year friendship treaty. Hostile crowds menaced the departing Russians as they clambered aboard aircraft, taking with them hastily gathered belongings. In every sense the departure was undignified.

In strategic terms the Soviet Union lost the use of Berbera, where it had dredged the harbour to accommodate larger vessels, at a time when it wished to build up an Indian Ocean naval presence to replace the British who had withdrawn west of Suez. Berbera had become the only facility for emergency repairs in the area and provided a communication centre which covered Soviet

operations throughout the entire Indian Ocean. A missile-handling facility had also been built and the Russians had also enjoyed the use of Somali airfields at Hargeisa and elsewhere.

In Ethiopia the Soviet Union displaced the Americans, who were bundled out as unceremoniously as the Russians themselves had been in Somalia. Although Soviet-bloc aid prevented Somalia from capturing the Ogaden, it has not pacified Ethiopia. Guerrilla warfare continues in the Ogaden, as it does in Eritrea. The Kremlin acted as king-maker – but cannot secure its candidate in power without a consistent presence, which may in the longer term provoke a hostile reaction.

The Ogaden War

SINCE 1960 it has been the policy of the Somali Republic to promote, by legal and peaceful means, the unity of Somali peoples living beyond its frontier. Such a claim, written into the country's constitution and represented on its flag, affected not only Ethiopia but Kenya and Djibouti too. Little wonder that President Siad Barre, seeing the giant empire to the north crumbling, seized the opportunity to invade Ethiopia and to incorporate the Ogaden into a Greater Somalia.

The invasion raised to a conventional level the guerrilla warfare which had been waged for a couple of years by the Western Somali Liberation Front (WSLF). The front's central committee met in Mogadishu, the Somali capital, and claimed all territory east of a line running from Moyale on the Kenyan border, through Awash, some 160km (100 miles) east of Addis Ababa, to the Djibouti border. The area consisted of almost one-third of Ethiopia. To back it up was a force numbering between 3000 and 6000 men, armed with Soviet weapons supplied by the Somali government.

In May 1977 these troops crossed the border to join forces with local resistance leaders, who had provoked numerous clashes in the past. The development of the conflict was seen in the capture of towns and in the claim to have put out of action Ethiopian tanks and armoured personnel carriers. The local population, being of the same stock, welcomed the newcomers and willingly collaborated in the supply of food and other essentials.

The invasion of 1977 was not merely an escalation of guerrilla warfare: it had the characteristics of a campaign, strategically planned and executed. The men had been trained in the Somali military, but had resigned their commissions in order to take part in the operation. One of the immediate targets was to cripple Ethiopia's foreign trade by cutting the country's only railway line, which links Addis Ababa to the port of

RIGHT *Ethiopian soldiers display a T54 tank and weapons captured from the Somalis.* BELOW *Women rebels, armed by the West Somali Liberation Front, show their support for Somalia.*

Djibouti. In June guerrillas attacked a train and shortly afterwards blew up five bridges, bringing a halt to all traffic.

Garrisons were attacked, too, in particular the air force base at Gode. Here, the fifth brigade of Ethiopia's fourth division was stationed in five military camps. Arms and ammunition depots fell to the attackers, who routed Ethiopian forces in rural areas in July. Yet the WSLF troops found it impossible to capture the provincial capitals of Sidamo and Bale. So they struck north from Hargeisa to take Jijiga, and came close to taking the strategic towns of Harer and Dire Dawa before the rains fell in November.

Heavy fighting in August took place around these two towns, which were vigorously defended by seasoned troops supported by a newly recruited and raw militia. The fighting was entirely conventional and cost both sides many casualties. The high point for Somalia came in September, when the Ethiopians abandoned the strategic Kara Marda Pass, allowing the invaders to capture Jijiga.

Soviet intervention

At this juncture the Soviet bloc came to Ethiopia's aid. Harer and Dire Dawa were held after the prompt arrival of BM-21 rocket launchers, long-range 155mm and 185mm artillery, T62 and T54 tanks and MiG-21 fighters. By mid-November over 500 Cubans had come to help train recruits for the People's Militia.

Military intervention on this scale turned the tide of the struggle in 1978. The counter-offensive was launched in January with far superior equipment, flown in before and after Christmas. More than 200 air transports were dispatched to Addis Ababa, the Marxist People's Democratic Republic of the Yemen as well as the Mozambique port of Maputo. They flew from bases in eastern Europe as well as the Soviet Union. Naval transport using the Suez Canal also set out from the Black Sea. For its part, the West supplied Somalia with defensive weapons to resist an invasion by Ethiopia but would not support the Somali thrust into the Ogaden.

The final repulse

A second counter-offensive began in February involving about 120 T54 and T62 tanks advancing from north of Dire Dawa and east of Harer. Possibly as many as 3000 Somalis died in the onslaught that resulted from encirclement by helicopter-borne tanks landed at their rear. General Barisov, who had been in Somalia until his expulsion in November 1977, commanded the operation.

Shortly afterwards, on 9 February 1978, Somalia proclaimed a general mobilisation followed by a State of Emergency. Troops were moved to the frontier after the border town of Hargeisa had been bombed, but no fighting occurred on the ground in Somalia. Large numbers of Somali-speaking refugees from the Ogaden crossed the border and with them came fleeing troops, dislodged from the positions they had won in 1977. Jijiga fell to the Ethiopians on 5 March and three days later Somali President Siad Barre announced that all troops would be withdrawn. The operation was completed by 14 March.

Such a reversal in fortune had come about because of the build-up of foreign forces, particularly Cubans, who were said to number at the end some 11,000 men, many of whom were engaged in the conflict. The 1500-strong Soviet contingent was under the command of General Vasily Petrov, first deputy commander of Soviet ground troops. South Yemenis were also involved, but not in great numbers. The campaign had been directed by a committee consisting of Ethiopia's President Mengistu Haile Mariam and five Ethiopians working alongside five Soviet officers, nine Cubans and two South Yemenis.

Soviet intervention in Ethiopia in defence of its interests in the Persian Gulf and Indian Ocean was largely made possible because the West did little when confronted by Soviet bloc involvement in Angola in 1975–76. The same principles were involved on each occasion – Cuba supplied the manpower, and the Soviet Union supplied the *matériel* and supervised the logistics of the operation. It is a formula which can be repeated in any African state where a weak contender for power espouses socialist policies and appeals for aid in the name of true revolution.

ABOVE *Somali troops are shown how to operate an anti-aircraft gun.*
BELOW *Recruits to the army of the West Somali Liberation Front undergo training in late 1977, when the guerrillas were making useful gains in Ethiopia.*

War in Eritrea

AFTER THE REVOLUTION in Ethiopia in 1974, the Eritrean separatists took advantage of the confusion in Addis Ababa to press claims that they had been fighting for since 1960. The secessionist cause presented the longest-standing threat to Ethiopian unity.

Once an Italian colony, Eritrea was administered by Britain from the end of World War II until 1952, when it was federated to Ethiopia. Ten years later the emperor abolished Eritrea's autonomous status, an act which fuelled the flames of rebellion by driving recruits into the Eritrean Liberation Front (ELF).

The ELF had been founded in Cairo by nationalists who demanded independence and who had been defrauded of it by the British and the United Nations. In time the younger ELF militants embraced socialist views and eventually split off in 1960 to form the Eritrean People's Liberation Forces (EPLF). The new Marxist stance was championed by radical Arab governments in Iraq, Libya and Syria and by the Palestinian Al Fatah guerrilla movement. Another group emerged from the Marxists in 1975. This was the ELF Popular Liberation Forces (ELF-PLF), led by Osman Saleh Sabbe. These three movements, despite alliances, were unable to agree upon a formula for independence. Had they united they might well have secured independence from a weakened central government.

Estimates vary as to the numbers involved, but reliable sources suggested some 22,000 ELF guerrillas operated in the Barka and Tessenei areas between Om Hajer and Keren. They enjoyed the support of Saudi Arabia, Kuwait and the Sudan and inflicted considerable losses on Ethiopian troops. Early in 1977 large battles involving the death of 1000 Ethiopian soldiers were reported.

Rebel activity

On 31 January 1977 the ELF claimed that Om Hajer, a town on the Eritrean frontier with Sudan, had fallen to the separatists. Fighting around the larger town of Tessenei was fierce until its fall on 12 April. Thousands of inhabitants were rendered homeless. Two further important towns to fall to the ELF were Keren and Agordat. Some 4000 soldiers were deployed in the defence of Agordat. The battle lasted 20 days and the ELF claimed 1900 Ethiopians were killed or wounded.

Farther north in Eritrea the EPLF controlled the countryside and set up elementary structures of a state. Military success also attended the efforts of the EPLF, which had 12,000 hardened guerrillas under arms. The EPLF were active all along the Red Sea coast, but were unable to take the ports of Mits'iwa in the north and Aseb in the south. Yet these cities were not considered safe, since in January 1975 Asmera (with a population of 250,000) had very nearly fallen to a joint ELF/EPLF attack.

Also active was the ELF-PLF, which sought a unified command with the parent ELF body under Ahmed Nasser. Osman Saleh Sabbe made several trips abroad in 1977 and was particularly welcomed in Syria and Iraq. Both countries supported the movement.

Government strategy

It is as vital to Ethiopia to maintain control of Eritrea as it is to prevent Djibouti from falling into the hands of the Somalis, for without it Ethiopia would be a landlocked state. By the end of 1977 there were said to be as many as 80,000 troops and reservists in Eritrea fighting a combined force of 40,000 guerrillas who knew the mountainous terrain and could count

An Ethiopian soldier in Eritrea. He carries a Soviet DP-28 light machine gun of World War II origin.

on the active sympathy of the countryside.

An attempt in 1976 by the government to raise a peasant army to fight in Eritrea had failed dismally after defeats in battle. A similar move was made in 1977 to cope with the Somali invasion in the south; but there, as in Eritrea, the deciding factor which turned around the guerrilla successes was military aid from the Soviet bloc.

The Soviet Union lent crucial naval support from the Red Sea to ensure that the harbours did not fall to the rebels. Because of this timely intervention the military situation was contained for six months whilst Mengistu Haile Mariam concentrated upon resisting Somalia's invasion of the Ogaden. Once these forces had been repulsed, he turned in 1978 to Eritrea.

Within a few weeks the substantial separatist gains of 1977 had been lost to a military campaign reinforced by Cuban training in Ethiopia, by Soviet military direction on the ground and by massive provision of military equipment. Furthermore, Eritrean forces were ill prepared to withstand the air raids started in January 1978. In May, Mengistu called for a victory in Eritrea similar to that in the Ogaden, and sent into battle the second liberation army. Many victories were recorded in June, but the big push came on 17 July, employing at least 300 tanks and four infantry divisions of 12,000 to 14,000 men supported by random bombing.

Having secured the north, a further drive in southern Eritrea brought much of the coast under government control. In mid-October the small ports of Thio, Edd and Beilul were recaptured. On 27 November, Keren, the last substantial separatist stronghold, was recaptured. It enabled the government to lift the siege of the Red Sea port of Mits'iwa.

TOP *The Eritrean Liberation Front (ELF) gave military instruction to children and women as well as adult men. The guerrilla war was waged with a new intensity after the 1974 revolution.*
ABOVE *Guerrillas receive weapons training in Eritrea. Both sides were equipped with Soviet arms.*
RIGHT *Soldiers of the ELF move against a government post near Barentu.*

These successes reduced guerrilla control to the countryside which, for the previous 15 years, they had largely controlled anyway. The campaign did not, however, eradicate the threat. In the far north the separatists held on to small towns near the Sudanese frontier. On the other side of the border at least 300,000 Eritreans had sought refuge from the conflict, which created enormous problems for local and international relief agencies.

Far from weakening the cause of independence the 1978 campaign increased it. The ruthless Soviet-backed assaults drove recruits into the arms of the EPLF, whose military commander, Ibrahim Affa, counted as many as 40,000 supporters in the field by mid-year. Certainly, the EPLF benefited more than the ELF, whose numbers dwindled to 7000 in 1979.

Although it no longer controlled the main roads and relied upon camels rather than trucks for supplies, this joint force successfully withstood a Soviet-devised offensive in mid-July 1979. Ilyushin and Antonov heavy bombers softened up the rebels who had then to confront 40,000 troops on two fronts in the Nakfa area. Some were landed on the Red Sea littoral and pushed inland while others attacked from the south, moving overland. In major confrontations, however, the Ethiopians were said to have lost 6000 men. It was a major set-back for government morale and vindicated EPLF tactics of a protracted people's war. The struggle was to continue as fiercely as ever.

International Terrorism

In the 1970s extremist groups adopted tactics of terror to achieve their political aims

David Rees

TERRORISM has been a significant international phenomenon since World War II, as the case-histories of British-ruled Palestine, Kenya, Cyprus and Malaya all show. But it is only since the late 1960s that international terrorism as such has become a major problem for the West's governments and security services.

There are three broad reasons for the escalation of international terrorism in the past decade. First, there is a tactical and technical context in that new techniques of electronically-detonated bombs, refined plastic explosives, and virtually instant international communications greatly facilitate the mobility and striking power of the terrorist.

A second reason for the growth of international terrorism is broadly strategic in that some Third World governments (such as Libya) support terrorist groups as a deliberate act of state policy. This is immensely significant in that it facilitates long-term funding of terrorism and provides terrorist 'base areas' or havens.

A third factor which facilitates international terrorism – albeit to an unquantifiable degree – is the political weakness of many Western governments. In the past decade these governments have been faced with a crisis of authority stemming from deep-rooted political, economic and minority problems.

ABOVE RIGHT *Yasir Arafat has been head of the Palestine Liberation Organisation, the co-ordinating body for Palestinian groups, since 1968.* BELOW *Members of the Palestine Liberation Army are shown cleaning weapons. The Palestinian question has been a major source of Arab-Israeli enmity.*

Motivation and ideology

Central to the effective functioning of any determined international terrorist group is its ideological or political programme. This programme invariably provides the intense, driving motivation that can overcome the defensive barriers and controls erected by national security services. Motivation thus gives the terrorist the initiative.

Although the precise ideological or political roots of some terrorist groups resist exact classification, three broad categories of international terrorism have emerged in the past two decades. Perhaps the most common

of these categories are the Marxist inspired left-wing revolutionaries who include the Baader-Meinhof group, the Italian Red Brigades and the Japanese Red Army.

A second important grouping of terrorism, found especially in Europe, is that of the nationalist or separatist organisation fighting against a metropolitan power. The Provisional IRA, the Basque ETA, and the Corsican separatists come under this heading. But both the IRA and the ETA have developed links with other international terrorists.

Finally, there is a third important category of terrorists who claim to be both nationalists and revolutionaries engaged in a liberation struggle. In practice, the most significant (and effective) group in this category is the Palestine Liberation Organisation (PLO), an umbrella group comprising about five separate bodies dedicated to the Palestinian cause.

The PLO can be distinguished from other international terrorist groups in that it is recognised by Arab states and some Soviet bloc countries. Moreover, while deploring its methods, a number of West European governments have developed contacts with the PLO, believing that the PLO's programme for a Palestinian state has at least some legitimacy. Hence the PLO operates in the arena of world politics on an increasingly *de facto* state-to-state basis.

Funding and sanctuaries

International terrorism would not be possible without two significant assets: large-scale funding and the provision of sovereign state 'base areas' or havens. These two factors give the international terrorist a sound logistics system.

A major source of revenue for the modern terrorist has been the ransom sums gained from kidnapping, the most notable example being the seizure of the Saudi and the Iranian oil ministers at the Vienna OPEC meeting in 1975 when, according to some reports, a sum of $50 million was exacted.

The provisional IRA has gained money from sympathisers in the United States and by bank robberies in the Irish Republic. Another major source of revenue has been from the Libyan leader, Colonel Gaddhafi, who is considered to be an important financial backer of the PLO and other terrorist groups.

Such financial support from a national leader merges into the even more significant policy of granting a national sanctuary to terrorists. The leading terrorist sanctuary is, of course, Libya, but Algeria, Syria and the People's Democratic Republic of Yemen (Aden) have also been used extensively as terrorist havens.

The Soviet connection

A refinement of the protection given to terrorists by Arab countries is the considerable cover support provided by the Soviet Union. While Arab support is basically for Palestinian nationalism, Soviet motives are more complicated. Until the 1960s, the Russians tended to support only Moscow-line parties and subversive groups. But since that time, Soviet clandestine aid to non-communist terrorist groups has escalated, usually well-disguised or 'laundered' by satellite intelligence services.

Looked at in this perspective, Soviet motives become clearer. International terrorism tends to 'destablise' Western societies at a time of political and economic crisis.

Despite the ravages of international terrorism in the 1970s, no terrorist group succeeded in achieving its stated national or ideological objectives. Even the aims of the PLO have not been achieved, although there has been a shift in world opinion on the Palestinian issue. But as far as Western countries are concerned this change of heart is probably due to the implied threat of the Arab oil weapon rather than terrorism itself.

A decade of terrorism 1968–78

1968 **26 December** El Al aircraft attacked at Athens, passenger killed

1969 **18 February** Attack on El Al plane at Zurich, pilot killed
18 July Bombs explode in Jewish-owned department store, London
4 September US ambassador kidnapped in Rio de Janeiro
8 September Grenade attacks on Israeli offices in Bonn, Brussels, The Hague

1970 **10 February** Grenade attack on bus at Munich airport, 1 passenger killed
21 February Swissair plane destroyed by mid-air explosion, 47 killed
31 July 2 diplomats kidnapped in Uruguay, 1 later killed
6 September 2 aircraft hijacked to Jordan, 1 to Cairo
5 October British diplomat James Cross kidnapped by French-Canadian separatists in Quebec
10 October Quebec cabinet minister kidnapped and killed
1 December Basque nationalists kidnap West German consul

1971 **8 January** British ambassador Geoffrey Jackson kidnapped in Uruguay
15 March Fuel tanks blown up in Rotterdam
17 May Israeli diplomat kidnapped and killed by Turks
27 July Bomb attack on Jordanian embassy, Paris
28 November Jordan's prime minister assassinated in Cairo
15 December Jordanian ambassador wounded in London

1972 **6 February** 5 Jordanians killed in Cologne
22 February Provisional IRA bomb attack on British Army base, Aldershot; 9 killed
21 March Fiat executive kidnapped in Buenos Aires then killed
11 May Bombs explode at US Army base in Germany, 1 officer killed
30 May Japanese Red Army kill 26 passengers at Tel Aviv airport
5 September Black September terrorists kill 2 Israeli athletes at Munich Olympic Games; 9 hostages and 5 terrorists later killed in airport shootout
8 December PLO Paris representative murdered

1973 **1 March** Saudi Arabian embassy in Khartoum is seized, 3 Western diplomats killed
10 April Israeli commandos attack Palestinian guerrillas' homes in Beirut, 17 killed
28 June Top Arab terrorist, Mohammed Boudia, killed by car bomb, Paris
1 July Israeli military attaché assassinated in Washington DC
5 August Palestinians kill 5 passengers from Tel Aviv–Athens flight
6 December US businessman Victor Samuelson kidnapped, later released on payment of $14.2 million ransom
17 December Aircraft set alight at Rome, 32 killed
20 December Spanish Premier Luis Carrero Blanco killed by Basque car-bomb
31 December E. Sieff, British businessman and Zionist, shot by Carlos

1974 **3 February** Suitcase bomb kills 11 British soldiers
8 September Airliner blown up over Agean; all 88 passengers killed

1975 **27 February** German politician Peter Lorenz kidnapped
24 April Baader-Meinhof kill 2 German diplomats in Stockholm and blow up German embassy
2 December South Moluccans capture train in Holland, kill 3
21 December Vienna HQ of OPEC seized, 3 men shot

1976 **27 June** German and Palestinian terrorists hijack airliner to Entebbe, Uganda, and seize Jewish passengers; Israeli paratroops conduct lightning rescue mission
19 July Argentinian troops kill Robert Santucho, revolutionary leader
21 July British ambassador to Ireland, Christopher Ewart-Biggs, killed in bomb blast

1977 **7 April** West Germany's chief prosecutor assassinated
10 April Ex-Yemeni prime minister and 2 others assassinated
23 May South Moluccans seize train in Holland; 2 hostages killed in army rescue mission
30 July German banker Juergen Ponto murdered
5 September Hans-Martin Schleyer, German businessman, kidnapped, 4 others killed
13 October Airliner hijacked, pilot killed; at Mogadishu, German commandos storm plane and release passengers
19 October Schleyer found murdered
6 December British journalist David Holden murdered in Cairo

1978 **4 January** PLO's London representative killed
10 March Red Brigades murder Italian judge and prison official
16 March Former Premier Aldo Moro kidnapped in Rome, 5 others killed
9 May Moro's body found in Rome
9 July Former Iraqi premier, General al-Naif, killed in London
20 August Israeli aircrew bus attacked in London, 1 killed

Terrorist Tactics

UNLIKE THE TERRORISTS of the earlier postwar period in, say, Cyprus or Kenya, today's terrorist has at his disposal a whole *ad hoc* network of international links. German, Spanish, Arab, Irish and Italian terrorists all pool intelligence and operational experience. Even if their ideologies differ, all share a common antipathy to international 'imperialism'. Most international terrorists, it is commonly agreed, are at least indirectly connected with the PLO. During 1980, for example, there were press reports that the PLO was now actually co-ordinating various national revolutionary groups through training camps in Syria.

Through such international co-operation, terrorists have developed a *de facto* tactical infrastructure in many Western countries. But the essence of this infrastructure is that there are no highly visible 'organisational' links such as connect the world's Soviet-line communist parties. The very absence of such formal links thus inhibits penetration and surveillance by the West's security services and counter-terrorist organisations. In this way a clandestine network of terrorist sympathisers exists in most Western countries as a 'back-up'.

The terrorists have other important tactical assets in their operational planning. Outstanding among these is the speed-up in international communications during the past ten to fifteen years. The relatively recent introduction of direct-dial telephoning from country to country materially assists terrorist planning because such calls are difficult to monitor by national security services. Another tactical asset is the progressive liberalisation of the Western banking and financial system, so making the transfer of terrorist funds an easy matter. Banking secrecy also protects the terrorist.

International jet travel means that the terrorist can fly in and out of a target country in a matter of hours. Closely related is the enormous increase in international tourism which gives excellent 'cover' to terrorists and at the same time prevents efficient surveillance by police forces in crowded airports. Moreover, once his attack is over, the international terrorist can expect immediate television coverage, often on a global basis, through the

TOP: *South Moluccan terrorists were active in Holland. In 1977 they occupied a train at Assen and after a 20-day siege two hostages and six terrorists were killed.* BELOW: *Spanish Premier Luis Carrero Blanco was killed when a bomb exploded in his car in December 1973.*

medium of satellite-linked TV. The very technical proficiency of Western society enables the terrorist to attack it all the more effectively.

But there is no one 'Terrorist International'. Central to terrorist flexibility is the fact that there is no single 'Godfather'. The essence of terrorist tactics is decentralisation. This decreases the risks, and increases the effectiveness of today's international terrorist.

Operational methods

Although sophisticated weapons such as remote-controlled bombs, the quick-firing MAC-11 machine pistol, and portable rocket launchers are important items in augmenting the strike power of the terrorist, such weapons technology has to be seen in the context of overall operational planning.

Unlike raiding parties in conventional military operations, a terrorist strike force cannot regroup and return if their attack fails. There is, therefore, an enormous premium on the carefully planned attack. The target must also be chosen to produce the maximum impact on world opinion and so advertise the existence and aims of the terrorist group. From such tactical conceptions spring such operations as the massacre of the Israeli athletes at the Munich Olympics of 1972, the assassination of the Spanish Premier, Admiral Carrero Blanco, by the Basque ETA (1973), and the murder of the British ambassador to Ireland, Christopher Ewart-Biggs, by the IRA (1976).

In these and other incidents there was intense surveillance of the future target by the terrorists to discover travel patterns and other routines. In addition, it is extremely rare for more than six to eight terrorists to attack a target. Small numbers maximise surprise, give the terrorists the initiative and facilitate the getaway.

Choice of targets

Operationally, the terrorist invariably avoids 'hard' targets such as closely guarded military installations. Although aircraft hijacking was a favourite terrorist tactic in the early 1970s, experience has shown that once grounded for refuelling, skyjackers are vulnerable to fatigue and hence to storming by the counter-terrorist squads which most Western countries have now created. The West German IG9 counter-terrorist group, for example, successfully tracked and then stormed a terrorist-held Lufthansa aircraft at Mogadishu in 1977.

The characteristic target of the terrorist is thus a 'soft' one such as a prominent national figure whose security is in practice minimal or vulnerable. Moreover, experience in both Northern Ireland and the Basque country has shown that even well-equipped troops, if they are on the move in difficult terrain, are extremely vulnerable to terrorist attack. The killing of 18 British soldiers at Warren Point, Northern Ireland, in 1979 by the IRA was a good example of this.

The choice of a 'soft' target, however, is not dictated solely by operational considerations. Above all the terrorist seeks instant publicity for his cause with the objective of discrediting his enemy and rallying his own supporters. In the Munich massacre of 1972, although five out of the eight Arab terrorists involved were shot by West German sharpshooters, the enormous publicity surrounding the incident, seen by hundreds of millions on prime-time TV, was rated an outstanding propaganda success. Despite the horrified reaction in the West and Israel, the sacrifice of the terrorists actually helped to mobilise support for the Palestinian cause in the Arab countries. For the terrorist, all publicity is good publicity.

An Al Fatah commando in training in Jordan. Al Fatah is the largest single group within the PLO.

Terrorists active in Europe 1968-78

ECLP–Executive Committee for the Liberation of Palestine, **ETA**–Basque Nation and Liberty, **IRA**–Irish Republican Army, **JRA**–Japanese Red Army, **NAYLP**–National Arab Youth for the Liberation of Palestine, **PFLP**–Popular Front for the Liberation of Palestine, **PLO**–Palestine Liberation Organisation, **UDA**–Ulster Defence Association.

Government Response

DURING THE PAST DECADE, a whole range of counter-terrorist strategies, tactics and methods have been developed by the Western powers, both collectively and individually. Given the existence of terrorist base havens and sanctuaries, especially in the Arab world, terrorism is unlikely to be eradicated in the foreseeable future. The result is that the responsibility for developing countervailing forces lies with the Western countries rather than the world community generally.

The United Nations General Assembly has remained deadlocked on the issue of counter-terrorism. Many of the Arab and African countries support terrorism in the name of 'national liberation', but the Western position is to condemn terrorism regardless of motive. The inevitable corollary is that West European countries, acting in co-operation with the United States and Canada, have developed their own intergovernmental measures for fighting terrorism.

In January 1977, the Council of Europe reached agreement on a Convention on Terrorism, which was signed by the 17 foreign ministers. Since that time, extradition measures and procedures have been concerted and tightened up by the 17, but the council remains only a consultative body. More effective are the counter-terrorist methods agreed by the nine EEC countries in June 1976. This six-point agreement covered the outlines of co-operation between the nine nations' security forces, while leaving detailed implementation to working parties.

During 1976–80, there was increasing and effective co-operation between Britain, France and West Germany in this EEC context. But there was also a growing network of bilateral anti-terrorist agreements such as those between Britain and the Irish Republic, West Germany and Austria, West Germany and Holland, France and Spain. There has been close bilateral co-operation between the British and American security services (MI5 and the FBI) since World War II.

Counter-terrorist measures

A US cabinet committee was created as a counter-terrorist measure in 1972 with a working group to report every two weeks. Although terrorism in America did not reach West European levels during the 1970s, Puerto Rican terrorists and the 'Weathermen', both backed by Cuba, were active. Throughout the decade, FBI statistics report that over 100 law enforcement officers were killed anually in terrorist and politically-motivated crimes.

Following the 1972 Munich massacre and the advent of Baader-Meinhof terrorism in West Germany, the Bonn government created a new federal counter-terrorist police department. Over 200 officers were seconded from other West German police agencies. Membership of terrorist groups in the German Federal Republic was made a criminal offence, while in Japan, the advent of the Japanese Red Army terrorist group led to the creation of a new anti-terrorist section of the National Police Agency during 1975. The same administrative trend was discernible in the United Kingdom during 1976 when a special constabulary to guard nuclear power stations was announced. This force was armed, and given powers of arrest.

TOP *Troops take cover behind army trucks during a search of areas in Assen, Holland, where South Moluccans were known to live. This occurred after the 1977 train seizure.* ABOVE *A West German poster seeks public help in capturing wanted terrorists.*

In addition to these administrative changes, new technical measures in the Western powers' fight against terrorism were developed during the 1970s. Essentially these measures involved the introduction of computerised 'memory banks' with the ability to store and analyse all available information involving international

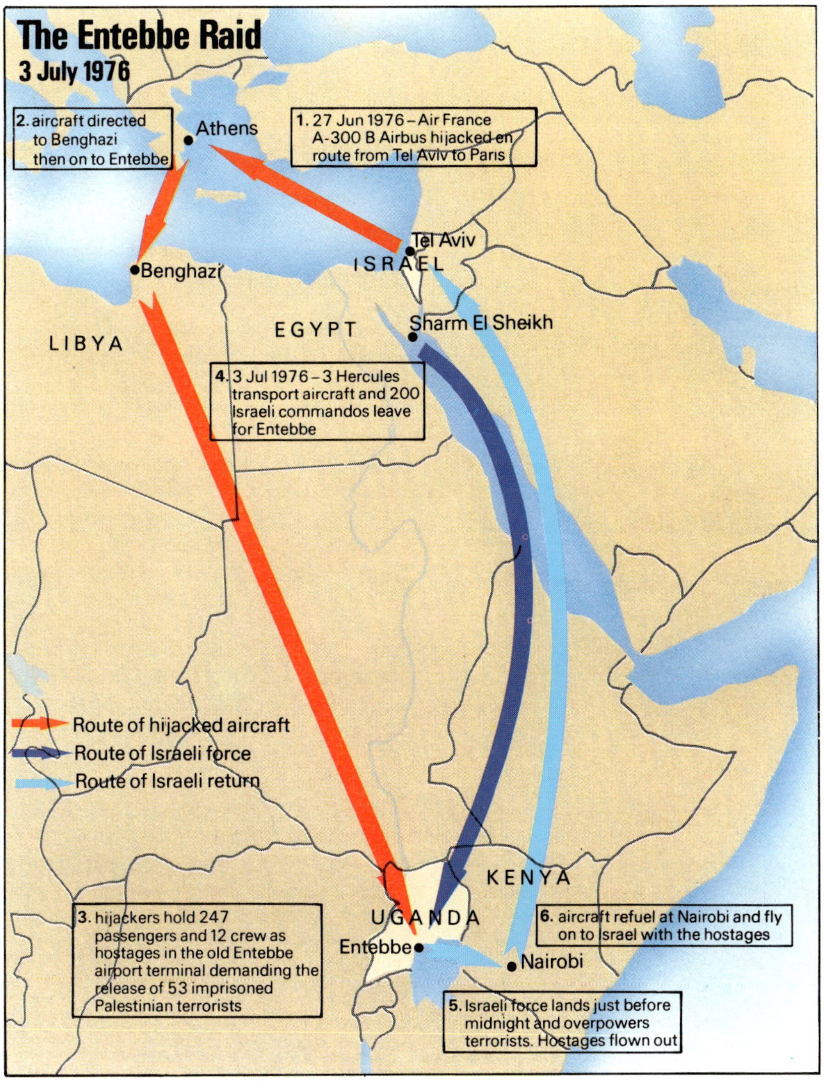

terrorism. The arrest and interrogation of terrorist suspects, combined with new international police measures, have to be seen in the light of these new data-retrieval systems.

In the early 1970s, the American government set up the Octopus Project which sought to amass in computer banks information from national and international sources on global terrorism. In the United Kingdom, a new British police computer, together with a new communications system, was organised to link Scotland Yard with regional police forces. In Northern Ireland, the British Army's Military Intelligence Department set up a separate computer system for monitoring in great detail not only the operations but the background of terrorists. Creation of the new federal anti-terrorist police department in West Germany was also linked to the development of a new, sophisticated computer system. These systems are under continuing development.

In the wider strategic context, the counter-terrorists must organise an efficient 'all-source' intelligence service which synthesises information from computer banks, security services, diplomatic sources and police informants. There must also be unified direction of this intelligence effort against the target terrorist group.

Above all, this 'strategic' intelligence effort must be applied in the context of a viable programme, or a strong defence of the democratic state. Only then will the intelligence process function efficiently as waverers and other faint-hearted terrorists turn to the security forces rather than to the terrorists for support. The will to win on the government's part is central at this juncture.

Meanwhile, the tactical application of the government's intelligence programme develops in three phases. First, the counter-terrorists minutely analyse their intelligence to pin-point individual terrorists, particular organisations and their international links. A complete intelligence 'profile' of the target terrorist organisation begins to emerge. Sometimes, tactical intelligence means that a terrorist attack can be pre-empted or ambushed. But even if a terrorist attack gains initial surprise, the arrest of a single terrorist is still a significant gain for the counter-terrorist forces.

In the second phase of the tactical intelligence process, the skilled interrogator enters the picture. He questions the terrorist prior to trial, extradition or deportation. Although democratic countries cannot legally use physical force – 'interrogation in depth', for example, was banned in Ulster by the British government in 1972 – persistent, non-violent questioning often elicits valuable information.

A third phase of the process involves some form of surveillance of the terrorist if he is detained. This would probably involve regular monitoring of the terrorist and his contacts while under detention. Counter-terrorist intelligence methods thus include a continuous assessment of the target terrorist group and its links. Many of these methods, of course, antedate today's counter-terrorist programmes. But the new technology has given an extra dimension to classic intelligence and interrogation procedures.

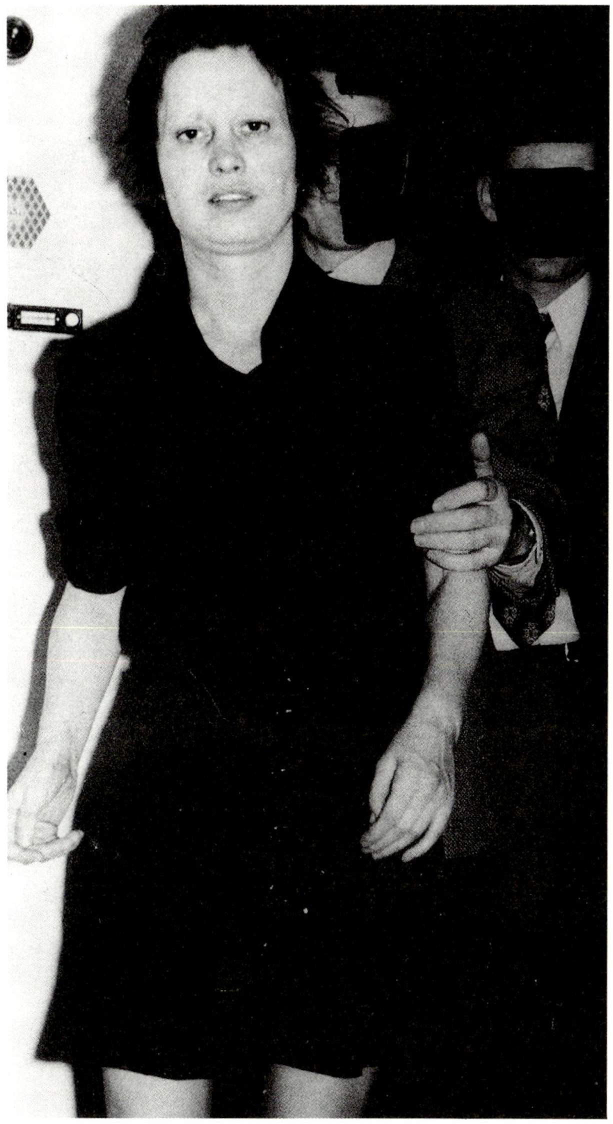

Ulrike Meinhof, head of the Baader-Meinhof gang, was arrested in June 1972 and later hanged herself.

Operational squads

The third phase in counter-terrorist activity has involved the creation of special squads to deal with outrages and to wrest the initiative from the terrorists on a tactical level.

A hostage escapes from the Iranian embassy in London as the SAS go in. The SAS assault that ended the six-day siege in 1980 was a spectacular operation. On 30 April six gunmen had taken 26 hostages, five of whom were later released. Two hostages were killed by the gunmen, all but one of whom were shot dead in the successful rescue mission, which fully justified the use of counter-terrorist squads.

Assault on the Iranian embassy
London 5 May 1980

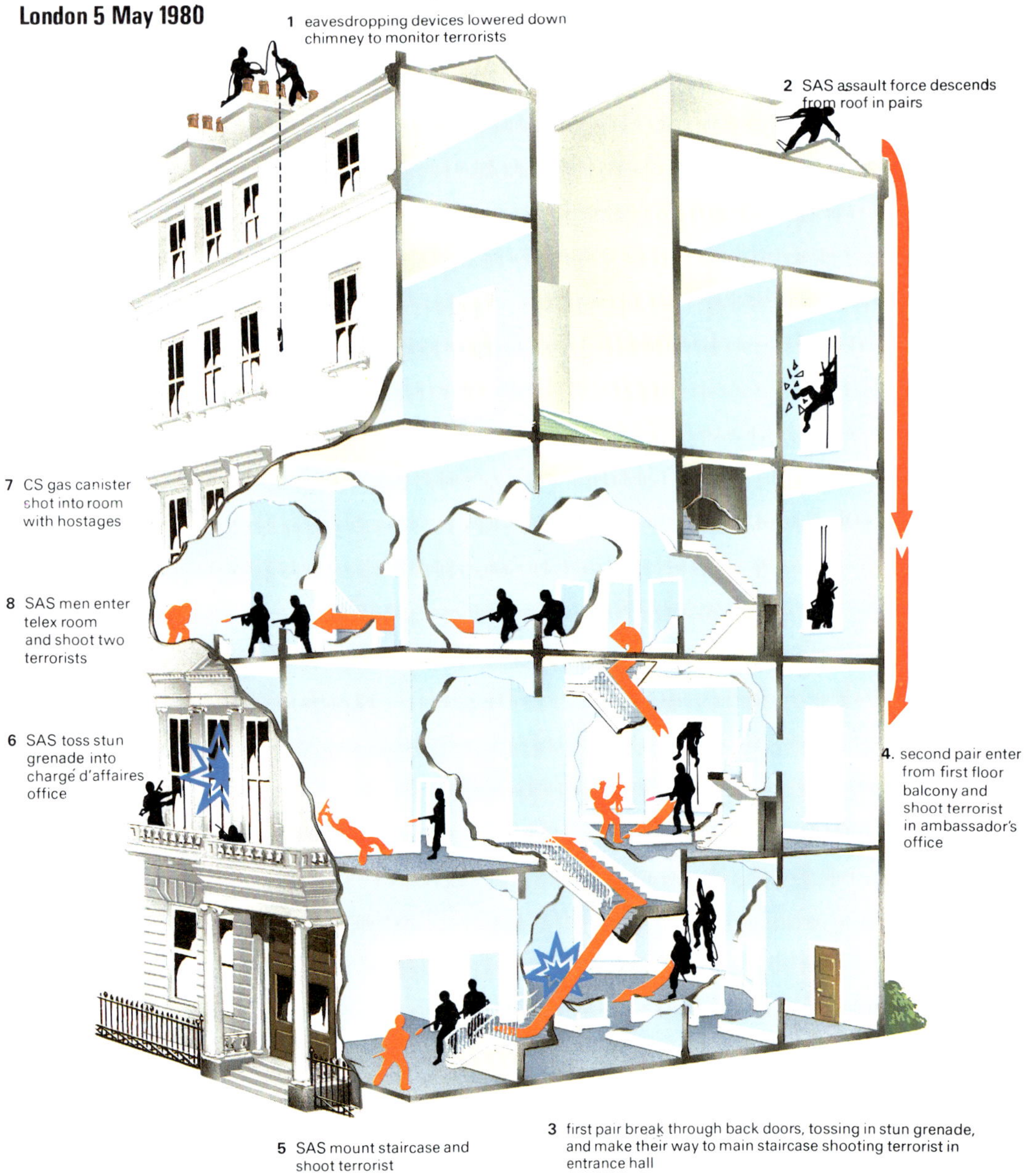

Besides the special squads of the Israeli Army, the West German IG9 and the units organised and trained by the British Special Air Service (SAS) are examples of these operational anti-terrorist groups. The SAS has been regularly used for undercover counter-terrorist work in Northern Ireland.

More prominently, an SAS squad stormed the Iranian embassy in London after its takeover by Arab terrorists in May 1980. Special counter-terrorist squads develop extremely close liaison not only with police and other intelligence authorities but with the political leadership of their country. Unity of command all the way down the operational channel is essential if the terrorist attack is to be countered effectively. Thus during the storming of the London Iranian embassy on 5 May, there was virtually instant communication between the SAS unit and the British Home Secretary.

The principles of action

In the past decade, many Western countries have learnt the hard way that counter-terrorism must be guided by four political guidelines. Only then will modern technical aids and intelligence procedures be fully effective. The first, and clearly the most important principle, is that there must be the political will to defeat terrorism. This determination must infuse the government's counter-terrorist apparatus from top to bottom. A second important guideline is that the target government must avoid overreaction which will alienate moderate opinion, dry up important intelligence sources and lead the people to equate the state with those who want to destroy it.

Thirdly, the target government must explain and project its counter-terrorist programme to the public at large. Necessary reforms must be expedited. But a democratic government which can successfully project the historic necessity of tough anti-terrorist measures can defeat the armed challenge – as did the Bonn government when faced with Baader-Meinhof terrorism in the 1970s.

The fourth principle is that any granting of 'political status' to the terrorist is completely counterproductive as it legitimises and encourages the terror. Denial of 'political status' thus goes to the heart of all successful counter-terrorist strategies.

The Military Balance

In the 1960s and 1970s the major nations had to adjust to constant changes in the balance of world power

Eric Morris

The nuclear-powered USS Enterprise, *a mainstay of the US Fleet, was commissioned in 1961. It has a displacement of 75,700 tonnes.*

IN THE EARLY 1960s, the period known as the Cold War came to an end, and war between the Soviet Union and the United States seemed a less likely possibility. The reasons for this have already been discussed in the chapter on the Cold War. By 1980, the military and economic balance in world politics was very different to what it had been in 1960. The end of the Cold War was not, however, followed by a lessening of minor wars, and there were various developments from the 1960s which made for instability, tension and conflict.

A major change was a more pluralistic international order. The Sino-Soviet split opened up completely new vistas as a new superpower, China, made its presence felt; the problem of the Sino-Soviet split affected areas such as Southeast Asia, where competing clients and Sino-Vietnamese hostility erupted into conflict. Other areas – notably the Middle East and the Persian Gulf – experienced a shifting balance which cut across the previous East-West divide. The final retreat of most of the colonial nations from Africa was accompanied by destabilising wars, and the introduction of Soviet influence in this continent led to a shift in the balance of power. War in the Indian subcontinent, too, changed the relative strength of the powers there.

In spite of changes in many areas, however, the most important confrontation in world politics was still that between the United States and the Soviet Union. And central to that was their relative military strength, which often lay behind smaller-scale wars.

In the aftermath of the Cuban missile crisis of October 1962 the two nuclear giants sought to pursue what at first sight must have appeared contradictory policies. On the one hand they sought by negotiation and treaty to reach an understanding about nuclear weapons, ban testing, and prevent the spread of such weapons to other states. Yet they each pursued the arms race with relentless determination, adding new and ever more destructive weapons to their strategic arsenals so that each had the ability to destroy the other many times over.

Greater complexity

Since the United States confronted the Soviet Union over Cuba, the balance of military power has changed dramatically. During the 1970s the Soviet Union spent $150 billion more than the United States on defence. This level of commitment is beginning to produce dividends, at least in military terms. The Soviet Union has achieved parity in nuclear weapons, and superiority in manpower and conventional weapons.

During America's preoccupation with Vietnam the Soviet Navy was feeling its way into long-range or deep-sea capability, and came of age in the mid-1970s when Russian warships became a common sight in the more distant waters of the world. All at once the Russians seemed to be deploying ships into oceans they had never used before and were building ships they had not needed before. Soviet warships from the fleet bases in Vladivostok appeared off the shores of Hawaii and Singapore while others ventured into the Indian Ocean. Western leaders looked with apprehension to their oil supply-lines from the Persian Gulf and along the Cape route.

By the end of the 1970s the Soviet Union had assumed all the characteristics of an armed leviathan in the full bloom of military expansion. The extension of her global power has seen Russian influence spread into Central America, Asia and Africa, supplying military force in the remotest regions of the world.

At the strategic level, technical progress in mid-course and terminal guidance systems has produced missiles of unerring accuracy. It is claimed that the superpowers are able to wage war with such weapons as particle-beam satellite killers and lasers. Science has taken us to the point where any target which can be located and identified can be hit regardless of size or distance – and where one shot can achieve a kill.

But the superpowers have been thwarted because there are now several centres of power in the world, no longer just two. International politics are infinitely more complicated than they were in the days of the Cold War, and fewer states are prepared to give automatic support to either the United States or the Soviet Union. The world has become more turbulent and complex; and international terrorists challenge the diplomatic order and cause new uncertainties.

Changes in the 60s

IN HIS INAUGURAL SPEECH in January 1961, President John F. Kennedy sounded the call to arms. Under his leadership the United States would play St George to her 44 allies, all of whom were confronted by communist 'dragons'. Kennedy's foreign policy, like his predecessors', firmly opposed aggressive moves by communist states against any independent nation that wished to choose its own form of government. In the three years of his presidency, the free world willingly looked to the United States for leadership, inspiration and protection. Compared with John Foster Dulles and President Dwight D. Eisenhower, Kennedy adopted a more discerning approach to foreign relations, for he acknowledged and respected the right of non-aligned states to pursue their own interests independent of the superpowers.

The Vietnam quagmire

Under Kennedy the United States became increasingly embroiled in Vietnam. He had inherited a commitment that was rapidly growing. The United States had sent supplies and advisers to help the South Vietnamese fight the communists but, as the regime of Ngo Dinh Diem lapsed into inefficiency and corruption, communist insurgency flourished. In 1961 Kennedy decided that more vigorous measures were necessary. Advisers assured him that military action alone would defeat the guerrillas and that the United States must increase its effort from advice to one of 'limited partnership'. Accordingly, American combat troops were committed.

The United States was faced with the choice of either sending substantial forces into Vietnam or abandoning it and admitting defeat by an army of ragged guerrillas. It was a war which had already spread into neighbouring Laos and Cambodia which in turn allowed communist forces, by way of the Ho Chi Minh Trail, to outflank the embattled regiments of Saigon and strike deep into the heart of the Mekong Delta.

Kennedy's successor, Lyndon B. Johnson, could not contemplate the prospect of defeat in Vietnam. In 1964 he used the Tongking Gulf incident, when North Vietnamese patrol boats fired on American warships, to persuade Congress to endorse a huge influx of combat troops into South Vietnam and to launch air attacks on the North. In March 1965 the 9th Marine Expeditionary Brigade was committed to South Vietnam.

In the midst of an escalating war in Asia, conflict erupted in the Middle East where an American ally, Israel, confronted Soviet-backed Egypt and Syria. On 5 June 1967, the Israeli Defence Minister, Moshe Dayan, ordered a pre-emptive strike against Egyptian airfields. The Six-Day War resulted in total victory for Israel, but Israel's triumph drove the Arabs still further into the Russian embrace. Ever since the mid-1950s the Soviet Union had sought greater influence in the Middle East by the use of military and economic aid. Moscow achieved no substantial gains until the outcome of the Six-Day War made the Arabs more reliant than ever on Soviet support.

Relations after Cuba

After the Cuban missile crisis of 1962 a new era of US-Soviet co-operation was signalled with the signing of the Nuclear Test Ban Treaty in 1963. Other measures followed as the two giants sought to improve their relations with each other. Yet the Soviet Union continued to pursue policies that encouraged instability outside Europe. It gave priority to relations with the United States, since that was

Demonstrators vent their anger at the presence of Soviet tanks in Prague, 1968. The invasion halted the Czechs' attempts to introduce liberal reforms.

the only power capable of destroying Russia single-handed. Nevertheless the Soviet leadership consistently worked to gain advantages for Russia and to weaken the United States, the main ideological enemy. The Soviet Union succeeded in matching the United States' military power in strategic nuclear weapons. It wished also to weaken the cohesion of the Western alliance but was thwarted in this aim by the development of the European Economic Community and the emergence of West Germany as a major power.

In 1968 the Soviet Union was disconcerted by trouble within its own camp. The 'Prague Spring' heralded a more liberal brand of communism in Czechoslovakia under Alexander Dubček, but for Moscow the reforms he introduced went too far. In August, Soviet and Warsaw Pact tank divisions rolled across the borders to depose the Dubček regime and replace it with one that was more in tune with Soviet thinking. In response to Western protests at this outrage Leonid Brezhnev, the Soviet leader, invoked the doctrine of 'limited sovereignty' of the satellite states to support the Soviet actions.

By then Moscow was being challenged from another quarter – China. Relations between these two communist giants had deteriorated over many years on ideology, policy and territorial boundaries. They conducted a propaganda war that became shrill and armed clashes occurred on the disputed frontiers. Moscow found itself confronted by an unpredictable foe and could devise no solution.

In the United States, meanwhile, the intractable war in Vietnam provoked widespread protest. Nightly TV coverage, the spiralling cost and increased questioning of America's seemingly open-ended commitment created the mood which carried Richard Nixon to the White House. He promised to end the war and to 'bring the boys home'. Along with his National Security Adviser, Dr Henry Kissinger, he realised that, with Soviet parity in nuclear weapons, the days of American dominance were over.

ABOVE *President Lyndon Johnson (left) was exhausted by the Vietnam War and did not seek re-election in 1968. Dr Henry Kissinger (centre), Secretary of State from 1973, helped formulate the policies of withdrawal from Vietnam and improved relations with China. Leonid Brezhnev (right) remained firmly in control in Russia throughout the 1970s. Relations with the West were strained over human rights and the invasion of Afghanistan.* RIGHT *A Soviet Tu-20 Bear is shadowed by a US Navy aircraft.* BELOW *Marines wait to be flown in to Khe Sanh. The withdrawal from Vietnam ushered in a new era in American foreign policy.*

World Strategy in the 70s

THE AMERICAN POLITICAL SYSTEM was in disarray in 1968. Richard Nixon, who for much of the 1960s had been shunned by the people and written-off by pundits, won the presidential election because he spoke for a nation which had grown weary and frustrated with the role of world policeman which dated from the Cold War years of the 1950s. The majority of Americans wanted an end to involvement in the Vietnam War and a few called vociferously for isolation. It was a time when the United States had suffered a relative decline in its wealth yet its allies, particularly in Europe and Japan, enjoyed strong economies.

In this climate of change the United States' leaders sought to make the biggest adjustment of all – to re-order the relationship with the Soviet Union. This new approach was called détente ('a relaxation of tension') and had its origins in the 1950s with Nikita Khrushchev's first halting steps towards 'peaceful co-existence'.

Détente did not imply that the ultimate intentions of either superpower had changed. The Soviet Union still sought to encourage the spread of communism throughout the world, but it now ruled out full-scale war as a means to its ultimate end of world revolution.

Through a series of bilateral negotiations, the two giants entered into what Americans called a 'limited adversary relationship'. Basic policies and interests were still in conflict, but neither side wished to use military power directly against the other. So détente emerged because of the nuclear stalemate and the frightening consequences that would result from an arms race that was allowed to continue unchecked. In 1972 the first Strategic Arms Limitation Treaty (SALT I) was signed.

The American decision to withdraw from Vietnam removed the last obstacle to another dramatic change in international affairs. The Chinese reduced their propaganda against the United States and began to put out peace feelers as tension with the Soviet Union increased. It occurred at a time when the American president wished to normalise relations between the two countries. In February 1972, Richard Nixon, master of the dramatic and an aggressive anti-communist in the 1950s, flew to Peking and met Chair-

A Trident missile is pad-launched during testing. This missile equips submarines and will replace Poseidon. TOP *President Richard Nixon shares a meal with China's Premier Chou En-lai (left) in 1972.* ABOVE *Jimmy Carter's four years as president saw American influence visibly diminished in Europe and the Middle East.*

man Mao Tse-tung. The *rapprochement* with China caused consternation among America's Asian allies, particularly Japan and Taiwan. The United States had now adopted a 'one China' policy, which largely meant abandoning the Chinese Nationalists on Taiwan. All American troops were to be removed from the island and the United States was to support Peking's entry to the United Nations.

The new balance

Such an about-turn in Sino-American relations, though interpreted in Peking as a necessary compromise more than anything else, has been of advantage to China. Chinese leaders recognised that the Soviet Union posed the greater threat and that it was to their advantage to end their isolation from world affairs. The Americans exploited their position in what was now the 'superpower triangle' and, with the possibility of war between Russia and China, Nixon and Dr Henry Kissinger (Secretary of State from 1973) hoped to lever further concessions from the Russians over such issues as the easing of tension in Europe and arms control.

This old-fashioned balance of power approach worked imperfectly, however. The Russians were simply not amenable to such pressure and, while they disliked the thought of China moving into the mainstream of world affairs, and perhaps disrupting the alignment of states, they knew that the diplomatic value of China was still limited because China was so much weaker than the Soviet Union.

From 1973 onwards Soviet-American relations deteriorated gradually. There was a clash of wills during the Yom Kippur War, during which America went onto strategic alert. In November 1974 President Gerald Ford (who had assumed office after Nixon's resignation over Watergate) met Leonid Brezhnev at Vladivostok, but it was clear that the second round of strategic arms limitation talks had stalled on difficulties which even the personal intervention of the two leaders could not resolve. The time-table for negotiation lost momentum with unfavourable consequences for the strategic balance.

LEFT *A Chinese soldier in training. China's emergence from isolation has added a new dimension to world affairs.* BELOW *The in-flight refuelling capability of the Soviet Tu-26 Backfire bomber gives it strategic importance.*

African involvement

In 1975 Cuba, backed by Russian arms, intervened in Angola and Moscow went on to manipulate the war between Somalia and Ethiopia in the Ogaden Desert. In Afghanistan and South Yemen, Moscow's friends came to power while Hanoi, having first secured South Vietnam, deployed forces against Peking's candidates in Laos and Cambodia.

Against this newly confident and assertive Soviet Union, American power seemed to be in decline and there were rumblings of concern among the Western allies. American enthusiasm for the techniques of containment had largely evaporated. The State Department clearly believed that the Soviet drive would be halted by some of the very forces that had thwarted the United States in the 1960s, such as the intractable nature of Third World nationalism.

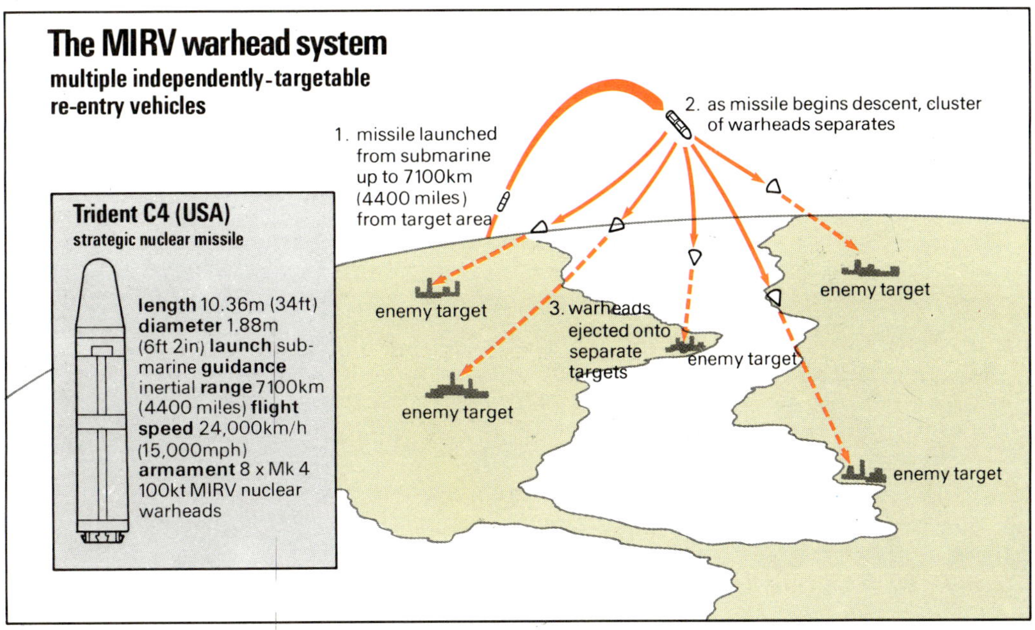

As the 1970s drew to a close détente seemed quite dead. The US Senate was clearly unhappy with SALT 2, which was quietly shelved, and American concern at Soviet assertiveness became widespread and played a large part in Jimmy Carter's defeat by Ronald Reagan in 1980. American helplessness at the downfall of the shah of Iran, a most abiding ally, and the Soviet invasion of Afghanistan had contributed to the impression of America as a crippled world power. It was an image reinforced by the inept attempt to rescue American hostages held in Tehran, a mission aborted on presidential orders as a result of mechanical failures and aircraft collision in a desert hundreds of miles from the objective.

Nuclear Confrontation

IN 1979 the United States and the Soviet Union reached a new agreement on the limitation of strategic nuclear arms. SALT 2 came more than five years later than the target date which the two superpowers had originally set themselves and was stillborn. The objective of the negotiations was straightforward: to prevent the two nations from spending vast amounts on new weapon systems while at the same time meeting their basic needs for security, and ensuring that each retained sufficient warheads to maintain a credible deterrent.

The difficulty in the first instance lay in the sheer complexity of negotiations, for whilst the objectives were laudable agreement proved elusive: the treaty framers could not come up with a form of words which would encompass the recent advances made in weapon technology. For example, the first treaty legislated on the number of missiles but this only encouraged the superpowers to use the loophole of multiple warheads. Because their ingenuity was concentrated on that aspect the scientists produced better and more accurate weapons, which in turn presented the prospect of one or other superpower being able, in time, to deliver a disarming blow.

American doubts

Perhaps if the Soviet Union had not adopted behaviour and policies which the United States found unreasonable then Congress might have been prepared to risk the compromise of SALT 2 and cast aside their doubts in favour of better relations. But without détente there can be no meaningful arms control because the vital element of trust in intentions is missing and leaders are not prepared to take risks with national security. When Soviet troops intervened in Afghanistan SALT 2 was finished. What caused this upset to the strategic balance was that a new, confident and seemingly aggressively-minded Russia had deployed its armies beyond what America was prepared to accept as the limit of Soviet military power.

American political leaders, supported by the military establishment, have also expressed concern at what they see as the considerable growth in the power of the Soviet Union com-

pared to the relative decline in American power. American discomfiture over Iran is compared to the increase in Soviet qualitative power in central Europe.

There are a number of intrinsic difficulties, however, in assessing the strategic balance between the superpowers. A purely quantitative analysis based on the number of missiles or the total megatonnage tells us very little about the qualities of weapon systems or how effective they would be in reaching their target. The United States, for example, has a great advantage over the Soviet Union in terms of the number of warheads deployed on missiles. Moreover, it is probably true that the American missiles can deliver their warheads more accurately than the Soviet ones. Yet this advantage is partly balanced by a new generation of Soviet intercontinental ballistic missiles (ICBMs) which have more accurate warheads than their predecessors and a greater throw-weight than the Minuteman.

As for the number of warheads carried by land-based ICBMs, the Soviet Union has nearly three times the number of warheads as the total number of American ICBM silos. In addition the Russian warheads tend to be bigger in terms of yield than those of the Americans. Almost 70 per cent of the warheads on all American missiles have an explosive yield of less than 50 kilotons while the Russians have that same percentage of their warheads in the megaton range. The new Soviet SS-18 ICBM can carry ten two-megaton warheads while the Minuteman 4 has three 170-kiloton warheads.

The underwater deterrent

The Russians initially put all their eggs in one basket, the bulk of their strategic nuclear force being their land-based ICBMs. These missiles are more accurate because their trajectory can be fixed precisely, but they are more vulnerable because they are immobile and their locations can be plotted by satellites. The US missile-armed nuclear submarines (SSBNs) have multiple warheads and generally a longer range than their Soviet counterparts. The Russian Delta II SSBNs have a missile, the SS-N-8, which can outrange Poseidon and has a greater throw-weight; but the Soviet missile has only a single warhead. Submarine-launched missiles (SLBMs) lack the accuracy of those fired from silos on land but because a nuclear-powered submarine is so difficult to detect, let alone destroy, they are virtually invulnerable and are ideal as a second strike force.

American dependence on this force is a reflection of a strategic doctrine which stresses the deterrence mission to the exclusion of virtually all else. The smaller American warheads are intended as a counter-value weapon to threaten Soviet cities in a retaliatory blow and thus ensure that mutual and assured destruction (MAD) remains the cornerstone of the strategic balance.

The third element of the strategic 'triad' are the bomber fleets deployed by both sides. The number of B-52s is slowly declining and the B-1 (the most expensive combat plane in history) has been cancelled as its replacement. The Soviet Backfire cannot attack America without in-flight refuelling, but it can hit targets in Japan, China and European NATO countries; and if present trends continue there will be more Backfires in the mid-1980s than B-52 Stratofortresses.

So-called 'grey weapons' are deployed by both sides. These are often referred to as 'theatre nuclear weapons' and are epitomised by the Soviet SS20 missiles, fired from a mobile launcher and armed with three warheads of frightening accuracy. Taken with the expanding force of Backfires these weapons present a threat which has prompted NATO to seek an answer. The fear is that in a war the American strategic deterrent could be neutralised by a massive threat from the Russians. In this sense the commitment to defend Europe with nuclear weapons if necessary has a hollow ring for those who believe that Europe could be 'decoupled' from the American strategic umbrella.

President Jimmy Carter offered new missiles to the Europeans to fill the gap in the deterrent forces. The Russians tried to thwart this move by the usual 'stick and carrot'. On the one hand Leonid Brezhnev offered to discuss troop reductions but at the same time threatened that any country which ignored his offer and accepted the missiles would find its position 'considerably worse'. The NATO alliance stood firm and resolute. In December 1979 it was announced that 108 American Pershing II medium-range missiles (MRBMs) and 464 ground-launched cruise missiles, all with single warheads, would be deployed in Europe.

There does seem to be a rough kind of strategic parity between the two superpowers. The Soviet Union emphasises heavy missiles and large warheads, but American weapons have greater accuracy; and all the other strategic nuclear forces – the British, French and Chinese – are targetted on Russia.

LEFT *The twin antennae of Cam Main radar station, a Canadian outpost on the Distant Early Warning line which stretches from Alaska to Greenland.* ABOVE LEFT *Minuteman land-based ICBMs are salvo-launched at a testing ground in the United States.* ABOVE RIGHT *A Poseidon multiple-warhead missile is launched from a still-submerged submarine.*

Nuclear Arsenals 1980

Missiles	United States	Soviet Union
ICBMs	1054	1398
ICBM warheads	2154	4306
IRBMs, MRBMs	—	600
SLBMs	656	1003
SLBM warheads	5120	1309
Aircraft		
LR Bombers	338	156
MR Bombers	65	518
Submarines		
Nuclear ballistic missile subs	41	87

Cruise missiles are also under development and the Soviet Union was estimated to have, in 1980, 68 nuclear submarines carrying cruise missiles.

American Air Power

THE INDOMITABLE B-52, though now more than 20 years old, lumbers on into the 1980s as the mainstay bomber force of Strategic Air Command. Millions of dollars have been spent to extend its service life and increase operational effectiveness. This is vital since the Soviet Union has now deployed some 10,000 anti-aircraft missiles and 2720 interceptors to defend herself. The United States has no such missiles and only 331 interceptors to defend its air space.

The final production model was the B-52H, of which 102 were built, bringing the total to 744 bombers. The main strike force comprises 13 wings equipped with 151 B-52G and H bombers. These planes carry up to 20 SRAMs (short-range attack missiles) with 200 kiloton warheads. At high altitude the missile has a 'stand off' range of 170km (105 miles) and low down it can be released 56km (35 miles) from the target.

Supporting the B-52 are four squadrons of FB-111 medium-range supersonic bombers. The highly versatile F-111 is also deployed in Europe where it is claimed to be the most effective tactical bomber in any Western air force. This swing-wing, variable-geometry aircraft has a speed in excess of Mach 2 and can be used in three roles: as an all-weather attack bomber, in electronic warfare, and as a strategic bomber.

The most expensive aircraft to enter service is the Boeing E-3A Sentry AWACS (airborne warning and control system). Derived from the Boeing 707-320B airliner this flying management station can watch every aircraft at a radius of more than 320km (200 miles). In addition it can command and control air operations over a beachhead or battlefield and direct a rescue helicopter onto a downed pilot.

Interceptors and close support

One of the smallest combat aircraft is the plane destined to be the mainstay of the interceptor force for the rest of this century, the General Dynamics F-16 fighter. It is small, with a wing span of 9.4m (31 feet), but the thrust from its single Pratt and Whitney turbo-fan engine can send it hurtling through the air at almost twice the speed of sound.

The war in Vietnam revealed a glaring deficiency in the American air arsenal – a close-support aircraft that could carry a heavy ordnance load and survive severe and punishing fire from the ground. The remedy is the Fairchild A-10A Thunderbolt II. The main armament, a 30mm anti-tank cannon, has a muzzle horsepower 20 times that of the 75mm gun which was fitted to some B-52s in World War II. It is the most powerful gun ever fitted to an aircraft and its magazine holds 1350 rounds, each the size of a milk bottle. The pilot's cockpit is encased in a thick titanium armour while the engines are located above the rear fuselage where they betray a lower infra-red signature on the enemy's radar. This ugly duckling will be deployed in Europe where, alongside the TOW-armed Cobra helicopters, it could provide an effective counter to Soviet tank superiority.

There is also the Grumman A-6 Intruder, a remarkable naval aircraft which can take into action a payload

ABOVE *By 1985 more than 500 Grumman F-14 Tomcats will be in service with the US Navy.* BELOW *The 'tank busting' Fairchild A-10.* RIGHT *The F-16 is the USAF's newest fighter.*

Fairchild A-10A Thunderbolt II

length 16.26m (53ft 4in) **span** 17.53m (57ft 6in) **combat speed** 716km/h (445mph) **combat range (close air support)** 463km (288 miles) **armament** 1 x 30mm 7-barrel rotary cannon (1350 rounds of ammunition) **available stores include** 907kg (2000lb) Mk84 bombs, 227kg (500lb) Mk82 bombs, Rockeye II cluster bombs (anti-armour), Paveway 1360kg (3000lb) laser guided bombs, AGM-65A Maverick air-to-surface missiles

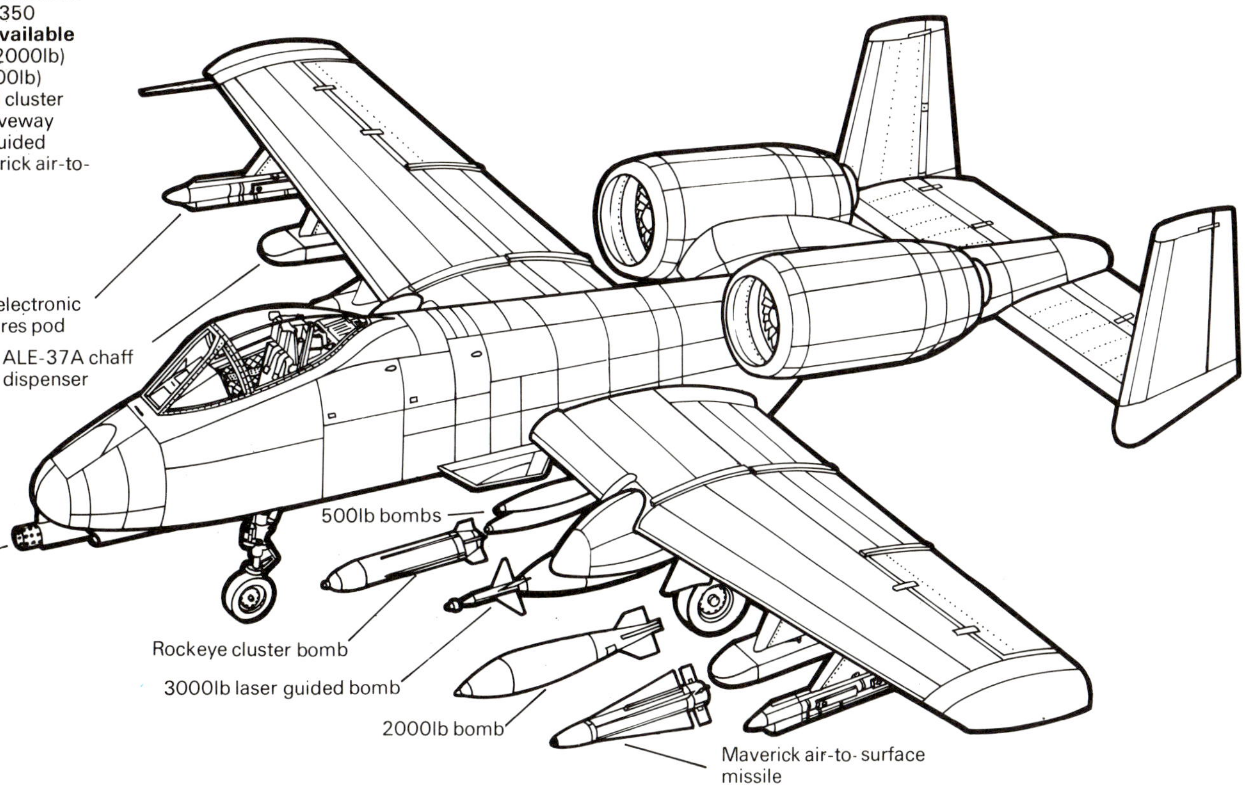

greater than that of the four-engined heavy bombers used in World War II.

On some counts the Lockheed C-5A Galaxy, which gives the American armed forces their strategic reach, is the world's largest aircraft. Though some of the late model Boeing 747 'jumbo jets' have a greater wing span and weight, nothing can compete with the cavernous hold of the Lockheed for sheer bulk or capacity. A normal complement of troops can be carried on the top deck, and beneath there is a hangar space that is big enough to carry two M60 battle tanks.

One of the most versatile aircraft is the C-130 Hercules. Built originally as a tactical transport and affectionately called the 'Herky bird', it has been adapted to be used as an RPV director, electronic warfare and tactical communications aircraft. Others have been used as tankers to refuel helicopters and retrieve spacecraft from the ocean. Another version is the AC-130H which was a night flying gunship in Vietnam. It carried forward-looking infra-red, low-level TV and lasers to identify its targets, and a 105mm howitzer, 40mm cannon, 20mm gatlings and mini-guns, in addition to rocket and grenade launchers.

The US Marine Corps relies on a British design for the aircraft to give them beach defence and fighter ground-attack. McDonnell Douglas build under licence the AV-8B which is a modified design of the Hawker Siddeley Harrier. This plane is intended to operate from amphibious assault ships like the Tarawa class. These 40,000-tonne monsters carry a battalion group of about 1800 marines and land them, together with all their equipment, by helicopter and landing craft.

World Security 1962-80

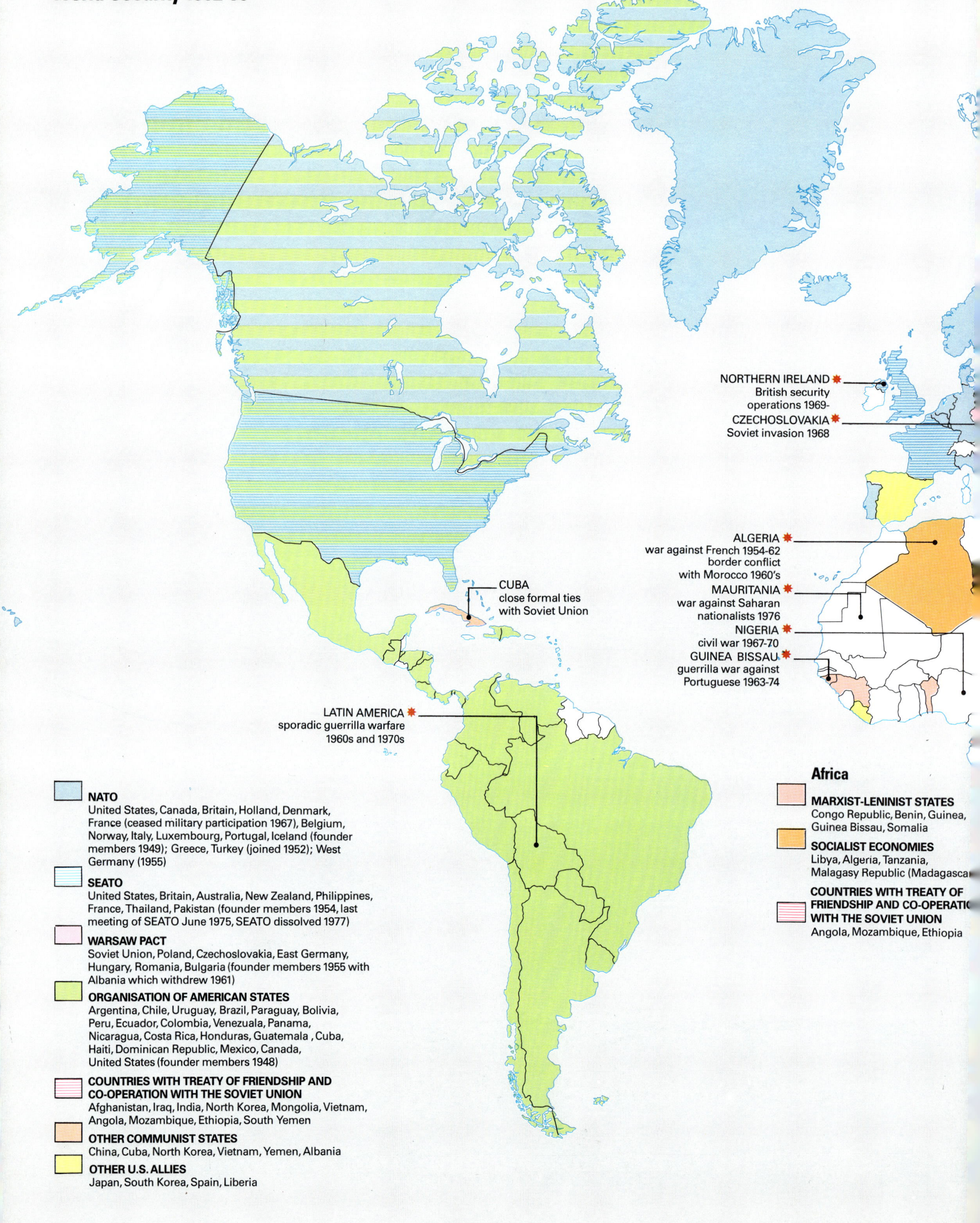

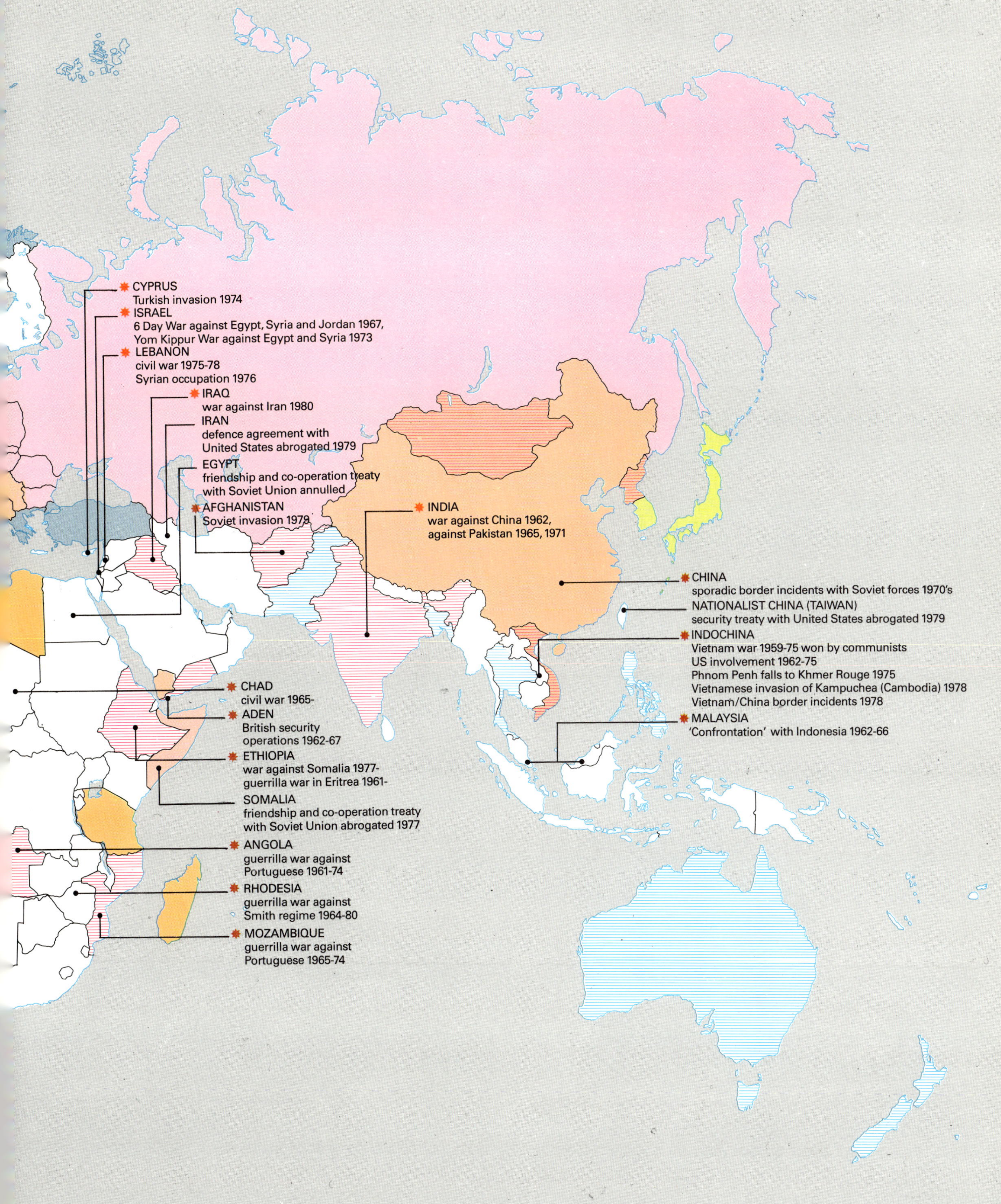

CYPRUS
Turkish invasion 1974
ISRAEL
6 Day War against Egypt, Syria and Jordan 1967,
Yom Kippur War against Egypt and Syria 1973
LEBANON
civil war 1975-78
Syrian occupation 1976
IRAQ
war against Iran 1980
IRAN
defence agreement with
United States abrogated 1979
EGYPT
friendship and co-operation treaty
with Soviet Union annulled
AFGHANISTAN
Soviet invasion 1979
INDIA
war against China 1962,
against Pakistan 1965, 1971
CHINA
sporadic border incidents with Soviet forces 1970's
NATIONALIST CHINA (TAIWAN)
security treaty with United States abrogated 1979
INDOCHINA
Vietnam war 1959-75 won by communists
US involvement 1962-75
Phnom Penh falls to Khmer Rouge 1975
Vietnamese invasion of Kampuchea (Cambodia) 1978
Vietnam/China border incidents 1978
MALAYSIA
'Confrontation' with Indonesia 1962-66
CHAD
civil war 1965-
ADEN
British security
operations 1962-67
ETHIOPIA
war against Somalia 1977-
guerrilla war in Eritrea 1961-
SOMALIA
friendship and co-operation treaty
with Soviet Union abrogated 1977
ANGOLA
guerrilla war against
Portuguese 1961-74
RHODESIA
guerrilla war against
Smith regime 1964-80
MOZAMBIQUE
guerrilla war against
Portuguese 1965-74

Soviet Land Forces

AT THE TACTICAL or battlefield level the Soviet Union has continued to improve the equipment available to all its three services. For the first time the Soviet tactical air forces have the operational capability to carry out long-range air superiority missions. Later models of the MiG-21 Fishbed, MiG-23 Flogger and MiG-25 Foxbat, together with the Su-17 Fitter and Su-24 Fencer, equip the frontline squadrons. These aircraft present a serious problem for NATO, whose strike aircraft would have to overcome this enhanced air defence in order to reach their targets.

Despite the need to maintain some 600,000 troops on the Chinese border and to support a further five divisions fighting in Afghanistan, the Soviet Army has 30 divisions at full alert in eastern Europe. Interior lines of communication and standardised equipment throughout the Warsaw Pact give it an edge over the more diffusely equipped armies of the Western allies. There are some 12,500 main battle tanks in these Russian divisions which, together with the Pact forces, gives the eastern block a 2 to 1 superiority over the West.

Until recently NATO could take comfort from the marked superiority in the quality of its armour but the appearance of the T72 has changed all that. This tank is dramatically superior to American armour and its 125mm gun is bigger even than that of the British Chieftain. With its much improved armour protection the T72

BELOW *Representatives of the seven Warsaw Pact countries participating in manoeuvres in East Germany in 1980 line up in front of their T62 battle tanks.* RIGHT *A Frog-7 surface-to-surface tactical missile is shown on its ZIL-135 transporter.* BOTTOM *T72 main battle tanks take part in a Moscow parade. This Soviet tank was put into production in 1974, and its 125mm gun is unequalled in calibre by any Western tank.*

represents a massive improvement in Soviet tank technology over the earlier T54, T55 and T62 models.

The three types of Soviet divisions – tank, motor rifle and airborne – have all benefitted from a renaissance in conventional weaponry. The infantry components in the tank and motor rifle divisions are carried in armoured fighting vehicles. The new BTR-50 series and BMP mechanised infantry combat vehicle are as good as anything which the Western armies possess.

It is in Afghanistan that much of the more sophisticated new equipment used by the Russians has been seen in action. Between 24 and 27 December 1979 some 6700 airborne troops were lifted into Kabul airport. The mainstay of the airlift were the An-12 (which can carry 90 men) and the larger An-22 with a capacity for 150 troops. By the end of February 1980 there were some 80,000 troops, mostly reservists called up from neighbouring Turkestan, Uzbekistan and other southern Soviet republics.

Vehicles travelling between the main towns were escorted by infantry in BMPs while main battle tanks, particularly the T62 but also it was rumoured T72s, escorted troop convoys and also acted as mobile pillboxes at crucial junctions. Above, the MiG-21 strike aircraft and the feared Mil Mi-24 Hind helicopter gunship carried the war to the embattled guerrillas in the foothills.

Tanks and artillery

Soviet armies have always relied heavily on the massed fire support provided by their artillery. In recent years they have acquired a decided superiority over the NATO forces in northern and central Europe. Field medium and heavy artillery together with mortars and multiple rocket launchers out-number by 3 to 1 those in Western forces. Nuclear shells have been developed for the full range of Soviet heavier artillery, including 152mm and 202mm towed artillery together with 152mm and 122mm self-propelled guns.

At least 700 T72B main battle tanks have now been assigned to the Soviet divisions in East Germany alone and this is in keeping with current Russian practice that the latest and the best is given to the central European front. Soviet and Warsaw Pact divisions train extensively for an off-the-mark, high-speed offensive where the momentum of the advance is maintained by heavy concentrations of firepower and local superiority in tanks and men. At present the Soviet armies are in need of reinforcements, but some observers in the West maintain that they are close to achieving local superiority in Europe so that they might soon be capable of the 'cold start' – an advance across the German border without reinforcements.

The strategic position of the Soviet Union

The Soviet Union is a powerful nation, which poses a constant threat to Western Europe. But from another perspective, it is itself vulnerable because it is almost encircled by hostile countries (the NATO powers and China) on its land frontiers, and by the US fleets and strategic air forces placed around the globe.

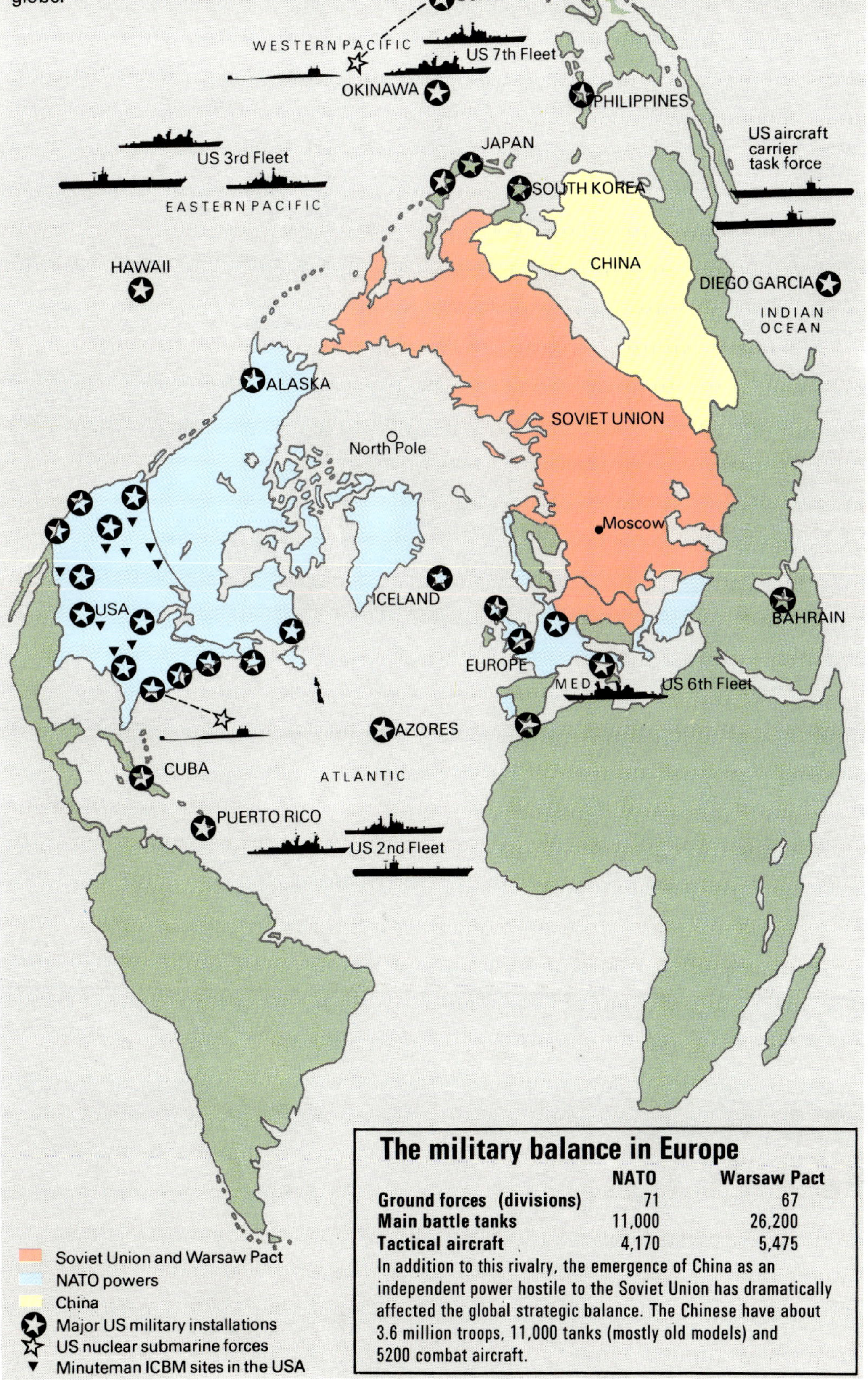

The military balance in Europe

	NATO	Warsaw Pact
Ground forces (divisions)	71	67
Main battle tanks	11,000	26,200
Tactical aircraft	4,170	5,475

In addition to this rivalry, the emergence of China as an independent power hostile to the Soviet Union has dramatically affected the global strategic balance. The Chinese have about 3.6 million troops, 11,000 tanks (mostly old models) and 5200 combat aircraft.

Growth of the Red Fleet

A SIGNIFICANT TREND since the end of World War II has been the emergence of the Soviet Navy to challenge the American monopoly of the sea. By the end of the 1960s the Soviet Union, once a naval power of little consequence, ranked alongside the leading maritime states. Then, on 18 July 1975, the *Kiev*, Russia's brand-new 40,000-tonne aircraft carrier and pride of the fleet, passed through the Bosporus and the Dardanelles en route to its first operational cruise. The arrival of the *Kiev* made complete the claim of the Soviet Union to be a global maritime power. The achievement is an impressive one and testimony to the work of Admiral Sergei Gorshkov, who for more than 30 years has held flag rank and moulded the Red Navy into a powerful force.

The prime mission of the Soviet Navy – shared by the navies of the United States, Great Britain and France – is to contribute to the strategic deterrence provided by the ballistic missile-armed submarines (SSBNs). The equally impressive surface units of the Red Navy support the missions of the ballistic-missile carrying submarines by sweeping the seas clear of Western anti-submarine forces and denying the West access to vital waters in a 'surge deployment'. In time of peace these ships are used to further Russian interests by appearing worldwide in ports which the Soviet government considers to be of importance. This in turn has meant the deployment of task forces, centred on the *Kiev* and her sister ships, including fleet escorts and support.

Except for the occasional sortie from the Mediterranean, or the odd ship en route from the Pacific, the Soviet warships which patrol off Britain's shores or are observed in the Atlantic are stationed in either the Baltic or the Barents Sea. There are four Soviet Fleets and of the two in these waters the more important is the Northern Fleet which has its base in the Kola Inlet.

Role of the Northern Fleet

The Northern Fleet has more than 60 major surface units and 160 submarines, and the majority are nuclear-powered. Close to 70 per cent of all Soviet SSBNs are based in the Kola Inlet, because the warm waters of the Gulf Stream keep the fjords and ports of northern Europe ice-free as far east as Murmansk. Moreover, the Arctic tip of Europe lies directly on the shortest route between the more densely populated centres of the United States and the Soviet Union. The polar trajectory is the missile flight-path not just of ICBMs but also of the submarine-launched missiles and helps to explain the heavy concentration of Soviet strategic naval power in the region. From the Barents Sea the Deltas, the latest class of Soviet SSBNs, can strike deep into the United States with their multi-warhead missiles.

So the Northern Fleet has to control the Barents Sea and the North Cape in order to sweep the passage clear for the SSBNs to move to their patrol stations at the first hint of war. There is, in addition, a regiment or more of naval infantry together with their landing craft and support ships stationed with the Northern Fleet. Should the need arise these forces would be used for amphibious operations along the maritime flank of Finnmark, Norway's most northerly province.

LEFT *Admiral of the Soviet Fleet Sergei Gorshkov has been instrumental in extending Russia's maritime capability since World War II.* BELOW *The aircraft carrier* Kiev, *here shadowed by* HMS Danae, *carries both VTOL fighters and helicopters.*

Baltic-based vessels

The Soviet warships stationed in the Baltic include many old and obsolescent vessels that are used for training. Together with the navies of Poland and the German Democratic Republic, there is a heavy emphasis on amphibious warfare in the Baltic. But for those surface units and submarines which operate on the high seas, the narrow exits of the Baltic via the Danish straits, overlooked by a 'belligerently neutral' Sweden, are a major constraint. Indeed, so hampered are the Russians by geography that they have recently sought a way out of this bottleneck by extending the canal and river network that links the Baltic with the White Sea.

In the event of war, Soviet warships operating from these bases would seek to interdict the sea lanes between North America and Western Europe. It is across this 'Atlantic Bridge' that the supplies of weapons and *matériel* must pass, though in an age of nuclear propulsion and missiles, convoy protection assumes a new dimension.

A global presence

The third Soviet fleet operates in the Black Sea with a squadron deployed forward into the Mediterranean. From the naval bases in the Crimea to the open anchorages which Russian ships use off Crete is a voyage of some 2400km (1500 miles). Throughout the year there are between 10 and 14 surface ships and possibly 12 submarines in the Mediterranean squadron. The wartime role of this force, which would then be considerably reinforced, is to prevent the West closing in on the Turkish straits and to counter the threat of the US Sixth Fleet and the navies of NATO's southern flank.

The presence of the Soviet Navy in the Indian Ocean is enigmatic in terms of motives and intentions. Vessels have fanned out across the ocean and pose a threat to the vital oil routes of many industrial states. To date the Soviet emphasis has been on the Persian Gulf and the Horn of Africa. From base facilities provided by compliant states Russian warships intervened in the war in Ethiopia and the Somali Republic. In 1980 a Soviet squadron shadowed an American task force off the entrance to the Persian Gulf, both uneasy bystanders during the conflict between Iraq and Iran.

The Pacific Ocean, the world's largest ocean, occupies a greater area of the earth's surface than all the land masses put together. Satellites have made navigation more precise than before and have reduced the sea's vastness to entirely manageable proportions. The Soviet Pacific Fleet operates out of two main bases, Vladivostok (close to the Korean frontier) and Petropavlovsk, about 1600km (1000 miles) to the north-east on the barren and inhospitable Kamchatka Peninsula. Petropavlovsk is the only significant Russian port which opens directly onto the high seas; all the others are dominated by narrow waters and potentially hostile shorelines. The Soviet Pacific Fleet has perhaps 60 major warships and 100 submarines and its main task in war would be to act against communist China.

The Soviet Navy 1977–80

	1977	1978	1979	1980
Submarines	321	333	338	344
Aircraft carriers	1	1	2	3
Cruisers	35	37	37	39
Destroyers	91	97	100	75
Frigates	103	107	136	173

A Soviet Whiskey class submarine lies at anchor with a Mil Mi-4 helicopter overhead. These vessels joined the Soviet Fleet in 1951. About 50 remained in service in the late 1970s, with a further 80 in reserve.

Fleets of the Soviet Navy-1980

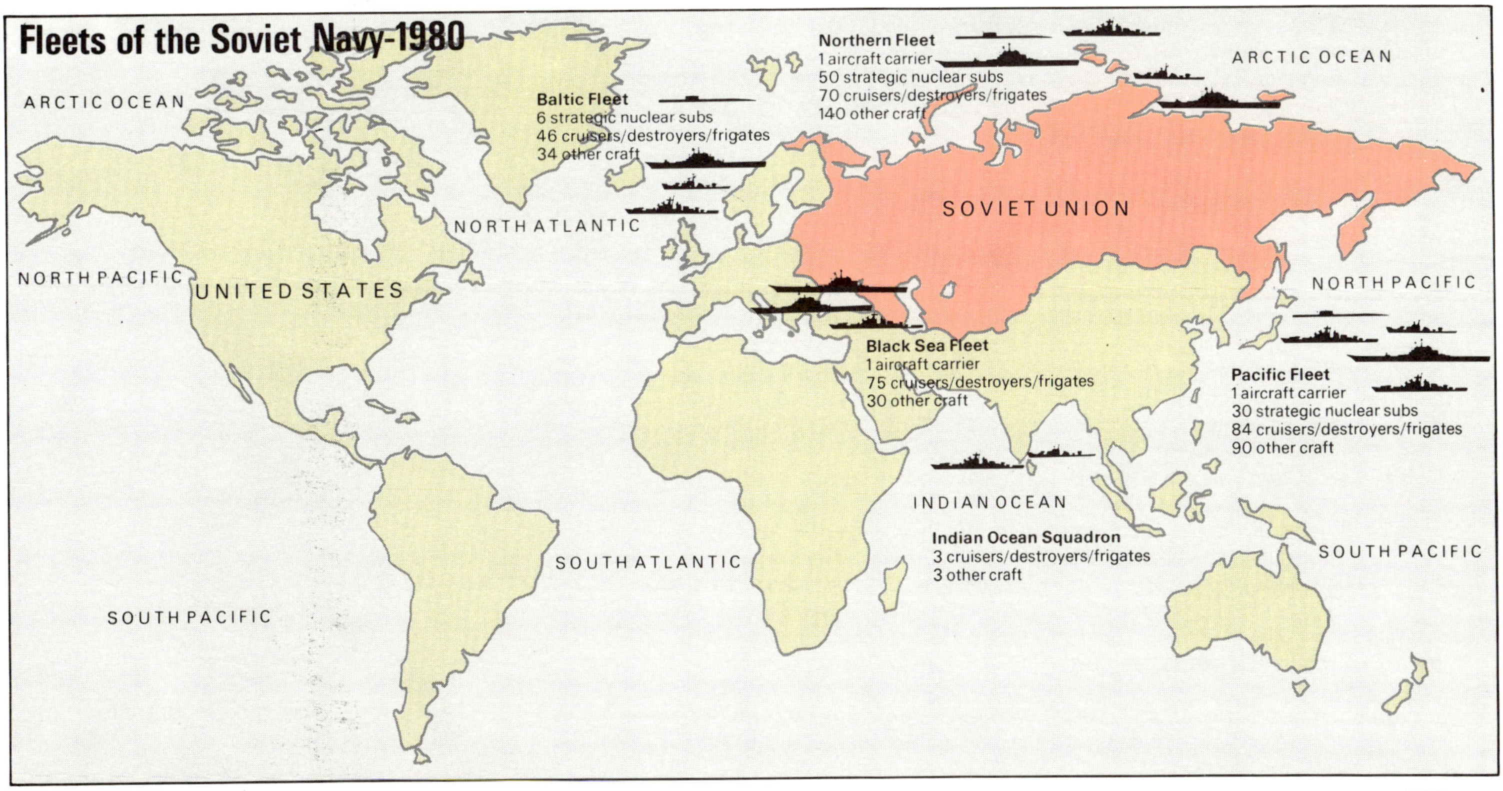

Scenarios for World War

UNLIKE THE AMERICANS, the Soviets do not see strategic nuclear war as distinct from other forms of warfare. The objective of Russian strategic forces is to develop the ability to fight, survive and possibly win a nuclear conflict. This commitment to fight a nuclear war in Europe has remained constant, and their conventional forces are better prepared to fight a nuclear land battle than those in the West. Soviet troops are equipped to detect radiological and chemical contamination and their headquarters are designed with this in mind.

NATO's forward defence strategy commits the alliance to defend West Germany at the inner German border or as far forward as possible. Such a political requirement could hamper the military planners by denying them the necessary flexibility over the positioning of troops on the battlefield. Soviet units are no closer to the 'front' than those of the Western alliance (in fact the average distance of Russian troops is about 125km or 80 miles while NATO forces are about 100km or 60 miles from the border). However, the Russian forces are better positioned and concentrated for a quick reaction to a crisis.

In contrast NATO formations compete for the same routes, and are more 'nationally self-conscious'; only on occasion do they practise reinforcing allies across national and corps boundaries. NATO supply lines are parallel to the front and thus in danger of being cut by penetrating Soviet or Warsaw Pact tank columns.

Should the Russians attack, there are two principal invasion routes on this front. The first and probably more important is the North German Plain which is defended by the Northern Army Group comprising Belgian, Dutch and West German divisions with the total fighting strength of the British Army of the Rhine and an American brigade. The second route, the Fulda Gap corridor, is defended by the American Army, German divisions and a Canadian Battle Group. A third and minor route, the Hof corridor, would lead Soviet forces towards Munich.

Strategy for limited war

NATO's strategy for limited war within this theatre relies on the forward defence to repel the invading divisions as close to the border as possible. Such a concept requires the defending forces to counter aggression at an appropriate level and then,

TOP *West Germany developed the Leopard II tank in the mid-1970s. Its 120mm gun, Chobham armour and exceptional mobility make the type one of NATO's most potent tanks.* ABOVE RIGHT *American troops armed with M16 rifles take part in a NATO manoeuvre in 1979.* RIGHT *Bird's-eye view of a Soviet tactical missile.*

T72 (Soviet Union)

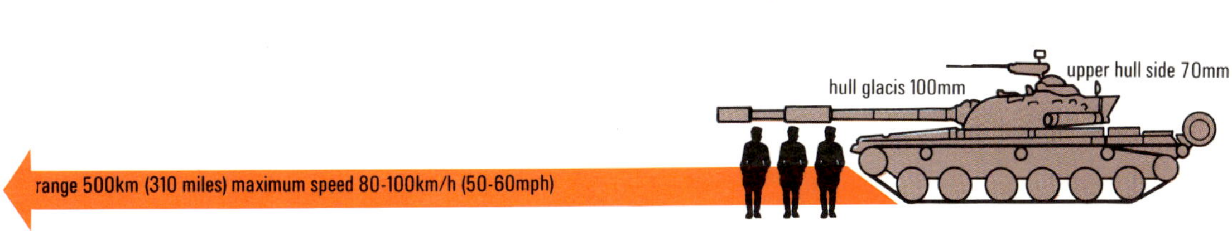

weight 39.3 tonnes (38.7 tons) **length** 9.02m (29ft 6in) **height** 2.265m (7ft 5in) **armament** 1 x 125mm smooth-bore gun, 1 x 7.62mm machine gun, 1 x 12.7mm machine gun **ammunition carried** 12 rounds of APFSDS, 6 rounds of HEAT and 22 rounds of HE (fin stabilised) for 125mm

Chieftain Mk5 (Britain)

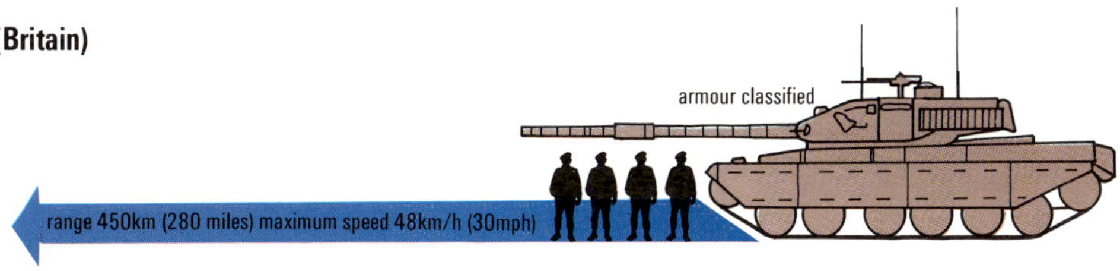

weight 55 tonnes (54.1 tons) **length** 10.795m (33ft 5in) **height** 2.895m (9ft 6in) **armament** 1 x 120mm gun, 2 x 7.62mm machine guns, 1 x 12.7mm machine gun, 2 x 6 smoke dishargers **ammunition carried** 64 rounds of HESH or APDS for 120mm, 6000 rounds for 7.62mm, 300 rounds for 12.7mm

if it proves impossible either to repel or contain, to escalate under full control. Nuclear weapons are held in reserve, ready to be used but only at the command of the political heads of the alliance. As part of this strategy, which combines a forward defence with a flexible response, the alliance has to control not only its own air space but also the vital sea routes across the Atlantic.

NATO's far northern flank overlooks the Soviet routes from the Kola bases into the open waters of the North Atlantic. Soviet naval activity is monitored by sensors on the sea bed and maritime air bases in Britain, Iceland, Greenland and northern Norway. The Norwegians fear a Russian 'smash-and-grab' raid to seize their northern province of Finnmark. From such captured air bases the Russians could extend the air cover for their own naval forces deep into the Atlantic.

A great alpine divide separates NATO's central and southern fronts into two distinct theatres of operation that lack mutual support and are only related at the most tenuous levels. The members of NATO's southern flank, principally Greece, Turkey and Italy, are not only isolated from the main forces on the central front but are cut off from one another. Common fronts are not feasible in southern Europe, but then common threats are unlikely for the same reasons.

The southern flank is divided into three sub-theatres, Italy, Greece plus Turkish Thrace, and Asia Minor. It is possible for Soviet and Warsaw Pact divisions to menace Greece and Turkey but so long as the alliance could hold the vital choke-point formed by the Sicilian narrows, Italy would be intact. Any Soviet contingencies must make considerable allowance for Yugoslavia and to a lesser extent Albania.

The Eastern front

Viewed from the Kremlin, the most dangerous confrontation apart from that in Europe is the deepening quarrel with Peking. There are still some 600,000 Soviet troops deployed along a 7250km (4500-mile) border in some of the most inhospitable terrain in the world.

The communist Chinese have embarked upon policies which cause concern in the Kremlin. Politically China has mended its fences with Japan and formalised its relations with the United States. The Russian nightmare of a Peking-Washington-Tokyo axis extending to the European Community is closer to reality. So tension remains high along the border while the Chinese nuclear forces, which are capable of reaching targets deep inside the Soviet Union, continue to grow.

The Sino-Soviet dispute has become more 'international' in recent years with their clients and proxies fighting in Southeast Asia. Hanoi relies on Moscow to watch its back while it seeks to impose its regime over China's candidate in Kampuchea. The United States meanwhile watches warily lest the conflict spreads across the borders of its client, Thailand.

Civil Defence

THE BOMB which exploded over Hiroshima in August 1945 had about 10,000 times as much power as the largest conventional bombs then in use. The level and extent of destruction to life and property completely overwhelmed the civil defence system in Japan. By the early 1960s the fusion or hydrogen weapons which were then stockpiled possessed increased destructive power by a factor of hundreds of thousands. The total yield of such weapons held by the superpowers when divided by the population of the world, is estimated today at over 40 tonnes of TNT per head for every man, woman and child on earth.

Such radical increases in the destructive power of weapons has caused equally radical changes in the civil defence policies pursued by most industrial states. In the past almost any shelter provided a modicum of protection against conventional bombs, but atomic bombs required an entirely new approach.

With a 10-megaton explosion, dwellings will suffer very severe damage from blast up to 10km (6 miles) or more from the detonation point; and if houses are made of timber, they will be engulfed in flames up to 25km (15 miles) from impact. From such a burst a man would receive second degree burns if caught out in the open 16km (10 miles) from impact. If there is a wind of 32km/h (20mph) over the detonation this would result in death from the effects of radiation on as many as 50 per cent of all people exposed, up to 240km (150 miles) from the point of impact.

The absence of adequate warning time, the sheer destructiveness of the warheads and a better understanding of the radiation hazards from fall-out rendered obsolete most plans for evacuation and meant that civil defence lost its momentum. In Britain, France and West Germany national plans have concentrated instead on the establishment of regional government which, in the advent of nuclear war, would be carried out by the normal branches of local government with a core of administrators aided by military direction. For some countries like Japan the spread of their populations made nonsense of any preparation for civil defence. Almost a third of Japan's population is located in three urban areas, Tokyo, Nagoya and Osaka. In Britain the urban spine, a corridor 65km (40 miles) wide which runs from Liverpool to London, presents a similar nightmare to civil defence planners. In China, by contrast, the thousand largest cities contain only 11 per cent of the population.

Diverse schemes

In the northern hemisphere only three states have really persisted with well-publicised plans for civilian evacuation and seem willing to invest the huge sums necessary to provide an adequate civil defence service. Surprisingly these states are Sweden, Switzerland and Yugoslavia, while Denmark and Norway have retained comprehensive civil defence schemes, but on a much smaller scale.

In Sweden the civil defence forces number about 230,000 people. This force is mostly composed of women between the ages of 16 and 67 years; men serve from 16 to 18 years and from 47 years, when they are released from military obligations, to 67 years of age.

Sweden's terrain and geology enable the building of rock-firm shelters. Most of the Baltic countries have in recent years placed a large proportion of their vital industries deep underground in specially constructed nuclear-proof caverns. Civil defence members are trained in peacetime to be responsible in war for first aid, damage clearance, and fire services as well as protection against chemical and biological warfare. The government has encouraged the construction of shelters and now more than 4 million of the population can use private shelters. In the cities there are extremely well-publicised evacuation schemes and communal shelters for another 100,000 of those who would need to remain behind to maintain essential services.

Switzerland in many respects is like Sweden, sandwiched between hostile power blocs and blessed with a formidable terrain that favours the construction of shelters. The Swiss have a most ambitious programme which aims by the turn of the century to provide places in nuclear shelters for all its 6 million citizens. At present it is estimated that 60 per cent can be protected. The mountains of Switzerland make it difficult to plan for a wholesale exodus of cities and so the Swiss employ what is known as 'vertical evacuation', which simply means the provision of shelters in people's homes and their places of work.

Under the terms of the national defence law all adults in Yugoslavia aged between 16 and 60 years who are not assigned to the armed forces or the militia are obliged to serve in civil defence organisations. Official government figures show there are 1.3 million employed in the provision of shelters, evacuation schemes, medical care and blackout precautions.

In Asia there are perhaps two prime

An American radar station in Greenland, part of the strategic early warning system. Such stations are an essential part of civil defence measures.

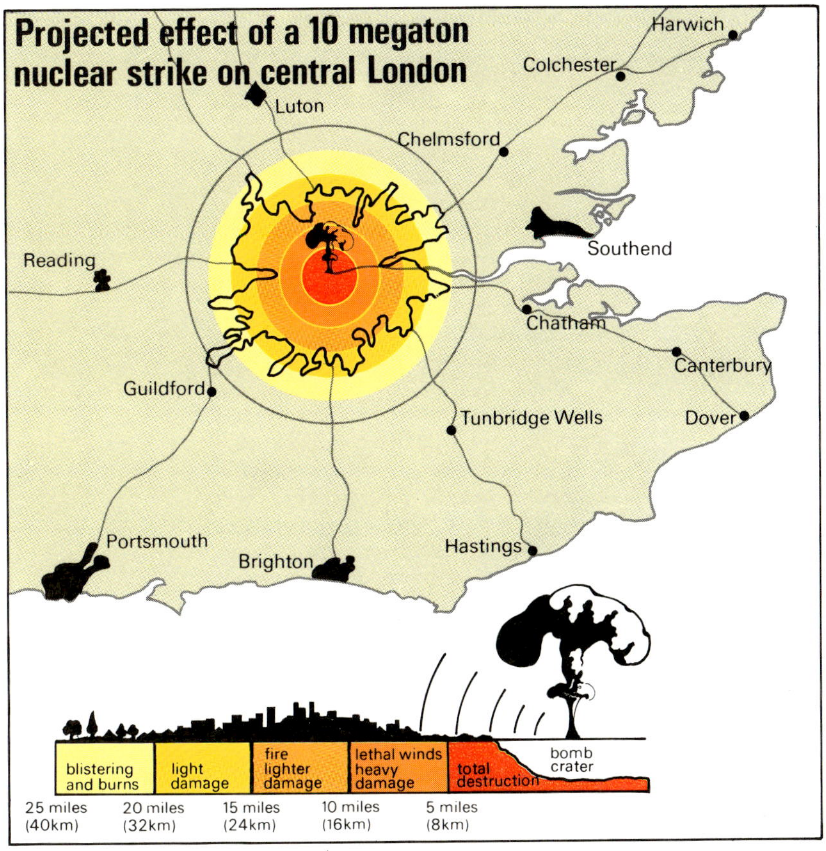

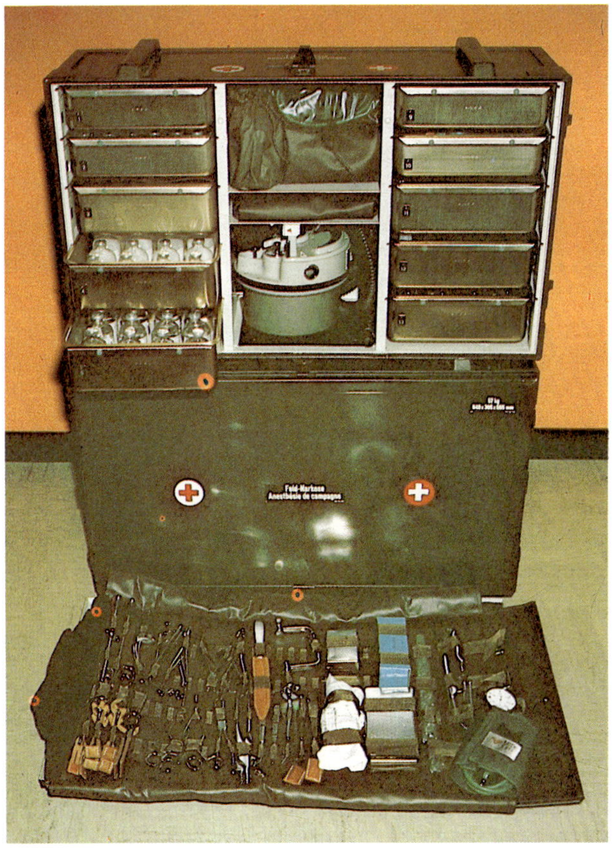

examples of civil defence. For ten years and more the cities and hamlets of North Vietnam experienced a steadily increasing tempo of American air raids. Despite the huge tonnage of high explosive that rained down (some reports indicate ten times the total dropped on Germany in World War II) much of the effectiveness of this was countered by such measures as evacuation and dispersion together with concealment and the building of underground shelters.

Seoul, the capital of South Korea, lies just a few miles from the front line with the communist enemy to the north. The North Korean war machine is in a constant state of alert with forces concentrated along the Demilitarised Zone. These troops could move in hours, and there would be very little warning. Consequently on one day each month the air raid sirens wail in Seoul and the capital rehearses its air-raid drills.

In the United States civil defence has received scant attention since the Cuban missile crisis, but the picture is quite the opposite in the Soviet Union. The objective of the Russian strategic nuclear forces is to achieve a capability to fight, survive and win a nuclear war. So there is a continued strengthening of Soviet effort to function during and after a nuclear war with the emphasis placed on ensuring the survival of the political and administrative leadership, as much of the industrial work force as possible and the military infrastructure. Experts in the West disagree on how effective the Soviet civil defence effort would be in war. Some argue that relocation procedures would limit Russian fatalities to 4 or 5 per cent during a general war whereas 50 per cent of the American population would die under similar circumstances.

TOP *An anaesthetic pack in a Swiss underground hospital.* ABOVE *A shelter for workers in a factory.* BELOW *The exit door of a domestic shelter. On the wall is an air filter, an essential protection against radioactive material.*

USA-main cities and densely populated areas

Future Possibilities

THE MILITARY BALANCE in the future will be influenced by the fact that the Americans, as much as the Russians, are moving away from sole dependence on mutual assured destruction and seeking to be able to fight a limited nuclear war. In such a scenario the aim would be to limit the collateral damage and limit the level of response by a very tight control over the degree of military escalation.

At the level of strategic weaponry the United States is now developing the MX (Missile Experimental) series, an ICBM which is deployed on a mobile launcher. The missile, which weighs 86,200kg (190,000 pounds), is 2.3m (92 inches) in diameter and is tipped with ten Mark 12A warheads each independently targetted and with an estimated yield of more than 300 megatons. The Mark 12A warhead which is currently being fitted to the Minuteman 3 missiles is sufficiently accurate to place about 50 per cent within 180m (600 feet) of their targets. The new ones for MX will achieve 50 per cent within 15m (50 feet) of the target, enough to be selective over a political target like a KGB provincial headquarters or a military base. But where would the remainder fall, and how many civilian casualties would they cause to lead to an unlimited nuclear response?

On the battlefield

Perhaps the most important aspect of each generation of new weapons at a tactical level is that they all reflect a greater killing power available to smaller units. Such a trend favours defence, because if a target moves it has a high probability of being destroyed. Costly investments like tanks or warships are increasingly vulnerable to an ever-widening spectrum of weapon systems. Weapons are increasingly accurate and destructive. In part this is due to 'weapon tailoring', matching targets with the most suitable weapons to destroy them.

In Vietnam, American aircraft carried instruments to neutralise the effectiveness of the radar-controlled anti-aircraft batteries of North Vietnam, and electronic warfare moved into a new phase. The first large-scale use of electronic counter measures (ECM) by the Soviets was in 1968 when Warsaw Pact ground and air formations masked their movement by massive jamming of radio frequencies as they descended on Czechoslovakia. Superpower allies took it one stage further to electronic counter counter measures (ECCM) in the Yom Kippur War of 1973.

Today the Soviets have surface-to-air missiles with variable radar frequencies which make them all the more difficult to jam. The Americans have produced aircraft variants which are employed in this eerie world of electronic warfare. The latest versions of the F-111 – designated the EF-111A – will escort bombers which are striking deep into eastern Europe and jam the air defences. Perhaps in time there will be no need for such tasks to be flown by man. The Americans have already tested remotely-piloted vehicles (RPVs) which can carry out many missions which previously were undertaken by aircraft such as reconnaissance, electronic warfare, and strike. They have even married an RPV with a precision-guided missile (PGM).

On the ground the soldier of today has to be prepared to fight the '24-hour battle'. No longer can weary combatants take shelter behind the cover of darkness. Rifles fitted with image-intensifier sights turn night into day and places all the emphasis on concealment. In his protective clothing the soldier may need to counter the effects not just of radiation or high explosive but also chemical and biological weapons.

Whatever new weapons are introduced there is one feature of the military balance which must remain constant and that is its equilibrium. The chances are that elements of instability will increase with the risks of nuclear proliferation and as the subject peoples of eastern Europe and in the Soviet Union become ever more restive. Even so, war by design – the deliberate act of aggression – will remain the most remote of possibilities provided the forces are balanced and mutual deterrence holds firm. What cannot be legislated against is inadvertent war when, in a period of high tension, increasing instability and spreading turbulence, a violent incident could so easily provide the catalyst to nuclear holocaust.

RIGHT *A Chieftain main battle tank of the British Army's 4/7 Dragoon Guards on winter exercises in West Germany. The Chieftain is now being replaced by the Challenger.* BELOW *The Tomahawk cruise missile's Tercom (Terrain Comparison) guidance system uses an electronic relief map to plot the missile's course.*

BGM-109 Tomahawk cruise missile

length 5.56m (18ft 3in) **propulsion** turbofan **launch** air, submarine, surface ship, ground **guidance** TERCOM **strategic range (submarine and surface launch)** 2735km (1700 miles) **strategic range (air launch)** 3600km (2240 miles) **speed** 885km/h (550mph) **armament** nuclear warhead

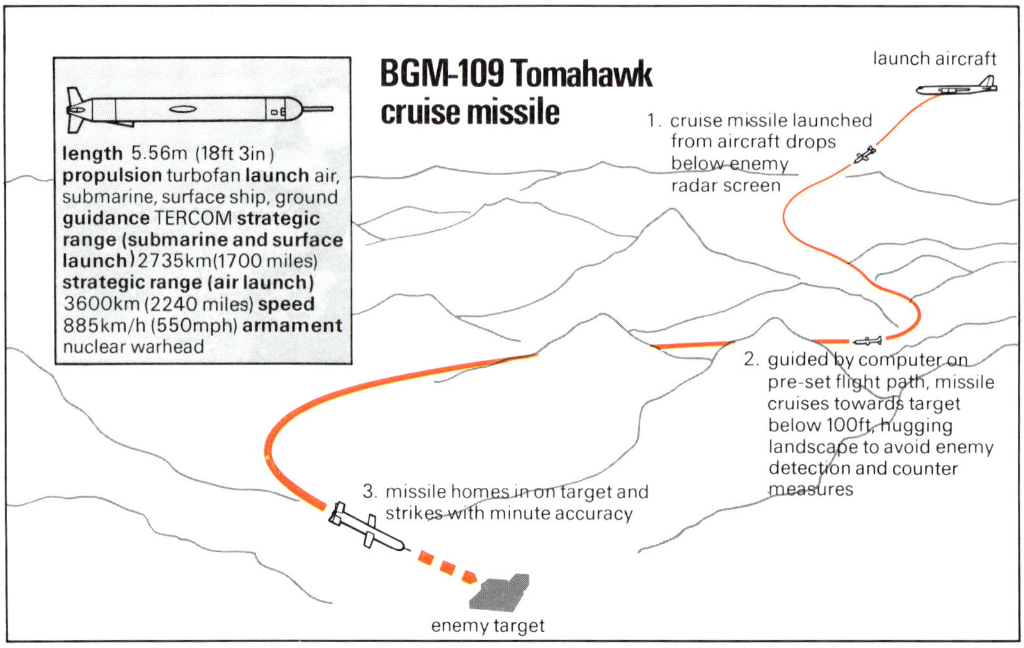

Projected nuclear strengths 1985

	United States	Soviet Union
ICBMs	1040	1180
ICBM warheads	2112	6232
ICBM megatonnage	1449	8904
SLBMs	774	976
SLBM warheads	5888	4356
SLBM megatonnage	431	1546
Bombers	340	90
warheads	4480	400
megatonnage	1600	400

Northern Ireland

During the 1970s the six counties of this province were rocked by a wave of terror

Peter Janke

THE PRESENT PHASE OF VIOLENCE in Northern Ireland has lasted for more than a decade. Starting with the civil rights marches of the late 1960s, it has developed into a vicious terrorist war in which there have been four main elements engaged: the Provisional IRA; Protestant paramilitary groups such as the Ulster Volunteer Force; the conventional forces of law and order in Northern Ireland (such as the Royal Ulster Constabulary); and the British Army. Although the Protestant paramilitary groups have had a decisive influence on events, the war since the early 1970s has been based on the campaign of terror waged by the IRA.

From 13 politically motivated deaths in 1969, the toll rose swiftly to a high of 468 in 1972, to drop back to an average of 250 deaths a year until 1977, when the figure was more than halved. In 11 years of slaughter (1969–79) there were 2000 killings, 14,600 injuries, 6582 bombings causing 555 deaths, and 27,000 shooting incidents. If these statistics convey little of the horror, those on kneecapping might.

Between 1973 and 1979 some 700 people have either been shot from behind or in the side of the knee, have felt the power of an electric drill on bone, or seen the kneecap break under a block of concrete dropped from a ladder. Such punishment was reserved to enforce discipline within the IRA ranks. Girls and women who may have gone out with British soldiers, or offended more seriously the code of secrecy, have been tarred and feathered.

The Provisional IRA campaign has been costly in terms of bomb damage, with a total bill at the end of 1979 of over £250 million. Much of the destruction was caused by incendiary devices – especially effective after the introduction in 1976 of the cassette incendiary. Earlier, introduction of the car bomb had not only doubled casualties in 1972 but increased damage. Drivers were forced to transport explosives to a target while a passenger or a relative was held hostage. Shopping centres suffered badly, and not only in Belfast, but in Armagh, Dungannon, Bangor and Lisburn. Banks escaped until March 1979, when 22 branches in 15 towns were bombed, although with only slight damage. Cinemas were singled out early on in the campaign, as were hotels, restaurants and bus stations. Bombs were exploded on the railway. On 21 January 1979 a computer at Queen's University, Belfast, was damaged.

More sophisticated attacks have been made with mortars on military bases and on Aldergrove airport. Radio-controlled bombs and long-delay timing devices make the future still more dangerous. Booby-traps are already set with great ingenuity. Other weapons in Provisional hands include the US M-16 Armalite rifle, the Remington Woodmaster equipped for sniping with telescopic sights, and the US M-60 machine gun. Although ammunition is scarce, terrorists have also used the Soviet RPG-7 rocket launcher.

The historical dimension

There have been various attempts to find a peaceful solution – in the aftermath of the Mountbatten murders in 1979 the visit of the Pope seemed to create a new atmosphere, for example – but peace initiatives have foundered upon the intransigence born of generations of prejudice and hatred. For there are two aspects to the Irish situation that together make it very different to other wars since 1945. The first is religion. The intensity of much of the terrorism has stemmed from religious bigotry of the worst kind, which provided a justification for some of the most hideous acts. Violence has, of course, been denounced by leading Protestant and Catholic churchmen; but the polarisation of certain classes of society into mutually hostile religious communities is at the very heart of the problem, and the churches must bear a considerable responsibility.

Masked against tear gas, a Belfast youth hurls a missile at police in the Falls Road, a predominantly Catholic area of the city.

This religious divide is, in its turn, conditioned by the second element: the weight of history. The often-brutal assertion of English rule over Ireland; the importation of Protestantism and Protestant settlers; the long struggle for Home Rule during the 19th century; and the bloody episodes from 1916 until the partition which created two Irelands after World War I – all these events left subsequent generations in Northern Ireland trapped in a web of tradition, sentiment and fear which prevented the development of a common identity between the Protestant and Catholic communities, particularly in the cities. By the late 1960s, Northern Ireland had a large Catholic minority which was still politically and economically disadvantaged.

Many of these disadvantages were officially removed in 1969, when discrimination in housing and employment was declared illegal, and Catholic political representation was guaranteed. But three factors combined to nullify the effects of these reforms and to start the spiral of violence. To begin with, Protestants took to violence against the Catholic community and against the state; the simple demand for civil rights for Catholics became linked to a more revolutionary programme of left-wing activists; and the Provisional IRA was formed.

Role of the Provos

The 'Official' IRA (Irish Republican Army), which had played such an important role in the events of the first third of the century, had begun to lose any widespread influence by the mid-1960s. It had become dominated by Marxists, and was unwilling to involve itself in sectarian conflict between what it saw as members of the same working class. But in 1969, under the threat of Protestant violence, a new IRA emerged in the northern cities: the Provisional IRA, known as the Provisionals or simply the Provos. The defensive intentions of this group soon merged into the more general hope for a united Ireland, and it became one of the most effective terrorist groups in western Europe, involving the British Army in a long and bitter campaign.

The Provisionals had two great advantages: their ability to obtain arms and money abroad, and their ability to operate across the border with the Irish Republic where, in spite of governmental opposition, they have many sympathisers. The amount of support the Provisionals enjoy in the Catholic community of the north is problematical. With their access to large sums of money and arms, they can be effective with a relatively small core of active support. The range of passive support is wide; it extends from those who feel sympathetic to their aims to those who dare not run the risk of reprisals, which taking a stand or helping the police would entail.

Funding is no problem for the IRA. A wealth of sympathetic but ill-informed opinion exists in the United States. Irish communities in Canada, Australia and New Zealand have similarly contributed. Yet all along the Southern Irish government has strongly discouraged fund raising in the republic and abroad.

Besides contributions, the Provisionals raise cash from armed robbery, protection rackets, fraud, blackmail and extortion. It costs the IRA something in the region of £500,000 a year to operate, and it is estimated that over the 1975–77 period more than £2.5 million was stolen for Republican ends.

ABOVE *The face of IRA power: masked gunmen stop a post office van in a 'no-go' area of Londonderry.* BELOW *A soldier falls to the ground as his patrol is pelted by rioters.*

Deaths in Ulster 1969–80

Year	RUC	Army and UDR	Civilian	Total
1969	1	0	12	13
1970	2	0	23	25
1971	11	48	115	174
1972	17	129	322	468
1973	13	66	171	250
1974	15	25	166	206
1975	11	20	216	247
1976	23	29	245	297
1977	14	29	69	112
1978	10	21	50	81
1979	14	48	51	113
1980	9	16	50	75
Total	140	431	1490	2061

But the depth of subversion can be best measured by the protection rackets which daily affect the lives of a significant proportion of the wealth-producing population of Belfast. Businessmen were first approached in the early 1970s: if they refused payment their staffs or their premises were threatened. Because of the seriousness of unemployment, the authorities in fact prefer a company to pay up and to continue in business, rather than to be bombed to a standstill or to have a workforce so cowed that it prefers to stay at home.

One of the most effective measures used to attract attention is the hunger strike. In 1916 Terence McSwiney died on hunger strike in jail. In 1920 Thomas Ashe determined on the same fate. In the present troubles Dolours and Marian Price, convicted for their part in London bombing activities, embarked upon such a strike in 1974 on the orders of the Republican movement. They gave up before death; but great propaganda was made of the deaths in 1974 of Michael Gaughan and in 1976 of Frank Stagg. In the republic, too, IRA prisoners have pursued the same course in Portlaoise jail. In 1981 the hunger-strike weapon was renewed when six republican prisoners at the Maze prison starved themselves to death. Despite winning world-wide publicity for their actions, the strikers were unsuccessful in gaining their objective of political status for republican prisoners.

The phases of violence

Looking back to the mid-1960s, four principal phases may be discerned in the political violence, but the phases superimpose themselves, building up into a complex terrorist phenomenon.

During the years immediately before the outbreak of communal violence in 1968 Protestant extremism operated in the ugly form of the Ulster Volunteer Force, which terrorised Catholic residents of Belfast from 1966. It was fear of reform masked by religious bigotry that drove the lower orders of Protestantism to violence in defence of privilege.

Tension rose throughout 1968. In January 1969 Protestants attacked a march by the People's Democracy group from Belfast to Londonderry. Further clashes followed as police entered the Bogside, Londonderry. For six days Stormont MP John Hume organised the local inhabitants into a Bogside police force to protect property, whilst the community utterly rejected the Royal Ulster Constabulary (RUC) as a force which could or should impartially uphold law. In early 1969 army units were made available for the first time to guard key installations from Protestant sabotage attacks.

The second phase can be detected in the sectarian disturbances that summer in Londonderry, Lurgan, Dungannon, Newry, Strabane, Omagh, Dungiven and Belfast. The capital experienced its worst riots for 30 years. A peace-line was erected between the two communities in the city centre to keep them apart. Barricades had been thrown up, shops looted, windows broken, cars overturned and burned. Gang fought gang, marchers fought marchers. From the communal violence grew the sectarian violence of paramilitary groups, which indiscriminately shot and killed citizens from across the religious divide.

As the army had been drafted in to keep the peace, it became the target for both sides and the friend of no-one. The campaign escalated in 1971 into a third phase with the murder of off-duty soldiers, attacks upon the homes of RUC members, gunfire from passing cars, gelignite bombings and the detonation of mines on country roads. Rocket launchers appeared that year in September. Letter bombs were first used in April 1973, followed shortly after by parcel bombs mailed to senior civil servants. This was war between the IRA and the security forces; and yet the Protestant paramilitaries only took a back seat from 1977, thanks to successful police ground work leading to convictions.

The most recent and fourth phase of the Ulster imbroglio is the European dimension, which grew from earlier international links and which could prove as intractable to solve as the political problem in the north. The IRA early established links with the Basque nationalists of ETA and Breton separatists, and had meetings with the Baader-Meinhoff groups. So far, this aspect has not been critical, however; Northern Ireland is a very specific terrorist war.

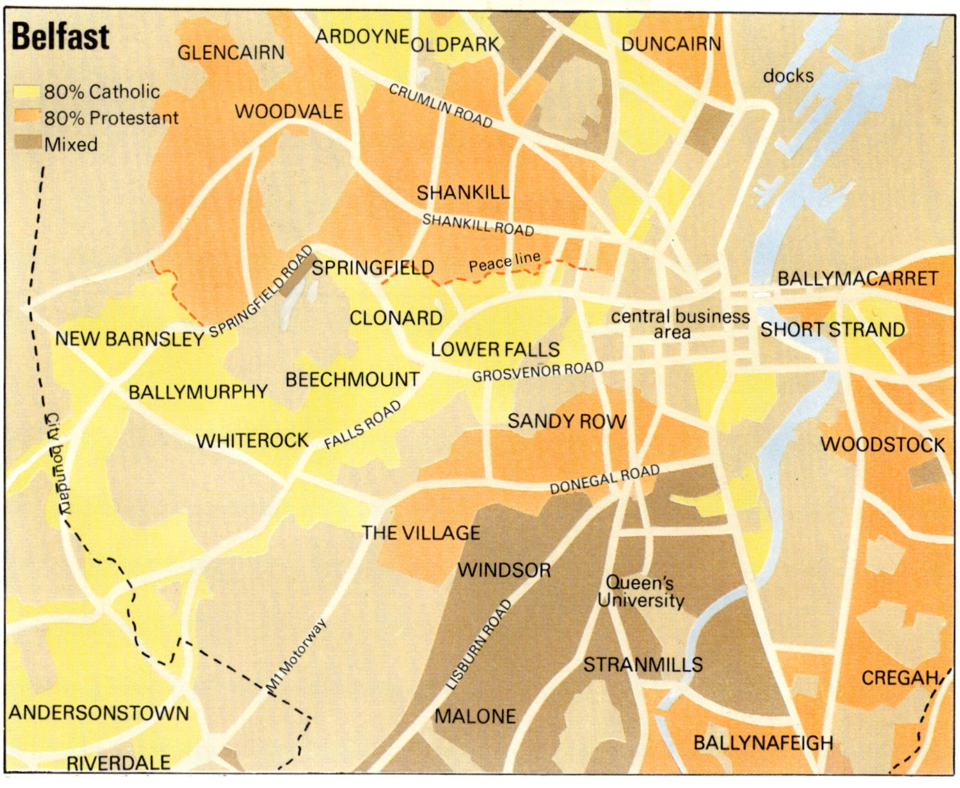

Army Tactics

AT HOME in Northern Ireland the British Army has been involved in peace-keeping duties since April 1969, when the first contingent of 500 troops was flown in to guard public installations such as reservoirs and electricity stations from Protestant sabotage attacks. In August that year 600 troops arrived in Belfast and established a 'peace-line', which separated the warring factions of Protestants and Catholics.

But by the end of that summer 7500 troops were on duty, and the role had changed from peace-keeping to one of active involvement in containing terrorism. In April 1970 it was decided that the permanent garrison should include five infantry battalions and an armoured car regiment. At this time the Ulster Defence Regiment undertook its first operational duties.

Fluctuating troop levels

To cope with the Orange marches, in July 1970 a further 3000 troops were drafted in. The force level was kept under continuous review and reduced to 6000 at the end of the year. By mid-1971 there were again some 14,000 troops in Ulster, but the level reached its peak in 1972, when Operation Motorman required a force of 21,000 in the province.

Shortly after midnight on 31 July, troops in 100 armoured vehicles preceded by Centurion tanks fitted with bulldozer blades, swept into the 'no-go' areas of Belfast and Londonderry. As the barricades were lowered there were few casualties, for the IRA backed down from outright confrontation with the military. The gunmen in Londonderry, including the Provisionals' leader, Martin McGuinness, crossed the border into Donegal. Those in Belfast went south to Dundalk, Drogheda and Portlaoise.

Thereafter the army reverted to low-intensity operations. Its strength by 1980 had been gradually reduced to 12,000 men, performing mobile and static tasks in a much-reduced area. The policy has been to return as much of the province as possible to the control of the Royal Ulster Constabulary (RUC), so that today the counties of Londonderry, Antrim and Down are very largely controlled by the RUC. The military presence remains on hand in Armagh, Fermanagh and Tyrone, with maximum military involvement in and around Belfast and Londonderry city and on the border in the southern rural area of Armagh.

Picking up a suspect

Stage 1
Car stopped at army checkpoint

Stage 2
Patrol checks driver's driving licence to establish identity. Car number and driver's identity radioed through to HQ for checking

Stage 3
While check is being made, patrol inspects bonnet and boot of car

Stage 4
If any suspicions aroused, more thorough search of car and occupants made

Stage 5
Any information on suspect or car radioed back to patrol

Stage 6
If any irregularity, suspect arrested

Stage 7
Should army want to interview suspect, suspect taken to army barracks where he can be held for up to 4 hours. After that if any further interrogation is required he is handed over to the RUC

Stage 8
If he has been arrested in connection with a police matter he will be taken to a police station and normal legal proceedings are then invoked

LEFT *The army moves in to seal off a Belfast street after a car-bomb explosion.* INSET *Troops conduct a search in the Shankill Road, Belfast, in October 1969 after a night of shooting in which three people were killed.* OPPOSITE BOTTOM *Troops fire tear gas grenades in Belfast in 1979.*

Mobile framework operations involving the routine checking of vehicles and people are carried on around the clock, using foot patrols, vehicles and helicopters. Static tasks include guard duties at power stations, docks and oil terminals, and surveillance from prominent and well-guarded urban observation posts. The army continues to collect intelligence (all of which the RUC collates), and undertakes operations in response to specific information.

Where the police have little or no expertise the army plays a specialist role. Obvious examples are air reconnaissance and photography. But it remains policy that the central role in security operations belongs to the police, with the army playing a supportive one. Even in this area it is hoped that the Ulster Defence Regiment, a part-time force, will assume increasingly broader and more effective duties.

Relations between the police and the military have not been easy over the years. At first the army imagined it could return the province to normality swiftly, without regard for or use of the police. There was no co-operation on the intelligence level between the one and the other. Gradually it was realised that the police had an essential role to play, in detection, in achieving convictions and in building bridges across the religious divide.

A further problem between the two forces was the type and personality of top army commanders and top police officers. Both excellent in their respective duties but very different from each other, they tended to compete rather than co-operate. Today the RUC is a young force armed when necessary with high-velocity weapons and using armoured vehicles. A Special Patrol Group operates in Belfast and Londonderry round the clock for saturation patrolling. Its members are volunteers, and much of their success in detecting terrorists derives from training which concentrates on facial identification.

Border patrols

In the Armagh border area the police are still rejected by the population and the army finds itself operating in a region in full rebellion against the crown. In every respect it is IRA territory. The military is reluctant to take visitors at all into the area. Transport by air is the safest and most frequently used method. The roads have been mined, with the most appalling consequences on military life and limb. Over the period 1969 to 1980 some 3000 soldiers have been wounded and in all more than 400 have died. Police losses amounted to only one-third of that figure, but they suffered many more injuries.

On the border both the RUC and the military co-operate with their opposite numbers in the republic. The majority of raids are planned in the republic and launched from there, so that joint border patrolling is essential. Until recently co-operation has not been all that it might have been, but today the republic spends considerably more on the anti-terrorist fight with marked results. Over 150 IRA terrorists are serving time in the republic's prisons. It is generally thought that the Provisionals can still count upon some 300 adherents, who are better organised than before and more aware of security.

Invasion of Afghanistan

The Soviet invasion of this backward Moslem country provoked a world-wide outcry

Michael Orr

THE SOVIET INVASION of Afghanistan in December 1979 was the first time since World War II that Soviet troops had intervened in a country which had not previously been considered part of the Soviet bloc. Some commentators saw it as an act of imperialist aggression, reminiscent of tsarist days. Others have considered the move a defensive measure to protect the long-standing but crumbling Soviet interest in Afghanistan.

The Russians' interest in Afghanistan dates back to the middle of the 19th century, when the tsarist empire was absorbing the ancient states of Central Asia. Britain, ever concerned for the safety of India, tried to impose a friendly government by force and two attempts to do so ended in disaster in 1840 and 1880. Once it was clear that the Russians did not intend to occupy Afghanistan, the British were content to leave it as a somewhat prickly neutral, although the constant guerrilla war with the border tribesmen flared into open warfare in 1919. This Third Afghan War led to the first Soviet interest in the country. The new Soviet state sent subsidies to King Amanullah and continued to back the anti-British and reforming king.

The year 1953 is a key date in Afghan history: the king's cousin, Mohammad Daoud Khan, seized power as prime minister, and in Russia Stalin died. Daoud was comparatively liberal and wanted to modernise Afghanistan. He asked for aid from the Soviet Union, which was eagerly granted.

Daoud hoped to benefit from both the capitalist and socialist blocs, and at first the United States competed with the Soviet Union in supplying economic aid. By the 1960s, however, America had decided that Afghanistan was not important and the country became dependent on Soviet aid. Daoud thought it was essential to preserve a neutral stance between the two superpowers and so he resigned in 1963.

Meanwhile a number of left-wing parties came into existence which were generally known by the names of the newspapers they published. The most important of the parties was Khalq ('The People'), led by Nur Mohammad Taraki. In 1967 Khalq split into two, with the breakaway faction, under Babrak Kamal, publishing the newspaper *Parcham* ('Banner') in 1968. The Parcham faction was more pro-Soviet than Khalq.

The April Revolution

In July 1973 Daoud returned to power in a coup which toppled both king and government. In 1978 Khalq and Parcham united to oppose Daoud and on 27 April, in an army-led coup, Daoud and 30 members of his family were killed.

This was the so-called April Revolution which brought Khalq to power with Taraki as president. At first Taraki included the Parcham faction in his government, but after a year the two parties split again. It seems unlikely that the Soviets instigated the April coup but they supported Taraki with

Nur Mohammad Taraki (BELOW LEFT) *became Afghanistan's president in the wake of the April Revolution of 1977. Hafizullah Amin* (BELOW CENTRE) *was president at the time of the invasion. After the Soviet intervention the Russians replaced him with Babrak Kamal* (BELOW RIGHT). BOTTOM *A Soviet soldier stands guard at an Afghan highway checkpoint. He is armed with a Kalashnikov AKM, the improved version of the AK47.*

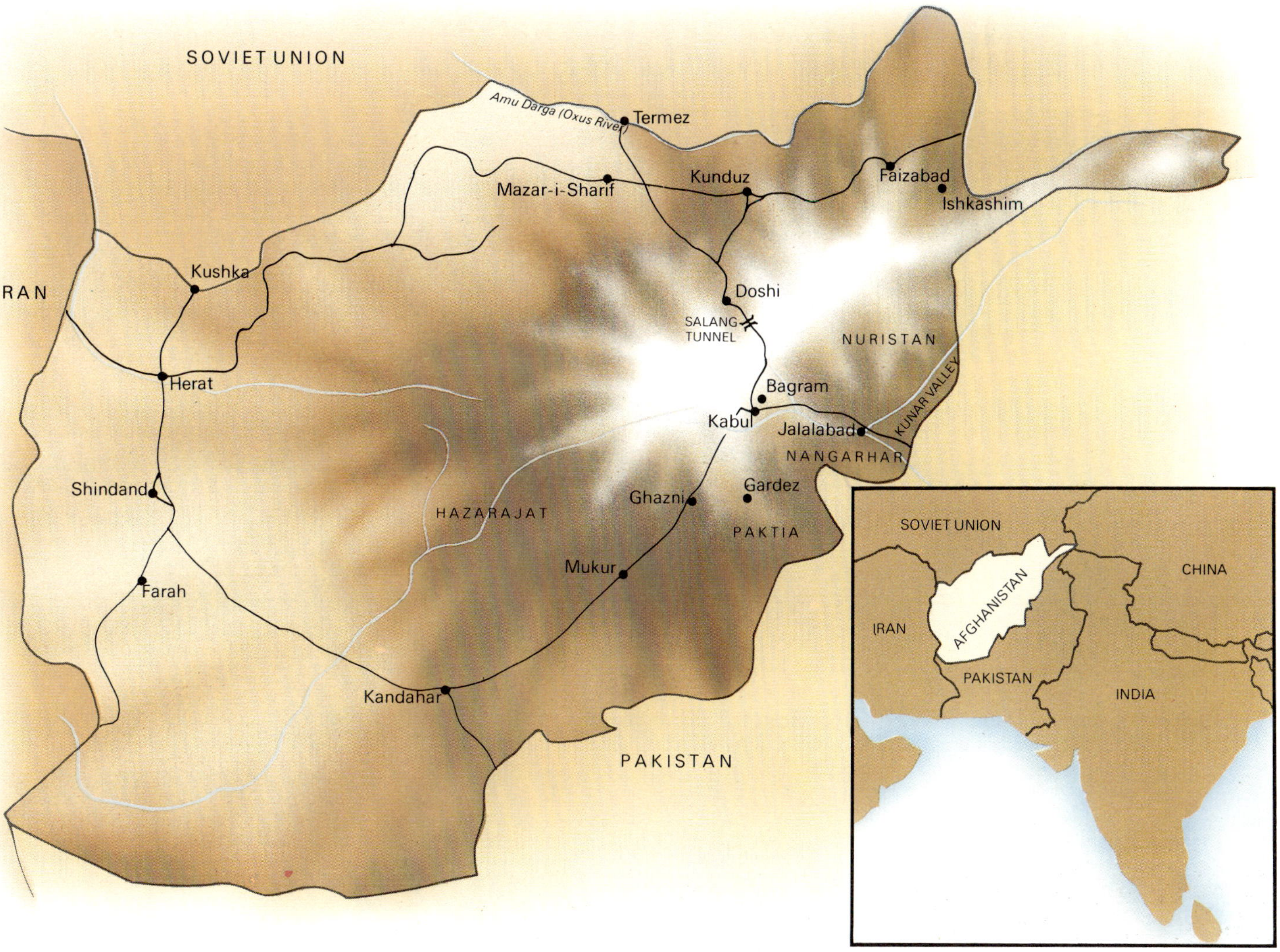

financial aid and thousands of 'advisers' in every field of Afghan life.

The new government introduced a sweeping programme of reform, designed to make Afghanistan a 20th-century state. Land was redistributed and peasant debts to the big landowners were cancelled. Attempts were made to emancipate women and abolish the system of dowries and arranged marriages. Many of these measures were forced through too quickly. The peasants had depended on loans from the landowners to buy seed and tools and these were no longer forthcoming, so the rural economy collapsed. Female emancipation did not please Moslem majority opinion. No real attempt was made to explain the reforms to the mass of the population, which was almost entirely uneducated, fiercely Moslem, suspicious of any government, and in particular suspicious of atheistic Soviet Marxism. The result was inevitable.

Open rebellion began in east Afghanistan, along the Kunar Valley north of Jalalabad. By April 1979 most of Afghanistan's provinces were in a state of rebellion. The government controlled the towns, but the most inaccessible parts of eastern and central Afghanistan were in the hands of insurgent groups. Government repression filled the prisons with political detainees. Hafizullah Amin became prime minister in March, proving himself the driving force behind reform and the suppression of opposition.

In the West there was little reaction to these developments but the Soviet Union was alarmed by the course of events after the revolution. Moslem insurgency in Afghanistan began just after the overthrow of the shah of Iran in January 1979. Islamic fundamentalism and resistance to change disturbed Moscow for two reasons. Firstly, it threatened the Soviets' influence within the Moslem world. Secondly, the Soviet Union has a large and growing Moslem population which might be disturbed by the Islamic revival. In particular the population of Soviet Central Asia has racial and linguistic as well as religious ties with the tribes of northern Afghanistan.

Soviet concern

The Soviet Union's reaction to the growing insurgency in Afghanistan was therefore to try to damp it down as quickly as possible. It supplied modern arms to the Afghan Army and Air Force and sent several thousand advisers to train and direct the armed forces. At the same time it seems to have favoured a moderate pace of reform within Afghanistan which was not acceptable to hard-liners such as Amin. Soviet concern grew as the anger of the Afghan resistance was increasingly concentrated on the Soviet presence.

Armed intervention was the Soviet Union's last resort. In September, Taraki stopped off in Moscow while returning from Havana. It is generally believed that he was persuaded to dismiss or demote Amin and introduce more moderates into his government. Amin must have got wind of the plot, and he struck first. On 14 September Taraki was attacked in the presidential palace and fatally wounded. He died on 17 September. Preparations for intervention were advanced.

The call-up of Soviet reserves began by mid-December. It seems probable that the Russians hoped that Amin would endorse the invasion and agree to make way for Babrak Kamal and more moderate policies. But Amin refused to co-operate and the Soviet invasion took place without invitation.

The Soviets were surprised by the strength of America's reaction. President Jimmy Carter asked Congress to postpone ratification of the SALT 2 treaty on arms limitation, he restricted the sale of grain and high technology to the Soviet Union and asked for a boycott of the Moscow Olympic Games. He also announced that America would improve her capability to intervene in the area, in case the Soviet Union tried to move from Afghanistan towards the vital oil-producing regions of the Persian Gulf.

The Soviets probably hoped that they would be accepted within Afghanistan as saving the country from the rigours of the Amin regime. However, they overlooked the Afghans' traditional hatred for foreign interference. Babrak Kamal was promptly installed as president, introduced moderate measures and released thousands of political prisoners. Nevertheless, he is regarded as a Soviet puppet by most Afghans and his government has won little allegiance.

The Soviet Intervention

SOVIET PREPARATIONS for the invasion of Afghanistan may have begun in the spring of 1979, although the final decision to invade was probably not taken until December. The operation followed conventional Soviet doctrine and has many similarities with the invasion of Czechoslovakia in 1968. Some reconnaissance and planning was probably done by General Ivan Pavlovsky during his visit to Afghanistan from August to October. There were also about 4000 Soviet military advisers in Afghanistan who could provide up-to-date intelligence about the country and the Afghan armed forces.

The forces involved in the invasion came from the Turkestan and Central Asian Military Districts. Soviet divisions in these districts are normally at a low state of readiness and little more than cadre strength. It was therefore necessary to recall civilian reservists to raise these formations to full strength. These reservists came from Turkestan and Central Asia and many of them were from the same religious and racial background as the northern Afghans. The mobilisation began in early December and may have involved as many as 100,000 men. The 40th Army headquarters based in Termez, on the Afghan border, was in local control but a satellite link enabled Moscow to supervise operations. It is believed that General Sergei Sokolov, a First Deputy Minister of Defence, was in overall command.

Lieutenant General Viktov Paputin was sent to Kabul on 2 December. Theoretically his mission was to advise Hafizullah Amin, the Afghan president, on internal security, but it is generally believed that his real objective was to persuade Amin to make way for Babrak Kamal and ensure that the Soviet Union was formally invited to send troops to Afghanistan's aid, in accordance with the Soviet-Afghan Treaty of December 1978.

RIGHT *Soviet soldiers on patrol in Kabul.* BELOW *Tank transporters rumble through the streets. The Soviet presence was strongly resented by many sections of the population, and even school children rioted in protest at the imposition of the new order. Yet Soviet control of the towns was largely secure; it was in the mountains that problems most often occurred.*

The first combat troops to enter Afghanistan came from the 105th Guards Airborne Division. An advance party were flown to Bagram military airfield, just north of Kabul, which they had secured by 24 December. The Afghans were probably expecting Soviet troops to assist them in the war against the tribal rebels. It has also been reported that Soviet advisers neutralised many Afghan Army units by persuading them that they were about to be re-equipped from the Soviet Union. The Afghans were tricked into disarming their tanks in preparation for recovery to Russia after the new equipment arrived.

On 25 and 26 December the main body of the 105th Guards Airborne Division, consisting of at least two regiments and supporting troops, in all about 5000 men, arrived at Bagram. This involved 280 missions by Ilyushin Il-76, Antonov An-22 and An-12 transport aircraft. The crucial day was 27 December. In the evening Soviet paratroopers in BMD armoured personnel carriers moved into Kabul and secured key points. Other units, backed by ASU-85 airborne assault guns, moved to surround the Darulaman Palace on the outskirts of the capital. Paputin had persuaded Amin to move there only a few days before, to guarantee his safety against disturbances in Kabul.

It is not clear what happened next. Paputin tried to persuade Amin to stand down. Amin refused and it is possible that one of his bodyguards shot Paputin. The Soviet paratroopers attacked the palace, which was defended by an Afghan tank regiment. Amin was killed in the fighting. This was disastrous for the Soviets because it made a nonsense of their claim that the Afghan government had asked for their help.

Arrival of ground troops

Soviet ground troops were already advancing into Afghanistan. The 357th and 66th Motor Rifle Divisions crossed the border at Kushka and occupied Kandahar and Herat in the west. The 360th and 201st Motor Rifle Divisions crossed from Termez, where a pontoon bridge had been built across the Amu Darya (the Oxus River). Paratroopers were pushed north from Kabul to secure the Salang tunnel, through which the 360th and 201st Divisions had to pass. The divisions travelled with their full complements of tanks, APCs, artillery and missiles and were given air cover by MiG-21 and MiG-23 fighter-bombers operating from bases in the Soviet Union.

In some places Afghan Army units resisted the invaders. The 8th Afghan Division is said to have fought particularly hard and over 2000 Afghans were reported killed during the invasion. However, most of the Afghan Army allowed itself to be disarmed by the Soviet troops. In the days after the invasion desertion from the 80,000-strong Afghan Army may have exceeded 40,000. Most of the deserters went home but some joined the Moslem freedom-fighters.

By the middle of January up to two more Soviet divisions, the 16th and 54th Motor Rifle, had entered Afghanistan and 40th Army headquarters had moved to Kabul. The Soviet troops were deployed along the circuit of the main road, holding the towns and strategic points such as bridges and the Salang tunnel. With the collapse of the Afghan Army, Soviet troops came into direct contact with the guerrillas, but operations were limited by winter conditions.

As the years have passed, the Soviet Army has settled in as an army of occupation. Its strength has risen to around 80,000 men with a further 30,000 stationed north of the border. While the guerrillas have scored isolated successes against Russian and Afghan government forces, the Soviet Army remains in control of the key urban areas.

TOP *An Antonov transport at Kabul airport.* ABOVE *A poster advertises flights to Moscow for the 1980 Olympic Games, which became a target for Western retaliation after the invasion.* BELOW *A T54 moves along one of Afghanistan's few efficient roads.*

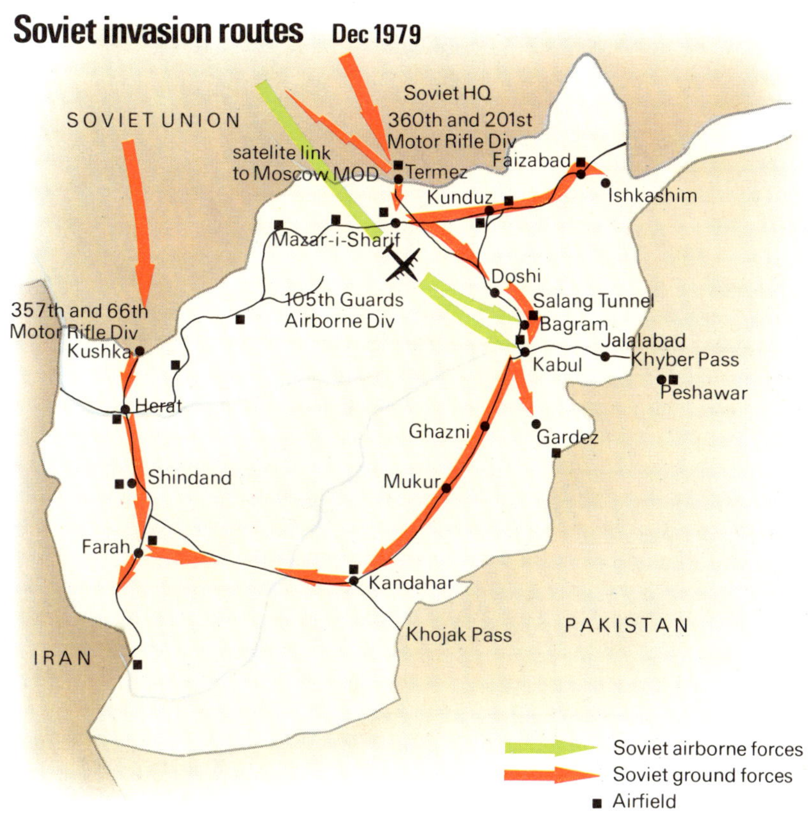

Moslem Guerrillas

THE AFGHANS have long been regarded as natural guerrilla fighters. At the best of times the government has a very loose hold on the country outside the towns, and ethnic and tribal loyalties are most important. Most Afghans carry weapons, they are naturally good shots and the tradition of the blood feud provides excellent training in ambushes and hit-and-run raids.

It is therefore not surprising that resistance to the Marxist regime began soon after the April Revolution of 1978. The government was trying to introduce strict central control of Afghan life and to modernise it, which threatened the Afghan's liberty, religion and his whole way of life. Resistance began among ethnic minorities and tribal confederations and by its very nature it lacked co-ordination.

Afghanistan is ideal country for guerrilla warfare, particularly in the mountains of the centre and north-east. The long border with Pakistan is almost impossible to police because of the number of tracks known only to locals. The border has provided a sanctuary, although Pakistan is determined not to become an active guerrilla base. By early 1979 the government had lost control of most of these inaccessible areas. The guerrillas were particularly strong in the eastern provinces of Paktia, Nangarhar and Nuristan, the central Hazarajat region and around Herat near the border with Iran in the west.

Tactics of defiance

Shortly after their arrival the Soviets imposed a night curfew in the towns. This was defied by many and soon after the fall of darkness Kabul and the other cities echoed with cries of 'Allahu akbar' ('God is great') from the roof-tops. In the morning crudely printed leaflets, the so-called 'night letters' or *shabnama*, would be scattered in the streets. The night letters called for a general strike, which began in Kabul on 21 February 1980. Most of the shops in the bazaars were closed and on the 22nd thousands of Afghans demonstrated in the streets, chanting anti-Soviet slogans. Soviet and Afghan troops moved in to disperse the demonstrators and in the fighting which followed up to 300 civilians were killed. Strikes also occurred in the other major towns but were ended after a few days. In May

The most reliable weapons used by the Moslem guerrillas (also known as Mujahideen) are those captured or stolen from Soviet troops and the Soviet-supplied Afghan Army. ABOVE *A rebel band cleans its weapons.* BELOW *Guerrillas proudly display captured Soviet arms.* OPPOSITE TOP *Mujahideen pose on top of an abandoned armoured car.* OPPOSITE BOTTOM *Rebels in the mountains near the border with Pakistan.*

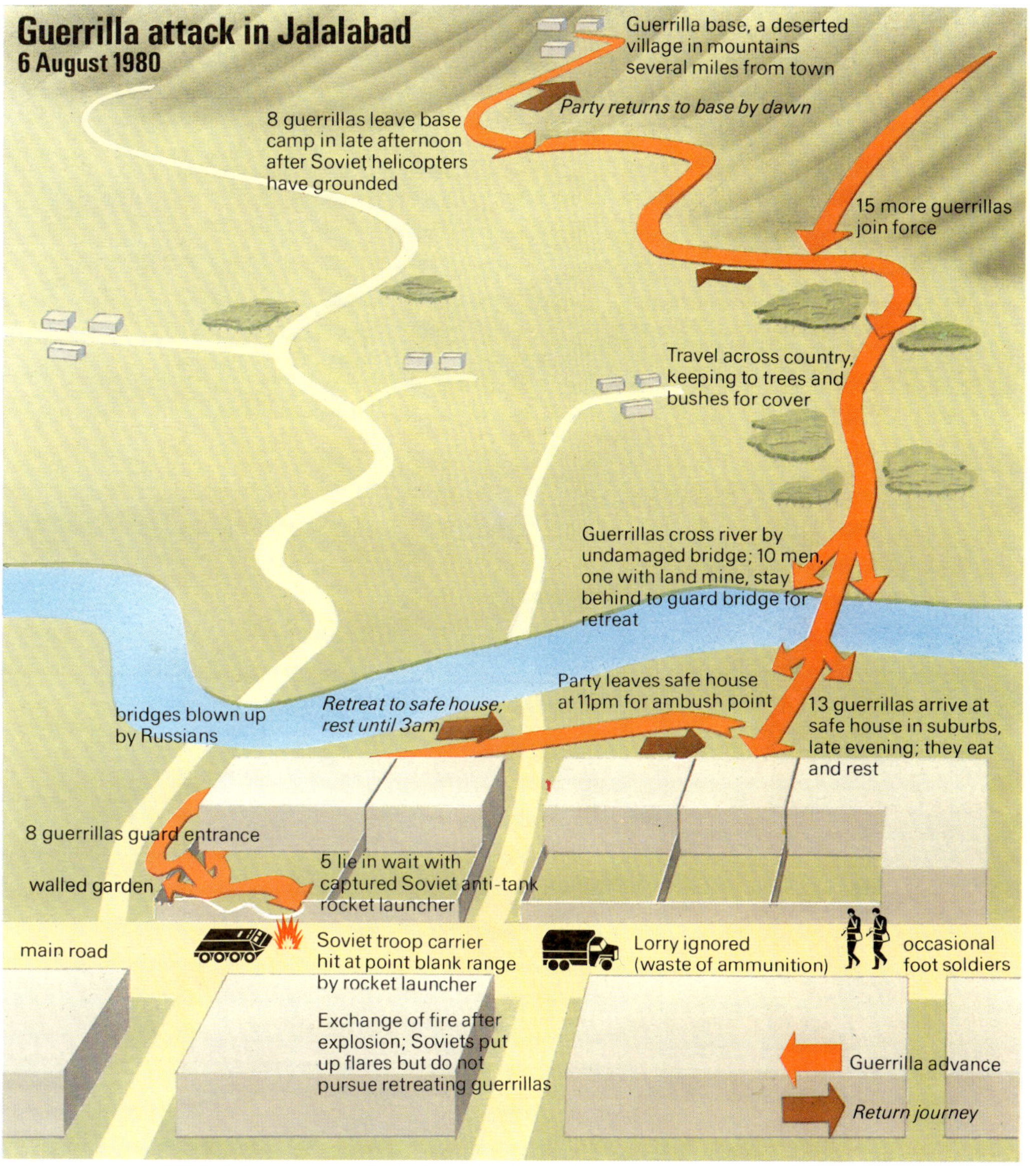

and June demonstrations by students and schoolgirls were broken up by the Afghan Army.

More violent resistance has followed traditional guerrilla lines. Soviet soldiers wandering alone around the towns have been killed with stones and knives. Such incidents are particularly damaging to morale. Elsewhere the guerrillas have concentrated on the roads and isolated military posts. In the narrow, winding valleys of Afghanistan there are many ideal sites for ambushes. A few men with a crowbar can lever out a boulder on the mountainside and start a land-slide which will block the road. Bridges and culverts can be mined or holes dug in the roads. Having stopped a column of vehicles the guerrillas wait for the troops to climb out of their armoured vehicles before opening fire. The guerrillas then vanish into the hills before the soldiers can deploy their full firepower. In the dark the guerrillas can keep outposts on the alert all night with just a few snipers, which wears down the soldiers' morale and fitness.

The guerrillas lack the co-ordination and weapons to make major attacks on military positions. For the same reason they have been very wary about trying to seize the main towns, although small groups often infiltrate the towns at night to terrorise government sympathisers or attack Soviet patrols.

Obstacles to insurgency

There are two basic weaknesses in the Afghan resistance. The first is the lack of co-ordination among the rival factions. The second is the shortage of modern weapons. Guerrilla bands use a bewildering variety of weapons. Some still carry jezails, the long muskets dating back over 100 years. The British Lee-Enfield rifle is still highly prized for its accuracy, although many Afghans carry beautifully made local copies of the rifle which lack its reliability. Through desertions and the capture of arms from the Afghan Army the AK47 Kalashnikov assault rifle is widely available. It is capable of a high rate of fire, but is a short-range weapon.

There are not enough small-arms for the guerrillas and the shortage of heavier weapons is even more acute. Some machine guns and mortars have been captured but ammunition is in short supply. The guerrillas really need modern, light-weight anti-tank and anti-aircraft missiles, which would even the odds against Soviet armoured fighting vehicles and helicopters. Proper mines would also be useful, instead of having to rely on explosive steamed from unexploded Russian bombs. Such weapons can only come from outside Afghanistan and have not been available in significant numbers.

Few analysts are prepared to predict the outcome. The Soviets do not have sufficient troops in Afghanistan to guarantee victory but it is likely that they could absorb the present rate of casualties for some time. (Soviet casualties are estimated as having been at least 5000 per year since 1980.) The guerrillas, on the other hand, lack the organisation and weapons to take on the Red Army in the open. A stalemate has developed, and there seems no way that it can be broken unless the Russians either quit Afghanistan or raise the military stakes.

Soviet Equipment

THE SOVIET ARMY has not yet developed special equipment and techniques for a counter-insurgency war. Therefore the Soviet forces in Afghanistan have been equipped and trained for conventional warfare, with some minor modifications to suit the Afghan terrain. The first Soviet combat troops to enter Afghanistan were from an airborne division. They arrived in transport aircraft of the Soviet Military Transport Aviation (VTA).

The VTA's basic aircraft are the Antonov An-12, the An-22 and the Ilyushin Il-76. The An-12 is a turboprop passenger and freight aircraft, which is now becoming somewhat dated. It can carry 100 troops or 20,000kg (44,000 pounds) of cargo (including light armoured vehicles) more than 3550km (2200 miles). It is being replaced by the Il-76, a four-engined jet with a maximum payload of 40,000kg (88,000 pounds) over a 5000km (3100-mile) range. The An-22 Antei is one of the world's largest aircraft and can carry 80,000kg (176,000 pounds) of freight over 5000km (3100 miles). It is well suited for tanks and missile carriers.

Soviet airborne troops have two specially designed armoured fighting vehicles which were particularly evident in Kabul in the first days of the invasion. The ASU-85 is an airborne assault gun with an 85mm anti-tank gun. Because of the limited traverse of the gun it is not well suited to street-fighting or mountain operations. The BMD is the only armoured personnel carrier in the world designed specifically for airborne troops. It has excellent firepower with a 73mm gun, three 7.62mm machine guns and a launch-rail for Sagger anti-tank missiles. Its armour is thin, however, and although it can carry an infantry section, most of the troops travel unprotected. A new version of the BMD was seen for the first time in Afghanistan. It is a command post vehicle and lacks the turret for the gun and missile launcher.

The Soviet motor rifle divisions in Afghanistan are equipped with T55 and T62 tanks. Early reports of the latest Soviet tanks, T64 and T72, have not been confirmed. The T55 and T62 are adequate for the task in Afghanistan, though they would be dated on a European battlefield. The Russians have used their tanks in groups of three or four, with infantry companies to picket the main roads and to escort convoys. The Soviet infantry in Afghanistan use the BTR60 and BMP APCs. The BTR60 is a wheeled APC with limited firepower, but the BMP is a tracked vehicle with better cross-country performance and a similar armament to the BMD.

Artillery weapons

The Soviets' range of artillery has given them a considerable advantage over the lightly equipped guerrillas. Many units in Afghanistan are still equipped with the M-38 122mm howitzer, a veteran of World War II. It is a towed weapon with a range of just under 12km (7 miles). The more modern D-30 is also available; it is another towed 122mm howitzer with a range in excess of 15km (9 miles). Soviet troops also have the new M-1973 152mm self-propelled gun, with an 18km (11-mile) range.

In mountain warfare mortars are one of the most useful weapons available. Their high trajectory makes

TOP *Soviet troops man field guns in typically inhospitable Afghan terrain.* ABOVE *Armoured personnel carriers have been widely employed to back up Russian tank divisions.* BELOW *The BMP infantry combat vehicle performs particularly effectively in Afghanistan's mountainous regions.*

them particularly suitable and they can also be broken down for man-packing over difficult country. The standard Soviet mortar is a 120mm weapon, but a 160mm mortar is often issued.

Most Soviet soldiers in Afghanistan carry the AKM assault rifle as their personal weapon. This is a 7.62mm calibre weapon, which is a modernised version of the AK47 widely used by the guerrillas. Some Soviet troops have been seen with the latest Soviet rifle, the AK74. Its 5.45mm bullet causes particularly unpleasant wounds.

Soviet air power has played a crucial part in operations in Afghanistan. MiG-21 and MiG-23 fighter-ground-attack aircraft have added to the firepower available and have used napalm bombs. However, there is little doubt that the most important Soviet weapon has been the helicopter. Transport helicopters such as the Mil Mi-8 have enabled Soviet infantry to be carried into the most inaccessible country. The Mil Mi-24 gunship has provided quickly reacting and devastating firepower. It can carry an infantry section and a mix of machine guns, rocket pods, missiles and bombs. It is greatly feared.

Soviet strategy

The basic Soviet operational technique has been to control the towns and roads. Large camps have been established outside the main towns to overawe the inhabitants. The roads have been protected by smaller bases, with sub-units of tanks and mechanised infantry guarding bridges and other key points. As conditions permit the Soviets, with what remains of the Afghan Army, have struck at the areas where the guerrillas are most active. The Kunar Valley, for example, was attacked in March and June 1980.

Soviet tactics in these operations would be familiar to British soldiers who served on the frontier in the last century. The main body, usually tanks and APCs, drive up a valley while artillery batteries occupy covering positions. Flank guards are sent along the crests of the ridges to prevent ambushes. Helicopters have greatly eased the laborious task of 'crowning the heights'. The guerrillas usually withdraw, leaving the Russians to carry out a 'scorched earth' policy of destroying villages and crops in the hope of starving the guerrillas into submission.

Owing to the volume of firepower used by the invaders, civilian casualties have been high. Irritant gases such as tear gas have been employed to clear the guerrillas out of their hideouts, but the use of lethal gases has not been confirmed.

ABOVE RIGHT *A Mil Mi-24 gunship (the Hind), with rocket pods and missiles underwing, on patrol over Afghanistan. A 12.7mm machine gun completes its armament.*

Equipment of the Soviet airborne forces

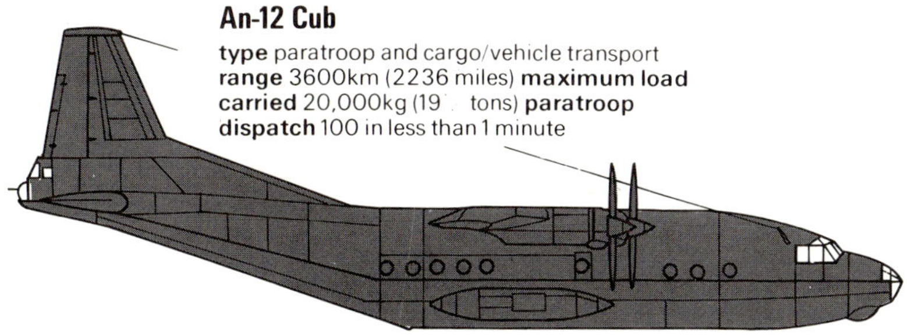

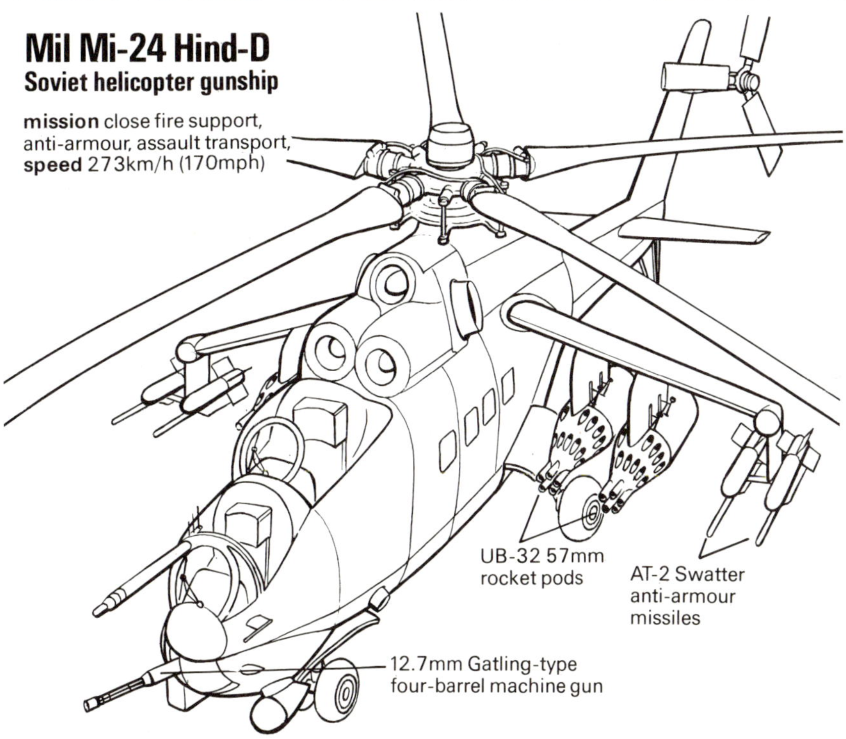

The Gulf War

In 1980 two rival Moslem states went to war and threw the Middle East into turmoil

Michael Orr

BELOW *The Ayatollah Khomeini embodies the new spirit of Islamic nationalism that has ruled Iran since 1979.* BOTTOM *Artillery in action near Kermanshah in Iran. Iraqi hopes of a swift victory quickly evaporated as the Iranian forces fought back doggedly.*

THE ORIGINS OF THE DISPUTE between Iran and Iraq go back centuries, but the causes of the war of 1980 are much more recent. Iran is the successor of the Persian Empire; Iraq was part of the former Turkish Empire. Until the 19th century the border between the two was badly defined but generally considered to run between the Mesopotamian flood plains and the higher ground of the Iranian plateau. In 1847 the Second Treaty of Erzurum gave Persia control of a triangle of land between the Shatt al Arab and the plateau which included the port of Khorramshahr and the island of Abadan. This area is now known as Khuzestan. Persia and Turkey continued to squabble about the exact border and control of navigation in the Shatt al Arab, and in 1937 a treaty fixed the river boundary along the eastern bank of the Shatt, except off Abadan and Khorramshahr, where it was to run along the deep-water channel in the middle of the river. The border quarrel continued, however, and in 1969 Iran abrogated the 1937 treaty and in the early 1970s hostility increased. The dispute was made fiercer by the fact that Khuzestan contains most of Iran's oil reserves although the original population was overwhelmingly Arab.

In 1975 the shah of Iran obtained concessions on the border issue from Iraq in the Treaty of Algiers. The deep-water channel became the boundary along the whole of the Shatt al Arab section and the land border was confirmed. In return the shah promised to withdraw his support for the Kurdish guerrillas in Iraq. The Kurds had been fighting for independence in north-east Iraq for several years but their resistance collapsed within a year of the treaty.

Revolution in Iran

Obviously the border question was a perpetual irritant but the immediate causes of the war are more concerned with the personal leadership of the two nations. In January 1979 the shah of Iran was driven out of the country. His authoritarian attempts to modernise Iran, exploiting the nation's vast oil wealth, had lost him the support of most Iranians. In the shah's place an Islamic republic was established, dominated by the clergy and particularly the Ayatollah Khomeini. He reacted against every form of Western influence and his Islamic fundamentalism alarmed most of his neighbours.

This was especially true of Iraq's leader, Saddam Hussein. His ruling Baathist Party follows a socialist and secular policy, far removed from Khomeini's ideals. Moreover the ruling clique in Iraq are members of the Sunni Moslem sect, while over half of the population follow the Shia sect to which Khomeini belongs. Saddam Hussein feared that Khomeini might export his revolution among the Shiite majority of Iraq. The two leaders have also loathed each other personally since Khomeini spent 14 years in exile in Iraq, under virtual house arrest. Saddam Hussein negotiated the Algiers Treaty on behalf of Iraq and its unfavourable terms no doubt still rankled.

The fall of the shah was followed by a purge of the Iranian government and armed forces to remove his supporters. Iran seemed to be falling into anarchy, with the nominal government of President Abolhassan Bani-Sadr unable to counter the real authority of Ayatollah Khomeini. Saddam Hussein probably considered that he would never have such a good opportunity to force concessions from Iran. He also hoped that an easy success against Iran would help him to assume the moral leadership of the Arab world which had been held by Egypt until President Anwar Sadat's peace treaty with Israel left him isolated.

Saddam Hussein therefore increased his grievances against Iran to include the shah's seizure in 1971 of three small islands, the Greater and Lesser Tumbs and Abu Musa, in the mouth of the Persian Gulf, which he hoped to restore to Arab rule. His other declared aims were to restore the Iran-Iraq border to the east bank of the Shatt al Arab and to reclaim some 500 square km (200 square miles) of desert further north which the Iranians were alleged to have occupied illegally since 1971.

The opposing forces

The balance of power in the gulf at the start of the war is not easy to assess. The shah had built impressive armed forces for Iran. The army possessed 875 Chieftain tanks and more than 800 American M48 and M60 tanks, with a range of British, American and Soviet support vehicles and artillery and over 600 helicopters. The air force had 188 F-4 Phantoms, 166 F-5 Tigers and 77 F-14 Tomcats. The navy was the largest and most modern in the gulf. All these weapon systems were dependent on the West for spares and maintenance, but since the revolution (and particularly the seizure of the American embassy in November 1979) the West had withdrawn its support for the Iranian armed forces. It was generally considered that no more than a third of the equipment of the army and air force was effective.

The Iraqi armed forces were mostly equipped with Soviet weapons. The army had 2500 T54 and T62 tanks, 50 of the latest T72s and about 1000 field guns. The air force had 332 combat aircraft, mostly MiG-21s and MiG-23s. The navy had a

number of Soviet-built missile-armed patrol boats. Generally Iraqi equipment was older than Iranian. Furthermore, relations between Iraq and the Soviet Union had cooled in recent years and Iraq could not be sure of re-supply.

During 1980 relations between Iran and Iraq grew steadily worse. Each encouraged subversive activity on the other side as both countries have Kurdish minorities ready to rise against the central government. The Iranian Army was drawn into a campaign in Iranian Kurdistan. Iraq trained Iranian Arabs to sabotage pipelines in Khuzestan. In April the Iraqi Deputy Prime Minister, Tariq Aziz, narrowly escaped assassination by Iranians. In July artillery fire was exchanged across the border and on 4 September the Iranians attacked the border villages of Khanquin and Zurbatiyah on the Baghdad road. This seems to have persuaded Saddam Hussein that he must act.

Iraq's offensive

The Iraqi attack began on 12 September with thrusts across the border. In the north the Iraqis made feints towards Mahabad but this was only designed to tie down Iranian forces in Kurdistan. In the centre a mechanised division captured Qasr-e-Shirin and blocked the passes out of the mountains. Its basic role seems to have been to forestall any Iranian counter-thrust along the Baghdad road. Further south a mountain division crossed the border near Mehran and occupied territory which Iraq claims is rightfully hers. One brigade thrust towards Ilam and another southwards towards Dezful.

The Iraqis made no real attempt to drive into the mountains. The most dramatic Iraqi gains were made in the south, where an armoured division swept eastwards from the Al Amarah-Basra road. The Iranians did not try to stop the Iraqi tanks in the open desert and the Iraqis made rapid progress until they approached the major towns of Dezful, Ahvaz and Khorramshahr. These first land moves were accompanied by Iraqi air strikes against targets throughout Iran, including Tehran airport.

It seems probable that Saddam Hussein expected that the air raids would start a civilian panic and that his early successes would be swiftly followed by the collapse of the Iranian government. He no doubt hoped for a new regime, probably military, which would see the need to make peace on the basis of Iraq's limited war aims. If so, it was a serious miscalculation. The war helped heal many of the divisions in Iranian society, and even in Khuzestan there was no upsurge against the Tehran government.

In the early stages the Iraqis used only three divisions (40,000 men) out of twelve in their army. Reinforcements were later poured down the Baghdad–Basra road until perhaps eight or nine divisions were committed to the war. The main Iraqi objectives were Khorramshahr, Abadan, Dezful and Ahvaz. Khorramshahr is Iran's main port and Abadan the largest oil refinery in the world; Dezful and Ahvaz are key points on the pipeline which supplies most of Iran's oil and are also important military bases.

At first the Iraqi attack concentrated on Khorramshahr. The town was held fanatically by small groups of Revolutionary Guards and the Iraqi armoured forces were ill-suited to house-to-house fighting. Only by destroying almost the whole city were the Iraqis able to capture Khorramshahr north of the Karun River. On 12 October they crossed the Karun onto Abadan Island, cutting the last road to Khorramshahr and isolating Abadan itself. A counter-attack by two Iranian battalions two weeks later was crushed and this marked the end of formal fighting in the area. Yet even in December the Iraqis had not crushed all resistance.

Further north the Iraqis did not try to assault Ahvaz and Dezful, preferring long-range bombardments. At first they by-passed the town of Susangerd, but during October the Iranian garrison there became a threat to their flank and rear which had to be eliminated. The other major Iraqi priority was building all-weather roads and flood embankments before the November rains could wash away the desert tracks and isolate the Iraqi front line. As winter closed in both sides seemed to have settled for a war of attrition and were building up their strength for the battles to come.

But 1981 brought few new developments and the military stalemate continued; it was not until 1982 that Iran felt confident enough to mount an offensive in the disputed Khorramshahr region. Although the Iranians were able to regain much of their territory, they failed to exploit this initial success. And while the balance of power now lies with the Iranians it is unlikely that they will be able to crush the Iraqis on the battlefield. A negotiated settlement seems the most likely outcome to the war.

Gains and Losses

THE IRAQI OBJECTIVE in starting the Gulf War was to win a quick but limited military victory, which would lead to public dissatisfaction in Iran with the Khomeini regime and its replacement by a new government prepared to negotiate a reasonable settlement to the border dispute. The international standing of Iraq and President Saddam Hussein would thus be increased and they would emerge as the dominant power in the Persian Gulf and possibly in the whole Arab world.

The tactics chosen to achieve this aim were a rapid advance across the desert by the ground forces to seize the disputed border areas and threaten, but not attack, the main towns in Khuzestan. Enemy strongpoints were to be by-passed and isolated. The Iraqis no doubt expected that if the Iranian Army did challenge battle in open country they would be too dispirited to fight effectively. Air strikes on targets throughout Iran were intended to cause civilian panic.

Iran holds firm

The Iraqis, however, underestimated their enemy. The Iranian government did not collapse, but was strengthened by the war. Although the Iraqis occupied territory they won no sweeping victories. The bulk of the Iranian Army withdrew intact to the eastern mountains, leaving stay-behind parties of regulars and Revolutionary Guards to engage the Iraqi forces. By October the Iraqis were on the outskirts of the cities of Dezful, Ahvaz and Khorramshahr and they were faced with a long, costly battle to capture them. At sea, patrol boats of both navies had clashed in the Shatt al Arab on 19/20 September and air strikes had been launched against the Iranian base of Khosrowabad and the Iraqi base at Khawr Abd Allah. Naval activity soon died away with neither side completely controlling the Shatt al Arab.

Thus the war quickly took on a peculiar character, with neither side making an all-out effort. The Iraqis were content to bombard the cities from a distance and seemed in no hurry to begin fighting within the cities or even to isolate them completely. The result has been considerable destruction within the towns and in the refinery complex at Abadan. The Iranians did not try to launch major counter-attacks. Neither air force made its presence felt over the battlefield, preferring to strike at airfields and economic installations such as refineries and pumping stations. The Iraqis may also have used some of their Frog and Scud surface-to-surface missiles against towns.

There are several reasons why the war should develop such a character. It is likely that Iraqi military doctrine is derived from Soviet sources and designed for a *blitzkrieg* attack in a European setting, where towns would be ignored as much as possible in order to maintain the speed of advance. There may well be weaknesses in the training of the Iraqi infantry and it is unlikely that junior leaders have the skill and initiative to operate freely in the confusion of house-to-house fighting. No doubt Saddam Hussein also wishes to minimise casualties for political reasons, preferring to spend artillery shells rather than lives. When the Iraqis were finally forced to begin fighting through Khorramshahr they showed little aptitude, clearing the town in an inefficient manner and leaving pockets of fanatical resistance which gave trouble for days after they should have been subdued.

RIGHT *Iranian M60 tanks near Shiraz.* BELOW *Ebullient Iraqi troops celebrate a successful encounter on the banks of the Shatt al Arab.*

There has been little fighting between armoured units, although the Iraqis have captured a considerable quantity of abandoned tanks and other vehicles. The Iranians have made effective use of their attack helicopters, the AH-1 Cobra, employing classic tactics – using dead ground, 'popping-up' for the briefest possible time to engage a target and dodging behind cover again. The Cobras were particularly effective around Susangerd and Dezful. However, the Iranians do not seem to have been able to co-ordinate operations at a higher level. This may be partly due to the purge of so many senior officers after the shah's fall in 1979. On the Iraqi side co-operation between the army and air force seems almost non-existent.

Another surprising feature is the number of aircraft that the Iranians have managed to keep operational. The strikes by Iranian Phantoms on Iraqi oil installations have been particularly threatening. Apparently the American airborne warning and control aircraft have seen no air-to-air combat, nor has any aircraft been lost to surface-to-air missiles. Anti-aircraft artillery and accidents have been responsible for the aircraft losses occurred. It is believed that the two air forces have kept away from battlefield support missions because of the impossibility of controlling their own anti-aircraft fire, but as the war drags on they have had to accept the need to take the risk.

It is possible that the Gulf War is the first of a new form of war in the Third World, where countries have been supplied with sophisticated equipment which it is beyond their skill to operate. Indeed one commentator has already attributed the indecisiveness of the war to the 'delicate balance of incompetence' on each side.

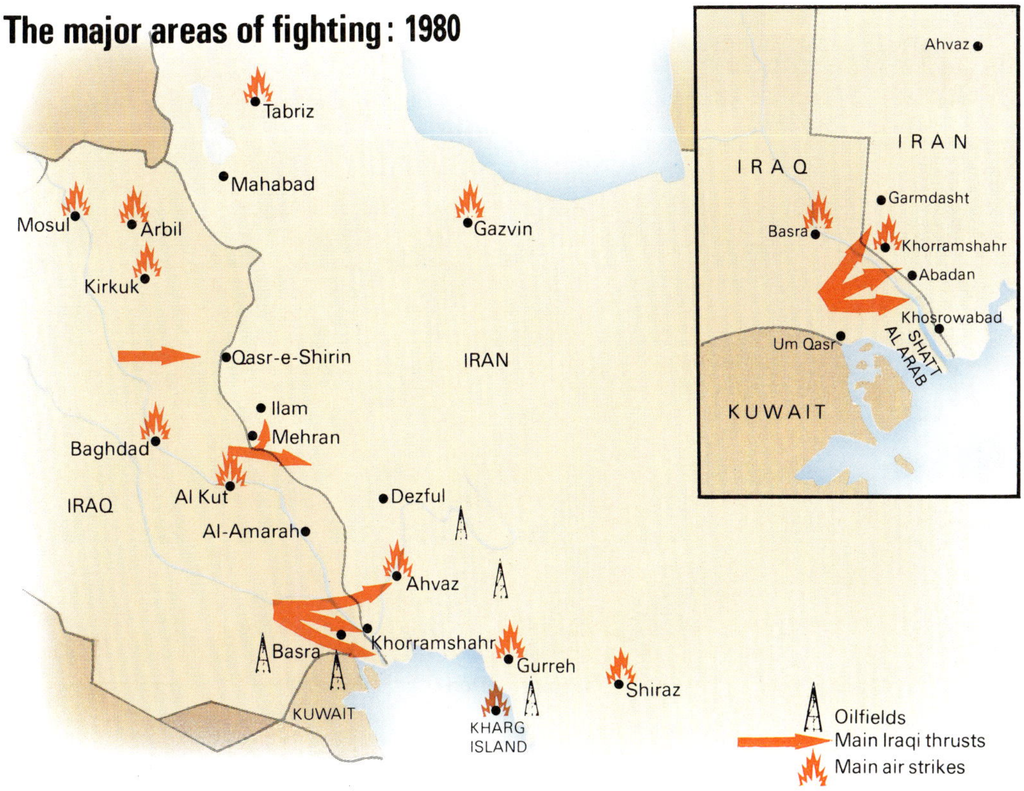

ABOVE *As the Iraqis pushed forward the refineries of Abadan were an early victim, which caused concern among Western oil importers.* RIGHT *Iraqi infantry armed with a rocket launcher during the fighting along the border.*

The Wider View

HELMUT SCHMIDT, former chancellor of West Germany, has compared the Persian Gulf of today to the Balkans before World War I as an unstable area which could involve the rest of the world in its crises. From the late 1970s the world's attention has been repeatedly drawn to this area. First came the overthrow of the shah of Iran in January 1979 and the Islamic terror which killed hundreds of people. In November the American embassy in Tehran was seized and the staff held as hostages. In December the Soviet invasion of Afghanistan was interpreted by some as a first step towards the gulf. The abortive American attempt to rescue the hostages in April 1980 continued the interest in the region. When the Iranian embassy in London was seized in May it was by terrorists demanding a 'Free Khuzestan'. In August there was speculation that the Iraqis were developing nuclear weapons with French assistance. Finally in September 1980 the war itself broke out.

Importance of oil

The reason for all this concern is oil. The countries bordering the Persian Gulf currently produce 16 million barrels of oil a day. This is 60 per cent of the world's oil imports and 35 per cent of the free world's oil consumption. To carry this oil, a hundred tankers a day pass through the narrow Strait of Hormuz at the entrance to the gulf.

The modern world is dependent on oil, not just as a fuel but also as a source of plastics, fertilizers and other chemicals. It is unlikely that this flow of oil would be stopped entirely but the price of oil is extremely sensitive to variations in supply and to any sort of instability which threatens that supply. The loss of most of Iran's production in 1979 caused world oil prices to double within the year. Such price rises are a major factor in the inflation which has so damaged the world economy in recent years. Many economists would say that these economic troubles in fact began with the steps taken by the Arab oil producers to raise prices and limit supplies in the aftermath of the 1973 Arab-Israeli War.

Reasons for instability

Why is the gulf so unstable? For one thing, there is no natural balance of power in the region. Iran is the largest state but has been in turmoil for the last two years. Iraq was for long a client of the Soviet Union and although Saddam Hussein is trying to

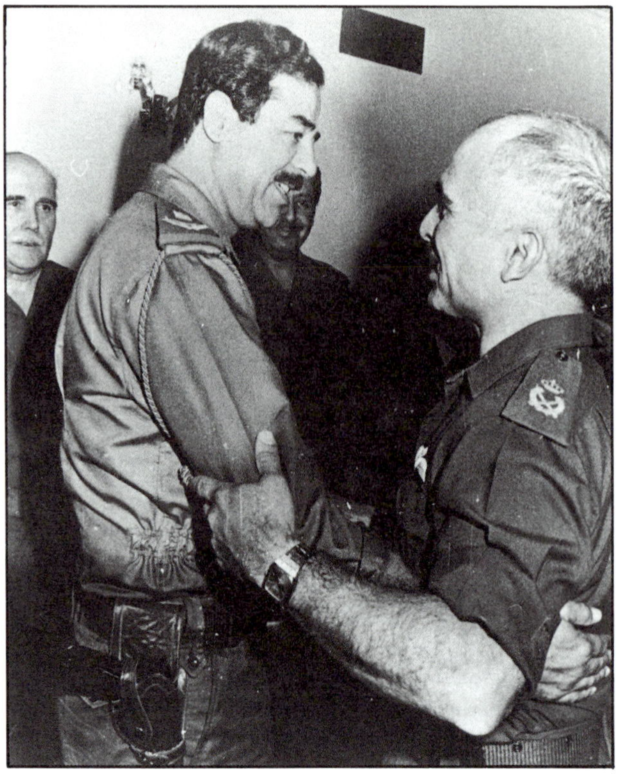

ABOVE *President Saddam Hussein of Iraq (left) is greeted by Jordan's King Hussein who arrived in Baghdad on 4 October 1980 to discuss the war against Iran.* BELOW *The arteries of the Western world: oil pipelines of the Middle East. Approximately 60 per cent of western Europe's oil comes from Middle East suppliers.*

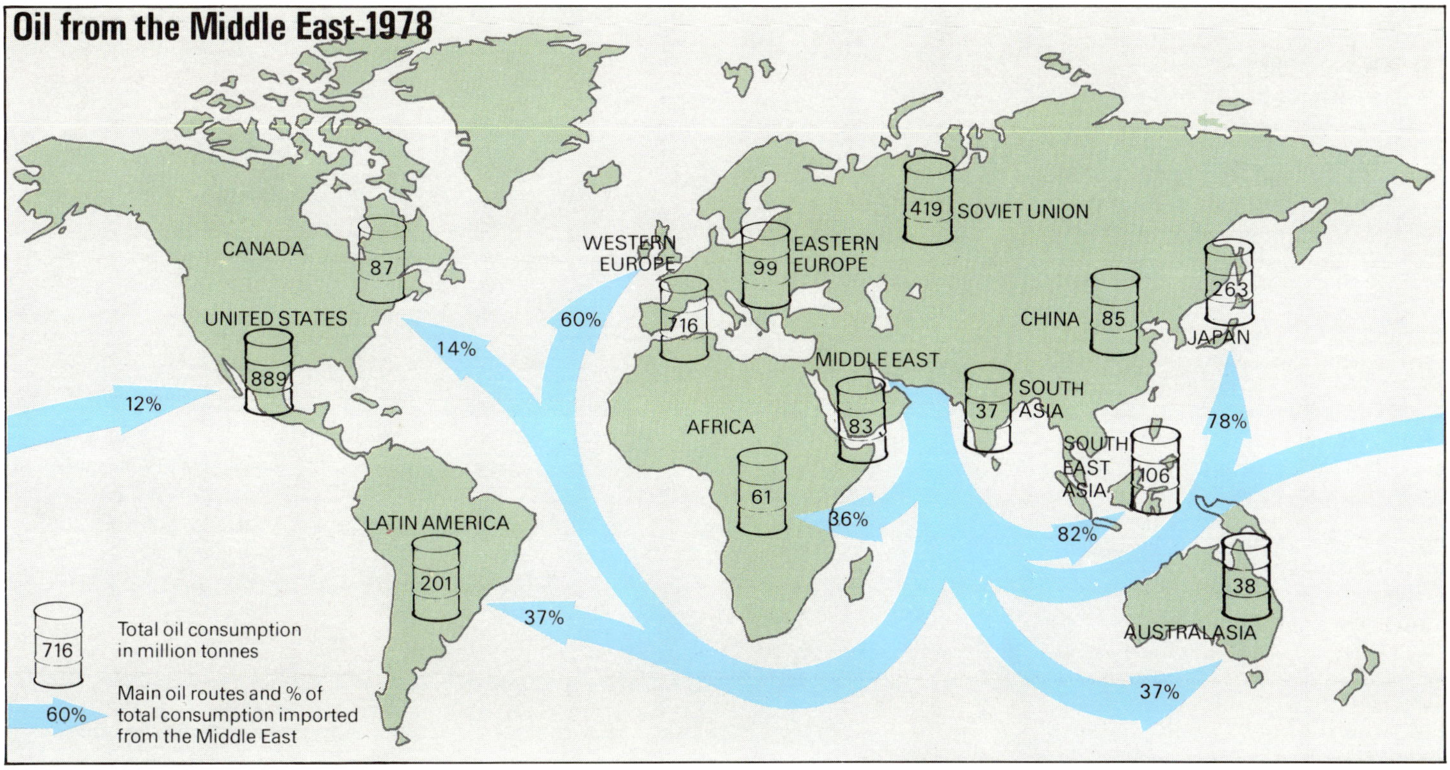

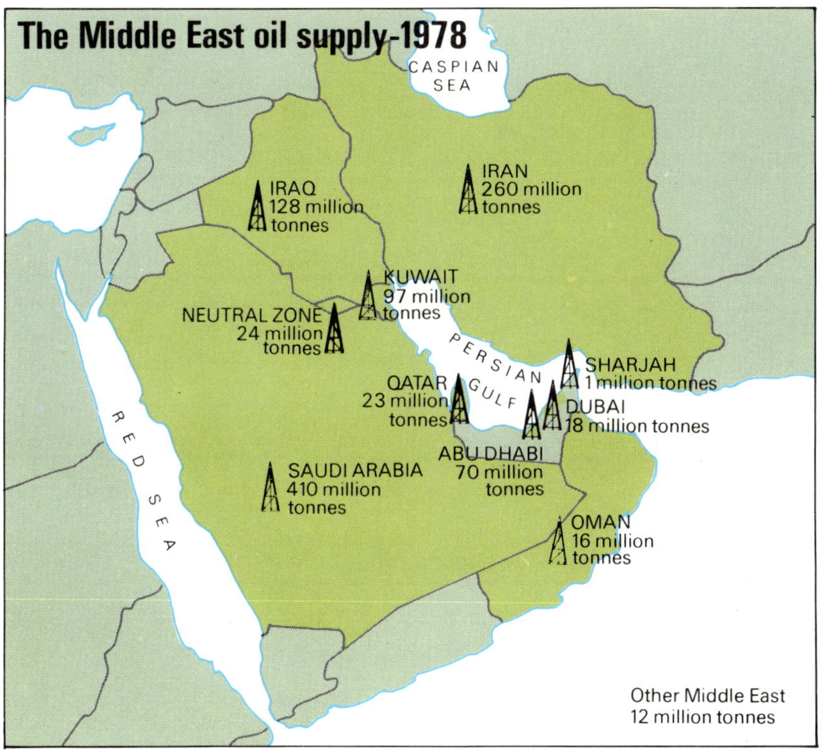

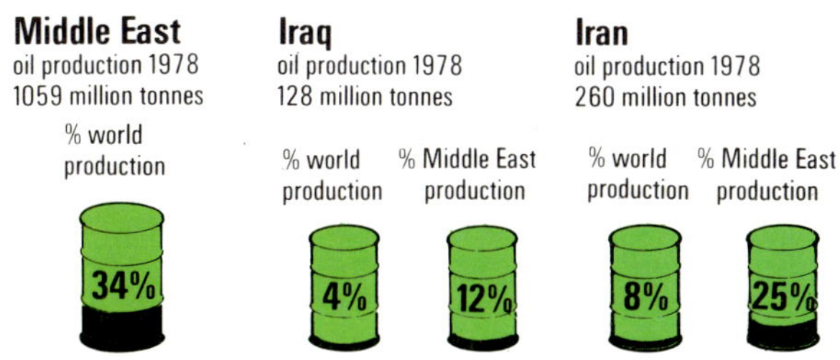

use his country's new-found wealth to pursue a more nationalist and independent role, both his past and his ambitions are regarded with suspicion by his neighbours. Saudi Arabia is the world's largest oil producer but her wealth is out of all proportion to her tiny population. The smaller states – Kuwait, Qatar, Bahrain and the seven United Arab Emirates – are in a similar position. Oman is not really a gulf state at all, but possession of the Musandam peninsula means that Oman has to police the tanker routes through the Strait of Hormuz, though it is really beyond its resources.

Until 1971 Britain was the dominant power in the gulf and a British military presence ensured stability. From 1971 to 1979 the shah of Iran tried to act as the 'gendarme' of the gulf but never won acceptance for this role. Since 1979 the region has been a power vacuum.

A number of traditional rivalries influence relations among the gulf states. That between Iran and Iraq is the most ancient, but other territorial claims exist between the states. For example, Iran has an old claim to Bahrain which could be revived to suit modern policies. Iran is also the major Shiite Moslem power, but the other gulf states have Sunni rulers, often with substantial Shia populations. This gives Iran a lever in all these countries and (outside the gulf) in Pakistan, which also has a Shia minority. In the summer of 1979 rioting broke out among Bahrain's Shia community, inspired by the Iranian Revolution. Add to this the racial antagonism between Persian and Arab and it is easy to see why the lesser gulf states have tended to side with Iraq in the conflict with Iran, despite their suspicions of Saddam Hussein, although Iranian threats of retaliation against their vulnerable oil industries, either by blocking the Strait of Hormuz or by direct military action against installations, has meant that their sympathy has stopped a long way short of actual involvement in the war.

Regional interest

Saddam Hussein's bid for leadership of the Arab world ensures that the Middle East has a general interest in the outcome of the war. Syria and Iraq both have Baathist regimes but the rivalry between the two is long-standing. When Jordan voiced its support for Iraq, Syria responded by concentrating troops along its border with Jordan. For a time it looked as though the Gulf War might spread, but after Saudi mediation both sides relaxed their military preparations.

Israel also has an interest. Iraq is a firm supporter of the Palestine Liberation Organisation and sent a division to fight against Israel on the Syrian front in the 1973 war. Iraq has usually been a powerful voice rallying the Arabs against Israel. It is therefore not in Israel's interest that Iraq should inflict a heavy defeat upon Iran and thereby increase her standing in the Arab world. Israel has supplied vital spares to Iran to help keep her Phantom fighter-bombers in the air. And, ever fearful for her security, Israel went so far as to bomb Iraq's Tamuz nuclear reactor on 7 July 1981 in order to forestall the admittedly remote possibility of an Iraqi nuclear strike against Israel in the distant future. In general the Israelis hope that the war will exhaust both sides for several years.

Superpower attitudes

The Gulf War placed the superpowers in a difficult position. Neither had a hand in starting the quarrel, nor could they control their former clients. There was no way that they could impose a ceasefire in the first months of the war, because each side had sufficient stocks of weaponry to last for some time.

After the Soviet invasion of Afghanistan the United States declared that the Persian Gulf was an area of vital interest to its security and that it would not tolerate a threat from outside the area. President Jimmy Carter repeated his concern when the Gulf War broke out. There was already a large American fleet in the area which was joined by British and French squadrons for exercises after the war started. The Americans then formed a Rapid Deployment Force to give them the capability of intervening quickly around the Indian Ocean.

The United States would like bases in the area to make it better able to defend its interests, and the gulf states probably want the ultimate assurance of American support. They do not, however, want a permanent American presence on their territory. The deployment of four airborne warning and control aircraft to Saudi Arabia indicates the limits of a desirable American presence. (This US equipment helped to intercept and destroy two Iranian Phantoms violating Saudi airspace in June 1984.)

Most of the states are worried that a permanent American presence would be matched by the Soviet Union, which would increase the danger of a confrontation between the two. Early US fears that Iran might disintegrate were soon replaced by worries that Iranian victory might destabilise the whole gulf region.

The Soviet Union's immediate interests probably favour stability in the gulf. It may soon become an importer of gulf oil itself, either for home consumption or for its east European satellites. Hence the plan announced by Leonid Brezhnev in Delhi on 10 December 1980 for a 'zone of peace' in the Persian Gulf and the Indian Ocean. The plan stressed joint action with the Western powers, China and Japan and opposed foreign military bases in the gulf area or adjacent islands.

The whole situation in the gulf took a new turn with the extension of naval action in 1983. In July it was discovered that Iraq had laid mines around the Iranian coast, and between March and May 1984 a number of ships were attacked and damaged by Iraqi aircraft in the gulf. Iran retaliated with two attacks on oil tankers in May, and although oil supplies were not at this stage seriously affected, by the end of 1984 world attention was still focused on this sensitive area.

Soldiers of an élite Iranian Army corps parade through Tehran carrying photographs of the Ayatollah Khomeini. Such enthusiasm helped to compensate for Iran's lack of spare parts for her armed forces' equipment.

The Falklands Conflict

The Argentinian invasion of the Falkland Islands led Britain to undertake a highly successful amphibious operation to regain her lost possessions

John Pimlott

BELOW RIGHT: *The fall of Port Stanley – British commandos are led away by an Argentinian soldier.*

BETWEEN 2 APRIL AND 14 JUNE 1982 Great Britain and Argentina fought for possession of the Falklands, a collection of wind-swept islands 770km (480 miles) north-east of Cape Horn in the South Atlantic. Despite a history of British rule since 1833 and an 1800-strong population which was almost entirely of British stock, Argentina claimed sovereignty over the islands under their Spanish name of Islas Malvinas. Diplomatic negotiations had been going on since 1965, with distinct signs that Britain was prepared to accede to Argentinian demands in the long-term, but when this was opposed by the democratically-elected Falkland Islands Council, deadlock ensued. In an effort to break this, while at the same time diverting domestic attention away from chronic economic and political problems, the Argentinian ruling junta led by General Leopoldo Galtieri determined to take the islands by force. They were convinced that the British government, thousands of miles away, would not react militarily.

The invasion began at 0430 hours (local time) on 2 April when Argentinian troops landed close to the Falklands capital Port Stanley. The islands were inadequately protected by a token force of 79 Royal Marines and although they fought bravely in defence of Government House, they stood no chance against an estimated 2500 invading troops. At 0925 the Governor, Rex Hunt, ordered surrender. The following day the Falklands dependency of South Georgia, 1290km (800 miles) to the east-south-east, was also overwhelmed.

Despite the junta's prediction, Britain responded to this 'humiliating affront' with a surprisingly formidable package of inter-related counter-measures. Diplomatically, Argentina was condemned and progressively isolated; while at the same time Argentinian assets were frozen, arms shipments to the junta were suspended and trade links severed. Most dramatically of all, a special naval task force was assembled for despatch to the South Atlantic.

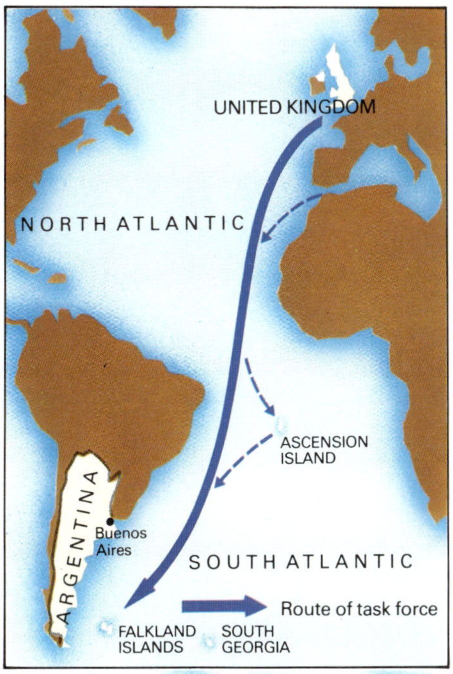

On 5 April the carriers HMS *Hermes* and *Invincible*, loaded with marines, helicopters and Sea Harrier 'jump-jets', left Portsmouth to join the command of Rear Admiral J. F. ('Sandy') Woodward. On 7 April, as the task force moved towards its assembly-point at Ascension Island in mid-Atlantic, it was announced that a 200-mile (320km) Maritime Exclusion Zone (MEZ) would be imposed around the Falklands from 0400 GMT on 12 April. By that time nuclear-powered submarines would be on station to interdict Argentinian supply lines to a Falklands garrison which was already estimated to exceed 10,000 men.

Royal Navy Task Force

ABOVE: *General Leopoldo Galtieri, the architect of Argentina's invasion of the Falkland Islands.* BELOW: *Dawn breaks over the flight deck of HMS* Hermes. *Behind the ranks of Sea Harriers is the ship's complement of Sea King helicopters; both aircraft types proved highly successful in combat.*

Diplomatic efforts, based upon the 'even-handed' approach of an American administration caught between two allies, failed to produce a peaceful settlement, and as the task force steamed towards the MEZ the governments of Britain and Argentina prepared themselves for military action. By late April, with more marines, plus 2nd and 3rd Battalions of The Parachute Regiment and full supporting arms also on their way from Britain, Woodward had at his disposal over 5000 troops organised into 3rd Commando Brigade under Brigadier Julian Thompson.

The land campaign began on 25 April when Royal Marines, spearheaded by elements of the Special Air Service (SAS) and its naval equivalent the Special Boat Squadron (SBS), recaptured South Georgia without personal loss. The Falkland Islands themselves were well defended by Argentinian troops; although a large proportion were poorly motivated conscripts, their very presence made an immediate land assault impossible. On 30 April, therefore, Woodward initiated a policy of isolation and steady military pressure with the imposition of a Total Exclusion Zone (TEZ) through which neither air nor sea craft would be allowed to pass. The next day – 1 May – a single Vulcan bomber flew 5550km (3450 miles) from Ascension to open the new campaign with a raid on Stanley airfield and Harriers from the fleet quickly followed suit. Retaliatory air attacks on the task force were effectively contained.

War at sea

The scale of the fighting soon escalated. Within twenty-four hours HM Submarine *Conqueror*, patrolling outside the TEZ, had torpedoed and sunk the Argentinian cruiser *General Belgrano* with the loss of 368 lives. The Argentinian Air Force, despite mounting losses caused by Harriers and anti-air defences, responded with heavier attacks, one of which was dramatically successful. On 4 May Super Etendard attack aircraft launched two Exocet sea-skimming missiles some 32km (20 miles) from the fleet: one failed to find a target but the other hit the destroyer HMS *Sheffield*. Twenty sailors died, *Sheffield* was abandoned and the task force suddenly seemed to be dangerously vulnerable; a decisive land campaign to bring the war to a swift end became ever more necessary. On 12 May the Cunard liner *Queen Elizabeth II* left Southampton with 5th Infantry Brigade (2nd Battalion Scots Guards, 1st Battalion Welsh Guards and 1st Battalion 7th Gurkha Rifles, plus supporting arms) on board, emphasising the new priority. As she sailed towards the South Atlantic, Argentinian positions on the Falklands were 'softened up', preparatory to the main assault.

When 3rd Commando Brigade went ashore on 21 May at San Carlos, on the northwest coast of East Falkland 80km (50 miles) from Stanley, the Argentinians were taken by surprise. Little ground opposition was encountered, enabling a beach-head of 16

square km (10 square miles) to be seized on the first day, but with the bulk of the task force unavoidably concentrated in support of the landing, air attacks were intense. British naval losses mounted steadily: on 21 May the frigate HMS *Ardent* was hit by rockets and abandoned; two days later her sister-ship HMS *Antelope* blew up spectacularly in San Carlos Water; on 25 May the destroyer HMS *Coventry* was lost and the requisitioned Cunard container-ship *Atlantic Conveyor*, loaded with supplies and heavy-lift helicopters, fell victim to an Exocet. Significant numbers of Argentinian aircraft were shot down, but the British could not absorb such losses indefinitely. Further military operations were imperative.

Assault on Goose Green

Major-General Jeremy Moore, British land commander, made his move on 27 May, sending 2 Para south out of the beach-head to take the settlements of Darwin and Goose Green, essential as flank-protection to the southern arm of an advance on Stanley. The operation took 14 hours, during which the Paras, early on 28 May, conducted an epic frontal assault against superior forces, losing 17 men but capturing 1400. Meanwhile 3 Para and the Marines pushed across the north of the island, advancing on foot over difficult terrain. By early June they had taken the settlements of Douglas and Teal Inlet and captured Mount Challenger and Mount Kent, the first in a series of ridges and hills overlooking the Falklands capital. In the south the advance reached Fitzroy and Bluff Cove, 32km (20 miles) from Stanley, on 6 June with 5th Infantry Brigade assuming responsibility as they became available. Unfortunately it was here, two days later, that the landing ships *Sir Galahad* and *Sir Tristram*, off-loading men of the Welsh Guards, were caught by Argentinian aircraft and bombed.

But this was not enough to disrupt the momentum of advance. Supported by intense artillery fire, the British closed in on Port Stanley. On the night of 11/12 June, 3 Para fought their way onto Mount Longdon while 42 and 45 Commando took Mount Harriet and Two Sisters respectively. Two nights later – 13/14 June – 2 Para overran Wireless Ridge in the north and the Scots Guards cleared Tumbledown in the centre. As the Gurkhas and Welsh Guards moved forward to take Mount William and Sapper Hill – the last high ground to the south of Stanley – the Argentinians broke and ran. At 2100 hours on 14 June General Moore accepted their surrender. The British had lost 255 dead and 777 injured since 2 April but the Falklands were, in Moore's words, 'once more under the government desired by their inhabitants'.

ABOVE RIGHT: *Argentinian soldiers.* RIGHT: *The sinking of the* Belgrano. BELOW: *Assault craft from HMS* Fearless.

Naval Operations

WHEN THE FALKLANDS conflict began, the Argentinians enjoyed a number of naval advantages. For a start, they completely outclassed available opposition, for although their fleet of 17 major combat vessels compared poorly to that eventually assembled by Britain, in early April it was a formidable local force. Centred upon the aged – but still potent – aircraft carrier *Veinticinco de Mayo*, with its complement of 14 A-4 Skyhawk fighter-bombers, the fleet was capable of projecting Argentinian influence over a wide area of the South Atlantic. Supporting the carrier was a respectable array of surface ships which included two British-built Type 42 destroyers, armed with Exocet surface-to-surface missiles (SSMs) and Sea Dart surface-to-air missiles (SAMs), as well as three French-built A-69 corvettes, also with Exocet missiles on board. In addition, four diesel-powered submarines provided underwater menace.

Nor was that all. Argentina, with its infrastructure of port facilities and air bases, was never very far away, enabling the fleet to fall back on its relatively short supply lines and – around the Falklands at least – to enjoy the benefit of shore-based air cover. When it is recalled that Britain had just one ice-patrol vessel in the region on 2 April, the ease of the Argentinian takeover is readily understandable. Furthermore, with the nearest British naval reinforcements some 12,870km (8000 miles) away, the junta's belief that no military response would be attempted was not unreasonable.

The task force sails

But Britain did respond – quickly and with surprising force. Within days of the invasion some of the most powerful fighting ships in the world – forerunners to a task force which was eventually to involve over 100 vessels – were on their way to the South Atlantic from bases in Britain and exercise locations in the Mediterranean. The aircraft carriers *Hermes* and *Invincible*, with 20 Sea Harriers on board, provided air support and command facilities. They were protected, at one time or another during the conflict, by a reported total of eight destroyers, 15 frigates and six submarines, armed with sophisticated weapon systems which included Sea Dart, Sea Wolf and Seacat SAMs, Exocet and Seaslug SSMs and Mark 8 and Tigerfish torpedoes. The assault ships *Fearless* and *Intrepid* supported by six logistic landing vessels gave the force an amphibious landing capability, while the Royal Fleet Auxiliary provided replenishment facilities. But the key to the long-term viability of the task force lay in

BELOW: *The British frigate HMS* Antelope *explodes off San Carlos Bay.* BOTTOM: *Another British victim, the destroyer HMS* Sheffield.

the creation of a continuous supply chain, stretching from Britain to Ascension Island and from there to the battle zone. This was achieved through the requisition or charter of 50 merchant ships, ranging from the luxury liner *Queen Elizabeth II* to a host of container ships, ferries and tankers, the first of which were operating by mid-April. Without them the task force could not have survived. Of the 113 vessels that constituted the task force, 39 were from the Royal Navy, 22 from the Royal Fleet Auxiliary, two from the Royal Maritime Auxiliary and 50 from the Merchant Navy.

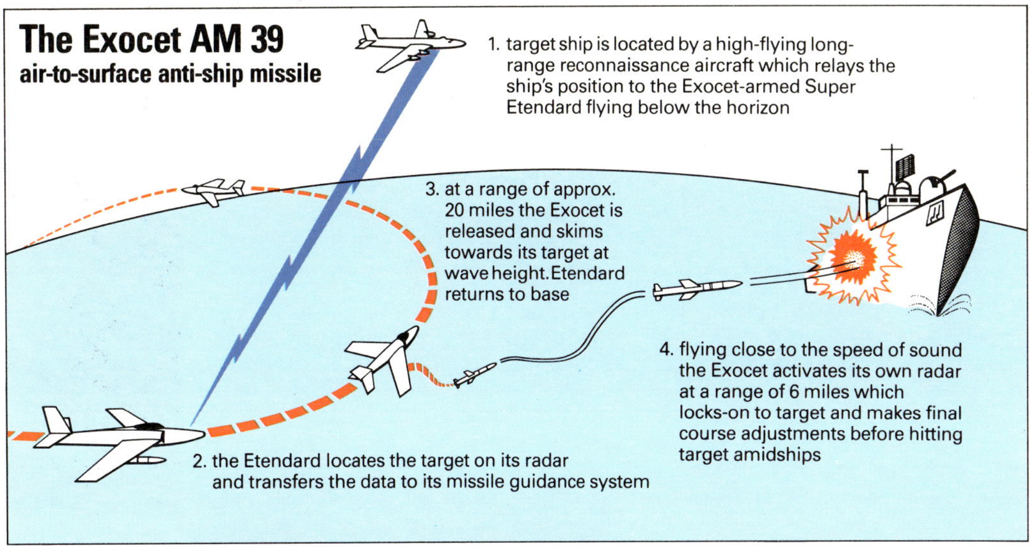

LEFT: *The French-manufactured Exocet missile which the Argentinian Air Force used to such good effect in the Falklands.* BELOW: *The British carrier HMS* Invincible *puts to sea. With the* Hermes, *the* Invincible *provided the air support that was crucial to the success of the Falklands campaign. Ironically the* Invincible *had been due to be sold to Australia, but fortunately for the task force the sale had not gone through and so the* Invincible *was able to fulfil her role in the South Atlantic.*

The Belgrano goes down

Once in position in and around the exclusion zone, the Royal Navy had three basic roles. Firstly, it had to prevent further Argentinian support to the Falklands garrison by sea, and in this it was successful. From as early as mid-April it was reported that British submarines were operating off the Argentinian coast, threatening to cut the enemy's supply line. Any doubts about their effectiveness were dispelled on 2 May when the *General Belgrano* went down, and thereafter the Argentinians were understandably wary about committing their surface ships to the conflict. A few light craft and unescorted supply vessels did try to breach the blockade, but few survived, especially after the arrival of the main body of the task force in the TEZ. On 3 May, for example, the Argentinian patrol boat *Comodoro Somellera* was sunk and her sister-ship *Alferez Sobral* badly damaged by helicopter attack within the exclusion zone; ten days later the frigate HMS *Alacrity* sank a supply ship in Falkland Sound. The latter incident implied that the occasional enemy vessel was reaching the Falklands, but to all intents and purposes the sea blockade was effective.

The absence of the Argentinian fleet from the battle area (a direct result of the success of the blockade) made the second role of the task force – self-protection against enemy attack – that much easier to carry out, for it meant that ship-to-ship contact was avoided. But this did not guarantee complete security, for whereas the Argentinian Navy clearly failed, her Air Force very nearly succeeded. By 14 June the task force had lost six of its ships and suffered damage to many more, all through air attack. The Argentinian pilots suffered grievously in the process, but the vulnerability of surface ships could not be disguised.

The task force should have been protected by a three-tier air-defence system: radar early-warning, air cover and ship-borne anti-air weapons. Deficiencies were apparent in all three during the Falklands conflict. Nimrod early-warning aircraft, based at Ascension, lacked the range to provide continuous cover, leaving the job to ship-borne radars which could not always cope – as the loss of HMS *Sheffield* implied. Similarly, although the Harriers operated well in air-to-air combat, there were never enough of them to intercept all incoming aircraft, creating gaps which, as the attacks on ships in San Carlos Water showed, could be exploited. And faced with the sophistication of the Exocet, many existing air-defence systems (notably Sea Dart) proved inadequate. Add to this the apparent ease with which modern ships burned when hit, and a disturbing catalogue of problems emerged.

The fact that the task force continued to operate under such pressure reflects well upon its professionalism. Without this, the final role of the force – the projection of military power ashore in a campaign of liberation – would have been impossible. But in this, the *raison d'être* of British actions, success was achieved. Whether on South Georgia, Pebble Island or East Falkland, the Royal Navy ensured the safety of assault landings and supported subsequent military operations to an extent which proved that, regardless of problems and initial Argentinian advantages, the British undoubtedly won the naval war.

Aerial Conflict

AIR OPERATIONS, whether offensive or defensive, were of prime importance to both sides in the Falklands conflict. To the British, it would have been unthinkable to dispatch a task force so far away from home without air cover and impossible to conduct land operations without an ability to hit enemy positions from the air or move men and supplies quickly over difficult terrain. Similarly, the Argentinians needed aircraft to attack the task force and to supply their beleaguered garrison, especially after the Navy had been neutralised by the British blockade. Air battles, involving air-to-air combat as well as struggles between aircraft and air-defence systems, were therefore an inevitable feature of the Falklands War and a key to eventual victory.

Strengths and weaknesses

On paper the balance of air strength favoured the Argentinians. With air bases on the mainland and, after 2 April, on the Falklands as well, they could deploy almost all of their not inconsiderable Air Force to the battle area. Their numerical strength lay in bombers: nine American-supplied B-62 Canberras, each capable of delivering up to 3000kgs (6610 lbs) of conventional bombs; 82 American-designed A-4P and A-4Q Skyhawks (14 of them carrier-based), armed with bombs, rocket pods and cannon; and 10 of the new French-built Super Etendards, equipped with Exocet sea-skimming anti-ship missiles. To protect them there were 47 French-designed Mirage III interceptors, manufactured in two main versions: the IIIEA, which was a pure fighter, armed with 30mm cannon and AIM-9B Sidewinder heat-seeking air-to-air missiles, and the IIICJ, an Israeli-built fighter-ground-attack modification known as the Dagger. Both types were capable of high speed (Mach 2.2, over twice the speed of sound) and had been proved in combat by the Israelis.

Although the primitive airfield at Stanley was too short for Argentinian Mirages and Skyhawks – forced to operate from the mainland at extreme range – it did not mean that the islands were devoid of aircraft: at least 15 Argentinian-built IA-58 Pucara counter-insurgency machines, armed with cannon and machine-guns for close ground support, were deployed at Stanley and at a number of grass airstrips elsewhere (notably Goose Green and Pebble Island); and about 25 Chinook, Puma and UH-1 helicopters, as well as various light aircraft, were also available. In addition, despite British air attacks, Stanley airfield remained open throughout to C-130 transports bringing in supplies.

The Harrier's role

By comparison the British were weak. With no land bases closer than Ascension the task force had to provide its own air cover, and although the carriers could accommodate 20 Sea Harrier FRS-1 V/STOL (vertical/short takeoff and landing) interceptors, this was hardly an overwhelming force. The Sea Harrier may have been sophisticated, with Blue Fox radar, 30mm Aden cannon and Sidewinder missiles, but there were never enough to satisfy the twin roles of air interception and ground attack. By early May, after three had been lost, 22 reinforcement aircraft were hurriedly sent out (some by the extraordinary method of direct flight using in-flight refuelling

ABOVE: *Argentinian Super Etendard aircraft fly into battle; it was one of these aircraft which launched the Exocet that sank the* Sheffield.
BELOW: *A rare battle picture of an Argentinian Mirage as it attacks a Royal Fleet Auxiliary ship.*

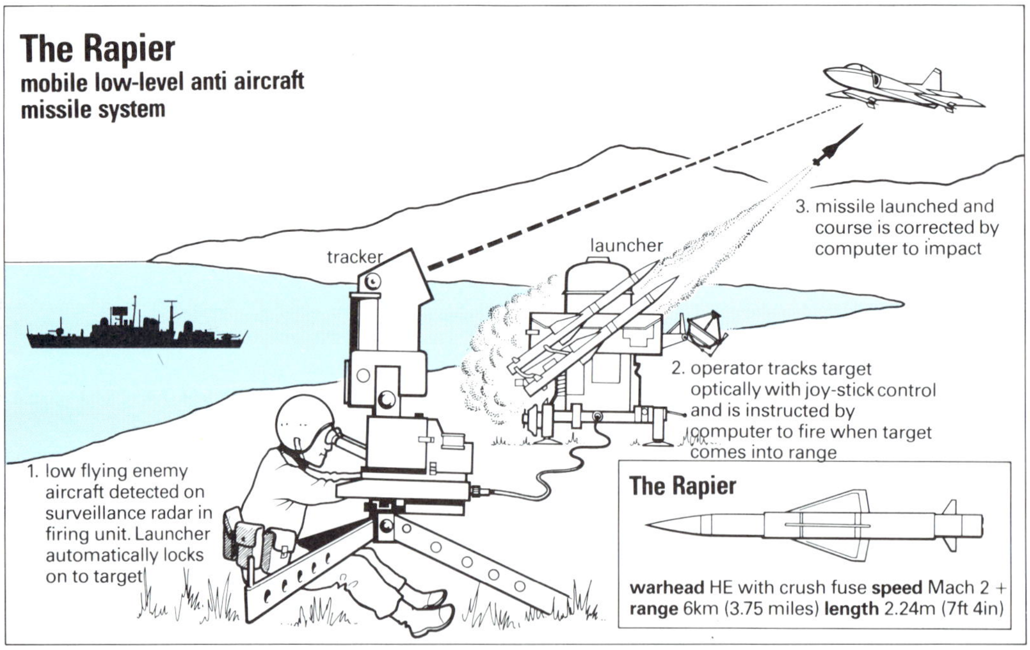

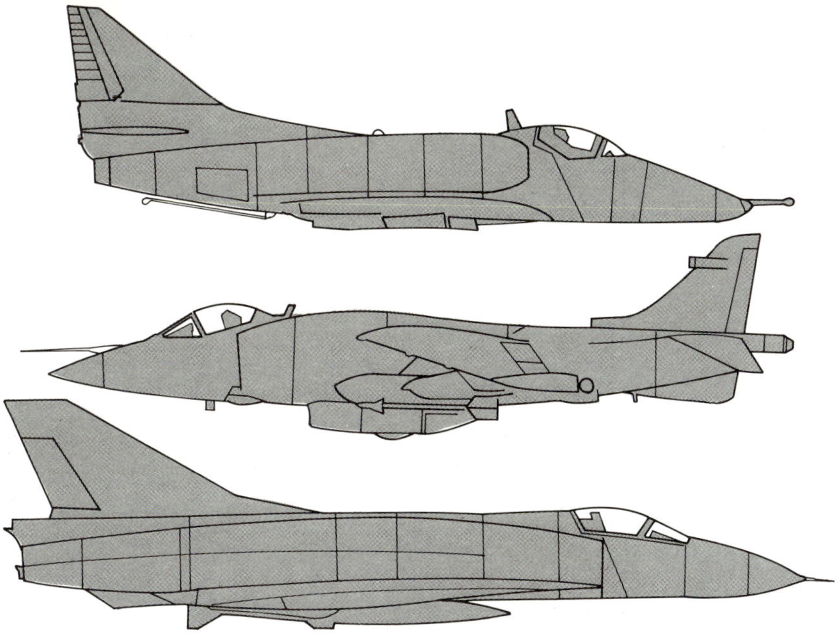

Skyhawk A-4P
type attack bomber **range (combat radius)** 3219km (2000 miles) **speed** 1040km/h (646mph) **armament** bombs, rockets, missiles, gunpods, 2 x 20mm guns **crew** 1

Sea Harrier FRS 1
type close support fighter bomber/interceptor **range (combat radius)** 667km (414 miles) **speed** 1186km/h (737mph) **armament** bombs, rockets, gunpods, flares, Sidewinder AAMs, provision for 2 x 30mm Aden guns **crew** 1

Mirage III
type air defence fighter with ground attack capability **range (combat radius)** 1200km (746 miles) **speed** (2112km/h) (1320mph) **armament** 2 x 30mm DEFA cannons, Sidewinder AAMs, provision for 2268kg (5000lb) bombload **crew** 1

RIGHT: *A Royal Navy Sea Harrier hovers over the flight deck of HMS* Hermes. BOTTOM: *A Harrier takes off from HMS* Invincible.

from Victor tankers), but as 14 of these were older RAF ground-attack Harriers, lacking Blue Fox and only recently fitted with Sidewinders, the force was still weak. Some support could be provided by Vulcan heavy bombers from Ascension, but as each of their sorties could take 18 hours, involving seven refuelling operations to cover the 11,270-km (7000-mile) round trip, they could not react quickly. Similarly, although the task force had about 200 Sea King, Wessex, Lynx, Scout, Wasp, Gazelle and even Chinook helicopters available, they were confined largely to ASW (anti-submarine warfare) and transport roles.

Yet the fact remains that the Argentinian Air Force, despite stunning success against individual ships, was effectively contained and very badly mauled over the Falklands, losing an estimated 26 Skyhawks, 24 Mirages, one Canberra, 15 Pucaras and about 30 light aircraft and helicopters to a combination of air, naval and military action.

In the air, the Harrier proved to be a superb fighting machine. Admittedly the range problem and the need to conserve fuel forced the Argentinian Mirages to sacrifice their advantage of speed, so that dogfights tended to take place at about 740 km/h (460 mph), ideally suited to the slower Harrier, but there was more to it than that. Because of its unique variable-thrust engines, the Harrier was extremely manoeuvrable, particularly if a skilled pilot used the so-called VIFF (Vector in Forward Flight) technique. If chased by a Mirage, he could suddenly select vectored (downward) thrust, slowing and lifting his aircraft in mid-flight. This caused the enemy to overshoot, exposing his tail exhaust to devastating Sidewinder attack. Even if the Mirage fired first, the lateral exhausts of the Harrier were poor targets for heat-seeking missiles.

But it would be wrong to attribute all the credit to the Harriers, for although precise figures are impossible to compute, a significant proportion of Argentinian losses were caused by air-defence systems. Naval SAMs, despite deficiencies in countering the Super Etendard/Exocet combination, operated well against Skyhawks and Mirages over San Carlos Water; the Argentinians began to find a hostile sky whenever they appeared. They continued to achieve individual successes throughout the conflict, as events at Bluff Cove as late as 8 June showed, but as their losses mounted, their chances of victory slipped away.

The Land Battle

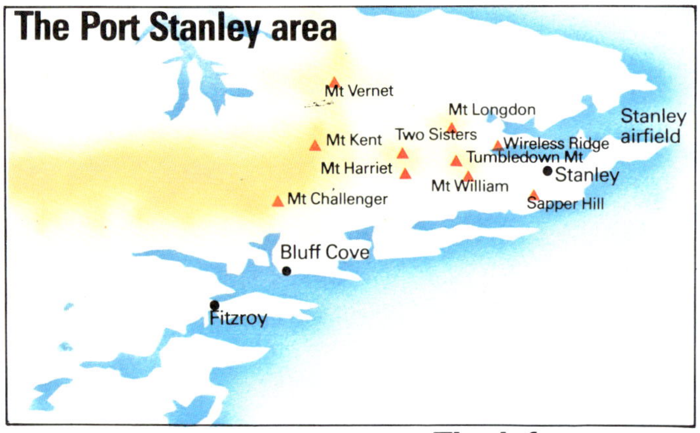

THE BATTLES WHICH took place at sea and in the air around the Falklands were undoubtedly important to the outcome of the war, but in the end it had to be land operations which decided the issue. After all, the conflict was about territory and whoever occupied it had the ability to impose a political solution. This was recognised by the Argentinians when they used overwhelming military force to usurp British rule in the islands on 2 April, just as it was by Britain when units of 3rd Commando Brigade accompanied the task force three days later. There may have been some hope that a British naval and air blockade would force the Argentinians to withdraw, but when this did not occur a land campaign became unavoidable.

The problems involved were immense. According to the accepted rules of war, the British needed a 3:1 advantage in men and equipment as well as mastery of both sea and air to take on a garrison in prepared positions. This they did not have. The Argentinians had used the four weeks before the task force arrived to build up their strength to over 10,000 troops, backed by light armour, artillery and stockpiles of supplies. For their part the British could barely muster 5000 men.

ABOVE: *The officer of an Argentinian unit radios back to base.* LEFT: *The survivors of the* Sir Galahad.

Such a disparity made the choice of a suitable landing site, free from enemy interference yet within striking distance of Port Stanley, especially important. Some possibilities could be dismissed immediately – landings on West Falkland would lead nowhere; the southern half of East Falkland comprised low-lying, impassable terrain; a direct assault on Stanley would be suicidal – but others had to be investigated. For this purpose, SAS and SBS covert reconnaissance teams were put ashore on the northern part of East Falkland, probably in early May. Their intelligence findings were crucial.

A conscript army

They soon discovered that the Argentinian garrison, despite its size, was badly organised and poorly deployed. Although some professional units – notably marines and artillery – were present, the majority of soldiers were conscripts or reservists, low on training, discipline and military expertise. It was probably because of this that the Argentinian commander, General Mario Menendez, chose to keep the bulk of his force around the supply base at Stanley, with only small outposts guarding grass airstrips at Darwin/Goose Green, Fox Bay (on West Falkland) and Pebble Island. Although this meant that the Falklands capital was heavily defended, it did give the British virtual freedom to land elsewhere, secure in the belief that immediate counterattacks were unlikely. The eventual choice of San Carlos – an undefended settlement which offered good landing beaches and a degree of shelter from air attack – reflected these findings exactly.

Even so, the decision to go ashore in strength was always a gamble and the odds had to be shortened as far as possible beforehand. Naval and air attacks on known Argentinian positions throughout the islands spread confusion and undermined morale, while specific targets which might pose a threat to the landing force were eliminated – the SAS raid on Pebble Island on 14 May, for example, destroyed six Pucara ground-attack aircraft. Nevertheless, when British troops landed at San Carlos on 21 May they were still vulnerable and were extremely lucky to face only a weak Argentinian response.

The reasons for this lack of Argentinian resolve lay in the physical conditions of life on the Falklands. Winter was setting in, bringing rain or snow nearly every day, the ground was waterlogged, temperatures were dropping (sometimes to as low as $-20°C$) and winds were gusting up to 60 knots. With 80km (50 miles) of peat bog and barren rocks between the British and Stanley, Menendez probably believed that any rapid advance would be impossible and he was certainly not prepared to commit his own men beyond existing defence lines. Also, he may have believed the San Carlos landings to be a feint, with the main assault on Stanley still to be delivered by 5th Infantry Brigade. In any event, what he did not expect was a British advance, following the northern and southern coasts of East Falkland in a pincer movement converging on Port Stanley, and when this began on 27/28 May it soon became apparent that his forces were outclassed. As 2 Para fought for Darwin/Goose Green and other elements of the British brigade 'yomped' towards Douglas and Teal Inlet, they displayed all the advantages of a highly-professional volunteer force: military expertise, high morale and superb physical fitness.

But it would be wrong to imagine that the British advance was easy, for problems still arose. The most critical concerned supplies, for although a logistic base was soon established at San Carlos, forward movement was difficult because of the adverse conditions. Helicopters were used extensively, but with the loss of three of the four available Chinook heavy-lift machines on *Atlantic Conveyor*, their capabilities were reduced, unavoidably affecting the rate of build-up in front of Stanley in early June.

The rate at which supplies and munitions could be brought up to the British forward positions around Stanley was a major factor in determining when the main assault could be launched. The land force commanders were determined to keep casualties to a minimum and as a means of softening up the Argentinian positions priority was given to the artillery.

In spite of the British artillery's sustained barrage the Argentinians still put up resistance, especially as the ring tightened around the capital, and their – at times – effective use of artillery, machine-guns and snipers continued to inflict casualties in the bitter battles for successive rock features, some of which were reduced to hand-to-hand fighting where the bayonet decided the outcome. They may have been outmanoeuvred and outclassed, but in the end the Argentinians had to be defeated using basic battlefield skills – courage, tenacity, leadership, discipline and all-arms cooperation, particularly between infantry and artillery.

TOP: *British troops move up to a forward position in the land campaign against the Argentinian Army.*
ABOVE: *Men of 2 Para grab a rations meal in a sheep pen at Fitzroy. Conditions were grim and the campaign soon became a test of endurance between the two opposing forces.*

The Invasion of Lebanon

In 1982 war erupted in Lebanon as Israeli armoured columns invaded the country in an attempt to crush the PLO

Eric Morris

BELOW RIGHT: *Israeli troops climb out of their armoured personnel carrier in the battered coastal town of Saida (Sidon). Many Lebanese towns were subjected to ferocious assaults by the IDF – from land, sea and air.*

THE THREE MONTHS prior to the Israeli invasion of Lebanon in June 1982 saw a series of guerrilla attacks in Europe, including the attempted assassination of the Israeli ambassador to Britain, Shlomo Argov. Despite Palestine Liberation Organisation (PLO) denials of responsibility, Israel proclaimed to the world that unless the PLO infrastructure based in Lebanon was destroyed, further attacks would be unavoidable. The resulting Israeli offensive was swift and lethal with more than 50 targets in Beirut and southern Lebanon coming under Israeli aerial assault. Under attack the PLO responded with rocket and long-range artillery strikes on targets in northern Israel. If these were to be halted, Israel claimed that it had no choice but to intervene on the ground.

Operation Peace for Galilee was launched on 6 June when armoured columns from Israel's fully-mobilised Northern Command crossed the Lebanese frontier. Their objective, in Prime Minister Menachim Begin's words, was to 'cleanse southern Lebanon' of its PLO strongholds, and as the armoured units moved deeper into Lebanon, sweeping aside the detachment of UN (United Nations) troops, they linked up with Major Saad Haddad's Phalangist militia groups. As they crossed the Litani River, however, the Israelis revealed the broader nature of their plans – nothing less than the complete elimination of the PLO from Lebanon and the formation of a pro-Israeli government in Beirut. The 'hawks' of the Cabinet, led by Defence Minister Ariel Sharon, were determined to secure a military solution to the Palestinian question, regardless of consequences.

From the first the Israeli Defence Forces (IDF) displayed an elegant strategy and meticulous planning. The Israeli Air Force (IAF) soon secured command of the air from Syrian hands and ground-attack squadrons, bombers and helicopters provided round-the-clock support. All-arms formations of tanks, self-propelled artillery and armoured infantry moved along two main axes of advance. On the coast Centurion tanks and M-113 half-tracks mounting élite paratroops secured the port of Tyre and then linked up with other forces that had stormed ashore in an amphibious assault and captured Sidon. A combined force under Colonel Eli Geva moved on to Damour and the very outskirts of Beirut. Inland, armoured columns drove northwards through the mountains. In classic

The Israeli invasion of the Lebanon
June 1982

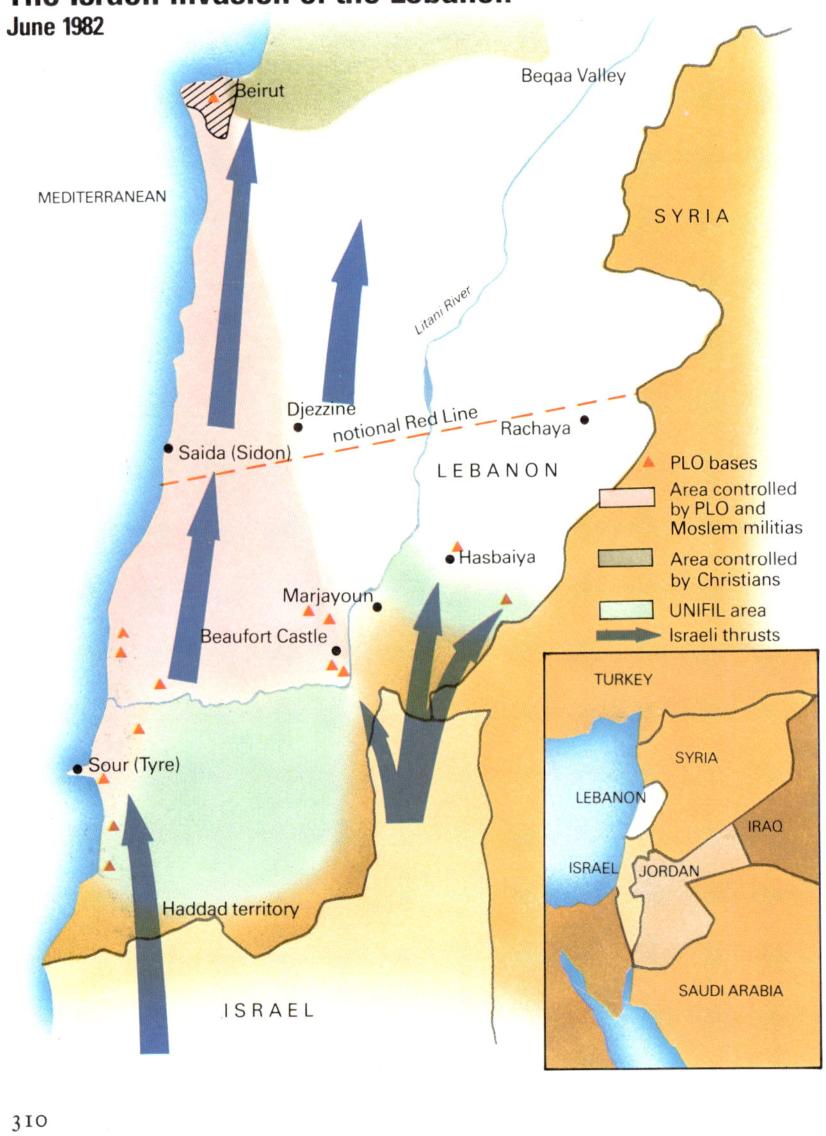

blitzkrieg fashion they either bypassed PLO strongholds or used special forces to overcome resistance, while supporting infantry mopped-up pockets of PLO survivors. On the second day Beaufort Castle, a formidable PLO stronghold, was bombarded by IAF Skyhawks while the infantry worked their way up to the battlements. After bitter hand-to-hand fighting the fortress surrendered and the road to the north lay open.

On 9 June the Israelis introduced a third axis: armoured columns, spearheaded by battalions of Merkava tanks, swung eastwards and outflanked elements of the Syrian 1st Armoured Division in the Beqaa Valley. Again, infantry secured the high ground while the tanks, ably supported from the air, moved through the passes and attacked Syrian defences. Syrian MiGs flew to protect their armoured division but by all accounts proved no match for IAF F-15s and F-16s.

PLO under siege

Meanwhile the main advance on Beirut had reached Khalde where the PLO defenders were supported by units of Lebanese Moslem militia, but as elsewhere they had no answer to the weight and quality of Israeli firepower. The speed and momentum of the IDF advance overwhelmed them and a few hours later Israeli tanks reached Baabda and moved on to cut the main Damascus–Beirut highway at Jamhur. Syrian armour, Lebanese Moslem militia and PLO units fell back into the city and were soon trapped by the encircling Israeli forces. Under increasing international pressure, the Israelis declared a ceasefire on 11 June and Sharon announced the successful completion of Operation Peace for Galilee. It was a premature claim, for although the IDF had outfought its rivals it had not destroyed them, and if a withdrawal was ordered then the PLO guerrillas would surely return. As a result, the Israelis decided to lay siege to Beirut and hope for a diplomatic settlement. Despite international and domestic pressure, Begin's cabinet stuck to its original objectives, and while President Reagan's special envoy Philip Habib shuttled from one Middle East capital to another, the battle raged for West Beirut.

On 19 August, with an estimated 11,000 dead since the first shots were fired, Habib finally secured the agreement of all parties to a ceasefire. Preparatory to an Israeli withdrawal, an estimated 14,000 PLO and Syrian soldiers, supervised by a multi-national force, had been evacuated from Beirut. The violence in Lebanon was not over, however. On 14 September the president-elect, Bashir Gemayel – a Phalangist whose sympathies lay with Israel – was assassinated and the Israelis used this as an opportunity to renew their offensive. Convinced that about 2000 PLO fighters had remained in hiding in Beirut and wary of Moslem militia groups which had not been included in the evacuation, the IDF advanced into West Beirut on 15/16 September amid cries of outrage from President Reagan and the Arab world. Israeli euphoria was short-lived, however, for it soon emerged that, in the latest advance, over a thousand Palestinian refugees had been massacred in camps at Sabra and Chatila. In retrospect it is clear that the killings were not carried out by the IDF but by Phalangist militiamen, although the fact that such forces were ostensibly under Israeli control reflected badly on the IDF. Israel stood condemned by association; domestic pressure forced Begin to convene a special commission of inquiry which, although exonerating most of the politicians, recommended Sharon's dismissal. When this failed to quieten international opprobrium, Begin agreed to withdraw the IDF from West Beirut and by 1 October the international peacekeeping force was back in Lebanon.

The continuing conflict

The resultant ceasefire has not been secure. Despite the Habib agreement of August 1982 the Israelis have refused to withdraw from Lebanon so long as Syrian and Palestinian forces remain in the Beqaa Valley; the Syrians, by the same token, have refused to evacuate their positions until the IDF has returned home. Indeed, in the first six months of 1983, both sides continued to deploy major military formations inside Lebanon, raising the spectre of a renewed Arab–Israeli conflict. The Americans have tried desperately to produce a settlement based on the so-called 'Reagan Plan' of early September 1982 whereby Israel would withdraw not just from Lebanon but also from the West Bank and Gaza, handing the latter over to the Palestinians who would enjoy self government 'in association' with Jordan. The Arab states rejected this at the Fez summit in Morocco in late September, calling for the establishment of a completely independent Palestinian state, although in early 1983 Yasir Arafat appeared to be negotiating with King Hussein of Jordan along the lines of Reagan's proposals. Such moderation only served to increase the level of opposition to Arafat within the PLO.

While the Syrians continued to build up their air defence and ground forces in the Beqaa Valley during 1983, the Israelis remained in occupation of most of southern Lebanon. By September 1983, civil war was again rife, in the wake of a sudden Israeli withdrawal to the line of the Awali River. The international peacekeeping force proved unable to cope, and both the US Marine and French Parachutist barracks were attacked by suicide bombers on 23 October, killing 318. The various national contingents began to pull out of Lebanon from February 1984, leaving this unhappy country once more prey both to its contending factions within and its more powerful neighbours.

BELOW: *A PLO fighter scans the burning tower blocks of central Beirut. Like most other PLO and Moslem troops he is armed with an AK assault rifle.* BOTTOM: *Beirut suffered from repeated Israeli bombardments which turned much of the city into rubble, and caused many civilian casualties. Since then, renewed fighting has only added to the casualty list.*

The Palestinians

THE 'PALESTINIAN PROBLEM' began with the creation of the state of Israel. Between 1948 and the Six-Day War of June 1967, Palestinians were dispersed into three main groups. Some 315,000 lived within the borders of Israel while a further 300,000 were settled in Syria, Egypt and Lebanon. The majority, however – an estimated 700,000 – were in Jordan, either in the Arab part of Jerusalem or in the squalid refugee camps of the West Bank.

The territories taken by the Israelis in 1967 (Sinai, the Gaza Strip, the West Bank and Golan) displaced a further 200,000 Palestinians, most of whom crossed into Jordan. Though the Israelis subsequently allowed some to return, this new influx placed an intolerable burden on Jordanian resources and in September 1970, in response to a spate of Palestine Liberation Organisation (PLO) sponsored aircraft hijacks which culminated in the spectacular destruction of three airliners at Dawson's Field in Jordan, King Hussein challenged and then defeated the military power of the Palestinians in his state. The PLO and its guerrilla units were expelled amid heavy fighting and bitter recriminations. Many fled, this time to Lebanon, the only remaining refuge within striking distance of Israel. By the mid 1970s some 700,000 Palestinians were living in Lebanon. They had become a state within a state, with their own schools, hospitals and a radio station. The majority lived in 14 large refugee camps, some in the south and close to the coast, others in shanty towns beyond the rich suburbs of Beirut. They posed a threat which Israel could not afford to ignore.

PLO and Palestinians

Since its creation in 1964 the PLO has come to be accepted by more and more states as the official representative of the Palestinian people. It is a loose alliance or grouping of eight main guerrilla organisations, the largest and most prestigious of which is Al-Fatah. Others include the Marxist Popular Front for the Liberation of Palestine (PFLP), which was created in 1967 by Dr George Habash. The PFLP has probably been the most active of the terrorist groups on the international scene in recent years. Two groups have broken away from the PFLP – the PFLP-General Command, led by Ahmed Jibril, and the People's Democratic Front for the Liberation of Palestine (PDFLP), led by Naif Hawatmeh. In 1966 the Syrian Baathist Party helped to create *Sa'iqa*, which represents the Palestinians living in Syria, and the Palestine Liberation Army (PLA), a Syrian-officered regular army force of some 6000 men. Later the Iraqis sponsored the Arab Liberation Front (ALF) along similar lines.

The nominal head of the PLO is Yasir Arafat. In part his power and authority rests on the belief that no other leading figure within the movement enjoys anything like his stature or reputation as Chairman of the Executive Council. He is however, by Palestinian standards, a moderate and by June 1983, having been seen to negotiate with King Hussein over a plan put forward by President Reagan to create a Palestinian 'homeland' under Jordanian tutelage in the West Bank and Gaza, his position was under attack. Radical PLO members – many of whom had suffered the humiliation of defeat in Lebanon a year earlier – began not merely to oppose his leadership but even to launch attacks on his followers.

International recognition

Arab attitudes towards the PLO and the Palestinians are ambiguous. In 1974 at a conference in Rabat, the Arab world unanimously acknowledged that the PLO spoke for Arab Palestine. From Rabat, Arafat went on to address the General Assembly of the United Nations, which in turn accorded the PLO 'observer status'. Thus a new state came into existence, one which had a people and a recog-

The Soviet 7.62mm AKM assault rifle

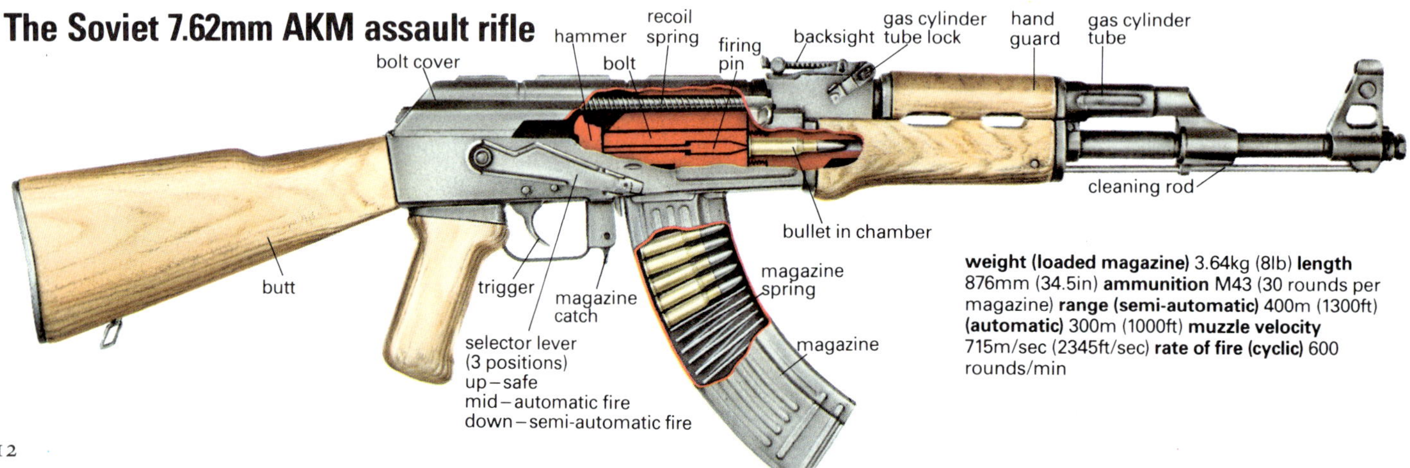

weight (loaded magazine) 3.64kg (8lb) **length** 876mm (34.5in) **ammunition** M43 (30 rounds per magazine) **range (semi-automatic)** 400m (1300ft) **(automatic)** 300m (1000ft) **muzzle velocity** 715m/sec (2345ft/sec) **rate of fire (cyclic)** 600 rounds/min

FAR LEFT: *PLO leader and statesman of the Palestinian cause, Yasir Arafat.* LEFT: *Palestinian and Syrian troops raise their Soviet-built weapons in salute near Khalda on the Lebanese coast.*

ABOVE: *Left-wing troops stand amidst the burning ruins of Beirut while the Israelis close in.* BELOW: *A security cordon is set up after an explosion in Beirut. Car bombs became a favoured terrorist weapon in the city.*

nised 'government' – but no territory. This was followed in 1976 by a further diplomatic victory when the PLO, in the face of American opposition and an Israeli boycott, attended a UN Security Council debate on the Middle East. It was only the US veto that prevented the Security Council from passing a resolution recognising the PLO as a state and calling for the establishment of an independent Palestinian homeland. Nevertheless the PLO continued to grow in diplomatic stature as more and more states accorded it various degrees of recognition.

Despite increasing international acceptance the Arab world must wish at times that the PLO had never been created. The Palestinian refugees are a constant reproach to Arab states, for they would not exist had the Arabs been more effective in preventing the emergence of the state of Israel in the late 1940s. At the same time, the Palestinian presents problems to his Arab host wherever he lives. Like displaced persons the world over, he has to be fed, housed, policed and requires both a passport and work permit. In some states like Kuwait, the government and the administration could not function without Palestinian expertise, but elsewhere the Palestinians are a dangerous element, particularly if they are actively engaged in the fight against Israel. Two Arab countries, Jordan and Syria, have fought battles against the PLO, while any state that plays host to Palestinian guerrillas invites Israeli retaliation.

Fundamentalist support

The conservative oil sheikdoms of the Gulf shudder at the revolutionary aspirations of the Palestinians, especially their endorsement of the Moslem fundamentalist regime in Iran. Even the ardent support of such radical states as Libya, which provides finance, organisation and training facilities, is balanced by their security forces keeping a very close watch on PLO activities within their borders.

Since the enforced withdrawal of the PLO from Beirut in August 1982, signs of a deep rift within the organisation have appeared. Arafat is fighting hard to maintain his leadership, looking to the moderate Arab powers and the Soviet bloc for support, but radicals such as George Habash of the PFLP are insistent that the time for negotiation is over. The PLO is in the process of 'hardening' and renewed terrorist activity, aimed either directly at Israel or, on the international level, at her allies, is likely. Once that happens, the 'Palestinian problem' will enter a new and more dangerous phase.

The IDF

THE CENTRAL OPERATIONAL concept behind the evolution of the Israeli Defence Forces (IDF) has always been the protection of Israel's borders. The Israeli view of defence, however, is flexible, and on a number of occasions aggressive preventative measures have been taken in the interests of long-term security. Such was the thinking behind the strike by Israeli Air Force (IAF) F-16s against the Iraqi nuclear powerplant at Tuwaitha in June 1981.

Defence of the border areas has involved not only preparation for a full-scale war launched against Israel by her Arab neighbours but has also included measures taken against limited-scale military aggression in the form of guerrilla attacks on Israeli settlements. With a population of just over three million Jews, one of the main problems for Israel has been a chronic shortage of manpower and the economic impossibility of maintaining a large standing army. The IDF relies on compulsory military service and the manpower problem has resulted in a heavy emphasis on the aquisition of up-to-date weapon systems and the training of personnel to a high level of proficiency in their usage. Military service comprises a basic three years full-time commitment with 28 days reserve duty a year thereafter to the age of 55.

The IDF deploys its border-protection forces at a constant state of readiness. Long-distance observation posts utilising anti-personnel radar and night-vision equipment, minefields, anti-tank ditches, earthworks, artillery emplacements and barbed-wire fencing provide the static defences while the units themselves are deployed in a manner capable of carrying out mobile blocking operations, making good use of firepower. This strategy aims to delay any oncoming enemy long enough for the reservists, who form the main body of the IDF, to be mobilised and to carry the battle back into enemy territory. In this context the IAF plays a crucial role, since without air superiority the numerically inferior ground forces would be hard pressed. Israel's seaboard is covered by coastal patrol boats and missile-armed ships patrolling the seas. Highly sophisticated radar and early warning aircraft warn of any incursion of Israeli airspace and the highly-trained interceptor squadrons can deal with any potential intruders.

Defence fictions

One of the main problems in making any assessment of the strength and capabilities of the IDF lies in the quality and quantity of available information. As Israeli Minister of Defence Moshe Dayan stated in the aftermath of the 1967 War: 'We have never revealed, and I hope we never shall, what the size and numbers of the Israeli defences are.' His successors have been remarkably consistent in achieving that aim. The Israelis have become masters of misinformation, making it virtually impossible for any military analyst to be at all precise about the exact size, composition, equipment scales or deployment of the IDF. Thus in any discussion of the role of the IDF in the Middle East it must be borne in mind that certain facts may not have been fully revealed or may have been subject to deliberate falsification.

Beirut under siege

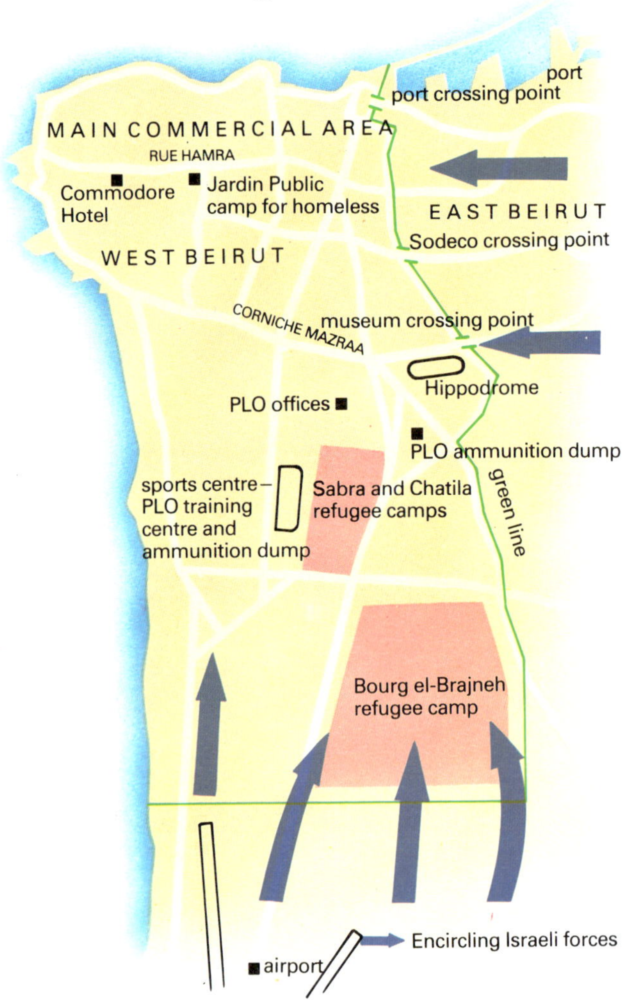

BELOW: *Israeli self-propelled artillery pounds the Lebanese capital of Beirut.* RIGHT: *The introduction of the Israeli-built Merkava MBT marked a significant trend towards home-manufactured weaponry, and with its advanced technology it soon proved itself in combat against the Soviet-built tanks and armoured vehicles of the Syrian Army.*

Having said that, however, some points are indisputable. It is clear, for example, that the bitter lessons learnt in the Yom Kippur War of October 1973 have been taken to heart. A new emphasis upon all-arms cooperation on the battlefield may be seen in the addition of mechanised infantry and self-propelled artillery to the armoured formations of the IDF; munitions and other war supplies have been carefully stockpiled, and a significant trend towards self-reliance and an indigenous armaments industry has emerged. The latter is perhaps the most important development, caused by fears that Arab economic or political pressure may in the future lead to the loss of traditional sources of supply, particularly from the United States. This trend can be seen in two distinct areas of Israeli policy. On the one hand, the IDF has adapted captured Arab weapons, almost entirely of Russian origin, for front-line service. Although the T54/55s of 1967 have been phased out, a number of IDF tank battalions still use the T62s captured in 1973, modifying them by the addition of diesel engines and the standard Israeli 105mm main armament. In addition, the Soviet-built BT series of armoured fighting vehicles (AFVs) and PT76 light tanks have found their way into Israeli armoured infantry and reconnaissance units.

Israeli armaments

But such weapons are difficult to replace without recourse to renewed war, so as the second part of the policy the Israelis have established their own armaments industry. The IDF's high ratio of tanks to infantry ensures a constant demand for main battle tanks (MBTs). In the past Israel was forced to look to many sources to supply this demand. During the 1948 war the IDF had little in the way of armour, relying on a few hastily-repaired near-derelict M4 Shermans, a handful of Cromwell and Hotchkiss tanks and some locally manufactured 'sandwich' armour-plated trucks. During the 1950s most of the IDF's armour came from the USA, France and the United Kingdom and included Shermans, AMX13s and Centurions. Tank modification on Israeli soil began to function in earnest in 1955 with the introduction of the Israeli-designated M50 Sherman and was followed by the 'upgraded' Centurion which was to see extensive combat experience in the 1973 Yom Kippur war as well as the invasion of Lebanon in 1982.

The outbreak of the Six-Day War saw the breakdown of secret negotiations with Britain for the purchase of the Chieftain tank and with other European nations similarly hesitant to supply the IDF, Israel's only remaining supplier became the USA from whom they bought M48, M60 and M60A1 tanks. Israeli defence planners clearly realised the necessity for a home-produced MBT if they were to maintain control over their military future. In 1970 government sanction was gained for the new Merkava MBT project; the tank which was first to see action against the Syrians in the Lebanon in 1982. The Merkava was designed to meet the particular needs of the IDF and while with a combat weight of 56 tonnes it is one of the heaviest tanks in service in the Middle East, it places heavy emphasis on the protection of the crew of four. The engine is located at the forward end of the hull, which allows the Merkava to incorporate a unique rear-hatch arrangement, thereby providing a rapid escape route from the combat compartment and even the capacity to carry infantry and extra ammunition.

Reconnaissance units are now receiving the RBY, an Israeli-built four-wheel drive scout car, specially designed to withstand the effects of a landmine detonation. It too has a four-man crew and is armed with 0.30 and 0.50-inch calibre machine guns. Artillery battalions still use the

The Merkava main battle tank

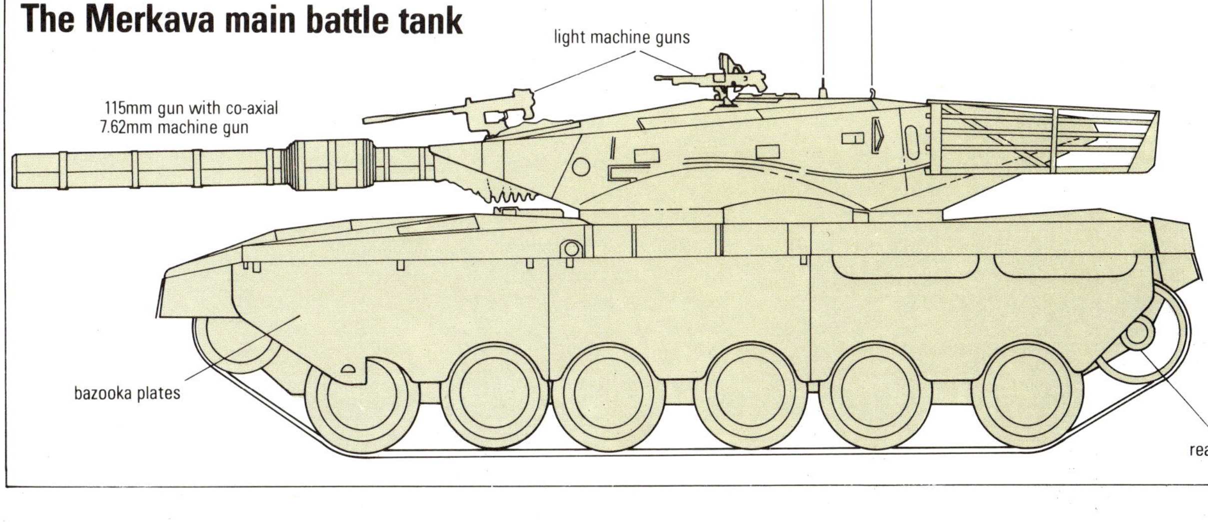

weight 55.9 tonnes (55 tons) **length** 8.63m (28ft 4in) **height** 2.64m (8ft 8in) **ammunition** APDS, HEAT, HESH, APFSDS, phosphorus **armour** 105mm **range** 450km (280 miles) **speed** 46km/h (28mph) **crew** 4

105mm howitzer mounted on the Super Sherman chassis, but they also have their own tracked Ziev surface-to-surface missile (SSM) alongside the American-supplied Lance. The Navy deploys Israeli-produced Gabriel ship-to-ship missiles and, most importantly of all, the IAF has over 200 Kfir fighter-bombers, designed around the French Mirage airframe and an American engine but produced without dependence upon outside sources of supply. Further developments in this area include the Israeli Aircraft Industries new Lavi programme. Some fifty million dollars was allocated by the Defence Ministry in early 1982 for the development of a new high-speed, long-range aircraft, primarily for ground-attack missions but with a secondary fighter role. Due to rising costs the Lavi programme now seems to be in jeopardy, but if it goes ahead it will serve as a replacement for the IAF Skyhawks and Kfirs and the first units will receive the aircraft in the early 1990s.

The US involvement

The move towards self-sufficiency is by no means complete and the IDF is still very dependent upon the United States for certain key areas of supply, particularly during times of war when spare parts and replacement vehicles are needed quickly. Since Israel became an independent state in 1948 the Americans have provided nearly 15 billion dollars in military aid alone. About a third of this has been outright 'gifts' in the form of grants; the remainder has been made up of loans with more than generous repayment terms. The net result has been a deep dependence upon the Americans and this is quite naturally reflected in the large amount of US equipment in the IDF. On the ground, the main firepower for the armoured striking force comes from the 800 advanced versions of the M60 MBT, while the armoured infantry rides into battle in M-113 armoured personnel carriers, of which the Israelis have over 4000 with a further 800 currently on order. In the air the situation is the same, for over 600 of the IAF's combat aircraft are American in origin. These include the formidable F-15 Eagles and F-16 Fighting Falcons, backed up by the redoubtable multi-role F-4 Phantoms and A-4 Skyhawks with their prodigious bomb-loads. In addition, Israel operates a sophisticated airborne early warning system, based upon the American E-2C Hawkeye surveillance aircraft equipped with electronic counter-measures, jamming and anti-jamming devices. Finally, despite a degree of self-sufficiency in ammunition and small-arms, which includes the Uzi sub-machine gun and Galil assault rifle, the Israelis look to the Americans for the more destructive weapons. One of the most lethal of these is undoubtedly the CBU-58 cluster bomb which, in the version deployed by the IAF and known as the Mark 20 Rockeye, scatter eight-inch steel darts from a host of small bomblets to devastating effect.

So long as these items remain available, augmented by the results of Israeli domestic efforts, the IDF maintains its formidable potential. Its primary role is still to protect the state of Israel from Arab attack – something which it has carried out with remarkable success since the war of 1948–49 – and for that reason it has to be prepared for immediate operations whenever a threat materialises. In many cases this has produced an emphasis upon the pre-emptive strike, designed to remove a threat before it has time to develop into an attack upon Israeli territory. The invasion of southern Lebanon in June 1982 fitted the pattern exactly.

A new warfare

In the Lebanon the IDF was faced with two kinds of opponent: on the one hand they were pitted against a semi-regular army and guerrillas in the form of the PLO and Moslem groups, while on the other they faced the regular Syrian Army. The guerrillas, although reasonably well equipped and experienced in urban warfare, clearly lacked the means to hold the Israeli mobile offensive in southern Lebanon and the towns were overwhelmed by superior firepower, while the Syrians were defeated by a combination of the sophisticated equipment and superior military efficiency of the IDF. The Israeli victory was an undoubted vindication of IDF policy but the decision to stay in southern Lebanon brought a new problem. As the Israeli Army settled in as a force of occupation then the tactical advantages of mobility and surprise, so ably exploited earlier in the campaign and in past Middle East conflicts, evaporated, leaving their units to face a war of attrition, a form of warfare totally at variance with Israeli military theory and experience. For their part, the Syrians and PLO continued to build up their forces in the Beqaa Valley while in Israel itself popular dissent against the prolonged presence of the IDF on foreign soil gathered momentum.

The withdrawal to the Awali Line on 2 September 1983, designed in part to counter such dissent, has not removed the IDF from the war zone. The Syrians remain in Lebanon and the fighting between Lebanese national and religious factions continues, and unless there is a dramatic turn around in Israeli foreign policy it seems unlikely that the IDF will relinquish its strategically favourable position in southern Lebanon.

TOP: *The formidable Israeli F-15 air-superiority fighter.* ABOVE: *An Israeli gunboat.* BELOW LEFT: *An Israeli infantryman on patrol.*

War in the US Backyard

In the 1980s bloody civil war was rife in Central America, with thousands dying in the struggle between right-wing juntas and guerrilla liberation armies

Jonathan Reed

SINCE THE mid-1970s and the communist victories in Indochina, the Central American isthmus has become the new focus for East–West Cold War tensions and hostilities. The stability and security of the region has been high on US foreign policy priorities since the 19th and early 20th centuries, when huge amounts of American investment were poured into Central America. US interests were mainly in mining and agriculture and it was during the years of investment that the massively lucrative fruit and coffee empires were built in the so-called 'banana republics'. The importance of the area was further consolidated when in 1914 the Panama Canal was opened. This linked the eastern and western seaboards of the US and opened up whole new vistas to the growing trade in the area. To protect these interests the US has maintained a substantial military presence in Panama, while also administering the Canal, and has frequently deployed interventionary forces throughout the Caribbean when local revolts and uprisings have threatened to damage US economic interests and undermine friendly regimes.

But while the US has pursued a 'good neighbour' policy in Central America, since the 1959 Cuban Revolution the level of communist interest in the area has also increased. The strategic importance of the Caribbean was fully realised with the Cuban Missile Crisis in 1962 when the Soviet Union attempted to base nuclear missiles on the US doorstep. For the US, Central America is the key to the vitally important shipping lanes of the Caribbean and the Panama Canal, while for the Eastern bloc, the Central American and Caribbean states provide excellent potential as staging points for Cuban and Soviet operations not only in the whole Latin American region, but also in Africa.

While each of the main Central American countries – El Salvador, Nicaragua, Honduras, Guatemala and Costa Rica – is beset with its own indigenous economic and political problems, they all share to a great extent the common factors of extreme social and ideological polarisation, grotesque poverty, violent instability, the continued pressure of guerrilla insurgency and the ever-present threat of revolution and protracted civil war. In the Caribbean as a whole, communism and armed revolutionary opposition have taken firm root. Between 1956 and 1959, Fidel Castro waged a successful guerrilla war and Cuba became the first communist state in the region. This was followed in 1979 by a bloodless coup in Grenada in which Maurice Bishop seized power and a People's Revolutionary Government took over control of the country. That same year after a bitter all-out civil war President

ABOVE LEFT: *Guerrilla units in El Salvador raise money by levying a war tax from motorists on the Pan American highway. This supplements the arms shipments they receive from Cuba and the Soviet Union.* BELOW LEFT: *'Contra' groups undergoing training with US weapons and US instructors in Panama after the 1979 Sandinista takeover in Nicaragua.* BELOW: *Fidel Castro enters Havana in triumph in 1959, at the end of his successful guerrilla campaign in Cuba. Castro's victory became the model for revolutionary struggle.*

Anastasio Somoza of Nicaragua was toppled and the Marxist Sandinista Junta of National Reconstruction came to power. Since 1980, El Salvador has been locked in a state of civil war with the military government and extremist right-wing death squads fighting a stalemated battle for the country against left-wing guerrillas of the FMLN (Farabundo Martí de Liberación Nacional). In Guatemala the poverty-stricken Indian population has fielded rebel guerrilla units and the military junta continues to pursue a campaign of repression and counter-insurgency against the dissident elements.

ABOVE: *Armed with US-supplied M16s and a recoilless rifle, a patrol of Salvadorean troops moves through the town of Berlin during a counter-insurgency operation against FMLN guerrillas. Increased US aid has not, however, resolved the conflict, and El Salvador's civil war remains deadlocked.* RIGHT: *The tables are turned in Nicaragua. A Sandinista militia woman stands guard over captured National Guardsmen at Managua's police headquarters three days after Somoza's flight to Miami.*

Bad neighbours

In addition to each country's struggle to maintain internal security against the steadily escalating level of armed insurgency, the region has been torn by a number of military disputes and political tensions between the countries themselves. In 1969 El Salvador and Honduras fought the so-called 'Football War', and the border between the two remained closed with frequent outbreaks of violence until 1980. Following the successful revolution in Nicaragua, relations between Honduras and Nicaragua rapidly deteriorated in the early 1980s and the possibility of an all-out war between the two countries still represents a major threat to the fragile security of the region as a whole. Only Costa Rica, which has no armed forces apart from a Rural Guard, has so far remained immune. Even there, however, although the people enjoy a substantial social welfare apparatus and a high level of literacy by Central American standards, stirrings of dissent are beginning to surface as economic stability is increasingly threatened by rising inflation and a sharp decline in coffee export prices.

By the mid-1980s the wars in Central America had escalated far beyond local outbreaks of insurgency, with both geographical and political boundaries of the countries being constantly violated. Salvadorean guerrillas operate out of Nicaragua and Honduras, anti-Sandinista US-sponsored counter-revolutionary 'Contra' groups fighting to retake Nicaragua are based in Honduras and Costa Rica, while Cubans train the Sandinista People's Army and Honduran anti-government guerrillas in Nicaragua. The Soviet Union supplies large quantities of arms and equipment to the guerrillas in all countries through Cuba and Nicaragua and there is a constant flow of weapons across the borders. Well over 100,000 people have died in the conflicts and more than a million made homeless. Fears of further communist successes, especially in El Salvador, have resulted in the US pursuing a high-profile presence in Central America, but the options now open to the US are far more limited than they were in the 1960s.

The US experience in Southeast Asia in the 1960s and 1970s has cast a new light on Cold War strategy. Prior to the defeat in Vietnam, direct US intervention had on a number of occasions effectively controlled the political turbulence in Central America. In 1954 the US intervened in Guatemala using a CIA-organised rebel force to overthrow the reformist government of President Jacobo Arbenz Guzman following his seizure of large landholdings owned by the American United Fruit Company. In 1961 a US-sponsored force of Cuban exiles attempted to overthrow the recently empowered Cuban Castro regime in the unsuccessful Bay of Pigs invasion, and four years later 20,000 US troops were committed in the Dominican Republic to quash an uprising against the ruling military junta. Between 1966 and 1968 US Special Forces aided the Guatemalan regime in a two-year counter-insurgency campaign against rebel guerrillas. The most recent act of open intervention by the US was in October 1983 when a force of Marines and Rangers invaded Grenada following the assassination of the Grenadian president, Maurice Bishop. This particular operation, however, was mounted in conjunction with six other Caribbean states and only after member countries of the Organisation of Eastern Caribbean States had appealed to President Reagan to provide direct military aid to restore order on the island.

Since Vietnam, the US has had to abandon overt gunboat diplomacy, and considerable

TOP: *A refugee camp in Guatemala housing the victims of the ruling junta's brutal campaign of counter-insurgency. It was the desperate poverty of the Indian population that sparked off a renewed guerrilla campaign in the 1980s.* ABOVE: *President Reagan meets President Cordova of Honduras, which has become the main US power base for the escalating battle against communism in Central America.*

pressure has been exerted on the Reagan administration from both inside and outside the US on the highly sensitive issue of US involvement in the affairs of Central America. The Contadora Group, composed of Mexico, Venezuela, Panama and Colombia, are looking into means of achieving a peaceful resolution to Central America's problems and have made it quite clear to the Reagan administration that the problems are essentially indigenous to the area and lie in social and economic inequalities, and as such should not enter into the context of an East–West struggle for control in the region. The US, however, has not viewed favourably the Group's proposals to date, especially concerning the numerical level of Nicaragua's armed forces and the participation of the FMLN guerrillas in El Salvador's government.

President Reagan's dictum that El Salvador will not be 'lost' under any circumstances and the continued US efforts to destabilise the Nicaraguan regime have resulted in the establishment of a strong US power base in Honduras. Honduras, the original 'banana republic', has become America's closest ally in Central America and the centre of US military activity in the region. Five airbases have either been built or modernised by the US in Honduras, and US Mohawk reconnaissance aircraft in conjunction with C-130s based in Panama fly regularly over El Salvador providing up-to-the-minute intelligence on FMLN movements. In 1984 more than 1500 US military personnel including 160 Special Forces advisors were stationed in Honduras while the number of advisors in El Salvador increased to just under 100. In El Salvador some are reported to have been seen carrying arms very close to the scene of counter-insurgency operations. Financial assistance for military actions in El Salvador shot up from some $82 million in 1982 to $136.3 million in 1983, and a Regional Military Training Centre for Salvadorean and Honduran army units has been established at Trujillo on the Caribbean coast of Honduras. In 1984 CIA-directed Contra operations against Nicaragua doubled from their 1983 levels, and a series of naval and joint US-Honduran military manoeuvres have been staged in the area.

The watchful eye of the US

The Reagan administration continues to stress the long-term economic aspects of US involvement in Central America and the Caribbean while playing down any suggestion that the US is seeking a purely military solution in the area. The official line is that the continued provision of military assistance is essential in the 1980s since while anti-government guerrilla forces continue to destabilise the various countries, economic, social and political development is impossible. In January 1984, the National Bipartisan Commission on Central America, a body of politicians and political scientists headed by former US Secretary of State Henry Kissinger, reported its findings to President Reagan after an in-depth study of the problems and possible courses of action in Central America. The Commission re-stressed the urgency of the communist threat in the US 'backyard' and the vulnerability of the vitally important Caribbean shipping lanes. Ratifying the policy of massive aid to the region, Kissinger recommended the spending of some $8 billion in economic aid in the area up to 1990, and that military aid to El Salvador should be 'significantly increased'. Concern in the US on the issue of human rights and the continued murderous activities of the death squads led him to emphasise that military aid should be linked to an improvement in human rights and the building of an effective judicial system – but that this should not be pursued to an extent that might allow a guerrilla victory in El Salvador. (As the war in El Salvador remained deadlocked, the first glimmer of a peace settlement emerged in October 1984 when President José Napoleón Duarte met with guerrilla leaders to discuss the political future of the country.)

The ambiguity of the US attitude to its involvement in Central America, however, is typified by the Bipartisan Commission's findings and recommendations on the issue of Nicaragua. While one commissioner called for a two-year suspension of US support to the Contras, another declared that any aid given should be overt. Extensive debate as to whether Central America will evolve into another Vietnam has made the US administrations wary of over-reacting. However, should war break out between Nicaragua and Honduras, or Nicaragua be tempted to interfere with neutral Costa Rica, the US will find it hard to sit on the sidelines.

Nicaragua

ON 17 JULY 1979, with rebel columns of the FSLN (Frente Sandinista de Liberación Nacional) surrounding Managua, the capital city of Nicaragua, President Anastasio Somoza Debayle boarded a plane for Miami. He was never to set foot in the country again. For Nicaragua it was the end of a bitter and bloody civil war and the beginning of a new political state in Central America. Yet although the brutal and repressive Somoza dictatorship had been replaced by a Sandinista Junta of National Reconstruction, for many in Nicaragua the revolution was not to live up to all its promises of freedom and non-alignment. While all-out civil war had been brought to an end with the FSLN victory, the battle for Nicaragua continued.

While the roots of the Sandinista revolution lay in nationalism, its success depended on a broad class alliance opposition to the political, economic and military stranglehold exercised over Nicaragua by the Somoza family for 44 years. In the late 1920s, Augusto César Sandino (from whom the FSLN took its name) waged a nationalist guerrilla war in the inhospitable Las Segovias mountains in the northwest of the country against a force of US Marines deployed to protect US interests in mining and agriculture. The Marines were withdrawn in 1933, leaving the country in the hands of the recently formed 2500-strong National Guard commanded by General Anastasio Somoza García. In 1934, during the ensuing peace negotiations, Sandino was murdered by the Guard, and in 1935, having effectively wiped out the guerrilla presence in Nicaragua, Somoza seized power in a coup. Somoza remained in power until his assassination in 1956, when he was succeeded by his son Luís Somoza Debayle. His other son, Anastasio Somoza Debayle (who became president in 1967), commanded the National Guard. Between them the Somozas wielded immense power; they were fabulously wealthy, they had a firm hold on the presidency and, in the National Guard, they controlled the means to keep it.

The National Guard

The role of the National Guard in Nicaragua extended far beyond that of a normal army. While it administered both internal and external security, it also controlled the national electricity grid and the postal and telecommunications networks. Its officers enjoyed great social prestige and by the 1970s the troops were well trained and equipped with modern US and Israeli weaponry. There were also several elite anti-guerrilla units such as the notorious Escuela de Entrenamiento Basico de Infanteria, a force indoctrinated with a fierce hatred of any opposition to Somoza, and whose savage brutality in the latter part of the war was to become legendary.

In July 1961 three former university students, Carlos Fonseca Amador, Silvio Mayorga and Thomas Borge, met in Honduras with the aim of establishing a revolutionary movement. Pinprick guerrilla raids across the border into Nicaragua had so far achieved little, and the FSLN, founded in 1962, began the arduous task of mobilising the working classes in opposition to Luís Somoza. Like their martyred hero Sandino, the FSLN operated from the northern mountains, and for five years they struggled to build support. In 1967 they judged the time right to consolidate a guerrilla army in central Nicaragua at Mount Pancasan. The National Guard, however, soon discovered the whereabouts of the FSLN columns and inflicted a severe defeat on the rebels, who were forced to go underground and continue their struggle through intermediary worker and student organisations.

On 27 December 1974 the FSLN broke cover, launching a daring commando raid against a reception given for the US ambassador in Managua, and taking hostage a number of senior politicians and friends of the president, now Anastasio Somoza.

ABOVE: *The charismatic father of the Nicaraguan revolution, Augusto Sandino.* BELOW: *President Anastasio Somoza, who was toppled from power in July 1979.* BOTTOM: *A young Sandinista guerrilla in the war-torn streets of Masaya in May 1979.*

He acceded to the ransom demands ($500,000 and the release of 59 jailed guerrillas) and the 13 commandos escaped to Cuba, leaving the regime badly humiliated. Somoza responded with a brutal reign of terror – martial law and tight censorship were imposed and a savage counter-insurgency campaign was mounted against the guerrillas. Peasant villages in guerrilla areas were destroyed, concentration camps established, and search-and-destroy operations were augmented with bombing, napalm attacks and the use of defoliants.

A popular rebellion

Over the next three years, opposition to the regime spread throughout Nicaraguan society. A split within the FSLN brought about a change of strategy, a war of popular insurrection replacing the prolonged guerrilla war of attrition they had been fighting. At the same time the FSLN's narrow Marxist base was broadened to embrace the disaffected Conservative and Liberal Party middle-class opposition to the regime. Taking advantage of Somoza's recent heart attack, the FSLN renewed their offensive in October 1977 with outright assaults on Guard units in Managua and the main towns. Two months later, rioting broke out in Managua after Somoza's assassination of the outspoken editor of the newspaper *La Prensa*, and this was immediately followed by a two-week general strike in which employers participated alongside their workers. Throughout 1978 hostilities flared in the towns, with barricades being erected and the inhabitants fighting in the streets against the National Guard. Another daring commando raid against the National Palace in Managua in August emboldened the populace still further, and the inhabitants of Matagalpa rose in an insurrection which spread rapidly through other major towns. Somoza succeeded in temporarily subduing the urban revolts but by now the regime and the FSLN were locked in an all-out civil war. The offensive was renewed in February 1979 and by May the FSLN was ready to launch its final offensive on seven main battle fronts. One by one the cities of Nicaragua fell, and on 9 June popular revolt broke out in the capital. Somoza took personal command of the counterattack in Managua, using artillery, rockets and helicopter bombers against the rebel positions, but by mid-July, with the Sandinista forces poised around the city, the war was effectively over, and Somoza was forced to seek refuge in the US. He was to be assassinated in Paraguay in September 1980.

On 20 July 1979 the Junta of National Reconstruction took over the government of Nicaragua. The National Guard was dissolved and replaced by the Sandinista People's Army, while various industrial reform, agrarian and educational programmes were introduced. By 1981, however, the political situation had begun to deteriorate. The promised elections had not materialised and opposition to FSLN rule in Nicaragua strengthened as the government became more radical and relations with the Church worsened. Along the border with Honduras some 2000 ex-National Guardsmen, known as the 'Contras', supported by the Honduran armed forces and US funding, launched raids into Nicaragua. Internal security was also threatened by a rebellion of Moskito Indians seeking the establishment of the province of Zelaya as an independent territory. In the face of joint US and Honduran military manoeuvres and Honduran air attacks on Nicaraguan petroleum plants the Sandinista junta declared a state of emergency in March 1982. In July another combined US–Honduran exercise, 'Big Pine', gave rise to fears of an imminent invasion of Nicaragua, which were exacerbated by a new offensive mounted by the Honduran-based Contras against Sandinista military installations and economic targets in January 1983. In April Edén Pastora Gómez ('Commander Zero'), senior Sandinista officer and leader of the 1978 National Palace raid, announced his opposition to the new state and began operations against Nicaragua from his base in Costa Rica. Relations with Honduras remained tense, and in July a naval clash between the two countries occurred in the Gulf of Fonseca. Meanwhile, another anti-Sandinista group, the FDN (Fuerzas Democráticos Nigaragüenses), announced that it had mined Nicaragua's Atlantic coast ports.

In the face of mounting opposition, in December 1983 Nicaragua adopted a more conciliatory attitude towards the opposition elements, announcing that the state of emergency would be lifted in 1984 and reaffirming its support for the Central American peace initiatives of the Contadora

ABOVE: *With modern weapons in short supply, Sandinista fighters often had to do battle with home-made equipment.* BELOW: *In contrast, the US-sponsored Contra groups are armed with modern assault rifles.*

Group (comprising Mexico, Venezuela, Panama and Colombia). Relations with the US, however, remained strained because of continued US financial aid to the Contras (amounting to $19 million in 1981 and 1982), and the Reagan administration's refusal to enter into direct negotiations with the junta. The junta, on the other hand, continued to supply arms to the rebel forces in El Salvador, and the situation was not improved by an incident in January 1984, when the Sandinista army shot down a US helicopter in the border region.

In Nicaragua itself the problems of internal opposition were to a certain extent allayed by promises of elections and reduced restrictions on political activity and on the tight press censorship imposed earlier in the junta's rule. The elections, held in October 1984, confirmed President Daniel Ortega's Sandinista leadership, but the external threat from the Contras and their US and Honduran backers remained as real as ever. Relations between Nicaragua and the US deteriorated as Soviet ships imported more military hardware in November 1984.

Grenada

THE TINY island of Grenada lies at the southernmost tip of the Caribbean Windward Islands, has a population of some 115,000, and with the smaller Grenadine Islands forms a state of 210 square km (133 square miles). A former British colony which achieved independence in February 1974, this seemingly insignificant plot of land became the focus of world attention when on 25 October 1983 US forces, along with token contingents from six other Caribbean countries, stormed the island at dawn. The reasons for the invasion, as outlined in a statement by the US Secretary of State, were the protection of the 1000 US citizens then resident in Grenada and 'to help Grenada re-establish governmental institutions capable of restoring order, protecting human rights and maintaining peace and stability'. Within the context of the Reagan administration's broader Central American and Caribbean policy, however, Grenada had been a growing source of US concern for some time.

Left-wing coup

On 13 March 1979, the left-wing New Jewel Movement (NJM) seized power in a bloodless coup, unseating the incumbent government and its prime minister, Sir Eric Gairy, and a new People's Revolutionary Government (PRG) was formed under Maurice Bishop. The PRG embarked on policies which emphasised education and welfare, but the country remained under fairly strong central control especially after an attempt by extreme left-wing elements to assassinate Bishop in 1980; the 1973 constitution was suspended, the PRG empowered itself to arrest people suspected of counter-revolutionary activities and all newspapers with the exception of the official government journal were closed down. Although the PRG had at first declared itself to hold non-aligned foreign policies, by 1982 the US and the more conservative Caribbean states were becoming increasingly concerned at the level of Soviet and Cuban influence in Grenada. Economic and scientific agreements had been signed with the Eastern bloc and aid teams had been sent out to Grenada. The People's Revolutionary Army (PRA) was supplied with Soviet AK-47 assault rifles, anti-aircraft guns and armoured personnel carriers. But although the PRA's arsenal dwarfed those of Grenada's immediate neighbours, the PRA itself only numbered 1000 men, and the real focus of US concern lay in the construction of a new airport at Point Salines, built with the assistance of Cuban construction workers. The airport was to have a 3km (2-mile) runway, long enough in the US view to accommodate any aircraft in the Soviet or Cuban Air Forces, and a potential staging and refuelling point for future Soviet or Cuban ventures in the western hemisphere and Africa. Tensions between the US and Grenada increased when in March 1983 Bishop put the armed forces on alert, announcing that he had discovered the existence of a US-backed plan for an invasion of Grenada by Cuban,

ABOVE: *US forces on the deck of the assault ship* Guam *from which the invasion was launched.* BELOW: *Maurice Bishop, whose murder in October 1983 prompted the US intervention.* BOTTOM: *US medical students take their leave of the island.*

Nicaraguan and Grenadian exiles.

Bishop, however, recognised the danger of overt intimidation of the US, and in a move to placate President Ronald Reagan, he visited America in June 1983 – only to be refused an interview with the president. But his 'soft' attitude towards the US, his own brand of socialism which allowed for the continued existence of private enterprise, and his seeming willingness to hold elections, reduce the Cuban presence and arrest the further development of links with the Eastern bloc brought him accusations of 'disgracing the revolution' at home. Hard-line elements in the NJM Central Committee (including Bishop's deputy Bernard Coard, and commander of the PRA General Hudson Austin) moved with the support of the majority of the Committee that Bishop share power with Coard. Bishop opposed this and subsequent rumours that Coard was planning to kill Bishop led to Coard's resignation. An investigation into the rumours traced them back to Bishop himself and he was placed under house arrest on 13 October. Six days later, Bishop's popularity came to his rescue and a crowd of 3000 marched to his house and released him, carrying him in triumph to Fort Rupert, the PRA headquarters. The struggle for power in Grenada then proceeded to take a violent turn – troops opened fire on Bishop's supporters outside the fort and Bishop and several ministers and trade-union leaders were taken away and executed. That same day General Austin announced the dissolution of the PRG and the formation of a 16-member Revolutionary Military Council. A 24-hour curfew was imposed and anyone found on the streets was shot on sight.

ABOVE: *US Rangers shell Cuban and PRA positions in the surrounding hills from the airstrip at Point Salines. Opposition to the invading forces was much heavier than expected.* RIGHT: *In the wake of the US intervention, former deputy prime minister Bernard Coard is brought to court to face charges of conspiring to murder Bishop.*

The US steps in

Outrage at the killing of Bishop and his supporters was widespread throughout the Caribbean and at a meeting of the Organisation of Eastern Caribbean States on 21 October it was decided to seek help from the US for action in Grenada. President Reagan responded to their appeals for aid and for the first time since the end of their involvement in the Vietnam War in 1973 US troops were committed to a combat assault.

The first party to land was a group of US Navy SEALs (Sea-Air-Land teams) whose task it was to secure Government House where Sir Paul Scoon, Governor-General of Grenada, was being held. Having achieved their objective, at 0536 hours on 25 October some 400 heliborne US Marines from the assault ship *Guam* were landed at Pearls airport, and half an hour later the main assault force of US Rangers supported by Cobra and AC-130 gunships parachuted into the half-built barricaded airport at Point Salines. As they landed the Rangers came under heavy fire from Cuban and PRA forces but by 0715 hours had succeeded in clearing and securing the runway to allow the larger fixed-wing transports to bring in more troops. Moving out from Point Salines the Rangers secured the nearby True Blue Medical School where several hundred US students were sheltering from the fighting. By now some 1900 US troops were on Grenada but as strong resistance continued reinforcements were flown in, bringing the invasion force up to 3000.

At 0730 hours a further 250 Marines made an amphibious landing just north of the capital, St George's, near where the PRA and Cuban forces were holding Fort Frederick and attacking Government House. Encountering heavy resistance the Marines were not able to secure these two objectives until the following morning when they finally succeeded in evacuating Sir Paul Scoon to the *Guam*. The next objective was to take the campus at Grand Anse. A force of Marines and Rangers in six helicopters broke through the ring of PRA and Cuban defenders and evacuated the students by helicopter under fire. The final objectives, Fort Frederick and the Richmond Hill prison, were stormed but had already been evacuated, and by late afternoon the invasion force was in control of Grenada, apart from isolated pockets of resistance where sporadic fighting continued.

At the close of the operation the US had committed some 7300 troops to Grenada. According to casualty figures 18 US soldiers, 24 Cubans and 16 Grenadians were killed in the fighting. Figures for civilians killed (including the casualties caused by an unfortunate US attack on a mental hospital) are unknown. US intelligence had severely underestimated the opposition, and figures based on captured Cuban documents put the total Cuban presence at 1100 men, while substantial quantities of Soviet and Cuban military equipment were also unearthed. US troop withdrawal commenced in mid-November, and by mid-December only 300 US support troops remained to aid the 400 Caribbean troops who had stayed on after the operation while a new defence force comprising police and a paramilitary section was being set up. On the political side Sir Paul Scoon established an interim advisory council; this was superseded by the US-backed New National Party, headed by Herbert Blaize, which came to power in the elections of December 1984.

TOP LEFT: *Mayhem breaks out in the streets of San Salvador immediately following the assassination of Archbishop Romero. It was Romero's killing which brought El Salvador to the brink of all-out civil war.* TOP RIGHT: *National Guards fighting the FMLN.* BELOW: *Well-armed guerrillas set off on a mission.*

El Salvador

THE REPUBLIC of El Salvador is the most densely populated and highly-industrialised state in Central America. It is also the poorest. Since the outbreak of civil war in April 1980, the Salvadorean economy has been ruined. Sharp falls in world prices, drought and continued rural warfare have devastated coffee production, El Salvador's most important source of export revenue, while the industrial sector was so severely damaged by guerrilla activity in 1981 that industry was reduced to operating at half its normal capacity. By 1982 unemployment had risen to 40 per cent in urban areas and up to 70 per cent in the main areas of fighting. This further inflamed the deep-rooted social and economic problems which had stimulated the growth of peasant and worker organisations and an armed guerrilla movement in the 1960s and 1970s, and soon El Salvador was gripped in the vice of chronic civil war, with the military government fighting full-scale pitched battles against the guerrilla forces.

Social problems

Since the late 1950s, El Salvador has been subject to a great deal of political instability and social polarisation. Its military government has seen a succession of coups while the Catholic Church and the tiny landowning elite have come to blows over the key issues at the heart of El Salvador's instability – agrarian reform, extreme poverty, the abuse of human rights and inadequate political representation. Various military governments have made modest efforts to deflect the threat of revolution by admitting civilians to the junta and introducing limited reform programmes, but these have been rejected by the left and have sparked off an extremely hostile reaction from the landowning elite. More recent governments have since pursued progressively harsher and more repressive policies in an attempt to maintain order in the country.

Although the civil war was the direct result of internal political and economic factors, its outbreak was accelerated by an external factor, namely El Salvador's relations with neighbouring Honduras. During the 1960s, El Salvador's acute shortage of land had led to an enormous exodus of landless peasants over the border into Honduras, whose population density was one-tenth that of El Salvador. By 1969 immigrant refugees constituted over 12 per cent of the Honduran population and despite intense protests from the Honduran government the flow continued unchecked. Hostilities flared up in 1969 during local World Cup soccer qualifying matches and on 14 July the Salvadorean Army invaded Honduras. Two weeks later international pressure forced it to withdraw, but this brief 'Football War' was to have serious consequences for the future of El Salvador. During the period of industrial expansion in the 1960s, El Salvador had viewed Honduras as a major market for its industrial sector, but with the permanent closure of the border following the Salvadorean withdrawal the market disappeared. Relations between the two countries were to remain tense, with frequent clashes along the border during the 1970s; it was not until 1980 that a peace treaty was signed and the 11-year period of hostilities finally brought to an end.

While border tension and a steady expansion of the Honduran armed forces during the 1970s threatened El Salvador's external security, widespread discontent with political processes at home threatened its internal stability. Coupled with a further decline in the economy, this resulted in the growth of peasant and labour unions and the emergence of a number of guerrilla groups committed to the overthrow of the increasingly repressive regime led by Colonel Arturo Molina. Molina, chosen candidate of the ruling PCN (Partido de Conciliación Nacional) had come to power in March 1972, replacing General Fidel Sánchez Hernández, to whom he had been private secretary. In opposition to the PCN at the 1972 elections the Christian Democrats (PDC) had formed a coalition with two of the main left-wing parties, nominating José Napoleón Duarte as

The 'Football War'

On 8 June 1969 El Salvador played Honduras in the first leg of a qualifying match for the World Cup soccer competition. The match, played at Tegucigalpa in Honduras, ended in a 1–0 victory for the home team, but there were accusations that the Salvadorean side had been poisoned. The second leg was held a week later amid vicious anti-Honduran riots. El Salvador won 3–0 and qualified to play Haiti for a place in the World Cup. Soon afterwards Salvadorean settlers were subjected to revenge attacks and forced to flee Honduras. El Salvador retaliated with an invasion force, and fighting continued for two weeks before the Organisation of American States (OAS) intervened with the threat of total economic sanctions against the aggressor. Some 4000 people – mostly civilians – died in the fighting.

their candidate. During the election campaigns, Duarte narrowly escaped an assassination attempt in which his aide was killed. Moreover, as the results of the vote began to come in from El Salvador's cities showing Duarte and the PDC coalition ahead, radio and television broadcasts suddenly ceased to carry any election news. Outcries and accusations of fraud greeted the victorious Molina, and within a month an attempted coup nearly unseated him. More than 100 people died in the fighting as the coup was suppressed, the capital San Salvador was bombed, and Duarte was arrested and exiled to Venezuela. Further blatant electoral engineering in the local and municipal elections of 1974 and 1976 intensified the climate of political disillusionment in El Salvador, and armed opposition to the Molina regime was established. Several guerrilla groups emerged, the largest and most active of which was the People's Revolutionary Army (ERP), but the groups were far from united, each having its own views as to how the revolution should be achieved. Guerrilla activity took the form of attacks on military outposts, police stations and convoys, and the assassination of government informers, but the number of operational guerrillas still remained small.

Government forces

To combat the growing unrest, the Salvadorean government fielded a well-armed, US-supplied and trained army, a National Guard and an 80,000-strong peasant paramilitary network. With these forces to hand, discontent was actively suppressed. In 1974 the National Guard attacked the town of La Cayetana where peasants were in dispute with a local landowner; six villagers were killed and 20 'disappeared'. A year later police opened fire on a student demonstration against the government's spending US $3 million on the staging of the Miss Universe competition, and a great many demonstrators were killed and wounded. Alarmed by the growing protest, Molina changed tack and attempted to mollify the opposition with a very limited programme of land reform. His proposals were immediately rejected by both sides; by the peasant unions who thought they did not go far enough, and by the powerful right-wing landowner associations who saw such pacifying tactics as opening the door to communist control in El Salvador.

By 1977 the situation had become critical. Another blatantly fraudulent general election in February brought former Minister of Defence General Carlos Humberto Romero Mena to power, and in the wake of the election police opened fire on a 70,000-strong demonstration against the new regime, killing between 50 and 100 people. Romero tried to calm the situation with appeals for reconciliation, but by now the landowning elite and the extreme right-wing elements in the armed forces had virtually declared war on the popular organisations. Catholic clergy, especially Jesuits, who had championed the cause of human rights and supported the peasant organisations in the 1960s were declared subversive, and a number of priests were tortured or murdered. A new element had entered the struggle for El Salvador – the extremist ultra-right-wing terrorist 'death squads'. Organisations such as the White Warriors Union, hostile both to the left and to any government attempts at land reform, systematically set about murdering suspected left-wing sympathisers in a brutal campaign of terror and sickening violence. Piles of mutilated corpses dumped by the sides of the road soon became a not uncommon sight in El Salvador; by the autumn of 1983, during a particularly intense period of death squad activity, the body-count had reached a weekly total of over 200.

In November 1977, as the guerrillas retaliated against the death squad atrocities, and strikes and occupations became more frequent, Romero's regime abandoned its attempts at unifying the country and applied itself to the task of stamping out the threat of revolution: strikes were banned, public meetings broken up and agitators arrested. But the developing situation was now also of

RIGHT: *General Carlos Romero, who became president in 1977. His attempt to stamp out the threat of revolution met with little success.* BELOW: *The tragic reality of civil war. The bodies lie where they fell, victims of an attack by one of the Salvadorean death squads which have liquidated whole families in their search for left-wing sympathisers.*

increasing concern to the US, and in line with the Carter administration's policies on human rights, considerable pressure was exerted on El Salvador to try to put an end to the violence and repression. Carter had hoped that a moderate centre could be nurtured in El Salvadorean politics, and when Romero was ousted by a coup in October 1979 and a new junta promising social and economic reform and an end to repression took his place, it appeared that a chance to head off a revolution had emerged. The promises failed to materialise, however, and the violence continued. In March 1980, Duarte, the former PDC coalition candidate in the 1972 elections, joined a new junta; large-scale agrarian reforms were announced and the US began to resume aid with supplies of finance and equipment for 'clean' counter-insurgency operations. Despite a seemingly more progressive attitude, however, the new junta continued to repress the left, and at the end of March 1980 the country was brought to the brink of all-out civil war by the assassination of the outspoken Roman Catholic Archbishop of San Salvador, Oscar Romero.

Archbishop Romero's death, however, served to unite the previously disparate elements of El Salvadorean opposition. A month later in April, the FDR (Frente Democrático Revolucionario) was formed from the political parties while later in the year in October, the five main guerrilla groups amalgamated and took to the field as the FMLN (Farabundo Martí de Liberación Nacional). On 10 January 1981, the new FMLN launched its so-called 'final offensive', strengthening its hold on the northern and eastern parts of the country, and throughout 1981 continued to attack major economic targets and military installations. By the end of the year some 300,000 refugees had fled the fighting and several of the northern provinces were almost totally depopulated. Despite the fact that the government was receiving substantial military aid from the US, the war continued, and in January 1982 a guerrilla attack on aircraft at Ilopango air base destroyed nearly 30 per cent of the air force's effective strength.

Right-wing rule

On the political front, the government moved further to the right. As a result of the fraudulent elections of March 1982, Duarte lost control of the country and the five right-wing parties came together to form a Government of National Unity under the effective rule of the extreme right-wing former chief of the National Guard, Major Roberto D'Aubuisson Arrieta. In May the agrarian reform initiated by the Duarte junta was suspended. Efforts to contain guerrilla activity, however, remained unsuccessful despite the rigorous methods employed – in three years some 35,000 civilians were killed – and in October the FMLN renewed its offensive. Following a successful FMLN campaign in the south in the province of Usulutan, the army counter-attacked with Operation Wellbeing in June 1983, but although limited successes were achieved, by the end of the year government forces had taken over 7000 casualties.

No political solution

The guerrillas continued to attack and in January 1984 the government suffered another major blow when the FMLN struck the garrison at El Paraiso and destroyed the important Cuscatlan bridge. A month later, the allied opposition front of the FDR and FMLN proposed the founding of a broad-based new government. The FMLN, however, refused to participate in the March 1984 presidential elections in which Duarte triumphed over the former leader D'Aubuisson.

By September 1984, government and guerrilla forces remained deadlocked in a civil war that had virtually destroyed the country. Despite aid of $233 million from the Carter and Reagan administrations and the training of rapid reaction forces in the US, the successive governments of El Salvador had failed to make any significant headway against the FMLN. In El Salvador human rights, poverty and democratic representation remained the fundamental issues of the continued war. However, fears in the US of a repeat of the Sandinista success in Nicaragua and Reagan's dictum that El Salvador would not be 'lost', guaranteed continued US support for the Duarte government in its war against the FMLN.

TOP: *Troops watch over a queue of voters in the 1982 election which brought Major Roberto D'Aubuisson to power. He was later ousted by José Napoleón Duarte* (ABOVE) *in the 1984 election.* BELOW: *The war continues. A helicopter gunship patrols the mountains in search of FMLN guerrillas.*

Glossary of terms

ASM Air to Surface Missile.

APC Armoured Personnel Carrier.

APDS Armour Piercing Discarding Sabot: high velocity anti-tank shot which discards part of its casing after leaving the barrel.

Assault gun Self-propelled gun with enclosed armoured protection for crew.

Attrition strategy The strategy of wearing down the enemy's will to fight by systematic destruction of his manpower and *matériel*; widely used in guerrilla warfare.

Ballistic missile Weapon which reaches its target under force of gravity after initial powered and guided stage.

Bangalore torpedo Explosive tube, particularly used against barbed-wire defences.

Blitzkrieg The strategy of lightning attack by air and mobile land forces developed by the Germans in World War II.

Cannon Automatic weapon firing explosive bullets.

Chaff Metallic strips scattered by aircraft to confuse enemy radar.

Claymore mine A directional mine which scatters steel balls over a 60 degree arc to an effective range of about 50 metres. Widely used by US forces in Vietnam.

Cold start The ability of an army to begin a full-scale offensive without prior reinforcement.

Cruise missile A long-range nuclear missile equipped with a sophisticated guidance system which provides pin-point accuracy and allows the missile to fly at exceptionally low altitudes, thereby avoiding radar detection.

Discharger cup Attachment fitted to small arms for the launching of grenades.

ECCM Electronic Counter-Counter-Measures: the attempt to minimise the effects of ECM on radar and defence systems.

ECM Electronic Counter-Measures: a method of electronic interference designed to jam enemy weapon systems and radar screens.

Fire-base Self-contained, self-defended artillery base, especially used by US Army in Vietnam.

FROG Free Rocket Over Ground: a series of Soviet tactical missiles, unguided artillery rockets armed with either nuclear or conventional high explosive warheads. They are road-transportable. The FROG-7 has a range of at least 60 kilometres (37 miles).

Gatling gun See Minigun.

Glacis Sloping hull section of tank designed to deflect shells.

Grey weapons See Theatre Nuclear Weapons.

HE High Explosive ammunition.

HEAT High Explosive Anti-Tank: a shell containing a shaped charge which explodes a short distance from the armour plate of an enemy vehicle and concentrates the force of the blast on a small area, sending a stream of molten fragments into the tank.

Herbicides and defoliants Chemicals used to destroy vegetation in order to deny the enemy natural cover. Widely used by the Americans in Vietnam against Vietcong guerrilla forces.

HESH High Explosive Squash Head: a shell which squashes against the target on impact and on detonation sends out shock waves which break off steel fragments on the inside surface of the tank.

ICBM Inter Continental Ballistic Missile: a nuclear missile with a range over 6440 kilometres (4000 miles).

Infra-red signature Heat emitted by aircraft's engine onto which a heat-seeking missile may home.

Interdiction The concentration of bombardment on specific areas in order to prevent enemy access to them.

IRBM Intermediate Range Ballistic Missile: a nuclear missile with a range of between 2400–6440 kilometres (1500–4000 miles).

Kilotonnage The explosive power of a nuclear warhead expressed in thousands of tons of TNT.

LAW Light Anti-tank Weapon (US).

Megatonnage The explosive power of a nuclear warhead expressed in millions of tons of TNT.

Minigun Machine gun of US manufacture with electrically-driven revolving barrels capable of a rate of fire of up to 6000 rounds per minute.

MIRV Multiple Independently-targeted Re-entry Vehicle: a nuclear missile warhead capable of striking a number of projected targets simultaneously. The American MIRV Poseidon is capable of striking up to 14 separate targets.

MRBM Medium Range Ballistic Missile: a nuclear missile with a range of between 800–2400 kilometres (500–1500 miles).

Napalm Oil-based anti-personnel incendiary bomb developed in 1943.

Paramilitary Civilian or police organisations organised on military lines. Such as the *Guardia Civil* in Spain.

PGM Precision Guided Missile.

Political status The treatment of convicted terrorists as prisoners of war, rather than criminals under the law.

Pre-emptive strike An offensive launched in anticipation of imminent enemy action, such as that launched by the Israeli armed forces in June 1967.

Recoilless rifle Lightweight artillery piece, often man-portable, with a compensating charge eliminating recoil.

RPV Remotely Piloted Vehicles: unmanned drones, frequently used as information gatherers.

SALT Strategic Arms Limitation Talks: an agreement to limit nuclear arms concluded between the Soviet Union and United States in 1972–4. A subsequent agreement, SALT-2, remained unratified.

SAM Surface-to-Air Missile.

Silo Subterranean installation used to store, protect and launch ICBMs.

SLBM Submarine-Launched Ballistic Missile.

'Smart' bomb Bomb fitted with a guidance system (either laser or electro-optical) which makes great accuracy possible.

SRBM Short Range Ballistic Missile: a nuclear missile with ranges up to 800 kilometres (500 miles).

SSBN Nuclear Ballistic Missile Submarine: US Navy designation.

Stand-off missile Missile launched at a distance from a target by aircraft.

Stand-off range The distance from a target at which an aircraft can release an air to surface missile (ASM).

STOL/VTOL Short Take-Off and Landing/Vertical Take-Off and Landing: fixed-wing aircraft with the ability to take off and land in a short distance or vertically.

Strategic hamlet A US strategy in Vietnam in which Vietnamese peasants were moved from their original location to defended positions ostensibly safe from Vietcong influence.

Strategic nuclear arms Missiles intended to destroy an enemy nation's centres of population and industry.

TERCOM TERrain COMparison radar carried by certain cruise missiles which enables them to correct course automatically in flight by comparing the ground below with a pre-programmed map.

Theatre nuclear weapons Missiles and artillery with nuclear warheads designed for tactical as opposed to strategic use (see SRBM).

Throw-weight Aggregate payload of a ballistic missile.

TOW Tube-launched, Optically-tracked, Wire-guided anti-tank missile.

The Major Wars since 1945

In the tables and chart which follow, we have listed the major wars since 1945, and the main incidents involving the use of large-scale armed force by one country in another state. Since 1945, of course, urban and rural guerrilla campaigns have become a sophisticated form of low-level warfare, and although the largest of them have been included, we have not put in others, such as the Naxalite revolt in India, the Tupamaros in Uruguay or the Red Brigades in Italy. Again, the military coup, usually involving armed force, has been common in many areas of the globe, but we have not included the vast majority of such incidents.

Asia

Chinese civil war
Date: 1945–December 1949
Combatants: Communists versus Nationalists
Main Engagements: Second battle of Szeping (1946), Fall of Mukden (1948), Hsuchow (1948–9)
Outcome: Communist victory, withdrawal of Nationalists to Taiwan
Casualties: Accurate figures not available; probably millions

French Indochina
Date: March 1946–21 July 1954
Combatants: Viet Minh versus France
Main Engagements: Fort Cao Bang (9 October 1950), Red River Delta (1951), Quinhon (January 1953), Dien Bien Phu (7 May 1954)
Outcome: Viet Minh victory; division of Vietnam on the 17th Parallel into communist North and US-supported South
Casualties: French metropolitan and colonial forces 75,000 dead. Viet Minh approximately 150,000 dead

Malayan Emergency
Date: June 1948–12 July 1960
Combatants: Great Britain versus communist MRLA
Outcome: Defeat of MRLA; creation of independent Malay state, 31 September 1957
Casualties: British and allied forces 2384 dead, 2400 wounded. MRLA 6711 dead, 1289 wounded, 2704 surrendered

Indonesian war of independence
Date: 14 October 1945–2 November 1949
Combatants: Indonesian People's Army versus the Netherlands
Main Engagements: Surabaya (29 November 1945), Jogjakarta (19 December 1948)
Outcome: Dutch withdrawal: Indonesian independence on 15 August 1950

Huk revolt in the Philippines
Dates: 1946–1954
Combatants: Government versus communist Hukbalahap rebels
Outcome: Government victory

Karen revolt in Burma
Dates: Spring 1948–Summer 1950
Combatants: Central government versus alliance of communists and Karen separatists
Main Engagements: Capture of Toungoo (March 1950)
Outcome: Government victory

Korea
Dates: 25 June 1950–27 July 1953
Combatants: North Korea (NKA) and China versus South Korea (ROK), United States and allies (UN forces)
Main Engagements: NKA invasion (25 June 1950), Inchon Landings (15 September 1950), Chinese Counter-Attack (25 November 1950), UN Counter-Offensive (22 May 1951)
Outcome: Military stalemate; formal division of Korea into North and South on the 38th Parallel (as pre-war division)
Casualties: UN forces 118,515 dead, 264,591 wounded, 92,987 captured. North Korea 500,000+ casualties. China 900,000 casualties

Tibetan revolt against Chinese occupation
Dates: Spring 1954–1959
Combatants: Tibetan nationalists versus China
Outcome: China quelled revolt
Casualties: Tibet estimated 105,000 dead, 10,000 deported

Indonesian civil war
Date: 1950–1965
Combatants: The constituent islands of Indonesia; also government forces versus communists
Outcome: Suppression of communists
Casualties: Estimated at 500,000

Malaysia-Indonesia confrontation
Date: 15 September 1963–11 August 1966
Combatants: Malaysia versus Indonesia
Outcome: Ceasefire agreement
Casualties: Commonwealth military and civilian services 150 dead, 234 wounded, 4 captured. Indonesia 590 dead, 222 wounded, 771 captured

Sino-Indian war
Date: October–November 1962
Combatants: Communist China versus India
Outcome: Chinese seizure of disputed border region
Casualties: India 1400 killed, 4013 captured. China unknown

Vietnam
Date: 1959–30 April 1975
Combatants: North Vietnam and South Vietnamese communists versus the Republic of South Vietnam and the US
Main Engagements: Khe Sanh (1968), the Tet Offensive (1968), Easter Offensive (1972), Final Offensive (1975)
Outcome: Communist victory
Casualties: North Vietnam 1 million killed. South Vietnam 400,000 killed and the USA 47,000 killed

Indo-Pakistan war of 1965
Date: April–27 September 1965
Combatants: India versus Pakistan
Main Engagements: Lahore
Outcome: UN-policed ceasefire
Casualties: India 2212 dead, 7636 wounded, 1500 missing. Pakistan estimated 5800+ dead

Sino-Soviet border incidents
Date: March–August 1969
Combatants: Soviet Union versus China
Main Engagements: Damansky Island (2 March 1969)
Outcome: Soviet occupation of Damansky Island
Casualties: Probably over 100 for each nation

Indo-Pakistan war of 1971
Date: 3–16 December 1971
Combatants: India versus Pakistan
Main Engagements: Dacca
Outcome: Independence for Bangladesh
Casualties: India 1426 killed, 3611 wounded, 2149 missing. Pakistan unknown

Indonesian invasion of East Timor
Date: 1975–
Combatants: Indonesian forces versus Timorese nationalists
Outcome: Undecided
Casualties: 100,000+ Timorese estimated killed

Moslem revolt in the Philippines
Date: 1972–1979
Combatants: Philippine government versus Moslem rebels
Outcome: Suppression of rebellion
Casualties: 30,000+ rebels estimated killed

Vietnamese invasion of Kampuchea
Date: Autumn 1978–Spring 1979
Combatants: Vietnam versus Khmer Rouge
Main Engagements: Vietnamese Invasion (25 December 1978), Phnom Penh (7 January 1979)
Outcome: PRK (People's Republic of Kampuchea) formed with aid from Vietnam

Chinese invasion of Vietnam
Date: February 1979
Combatants: China versus Vietnam
Outcome: Chinese withdrawal
Casualties: China 20,000 killed and wounded. Vietnam 27,000 killed and wounded (estimates)

Europe

Greek civil war
Date: 1945–16 October 1949
Combatants: Nationalists (GNA) versus communists (ELA)
Main Engagements: Relief of Konitsa (January 1948), clearing of Mount Grammos (August 1948)
Outcome: Nationalist victory; suppression of communists
Casualties: Communists 38,000 dead, 40,000 captured/surrendered. Nationalists 12,777 dead, 37,732 wounded, 4527 missing

East German revolt
Date: June 1953
Combatants: Demonstrators versus government and Soviet forces
Outcome: Disturbances suppressed

Hungarian revolt
Date: 23 October–4 November 1956
Combatants: Hungary versus Soviet Union
Main Engagements: Budapest
Outcome: Hungarian revolt suppressed
Casualties: Hungary 25,000 dead. Soviet Union 7000 dead

Polish revolt
Date: 28–29 June 1956
Combatants: Polish workers versus Soviet troops
Outcome: Riot suppressed
Casualties: Poland 50+ dead, 1000+ imprisoned

Invasion of Czechoslovakia
Date: 20 August 1968–20 March 1970
Combatants: Czechoslovakia versus Warsaw Pact forces
Outcome: Change of government in Czechoslovakia
Casualties: 70 dead, 1000 injured

Northern Ireland
Date: 1968–
Combatants: Great Britain versus Republican insurgents
Outcome: Continues
Casualties: (total to October 1984) 2412 dead

Latin America

Cuban revolution
Date: 2 December 1956–1 January 1959
Combatants: Government versus communist insurgents
Main Engagements: Santa Clara
Outcome: Communist victory
Casualties: Army 2000 dead. Insurgent figures not available

The Bay of Pigs
Date: 16–17 April 1961
Combatants: Cuban government versus invading exiles (with US backing)
Outcome: Invaders quickly rounded up
Casualties: 1200 invaders killed or captured

Civil war in Guatemala
Date: 1967–
Combatants: Right-wing terrorists versus reformist elements
Outcome: Undecided
Casualties: 20,000+ killed

Occupation of San Domingo
Date: April–May 1965
Combatants: US forces intervene in civil war
Outcome: Restoration of peace

Nicaragua
Date: May–July 1979
Combatants: Government forces versus Sandinista guerrillas
Main Engagements: Managua
Outcome: Sandinista victory, but war continues between Sandinista forces and US-sponsored counter-revolutionary forces
Casualties: Estimated at 10,000+ killed

El Salvador
Date: February 1980–
Combatants: Right-wing terrorists and government forces versus guerrilla insurgents
Outcome: War continues

'The Football War'
Date: July 1969
Combatants: El Salvador versus Honduras
Outcome: Salvadorean invading force withdraws under international pressure; border hostilities continue until 1980
Casualties: 4000

Grenada
Date: October 1983
Combatants: US and Caribbean forces versus Cuban and People's Revolutionary Army (PRA) troops
Outcome: Revolutionary Military Council deposed; stability restored

The Major Wars since 1945

Falklands
Date: 2 April–14 June 1982
Combatants: Great Britain versus Argentina
Main Engagements: San Carlos, Goose Green, Port Stanley
Outcome: British victory, expulsion of Argentinians from the Falklands
Casualties: British 255 killed, 777 wounded. Argentina 1000+ killed, 11,400 captured

Africa

Malagasy revolt
Date: 1947–1948
Combatants: French government versus Malagasy Nationalists
Outcome: French quelled revolt

Mau Mau revolt
Date: 20 October 1952–January 1960
Combatants: Mau Mau insurgents versus Great Britain
Main Engagements: Aberdare Forest
Outcome: British withdrawal, Kenyan independence in 1963
Casualties: British security forces 600 dead. Insurgents 11,500 dead, 2500 captured.

Tunisian war of independence
Date: 1952–June 1955
Combatants: France versus Tunisian Nationalists
Outcome: Full autonomy, then independence in March 1956

Moroccan war of independence
Date: 1953–1956
Combatants: France versus Moroccan Nationalists
Outcome: 5 November 1955, France agreed to independence

Suez
Date: 31 October– 7 November 1956
Combatants: Egypt versus Great Britain and France
Main Engagements: Port Said (6 November 1956)
Outcome: UN ceasefire imposed; Anglo-French forces evacuated
Casualties: Anglo-French 33 dead, 130 wounded. Egyptian casualties unknown

Algerian war of independence
Date: 1 November 1954–March 1962
Combatants: Algerian Nationalists (FLN/ALN) versus France
Main Engagements: Battle of Algiers (January–October 1957), Challe Offensive (February–April 1959)
Outcome: French withdrawal; Algerian independence on 3 July 1963
Casualties: French 17,456 dead. Colons 2788 dead. Algerian Moslems approximately 1 million dead

The Congo
Date: 1 July 1960–December 1967
Combatants: Nationalist factions
Main Engagements: Katanga secession (February 1961 to January 1962)
Outcome: Military coup ended conflict
Casualties: UN forces 126 dead. Congolese military and civil casualties numbered some tens of thousands

Biafra
Date: 30 May 1967–15 January 1970
Combatants: Nigeria versus Biafra
Main Engagements: Umahia
Outcome: Nigerian victory
Casualties: Estimated at 600,000 killed on both sides

Angolan war of independence
Date: 1961–11 November 1975
Combatants: Portugal versus Nationalists
Outcome: Independence

Angolan civil war
Date: November 1975–November 1976
Combatants: MPLA (with Soviet and Cuban support) versus FNLA and UNITA
Outcome: MPLA recognised by UN as government of Angola
Casualties: Estimated at 20,000 killed for all sides

Mozambique war of independence
Date: 1964–June 1975
Combatants: Portugal versus Nationalists
Outcome: Independence

Guinean war of independence
Date: 1963–September 1974
Combatants: Portugal versus Nationalists
Outcome: Independence

Somalian invasion of the Ogaden
Date: May 1977–March 1978
Combatants: Ethiopia versus Somalia
Main Engagements: Harer and Dire Dawa (August 1977)
Outcome: Ethiopia repelled invasion

Chadian civil war
Date: August 1960–
Combatants: Rebels versus government, with French and Libyan intervention
Main Engagements: Ati (May 1978)
Outcome: War continues

Eritrean revolt
Date: 1960–
Combatants: Ethiopian government versus Eritrean separatists
Main Engagements: Siege of Mits'iwa (Summer 1977–November 1978)
Outcome: War continues

Rhodesia
Date: 1957–March 1980
Combatants: Nationalists versus British/Rhodesian governments
Outcome: Nationalist victory and independence
Casualties: 20,000 killed on both sides

Sahel war
Date: 1978–
Combatants: Morocco versus Algerian-backed Sahel Nationalists
Outcome: War continues

Namibia
Date: 1976–
Combatants: South African forces versus SWAPO
Outcome: War continues

Tanzanian invasion of Uganda
Date: February 1979
Combatants: Tanzania versus forces of General Amin
Outcome: New government in Uganda

Middle East

1948 Arab-Israeli war
Date: 14 May 1948–5 January 1949
Combatants: Egypt, Jordan, Syria, Iraq and Lebanon versus Israel
Main Engagements: Jerusalem (May 1948)
Outcome: UN mediation brings about armistice
Casualties: Israel 6000. Arabs 6000+

Cyprus
Date: November 1955–December 1959
Combatants: Great Britain versus Greek Cypriots
Outcome: British withdrawal, followed by independence
Casualties: Britain 142 dead, 684 wounded. Greek Cypriots 278 dead, 295 wounded. Turkish Cypriots 84 dead, 258 wounded

Israeli invasion of Sinai
Date: 29 October–15 November 1956
Combatants: Israel versus Egypt
Main Engagements: Mitla Pass (29 October 1956), Abu Aweigila (29/30 October 1956)
Outcome: UN intervention halted hostilities
Casualties: Israel 181 dead, 600+ wounded. Egypt 1500 dead, 6000 taken prisoner

Occupation of the Lebanon
Date: 14 April–15 July 1958
Combatants: Lebanon versus UAR-supported communist forces
Main Engagements: Beirut (14–16 June), Tripoli (25–27 June)
Outcome: US Marines stabilised situation

Cypriot civil war
Date: December 1963–August 1964
Combatants: Greek versus Turkish Cypriots
Main Engagements: Kyrenia mountains
Outcome: UN imposed ceasefire

Yemeni civil war
Date: 26 December 1961–May 1970
Combatants: UAR-supported communists versus Saudi-supported Royalists
Main Engagements: Siege of San'aa (December 1967–March 1968), Capture of Sa'dah (September 1968)
Outcome: Peace treaty signed

Aden
Date: December 1963–29 November 1967
Combatants: Great Britain versus NLF and FLOSY
Outcome: British withdrawal, followed by independence for FSA
Casualties: Britain 57 dead, 651 wounded. Local civilians 280 dead, 922 wounded

Six Day War
Date: 5–10 June 1967
Combatants: Israel versus Egypt, Jordan and Syria
Main Engagements: Rafah-Khan Yunis, Golan Heights
Outcome: Israeli victory
Casualties: Israel 689 dead, 2563 wounded. Arab states 13,500 dead, 27,000 wounded

Yom Kippur war
Date: 6–24 October 1973
Combatants: Israel versus Egypt and Syria
Main Engagements: Golan Heights, Sinai
Outcome: Ceasefire
Casualties: Israel 1854 dead, 1850 wounded, 450 taken prisoner. Arab figures not available

Turkish invasion of Cyprus
Date: July 1974
Combatants: Turkey versus Greek Cypriots
Outcome: Division of island

Lebanese civil war
Date: September 1975–
Combatants: Christian factions versus Moslems; Syrian intervention
Outcome: War continues
Casualties: 50,000+ killed

Soviet invasion of Afghanistan
Date: 24 December 1979–
Combatants: Afghan Moslem guerrillas versus Soviet Union
Outcome: Soviet occupation of towns/urban areas; war continues
Casualties: Estimated at 100,000+ killed

Gulf War
Date: 12 September 1980–
Combatants: Iran versus Iraq
Main Engagements: Khorramshahr, Abadan
Outcome: War continues

Israeli invasion of Lebanon
Date: June 1982–
Combatants: Israeli and Phalangist militias versus PLO, Syria and Moslem militias
Main Engagements: Beaufort Castle, Beqaa Valley, Beirut
Outcome: PLO defeat, fighting continues

Bibliography

Afghanistan
Furlong, R. D. and Winkler, T. 'The Soviet Invasion of Afghanistan', *International Defence Review*, No 2, 1980
Rees, David 'Afghanistan's Role in Soviet Strategy', Institute for the Study of Conflict, Study No 118, 1980

Algeria
Horne, Alistair *A Savage War of Peace*, London 1977
O'Ballance, Edgar *The Algerian Insurrection*, London 1967
Paret, P. *French Revolutionary Warfare from Indochina to Algeria*, London 1964
Roy, Jules *The War in Algeria*, Westport 1975

Arab-Israeli Wars 1967, 1973
Herzog, Chaim *The War of Atonement*, London 1975
Monroe, Elizabeth and Farrar-Hockley, A. H. 'The Arab-Israeli War, October 1973: Background and Events', International Institute for Strategic Studies, Adelphi Paper No 111, 1975
O'Ballance, Edgar *The Third Arab-Israeli War*, London 1972
Sunday Times *Insight on the Middle East War*, London 1974

China
Chassin, Max *The Communist Conquest of China*, London 1965
Crozier, Brian *The Man Who Lost China: The First Full Biography of Chiang Kai-shek*, New York 1976
Schram, Stuart *Mao Tse-tung*, London 1966
Tsou, Tang *America's Failure in China 1941–50*, Chicago 1963

Cold War
Abel, E. *The Missiles of October*, London 1966
Bell, C. *The Conventions of Crisis*, London 1971
Calvocoressi, P. *World Politics since 1945*, London 1971
Martin, L. *Arms and Strategy*, London 1973
Morgan, Roger *The Unsettled Peace*, London 1974
Spanier, J. W. *American Foreign Policy since World War II*, London 1972

Congo
Kanza, Thomas *Conflict in the Congo*, London 1972
Lumumba, Patrice *Congo My Country*, London 1969
O'Brien, Conor Cruise *To Katanga and Back*, London 1962
Young, Crawford *Politics in the Congo*, Princeton 1965

Cuban Revolution
Guevara, Ernesto ('Che') *Reminiscences of the Cuban Revolutionary War*, London 1968
Thomas, Hugh *Cuba or the Pursuit of Freedom*, London 1971

Cyprus and Aden
Blaxland, G. *The Regiments Depart*, London 1971
Grivas, George *Guerrilla Warfare*, London 1964
Paget, Julian *Counter-insurgency Campaigning*, London 1967

Falklands Conflict
Fox, Robert *Eyewitness Falklands*, London 1982
Hastings, Max and Jenkins, Simon *The Battle for the Falklands*, London 1983
Kon, Daniel *Los Chicos De La Guerra*, London 1983

Greece
Kousoulas, D. George *Revolution and Defeat*, London 1965
Matthews, Kenneth *Memories of a Mountain War: Greece 1944–49*, London 1972
O'Ballance, Edgar *The Greek Civil War 1944–49*, 1966

Horn of Africa
Gilkes, Patrick *The Dying Lion*, London 1975
Hamilton, David 'Ethiopia's Embattled Revolutionaries', Institute for the Study of Conflict, Study No 82, 1977
Janke, Peter 'Marxist Statecraft in Africa, What Future?', Institute for the Study of Conflict, Study No 95, 1978
Ottaway, Marina and David *Ethiopia and Revolution*, New York 1978

Hungarian Uprising
Barber, Noel *Seven Days of Freedom*, London 1974
Lomax, Bill *Hungary 1956*, London 1976
Pryce-Jones, David *The Hungarian Revolution*, London 1969

Kenya
Clayton, T. *Counter-insurgency in Kenya*, Nairobi 1976
Condit, D. et al *Challenge and Response in Internal Conflict*, Washington 1967
Rosberg, Carl and Nottingham, John *The Myth of Mau Mau: Nationalism in Kenya*, New York 1966

Indochina War
Fall, Bernard *Street Without Joy*, Harrisburg 1966
Fall, Bernard *Hell in a Very Small Place: The Siege of Dien Bien Phu*, London 1966
O'Ballance, Edgar *The Indo-China War 1945–54*, London 1964
Rosie, G. *The British in Vietnam*, London 1970
Roy, J. *The Battle of Dien Bien Phu*, London 1965

Indo-Pakistan War
Ayoob, M. and Subrahmanyam, K. *The Liberation War*, New Delhi 1972
Jackson, R. *South Asian Crisis*, London 1975
Palit, D. *The Lightning Campaign*, Salisbury 1972

International Terrorism
Barron, John *KGB*, London 1974
Laski, Melvyn J. 'Ulrike Meinhof and the Baader-Meinhof Gang' *Encounter*, June 1975
Moss, Robert *Urban Terrorism*, London 1973
Smith, Colin *Carlos: Portrait of a Terrorist*, London 1976

Israeli attack on Sinai
Dayan, Moshe *Diary of the Sinai Campaign*, New York 1966
Love, Kenneth *Suez, The Twice-Fought War*, London 1970
Luttwak, Edward and Horowitz, Dan *The Israeli Army*, London 1975
O'Ballance, Edgar *The Sinai Campaign*, London 1959
Pimlott, John *The Middle East Conflicts*, London 1983

Israeli Invasion of Lebanon

Dimbleby, Jonathan *The Palestinians*, London 1980
Hogg, Ian V. *Israeli War Machine*, London 1983
Randal, Jonathan *The Tragedy of Lebanon*, London 1983
Rothenburg, Gunther E. *The Anatomy of the Israeli Army*, London 1979

Korea

Appleman, Roy E. *US Army in the Korean War, Jun–Nov 1950*, Washington 1961
Barclay, C. N. *The First Commonwealth Division*, Aldershot 1954
Rees, David *Korea, the Limited War*, London 1964
Rees, David *The Korean War: History and Tactics*, London 1984
Ridgway, Matthew B. *The War in Korea*, London 1968

Malayan Emergency

Clutterbuck, Richard *The Long Long War*, London 1966
Miller, Harry *Jungle War in Malaya*, London 1972
Short, Anthony *The Communist Insurrection in Malaya 1948–60*, London 1975
Thompson, Sir Robert *Defeating Communist Insurgency*, London 1966

Military Balance

Baylis, Booth, Garnett and Williams *Contemporary Strategy*, 1976
Bidwell, Shelford (ed) *World War 3*, London 1978
Bonds, Ray (ed.) *The Soviet War Machine*, London 1980
Bonds, Ray (ed.) *The US War Machine*, London 1978
International Institute for Strategic Studies *The Military Balance*, London annual
International Institute for Strategic Studies *Strategic Survey*, London annual
Martin, L. (ed.) *Strategic Thought in the Nuclear Age*, London 1979
Sampson, A. *The Arms Bazaar*, London 1977

Nigeria

Forsyth, Frederick *The Biafra Story*, London 1969
Niven, Rex *The War of Nigerian Unity*, London 1970
St Jorre, John de *The Nigerian Civil War*, London 1972

Northern Ireland

Coogan, Tim Pat *The IRA*, London 1970
Darby, John *Conflict in Northern Ireland*, London 1976
Fisk, Robert *The Point of No Return*, London 1975
O'Brien, Conor Cruise *State of Ireland*, London 1972
Winchester, Simon *In Holy Terror*, London 1974

Portuguese Africa

Bruce, Neil *Portugal: The Last Empire*, Newton Abbot 1975
Calvert, Michael 'Countery-insurgency in Mozambique', *Journal of the Royal United Services Institute for Defence Studies* Vol CXVIII, March 1973
Davidson, Basil *The Liberation of Guinea*, London 1969

Marcum, John *The Angolan Revolution* (2 vols), Cambridge, Mass. 1969, 1978
Porch, Douglas *The Portuguese Armed Forces and the Revolution*, London 1977

Rhodesia

Arbuckle, Thomas 'Rhodesian Bushwar Strategies and Tactics', *Journal of the Royal United Services Institute for Defence Studies* Vol CXXIV, December 1979
Blake, Robert *A History of Rhodesia*, London 1977
Keegan, John (ed.) *World Armies*, London 1979
Raeburn, Michael *Black Fire*, London 1978
Wilkinson, Anthony R. 'Insurgency in Rhodesia 1957–73: An Account and Assessment', International Institute for Strategic Studies, Adelphi Paper No 100, 1973

Suez

Barker, A. J. *Suez: The Seven Day War*, London 1969
Baufre, A. *The Suez Expedition of 1956*, London 1969
Nutting, Anthony *No End of a Lesson*, London 1966
Thomas, Hugh *The Suez Affair*, London 1966

Urban Guerrillas of South America

Asprey, Robert *War in the Shadows*, New York 1975
Gott, Richard *Rural Guerrillas in Latin America*, London 1973
Guevara, Ernesto ('Che') *Bolivian Diaries*, London 1968
Labrousse, Alain *The Tupamaros*, London 1973
Marighela, Carlos *For the Liberation of Brazil*, London 1971

Vietnam War

Charlton, Michael and Moncrieff, Anthony *Many Reasons Why: The American Involvement in Vietnam*, London 1978
Duncanson, Dennis *Government and Revolution in Vietnam*, London 1968
Pimlott, John *Vietnam: The history and the tactics*, London 1982
Thompson, Sir Robert *Peace is Not at Hand*, London 1974
Turner, Robert F. *Vietnamese Communism, its Origins and Development*, Stanford 1975
Warner, Denis *Certain Victory: How Hanoi Won the War*, Mission, Kansas, 1978
West, F. J. *The Village*, New York 1972

Index

Page numbers in *italics* refer to illustrations.

ACKNOWLEDGMENTS

We should like to thank the following for providing the photographs used in this volume: Anglo-Chinese Educational Institute, Associated Press, BBC Hulton Picture Library, Black Star, Camera Press, Central Press, Colorific, Communist Party of Great Britain, C. G. Croft/Federation of Nuclear Shelter Consultants and Contractors, René Dazy, John Fricker, John Frost Newspaper Library, General Dynamics, Greek Embassy, London, Grumman Corporation, Robert Hunt Library, Imperial War Museum, Keystone Press, League for Democracy in Greece Archive/King's College University of London, Lustige Blätter, Berlin, MacClancy Press, Marx Memorial Library, London, Military Archive and Research Services, London, Ministry of Defence, National Film Archive Stills Library, NATO, Novosti, Photri, Popperfoto, Rex Features, School of Slavonic Studies, London, Soldier magazine, Frank Spooner Pictures/Gamma, Sunday Times, Tass, Sir Robert Thompson, Times Newspapers, Topham Picture Library, Topix, United Press International, US Air Force, US Army, US Defense Department, US Marine Corps, US National Archives, US Navy, Roger Viollet, Xinhua News Agency.

We also wish to thank the artists and illustrators who drew the maps and diagrams: Arka Graphics, Graham Bingham, Paul Bryant, Colin Edwards, Tony Gibbons/Linden Artists, James Goulding, Keith Harmer, Mike Holland, Pavel Kostal.